THE BARBARA

Barbara Pym was born in Oswestry, Shropshire, in 1913. She was educated at Huyton College, Liverpool, and St Hilda's College, Oxford, where she gained an Honours Degree in English Language and Literature. During the war she served in the WRNS in Britain and Naples. From 1958 to 1974 she worked as an editorial secretary at the International African Institute, and from 1958 had been assistant editor of the anthropological journal *Africa*. Her first novel, *Some Tame Gazelle*, was published in 1950, and was followed by *Excellent Women* (1952), *Jane and Prudence* (1953), *Less than Angels* (1955) and *A Glass of Blessings* (1958).

During the sixties and early seventies her writing suffered a partial eclipse and, discouraged, she concentrated on her work for the International African Institute, from which she retired in 1974 to live in Oxfordshire. A renaissance in her fortunes came in 1977, when both Philip Larkin and Lord David Cecil chose her as one of the most underrated novelists of the century. This stimulated renewed interest in Miss Pym's work and encouraged her to recommence writing. *Quartet in Autumn* was published in 1977, and was shortlisted for the Booker Prize. *The Sweet Dove Died* was published in 1978; *A Few Green Leaves* was published posthumously.

Barbara Pym died in January 1980.

ALSO BY BARBARA PYM IN PAN BOOKS

Less Than Angels
No Fond Return of Love
An Unsuitable Attachment
A Glass of Blessings

THE BARBARA PYM OMNIBUS

Some Tame Gazelle

Excellent Women

Jane and Prudence

PAN BOOKS
in association with
JONATHAN CAPE

Some Tame Gazelle first published 1950 by Jonathan Cape Limited:
first published in Pan Books 1993 in association with
Jonathan Cape Limited
Excellent Women first published 1952 by Jonathan Cape Limited:
first published in Pan Books 1989 in association with
Jonathan Cape Limited
Jane and Prudence first published 1953 by Jonathan Cape Limited:
first published in Pan Books 1993 in association with
Jonathan Cape Limited

This omnibus edition published 1994 by Pan Books
an imprint of Macmillan Publishers Ltd
25 Eccleston Place, London SW1W 9NF
and Basingstoke

in association with Jonathan Cape Limited

Associated companies throughout the world

ISBN 0 330 33966 4

5 7 9 8 6

A CIP catalogue record for this book is available from the British Library.

Phototypeset by Intype, London
Printed and bound in Great Britain by
Mackays of Chatham PLC, Chatham, Kent

CONTENTS

Some Tame Gazelle

Some tame gazelle, or some gentle dove:
Something to love, oh, something to love!

THOMAS HAYNES BAYLY

CHAPTER ONE

THE NEW curate seemed quite a nice young man, but what a pity it was that his combinations showed, tucked carelessly into his socks, when he sat down. Belinda had noticed it when they had met him for the first time at the vicarage last week and had felt quite embarrassed. Perhaps Harriet could say something to him about it. Her blunt jolly manner could carry off these little awkwardnesses much better than Belinda's timidity. Of course he might think it none of their business, as indeed it was not, but Belinda rather doubted whether he thought at all, if one were to judge by the quality of his first sermon.

'If only we could get back some of the fervour and eloquence of the seventeenth century in the pulpit today,' she had said to her sister Harriet, a plump elegant spinster in the middle fifties.

'Oh, we don't want that kind of thing *here*,' Harriet had said in her downright way, for she had long ago given up all intellectual pursuits, while Belinda, who had never been considered the clever one, still retained some smattering of the culture acquired in her college days. Even now a light would shine in her mild greenish eyes, so decorously hidden behind horn-rimmed spectacles, at the mention of Young's *Night Thoughts* or the dear Earl of Rochester's *Poems on Several Occasions*.

Neither she nor Harriet had ever married, but Harriet was making her usual fuss over the new curate and was obviously prepared to be quite as silly over him as she had been over his predecessors. She was especially given to cherishing *young* clergymen, and her frequent excursions to the curates' lodgings had often given rise to talk, for people did like a bit of gossip, especially about a respectable spinster and church worker like Miss Harriet Bede. There was naturally nothing scandalous about these visits, as she always took with her a newly baked cake, some fresh eggs or fruit – for the poor young men always looked half starved – or even a hand-knitted pullover or pair of socks, begun by her in a burst of enthusiasm and usually finished, more soberly, by Belinda. And then of course she would ask them to supper.

Was it tonight he was coming? Belinda wondered vaguely. It must be tonight, she decided, catching sight of a bowl of exceptionally fine pears on the little table by the window, and expensive bought chrysanthemums in the vases when there were perfectly good Michaelmas daisies in the garden. Dear Harriet, she wasn't really extravagant, only rather too lavish in her hospitality. The Reverend Edgar Donne was surely a simple young man and would not expect much. Naturally one did not think of the clergy as expecting anything in the way of material luxuries . . . Belinda paused, for she was remembering the vicar, Archdeacon Hoccleve, and how one couldn't really say that about him. But then dear Henry was different, in some ways not like a clergyman at all. For although Belinda had loved him faithfully for over thirty years, she sometimes had to admit that he had very few of the obvious virtues that one somehow expected of one's parish priest. His letter in this month's parish magazine, announcing the arrival of the new curate, had a peevish and condescending tone that a stranger might have thought not quite the thing for an archdeacon. But the village was used to it.

'The Reverend Edgar Donne – the name is of course pronounced *Dunne* – will be with us by the time you read these words,' he wrote. 'Nobody will be more glad to welcome him than I myself, for whom these last few weeks have been more trying than any of you can possibly imagine. Without a curate it has been impossible for me to take the holiday I so badly need and I have been forced to cancel some of the services because I have not felt equal to taking them, as the ready help I looked for from fellow priests in neighbouring parishes has not been forthcoming. . . .'

Of course that was a dig at the Reverend Edward Plowman, who disliked the Archdeacon so much, and as he had quarrelled with Canon Glover what could he expect? thought Belinda, almost wishing that she were Deaconess Bede and could enter the pulpit herself. But even a deaconess was not permitted to celebrate Holy Communion – it was of course the *early* services which had been cancelled – whereas in the Nonconformist churches, she believed, women ministers had equal status with men. . . .

'B'*linda*!' Harriet's impatient voice interrupted her thoughts, 'it's nearly seven and Mr Donne will soon be here.' Harriet appeared in the doorway, wearing only a celanese vest and knickers, as if her actual presence in the room would make Belinda realize more fully how late it was.

'Why, Harriet, the curtains aren't drawn,' exclaimed Belinda in an agitated tone. 'Anybody might see into the room! And you know I never take as long to get ready as you do.'

'All the same Mr Donne will probably be punctual,' said Harriet, 'and it would be terrible if neither of us was ready. I've borrowed your lace scarf, as I must have something to cover up the neck of my green frock. Perhaps it would have been better if I hadn't tried to alter it to a Vee.'

'Yes, dear.' Belinda spoke rather absently, for by now she was occupied with the problem of what *she* should wear. She hoped that Harriet had not also borrowed her black velvet bridge coat, as she wanted it herself on these late September evenings. But then Harriet was probably too stout for it, although she liked her clothes to fit tightly and always wore an elastic roll-on corset.

In her room Belinda took out her blue marocain, a rather dim dress of the kind known as 'semi-evening'. Quite good enough for the curate, she decided, though if the Archdeacon had been coming as well she would probably have worn her velvet. She did hope that Harriet wouldn't put on a lot of lipstick, it was so unsuitable. . . .

At that moment there was a ring at the bell and an agitated call from Harriet.

'Belinda, you go! I haven't finished doing my hair.'

'But surely Emily will go?' said Belinda. She was wondering whether to wear her little seed-pearl brooch or not.

'No, Emily can't go. She's putting the sauce on the chicken.'

Belinda hurried downstairs without the little brooch. She felt flustered and incomplete.

The figure on the doorstep might have been any of the other curates, except that Mr Donne favoured a rather unfashionably high clerical collar. He doesn't remember me, thought Belinda, as she replied to his rather puzzled greeting.

'This *is* Miss Bede's house?' he asked, hesitating on the threshold.

'Yes, I am Miss Bede,' said Belinda with simple dignity, 'but I expect you know my sister better.'

'Ah, you must be Miss *Belinda* Bede,' he announced, triumphant at having placed her. 'I've heard a lot about you from the Archdeacon.'

'Oh, really? What did he say?' Belinda tried not to sound too coy and eager.

'He – er – said you did a lot of good work in the parish,' replied the curate primly.

'Oh . . .' Belinda could not help feeling disappointed. It made her sound almost unpleasant. If that was what he had really said, of course. It didn't sound at all like the Archdeacon, who never said the sort of things clergymen ought to say. It was so odd to think of him as being a clergyman at all . . . Belinda's thoughts slipped back to her college days when they had been students together. *Most* odd . . . and yet there was no sadness or bitterness in her mind as she thought of him. It was obvious that poor Agatha had a very difficult time with him, although by her scheming she had made him an archdeacon. Their cook had told the Bedes' Emily who had told Harriet that the Archdeacon was very difficult to get up in the mornings, and of course one knew that he always made his curates do the early services, which was really rather slack because it wasn't as if he were very old or weak in health. And yet he had such charm, even now. . . .

The curate coughed nervously and ventured a remark about the weather.

'Yes, I love September,' agreed Belinda, guilty at having let her thoughts wander from her guest. 'Michaelmas daisies and blackberries and comforting things like fires in the evening again and knitting.'

'Ah, knitting,' he smiled, and Belinda could see him glancing round the room as if he already expected to see the beginnings of a pullover for himself. But all that Belinda's cretonne work-bag contained was a pink lacy-looking garment, a winter vest for herself. It was so annoying of Miss Jenner not to have any more 'Perliknit' left. She had had to buy a slightly thicker wool of a rather brighter pink to finish it off.

Fortunately at this moment, for the conversational going was heavy, a firm step was heard on the stairs and Harriet came into the room, radiant in flowered voile. Tropical flowers rioted over her plump body. The background was the green of the jungle, the blossoms were crimson and mauve, of an unknown species. Harriet was still attractive in a fat Teutonic way. She did not wear her pince-nez when curates came to supper.

The curate sprang up eagerly and seemed suddenly to lose some of his shyness.

'Good evening, Mr Donne,' said Harriet, 'I'm afraid I haven't my sister's punctual ways, but I'm sure she has been entertaining you better than I could have done. I had a classical education and it isn't a very good training for scintillating conversation.' She sat down rather heavily on the sofa beside him. 'Now we must not forget that the name is pronounced *Dunne*,' she declared roguishly.

'Well, actually, as a matter of fact . . .' the curate looked embarrassed, 'I don't pronounce it that way. I can't imagine why the Archdeacon thought I did.'

'He was of course thinking of the seventeenth-century poet of that name,' said Belinda stoutly. The truth was, of course, that dear Henry could never resist a literary allusion and was delighted, in the way that children and scholars sometimes are, if it was one that the majority of his parishioners did not understand.

'He will have to put a correction in the magazine next month,' chortled Harriet. 'I should like to see the Archdeacon having to climb down.'

'It makes one feel quite odd to have one's name mispronounced or misspelt,' said Belinda evenly. 'Almost like a different person.'

'Oh, yes,' agreed Harriet, 'like Gorringe's catalogue.'

The curate looked politely interested but puzzled.

'You see,' Harriet explained, 'they once sent me a catalogue addressed to Miss *Bode*, and somehow I'm so lazy that I never bothered to correct it. So now I have a dual personality. I always feel Miss Bode is my dowdy self, rather a frumpish old thing.'

'She must certainly be most unlike Miss *Bede*,' blurted out Mr Donne with surprising gallantry.

Harriet protested amid delighted giggles. Belinda felt rather left out and found her eyes fixed on the curate's combinations, which still showed. Surely it was much too warm for such garments, unless perhaps he wore them all the year round?

During the short silence which followed, the tinkling of a cowbell was heard. The sisters had brought it back from a holiday in Switzerland and it was now used as a gong.

'Ah, dinner,' said Harriet. 'Come, Mr Donne, you shall take me in,' she added with mock solemnity.

Mr Donne was quite equal to the occasion, for he had all the qualifications of a typical curate. Indeed, his maternal grandfather had been a bishop.

In the dining-room Harriet sat at one end of the table and Belinda at the other, with the curate in the middle. Harriet carved the boiled chicken smothered in white sauce very capably. She gave the curate all the best white meat.

Were all new curates everywhere always given boiled chicken when they came to supper for the first time? Belinda wondered. It was certainly an established ritual at their house and it seemed somehow right for a new curate. The coldness, the whiteness, the muffling with sauce, perhaps even the sharpness added by the slices of lemon, there was something appropriate here, even if Belinda could not see exactly what it was.

'I called at the vicarage on the way here,' said the curate. 'Mrs Hoccleve very kindly promised me some apples.'

Harriet looked rather annoyed. 'Their apples haven't done at all well this year,' she said, 'and I always think those red ones are rather tasteless. You must take some of our Cox's Oranges with you when you go.'

The curate murmured grateful thanks.

'How is Mrs Hoccleve's rheumatism?' asked Belinda.

'Not very much better,' he replied. 'I hear she is going to Karlsbad in October. Apparently the waters there are very good.'

'Nettles are an excellent thing, I believe,' said Harriet.

'Indeed?' Mr Donne looked so interested that he must have found it quite a strain. 'How should they be used?'

'Oh, I don't really know,' Harriet beamed. 'Just nettles. Boiled, perhaps. People will try all sorts of odd remedies,' she added, with the complacency of one who is perfectly healthy.

'Poor Agatha,' murmured Belinda, although she could not really feel very sympathetic.

There was a slight lapse in the conversation.

'I hear you are a rowing man,' said Belinda, with what she felt was rather forced enthusiasm.

'Oh, how splendid!' Harriet was of course delighted, as she would have been with any piece of information. 'I can just imagine you stroking an eight.'

'Well, actually, I haven't done any for some time, but I used to be very keen.' The curate looked down at his chicken bone as if he would like to take it up in his fingers and gnaw it. He was not very well fed at his lodgings and the evening meal was particularly scrappy.

Harriet picked up her bone and began to eat it in her fingers. She beamed on Mr Donne and said brightly, 'Like Queen Victoria, you know, so much more sensible and convenient.'

He followed her example eagerly. Belinda looked on with some distaste. If only Harriet could see how foolish she looked. The white sauce was beginning to smear itself on her face.

'I expect you are quite bewildered meeting so many new people,' she said, leading the conversation back into suitable channels.

'Yes, in a way I am, but I find it fairly easy to remember them so far. I came across Miss Liversidge this afternoon in the village and have persuaded her to address a meeting of the Mothers' Union. She seems to have had a great many interesting experiences.'

Belinda smiled. The idea of Edith Liversidge addressing the Mothers' Union amused her. One never knew what she might say to them and she would hardly set them a good example of tidiness. Dear Edith, she was always such a mess.

'She's a kind of decayed gentlewoman,' said Harriet comfortably, helping the curate to trifle.

'Oh *no*, Harriet,' Belinda protested. Nobody could call Edith decayed and sometimes one almost forgot that she was a gentlewoman, with her cropped grey hair, her shabby clothes which weren't even the legendary 'good tweeds' of her kind and her blunt, almost rough, way of speaking. 'Miss

Liversidge is really splendid,' she declared and then wondered why one always said that Edith was 'splendid'. It was probably because she hadn't very much money, was tough and wiry, dug vigorously in her garden and kept goats. Also, she had travelled abroad a good deal and had done some relief work after the 1914 war among refugees in the Balkans. Work of rather an unpleasant nature too, something to do with sanitation. Belinda hoped that Harriet wouldn't mention it in front of Mr Donne. 'Of course she has made a home for poor Miss Aspinall, who's a kind of relation,' she said hastily. 'I always think it's very unselfish to have a comparative stranger to live with you when you've been used to living alone.'

'Ah, well, we ought to share what we have with others,' said Mr Donne with rather disagreeable unctuousness.

'Oh, Mr Donne, I can't imagine you sharing your home with Connie Aspinall,' Harriet burst out, 'she's so dreary.'

Mr Donne smiled. 'Well, perhaps I didn't mean to be taken quite literally,' he said.

'Now she's a decayed gentlewoman if you like,' said Harriet. 'She can talk of nothing but the days when she used to be companion to a lady in Belgrave Square who was a kind of relation of one of Queen Alexandra's Ladies-in-Waiting.'

'She plays the harp very beautifully,' murmured Belinda weakly, for poor Connie was really rather uninteresting and it was hard to think of anything nice to say about her.

'Let's have coffee in the drawing-room,' said Harriet rather grandly. At one time she had wanted to call it the lounge, but Belinda would not hear of it. She had finally won her point by reminding Harriet of how much their dear mother would have disliked it.

In the drawing-room they arranged themselves as before, Harriet on the sofa with the curate and Belinda in one of the armchairs. Belinda took out her knitting and went on doing it rather self-consciously. It was beginning to look so very much like an undergarment for herself. The curate's combinations must be 'Meridian', she thought. It was nice and warm for pyjamas, too, in fact Harriet herself wore it in the winter. The close fabric fitted her plump body like a woolly skin.

While they were drinking their coffee, Harriet went to the little table by the window and took up the bowl of pears which Belinda had noticed earlier in the evening.

'Now you must have a pear,' she insisted. 'Do you know, when we were children our mother used to say that we could never keep fruit on the sideboard.'

Belinda would have liked to add that they couldn't now, and that it was only because they had been having the curate to supper that there had been anything more than a withered apple or orange in the bowl this evening. Harriet's appetite was just as rapacious in her fifties as it had been in her teens.

The curate helped himself to a pear and began to peel it. He seemed to be getting rather sticky and there was some giggling and interchange of large handkerchiefs between him and Harriet.

Belinda went on quietly with her knitting. The evening promised to be just like so many other evenings when other curates had come to supper. There was something almost frightening and at the same time comforting about the sameness of it all. It was odd that Harriet should always have been so fond of curates. They were so immature and always made the same kind of conversation. Now the Archdeacon was altogether different. One never knew what he might say, except that it was certain to be something unexpected and provocative. Besides, it was really more suitable to lavish one's affection on somebody of a riper age, as it was obviously natural that one should lavish it on somebody. Indeed, one of Belinda's favourite quotations, taken from the works of a minor English poet, was

Some tame gazelle, or some gentle dove:
Something to love, oh, something to love!

Belinda, having loved the Archdeacon when she was twenty

and not having found anyone to replace him since, had naturally got into the habit of loving him, though with the years her passion had mellowed into a comfortable feeling, more like the cosiness of a winter evening by the fire than the uncertain rapture of a spring morning.

Harriet's tittering laugh disturbed Belinda's quiet thoughts. 'Oh, Mr Donne, I'm not quite as stupid as you think! I used to know some Latin. *Ah quotiens illum doluit properare Calypso*,' she retorted, flinging at him triumphantly the last remnants of her classical education.

Can she be hinting at me to go? he wondered, but then decided that she had probably long ago forgotten the meaning of the line. All the same it was getting late. He mustn't outstay his welcome and the elder Miss Bede had yawned once or twice, although she stifled it very politely.

Despite protests from Harriet, they were soon in the hall and the curate was putting on his overcoat. Harriet was fussing round him like a motherly hen.

'Why, of course, it's the garden party tomorrow,' said Belinda, suddenly feeling very tired. 'There will be such a lot to do.'

The curate sighed with an affectation of weariness. 'I shall be almost glad when it is over,' he said. 'These functions are always very tiring for us.'

Harriet smiled understandingly, as if including herself in the select brotherhood of the clergy. 'Never mind,' she said, 'there will be the coconut shies. I always love them. And you'll get a good tea. *I* am in charge of the tea garden.'

'Oh, *well*, Miss Bede . . .' the curate moved towards the front door and Belinda was able to slip quietly into the background. She went into the drawing-room and began to tidy it, plumping up the cushions and removing the remains of the pears they had eaten. She put her knitting into its cretonne bag and took the parish magazine to read in bed. There was a nice new serial in it, all about a drunken organist and a young bank clerk, who was also a lay reader and had been wrongfully accused of embezzlement. And of course the Archdeacon's letter was always worth a second reading.

CHAPTER TWO

ALTHOUGH the Misses Bede had a maid they were both quite domesticated and helped her in various small ways, clearing away the breakfast things, dusting their own bedrooms and doing a little cooking when they felt like it. On this particular morning, however, which was the day of the vicarage garden party, Belinda decided that she could miss doing her room with a clear conscience, as there were so many more important things to be done. It was unlikely that Miss Liversidge would be visiting them and putting them to shame by writing 'E. Liversidge' with her finger, as she had once done when Emily had neglected to dust the piano. Typical of Edith, of course, going straight to the point with no beating about the bush. Not that she could talk either, with dog's hairs all over the carpet and the washing-up left overnight.

This morning, as she went about humming *God moves in a mysterious way*, Belinda wondered what to do first. She had to arrange for some deck-chairs they had promised to be taken over to the vicarage. The cake she had made to be raffled – the Archdeacon was broad-minded and didn't disapprove of such things – must be finished off with its mauve paper frill. The seams of Harriet's crêpe de Chine dress had to be let out, as Harriet seemed to have grown stouter since she had last worn it. Perhaps that was the most important thing of all, for Harriet intended to wear it that afternoon.

While she was sewing, Belinda began to wonder what everyone would be wearing at the garden party. Agatha Hoccleve would of course wear a nice suitable dress, but nothing extreme or daring. As the wife of an archdeacon she always had very *good* clothes, which seemed somehow to emphasize the fact that her father had been a bishop. Then there was Edith Liversidge, who would look odd in the familiar old-fashioned grey costume, whose unfashionably narrow shoulders combined with Edith's broad hips made her look rather like a lighthouse. Her relation, Miss Aspinall, would wear a fluttering blue or grey dress with a great many scarves and draperies, and she would, as always, carry that mysterious little beaded bag without which she was never seen anywhere. Undoubtedly the most magnificent person there would be Lady Clara Boulding, who was to perform the opening ceremony. It was of course fitting that this should be so, as she was the daughter of an earl and the widow of their former Member of Parliament, an excellent man in his way, although he had never been known to speak in the House except on one occasion, when he had asked if a window might be opened or shut.

By now Belinda had tacked the seams of the dress and was fitting it on her sister, who twitched about impatiently, while Belinda ran round her with her mouth full of pins.

Harriet was having one of her tirades against the Archdeacon.

'All that nonsense in the parish magazine about him needing a holiday,' she stormed. 'If that's so, why doesn't he go to Karlsbad with Agatha? Unless she wants a holiday away from him – you could hardly blame her if she preferred to go alone. *I* certainly would.'

'But surely Agatha isn't going to Karlsbad *alone*?' asked Belinda eagerly.

'Well, their Florrie told Emily that she and cook aren't looking forward to managing the Archdeacon by themselves, so it looks as if he isn't going with her. I think it would be nicer if he went too, then we might have a good sermon for a change. I never heard anything so depressing in my life as that horrid thing he read last Sunday – all about worms, and such stilted language. Edith Liversidge walked out in the middle, and' – Harriet chortled at the memory of it – 'one of the churchwardens ran after her with a glass of water, thinking she felt faint or something.'

'But Harriet,' said Belinda gently, 'Henry was reading a passage from *Urn Burial*, I thought he read it magnificently,' she sighed. Of course the real truth of the matter was that poor Henry was too lazy to write sermons of his own and somehow one didn't think of him as being clever in a theological kind of way. That is, no scholarly study of any of St Paul's Epistles had as yet appeared under Archdeacon Hoccleve's name, although he had once remarked to Belinda that he thought the Apocalyptic literature remarkably fine.

Harriet continued her tirade. 'If it weren't so far to walk,' she said, 'I should certainly go to Edward Plowman's church; he does at least preach good homely sermons that everyone can understand. He works systematically through the Ten Commandments and the Beatitudes, I believe; much the most sensible thing to do. Besides, he's such a nice man.'

'But Harriet,' said Belinda anxiously, 'he *is* rather high. He wears a biretta and has incense in the church. It's all so – well – *Romish*.' Broad-minded as she was, Belinda was unable to keep a note of horror out of her voice.

Harriet became defiant. 'Edward Plowman is such a fine-looking man, too,' she declared. 'Like Cardinal Newman.'

'Oh, no, Harriet,' protested Belinda. 'Cardinal Newman had a much bigger nose. And besides, he really did go *over*, you know, and I'm sure Edward Plowman would never do that.'

'Oh, then I must have been thinking of somebody else,' said Harriet vaguely. 'Anyway,' she went on, 'Mr Donne could certainly preach better sermons than the Archdeacon, I'm sure.' She pulled the dress off over her head. 'You needn't bother to oversew the seams – they won't show.'

When Belinda had finished the sewing she decided that she had better go over to the vicarage to see if she could help Agatha in any way. It did not take her long to reach the vicarage gate, as it was very near her own house. When they had finally decided to spend their old age together, Harriet had insisted that they should be well in touch with the affairs of the parish. Belinda had not felt so strongly about it, although when Archdeacon Hoccleve had been made vicar she was naturally glad that their house was so near his. She imagined friendly poppings in and out but somehow, dear Henry not being quite like other clergymen, it hadn't worked out like that. And then of course there was Agatha. It was difficult to be completely informal with her, either because of her father having been a bishop or for some more subtle reason, Belinda had never been quite sure which.

She walked up the vicarage drive. The Archdeacon had a hankering after the picturesque and would have liked a ha-ha, a ruined temple, grottoes, waterfalls and gloomily overhanging trees. He fancied himself to be rather like one of those eighteenth-century clergymen suffering from the spleen, but Agatha was a practical woman, who liked neat borders and smooth lawns, flowers in the front garden and vegetables at the back. So the vicarage garden, as Belinda saw it on this September morning, was admirably suited to a garden party but there were no grottoes.

Belinda walked up to the front door, but before she had time to ring the bell Agatha appeared, carrying many bundles of brightly coloured paper. She was wearing a plain but well-cut dress of striped Macclesfield silk and looked rather harassed.

'How are you, Agatha?' asked Belinda. 'I've come to see if there's anything I can do to help and I must see the Archdeacon about the Sunday School children's recitations.'

'Henry is having a bath,' said Agatha shortly.

Surely rather late? thought Belinda. It was past eleven and oughtn't an archdeacon to rise earlier than that?

'So of course you can't see him now,' continued Agatha in the same tone of voice, which implied that she had the privilege not allowed to Belinda of seeing an archdeacon in his bath. 'You will have to wait,' she concluded, with a note of something like triumph in her voice.

'Why, of course,' said Belinda meekly. Agatha always seemed to be most formidable in the mornings. In the evenings she was often quite affable and would talk about begonias and the best way to pickle walnuts.

'You seem very busy,' said Belinda, moving towards Agatha as if to help her. 'Can't I do something while I'm waiting for the Archdeacon?'

Agatha nodded reluctantly. 'I was going to arrange the garden-produce stall,' she said, thinking that Belinda Bede was rather a nuisance although she no doubt meant well. 'You might help me to pin the coloured paper round it. I thought green and orange and perhaps red would show off the vegetables rather nicely.'

'What lovely marrows!' exclaimed Belinda, catching sight of them among a heap of miscellaneous garden produce. They were gleaming yellow and dark green, with pale stripes. Surely the poor soil of the vicarage garden could not have produced such beauties?

'Yes, they are fine,' agreed Agatha. 'They are from Count Bianco's garden. He brought them round himself early this morning.'

'Poor old Count Bianco,' said Belinda gently. Ricardo Bianco was an Italian count, who for some unexplained reason had settled in the village many years ago. He was a gentle melancholy man, beloved by everyone for his generosity and courtly manners and he had admired Harriet Bede for more years than could now be remembered. He had the habit of asking her to marry him every now and then, and Harriet, although she always refused him, was really very fond of him and often asked his advice about her gardening problems. Gardening and his childhood in Naples were his chief topics of conversation, though he would occasionally enjoy a melancholy talk about his old friend John Akenside, who had been killed in a riot in Prague, when he had just been sitting at an open-air café taking a glass of wine, as was his custom in the evening, doing no harm to anybody. 'Ricardo is so *devoted* to Harriet,' said Belinda, giving the words a full meaning which was not lost on Agatha Hoccleve.

Agatha went rather pink and said angrily, 'Count Bianco comes of a very old Italian family. I always think he and Lady Clara Boulding would be very suited to each other, but of course her father's earldom was only a nineteenth-century creation,' she mused.

Belinda was rather annoyed at this. 'I don't think Lady Clara and Ricardo would be at all suited to each other,' she said, repeating his Christian name with triumph. 'Harriet and Ricardo have a great many tastes in common, especially gardening. Why, whenever he comes to our house he nearly always brings with him some roots or seeds . . .' here Belinda broke off, aware that this sounded rather ridiculous, but Agatha did not seem to have noticed. She was just opening her mouth to say something else, when their attention was diverted by somebody calling out in a loud voice.

Belinda recognized the voice as that of the Archdeacon. He was leaning out of one of the upper windows, calling to Agatha, and he sounded very peevish. Belinda thought he looked so handsome in his dark green dressing-gown with his hair all ruffled. The years had dealt kindly with him and he had grown neither bald nor fat. It was Agatha who seemed to have suffered most. Her pointed face had lost the elfin charm which had delighted many and now looked drawn and harassed. She had rheumatism too, but Belinda realized that she would have to have something out of self-defence and perhaps with the passing of the years it had become a reality. One never knew.

The voice went on calling. It seemed that the moths had got into the Archdeacon's grey suit and why had Agatha been so grossly neglectful as to let this happen? The tirade was audible to anyone in the garden or in the road beyond.

Belinda turned away from the window and began to hang festoons of green paper along the top of the stall. The gardener, who was weeding one of the flower beds near by, also turned away. He could not bear the Venerable Hoccleve, as the servants called him. He was a bit mad in his opinion, wanting yew trees on the lawn and something he called a ha-ha, which no gardener had ever heard of.

Eventually Agatha returned to the business of decorating, looking extremely annoyed, but not mentioning the incident. She began to take down all Belinda's decorations and arrange them another way. Belinda thought it better to say nothing, so they went on with their work in silence. At last Belinda, who felt rather uncomfortable, drew Agatha's attention to the arrangement of the marrows.

'I think they would look rather effective in a kind of pyramid, if it could be managed,' she suggested, thinking to herself that it would obviously be better if Agatha were to humour dear Henry a little more. But of course Belinda could hardly give an archdeacon's wife a few hints on how to manage her husband.

At that moment one of the marrows fell over and the pyramid had to be rebuilt. While they were doing this, the Archdeacon came out on to the lawn.

'Good morning,' he said, ignoring his wife. 'I see that I have kept you waiting, but so many annoying things have happened that it was quite impossible to be ready any sooner.' He darted a quick, angry glance at Agatha.

Belinda spoke hastily in order to change the subject.

'I've brought a list of the recitations the children have

learnt, so you can choose which ones you think best from it,' she said, knowing perfectly well that he would find fault with the pieces and ask why they had not been taught more Middle English lyrics or passages from Gower and Chaucer.

He smiled with an affectation of weariness and then sighed. 'Ah, yes. There is so much to be done before this afternoon. I haven't been able to sleep for thinking about it. Nobody can possibly know how much I have to do,' he went on, with another meaning glance at Agatha.

'Perhaps if you had got up earlier, Henry,' she said sharply. 'Florrie called you at eight. I was up at *seven*.'

The Archdeacon laughed and began to pace about the lawn with his hands in his pockets. Belinda was embarrassed and began to walk slowly towards the house. Eventually the Archdeacon followed. They walked together into his study. He was smiling to himself in a sardonic way that Belinda found very disconcerting. It was unsuitable for a clergyman to look sardonic. Perhaps Harriet was right to prefer the more conventional Mr Plowman and Mr Donne.

There was an awkward silence and to break it Belinda descended weakly to flattery.

'I did enjoy hearing you read *Urn Burial* last Sunday,' she said. 'It is so *very* fine and you read it so well.'

'Ah, yes. Do you remember when I used to read Milton to you?' he said, his thoughts going back to the days when Belinda's frank adoration had been so flattering. By this time he had forgotten how bored he had been by her constancy. Agatha never asked him to read aloud to her when they were alone together in the evenings. 'Do you remember the magnificent opening lines of *Samson Agonistes*?' he asked, warming to his subject and looking dangerously on the brink of reminding her of them. Indeed, the first words were already out of his mouth when Belinda interrupted him, and directed his attention to the matter in hand. There was of course nothing she would have liked better than to hear dear

Henry reciting Milton, but somehow with Agatha outside and so much to be done it didn't seem quite the thing. Also, it was the morning and it seemed a little odd to be thinking about poetry before luncheon.

'Now,' she said, 'what about these recitations? I have a list of the ones they know, so I think perhaps you'd better let me choose the most suitable ones. I know you must be very busy with other things,' she added soothingly, 'and even though Mr Donne can help you, I know that you like to see to everything personally.'

'I doubt whether our friend Donne will be much help,' said the Archdeacon. 'His sermons are very poor. He and Edward Plowman are about a match for each other.'

'Oh, but one must be tolerant,' said Belinda, 'and many people prefer a simple sermon. I've heard people say that Edward Plowman is considered quite a saint in his parish.'

The Archdeacon laughed rather bitterly. 'Do you wonder when his parish consists almost entirely of doting spinsters?' he said. It was one of the Archdeacon's grievances that people never made a fuss of him as they did of Father Plowman or of the younger curates, although he pretended to despise such adulation. And then too, Lady Clara Boulding, whose country seat lay midway between the two villages, had chosen to attend Plowman's church rather than his. The Archdeacon could not help feeling bitter about this, for although Belinda might put a pound note into the collection bag on Easter Sunday, it was hardly the same as Lady Clara's five or ten. In these days of poverty the spirit in which it was given counted for very little.

'You need not make fun of doting spinsters,' said Belinda, roused by his mockery. 'After all, it isn't always our fault . . .' she stopped in confusion, fearing that he might make some sarcastic retort.

'No, women like to have something to dote on,' he said mildly enough. 'I have noticed that. And we in the Church are usually the victims.'

'We are *all* in the Church,' said Belinda gently. 'I think I should go out into the garden again and help Agatha. There must still be a great deal to do.'

Out in the garden, Agatha, surrounded now by several willing helpers, for she was popular among the church workers because of her distinguished ecclesiastical connections, had finished decorating and arranging the garden-produce stall.

The vicarage garden was beginning to look like a fair-ground. Stalls, coconut shies, bran-tubs and even a fortune-teller's booth had taken root on the lawn. The Archdeacon always hated this annual garden party and tried to have as little to do with it as possible, although he had to put in an appearance to fawn on the more distinguished visitors. There was always a possibility that Lady Clara Boulding might decide to come to his church, which was really nearer if one walked across the fields, although it was difficult to imagine anyone as impressive as Lady Clara doing that.

'It looks as if everything is finished,' said Belinda. 'I don't feel as if I have done my share.'

'You have put up with my ill-humour for ten minutes,' said the Archdeacon, 'which is more than anyone else could have done.'

Belinda flushed with embarrassment and secret pleasure. She felt herself to be somehow exalted above the groups of busy women, who had been arranging pyramids of apples, filling bran-tubs and decorating stalls with coloured paper. Once, she knew, she *had* been different, and perhaps after all the years had left her with a little of that difference. Perhaps she was still an original shining like a comet, mingling no water with her wine. But only very occasionally, mostly she was just like everyone else, rather less efficient, if anything. Even her paper decorations had been taken down and rearranged. There was nothing of her handiwork left on the garden-produce stall.

'Why, look,' she exclaimed, unable to deal with the Archdeacon's curious compliment, 'there's Edith Liversidge. Whatever is she doing?' For Miss Liversidge, looking even more dishevelled than usual, was pushing her way through a thick clump of rhododendrons on the opposite side of the lawn.

'Oh, Archdeacon,' she called in her rough, mannish voice, 'there you are! I've been looking everywhere for you.'

'Well, Miss Liversidge, I hardly see why you should have expected to find me in the rhododendrons,' he said.

'Oh, that's the treasure hunt,' she explained. 'I've just been arranging some of the clues. We shall have everybody tied up in knots this afternoon.'

'That will certainly be diverting,' said the Archdeacon politely, 'but I had imagined it was only for the younger people.'

'Oh, nonsense, everyone will be encouraged to join in. Now, what I really wanted to see you about was the cloakroom arrangements. Lavatories, you know. What has been done?' Edith rapped out the question with brusque efficiency.

Belinda turned away in embarrassment. Surely Edith could have asked Agatha and need not have troubled the Archdeacon with such an unsuitable thing? But he appeared to be enjoying the conversation and entered into the discussion with grave courtesy.

'I cannot really say. I had imagined that people would use their own discretion,' he ventured.

'Children are not noted for their discretion,' said Edith bluntly, 'and even grown-ups aren't angels.'

The Archdeacon smiled. 'No, not even the higher orders of the clergy would claim to be quite that. Perhaps you can help us, Miss Liversidge, we all know your experience in these matters.'

'Yes, but of course it wasn't at all the same thing in the Balkans after the war,' said Edith, perhaps unnecessarily. 'Still, I have been thinking things over. We must have clear notices put up. I've got Mr Matthews from the Art School at work on them now.'

'Poor Matthews, a prostitution of his talents, I feel,' said the Archdeacon. 'I think Gothic lettering would be most suitable. What is your opinion, Miss Bede?'

Poor Belinda, confused at being drawn into the conversation, could only murmur that in her opinion the largest and clearest kind of lettering would obviously be the best.

Miss Liversidge looked from one to the other impatiently.

'I thought the ladies should use the ground-floor cloakroom and the gentlemen the place behind the toolshed.'

'The Place Behind the Toolshed, what a sinister sound that has,' mused the Archdeacon. 'I'm sure your arrangements will be admirable, Miss Liversidge, though perhaps hardly necessary.'

'We shall see about that,' she said in a dark tone, and then stumped off in search of her relative, Miss Aspinall, calling her as if she were a dog, 'Connie! Connie! Come along! Time to go home to lunch.'

Miss Aspinall, who had been enjoying a snobbish little talk with Agatha, hurried after her. She could never keep pace with Edith and was always a few steps behind her.

'I think Edith Liversidge is really disgusting,' said Harriet indignantly. 'Mr Donne and I could overhear what she was saying from the tea garden. He seemed most embarrassed.'

'Ah, what it is to be young,' sighed the Archdeacon. 'Or perhaps he is what the higher orders of the clergy would not claim to be. One never knows.'

'He is an excellent preacher,' said Harriet stoutly, if irrelevantly, 'and he seems to have the coconuts *very* well organized. Now Mr Donne,' she called, bringing him into the group, 'don't forget that you promised to let me win a coconut.'

'Ah, Miss Bede, I'm sure your skill will win the biggest one of all,' said Mr Donne gallantly.

At this point Belinda thought it would be as well if they went home to luncheon. They would need to reserve all their strength for the afternoon, she explained.

CHAPTER THREE

'DON'T YOU think you would be more comfortable in low-heeled shoes, dear?' suggested Belinda tentatively. 'One's feet always get so tired standing about.' She glanced down at her own – long, English gentlewoman's feet she always thought them, sensibly clad in shoes that were rather too heavy for the printed crêpe de Chine dress and coatee she was wearing.

Harriet glanced down too. 'I always think low heels are so dowdy,' she said. 'Besides, high heels are definitely the fashion now.'

'Yes, I suppose they are,' agreed Belinda, for Harriet always knew things like that. And yet, she thought, at our age, surely all that was necessary was to dress suitably and if possible in good taste, without really thinking of fashion? With the years one ought to have grown beyond such thoughts but somehow one never did, and Belinda set out for the afternoon conscious that she was wearing dowdy shoes.

As they walked to the vicarage, Belinda regulating her normally brisk step in consideration for Harriet's high heels, they were overtaken by Count Bianco, who was escorting Miss Liversidge and Miss Aspinall, both of whom were dressed exactly as Belinda had anticipated. Count Bianco wore a light grey suit and a panama hat. He carried a stick and grey gloves and there was a fine rose in his buttonhole. As they came together he gave them a courtly bow, which, from anybody else, might have seemed exaggerated.

'How charming you are looking, Miss Harriet,' he said,

'and you also, Miss Belinda,' he added, as a courteous afterthought. 'Poor old John Akenside,' he went on meditatively, 'how he loved the hot weather.'

'Nonsense, Ricardo,' said Edith Liversidge, 'he always went as red as a lobster in the sun.' She had known the Çount's friend in what she called her Balkans Days and it was rumoured that he had been very fond of her, but had been too shy to declare himself. It seemed odd to think that anyone could have loved Edith, who seemed a person to inspire fear and respect rather than any more tender emotion, but, as Belinda had once suggested, perhaps the unpleasant nature of her work in the Balkans had hardened her and she had once been more lovable.

They walked on to the lawn where a group of people had assembled. Belinda could see the Archdeacon standing at the top of the front-door steps, against a background of Victorian stained glass, the vicarage being built in the Gothic style. She thought he looked splendid, and somehow the glass set off his good looks.

Lady Clara Boulding was to open the garden party officially at half-past two and as she had now arrived, there seemed no reason why she should not get on with it at once. But the crowd was obviously waiting for something. Agatha Hoccleve, who was standing by her husband, nudged him and said in an agitated and audible whisper, 'Henry, a *prayer*.'

The Archdeacon started. He had been wondering whether Lady Clara would give some definite contribution to the church-roof fund as well as buying things at the stalls. He cleared his throat.

'Let us ask for God's blessing on our endeavours,' he said, in a loud voice which quite startled some people.

Belinda looked down at the grass and then at Agatha's neat suede shoes, so much more suited to the occasion than her own.

The Archdeacon began to recite a prayer. *O Lord God, who*

seest that we put not our trust in anything that we do, mercifully grant that by Thy Power we may be defended against all adversity. . . .

Harriet looked at Belinda and frowned. The Archdeacon always chose such unsuitable prayers. *Prevent us O Lord in all our doings*, was the obviously correct one for such an occasion. These little departures from convention always annoyed her.

Belinda, on the other hand, was thinking loyally, what an excellent choice! It strikes just the right note of humility. When Henry prays for defence from adversity, he must mean too much confidence in our own powers. One knew that pride often came before a fall. Or perhaps he was not referring to the garden party specifically, but taking in the larger sphere of life outside it . . . here Belinda's thoughts became confused and a doubt crept into her mind, which was quickly and loyally pushed back. For it could not be that dear Henry had just said the first prayer that came into his head. . . .

There was a short pause. Count Bianco replaced his panama hat and everyone began to move, relieved to be normal once more.

But they were not to be released yet. Lady Clara enjoyed opening garden parties and bazaars. Indeed, apart from attending memorial services in fashionable London churches, it was her chief recreation. She stood on a grassy bank, slightly raised above the rest of the crowd. She was still a handsome woman, and if her speech contained rather too much of her late husband's meaningless parliamentary phraseology, her voice was nevertheless pleasant and soothing. Miss Aspinall, who had detached herself from Miss Liversidge in order to be among the foremost of the little group who would go round the stalls with Lady Clara, was listening with a pathetically eager expression on her thin face. Nobody knew how much Edith got on her nerves and how different it all was from the days when she had been companion to Lady Grudge in Belgrave Square. Treated like one of the family, *such* kindness . . . Connie's eyes filled with tears and she had to turn away.

At last Lady Clara stepped down from her grassy platform and made her way towards the stalls, accompanied by Agatha and the Archdeacon, who had a particularly ingratiating smile on his face. At a respectful distance behind them came Miss Aspinall with a group of lady helpers, who were hurrying to get to their places at the stalls. Lady Clara's progress was slow and stately but profitable. She bought some jam, two marrows, half a dozen lavender sachets, a tea cosy, a pair of bed socks, some paper spills in a fancy case and an embroidered *Radio Times* cover.

Belinda, now busy at the garden-produce stall, was wondering whether she ought to wrap Lady Clara's marrows up, and if so what was the best way of doing it. They had only newspapers for wrapping, so she chose *The Times* as being the most suitable and made them up into a rather clumsy parcel. Lady Clara's chauffeur was to collect them later.

Not long after this Agatha came back to the stall and began to fluster the helpers by rearranging them and collecting all the money together into one tin, so that they were all tumbling over each other to get change instead of each one having her own little pile.

'What's this?' asked Agatha sharply, pointing to the *Times*-shrouded parcel which Belinda had put into a corner.

'Oh, that's Lady Clara's marrows,' Belinda explained.

'Wrapped in newspaper?' Agatha's tone was expressive. 'I'm afraid that won't do at all.' She produced some blue tissue paper from a secret hiding-place and began to undo Belinda's parcel.

'Oh, dear, I'm so sorry, I didn't know there was any other paper,' said Belinda in confusion. 'I saw them lying there and I thought perhaps they ought to be wrapped up and put aside in case anybody sold them by mistake.'

'I don't think anybody would be so stupid as to do that,'

said Agatha evenly. 'They were the two finest marrows on the stall, I chose them myself.'

'Oh, well . . .' Belinda gave a weak little laugh. All this fuss about two marrows. But it might go deeper than that, although it did not do to think so.

'Perhaps you would like to go and have tea,' said Agatha, who was having difficulty with the bulk of the marrows and the fragility of the tissue paper and did not want Belinda to see. 'We may as well go in turns.'

'Well, yes, if it isn't too early,' said Belinda.

'Oh, no, Lady Clara is already having hers. She has gone with Count Bianco.' Agatha stood up and reached for a ball of string.

Belinda felt herself hurrying away, routed was perhaps the word, Agatha triumphant. It was a pity they sometimes had these little skirmishes, especially when Agatha was so often triumphant. All over two marrows, even if they were the finest on the stall.

Belinda looked around to see if she could find Harriet. She felt that she wanted to tell somebody about the marrows and perhaps laugh over them. Harriet's healthy indignation would do her as much good as a cup of tea, she thought. But Harriet was nowhere to be seen. And where was the Archdeacon? It would be just like him to retire to the house and have a bath. But he had already had one today, as Belinda knew, so she guessed that he was probably attending on some of the more distinguished visitors.

As she entered the tea garden she saw Harriet sitting at a table with the curate. Harriet was handing him a plate of cakes and urging him in her penetrating voice to try one of the pink ones which she had made specially for him. Perhaps it will be better if I don't disturb them, thought Belinda, turning round to look for a vacant place at one of the other tables. And then she came face to face with the Archdeacon. He also wanted his tea, and as they had so often had tea together in the past what could be more natural than that they should have it together this afternoon?

They sat down at a table for two. Belinda began to be assailed by various doubts. What would people think to see her having tea with the Archdeacon while his wife was still working tirelessly at the garden-produce stall? It was a pity really to worry about what people thought, but, Belinda flattered herself, she wasn't entirely old and unattractive, even in her sensible shoes, and she still had the marrows on her conscience, although she did not feel that she could tell the Archdeacon about them.

He on the other hand had no such scruples. Belinda began to wish that he wouldn't talk so loudly, for although she knew that it was only one of his little oddnesses to complain about his wife, other people might not realize this. So she put two lumps of sugar into his tea, and tried as tactfully as she could to change the subject of the conversation.

'But Agatha has been so busy arranging things for the garden party and the concert tonight,' said Belinda in a low voice. 'She can't see to everything at once.' Raising her voice, she went on, 'Speaking of the concert reminds me that Harriet is still undecided as to what she is going to play. Of course she has a large repertoire, but one must choose something suitable and not too long . . .' Belinda babbled on. ' . . . she's very anxious to play a Brahms intermezzo, but it may be a little heavy for a village concert. I thought perhaps some Mendelssohn, some of the *Songs without Words* are so charming . . .' She looked at the Archdeacon anxiously, to see if he had yet forgotten Agatha's negligence in letting the moths get into his grey suit.

His face betrayed that he had not. In fact all the bright conversation about the concert seemed to have been wasted on him. 'I don't think you'd have done that,' he said thoughtfully, gazing at a piece of bread and butter on his plate.

Belinda saw that it was no good trying to change the

subject yet. He must be humoured out of it. She seemed to be having a difficult afternoon altogether, what with the episode of the marrows and now having to humour the Archdeacon. Archdeacons ought not to need humouring, she told herself angrily. Supposing Henry were a bishop, could one still expect no improvement?

'What are you smiling at?' asked the Archdeacon crossly. 'People look very foolish smiling at nothing.'

'I wasn't smiling at nothing,' retorted Belinda. 'I was wondering if you'd still make such a fuss about unimportant trifles if you were a bishop.'

'Unimportant trifles! The only good suit I have ruined, and you call it an unimportant trifle.'

'We are supposed not to take heed of what we shall wear,' said Belinda unconvincingly.

'My dear Belinda, we are not in the Garden of Eden. That is no solution to the problem. We may as well face the facts. Agatha ought not to have let the moth get into that suit. It was her duty to see that they didn't. I am sure that you would have seen that it was put away with moth balls . . .' the Archdeacon's voice had now grown so loud that people at the other tables were beginning to look at them with interest and amusement. Belinda felt most embarrassed.

'It would have smelt of camphor then and you would probably have disliked that,' she said, almost in a whisper.

The Archdeacon gave a shout of laughter at this. Suddenly he was in a good temper again, fell on a plate of cakes and began to eat ravenously. 'I was too busy to have any luncheon,' he explained. 'So many tiresome things to do.'

'It will be nice for you to go away for a holiday,' ventured Belinda.

The Archdeacon sighed heavily. 'Ah, if only I could.'

'But now that Mr Donne is here, surely it can be managed?'

'One cannot leave the flock without a shepherd,' said the Archdeacon in a mocking tone.

'But he said – I mean we heard – that Agatha was going to Karlsbad in October,' said Belinda, urged on by curiosity. 'Surely you will be going too?'

'Alas, no.' The Archdeacon finished the last cake. 'And even if I were, it would hardly be a holiday for me.'

Belinda could think of no reply to make to this and none seemed to be expected. She could neither agree nor protest, she felt, but did what seemed to her the best she could by getting up from the table and saying that she really must get back to the stall. 'I must go and relieve Agatha,' she said. 'I see she hasn't been for her tea yet.'

'It will please her not to have any,' said the Archdeacon. 'I wonder that you have had any. I thought women enjoyed missing their meals and making martyrs of themselves.'

'We may do it, but I think we can leave the enjoyment of it to the men,' said Belinda, pleased at having thought of an answer. But Henry was really too bad, there was no knowing what he might say next. And he was *not* going to Karlsbad . . . She hoped nobody had overheard their conversation. It had really been most unsuitable, but somehow she felt better for it and had almost forgotten the episode of the marrows.

Back at the garden-produce stall, Belinda saw Agatha, looking rather tired and flustered, bundling what remained of the flowers, fruit and vegetables on to the front of the stall.

'Oh, there you are,' she exclaimed, making Belinda feel that she had been away too long.

'Yes, you must be longing for your tea, but surely you could have gone before now? Wouldn't Miss Liversidge or Miss Aspinall have taken charge of the stall?' said Belinda, doing the best she could.

'Oh, well, I may as well go now,' said Agatha grudgingly, 'we seem to have taken quite a lot of money.'

'Yes, and the tea garden has been crowded. The Archdeacon was still there when I left,' Belinda added, thinking that this might encourage Agatha.

'I have had no luncheon,' she said. 'I shall really be glad of a cup of tea.'

'Oh, dear, I wish I'd known that, then you could have gone first,' said Belinda. Had there been no luncheon at all at the vicarage today? Surely a bad arrangement, or had the Archdeacon and his wife wished to outdo each other in self-denial?

'Well, Belinda, I expect *you* enjoyed your tea,' said Harriet, advancing towards the stall.

Belinda was thankful that Agatha was out of hearing. 'Yes, I thought the cakes were lovely,' she said.

'You and the Archdeacon looked so cosy. Having a nice conversation about moth balls, too, most domestic. What a *pity* it is about Agatha. They have really nothing in common.'

'Oh, Harriet, you're quite wrong,' said Belinda stoutly. 'Agatha is a most intelligent woman. She knows a great deal about medieval English literature. And then there's *palaeography*,' she continued, as if her emphatic tone would explain its importance in the married life of Agatha and the Archdeacon.

'Oh, yes, that's about apes, isn't it?' said Harriet, losing interest in the subject. 'Do you think a fur cape would be too hot for the concert this evening? The gold lamé jacket doesn't really go so well with my blue as the white fur. Besides, it's rather severe and needs something to soften it.'

Eventually Harriet decided to wear the white fur cape, and everyone agreed that she looked very handsome, although one of the more spiteful Sunday School teachers whispered to her friend that she suspected it was not real ermine, but only shaved coney.

At the beginning of the concert, the Archdeacon, looking very striking in clerical evening dress, made a charming little speech. He seemed to have recovered completely from his bad temper of the afternoon, because they had made a splendid lot of money at the garden party and there was a good attendance at the concert. He beamed on the crowd of zealous church workers, as he praised their untiring efforts, and they in their turn were so greatly carried away by his charm that they forgot all his annoying oddities and began to think themselves fortunate to have such a distinguished-looking vicar.

Belinda was sitting by Count Bianco. She had seldom seen him so animated. He did not refer even once to the sad death of his friend John Akenside. After Harriet had played her Brahms intermezzo, he declared in an enthusiastic mixture of English and Italian that for him everything would be an anticlimax after this.

Belinda found herself thinking, as she often did, that it would be an excellent thing if Harriet would marry the Count. He was wealthy and he had a beautiful house and garden: and, moreover, as Agatha had remarked that morning, he came of a very old Italian family. Belinda was sure that he would have no objection to Harriet making cakes and other dainties for the curates. He was such a kind-hearted man.

In the meantime a child was reciting, rather too fast, but Belinda caught one or two lines.

In dingles deep and mountains hoar
They combated the tusky boar.

She tried to remember why the Archdeacon had been anxious to include this, for it was not a particularly suitable poem. Then she realized that it was in order that he might explain to an audience not really interested in such linguistic niceties, the history of the rare word *dingle*. How it is first known in the twelfth or thirteenth century in a work called *Sawles Warde*: then it is revived by the Elizabethans, who gave it to Milton – you remember it in *Comus*, of course. . . .

The Reverend Edward Plowman, sitting in the front row by Agatha, listened to the explanations jealously. How like

Hoccleve to show off his knowledge on such an unsuitable occasion! Father Plowman, as he was called by his devoted parishioners, was not a clever man. He had failed to take Honours in Theology, but he worked hard in his parish and the elaborate ritual of his services was ample compensation for the intellectual poverty of his sermons. He was greatly beloved by his flock and one Christmas he had received so many pairs of hand-worked slippers that he gave the Archdeacon a pair. The gift was accepted rather grudgingly, especially as they were a size too small. This evening Father Plowman was not wearing his usual costume of cassock and biretta and his evening dress was less well cut than the Archdeacon's. He shifted uneasily, reflecting that even the best seats were hard. But soon there would be an interval. Would there be refreshments? he wondered. He tried to remember whether they had had refreshments at the last concert. He could hardly ask Mrs Hoccleve. These recitations were really rather heavy going, though this was better. *Time wasted is existence, used is life* . . . one might almost use a line like that for a text. He began to meditate on the theme, although he did not really approve of these literary sermons. Still, he had no doubt that he could do them as well as Hoccleve.

In the interval, during which he enjoyed some excellent coffee and cakes, Father Plowman talked to the elder Miss Bede about the death-watch beetle and gave her a short dissertation on its habits. This put Belinda into an elegiac mood and somehow prepared her for the next item on the programme, which was a harp solo by Miss Aspinall. There was certainly something elegiac about poor Connie. Her thin, useless hands, her fluttering grey dress – surely a cast-off from Belgrave Square? – even the instrument itself with its Victorian association, made Belinda think of past glories, of more elegant gatherings than this one, at which Connie might have played. The little beaded bag came with her on to the platform and she took out of it a little lace-edged handkerchief, on which she wiped her hands before she started to play. What she played Belinda hardly knew, but it had a melancholy air and the applause which greeted it was restrained though sincere. The village people thought poor Miss Aspinall was not quite right in the head and considered it very clever of her to be able to play at all.

Certainly their most noisy enthusiasm was reserved for the curate, who appeared last on the programme and had a sensational success. Belinda read in her programme that he was to sing *Believe me if all those endearing young charms* and *The Lost Chord*, both very suitable songs and particular favourites of hers. Like all sentimental people she cherished the idea of loving a dear ruin, and found her eyes filling with tears as he sang the affecting words. Count Bianco too was very much moved, except that he thought of himself as the ruin, perhaps being loved by Harriet.

Belinda could not see the Archdeacon very well, but she could not help feeling that he was a little displeased at the tumultuous applause which greeted Mr Donne's songs. Some of the rougher members of the audience, accommodated on benches at the back of the hall, were even stamping their feet and whistling. There was no doubt of his success and popularity.

'The Archdeacon was looking quite annoyed,' said Harriet with satisfaction, as they drank their Ovaltine before going to bed that evening. 'Imagine *him* singing, though. I think Agatha was pleased at Mr Donne's success, she would do anything to disagree with the Archdeacon.'

Belinda was too tired to argue. 'I thought poor Connie played very nicely,' she said.

'Oh, yes,' agreed Harriet, 'and you should have heard Edith talking. She seems to think the whole success of the garden party was due to her arrangements. I didn't see anybody disappearing behind the toolshed though, did you, Belinda? At least, nobody we know, that is.'

'No, Harriet, I did not,' said Belinda in a weary but firm tone. 'After all, most of us were there only two or three hours.'

'Yes, I suppose that's really nothing,' said Harriet yawning.

CHAPTER FOUR

'I THOUGHT we might have a cauliflower cheese for lunch today,' Harriet announced at breakfast one morning. 'We shall only need a light meal as we are having the duck this evening.'

'Oh, of course, Mr Donne is coming again, isn't he,' said Belinda. 'I think perhaps it's a mistake to ask him *too* often, you know. It seems no time since he was last here.'

'Why, Belinda, it's nearly three weeks,' said Harriet indignantly.

'Yes, I suppose it must be. How quickly the time goes.' Belinda began piling up the plates, scraping fish bones from one to another. Suddenly she stopped, and an expression almost of horror came over her face. 'But Harriet,' she said, 'Miss Prior is coming today. Had you forgotten that?'

'Yes, I had, but I don't see what difference it makes,' said Harriet. 'It's rather a good thing, really. She'll be able to patch that chair cover that's getting so worn, and perhaps start on my new velvet dress.'

'But, Harriet, we *can't* give her only cauliflower cheese,' went on Belinda with unusual persistence. 'You know how she enjoys her meals and we always give her meat of some kind.'

'You surely aren't suggesting that we should have the duck for lunch, are you?' asked Harriet with a note of challenge in her voice.

'Well, I don't know, really . . .' Belinda hesitated. She was a little afraid of her sister sometimes. 'Would it matter if we gave Mr Donne cauliflower cheese? I'm sure he wouldn't mind. We could have some soup and a fairly substantial sweet, and with coffee afterwards it would be quite a nice little meal. I'm sure I would think it very nice. After all, when we had supper with Edith Liversidge on Friday we only had baked beans and *no* sweet, as far as I remember, just some coffee and biscuits . . .' poor Belinda floundered on, disconcerted by Harriet's stony silence.

'Miss Prior will just have to put up with cauliflower cheese,' said Harriet firmly. 'If you expect Mr Donne to, why shouldn't she?'

'Oh, dear, I can't explain exactly. We always seem to have this argument every time she comes,' said Belinda. 'But one feels that perhaps Miss Prior's whole life is just a putting up with second best all the time. And then she's so easily offended. I suppose it's cowardly of me, but I do hate any kind of *atmosphere*.'

The trouble was that Miss Prior wasn't entirely the meek person one expected a little sewing woman to be. Belinda had two feelings about her – Pity and Fear, like Aristotle's *Poetics*, she thought confusedly. She was so very nearly a gentlewoman in some ways that one felt that she might even turn out to be related to a clergyman or something like that. She could never have her meals with Emily in the kitchen, nor would she presume to take them with Belinda and Harriet. They must be taken in to her on a tray. She was so touchy, so conscious of her position, so quick to detect the slightest suspicion of patronage. One had to be *very* careful with Miss Prior.

She arrived at ten o'clock punctually, a little dried-up woman of uncertain age, with a brisk, birdlike manner and brown, darting eyes. Her dress was drab and dateless, but immaculate, and she wore what appeared to be rather a good cameo brooch at the neck.

She did her work in the little morning-room on the

ground floor, where Belinda usually did the flowers. This was generally tidied beforehand, but today, on showing her in, Belinda noticed to her dismay that it had not been done. Everything looked dusty, there were bits of cotton on the carpet, and worst of all, two vases of dead chrysanthemums. Their stems showed black and slimy in the yellow water.

'Good morning, Miss Prior,' Belinda's tone was bright and welcoming, but she looked a little harassed, wondering why Emily had not dusted the room and how the dead flowers could have been forgotten. She had taken them out of the drawing-room hastily the day before, when Lady Clara Boulding had been seen coming to the door.

'I think I would like the window open,' declared Miss Prior. 'I'm afraid the smell of chrysanthemums always upsets me.'

'I'm so sorry . . .' Belinda moved in the direction of the window.

'Oh, don't trouble, Miss Bede, I can manage perfectly well.' To Belinda's anxious eyes Miss Prior looked unusually fragile as she lifted the heavy frame.

'There . . .' Miss Prior took a deep breath of the sharp October air, then glanced round the room, alert and birdlike. 'And perhaps I could have a duster?'

'Oh, *dear* . . .' Belinda was almost speechless with confusion. 'I'm afraid Emily doesn't seem to have done it this morning' – that was obvious – 'and I know how particular you are.'

Miss Prior smiled. 'Well, I wouldn't like to say that, Miss Bede. I can hardly afford to be in *my* position, but I think we all work better in bright, clean surroundings, don't you?'

'Yes, of course, I'm *so* sorry . . .'

'That's quite all right, Miss Bede. You will make me think I am being a nuisance.' Miss Prior went to the sewing machine and drew off the cover with a brisk movement. 'Now, what is it to be this morning?'

'I think the chair covers are the most important, and then there are the new bathroom curtains and some sheets to be put sides to middle . . .' Belinda went on rapidly, as if speaking quickly would make the work seem less, 'and my sister was wondering whether you could start on a dress for her out of some brown velvet she's got. Perhaps you could begin to cut it out?'

'Very good, Miss Bede, I will commence with the chair covers,' said Miss Prior.

Belinda was saved any further explanations by the appearance of Harriet, who strode into the room with a bundle of silky velvet in her arms.

'Good morning, Miss Prior,' she said. 'Now I want you to start on this dress first of all, if you will.'

Belinda waited rather fearfully, but she need not have been afraid, for Miss Prior seemed much meeker with Harriet and began to admire the stuff and ask her what kind of style she had in mind.

'Oh, I've bought a *Vogue* pattern,' said Harriet, 'size 38, so you can just follow that.'

Miss Prior darted a doubtful upward glance at the bulk of Harriet towering over her. 'I wonder if it's going to be big enough on the *hips*?' she ventured. 'That's where you usually need it, isn't it?' She took out her familiar tape-measure which was in a little case shaped like a frog. 'Lady Boulding on the bust, Miss Harriet on the hips, that's what I always say to myself,' she chanted brightly.

Belinda laughed. 'Don't you say anything for me, Miss Prior?'

'Oh, well, Miss Bede, you never wear very *fitting* dresses, do you, if you see what I mean? A few inches here or there doesn't make much difference.'

'No, I suppose it doesn't,' said Belinda, depressed by this picture of herself in shapeless, unfashionable garments.

'Now, Mrs Hoccleve,' went on Miss Prior, turning the

knife in the wound, 'she *has* got some lovely things. Not that I make much for her, you know, except a few summer dresses, like I do for Lady Clara. But her clothes are from the *best* houses. She's just got a lovely navy two-piece with a lemon blouse . . .' Miss Prior's voice trailed off into a kind of rapture.

It isn't right, thought Belinda indignantly, for a clergyman's wife to get her clothes from the best houses. She ought to be a comfortable, shabby sort of person, in an old tweed coat and skirt or a sagging stockinette jumper suit. Her hats should be shapeless and of no particular style and colour. Like my old gardening hat.

'Would you like a cup of tea, Miss Prior?' she said aloud. 'I am just going to make some.'

'Thank you, Miss Bede, I was just thinking I should like a cup. I find I can start my work better after a cup of tea. There's quite a nip in the air these mornings and I had to breakfast earlier than usual today.'

Miss Prior's tone was uncomplaining, even bright, but Belinda felt she could bear no more and hurried out of the room to put the kettle on.

'I don't think today is going very well,' she remarked to Harriet, when they were alone drinking their own tea. 'First of all the room wasn't dusted and I'd forgotten to throw away those dead chrysanthemums, and then Miss Prior made me feel as if I really ought to have offered tea sooner. I wonder whether she would have preferred cocoa?' Belinda looked worried. 'It's more sustaining if one has had an early breakfast. Still, she is having a piece of cake with her tea.'

'Oh, and there was no paper in the downstairs lavatory,' chortled Harriet. 'She came to me just now, *so* confidential. I couldn't think what she was going to say.'

'Oh, dear,' sighed Belinda, 'I meant to get some more toilet rolls yesterday.'

'I just gave her an old *Church Times*,' said Harriet airily.

'Oh, Harriet, I wish you hadn't done that. I feel Miss Prior is the kind of person who wouldn't like to use the *Church Times*. And I'm still not quite happy about giving her cauliflower cheese.'

Belinda continued to be anxious about Miss Prior's lunch, even though she herself supervised the laying of the tray which Emily was to take in to her.

'It certainly *looked* very nice,' she said, helping herself to a rather smaller portion of the cauliflower cheese than she had given to Miss Prior, 'and I asked Emily to be sure to wash the cauliflower *very* well and to put plenty of cheese in it.'

Harriet helped herself liberally and ate with enjoyment.

'I think the damson flan will make quite a good contrast,' went on Belinda. 'I know she will like that.'

'Oh, I wish you'd stop worrying about Miss Prior,' said Harriet in exasperation.

'I think I will just look in and see if she is all right,' said Belinda when she had finished her meal. 'I expect she would like some coffee.'

Belinda hesitated for a moment outside the door of the morning-room. She could hear the whirr of the sewing machine inside, but Miss Prior never spent very long over her meals. She did not like to be seen in the act of eating or drinking, it seemed to make her more conscious of her position.

Belinda opened the door and went in. Her heart sank when she saw the tray on the little table, for although everything else had been eaten, the cauliflower cheese had been pushed to one side of the plate and was almost untouched.

'Oh, dear, I'm afraid you haven't enjoyed your lunch, Miss Prior,' said Belinda, who now felt near to tears. 'Don't you like cauliflower cheese?'

'Oh, yes, Miss Bede, I do sometimes,' said Miss Prior in an offhand tone, not looking up from her work.

Belinda went on standing in the doorway watching Miss

Prior negotiating an awkward bit of chair cover. Then she looked again at the tray, wondering what she could say next. And then, in a flash, she realized what it was. It was almost a relief to know, to see it there, the long, greyish caterpillar. Dead now, of course, but unmistakable. It needed a modern poet to put this into words. Eliot, perhaps.

Belinda burst into a torrent of apologies. How careless of Emily not to wash the cauliflower more thoroughly! How unfortunate that it should have been Miss Prior who had got the caterpillar!

'I'm afraid I didn't feel like going on with it after that,' said Miss Prior almost smugly.

'No, of course not, I quite understand,' said Belinda. But she did not really understand. If this had happened to her in somebody else's house she would have pretended she hadn't seen it and gone on eating. It might have required courage, but she would have done it. 'You must be hungry still,' she went on, 'perhaps you would like a poached egg, or two poached eggs? Emily could easily do them.'

Miss Prior gave a little laugh. 'Well, no, Miss Bede, thank you all the same. It would seem funny to have a meal the wrong way round like that, wouldn't it? You wouldn't fancy that yourself now, would you?'

'If I were really hungry I don't think I should mind,' said Belinda bravely. 'But you must have an egg with your tea. Perhaps that will make up for it.'

'Thank you, Miss Bede, that would be very nice. I am going to the vicarage tomorrow,' Miss Prior went on conversationally, putting down her work for a moment. 'Mrs Hoccleve wants one or two things done before she goes away.'

'I'm sure you wouldn't get a caterpillar in your cauliflower cheese there,' said Belinda lightly.

Miss Prior made a noise like a snort. 'It might be about all I *would* get,' she said. '*Very* poor meals there.' She lowered her voice, 'Between ourselves, Miss Bede, Mrs Hoccleve doesn't keep a good table. At least, *I* never see any proof of it. An old dried-up scrap of cheese or a bit of cottage pie, *no* sweet, sometimes. I've heard the maids say so, too, you know how these things get about. Scarcely any meat except at the week-end, the Sunday roast, you know. You always have such nice meals, Miss Bede, and you give me just the same as you have yourselves, I know that. After all, it might just as easily have been you or Miss Harriet that got the unwelcome visitor today,' she concluded with a little giggle.

Belinda's eyes filled with tears and she experienced one of those sudden moments of joy that sometimes come to us in the middle of an ordinary day. Her heart like a singing bird, and all because Agatha didn't keep as good a table as she did and Miss Prior had forgiven her for the caterpillar, and the afternoon sun streaming in through the window over it all. 'You're doing that chair cover *beautifully*, Miss Prior,' she said warmly, 'and how well you've got on with Miss Harriet's dress.'

'It really does pay to show her a little consideration,' she said to Harriet afterwards. 'I'm sure she works better when one does. Besides, I'm afraid she's sometimes made to feel inferior, poor soul. Next time she comes we'll have something really nice for lunch, perhaps even a chicken,' she mused.

But Harriet's thoughts were already with Mr Donne and the duck they were to have that evening. Could they perhaps have something original served with it, like the orange salad they had had at Count Bianco's? One wanted to give people really interesting food.

'It was a good idea to give Miss Prior an egg for her tea,' went on Belinda, 'I think it made up for the caterpillar.'

'Of course, Mr Donne *may* prefer apple sauce, though it would be more ordinary,' said Harriet thoughtfully.

So the sisters continued antiphonally, each busy with her own line of thought. But at last they found themselves in agreement on the subject of Harriet's brown velvet dress. It was going to be very successful and the new bracelet-length sleeves were most becoming. 'Not even Agatha has a dress with the new sleeves,' said Harriet proudly.

Belinda felt a little depressed at being reminded of Agatha and her clothes from the 'best houses', but soon brightened up when she remembered Miss Prior's remarks about her poor table.

'Do you know, Harriet,' she said, 'Miss Prior told me that the only time they have meat at the vicarage is at the week-end? I can't believe that, really, and yet I've always had a suspicion that Agatha was just the tiniest bit mean.'

'Well, it's a good thing Mr Donne doesn't have to live there,' said Harriet stoutly.

CHAPTER FIVE

ONE AFTERNOON Harriet set out for the curate's lodgings, carrying a large basket. Besides a cake and some apple jelly, she was taking some very special late plums which she had been guarding jealously for the last few weeks. She hurried along, hoping that she would not meet anybody on the way, as she and Belinda were going to tea with Count Bianco and she had not much time. She therefore felt very annoyed when she saw the Archdeacon coming towards her, and would have hurried on, had they not come face to face on the pavement.

The Archdeacon had been visiting a rich parishioner, who was thought to be dying. The poor were much too frightened of their vicar to regard him as being of any possible comfort to the sick, but the Archdeacon liked to think of himself as fulfilling some of the duties of a parish priest and there was something about a deathbed that appealed to his sense of the dramatic. He had also taken the opportunity of visiting the workhouse that afternoon and was altogether in a pleasant state of melancholy.

'When I visit these simple people,' he said affectedly with his head on one side, 'I am reminded of Gray's *Elegy*.' He began to quote:

> *Far from the madding crowd's ignoble strife,*
> *Their sober wishes never learn'd to stray;*
> *Along the cool sequester'd vale of life*
> *They kept the noiseless tenor of their way.*

'Oh, *quite*,' agreed Harriet, annoyed at being delayed. 'One of the finest poems in our language,' she pronounced, hoping that there the matter would end.

But the Archdeacon had had a tiring afternoon and was in no hurry to return to his good works.

'Indeed it is,' he agreed. 'Johnson's criticism of it is so apt, as you will remember – "Sentiments to which every bosom returns an echo." '

But Harriet could stay no longer. 'Oh, yes, like the Apes of Brazil,' she remarked, and moved off, leaving the Archdeacon puzzling over what she meant. He thought it unlikely that it would be a literary quotation and yet it seemed somehow Elizabethan. Perhaps Belinda would know it. She often wasted her time reading things that nobody else would dream of reading.

Harriet walked away in the opposite direction. It would be very annoying if the curate was out, although she supposed she could always leave the things in his sitting-room with a note. His lodgings were situated in what Harriet considered one of the more sordid streets of the village, a row of late Victorian red brick villas called Jubilee Terrace. Every window had its lace curtains and she imagined that she detected stealthy movements behind them as she walked along to the house where the curate lodged. Well, let them watch her and gossip about it too if they liked, she thought stoutly, it would do some of them good to realize that charity began at home. That Miss Beard, a Sunday School teacher too, pretending to be watering the ferns in the front room – Harriet called out 'Good afternoon!' to her, and was pleased to see her scuttle furtively back into the shelter of the lace curtains.

The curate's house was called 'Marazion'. Harriet walked up the little path bordered with shells and rang the front-door bell. Mr Donne himself answered it. He expressed himself delighted to see her and was quite overwhelmed with gratitude when she presented her gifts.

He gazed at the jelly in wonder as if he had never seen anything like it before, but then recovered sufficiently to show Harriet into his sitting-room. This was quite a nice room, not as meanly furnished as Harriet could have wished, though Belinda was relieved that they did not have to provide the curate with furniture as well as food.

Harriet looked eagerly round, searching for those personal touches that make a room interesting. Other curates had lodged here, but this was the first time Harriet had visited Mr Donne and there were bound to be differences of detail. The first thing she noticed was a large oar, fastened on the wall over the mantelpiece, with photographs of rowing groups hanging underneath it.

'Ah, now which one is you?' she asked, going up to one of the groups and peering at it. They all looked so alike but at last she discovered Mr Donne and he pointed out to her his best friend who was a curate in London and another who had been called to the Mission Field.

'Oh, dear,' she said, her face clouding, 'I hope you will not go overseas. I mean, you aren't *commanded* to go by your bishop, are you?'

'Oh no, it is a personal matter. The call comes from within, as it were,' explained Mr Donne, rather red in the face.

Harriet seemed satisfied with this explanation and turned her attention to his books, which were not a particularly original selection. Shakespeare, some standard theological works, a few paper-backed detective novels and the *Oxford Book of English Verse*.

'I do hope your electric light is good,' she said anxiously. 'You know how harmful it is to read in a bad light, like Milton or whoever it was, although of course he went blind, so perhaps his eyes were weak to begin with. Oh, good, you have a reading-lamp – I was thinking that I could let you have one that we don't use very much.'

Mr Donne thanked her for the kind thought. 'As a matter of fact,' he assured her, 'I don't work very much in the evenings, except when I'm preparing a sermon. The Boys' Club and the Scouts take up most of my time.'

Scouts seemed to remind Harriet that she had thought of knitting him a pair of socks or stockings.

'That's very kind of you,' he said, 'I wear them out terribly quickly and can never have enough. I've just had two pairs sent me today, so I shall be quite well off.'

Harriet bristled with indignation. 'Oh? Who made those for you? Your mother or an aunt perhaps?' These occurred to her as the only people who could legitimately be allowed to knit socks for a curate whom she regarded as her property.

'No, as a matter of fact, it was a relation of Mrs Hoccleve's, she was up at the University when I was, at least she was doing research. She's a kind of female Don.'

'Oh, I see.' Harriet was a little pacified, but the whole thing was unsatisfactory and needed to be looked into. It was not somehow natural for a female Don to knit for a curate, especially as she sounded to be quite a young woman.

'Her name's Olivia Berridge and she's awfully nice,' said the curate in a kind of burst.

'Well, I shall have to be going now,' said Harriet, putting on her gloves. 'My sister and I are going to tea with Count Bianco.'

The curate thanked her once more for her gifts and came to the front gate with her. Nevertheless Harriet could not help feeling that the visit had been disappointing. This Olivia Berridge knitting socks for him, that was the trouble. Harriet wondered if there could be anything more between them than that. Of course there had been no photographs other than the rowing groups in his sitting-room, though she had not been able to see his bedroom. There might well be a photograph of Miss Berridge there. And yet it seemed that she must be several years older than he was, so perhaps there was nothing in it after all. Mr Donne was so *very* young, not more than twenty-three or four, and there was really nobody here in whom he could confide. Agatha was so unsympathetic and the Archdeacon was definitely peculiar, perhaps even the tiniest bit *mental*. He had that odd sloping forehead which was supposed to be a sign of mental deficiency. Harriet had read about it in *Harmsworth's Encyclopaedia*. She let her thoughts wander at random on this interesting point, but by the time she reached home the worry of Olivia Berridge was again uppermost and as soon as she saw Belinda she asked her what she knew about 'a relation of Agatha Hoccleve's doing research at the University'.

Belinda frowned. 'I believe she has a niece who does research in Middle English,' she said. 'Something to do with *The Owl and the Nightingale*, I think, but I'm not sure what aspect. Of course there is still much that is obscure in that poem and several disputed readings. . . .'

Harriet interrupted her impatiently. 'Oh, I dare say,' she said, 'but how old is this girl?'

'Oh, I don't think she's very young,' said Belinda, 'at least, she's about thirty, I think, which is young really, isn't it?'

Harriet seemed satisfied and hurried away to change for tea at Count Bianco's. She came downstairs again looking very elegant in a green suit with a cape trimmed with monkey fur. She had decided to break in her new pythonskin shoes.

After some delay, because Harriet couldn't walk very fast in her new shoes, they arrived at Count Bianco's house.

They had tea almost at once. The Count had ordered his cook to make all Harriet's favourite cakes and there were four different kinds of jam.

Belinda enjoyed her tea quietly while Harriet and the Count talked. Every time they visited Ricardo's house, Belinda was struck by the excellence of everything in it. The house itself was an interesting continental-looking building with a tower at one end and balconies and window-boxes, filled at all times of the year with suitable flowers. And the garden was delightful, with its perfectly tended herbaceous borders and rockeries, a grove of lime trees and some fine Lombardy poplars. The joys of the vegetable garden, too, were considerable. Belinda wondered how anybody could remain unmoved at the sight of the lovely marrows, and the magnificent pears, carefully tied up in little cotton bags, so that they should not fall before they were ripe or be eaten by the birds. At the bottom of the vegetable garden was a meadow, which Ricardo had planted with such of his native Italian flowers as could be induced to grow in the less sunny English climate. This part of the garden was his especial delight, and on fine evenings he would sit for hours in a deck-chair reading Tacitus or Dante, or brooding over the letters of his friend John Akenside.

This afternoon he was anxious that they should see a fine show of Michaelmas daisies, eight different varieties, each one a different colour and one a particularly rare one which he had brought back from the south of France, when he was there in the spring. And he was thinking of having a pond made, for water-lilies and goldfish, and where did Harriet think would be the best place to have it?

'Oh, Ricardo, how lovely!' said Harriet, in raptures at the thought of the pond. 'Will you swim in it? If it had a nice concrete bottom it would be quite clean, and so romantic to swim in the moonlight with the fishes.'

Belinda shivered. The fishes would be so cold and slimy and besides, Ricardo didn't do romantic things like that. 'Leigh Hunt writes rather charmingly about a fish,' she said aloud, '*Legless, unloving, infamously chaste*'; she paused. Perhaps it was hardly suitable, really, and she was a little ashamed of having quoted it, but these little remembered scraps of culture had a way of coming out unexpectedly.

'Swans would be nice,' Harriet went on, 'or would they eat the fishes?'

Ricardo was uncertain, but said that he had thought of getting some peacocks, they would look so effective on the terrace.

Harriet agreed that they would, and they moved off together, leaving Belinda bending over the Michaelmas daisies. She did not want to listen to another proposal of marriage and probably a refusal as well. It was some months since Ricardo had last proposed to Harriet and Belinda could feel that another offer was due.

When they came back to the house she could tell that he had once more been disappointed. It seemed a suitable time to talk about Ricardo's old friend John Akenside, and how he must miss him, even after all these years.

Yes, indeed, Ricardo wondered at times whether his own end was near. Would Belinda come into his study and see the photograph which he meant to have as the frontispiece to his long-awaited edition of the letters of John Akenside?

They went into the house, leaving Harriet to collect some plants from the gardener.

Ricardo's study gave the impression that he was a very studious and learned man. The walls were lined with very dull-looking books and the large desk covered with papers and letters written in faded ink. His task of collecting and editing the letters of his friend took up most of his time now, and it was doubtful whether he read anything but a few lines of Dante or a sentence of Tacitus.

A large photograph of John Akenside stood in a prominent position on the desk, showing him in some central European court dress. He looked uncomfortable in the white uniform and faintly ridiculous, like something out of a musical comedy. Perhaps his collar was crooked or the row of medals too ostentatious to be quite convincing, for there was something indefinably wrong about it, which marred the grandeur of the whole effect. Belinda never minded laughing at this photograph, because she felt that somehow John would understand. Indeed, as she looked at the face, she thought she detected a twinkle in the eyes, which seemed to look slyly round the corners of the rimless glasses, and the mouth was curled into a half smile, self-conscious, but at the same time a little defiant.

Together Belinda and Ricardo studied the portrait and for some minutes neither spoke. Then Ricardo said rather sadly, 'I think he would have wished the world to see this one.'

Belinda agreed. 'Yes, perhaps you're right. And yet he never sought worldly glory, did he . . .' she mused sentimentally. 'He was always so humble – hardly downtrodden,' she added hastily, remembering his rather shambling gait and his fingers stained with red ink, 'but I think he never realized his unique gifts, from which we, who were privileged to be his friends, received so much benefit . . .' Belinda stopped, rather tied up in this sentence of appreciation. She felt as if she were writing his obituary notice in *The Times*. Being with Ricardo often made her talk like this. Of course, she thought, I believe John Akenside had a finger in nearly every European political pie at the time of his death, and yet one had never been sure what it was that he actually *did*.

Ricardo continued the funeral oration. 'At the beginning of my edition of the letters,' he said, 'which will also contain a short biographical memoir, I am going to quote that beautiful opening sentence from the *Agricola* of Tacitus – *Clarorum virorum facta moresque posteris tradere, antiquitus usitatum, ne nos-*

tris quidem temporibus quamquam incuriosa suorum aetas omisit . . .' he recited solemnly in his quaint Italian pronunciation.

Belinda waited patiently while Ricardo finished the complicated Latin sentence. She had never been much of a classical scholar.

After he had finished there was a long silence. At last Belinda noticed that it was nearly seven o'clock and at that moment Harriet came into the room, bustling and cheerful, and carrying a basket full of rare rock plants. Her appearance seemed to cheer Ricardo and they began to talk about the care of woolly-leaved alpine plants, a conversation in which Belinda was glad to join.

CHAPTER SIX

ON THE WAY home Belinda decided to call at the vicarage to see Agatha. Harriet, calculating that the curate would probably not be there, went home to make some sardine eggs for supper, as it was Emily's evening out.

Belinda found Agatha sitting in the drawing-room, mending the Archdeacon's socks. It was a gloomy, unhomely kind of room, though Belinda could never quite decide why she did not like it. The electric light was too dim or the chair covers too drab or perhaps it was just that Agatha was there and that behind her was a bookcase, where, behind glass, was a complete set of the publications of the Early English Text Society. Belinda noticed rather sadly that the crimson socks Henry had bought in Vienna were not among the pile on Agatha's sewing table. But how stupid of me, she thought, socks don't last thirty years, and how could a man in Henry's position wear crimson socks! The ones Belinda noticed tonight were of the most sober archidiaconal colours. She wanted to say, 'Oh, Agatha, let me help you,' but thought better of it. Agatha might consider it a reflection on her darning, and certainly would not care to be reminded that Belinda had darned socks for Henry before she had ever set eyes on him. 'Never interfere between husband and wife', as Belinda remembered her dear mother telling her, and one could not be too careful, even about an apparently trivial thing like a sock.

Agatha seemed pleased to see her and they began to talk of parish matters. There would be a great deal to do when Agatha went away, indeed, she was beginning to wonder whether it would be possible to go after all.

Belinda reflected on the truth of the saying that husbands and wives grow to be like each other, for it might almost have been Henry talking. So badly in need of a holiday, and yet who could be left in charge of the Mothers' Union and there was that rather delicate affair of the altar brasses and the unpleasantness between Miss Jenner and Miss Beard . . . listening to her Belinda began to feel very gloomy indeed. It seemed almost as if Agatha had decided not to go.

'I'm sure I should be very willing to do what I could,' she said doubtfully, aware that she was not a mother and was far too much of a moral coward to deal satisfactorily with even the slightest unpleasantness. 'I often go into Miss Jenner's shop to buy knitting wool,' she added, 'perhaps I could say a word. . . .'

To Belinda's surprise, Agatha seemed grateful for her offer of help and they found themselves talking about Mr Donne and what a great asset he was to the parish, after which it was the most natural thing in the world for Belinda to ask after the Archdeacon.

Agatha smiled indulgently. He was well, considering everything, she said.

Considering what? Belinda wondered, and ventured to

remark that men were really much more difficult to please than women, who bore their burdens without complaining.

Agatha nodded and sighed. There was a short pause during which Agatha seemed to be intent on finding a piece of wool to match the sock she was mending. Belinda took up the *Church Times* and began glancing idly through the advertisements. A priest's cloak for sale, 44-inch chest – clerical evening dress, tall, slim build, never worn – she paused, wondering what story, sad or dramatic, lay behind those words. She had just turned to the back pages and was wondering whether Harriet would care to spend part of their summer holiday at a Bright Christian Guest House at Bognor, when the door opened and the Archdeacon came in.

He kissed Agatha in a hasty, husbandly way, which rather surprised Belinda, who had not thought that any outward signs of affection ever passed between them. Perhaps it distressed her a little, too, but he seemed so genuinely pleased to see her that she soon recovered and was listening happily to his account of how he had spent the afternoon, visiting a deathbed and then going on to see the old people in the workhouse.

'These humble people remind me of Gray's *Elegy*,' he said affectedly with his head on one side.

Neither Belinda nor Agatha had heard his conversation with Harriet, so that they listened with respectful interest while he quoted the appropriate verse. Nor were they in a hurry to be gone, as Harriet had been, and so did not say 'Oh, *quite*' when he had finished but enlarged intelligently on the charming theme. Agatha was reminded of *Piers Plowman*, Belinda of the poetry of Crabbe, which she could not remember very exactly, but she felt she had to be reminded of something out of self-defence, for Agatha had got a First and knew all about *Piers Plowman*. Indeed, she seemed about to quote from it and would probably have done so had not the Archdeacon suddenly been reminded of Wordsworth and some suitable lines in *The Excursion*. Then he began to read from *The Prelude*. Belinda thought Agatha looked rather bored and fidgety, but she herself was delighted and lived happily in the past until the entry of Mr Donne brought her back into the present.

'Your sister brought me some delicious plums this afternoon,' he said, addressing Belinda, 'and some homemade cake and jelly. I'm afraid I'm getting quite spoilt.'

The Archdeacon looked envious. The plums in their garden hadn't done particularly well this year and Agatha was always too busy with parochial work to make jelly or cakes or even to ask the cook to make them.

'Ah, well, you won't always be a curate,' said Belinda indulgently.

'That doesn't follow at all,' said the Archdeacon. 'Look at Plowman and all the gifts he gets. I suppose it has something to do with celibacy.'

Agatha smiled complacently. 'Well, dear, people know that you are not in need of these things,' she said.

'I will bring you some of the plums tomorrow,' said the curate nobly.

'Now, you see, I have given Donne a chance to be unselfish,' said the Archdeacon, 'so good comes out of everything.'

Belinda was silent, wondering if by any chance there were any plums left and whether she would have the courage to bring the Archdeacon a pot of the blackberry jelly which she herself had made a week or two ago. Perhaps when Agatha went away . . . a cake, too, perhaps with coffee icing and filling and chopped nuts on the top, or a really rich fruit cake. . . .

'We really must do something about the Harvest Festival,' said the Archdeacon wearily. 'I suppose I shall have to get Plowman to preach. A pity Canon Harvey is such a difficult man, he's really a better preacher.'

'Ah, yes,' Agatha nodded sympathetically.

Belinda did not join in the conversation. She remembered that the Archdeacon and Canon Harvey had a long-standing quarrel about the use of *Songs of Praise* in church, which the latter considered 'savoured of Pantheism in many instances'. They had had a heated correspondence about it in the local paper.

'Of course Plowman knows a good deal about the technical side of farming,' said the Archdeacon. 'That is some advantage.'

'Yes, indeed,' said the curate earnestly. 'He believes that digging is a kind of worship and that we get nearer to God by digging. At least, it may not be exactly that,' he stammered in confusion, 'but of course one does feel that the countryman is nearer God, in a way.'

'Nature's cathedral,' retorted the Archdeacon scornfully. 'One sees what you mean, of course.'

'I think Mr Donne was remembering the Latin *colere*, which has the double meaning of dig and worship, as in cult and agriculture,' said Agatha helpfully. 'You explained it so well in your sermon about the spiritual meaning of harvest time,' she added, turning to her husband. 'It would be nice to hear that again.'

The Archdeacon nodded and looked pleased. 'Yes, I think that may be the solution,' he said. 'I felt at the time that it was perhaps too subtle for some of the congregation.'

Belinda was silent with admiration. What a splendid wife Agatha was! She could never have dealt with him half so cleverly herself, she thought humbly. She remembered the sermon, of course, but it had been so obscure, that even she had been forced to abandon all efforts to understand it.

'Oh, Mrs Hoccleve,' burst out the curate eagerly, 'I nearly forgot to tell you, I had a pair of hand-knitted socks from Olivia Berridge. Wasn't it nice of her?'

'Yes, she mentioned you the last time I heard from her,' said Agatha thoughtfully, and then began to explain to

Belinda that Olivia Berridge was a niece of hers whom Mr Donne had met when he was an undergraduate.

'We both used to sing in the Bach Choir,' explained the curate, making the acquaintance sound respectable, even dull, Belinda thought.

'She's a very clever girl,' Agatha went on, 'and she's doing some really excellent work on certain doubtful readings in *The Owl and The Nightingale*.' She sighed, and looked down at the sock she was mending. 'I envy her that opportunity.'

'Well, my dear, there is no reason why you shouldn't get down to something like that yourself,' said the Archdeacon. 'I am sure you have more time to spare than I have.'

'I do so admire people who do obscure research,' said Belinda. 'I'm sure I wish I could.'

'Of course I have done a good deal of work on Middle English texts myself in the past,' said Agatha, smiling.

'Now, Agatha, Belinda does not wish to be forced to admire you,' said the Archdeacon. 'After all, academic research is not everything. We must remember George Herbert's lines:

A servant with this clause
Makes drudgery divine,
Who sweeps a room as for Thy laws,
Makes that and the action fine.'

'Yes, they are comforting,' Belinda agreed. 'And yet,' she went on unhappily, 'I don't sweep rooms, Emily does that. The things I do seem rather useless, but I suppose it could be applied to any action of everyday life, really.'

'Oh, certainly, Miss Bede,' said Mr Donne, with curately heartiness. 'We cannot all have the same gifts,' he added, with what Belinda felt was an insufferably patronizing air.

'Olivia is a very forceful young woman,' said the Archdeacon, 'and rather a bluestocking in appearance. What do you think, Donne?'

'Well, I can't say that I've really noticed,' said the curate. 'I mean, it's what a person *is* that matters most, isn't it?'

'Ah, yes, the clergy at any rate should feel that,' said the Archdeacon sardonically. 'It might be an idea for one of your sermons, Donne. You could take the lilies of the field text and work it out quite simply. I'm not sure that I won't take it myself, though. It might be a way of reaching the evening congregations, they like something of that kind. Never waste your erudite quotations on them, they don't appreciate or understand them.'

The curate murmured something about not really knowing any erudite quotations, at which the Archdeacon nodded and looked satisfied.

Agatha rolled up the last pair of socks, and there was a pleasant silence, during which Belinda became rather sentimental as she contemplated the cosy domestic scene. Agatha, surrounded by the socks and her affectionate husband, dear Agatha, almost; it was very seldom that Belinda was able to think of her like that. We really ought to love one another, she thought warmly, it was a pity it was often so difficult. But as she walked home, her thoughts took a more definite and interesting turn. She began to wonder if perhaps Mr Donne loved Olivia Berridge. By the time she had reached her own house, however, she had decided that the whole idea was so upsetting that it could not possibly be so. In any case, he would not have the chance of seeing her very often, and a few pairs of socks through the post could not really do very much.

CHAPTER SEVEN

WHEN THE day came for Agatha to go away, Belinda and Harriet watched her departure out of Belinda's bedroom window. From here there was an excellent view of the vicarage drive and gate. Belinda had brought some brass with her to clean and in the intervals when she stopped her vigorous rubbing to look out of the window, was careful to display the duster in her hand. Harriet stared out quite unashamedly, with nothing in her hand to excuse her presence there. She even had a pair of binoculars, which she was now trying to focus.

The sisters had said goodbye to Agatha the day before. Belinda was sure that she would rather be alone on her last morning to say goodbye to her husband, and there were always so many last-minute things to see to that the presence of strangers could be nothing but a hindrance, she thought. She really felt quite unhappy to think of Agatha and the Archdeacon being parted, for the cosy domestic scene which she had witnessed on her last visit to the vicarage had made a deep impression, and she felt that she ought to keep reminding herself of it. Of course they did have their little differences, there was no denying that, but it was equally certain that they were devoted to each other and that Agatha was an admirable wife.

Belinda and Harriet had been at their posts by the window for about ten minutes before there was any sign of life at the vicarage. Harriet had suggested that they should be there early, as, according to her calculations, Agatha would have to start for the station at least twenty minutes before the train went at half-past eleven. To watch anyone coming or going in the village was a real delight to them, so that they had looked forward to this morning with an almost childish excitement. And yet it was understandable, for there were so many interesting things about a departure, if one could watch it without any feeling of sorrow or regret. What would Agatha wear? Would she have a great deal of luggage or just a suitcase and a hat-box? Would the Archdeacon go with her to the station in the taxi, or would he be too busy to spare the time? If he did *not* go to the station would he kiss Agatha goodbye before she got into the taxi, or would he already have done that in the house? Belinda and Harriet were busy discussing these interesting questions when Harriet gave a little cry of pleasure and amusement.

'Oh, look,' she exclaimed, 'the curate in his shirt-sleeves!'

Belinda looked. It was indeed the curate, wearing no coat and carrying a large round hat-box. As far as she could see he looked flushed and dishevelled.

'I do hope they didn't make him carry the trunk downstairs,' she said, peering anxiously through the field-glasses. 'He looks rather tired.'

The next person to appear in the drive was the Archdeacon. He was carrying a suitcase and looking round him uncertainly, as if he did not know what to do with it. But at this moment a taxi appeared, so he advanced towards it with a threatening air.

'That old car of Palmer's!' exclaimed Harriet in disgust. 'All the stuffing's coming out of the seats! I suppose the Archdeacon was too mean to order Haines.'

'Oh, Harriet, I'm sure it wasn't that,' said Belinda loyally. 'Probably Haines was engaged for this morning, and anyway, I don't think Palmer is any cheaper.'

'They've got plenty of time,' said Harriet, looking at her watch, 'but I expect the Archdeacon wants to make quite sure she doesn't miss the train. I expect they'll be glad to get away from each other for a bit,' she added.

Belinda was about to contradict her sister and remind her of what a devoted couple the Hoccleves were, when Agatha herself appeared, carrying a fur coat over her arm and a small dressing-case.

'Oh, that's the case with gold fittings, isn't it?' said Harriet. 'I always think it must be so heavy, though. I don't like her hat very much, it makes her face look too sharp.'

Belinda suddenly felt that there was something indecent about their curiosity and turned away to clean the brass candlesticks on the mantelpiece. But nothing would move Harriet from the window. She kept up a flow of comments on Agatha's clothes, the behaviour of the Archdeacon and the curate. Belinda only hoped nobody could see her, with the field-glasses glued to her eyes. It would look so bad, somehow, though she did not doubt that others in the village were doing exactly the same thing.

Belinda went downstairs, humming *God moves in a mysterious way,* and telling herself that it was not right that she should feel relieved because Agatha was going away. Of course she was glad that Agatha was to have a well-deserved holiday and the waters would undoubtedly help her rheumatism, so there was room for gladness, but she ought not to have to tell herself this after the first thought that came into her mind had been how nice it would be to be able to ask Henry in to tea or supper without having to ask Agatha as well.

She went into the kitchen with a rather firmer step than usual and quite startled Emily, who was reading the *Daily Mirror* over her mid-morning cup of tea.

'Oh, Emily, I hoped you would have got on to the silver by now,' she said. 'Miss Harriet and I have done the bedrooms' – she paused guiltily – 'and I think I will see to the lunch myself. I am going to make a risotto out of the chicken that was left over.'

'Yes, Miss Bede.' Emily began to assemble the materials for silver cleaning. 'I see Mrs Hoccleve's gone,' she remarked.

'Oh, yes, it was today she was going,' said Belinda casually.

'I hope she won't come to any harm, you never know with foreigners, do you?' said Emily.

'An English gentlewoman can never come to any harm,' said Belinda, more to herself than to Emily.

'But you do hear of people having nasty things happen to them,' persisted Emily. 'I've read it in the papers. But of course Mrs Hoccleve's elderly, really, isn't she, so it's different?'

Belinda was silent. She felt she could hardly agree that

Agatha was elderly when she herself was a year older and thought of herself as only middle-aged. And yet, middle-aged or elderly, what was the difference really? *Calm of mind, all passion spent* . . . she had known that before she was thirty. 'Don't waste the Silvo like that, Emily,' she said with unaccustomed sharpness, 'you won't get a better polish. It's the rubbing that does it.'

The sound of heavy footsteps on the stairs told Belinda that Harriet had finished her business there, and as the kettle was boiling, she made a pot of tea and took it into the dining-room.

'I think I shall see if I can alter my black coat and make the sleeves like Agatha's,' Harriet was saying, half to herself. 'Do you think there is anything to let out on the seams?'

'Your coat is so nice as it is,' said Belinda doubtfully, for she had had experience of Harriet's attempts at alteration. 'Altering a coat is so much more difficult than a dress.'

'Yes,' agreed Harriet gravely, 'I think you're right. I might buy some of that leopard-skin trimming though and put it on the cuffs and pockets. That would be a change, and sleeves are going to be *important* this winter, I believe.'

'Have they got Agatha away safely?' asked Belinda casually.

'Oh, yes,' said Harriet, in a more cheerful tone of voice. 'Mr Donne went in the taxi with her. I suppose he would see her off at the station. And do you *know*,' she leaned forward eagerly, 'the Archdeacon didn't even kiss her. He just waved his hand, like this.' Harriet gave a rather improbable imitation of how the Archdeacon had said goodbye to his wife.

'I expect they said their real goodbyes in the house,' said Belinda. 'After all it's rather upsetting, isn't it, a parting like that?'

'The Archdeacon didn't look in the least bit upset,' said Harriet. 'After the taxi had gone he stood in the drive grinning and rubbing his hands, looking as pleased as Punch.'

'Oh, no, Harriet, I can't believe that,' said Belinda, and

so, comfortably arguing, they drank their tea and were just finishing it when there was a cry from Harriet, who pointed in the direction of the window.

'Look,' she cried, for she had been so absorbed in her task of 'strengthening' a pair of corsets with elastic thread that she had not noticed the Archdeacon creeping up the drive. Neither had Belinda, but she was less observant and sharp.

'I thought I would take you by surprise,' he said. 'I am glad to find you both engaged in the trivial round, the common task.'

Belinda was too agitated to think of any clever reply, while Harriet was bundling the corsets under a cushion in one of the armchairs. Belinda noticed to her horror that they were imperfectly hidden and planted herself firmly in front of the chair. It was too bad of Harriet to make these little embarrassments. The two cats were curled up in the basket-chair on the other side of the fire, so it was quite a problem to know where to seat the Archdeacon. But Harriet recovered her composure more quickly than Belinda, turned out the cats with a quick movement and offered him the chair.

'I'm afraid we have annoyed them,' said the Archdeacon, 'they are looking positively baleful. And yet I feel that I need rest more than they do.' He sighed and stretched out his hands to the warmth of the fire.

'We always call them the brethren dwelling in unity,' said Harriet. '*Behold how good and joyful a thing it is, brethren, to dwell together in unity*,' she quoted, as if by way of explanation. 'The psalm, you know. . . .'

'Of course he knows,' said Belinda rather sharply, and yet it was odd how one sometimes felt that he might *not*. She began to wonder why he had come; it was unusual for him to call in the morning.

'I expect you know Agatha has just gone,' said the Archdeacon, in answer to her thoughts. 'Such a business getting her to the station, I really feel quite exhausted. These departures are always more tiring for those who are left behind.'

'Oh, dear, we should have offered you some tea,' said Belinda reflecting that it was in fact Mr Donne who had gone to the station with Agatha. 'We had ours some time ago so it won't be very nice. I'll get Emily to make you some more.'

'Well, that is kind of you, but I had some refreshment at the vicarage,' said the Archdeacon. 'I really felt justified in having something.'

Belinda nodded sympathetically, but she could see Harriet looking scornful and so began talking quickly about the Harvest Festival and the decorations which were to be done the next day.

'We must have more corn this year,' said the Archdeacon. 'Corn is an essential part of harvest, perhaps the most important part of all.'

'Ah, yes, bread is the staff of life,' said Harriet solemnly. 'But we mustn't forget the other fruits of the earth. Ricardo Bianco has some very fine marrows and pumpkins, and bigger things really show up better.'

'The church always looks very nice,' said Belinda, fearing they were going to have an argument.

'Yes, there are always plenty of willing helpers,' said the Archdeacon complacently.

'I do hope there won't be any unpleasantness this year,' said Belinda, her face clouding. 'Last year there was the embarrassment of Miss Prior, if you remember.'

'The Embarrassment of Miss Prior,' said the Archdeacon, savouring the words. 'It sounds almost naughty, but I fear it was not. I cannot recall the circumstances.'

'Oh, I remember,' said Harriet. 'When Miss Prior came to decorate it was found that somebody else had already done the lectern and she's always done it for the last twenty years or more.'

'Yes, poor little soul,' said Belinda reminiscently, 'she was rather late. She had been finishing some curtains for Lady

Clara Boulding – you know, those heavy maroon velvet ones in her morning-room – and she was nearly crying. She does so enjoy doing the lectern and making a bunch of grapes hang down from the bird's mouth. Of course the only disadvantage is that they do distract the Sunday School children's attention so; last year they were very much inclined to giggle – Miss Jenner and Miss Smiley had a very difficult time with them.'

'If only they would try to teach them that it is perfectly right and fitting that we should bring the fruits of the earth into God's House at Harvest Time,' said the Archdeacon rather peevishly.

'But children don't understand things like that,' said Belinda, 'and in any case young people are so prone to giggle. I can remember I was.'

Harriet chortled reminiscently at some schoolgirl joke, but would not reveal it when asked.

Eventually the Archdeacon stood up to go and Belinda was about to hurry to the kitchen to start preparing the risotto, when Harriet pointed towards the Archdeacon's left foot and exclaimed loudly, 'Oh, you've got a hole in your sock!'

'Damn,' said the Archdeacon firmly and unmistakably. 'I suppose it was too much to hope that my clothes would be left in order.'

'I expect Agatha doesn't like darning,' said Harriet tactlessly. 'I'm not at all fond of it myself, so I can sympathize.'

'Oh, but a sock is liable to go into a hole at any time,' said Belinda hastily. 'It doesn't look a very big one. Perhaps it could be cobbled together . . .' she was already rummaging in her work basket for some wool of the right shade. 'I'm afraid this grey is rather too light,' she said, 'but I don't think it will show very much.'

'Oh, that doesn't matter,' said the Archdeacon impatiently. 'What a fuss it all is over such a trifling matter.'

Belinda smiled as she threaded her needle. Dear Henry, he

was so inconsistent, but perhaps a hole in a sock was hardly as important as moths in a suit. 'I think it would be best if you put your foot up on this little chair,' she said, 'then I can get at your heel to mend the sock.'

The Archdeacon submitted himself to her ministrations with rather an ill will, and there was one anxious moment when Belinda inadvertently pricked him with the needle and it seemed as if he would lose his temper.

Harriet did her best to divert him with conversation and eventually he recovered his good humour and began to ask her the origin of her elusive quotation about the Apes of Brazil. He thought that it might be Elizabethan, it reminded him of that poem with the lines about making Tullia's ape a marmoset and Leda's goose a swan.

'I don't remember anything about the Apes of Brazil,' said Belinda anxiously, for the darning of the sock was an all-engrossing occupation.

'Do you mean what I said that afternoon we met in the village?' asked Harriet. 'That's not a quotation, that's natural history.' She laughed delightedly.

The Archdeacon seemed surprised and Harriet began to explain.

'It's quite simple, really,' she said. 'When the Apes of Brazil beat their chests with their hands or paws, or whatever apes have, you can hear the sound two miles away.'

'Oh, Harriet,' said Belinda, as if reproving a child, 'surely not two *miles*? You must be mistaken.'

'Two miles,' said Harriet firmly. 'Father Plowman told me.'

The Archdeacon laughed scornfully at this.

'It was at Lady Clara Boulding's house,' said Harriet indignantly. 'We were having a most interesting conversation, I can't remember now what it was about.'

'I cannot imagine what the subject of it can have been,' said the Archdeacon, 'and I did not know that Plowman had ever been in Brazil.'

'You said something about sentiments to which every bosom returns an echo,' said Harriet, 'so I naturally thought of the Apes of Brazil.'

'I think the minds of the metaphysical poets must have worked something like that,' said Belinda thoughtfully. 'Donne and Abraham Cowley, perhaps.'

'Cowley was a very stupid man,' said the Archdeacon shortly. 'I cannot understand the revival of interest in his works.'

'I think the hole is mended now,' said Belinda. 'It doesn't look so bad now; of course the wool *is* just a little too light.'

'My dear Belinda, you have done it quite exquisitely,' said the Archdeacon. 'I must take care to be passing your house every time I have a hole in my sock.'

Belinda smiled and went quite pink with pleasure and confusion. She went with him to the front door and then returned to the dining-room where Harriet had collapsed heavily into a chair and was fanning herself with the parish magazine.

'Thank goodness, he's gone,' she said. 'I really don't know how Agatha manages to put up with him all the time. No wonder she's gone away.'

'Harriet, *do* speak more quietly,' said Belinda in an agitated whisper, for Emily had just come into the room to lay the table. 'I must go and start the risotto,' she said and went into the kitchen, where she walked aimlessly about in circles trying to assemble all the ingredients she needed. For somehow it was difficult to concentrate. The mending of the sock had been an upsetting and unnerving experience, and even when she had made the risotto she did not feel any pleasure at the thought of eating it.

'Nearly twenty-past one!' said Harriet, as they sat down to their meal. 'The Archdeacon has delayed everything. I suppose he imagined Emily would be cooking.'

'I don't suppose he thought about it at all, men don't as a

rule,' said Belinda, 'they just expect meals to appear on the table and they do.'

'Of course Emily usually does cook,' went on Harriet, 'it's only that she can't manage foreign dishes.' She took a liberal second helping of risotto. 'This is really delicious.'

'It was Ricardo's recipe,' said Belinda absently.

'We really must go and get some more blackberries soon,' said Harriet. 'Although in October the devil will be in them. You know what the country people say.'

Belinda smiled.

'Mr Donne is very fond of blackberry jelly,' said Harriet. 'Apparently he very much enjoyed the apple jelly I took him. He said he really preferred it for breakfast – instead of marmalade, you know.'

'I wonder what it would be like to be turned into a pillar of salt?' said Belinda surprisingly, in a far-away voice.

'Belinda!' Harriet exclaimed in astonishment. 'Whatever made you think of that? Potiphar's wife, wasn't it, in the Old Testament somewhere?'

'I think it was Lot's wife,' said Belinda, 'but I can't remember why. I should imagine it would be very restful,' she went on, 'to have no feelings or emotions. Or perhaps,' she continued thoughtfully, 'it would have been simpler to have been born like Milton's first wife, an image of earth and phlegm.'

'Oh, Belinda, don't be disgusting!' said Harriet briskly. 'And do pass the cheese. You are hopelessly inattentive. When Mr Donne was here the other night you never passed him anything. If it hadn't been for me he would have *starved*.'

Belinda came back to everyday life again. How many curates would starve and die were it not for the Harriets of this world, she thought. 'I'm sorry, dear,' she said. 'I must try not to be so absent-minded. Today has been rather trying, hasn't it really – too much happening.'

'Yes,' agreed Harriet. 'Agatha going and the Archdeacon coming. Who knows what he may be up to now that she's gone?'

'Oh, Harriet, I wish you wouldn't talk like that,' said Belinda. 'It's really most unsuitable. And besides,' she went on, half to herself, 'what could he be up to when you come to think of it?' Her voice trailed off rather sadly, but she rose from the table briskly enough and spent the afternoon doing some useful work in the garden.

CHAPTER EIGHT

THE NEXT day Belinda had a letter from Dr Nicholas Parnell, a friend of her undergraduate days and the Librarian of her old University Library. He wrote of the successful tour which Mr Mold, the deputy Librarian, had made in Africa. 'He has penetrated the thickest jungles,' wrote Dr Parnell, 'where no white man, and certainly no deputy Librarian, has ever set foot before. The native chiefs have been remarkably generous with their gifts and Mold has collected some five thousand pounds, much of it in the form of precious stones and other rarities. I suspect that a great many of them have not the slightest idea to what they are contributing, but, where Ignorance is bliss . . .'

Belinda sighed. Dear Nicholas was really quite obsessed with the Library and its extensions. She wished he would remember that the two things which bound them together were the memory of their undergraduate days and our greater English poets. She turned to the end of the letter, where she found more cheering news. The Librarian thought he might be able to come and spend a few days with the Archdeacon while Agatha was away. Perhaps Mr Mold would come too. 'The Library can safely be left in charge of old Mr Lydgate,' he concluded. 'He is a little wandering now and is continually worrying about the pronunciation of the Russian "l". However, his duties will be light.'

How nice it would be to see dear Nicholas again, thought Belinda, eating her scrambled egg and feeling happy and proud that she, a middle-aged country spinster, should number famous librarians among her friends. At least, the Library was famous, she emended. Dear Nicholas had rather sunk into obscurity since his scholarly publications of twenty years ago, and now that he had definitely abandoned all intellectual pursuits, she assumed that no more in that line was to be expected from him. Still, *Floreat Bibliotheca*, and she was sure that under his guidance it would. And, what was perhaps even more important, the Library would be adequately heated and the material comfort of the readers considered. For who can produce a really scholarly work when he is sitting shivering in a too heavy overcoat, struggling all the time against the temptation to go out and get himself a warming cup of coffee?

The same afternoon Belinda went into the village to do a little shopping. She had to give an order at the grocer's and the butcher's, and, if there was time, she would go and choose some wool to make Ricardo Bianco a nice warm pair of socks. She wondered if he had tried taking calcium tablets for his chilblains; they were supposed to be very good.

She entered the wool shop, kept by Miss Jenner, who was also a Sunday School teacher. She always liked going to Miss Jenner's as the attractive display of different wools fired her imagination. Harriet would look splendid in a jumper of that coral pink. It would be a good idea for a Christmas present, although it was impossible to keep anything secret from Harriet owing to her insatiable curiosity. And here was an admirable clerical grey. Such nice soft wool too . . . would she ever dare to knit a pullover for the Archdeacon? It would have to be done surreptitiously and before Agatha came back. She might send it anonymously, or give it to him casually, as if it had been left over from the Christmas charity parcel. Surely that would be quite seemly, unless of course it might appear rather ill-mannered?

'This is a lovely clerical grey,' said Miss Jenner, as if sensing her thoughts. 'I've sold quite a lot of this to various ladies round here – especially in Father Plowman's parish. I was saying to the traveller only the other day that I knew this would be a popular line. He even suggested I might knit *him* a pullover' – she laughed shrilly – 'the idea of it!'

Belinda smiled. She could well imagine the scene. Miss Jenner was so silly with the travellers that it was quite embarrassing to be in the shop when one of them arrived. Still, poor thing, Belinda thought, the warm tide of easy sentimentality rising up within her, it was probably the only bit of excitement in her drab life. She was getting on now, and with her sharp, foxy face and prominent teeth had obviously never been pretty. Living over the shop with her old mother must be very dull. And perhaps we are all silly over something or somebody without knowing it; perhaps her own behaviour with the Archdeacon was no less silly than Miss Jenner's with the travellers. It was rather a disquieting thought, especially when Miss Jenner, with a smirk on her face, began to tell her that eight ounces was the amount of wool that ladies usually bought.

'It will go very well with my Harris tweed costume,' said Belinda firmly. 'I think I will have *nine* ounces, in case I decide to make long sleeves.' After all, she *might* make a jumper for herself, now that she came to think of it she was certain that she would, either that or something else equally safe and dull. When we grow older we lack the fine courage of youth, and even an ordinary task like making a pullover for somebody we love or used to love seems too dangerous to be undertaken. Then Agatha might get to hear of it; that was something else to be considered. Her long, thin fingers might pick at it critically and detect a mistake in the ribbing at the Vee neck; there was often some difficulty there. Agatha was not much of a knitter herself, but she would have an unfailing eye for Belinda's little mistakes. And then the pullover might be too small, or the neck opening too tight, so that he wouldn't be able to get his head through it. Belinda went hot and cold, imagining her humiliation. She would have to practise on Harriet, whose head was fully as big as the Archdeacon's. And yet, in a way, it would be better if Harriet didn't know about it, she might so easily blurt out something . . . Obviously the enterprise was too fraught with dangers to be attempted and Belinda determined to think no more about it. *God moves in a mysterious way*, she thought, without irreverence. It was wonderful how He did, even in small things. No doubt she would know what to do with the wool as time went on.

This afternoon Belinda had naturally hoped that she might meet the Archdeacon, but it was now nearly teatime, and although she had been through the main street and all the most likely side streets, Fate had not brought them together. She decided that there was nothing for it but to go home; after all, there would be many more opportunities.

But when she had got as far as the church, she saw a familiar figure wandering about among the tomb-stones, with his hands clasped behind his back and an expression of melancholy on his face. It was, of course, the Archdeacon. But what was he doing in the churchyard when it was nearly teatime? Belinda wondered. This would hardly be a suitable time to interrupt his meditations by telling him that she had had a letter from Nicholas Parnell and that she did hope they would both come to supper when he came to stay. She began to walk rather more slowly, uncertain what to do. She looked in her shopping basket to see if she had forgotten anything. She remembered now that the careful list she had made was lying on top of the bureau in the dining-room, so she could hardly expect to check things very satisfactorily. There was no reason why she should not hurry home to tea.

'These yew trees are remarkably fine,' said a voice quite close to her, 'they must be hundreds of years old.'

Belinda looked up from her basket. The Archdeacon had now come to the wall.

'Oh, good afternoon,' she said, hoping that he had not noticed her obvious reluctance to go home. 'You quite startled me. I didn't see you,' she added, hoping that she might be forgiven or at least not found out, in this obvious lie.

The Archdeacon smiled. 'I was thinking out my sermon for Sunday,' he said. 'I find the atmosphere so helpful. Looking at these tombs, I am reminded of my own mortality.'

Belinda contemplated a design of cherubs' heads with a worn inscription underneath it. 'Yes, indeed,' she said, hoping that the gentle melancholy of her tone would make amends for her trite reply.

'I have lately been reading Young's *Night Thoughts*,' went on the Archdeacon, in his pulpit voice. 'There are some magnificent lines in it that I had forgotten.'

Belinda waited. She doubted now whether it would be possible to be back for tea at four o'clock. She could hardly break away when the Archdeacon was about to deliver an address on the mortality of man.

He began to quote:

We take no note of time
But from its loss. To give it then a tongue
Is wise in man. As if an angel spoke,
I feel the solemn sound. If heard aright
It is the knell of my departed hours. . . .

'I thought of those lines when I heard the clock strike just now,' he explained.

'It must be wonderful, and unusual too, to think of time like that,' said Belinda shyly, realizing that when she heard the clock strike her thoughts were on a much lower level. She suspected that even dear Henry was guilty of more mundane thoughts occasionally. At four o'clock in the afternoon, surely the most saintly person would think rather of tea than of his departed hours? She stood silent, looking into her basket.

'Not that Young was a great theologian, or even a great poet,' the Archdeacon went on hastily. 'Much of the *Night Thoughts* consists of platitudes expressed in that over-elaborate and turgid style, which the minor eighteenth-century poets mistakenly associated with Milton.'

'Oh, yes, the style is certainly rather flowery,' said Belinda, doing the best she could, for she was beginning to be uneasily conscious of Harriet waiting for her tea, the hot scones getting cold and Miss Beard, that excellent church worker and indefatigable gossip, passing by on the other side of the road.

'That may be, but I do find in it a little of the wonder and awe which is generally supposed to be absent from the literature of that age.' The Archdeacon stood looking at Belinda with his head on one side, as if he expected her to agree with him.

But Belinda said nothing, for she was thinking how handsome he still was. His long pointed nose only added to the general distinction of his features. There was quite a long pause until the clock struck a quarter-past four.

'Tea,' said the Archdeacon, suddenly human once more. 'I'm all by myself,' he said rather pathetically. 'Won't you come and share my solitary meal? I don't know if there will be any cake,' he added doubtfully.

Belinda started. 'Oh, *no*,' she said, drawing back a little, and then remembering her manners, she added: 'Thank you very much but Harriet will be expecting me.' She did not dare to invite him to share their undoubtedly more appetizing meal and almost smiled when she pictured what Harriet's reaction would be were she to bring him home unexpectedly. All the same it would have been very nice to have had tea with him, she thought regretfully, quite like old times. Perhaps he would ask her again, though it was the kind of spontaneous invitation that comes perhaps only once in a lifetime. 'You must come to tea with us some time,' she said, doing her best to assume a light, social manner. 'I will ask Harriet what is the best day, though,' she added hastily, 'I expect you are very busy.'

'Ah, yes,' he sighed, 'nobody can possibly know how busy.'

'Then I mustn't keep you any longer,' said Belinda, moving away.

'Well, the tombs are always with us,' he replied enigmatically, raising his hat with a sweeping gesture.

Belinda could think of nothing to say to this, so she smiled and walked home very quickly. As she had expected, Harriet was waiting impatiently in the drawing-room. The tea was already in, and the hot scones stood in a little covered dish in the fireplace.

'Oh, Belinda, when *will* you learn to be punctual,' she said, in a despairing voice.

'I'm so sorry, dear,' said Belinda humbly. 'I should have been here by four, but I met the Archdeacon.' She looked about her rather helplessly for a place to put her coat. 'I'm sorry you waited tea for me.'

'Well, I was rather hungry,' said Harriet nobly, 'but having to wait will make me enjoy it all the more. What meat did you order?'

'Mutton,' said Belinda absently.

'But we haven't any red-currant jelly,' said Harriet. 'One of us will have to go out tomorrow morning and get some. Mutton's so uninteresting without it.'

Belinda sat down by the fire and began to pour out the tea.

'Where did you see the Archdeacon?' asked Harriet.

'In the churchyard,' said Belinda. 'He was walking about among the tombs.'

Harriet snorted.

'But, Harriet,' Belinda leaned forward eagerly, 'he asked me to go to tea with him, but of course I couldn't very well have gone.'

'I don't see why not,' said Harriet. 'I can't believe you didn't want to.'

'No, it wasn't exactly that,' said Belinda slowly. 'I didn't really mind one way or the other,' she lied, 'but I knew you would be expecting me back and I thought you might wonder where I was. And then Florrie and the cook might have thought it funny if I went there the minute Agatha was out of the house. You know how servants gossip, especially in a small place like this. I don't want to be silly in any way, of course there would have been nothing *in* it, but I decided it would be better if I didn't go.' She put the rest of her scone into her mouth with an air of finality.

Harriet was obviously disappointed. 'I do wish you'd gone,' she lamented. 'So little of interest happens here and one may as well make the most of life. Besides, dear,' she added gently, 'I don't think anybody would be likely to gossip about you in that old tweed coat.'

'No, you're quite right. I suppose it will have to go to Mrs Ramage next time she comes.' She got up and rang the bell for Emily to clear away the tea things. When she was going out with the tray, Emily turned to Harriet rather nervously and said, 'Excuse me, m'm, but would you mind if I just slip out to the post?'

'Oh, no, Emily,' said Harriet firmly, 'there's no need for that. I shall be writing some letters myself, so I can take yours as well. There is plenty for you to do here.'

Emily went out of the room with a sulky expression on her face, and was heard to bang the tray rather heavily on the table in the passage.

'She only wants to go and gossip with the vicarage Florrie,' said Harriet, triumphant at having frustrated her. 'And we can't have that, can we?' she said turning to Belinda for support.

But Belinda was not listening. She was wondering what they would have talked about if she *had* gone to tea, or rather what Henry would have talked about. It had started to rain outside, and the soft patter of the rain in the leaves, combined with the rapidly falling darkness, made her feel pleasantly melancholy. She wondered if Henry were looking at the twilight, missing Agatha, she thought dutifully, or even regretting that she had not stayed to tea. It *would* have been nice to go . . . Belinda put down her knitting and sat dreaming. Of course there was a certain pleasure in not doing something; it was impossible that one's high expectations should be disappointed by the reality. To Belinda's imaginative but contented mind this seemed a happy state, with no emptiness or bitterness about it. She was fortunate in needing very little to make her happy.

She was still sitting idly with her knitting in her lap, when the front door-bell rang, and Miss Liversidge and Miss Aspinall were shown into the room.

'We were just passing and thought we'd drop in,' Edith explained.

They stood in the doorway, a tall drooping figure and a short stout one, both wearing mackintoshes, and that wet-weather headgear so unbecoming to middle-aged ladies and so incongruously known as a 'pixie hood'.

'Do take off your wet things,' said Belinda rousing herself.

'You had better stay to supper,' said Harriet rather too bluntly. 'It won't be very much but we shall be having it soon.'

Why yes, it will be a good chance to repay the baked beans, thought Belinda. She wondered whether they ought perhaps to open a tin of tongue and get Emily to make a potato salad. Or would a macaroni cheese be better? With some bottled fruit and coffee to follow that should really be enough.

'I think I'll just go and tell Emily about supper,' she said.

'Oh, please don't trouble to make any difference for us,' said Connie. 'Bread and cheese or whatever you're having will do for us, won't it, Edith?'

Edith gave a short bark of laughter. 'Well, I must say that I should like to feel an effort was being made, even if only a small one,' she said in a jocular tone. 'I think we all like to feel that.'

'But we only came to see you,' said Connie. Her eyes brightened a little and she said in a low voice, 'We think we have a piece of news.'

'News? What kind of news?' asked Harriet rather sharply.

'We have heard that Mr Donne is engaged,' said Edith, in a loud triumphant tone.

'To a niece of Mrs Hoccleve's, a Miss Berry,' chimed in Connie.

'Miss Berridge, I think, if it's the niece who's doing research,' said Belinda, looking rather fearfully at her sister.

'Oh, I don't think that can be true,' declared Harriet indignantly. 'She has made him a pair of socks, but I don't think there is anything more than that between them.'

'Miss Prior told us,' persisted Edith, 'and she is usually very accurate. She has been a good deal at the vicarage lately, getting Mrs Hoccleve's clothes ready to go away. She may very well have heard something.'

'But Miss Berridge is some years older than Mr Donne,' said Harriet, equally persistent. 'It would be a most unsuitable marriage. Besides,' she added, her tone taking on a note of disgust, 'she's doing some research or something like that, isn't she, Belinda.'

'Yes, on some doubtful reading in *The Owl and the Nightingale*. It doesn't seem a very good training for a wife,' said Belinda uncertainly, thinking of Agatha and her inability to darn. 'Still, if she has knitted him a pair of socks perhaps she is not entirely lacking in the feminine arts.'

Edith gave a snort. 'I believe some of these old poems are very *coarse*, so she may not be such a blue stocking as we think.'

There was a short silence during which the front-door bell rang again and Mr Donne was shown into the room carrying a bundle of parish magazines.

'Miss Jenner couldn't manage to deliver them this month,' he explained, 'so I am doing it.'

'Just the person we wanted to see,' said Harriet. 'Now, *you* can surely tell us. Is it true that you are engaged to be married?' The words rang out as a challenge.

'I – engaged?' Mr Donne made a kind of bleating noise and a movement with his arms which scattered the parish magazines all over the floor. 'It's certainly the first I've heard of it,' he went on, recovering something of his usual manner. 'Who is the fortunate lady?'

'Miss Berridge,' said Edith Liversidge firmly.

'Miss Berridge?' he echoed in a puzzled tone. 'Well, of course, she's a very good sort, and I like her very much . . .' he hesitated, perhaps feeling that he was being ungallant.

'But you think of her more as an elder sister, I expect,' prompted Harriet with determination.

'Well, yes, I suppose I do,' he agreed gratefully. 'Anyway she's much too clever to look at anyone like me.'

'Is she beautiful?' persisted Edith.

'Well, not exactly *beautiful*,' he said, looking embarrassed, 'but very nice and so kind.'

Ah, had she been more beauteous and less kind,
She might have found me of another mind.

thought Belinda, but decided it might be better not to quote the lines.

'Well, that's that,' said Harriet. 'There is no truth in the rumour. Isn't it amazing how people will gossip?'

'I never thought there was,' said Connie to Belinda. 'I think Mr Donne will marry some pretty *young* thing.' She sighed and her eyes bulged sentimentally.

'I may not get married at all,' said Mr Donne almost defiantly. 'Many clergymen do not.'

'No, a single curate is in many ways more suitable,' said Belinda thoughtfully. 'More in the tradition, if you see what I mean. And then of course there's the celibacy of the clergy isn't there?' she added quickly.

'Is there?' said Edith scornfully. 'I thought St Paul said it was better to marry than burn.'

'Well, it is hardly a question of that,' said Belinda in a confused way. 'I mean, of burning. One would hardly expect it to be.' She felt rather annoyed with Edith, who must surely know less than anybody about what St Paul had said, for introducing this unsuitable aspect of the question.

Fortunately, Harriet, who had disappeared from the room while she was speaking, now came back with the news that supper was ready.

'You will stay, won't you, Mr Donne?' she asked, turning to him with a beaming smile. 'I'm afraid it won't be much of a meal . . .' she waved her hands deprecatingly.

Edith Liversidge moved into the dining-room with a confident step. They would all benefit from Mr Donne's presence, she knew, and noted with sardonic approval that there was a large bowl of fruit salad on the table and a jug of cream as well as a choice of cold meats.

Oh dear, thought Belinda, recognizing tomorrow's luncheon, surely the tin of tongue would have been enough?

'Let's all have a glass of sherry,' said Harriet, going over to the sideboard, where a decanter and glasses had been set out on a tray. 'After all, we *might* have been going to drink to Mr Donne's engagement.'

CHAPTER NINE

'I SUPPOSE they really *have* come,' said Harriet doubtfully. 'Emily is usually quite accurate in her information and she had this from the vicarage Florrie, who ought to know if anyone does. She told her that two gentlemen had arrived to stay at the vicarage last night, but of course we have no proof that it is Dr Parnell and Mr Mold. It might be two clergymen coming to see the Archdeacon about something.'

'Yes, I suppose it might be,' said Belinda, 'but somehow clergymen *don't* come to see him about things, do they? I don't know why.'

'They came by night,' declared Harriet, 'like Nicodemus. Isn't Mr Mold called Nicodemus?'

'Oh, *no*, Harriet, his name is Nathaniel.'

'Nathaniel Mold,' said Harriet, trying it. 'Nat Mold. I think that sounds rather common, doesn't it?'

'Well, we shall just call him Mr Mold,' said Belinda, 'so I don't think we need worry. I believe Nicholas always calls him Nathaniel. He hates abbreviations.' She got up from the table and went to the window. 'It seems quite a nice morning after all that heavy rain,' she said. 'I think I shall go out into the village a little later on. I expect Nicholas will be taking a stroll and I am so looking forward to seeing him. Perhaps we shall meet.'

'I won't come with you,' said Harriet nobly. 'After all, he is really your friend, not mine, and I expect you will have a lot to talk about.' Privately, Harriet thought him rather a boring little man, but she hoped for great things from Mr Mold, who was reputed to be something of a 'one for the ladies'. This piece of information had also been gleaned from the vicarage Florrie, but Harriet had thought it wiser not to tell her sister. She wondered how Florrie, a plain, lumpish girl, had managed to find it out in so short a time.

Belinda was fortunate enough to come face to face with Dr Parnell before she had gone very far, and as they were just outside the Old Refectory, a tea shop run by gentlewomen, it seemed a good idea to go inside and have a cup of coffee. Dear Nicholas looked rather cold and peevish, she thought, wondering if he had had an adequate breakfast at the vicarage.

'I don't suppose you are really in need of anything,' she said, as they sat down, 'but morning coffee is a pleasant, idle habit, I always think.'

'Good morning, Miss Bede.' Mrs Wilton, a pleasant-faced woman with rather prominent teeth, and wearing a smock patterned with a herbaceous border, stood before them. She stared at Dr Parnell with frank interest and then at Belinda. Nicholas Parnell was small and bearded and did not somehow look the kind of person one would marry, Belinda realized. All the same, she felt proud of his distinction and could not resist introducing him to Mrs Wilton, who was, after all, a canon's widow.

'Oh, the *Library*,' said Mrs Wilton in a reverent tone. 'My husband used to read there when he was an undergraduate. I've heard so much about it.'

'Of course we have central heating there now,' said Dr Parnell. 'There have been great improvements in the last ten years or so. We also have a Ladies' Cloakroom in the main building now,' he added, his voice rising to a clear, ringing tone. 'That is a very great convenience.' He chuckled into his beard as Mrs Wilton went away to fetch their coffee. 'I do not approve of this hushed and reverent attitude towards our great Library. After all, it is a place for human beings, isn't it?'

'Yes, I suppose it is,' said Belinda doubtfully, for she was remembering some of the strange people who used to work there in her undergraduate days, many of whom could hardly have been called human beings if one were to judge by their looks.

'These are excellent cakes,' said Dr Parnell, eating heartily, 'although I had such a late breakfast that I can hardly do them justice. I must say I was surprised that dear Henry was not up before me. I had quite expected that there would be a Daily Celebration. Now that I come to think of it, I distinctly remember seeing 'D' against the church in *Mowbray's Guide*. I hope I shall not have to write and correct them.'

'Oh, no,' said Belinda, always anxious to defend the Archdeacon. 'There is always a Daily Celebration but I expect Mr Donne – he's the curate – would be taking it. Probably Henry thought it would be more courteous to breakfast with you on your first morning here.'

'Ah, Belinda, I see you have not changed. We did not breakfast until half-past nine, so your argument falls to pieces. I left poor Henry in the churchyard, as I came out just now. He said the tombs put him in mind of his own mortality.'

'And did he quote Young's *Night Thoughts* to you?' asked Belinda, suddenly disloyal.

'Indeed, he did. I left him because he was so tiresomely melancholy. And then he has been trying to make me subscribe to some fund for the church roof,' said Dr Parnell.

> *'. . . but perforated sore,*
> *And drill'd in holes the solid oak is found*
> *By worms voracious, eating through and through. . . .'*

he quoted solemnly, so that Belinda could hardly help smiling, although she knew it was very naughty of her. As they walked out of the Old Refectory towards the church she tried to remember what it was that Father Plowman had told her about the death-watch beetle and its habits, as if to make amends for her lapse. But before she had got very far, they had reached the churchyard wall and Belinda could see that the Archdeacon was sitting in his favourite seat under the yew trees. She felt a faint irritation to see him sitting there in the middle of the morning when so many people, women mostly, were going about their household duties and shopping. She supposed that men would be working too, but somehow their work seemed less important and exhausting.

'What is he doing in the churchyard, I wonder?' she asked Dr Parnell, but she did not really expect him to be able to tell her. The Archdeacon's affected eighteenth-century melancholy failed to charm her this morning.

'I think he's meditating on his sermon for Sunday morning,' said Dr Parnell. 'I understand that it is to be something rather out of the ordinary.'

When the Archdeacon saw them he smiled benevolently, but at the same time condescendingly. It was as if he were letting them see how fortunate they were to be able to stroll in the village on a fine October morning, while he was condemned to sit among the tombs thinking out his sermon.

'Isn't that seat rather *damp*?' enquired Belinda sharply. 'We had some very heavy rain during the night, and you know how easily you catch cold.' She felt that as Agatha was so many miles away she was justified in adopting this almost wifely tone towards him.

He looked up irritably; Belinda had spoilt the romance of his environment. It was just the kind of remark that Agatha would make and, now that he came to think of it, he supposed the seat *was* rather damp. He felt a distinct chill striking up through his bones and began to wonder if he were perhaps catching cold. He would never have noticed it if Belinda had not put the idea into his head. He rose rather ungraciously and came towards them.

'It seems impossible to find peace and quiet anywhere,' he remarked. 'I had settled down in my study after breakfast when the girl came in with the vacuum cleaner and drove me into the churchyard. Now I am interrupted again.'

Belinda smiled at this picture: 'I'm sorry if we have disturbed you,' she said. 'I think we should really have walked past if you had not got up and come to us.'

'That would have been most unfriendly,' said the Archdeacon unreasonably. 'Besides, it is not every day that we have visitors. We should really make some effort to entertain them.'

'Belinda has been doing her best,' said Dr Parnell. 'She has given me an excellent cup of coffee and introduced me to a charming lady who showed great reverence when the Library was mentioned. It is really rather gratifying. I should be delighted to show her round,' he added. 'She would find every convenience. The next thing will be to have some kind of a restaurant where readers can take luncheon or tea together. Do you know,' – he tapped his walking stick on the ground – 'I have had to have notices printed requesting readers not to *eat* in the Library? One would hardly have thought it possible.'

During this time an idea had been taking shape in Belinda's mind, and it was one which she knew her sister would approve. The talk about eating had made her think how nice it would be if they had a little supper party on Sunday evening. So, with unusual boldness, she issued the invitation, though she realized that her own rather timid way did not compare with Harriet's careless joviality. 'If you have no other engagement on Sunday evening,' she began, 'I was wondering if perhaps . . . I mean, would you care to come to supper at our house after Evensong? And Mr Mold too, of course.'

'That would be delightful,' said Dr Parnell. 'One feels somehow that Sunday evening should be spent *away* from a vicarage if at all possible.'

'Sunday is always a heavy day for me,' said the Archdeacon, 'and this Sunday will be particularly so. I intend to preach myself both morning and evening. These people are so sunk in lethargy that they do not know their own wickedness.'

Belinda looked a little startled. 'I know,' she said inadequately. 'I mean, one is.' All the same it was uncomfortable to be reminded of one's sinfulness in the middle of a bright morning.

'Sloth and lethargy,' said Dr Parnell, with relish. 'But I take it you will accept Belinda's invitation, I know Nathaniel will want to.'

'I shall come if I possibly can,' said the Archdeacon, passing his hand over his eyes with a gesture of weariness, 'but it may be that I shall be completely exhausted by the evening.'

'But you will need a meal,' said Dr Parnell, 'and I expect Belinda will want to know the numbers. It makes some difference with the catering, the arrangement of the table and that kind of thing.'

'Ah, yes, I do not understand these mysteries,' said the Archdeacon. 'I think you can take it that I shall come,' he added, turning to Belinda with almost a smile.

'You would hardly believe what I found Henry doing when we arrived last night,' said Dr Parnell, in an easy, conversational tone.

Belinda, who was of a credulous nature, refrained from making a guess.

'Playing Patience on the floor of his study,' he went on. 'A complicated variety called Double Emperor.'

'Patience is a very intelligent relaxation,' said Belinda, her usual loyalty coming to the rescue. 'You don't realize how hard Henry works. I mean,' she added obscurely, 'there are things to do in a country parish that people don't know about unless they live in one. Your work in the Library has its fixed hours, but a clergyman is at everybody's beck and call.' Of course, she reflected sadly, people would never dare to trouble the Archdeacon with their worries; they would go hurrying along Jubilee Terrace to Mr Donne. Still, the smile that Henry gave her made her realize that being a little untruthful sometimes had its compensations.

The church clock struck half-past twelve.

'Ah, lunch-time,' said the Archdeacon, and the party broke up to return to their respective houses.

When Belinda got home she found Harriet in a state of great excitement.

'Oh, Belinda,' she said, in a loud voice, 'he really is *charming*.'

As Emily was at this moment bringing in the meat, Belinda waited until they were settled at the table before she made any further enquiries.

'Harriet, I wish you *wouldn't* talk in front of Emily,' she began, but her own curiosity prevented her from saying any more. 'Who's charming?' she asked.

'Why, Mr Mold,' declared Harriet with enthusiasm. 'I saw him this morning.' Should she tell Belinda that she had seen him coming out of the Crownwheel and Pinion? she wondered. Better not, perhaps, and yet it would spoil the story to leave out such a piece of information.

'But, Harriet, how could you have seen him?' asked Belinda rather impatiently. 'I understood from Nicholas that he was tired and was spending the morning in bed.'

'Well, he must have got up because I saw him in the street,' said Harriet defiantly. She wished Belinda would not always behave quite so much like an elder sister. She decided that she would not tell her story in full. 'I spoke to him,' she declared.

Belinda was incredulous. 'But, Harriet, you don't *know* him,' she said.

'Oh, of course he didn't realize who I was,' she explained. 'I met him coming out of the Crownwheel and Pinion, and he asked me the way to the Post Office; and as I happened to be going along to buy some stamps, we walked there together.' She paused, triumphant.

Belinda put down her knife and fork in astonishment. The Crownwheel and Pinion in the morning! Surely Harriet had been mistaken? It sounded as if she had been 'picked up' by some commercial traveller. Most distasteful.

'I don't think it can have been Mr Mold,' she declared, looking very worried. 'After all, I've only met him once many years ago and you've never met him. I don't think it *can* have been him,' she repeated, with a puzzled frown on her face.

'It *was* Mr Mold,' said Harriet patiently. 'He said he was a stranger here, and that he had arrived last night and was staying at the vicarage.'

'Oh, well, if he said that . . .' Belinda had to admit that it probably had been Mr Mold. But for a deputy librarian to go to the Crownwheel and Pinion in the morning . . . surely it was unthinkable! And yet perhaps it was not so surprising, when one came to consider it, for after all Mr Mold was not *quite* . . . He had started his career in the Library as a boy fetching books for readers, and although one didn't want to be snobbish and his ability had undoubtedly brought him to a distinguished position, it was certainly true that lack of breeding showed itself. Belinda could not help wishing that it had not been Harriet who had seen Mr Mold. She would be sure to tell people and the whole situation was so embarrassing. She wondered if Nicholas knew, because really he was to blame for bringing such a man to the village.

'Of course,' she said, more to herself than to Harriet, 'he may have felt ill or something. One must be careful not to judge people too hardly, and I dare say that in a town there is really no harm in a man going into a public house for a pint of beer in the morning, but these things *are* regarded rather differently in a village and I should have thought he would have realized that.'

'He certainly didn't look ill,' said Harriet, 'in fact quite the contrary. Rather a rosy complexion really and a well-built figure, not *fat*, of course . . . his suit was very well cut, a dark blue with a narrow stripe and a maroon tie. He didn't look at all *flashy*, though.'

'Oh, no,' said Belinda, 'one would hardly expect an official of one of the greatest libraries in England to look flashy.'

'And he had the most delightful manners,' Harriet went on. 'He didn't try to take advantage of me in any way,' she explained.

Had she not thought it would be rather indelicate, Belinda would have laughed at this remark. The idea of anybody taking advantage of a respectable spinster, plumply attractive it must be admitted, in the main street of a respectable village in daylight, struck her as being rather ridiculous. But she thought it wiser not to let Harriet see that she was amused. Instead, she went on to tell her how she had invited the Archdeacon and his visitors to supper on Sunday evening.

Harriet was delighted. She enjoyed entertaining and often complained that they did not do enough. 'I will see if Mr Donne is free,' she said. 'I expect he would like to come.'

'Yes, if you like,' said Belinda doubtfully, 'but I had thought it would be nice to ask Ricardo, then we shall all be more of an age, as it were.'

'Oh, but I think we need youth, and Mr Donne is so amusing,' persisted Harriet.

'We shall be rather short of women of course,' said Belinda. 'I suppose we could ask Edith and Connie. I have a feeling Edith and Nicholas would get on rather well together. They are both interested in the same kind of thing.'

'What, in lavatories?' asked Harriet bluntly.

Belinda, who had been going to say 'conveniences', was forced to agree that this was what she had in mind, and told Harriet about his pride in the Ladies' Cloakroom which had recently been added to the Library.

'I should have thought he had better things to think about,' retorted Harriet, 'and we certainly don't want to encourage Edith. Mr Donne was so embarrassed when she was talking like that to the Archdeacon on the morning of the garden party. And then poor Connie is so dreary, isn't she? Does it really matter if we don't have equal numbers? After all I can manage Ricardo and Mr Donne and you can have the Archdeacon and Dr Parnell.'

'Well, we shall have to think about it,' said Belinda. 'After all, Edith and Connie are always free and don't mind being asked at the last minute. The Archdeacon is preaching rather a special sermon on Sunday morning,' she added, getting up from the table, 'and he said he was preaching in the evening too and will be very tired. So I should like the supper to be particularly nice.'

'Oh, of course,' Harriet agreed, 'but whatever we give him will be better than what he would get at the vicarage. We must be careful not to have the same as we had the last time Mr Donne was here.'

'I know Henry is fond of chicken,' said Belinda thoughtfully. 'Perhaps that would be the best.'

'I really must look it up in my diary,' said Harriet, 'but I *think* we had chicken the last time Mr Donne was here.'

CHAPTER TEN

IT WAS ON the next Sunday morning that the Archdeacon preached his famous sermon on the Judgment Day.

The day had begun as other Sundays did. After breakfast Belinda had consulted with Emily about the roast beef, and together they had decided what time it ought to be put into the oven and how long it ought to stay there. The vegetables – celery and roast potatoes – were agreed upon, and the pudding – a plum tart – chosen. In addition, the chickens for the supper party were to be put on to boil and Emily was to start making the trifle if she had time. The jellies had been made on Saturday night and were now setting in the cool of the cellar. Belinda had suggested that they might have a lighter luncheon than usual, as there was so much to do, but Harriet was not going to be cheated of her Sunday roast, and had managed to persuade her sister that there would be plenty of time to get things ready in the afternoon and early evening. It was of course out of the question that either of them should attend Evensong.

At half-past ten Harriet began to prepare herself for church. This morning she was taking particular care with her appearance. On ordinary Sundays she had to look nicer than

Agatha, as well as wearing something that would cause Count Bianco to burst into ecstatic compliments, and she liked the curate to see that his generation still had something to learn from hers in matters of elegance and good taste. But this Sunday was a particularly important one, for Dr Parnell and Mr Mold would be among the congregation and it was most important that she should make a good impression. She could not help regretting that when she had met Mr Mold in the village and directed him to the Post Office, she had been wearing rather a countrified tweed coat, as was perhaps only to be expected on a weekday morning in a country village. This morning she was determined to make amends for this. Mr Mold would hardly recognize the plump woman he had met outside the Crownwheel and Pinion in the elegant creature he was to see this morning. Once or twice, though, she felt a twinge of anxiety. Supposing he were not there?

'Belinda,' she called down the stairs, 'Mr Mold isn't a Roman Catholic or a Methodist, is he?'

'No, I don't *think* so,' Belinda called back, wondering why her sister should want to know. Perhaps Harriet had some doctrinal difficulty to be solved, although she had never before betrayed any interest in that direction. The Church of England had been good enough for a long line of dear curates; it would have been presumptuous of her to attempt to go further than that.

'What I meant was, will he be in church this morning?' Harriet explained.

'Oh, surely,' said Belinda. 'I expect everyone will want to hear the special sermon.'

Harriet snorted, as if expressing her contempt for anyone who would go to church to hear the Archdeacon preach.

'Henry is very particular about the observance of Sunday,' Belinda went on. 'I'm sure he wouldn't like anyone staying at the vicarage not to attend Divine Service.'

Harriet, who had got to the stage of arranging the veil on

her hat, was too preoccupied to make any answer, but she could not help wondering if Belinda had forgotten one occasion when the Archdeacon himself had not been in church, and had later been seen in the vicarage garden, obviously in excellent health.

By ten minutes to eleven Harriet was ready, and waiting impatiently in the hall.

'Belinda!' she called in an agitated voice. 'If you don't hurry up somebody might take our pew.'

Belinda reflected unhappily that the church was never likely to be full enough for that to happen, unless there was a bishop or somebody very special preaching, like that time when, she could only imagine through some mistake, they had had a handsome Brother from a religious community, obviously intended for Father Plowman's church. She looked quickly in her bag to see if she had a half-crown and a clean handkerchief, picked up her prayer book, and hurried downstairs.

By this time Harriet was halfway out of the gate. Belinda received her scolding meekly and was still silent when Harriet, quite kindly of course, began to criticize the clothes she was wearing.

'You ought to have tied your scarf in a bow,' she said, 'it's much smarter, and you know that hats are turning *up* at the back this winter, don't you?'

'Yes, dear,' said Belinda. 'I like yours very much, but I don't think I could wear one like that myself.'

'Oh, it's quite easy,' said Harriet airily, tipping her hat forward to an angle which Belinda considered a little too rakish for church, 'but you'd have to have your hair curled up at the back,' she added.

'Yes, I know,' said Belinda hopelessly, looking at Harriet's carefully arranged ringlets. But I doubt whether Henry would like me any better, she thought.

This worldly conversation had carried them almost to the

vicarage. There was as yet no sign of the important visitors. Harriet looked in at the gate rather anxiously; of course it was not quite five minutes to eleven, there was plenty of time for them to appear. It would perhaps be better to be settled in their own pew before they arrived. She hurried Belinda into the church.

When they were inside Belinda knelt down hastily to say a prayer, but Harriet waited until she had arranged her bag and umbrella, removed her gloves and loosened her silver-fox fur. The next moment Belinda found herself being nudged by her sister, who whispered rather loudly, 'Here they come, they're going to sit by Ricardo.'

When they were sitting down again, Harriet assured Belinda triumphantly that she had not been mistaken, it *had* been Mr Mold whom she had seen in the village. It was rather difficult to study them at all intently, because they were sitting behind Harriet and Belinda, but it was possible to do it not too obviously by putting your umbrella in the stand behind and taking some time in doing it. When Harriet had gone through this process, she was able to inform Belinda that Dr Parnell was wearing a dark tie and that Mr Mold had on the same suit she had seen him in before.

The service began quite uneventfully with one of the usual morning hymns, *New every morning is the love.* As they sang, Belinda noticed that the Archdeacon was not joining with them, but looking rather sternly round the church. As she did not want to catch his eye, Belinda looked down at her prayer book and concentrated on Keble's fine lines

Through sleep and darkness safely brought,
Restored to life, and power and thought.

Not that she ever thought of herself as having much *power*, but she was certainly alive and might be considered capable of a small amount of thought. She could at least thank God for that. The curate was joining heartily in the singing and

Belinda hoped he was saving enough voice to read the lessons.

Obviously the Archdeacon was out to impress his visitors, for the *Te Deum* and the *Benedictus* were sung to elaborate, unfamiliar settings, which the congregation could not attempt and which seemed rather beyond the choir at some points. The Archdeacon himself read the first lesson and the curate the second. The Archdeacon also intoned many of the prayers and his voice went up and down in the oddest way. Of course the voice should go up or down, Belinda couldn't quite remember which, at the end of a line, but there seemed to be something wrong somewhere and so much disturbance was caused among the choir boys that Mr Gibson, the organist, had to hurry out of his place to control them.

Belinda thought that as the Archdeacon was going to preach, he was perhaps doing too much of the service himself, and what with the curious intoning and the curate's church voice, which was like nothing so much as a bleating sheep's, it was difficult for Belinda to keep from smiling. And even she was forced to admit to herself that they were getting a little too much for their money, when she realized that they were going to have the Litany.

Just before he went to the Litany desk, the Archdeacon glanced round the congregation with what appeared to be a look of malicious amusement on his face. At least, that was how it must have seemed to most people, but perhaps it could hardly have been amusement. Indulgence for his sinful flock was more likely and certainly more fitting. Everyone knelt down rather angrily. They had had the Litany last Sunday and the Archdeacon never made any attempt to shorten it. As he could not sing, he made up for it by making his voice heard as much as possible in other ways.

Belinda was trying hard to concentrate on her sins, but somehow the atmosphere was not very suitable this morning and she was at last forced to give it up. Staring at the Archdeacon's back, she reflected that he was still very handsome. Perhaps he would read aloud to them when he came to supper tonight, though, as she would be the only person who wanted to listen, it might be rather difficult to arrange. Harriet could play the piano and the curate might be asked to sing, but the main entertainment of the evening would be the conversation. Dear Nicholas was so delightfully witty and Mr Mold would no doubt be able to tell them many interesting things about the Library. By the time the Archdeacon had ascended the pulpit steps, Belinda had forgotten all about the special sermon, and settled herself comfortably in her pew, as did the rest of the congregation, having just sung with great vigour that the world was very evil.

The text was given out, quite a usual one from the Revelation. *And I saw a new heaven and a new earth, for the first heaven and the first earth were passed away.*

Harriet looked at her watch. She supposed they would have to endure the Archdeacon for at least twenty minutes, possibly twenty-five minutes or even half an hour. She sighed and tried to listen to what he was saying. It was some consolation that he was preaching a sermon of his own composition instead of one of those tedious literary things that Belinda said he read so magnificently.

'We are apt to accept this vision of the new heaven and the new earth with too much complacency,' he declared.

Oh, well, thought Harriet, clergymen are always saying things like that.

'But do we realize all that must happen before we can hope to share in this bliss? If, indeed, we are found worthy. I say again, do we realize? Have we any idea at all?' The Archdeacon paused impressively and peered at his congregation; a harmless enough collection of people – old Mrs Prior and her daughter, Miss Jenner, Miss Beard and Miss Smiley in front with the children, ever watchful to frown on giggles or fidgets – the Bank Manager, who sometimes read the lessons – the Misses Bede and the guests from the vicarage – Count Bianco – Miss Liversidge and Miss Aspinall – of course they did not realize but he was going to tell them. 'The *Judgment Day*,' he almost shouted, so loudly that Harriet had to take out her handkerchief to stifle her inappropriate amusement, and old Mrs Prior let out a kind of moan. 'That day may be soon,' he went on, 'it may even be *tomorrow*.'

The congregation shifted awkwardly in their seats. It was uncomfortable to be reminded that the Judgment Day might be tomorrow.

'*Dies Irae*,' he continued, lingering on the words with enjoyment. Belinda saw Edith Liversidge purse her lips disapprovingly at this Romish expression. 'Day of Wrath,' he translated. 'And what a terrible day that will be!'

The congregation, still rather uneasy and disturbed, reminded themselves that of course such a thing couldn't *really* happen. Why, scientists told us that it would take millions of years for the sun to move sufficiently far away from the earth for life to become extinct. At least it was perhaps not exactly that, but something very like it. They knew enough to realize that the Archdeacon was being ridiculous and that the Judgment Day could not possibly be tomorrow. When the first uncomfortable shock had passed they were able to laugh at themselves. How could they have been so silly as to be alarmed!

But even as they were thinking thus, the relentless voice from the pulpit was pouring scorn on those scientists who thought they knew how the world had begun and how it would end. How *could* they know? These matters were incomprehensible mysteries known to God alone. The Judgment Day was as likely to be tomorrow as at any time in the far distant future. The world was indeed very evil, as they had just been singing in that fine hymn translated from the Latin, the times were waxing late. All through our literature poets had been haunted by the idea of the Last Day and what it would be like. . . .

The congregation suddenly relaxed. It was just going to be one of the Archdeacon's usual sermons after all. There had been no need for those uncomfortable fears. They settled down again, now completely reassured, and prepared themselves for a long string of quotations, joined together by a few explanations from the Archdeacon.

He began at the seventeenth century. Belinda reflected that if he had gone back any further, the sermon would have assumed Elizabethan proportions. As it was, it promised to be longer than usual. She listened admiringly. The Archdeacon was quoting Thomas Flatman's lines written in 1659, to show how poets of the latter half of that century had imagined that the Judgment Day was near.

'Tis not far off; methinks I see
Among the stars some dimmer be;
Some tremble as their lamps did fear
A neighbouring extinguisher. . . .

And curiously enough one of the oldest inhabitants of the parish had remarked to him only the other day that the stars did not seem to be as bright as they were when he was a boy. It was very significant. The Archdeacon liked the sound of his own voice and so did Belinda, and she was delighted to hear him read about thirty more lines of Flatman's poem.

Those of the congregation who were still listening – Harriet's attention had long since wandered – smiled complacently. That had been in 1659, they thought, and nothing had come of this man's noticing that some of the stars were dimmer. Why even the Archdeacon himself was forced to admit it! 1659. 1660. What had happened in 1660? His hearers resented this history lesson. The Restoration. Everyone knew that. But here was the Archdeacon trying to tell them that the Restoration was itself a kind of Judgment Day.

Belinda tried hard to follow, but she found this point rather obscure. She was frowning slightly with the effort of concentration. Harriet was looking at the curate, but he had sunk so deeply into his stall that very little of him was visible. By looking out of the corner of her left eye and turning her head slightly, she could see Dr Parnell and Mr Mold. Mr Mold was looking at his watch and Dr Parnell appeared to be smiling at some private joke. Count Bianco, sitting in front of Dr Parnell, had long ago given up any attempt to follow the sermon. A Roman Catholic by upbringing, he still found the service confusing and only attended the Archdeacon's church because he felt it might bring him nearer to Harriet. This morning she had looked in his direction; she had distinctly turned her head. Could it be that she was looking at *him*?

When the Archdeacon reached the eighteenth century, the going was a little easier. Several people smiled at the lines he quoted from Blair's poem *The Grave*:

When the dread trumpet sounds, the slumb'ring dust,
Not unattentive to the call shall wake,
And ev'ry joint possess its proper place,
With a new elegance of form unknown
To its first state. Nor shall the conscious soul
Mistake his partner. . . .

Belinda liked this very much, but she was uneasily conscious that the Archdeacon had already been preaching for nearly half an hour, and she began to worry about the beef. It would be roasted to a cinder by now, unless Emily had had the sense to turn down the oven. Harriet did so like it underdone, and they were usually well out of church and sitting down to their meal by half-past twelve. And Henry had only got as far as the eighteenth century without yet having mentioned Edward Young, who was sure to be brought into the sermon somehow. She had rather lost the thread of what he was saying now, but suddenly felt herself on safer ground when she heard him mention the *Night Thoughts*. He seemed to be implying that each person listening to him this morning was little better than the unknown Lorenzo, for whose edification the poem had been written. Even Belinda thought the Archdeacon was going a little too far when he likened his congregation to such as '*call aloud for ev'ry bauble drivel'd o'er by sense*'. Whatever it might mean it certainly sounded abusive. He concluded his reading from Young by flinging a challenge at them.

> *. . . Say dreamers of gay dreams,*
> *How will you weather an eternal night,*
> *Where such expedients fail?*

He paused dramatically and the sermon was at an end. There was quite a stir in the congregation, for some of them had been dreaming gay dreams most of the morning, although many of them had given the sermon a chance, and had only allowed their thoughts to wander when it had passed beyond their comprehension. They now fidgeted angrily in bags and pockets for their collect-money. One or two even let the plate pass them, waving it on with an angry gesture.

Belinda soon recovered from her first feeling of shocked surprise. Of course dear Henry had not really meant to insult them. He had obviously been carried away by the fine poetry, and naturally he must have meant to include himself among those he condemned. It had really been one of the finest sermons she had ever heard him preach, she told herself loyally, even if the ending had been rather sudden and unusual. It didn't do people any harm to hear the truth occasionally. We were all inclined to get too complacent sometimes. She thought rather vaguely of great preachers like Savonarola, Donne and John Wesley. No doubt they had not spared the feelings of their hearers either, but as she was unable to think of anything that any one of them had said, she could not be absolutely sure. As they were singing the last hymn, *Ye servants of the Lord*, Belinda tried to think of some intelligent criticisms, for she did not want her praise of dear Henry to be lacking in discernment. He might welcome intelligent criticism, she thought, knowing perfectly well that he would not. Perhaps there had been rather too many literary quotations, and she had the feeling that it was not quite the thing to read bits of Restoration drama in church but it had certainly been a fine and unusual sermon. She could not help wondering whether he would continue it this evening, going through the Victorians and the modern poets and so bringing it up to date. But that would hardly be suitable for the evening congregation, who, as he had admitted himself, liked simpler stuff.

As they came out of church they passed the time of day with Dr Parnell and Mr Mold, but Belinda hurried Harriet away before they could get involved in conversation. Mr Mold's manner seemed very free and he had looked almost as if he were going to *wink* at Harriet. Ricardo, who was hovering hopefully by a tomb-stone, saw her whisked away before he could do more than bow and say good morning. But he comforted himself with the prospect of seeing her that evening.

'I was sorry not to stop and talk to Ricardo,' said Belinda, 'but we are so late as it is.'

'Yes,' said Harriet, 'I expect many people's Sunday dinner will be ruined. I wonder what they are having at the vicarage?'

'I think they are having duck,' said Belinda. 'At least, I saw one in Hartnell's on Saturday which was labelled for the vicarage. And of course,' she said thoughtfully, as she watched her sister carve the over-cooked beef, 'duck needs to be *very* well done, doesn't it? It can't really be cooked too much.'

CHAPTER ELEVEN

THE GUESTS were due to arrive at about eight o'clock, by which time Evensong would be over. Both Belinda and Harriet had of course been much too busy with their preparations to attend it. Belinda had felt very much tempted, indeed, the thought of missing one of the Archdeacon's sermons was almost unbearable, but she consoled herself with the reflection that looking after his material welfare was just as important as her own spiritual welfare, if such it could be called, and that she was making the sacrifice in a good cause.

A very nice supper had been prepared. It had to be so, for not only must the Archdeacon be pleased, but Harriet had thought the curate needed feeding up as he had been looking especially thin and pale lately. She could only hope it was nothing to do with that Miss Berridge. There were to be cold chickens with ham and tongue and various salads, followed by trifles, jellies, fruit and Stilton cheese. An extra leaf had been put in the dining-room table as, much against Harriet's will, Belinda had decided to invite Miss Liversidge and Miss Aspinall. She really thought that five men and two women was a little disproportionate and such a party might give rise to talk. Emily would think it so funny. It was rather an undertaking to have seven people to supper, but as most of the food was cold and could be prepared well in advance there was no reason why everything should not go very well.

Harriet was a little inclined to worry about what they should drink. Mr Mold would be used to living in style, she thought, and would surely expect whisky or gin.

'But we have a very good sherry,' said Belinda. 'I am sure that is quite correct, and there will be the hock and afterwards port.' Whisky was to Belinda more a medicine than a drink, something one took for a cold with hot milk or lemon. It was not at all suitable for a Sunday evening supper party at which there were to be clergymen and ladies present.

'We must be sure that the hock is *chilled* enough,' said Harriet. 'Not iced, of course, that would be a serious error; I shouldn't like Mr Mold to think that we didn't know about wine.'

'Nicholas is a great connoisseur,' said Belinda. 'It seems right that a librarian should be, I think. Good wine and old books seem to go together.'

'And of course the Archdeacon likes a drop,' said Harriet rather vulgarly. 'We shall have to watch him. I don't suppose Agatha lets him have much. Good heavens, it's nearly seven o'clock. We must go and change.'

Harriet was determined that this evening should see the climax of her elegance and only lamented the fact that she could not wear full evening dress. Still, her new brown velvet would be magnificent with her gold necklace and long ear-rings. Belinda had decided to wear her blue chiffon. Henry had once said that he liked her in pale colours, and although that had been over thirty years ago it was possible that he still might. Her crystal beads and ear-rings went quite well with it, and when she had put on a little rouge the whole effect was rather pleasing. She went into the bathroom where Harriet was splashing about in the bath like a plump porpoise. Her curls were protected by a round cap of green oilskin and the room was filled with the exotic scent of bath salts.

Harriet looked at Belinda critically. 'Yes, you look very nice,' she said, 'but I think I should use some more lipstick if I were you. Artificial light is apt to make one look paler.'

'Oh, no, Harriet, I don't think I can use any more,' said Belinda. 'I shouldn't really feel natural if I did. *Thou art not fair for all thy red and white*,' she quoted vaguely, leaving Harriet to wallow in her bath.

At five minutes to eight Belinda was downstairs in the drawing-room, waiting for somebody to arrive. She was sitting in a chair by the fire with a book on her knee, which she was not reading. It was something by an old friend of Harriet's – a former curate – Theodore Grote, now Bishop of Mbawawa in Africa. Dear Theo, he had certainly done splendid work among the natives, at least, that was what everyone said, although nobody seemed to know exactly what it was that he had done. Certainly they still *looked* very heathen, grinning away in their leafy dress. But perhaps that was before he converted them. She opened the book with a view to finding out, but she could not settle to reading and walked restlessly round the room, moving the flowers, rearranging the cushions and altering the position of chairs. She brought out a photograph of Nicholas Parnell in his academic robes and put it on the mantelpiece; she also displayed on a small table a little pamphlet he had written about central heating in libraries. It was prettily bound and had a picture of a phoenix on the cover with a Greek inscription underneath it. Something about Prometheus, Harriet had said, for Belinda was like Shakespeare in having little Latin and no Greek.

At eight o'clock the bell rang. Men's voices were heard in the hall and a minute or two later Emily showed the Archdeacon, Dr Parnell, Mr Mold and the curate into the room. Belinda shook hands with them rather formally. The Archdeacon advanced towards an armchair by the fire and sank down into it rather dramatically, as if exhausted. Dr Parnell took up his own pamphlet and said that he was glad to find somebody who had cut its beautiful pages.

'I'm afraid you're hardly a best seller,' said Mr Mold jovially. 'Nor even as much ordered in the Library as Rochester's poems,' he added.

Belinda frowned and looked embarrassed when the curate asked, with his usual eager interest, what poems those were.

'I am afraid they are rather *naughty*,' said Dr Parnell. 'We have had to lock them away in a special place, together with other books of a similar nature. All the same, they are quite often asked for by our readers.'

'Oh, well, I suppose people have to study them,' said Belinda, handing round cigarettes and wondering how she could change the subject.

'We should not like to think that they ordered them for any other reason,' said Dr Parnell, chuckling and rubbing his hands in front of the fire.

Belinda was greatly relieved when Miss Liversidge and Miss Aspinall arrived and she was able to introduce them. She was so afraid that Nicholas and Edith would discover their common interest in sanitary arrangements too soon, that she resolutely kept them apart. It was all very difficult and she wished Harriet would hurry up and come in. Only the curate was making what Belinda considered to be suitable conversation for the awkward interval between arriving and sitting down to eat.

'Do you know,' he was saying eagerly, 'there was quite a *nip* in the air this evening? I shouldn't be surprised if we had frost.'

'And the later the frost the harder the winter,' said a cheerful voice in the background. 'I do hope you're all wearing warm underclothes.'

It was Harriet, ready far sooner than Belinda had hoped was possible, looking splendid too, in her brown velvet and gold ornaments.

The curate laughed heartily and assured her that he had his on.

Harriet was in excellent form and soon had everybody laughing, except for the Archdeacon, who went on reclining in the armchair, not speaking.

'Well, what did you preach about this evening?' asked Harriet. 'I haven't heard any comments on the sermon yet.'

The Archdeacon roused himself. 'It was a continuation of this morning's, brought up to date as it were,' he explained.

'Oh, it was beautiful,' gushed Connie Aspinall, 'I did so enjoy it.'

The Archdeacon looked pleased. 'I had feared it might be rather too obscure,' he said. 'Eliot is not an easy poet.'

Belinda gasped. Eliot! And for the evening congregation! But it must have been magnificent to hear him reading Eliot. 'Perhaps you will give the sermon again,' she suggested timidly, 'for the benefit of those who were not at Evensong.'

'Perhaps I will,' said the Archdeacon, 'perhaps I will.' He paused. 'I have been considering giving a course of sermons on Dante,' he mused. 'Not of course in the original – Carey's translation, perhaps.'

'It would be a fine and unusual subject,' said Belinda doubtfully.

'Well, you can count me out,' said Edith bluntly. 'I couldn't make much of the sermon this morning. Too full of quotations, like *Hamlet*.' She gave her short barking laugh.

'I think people prefer the more obvious aspects of the Christian teaching,' said Nicholas regretfully. 'I mean, I am afraid that they do. Simple sentiments in intelligible prose. A great pity really. I can see how it limits the scope of the more enterprising clergy.'

'*Sentiments to which every bosom returns an echo*,' said the Archdeacon. 'Yes, one appreciates that, and yet, why shouldn't Eliot express those sentiments?'

'Do the bosoms of people nowadays return any echo?' said Mr Mold. 'One wonders really.'

'Well, if they do, it certainly isn't as loud as the echo made by the Apes of Brazil,' chortled Harriet, and in response to a very pressing appeal by Mr Mold, she began to explain it all over again.

'Can the sound really be heard two *miles* away?' said Connie, whose voice held just the same note of rapt awe as when she had praised the Archdeacon's sermon. 'Isn't that wonderful?'

The Archdeacon looked rather annoyed. 'Oh, it is nothing very unusual,' he said shortly, so that Belinda began to wonder whether he was about to embark on some tale of his own. But he lapsed into silence again, so that she was forced to continue the conversation with a bright and rather insincere remark about Agatha, and what a pity it was that she was not with them that evening.

'I had a postcard from her yesterday,' said the Archdeacon. 'She says she is getting on quite well speaking Anglo-Saxon and Old High German in the shops.'

'Ah, well, Agatha is so clever,' said Belinda, without bitterness. 'I'm afraid I've forgotten all my Anglo-Saxon. But surely the vocabulary is rather limited?'

'Yes, quite ridiculous,' said Edith shortly. 'Like trying to talk Latin in Italy.'

'Why, Ricardo isn't here yet,' said Belinda. 'What do you say to a glass of sherry while we are waiting?'

'I say yes,' said Mr Mold promptly.

'Yes *please*, Nathaniel,' Dr Parnell reminded him. 'We should not like it to be thought that an official of our great Library was lacking in manners.'

'I feel that *I* have been lacking in manners for not offering it sooner,' said Belinda quite sincerely, thus taking upon herself the blame for all the little frictions of the evening. But it was so obvious that women should take the blame, it was both the better and the easier part, and just as she was pouring out the sherry, Ricardo arrived, with such profuse and gallant apologies for being late that everyone was put into a good humour. He was a little encumbered by a magnificent pot of chrysanthemums, which he presented with a ceremonious gesture.

Shortly after this they went into supper, Edith and Harriet followed by Mr Mold and the curate, making for the dining-room with what Belinda considered indecent haste. But even those who followed more slowly moved with confident anticipation. Belinda had taken care to arrange the table so that Harriet should sit between Ricardo and Mr Mold, when she might see how superior dear Ricardo was. Belinda herself sat by the Archdeacon and Dr Parnell, while Miss Liversidge and Miss Aspinall were fitted in where there happened to be spaces.

'Why, the table is groaning!' exclaimed Dr Parnell. 'I like that expression so much, but one is hardly ever justified in using it or even expecting it. Certainly not at Sunday supper.'

Belinda looked pleased. 'I hope everything will be nice,' she said. 'I never see why Sunday supper should be the dreary meal it usually is. I mean,' she added hastily, remembering that they had had just such a dreary Sunday supper at the vicarage a few weeks ago, 'that it can sometimes be.'

'We always have cold meat with beetroot and no potatoes,' said the Archdeacon, as if reading her thoughts. 'Nothing could be more unappetizing.'

'Of course the servants are often out on Sunday evening,' said the curate, 'and one likes to feel that they are having an easier time.'

'I don't feel that at all,' said the Archdeacon. 'I like to feel that somebody has taken a little trouble in preparing a meal for me. I think we deserve it after the labour of Sunday.'

'Especially after that magnificent sermon this morning,' murmured Belinda loyally, giving him some of the best of the chicken.

'All that reading must be very tiring,' said Dr Parnell spitefully.

'It was some very fine poetry,' said Ricardo vaguely, for he had not grasped much of the sermon apart from the bare fact that it was supposed to be about the Judgment Day.

'We certainly thought it magnificent, didn't we, Harriet?' said Belinda, turning towards her sister rather urgently. It was tactless of Harriet not to have made any comment. But then she herself was rather to blame for introducing the subject when they had already discussed it once. It was a pity that her loyalty had got the better of her.

'Oh, splendid,' said Harriet, rather too enthusiastically.

'But of course I'm *not* a theologian,' she added, with a brilliant smile.

Mr Mold laughed at this and so did Dr Parnell, but the Archdeacon looked rather annoyed.

'Few of us are true theologians,' said the curate sententiously. 'But after all, the real knowledge comes from within and not from books.'

Belinda looked at him rather apprehensively. She hoped the wine wasn't beginning to have its effect on him. White wine wasn't really intoxicating and he had only had one glass of sherry.

'That is rather a disconcerting thought,' said Dr Parnell. 'You are preaching sedition. I maintain that the true knowledge comes from *books*. It would be a poor prospect for me and for Nathaniel if everybody thought as you do.'

'Ah, but it is true what Mr Donne says,' said Ricardo thoughtfully. 'My dear friend John Akenside used to say that he learned more about the political situation in central Europe in those quiet moments with a glass of wine at a café table than by all his talks with Pribitchevitch's brother.'

'Oh, yes, I can believe that,' said Edith Liversidge, 'John liked his glass of wine.'

'But surely the intrigues of Balkan politics can hardly be compared with the true knowledge that comes from within?' Dr Parnell protested. 'I hardly think it is the same thing.'

Belinda, too, thought Ricardo's remarks hardly relevant, but one could not argue the point. Perhaps it was a mistake to have any kind of serious conversation when eating, or even anywhere at all in mixed company. Men took themselves so seriously and seemed to insist on arguing even the most trivial points. So, at the risk of seeming frivolous, she turned the conversation to something lighter.

'I can never think of Belgrade without thinking of the public baths,' she said.

Mr Mold looked across the table expectantly. Perhaps this

would be more amusing than the knowledge that comes from within.

'Why does it remind you of public baths?' said the Archdeacon. 'It seems most unlikely.'

'Oh, well,' said Belinda, who hadn't really a story to tell, 'I once heard somebody describing them and I thought it was rather funny. A lot of old men all swimming about in a pool of hot water,' she concluded weakly, hoping that somebody would laugh.

Most of them did, especially the Archdeacon, who seemed to be in a good temper again.

'I never heard of there being any hot springs in Belgrade,' said Ricardo seriously.

'Oh, I expect the water was artificially heated,' explained the curate, turning earnestly to Belinda for further information on this interesting point.

Belinda felt rather flustered at the interest which everyone was taking in her silly little story. 'I don't really know,' she said. 'I've never been to Belgrade myself, and even if I had I don't suppose I should have visited the public baths.'

'Not the ones with the old men in them, we hope,' said Mr Mold, with almost a wink.

Belinda was rather taken aback. She didn't think she liked Mr Mold very much. Of course one didn't want to be snobbish, but it really was true that low origin always betrayed itself somewhere.

'Oh, Belinda never remembers where she's been,' said Harriet, hardly improving the situation. 'Now, Mr Mold, do have some more trifle,' she said, favouring him with a brilliant smile.

'Perhaps I may have some too,' said the Archdeacon. 'It really is delicious. I don't know when I've tasted anything so good.'

But Belinda hardly noticed his praise. She was thinking indignantly that Nicholas had always encouraged Mr Mold too much as a boy, although one would have thought that moving in a cultured intellectual society would have cured him of any tendency to make jokes not quite in the best of taste. And yet, she thought doubtfully, the Library, great though it was, did not always attract to it cultured and intellectual persons. Nicholas himself, obsessed with central heating and conveniences, was perhaps not the best influence for a weak character like Mr Mold. Belinda began to wish that she were in Karlsbad with dear Agatha, helping her to get cured of her rheumatism. She imagined herself in the pump-room, if there was one, drinking unpleasant but salutary waters, and making conversation with elderly people. Perhaps taking a gentle walk in the cool of the evening with an old clergyman or a retired general . . .

All around her the conversation buzzed pleasantly. Mr Mold's little lapse was quite forgotten, if indeed it had ever been noticed by anyone except Belinda. Harriet was asking Ricardo if it was true that the fleas on the Lido were so wonderful. She had heard that they bounced balls and drew little golden carriages.

'Indeed, they are,' said Ricardo gravely. 'I have seen them myself.'

The curate leaned forward eagerly. 'It is wonderful what things animals and even insects can be made to do if they are trained with kindness,' he said, his face aglow with interest.

Everyone agreed with this very just remark. Dr Parnell even went so far as to observe that it was also true of people.

'I should love to go to Venice,' said Belinda. 'I think there is something very special about Italy. It is so rich in literary associations.'

'Ah . . .' Ricardo put down his spoon and was obviously on the point of bursting into a flow of Dante, but the Archdeacon was too quick for him and got in first with Byron:

I stood in Venice on the Bridge of Sighs
A palace and a prison on each hand:

he quoted, and remarked that he had thought of visiting Italy in the spring, but that of course it was almost impossible for him to take a holiday however much he might need it.

'Oh, but I don't see why you shouldn't,' said Harriet, loudly and tactlessly. 'It isn't as if you had a frightful lot to do, and I'm sure Mr Donne could manage perfectly well when you were away.'

There was an uncomfortable silence.

'You know, you really should take a holiday,' said Edith Liversidge. 'A change does everyone good. Everyone would benefit.'

'You would feel you were doing good to others as well as yourself,' said Dr Parnell, 'so you would have a double satisfaction.'

'I doubt whether I could allow myself that luxury,' said the Archdeacon quite good-humouredly. 'Of course a change can sometimes be a good thing. I have often wondered whether I ought to have a town parish. There is more scope for preaching.'

'Oh, yes,' Connie Aspinall broke in eagerly. 'I remember when Canon Kendrick was rector of St Ermin's there wasn't a vacant seat at Evensong – you had to be there half an hour before it started. He said some very shocking things.'

'Well, of course, people like that,' said Dr Parnell. 'Kendrick was a contemporary of mine. He got a very poor degree, I believe, but he found out what his line was and made a success of it.'

'What a cynical way to talk,' said Harriet indignantly. 'He was probably a very sincere man.'

'Oh, he was,' said Connie, 'but I suppose he thought it his duty to say those things, unpleasant though they were.'

'Yes, there is evil even in Belgravia,' said Dr Parnell.

'There is evil everywhere,' said the curate.

Belinda looked around her uncomfortably as if expecting to find the devil sitting at the table, but by the time they were drinking their coffee in the drawing-room that solemn subject had somehow been forgotten and Ricardo, talking about the picturesque costume of the ancient Etruscans, was the centre of the little group. Belinda marvelled at the way conversation rushed from one subject to another with such bewildering speed, but decided that this was one which could give offence to nobody and was therefore to be encouraged. So she appeared interested although she knew nothing whatever about the ancient Etruscans. It was hardly the kind of thing one would know about, unless one had had the advantage of a classical education, as Nicholas and Ricardo had.

'Was their dress anything like that of the Germanic tribes?' she asked. 'I mean the ones Tacitus described in his *Germania*,' she added vaguely, for it was a long time since she had taken her first University examination in which it had been one of the set books.

Ricardo paused and looked thoughtful, but before he had time to answer, Harriet let out a cry of joy, as if she had suddenly come upon something which she had long ago given up for lost.

Locupletissimi veste distinguuntur, non fluitante . . .

she paused appealingly, and waved her plump hands about, searching for the rest of the quotation. While she did so, Belinda and Dr Parnell began to laugh, the curate and Miss Aspinall looked amazed and expectant, while the Archdeacon smiled a little doubtfully, for he was not a very good Latinist, nor had he known his Tacitus very well as an undergraduate. Mr Mold looked frankly bored, although he could not help thinking that Harriet looked very attractive, waving her hands about in the air.

Ricardo was frowning, but only for a moment. How

terrible it would be if he were to fail her! He cleared his throat . . .

non fluitante sed stricto et singulos artus exprimente,

he recited.

Really, reflected Belinda, Ricardo's faculty for quoting Tacitus is quite frightening!

'I suppose *veste* means vest,' said the curate earnestly, with an expression of painful intelligence on his face.

'Hardly in the modern sense, perhaps,' said Ricardo thoughtfully, 'although it was a tight-fitting garment, as you hear from the description.'

'More like men's long pants,' said Edith Liversidge bluntly. 'They must have looked rather comic.'

'Yes, it is strange that the rich men should have been distinguished by the wearing of underclothes,' said Belinda thinking that the conversation was getting more than usually silly. She was herself smiling, as she could not help thinking of the curate's combinations. It was a good thing, she felt, when Ricardo suggested that Harriet might honour them by playing something on the piano.

'How very talented your sister must be,' said Mr Mold, who was sitting on the sofa by Belinda. 'She would be an asset to any household,' he declared pompously.

Belinda tried to think of something to say which would put him off, but could think of nothing without being disloyal to her sister. Certainly she looked very splendid sitting at the piano; it was not surprising that he should admire her.

The first chords of *The Harmonious Blacksmith* jangled forth. Belinda wondered why Harriet had chosen this particular piece, and began to be a little anxious about the later variations, which she knew were rather tricky. But Harriet avoided this difficulty by playing only the first two variations.

'I don't want to bore you with the whole lot,' she said, and broke into a gay Chopin mazurka.

There was now an atmosphere of peace and contentment in the room. Everyone had eaten well, there was a good fire and comfortable chairs. The Archdeacon, in the best chair, was nodding now. Miss Aspinall had found a polite listener in the curate, who was asking her just the kind of questions she liked about the past glories of her life in Belgrave Square. Dr Parnell and Miss Liversidge were talking, but in a low voice, about the 'improvements' in the Library and what further ones could conveniently be made. Ricardo and Mr Mold were both admiring Harriet and vying for her attention. Only Belinda was unoccupied, but she was quite happy in the knowledge that the party had really been quite successful. Of course, if the Archdeacon had not been asleep, she could have had some conversation with him, but it was nice to know that he felt really at home, and she would not for the world have had him any different.

CHAPTER TWELVE

THE NEXT day Harriet could talk of nothing but Mr Mold. At breakfast she declared that he was remarkably young-looking for his age.

'I suppose he must be in the early fifties, but that's really the Prime of Life, isn't it?' she said to Belinda, who had not so far contributed anything to her sister's eulogy apart from the observation that he certainly had rather a high colour. Harriet repeated 'the Prime of Life', and went on eating her sausage.

'Yes, I suppose he is,' agreed Belinda, but rather doubtfully, for she was not really sure what the Prime of Life was. She had always thought that her own prime was twenty-five, so that by her reckoning Mr Mold must be nearly thirty years past it. 'Personally he isn't a type that appeals to me very much,' she added, remembering the joke about the public baths in Belgrade.

'Oh, I know he isn't always quoting Gray's *Elegy*,' said Harriet pointedly, 'but he's so amusing, such a Man of the World,' she added naïvely. 'I wonder how long he will be staying?'

'I expect he will have to get back to the Library soon,' said Belinda. 'Old Mr Lydgate is in charge now, but I should think he is hardly up to the work really, though,' she added irrelevantly, 'he had some very interesting experiences in Ethiopia.'

With that she went upstairs, thinking that it would really be a good thing when both the Librarian and Mr Mold went back. Although it was nice seeing different people, especially if they were old friends as dear Nicholas was, Belinda found it rather unsettling. The effort of trying to talk to so many people last night and keep them at peace with each other had quite exhausted her. But there was some satisfaction mixed with her tiredness, for she felt it had been quite a successful party. Edith and Connie had obviously enjoyed both the food and the company, and as inviting them had been something in the nature of a duty, one could feel special satisfaction there. Nicholas and Edith had had a very full conversation about conveniences and he had invited her to come for a personally conducted tour of the Library, where her advice on certain points would be much valued. The curate, Count Bianco and Mr Mold had seemed quite happy, though perhaps the word was scarcely applicable to the Count, who preferred his gentle state of melancholy which must have been enriched by Harriet's attentions to Mr Mold and the curate. Belinda's only fear was that the Archdeacon had been bored, though she had decided that his going to sleep showed rather that he felt at home in her house and she was determined to go on thinking so. As she dusted her dressing-table, she broke into Addison's noble hymn, *The spacious firmament on high*.

In Reason's ear they all rejoice . . . How admirable that was! Belinda began to think rather confusedly about the eighteenth century, and what in her undergraduate essays she had called its 'Rationalism'. Had not her favourite, Young, said something about his heart becoming the convert of his head? How useful that must have been! Belinda began to look back on her own life and came to the regretful conclusion that she had admired the great eighteenth-century poet without really taking his advice. She comforted herself by reflecting that it was now too late to do anything about it, but as she opened a drawer she came upon some skeins of grey wool, the wool she had bought to knit the Archdeacon a pullover. She knew now that she would never do it. She would make a jumper for herself, safe, dull and rather too thick. Surely this was proof that her heart had now become the convert of her head? Or was it just fear of Agatha?

She shut the drawer and turned her attention to other work, preparing to live this day as if her last. As it was a nice bright morning, she felt that it would be a good opportunity to do some gardening, and later, if she had time, she might write a letter to poor Agatha, who was probably feeling rather lonely all by herself in Karlsbad. It was quite a luxury to be able to think of her as 'poor Agatha'; it showed that absence could do more than just make the heart grow fonder.

Belinda went downstairs and put on her goloshes and an old mackintosh. She decided to put some bulbs in the beds in the front garden and then move round to the back. If people came to the door it was more likely that they would come later, and by then she would be out of sight. She began to plant tulip bulbs in between the wall-flower plants. They would make a pretty show in the late spring. She noticed how splendidly the aubrietias had done; they were spreading so much that they would soon have to be divided. Belinda remembered when she had put them in as little cuttings. They had had a particularly hard winter that year, so that she had been afraid the frost would kill them. But they had all lived and flourished. How wonderful it was, when one came to think of it, what a lot of hardships plants could stand! And people too. Here Belinda realized how well her own heart, broken at twenty-five, had mended with the passing of the years. Perhaps the slave had grown to love its chains, or whatever it was that the dear Earl of Rochester had said on that subject. Belinda was sure that our greater English poets had written much about unhappy lovers *not* dying of grief, although it was of course more romantic when they did. But there was always hope springing eternal in the human breast, which kept one alive, often unhappily . . . it would be an interesting subject on which to read a paper to the Literary Society, which the Archdeacon was always threatening to start in the village. Belinda began to collect material in her mind and then imagined the typical audience of clergy and female church workers, most of them unmarried. Perhaps after all it would hardly be suitable. She must consider, too, what was fitting to her *own* years and position.

By this time she had planted most of the bulbs, and her back was aching. She stood up to rest herself, and looked idly over the wall. The road was deserted and there was no sign of life at the vicarage, but of course it was barely half-past ten, and in the village the best people did not appear till later, when they would start out to do their shopping or to meet a friend at the Old Refectory for coffee. Belinda leaned her arms on the wall, apparently lost in thought. It did not occur to her that she would look odd to anyone passing by. Absent-mindedly she scraped the moss off the wall with a trowel. She would rest for a few minutes and then put some scyllas in the rockery. It was nice to think that she had the whole morning before her. She must go into the cellar and see if the bulbs she had planted in bowls were showing any shoots yet. It would be fatal if they were left in the darkness too long. . . .

She looked up from the moss and glanced in the direction of the vicarage, to see if anything had happened since she last looked. In the next instant she knew that a great deal had happened. Mr Mold had come out of the gate and was walking rapidly towards her.

He must be coming *here*, thought Belinda, in a flurry of agitation. For some seconds she wondered whether she ought to go and warn Harriet, but even now she could hear his step on the pavement. How quickly he walked! It would be as much as Belinda could do to hide herself before he came through the gate and walked up the drive.

She looked around frantically. There was no time to run back to the house, as he would see her, and even if he did not recognize her in her gardening clothes it would look so conspicuous. So Belinda concealed herself as best she could behind a large rhododendron bush, which grew on one side of the little drive leading up to the front door. She was fully aware how foolish she would feel if she were discovered in this undignified crouching position, but she could not imagine that Mr Mold would take the trouble to penetrate the thickness of the bush before he rang the bell and announced himself. She wished he would hurry, for it was very uncomfortable behind the bush and rather dirty. Also, Belinda felt like laughing and it would indeed be terrible if Mr Mold were startled on the doorstep by a sudden burst of laughter coming out of a bush.

The crunching of the gravel told Belinda that her ordeal was nearly over. Fom her hiding-place she could observe him quite well, and she noticed that he looked unusually smart. He seemed to be dressed all in grey and carried very new gloves and a walking-stick. Belinda could not see whether he had a flower in his buttonhole or not, but she thought it was not unlikely.

When he was safely in the house, Belinda took the opportunity to run as fast as she could into the back garden, where she arrived rather out of breath. She sat down on an upturned box in the tool-shed and began to consider the situation.

What could bring him to their house so early in the day? It seemed unlikely that he was the kind of person who would call to thank them for the supper party. It was more probable that he had come to demand a subscription for the Library extensions. It might be that he was calling on several people for this purpose and had come to their house first because it was nearest. Belinda hoped Harriet was not going to be disappointed. She seemed to have taken quite a fancy to Mr Mold, and it would be so unfortunate if she got any *ideas* about him. For Belinda was sure that if Mr Mold ever did decide to marry he would choose for his bride some pretty, helpless young woman, perhaps a reader in the Library, who asked him in appealing tones where she could find the *Dictionary of National Biography.* In any case, he was certainly not good enough for Harriet, who would soon tire of his florid complexion and facetious humour. Also, he was not really a gentleman; that seemed to matter a great deal. All the same, it would be interesting to know why he had called.

Harriet, who had been sitting over the fire in the dining-room at her usual task of 'strengthening corsets' with elastic thread, had not been so slow in finding an answer to this important question. It was quite obvious that he had come to see *her.* She had no time to go into this question more deeply, for almost immediately after she had heard the front-door bell, Emily had come into the dining-room and announced Mr Nathaniel Mold.

'Tell him I shall be with him in a minute,' said Harriet, rolling up the corsets and putting them under a cushion. It would never do for him to see her with her face all flushed and shining from sitting over the fire. 'Oh, and Emily, I hope you have switched on the electric fire in the drawing-room?'

Five minutes later she walked down the stairs looking considerably more elegant, her face rather heavily powdered and her hair neatly arranged. There was no need to hurry, she decided, as she paused for a moment in the hall to take a final look at herself in the mirror.

She opened the drawing-room door quietly. Mr Mold was standing with his back to her. At Harriet's entry he turned round, rather startled. He was holding in his hand a copy of *Stitchcraft*, in which he had been reading how to make a table runner. It is always difficult to know how one ought to be occupied when waiting for a lady in her drawing-room, and he had resisted the temptation to probe into the pigeon-holes of the large desk, which stood invitingly open. *Stitchcraft* was dull but safe, he felt.

'Good morning,' said Harriet, advancing towards him with hands outstretched in welcome and a brilliant smile on her face. 'I'm so sorry to have kept you waiting. I'm afraid you didn't find anything very interesting to read, but it must be a change for you to look at a frivolous feminine paper.'

'A very pleasant one,' he said gallantly, 'but of course we do take all these papers in the Library. I was in charge of cataloguing them at one time. I learnt quite a lot about needlework and beauty culture.'

'How wonderful – to think that these papers are preserved,' said Harriet, laughing. 'But I suppose you would be much too important to have anything to do with them now.'

'Oh, no!' Mr Mold smiled and laughed and looked generally rather coltish.

'Do sit down,' said Harriet, sinking into the softness of the sofa. 'It's very nice of you to have called,' she went on, hoping that he would soon give her some clue as to why he had come.

She was even more handsome in daylight than she had been in the evening, he decided, which was indeed very surprising. He had almost expected to be disappointed at their second meeting and had planned an alternate course of action should this happen.

'It is a very great pleasure to see you again,' he said rather stiffly. 'I felt I wanted to call and thank you and your sister for the very delightful party last night. I enjoyed it immensely.'

'Oh, I'm afraid my sister is out in the garden,' said Harriet, half rising, 'but I'm sure she would like to see you.'

'Oh, well perhaps you could convey my thanks to her. I expect she is busy and I shouldn't like to bother her,' said Mr Mold quickly. He had not been at all taken with the sister, and the last thing he wanted was to have to sit making conversation with her.

There was quite a long pause. Mr Mold began to feel rather uncomfortable. This was not at all his usual style. Perhaps it would have been better if he'd had a whisky before he came out, though half-past ten was a little early even for him. Still, it might have given him courage, though he could not help feeling that he might be more successful if there were a certain diffidence or nervousness about his bearing. He could not draw upon his experience in such matters because he had never before proposed marriage to anyone. His intrigues had been mostly with the kind of women who would hardly make suitable wives for the deputy Librarian of one of England's greatest libraries; nor had they ever been considered as such.

What *is* the matter with him? Harriet was wondering. He was not at all like his usual self, in fact he seemed quite nervous, almost like poor Ricardo when he was about to propose to her. She determined to put him at his ease, so she said in a light joking way, 'Now, I do hope you haven't come to say goodbye. It will be very naughty of you to run off and leave us so soon.' She found this way of talking very good with curates and it certainly seemed to make Mr Mold less shy.

'Unfortunately my work demands that I should go back this afternoon, or tomorrow at the latest,' he said, gaining courage from her manner. 'But before I went I hoped I should be able to have a talk with you.' He looked at her plump, handsome profile expectantly.

Very much what I expected, thought Harriet complacently, but she was pleased and flattered to discover that she had been right. It was gratifying to feel that such a Man of the World as Mr Mold obviously was should want to marry her. But should she accept him? When it came to the point, Harriet found herself surprisingly undecided, considering how well she had spoken of Mr Mold to Belinda. She began to see that there were many reasons why she should refuse his offer when it came. To begin with she had known him for such a short time; indeed, this morning was only their third meeting. Harriet was not the kind of person to believe with Marlowe that

Where both deliberate, the love is slight:
Whoever loved, that loved not at first sight?

Obviously that was quite ridiculous. How could one possibly know all the things that had to be known about a person at first sight? Belinda had said she believed Mr Mold had a very nice house, but then poor Belinda was so vague, and for all that the house might be semidetached and not at all in an advantageous position. If Mr Mold were very much in love with her it might be unkind to hurt his feelings – Harriet did not stop to consider how many times she must have hurt the feelings of her faithful admirer Count Bianco – but a smart and floridly handsome admirer in the Prime of Life would be much more acceptable to her than a husband of the same description. In her girlhood imaginings Harriet had always visualized a tall, pale man for her husband, hence her partiality for the clergy. People of Mr Mold's type could never look well in a pulpit. And finally, who would change a comfortable life of spinsterhood in a country parish, which always had its pale curate to be cherished, for the unknown trials of matrimony? Harriet remembered Belinda once saying something about people preferring to bear those ills they had, rather than flying to others that they knew not of, or something like that. It had been quite one of Belinda's most sensible observations.

Thus Harriet's mind was practically made up to refuse Mr Mold's offer when it came. In the meantime, she waited for him to declare himself. He was nearly as slow as poor Ricardo, who always took so long to come to the point that Harriet sometimes found herself helping him out.

There was a pause. Harriet sighed. Perhaps even Mr Mold needed to be helped a little; she had thought he might be better at coming to the point than Ricardo.

'How I envy you living in that lovely town,' she said, looking at him rather intensely. 'Your house is in the Woodbury road, isn't it? I always think that's the very nicest part.'

'Yes, it is pleasant. My house is on a corner, so it has a rather larger garden than the others.' Again there was a short pause, then Mr Mold burst out with rather forced joviality, 'You know, I feel that you and I have so much in common . . .'

Harriet said nothing. She was going rapidly over her own interests and comparing them with those that Mr Mold might be supposed to have. A certain standard of living, comfort, good food, all these they might share, but as before her mind went back to what was undoubtedly her greatest interest – curates. Perhaps she did not define it in that one simple word, but the idea was there, and with it the suspicion that Mr Mold was the kind of person who was not entirely at his ease with the clergy.

Encouraged by her silence Mr Mold went on: 'What I mean to say is, that I think we should be very happy if we married. My house is large and comfortable and my financial position is sound . . . and,' he added, rather as an afterthought, 'I loved you the moment I saw you.'

Harriet almost laughed when she remembered their first meeting in the village, when she had been wearing that awful old tweed coat, too! It was really amazing how blind love made people. Nevertheless, she was disappointed. Proposals from Ricardo several times a year had accustomed her to passionate pleadings, interspersed with fine phrases from the greater Italian poets. Besides, Ricardo never proposed sitting down. Always standing or even kneeling, indeed, his courtly manners had often caused Harriet some amusement. Compared with Ricardo, Mr Mold sounded so prosaic and casual. He didn't sound as if he really *cared* at all. She glanced at him hastily; little beads of sweat were glistening on his forehead and his face was crimson. Harriet could not help remembering that Ricardo always looked pale, and although these differences were rather trivial, they seemed somehow to add themselves to the list of reasons why she should not accept Mr Mold's proposal.

'Dear Mr Mold,' she began, not quite as certain of herself as usual, for she was not yet used to rejecting *him*, and did not know how he would take it. 'It is really charming of you to say such kind things, and I am deeply honoured by your proposal, but I feel I cannot accept it. It would not be fair to *you*,' she added hastily, not wishing to appear unkind.

Mr Mold looked genuinely disappointed. 'Of course I know this must be a shock to you,' he ventured. 'Perhaps you would like to wait a few days and decide after thinking it over?'

But Harriet didn't think she would like to do that. Thinking things over was so tiring, and really there was nothing to think about. The more she considered it, the less attractive the prospect of this marriage seemed to be. He had been so jolly last night, that was what she had liked. Perhaps that was because he had been a little drunk? And somehow he didn't look so handsome at close quarters. Was it possible that he was just *past* the Prime of Life? she wondered.

So she smiled at him very charmingly and repeated that although she was flattered and deeply touched by his proposal she thought it would be kinder to give him his answer now.

'I'm afraid my sister and I are *very* confirmed spinsters,' she added, in a lighter vein.

Mr Mold felt like saying that he had not intended to marry her sister as well, for he was now annoyed rather than hurt at her refusal, and did not consider that she had sufficiently realized the compliment he had paid her in asking her to be his wife. He muttered something about it being a great pity, and then Harriet said she hoped that he would have a pleasant journey back; the afternoon train was a very convenient one and she believed there was a restaurant car on it. Dr Parnell would be staying a little longer, perhaps? It was such a real pleasure for them to see visitors as they lived such uneventful lives in this quiet village. She did hope that Mr Mold would come and see them again next time he was in the neighbourhood.

As he stood on the front doorstep, Mr Mold extended a cordial invitation to her to come and visit him some time. 'You'll always find me in the Library,' he added jovially, almost his old self again.

'Reading *Stitchcraft*, I suppose,' said Harriet, on a teasing note.

As he went out of the gate, he even waved one of his new gloves at her. Perhaps after all the Librarian was right when he said that marriage was a tiresome business and that he and Mold were lucky not to have been caught. He looked at his watch. There would be plenty of time for a chat with the landlord of the Crownwheel and Pinion before lunch. Marriage might put a stop to all that kind of thing.

While Mr Mold's proposal was being rejected in the drawing-room, Belinda was in the dining-room, writing a letter to Agatha. 'We have had remarkably mild weather lately,' she wrote, 'and I have been able to do a lot of gardening, in fact I have just been putting in the last of the bulbs. I have noticed your pink chrysanthemums showing buds, which is very early for them, isn't it?

'The Archdeacon preached a very fine sermon on Sunday, about the Judgment Day. We were all very much impressed by it. You will be glad to hear that he is looking well and has a good appetite.'

Here Belinda paused and laid down her pen. Was this last sentence perhaps a little presumptuous? Ought an archdeacon to be looking well and eating with a good appetite when his wife was away? And ought Belinda to write as if she knew about his appetite?

She turned to the letter again and added 'as far as I know' to the sentence about the appetite.

'It was so nice to see Nicholas Parnell again, and I think he enjoys coming here for a quiet holiday. He brought the deputy Librarian, Mr Mold, with him. I don't know whether you have met him? Personally, his type does not appeal to me very much. He is supposed to be a great ladies' man, and is too fond of making jokes not always in the best of taste. Harriet saw him coming out of the Crownwheel and Pinion in the morning, which I thought a pity.'

Here Belinda laid down her pen again. Was she being quite fair to Mr Mold? She had allowed herself to get so carried away by her own feelings about him that she had rather forgotten she was writing to Agatha, in whom she did not normally confide.

'Still, I daresay he is a very nice man,' she went on, 'when one really knows him.'

This last sentence reminded Belinda that he had now been closeted in the drawing-room with Harriet for some considerable time. Belinda had not yet been able to decide why he had come, indeed, she had rather forgotten about the whole thing. Nothing was further from her mind than a proposal of marriage, and had she known what was going on, she would probably have rushed into the drawing-room, even if she had still been wearing her old gardening mackintosh and goloshes, and tried her best to stop it, for one was never quite sure what Harriet would do. Especially after her apparent admiration of Mr Mold and her continual harping on the Prime of Life. Belinda went so far as to go into the hall, but could not bring herself to listen at the drawing-room door. From where she stood she could hear a low murmur of voices. It was no use being impatient, and the last thing she wanted was to see Mr Mold herself, so she went back to her letter. Writing to Agatha was not easy, more of a duty than a pleasure, but Belinda felt that she might like to hear some of the details of the parish life which the Archdeacon probably would not give her, so she wrote about the autumn leaves and berries they had used to decorate the church, the organist's illness and Miss Smiley's brave attempt to play at Evensong, the success of the Scouts' Jumble Sale and other homely matters.

At last she heard the sound of a door opening, then conversation and laughter. Harriet and Mr Mold had come out of the drawing-room. Belinda waited until she judged him safely out of the front door and then went eagerly into the hall to hear the result of his visit.

She found Harriet standing in front of the mirror, rubbing her hands together and looking pleased with herself. Her face was rather red and she looked more elegant than was usual at such an early hour of the day.

'Well,' she said, with a hint of triumph in her voice, 'that's that.'

'Yes,' said Belinda, 'but what? I hope you didn't promise him anything for the Library Extension Fund. There are far more deserving causes in the parish.'

'But, Belinda, surely you guessed why he had come?' said Harriet patiently, for really her sister was very stupid. 'He came to ask me to marry him,' she declared, smiling.

'Oh, *Harriet* . . .' Belinda was quite speechless. She might have known that something dreadful like this would happen. As if he would bother to come and ask for a subscription to the Library funds! Her supposition seemed very vain and feeble now. Still, as Belinda would not have to live with them, perhaps she need not see very much of her over-jovial brother-in-law – that would be some consolation, though it would hardly make up for the loss of her sister. Of course, she supposed, she could always have a companion to live with her, some deserving poor relation like Connie Aspinall, or she might advertise in the *Church Times*; somebody with literary interests and fond of gardening, a churchwoman, of course. Belinda shuddered as she thought of the applications and the task of interviewing them; she was sure she would never have the strength to reject anyone, however unsuitable. Perhaps, after all, it would be better to live alone.

'Of course, I couldn't accept him,' said Harriet, rather loudly, for she had expected Belinda to show real interest, instead of just standing and staring at the floor.

The look of relief that brightened Belinda's face was pathetic in its intensity.

'Oh, *Harriet* . . .' again she was speechless. However could she have thought for a moment that her sister would do such a thing?

'Indeed I couldn't,' said Harriet calmly. 'Why I hardly know him, and you remember what Shakespeare said about when lovely woman stoops to folly . . .' she made a significant gesture with her hand.

Belinda frowned. 'I don't think it was *Shakespeare*, dear,' she said absently. 'I must ask Henry. I have an idea it may be Pope.' But what did it matter? Belinda was so overcome with joy and relief at Harriet's news that she kissed her impulsively and suggested that they should have some meringues for tea, as Harriet was so fond of them.

Together they went into the dining-room, where Harriet with many ludicrous and exaggerated imitations, gave a demonstration of how Mr Mold had proposed to her.

'Oh, Harriet, you mustn't be so unkind!' protested

Belinda, in the intervals of laughing, for her sister was really much funnier than Mr Mold could possibly have been. They laughed even more when the corsets were discovered under a cushion.

'Just imagine if Emily had brought him in here and he had discovered them while he was waiting. Or if the Archdeacon had when he came the other day,' chortled Harriet.

'Oh, Harriet,' said Belinda faintly. There was a vulgar, music-hall touch about it all that one could associate with Mr Mold but hardly with the Archdeacon.

'I expect he's consoling himself in the Crownwheel and Pinion,' said Harriet, 'so we needn't really pity him.'

She was perfectly right; so much so that, when he arrived at the vicarage rather late for lunch, Dr Parnell was constrained to whisper to his friend the Archdeacon, 'I fear poor Nathaniel is not entirely sober.'

CHAPTER THIRTEEN

AS MR MOLD settled himself comfortably in his first-class corner seat he decided that he had probably had a lucky escape. And indeed, he reflected, *Love is only one of many passions and it has no great influence on the sum of life*, as the Librarian was so fond of quoting.

A few days later Belinda and Harriet were invited to tea at the vicarage. It was hardly surprising that Mr Mold's proposal, which appeared to be known to the Archdeacon and Dr Parnell, should be the chief topic of conversation.

Dr Parnell was inclined to think it a pity that Harriet had refused his colleague, for although he had always been of the opinion that it must be very tiresome to be married, he did not deny that it was an interesting state. Indeed, he often regretted that the Archdeacon was the only one of his friends who had a wife. As a young man Dr Parnell had looked forward to the time when Belinda would come to him for advice on the trials of matrimony. In those days he had hoped that she might marry the Archdeacon, and was almost as disappointed as she had been at her failure to captivate him. He had never liked Agatha, but he could not help admiring her skill, and when by her powers her husband was raised to the dignity of archdeacon, Mr Parnell, as he then was, had aptly remarked that Henry was indeed fortunate in having won the love of a good woman. Nevertheless, he considered himself almost equally fortunate in *not* having done so, and often used to remark to John Akenside that he did not think poor Henry was quite as *free* as he had been.

But there was no denying that Harriet and Mr Mold would have made an admirable couple. They had both reached an age when temperament and character were settled, and instead of one dominating the other they would have been able to live in comfortable harmony. Besides, there would be plenty of money, so that if there had been love, which Dr Parnell rather doubted, it would have been less likely to fly out of the window, as he had been told it did when poverty came in at the door.

Sitting round the fire in the Archdeacon's study, they considered the problem.

'Of course I never advise anyone to enter into that state without long and careful thought,' said Dr Parnell, 'but I should be the last to admit impediments to the marriage of true minds, and it seems to me that you and Nathaniel have a great many tastes in common.'

Harriet denied this indignantly: perhaps she was still thinking of curates. 'The only thing we have in common is a love of good food,' she said, thinking that Dr Parnell was being more than usually interfering. 'I could never marry Mr Mold.'

'But surely liking the same things for dinner is one of the deepest and most lasting things you could possibly have in common with anyone,' argued Dr Parnell. 'After all, the emotions of the heart are very transitory, or so I believe; I should think it makes one much happier to be well-fed than well-loved.'

Belinda did not trouble to contradict this statement, romantic and sentimental though she was. She was feeling much too happy and peaceful to indulge in any argument. For here she was sitting on the sofa with the person she had loved well and faithfully for thirty years, and whom she still saw as the beautiful young man he had been then, although he was now married and an archdeacon. And as if this were not enough, had she not just escaped having a brother-in-law who was not really a gentleman, and made jokes not always in the best of taste? When one reached middle age it was even more true that all change is of itself an evil and ought not to be hazarded but for evident advantage. She smiled at Dr Parnell indulgently, but said nothing. The Archdeacon in his turn smiled affectionately at her, and thought what a nice peaceful creature she was, so different from his own admirable wife, with her busy schemes for his preferment.

Dr Parnell was still regretting Harriet's hasty action, and suggested that she might write Mr Mold a letter giving him some *hope*, for he had heard that even hope was better than nothing.

But Harriet, who knew she was being teased, merely listened with a smile on her face and said with dignity that she believed she could do a great deal better for herself. She looked at the three of them rather mysteriously, and Belinda wondered whether she could be making plans to captivate Dr Parnell.

'You would have kept poor Nathaniel out of mischief,' he said, still harping on the same subject.

'I daresay,' remarked Harriet, 'and I expect he needs it. Do you know,' she leaned forward confidentially, 'I believe he *drinks* . . .' she said, pronouncing this last word in a suitably hushed whisper.

'Oh, Harriet,' protested Belinda, for she could now afford to feel kindly towards Mr Mold, 'I don't think you should say that. We all like to take something occasionally, a drink can be a great comfort at times.'

'I am glad to hear that you are so broad-minded,' said the Archdeacon. 'I remember Agatha being quite shocked when I said something of the kind to the Mothers' Union once.'

'Well, I suppose it is a dangerous thing to say,' said Dr Parnell. 'They might abuse the comfort of drink.'

'Whereas *we* know how to be moderate,' said Harriet primly.

'I cannot imagine Agatha taking too much,' said Dr Parnell. He chuckled. 'No, I'm afraid I can't.'

Belinda gave him a shocked glance. 'Have you heard from Agatha again?' she asked the Archdeacon brightly.

'Yes, as a matter of fact I had a letter by the lunch-time post,' he said. 'You can read it if you want to,' he added, taking a letter out of his pocket and handing it to her.

Belinda took the letter rather gingerly, thinking it odd that he should hand it to her so willingly. But when she came to read Agatha's neat handwriting, she saw that the letter contained nothing private. It seemed to be a long list of things he must not forget to do. It was admirably practical, but unromantic. And yet, after so many years of being married to a charming but difficult man like the Archdeacon, perhaps it was rather too much to expect that Agatha should dwell on the desolation of life without him. All the same, Belinda could not help remembering her own letters, and she was sure that even now she could have found something a little more *tender* to write about than Florrie's and cook's wages and the Mothers' Union tea. She was just going to hand the letter back when she noticed that there was a postscript over the page.

'I forgot to tell you that among the people staying here is the Bishop of Mbawawa. I believe the Bedes know him. He is a delightful man, so friendly, and he tells many interesting stories about the splendid work he has been doing among the natives. I am trying to persuade him to come home with me, as I am sure everyone would be interested to meet him.'

Belinda stopped short in amazement as she read these words. 'Harriet,' she said, '*who* do you think is there?'

Harriet, who was quietly enjoying a substantial tea, looked up and asked who was where.

'In Karlsbad,' said Belinda.

'I don't know,' she said, not very interested. 'It's the sort of place where King Edward VII might be, only of course it could hardly be him.'

'It's an old friend of yours,' said Belinda.

'Is he an old friend?' asked the Archdeacon.

'I should like to number bishops among my friends,' said Dr Parnell.

Harriet seemed to brighten up at this. 'Bishops? Well, of course I know quite a number,' she mused. This was not really surprising, for after all every bishop has once been a curate. 'It couldn't be Willie Amery, I suppose, or Oliver Opobo and Calabar – isn't that a lovely title? – no, he's in Nigeria, I believe. Of course it might be Theo Grote, Theodore Mbawawa, as he signs himself,' she smiled to herself. '*That* would be the nicest of all.'

'Yes, Harriet, it's Theo Grote,' said Belinda. 'I knew you would be interested to hear that.'

'Oh *ho*,' said Dr Parnell, seeing that Harriet had gone quite pink in the face. 'I believe we are going to see some old broth being warmed up. I like to see that.'

'Agatha talks of bringing him to stay here,' said the Archdeacon distastefully. He disliked other members of his calling.

Clean sheets on the spare bed and a tin of biscuits on the little table in case he should feel hungry in the night, thought Belinda irrelevantly.

'He must be about fifty-seven or fifty-eight,' said Harriet, who seemed to have been doing a little calculation. 'It *will* be nice to see dear Theo again.'

'On the threshold of sixty,' mused Dr Parnell. 'That's a good age for a man to marry. He needs a woman to help him into his grave.'

'But that's just the Prime of Life,' said Harriet indignantly. 'I'm sure we shan't find Theo at all *doddery*.'

Belinda began to suspect that Harriet regarded the Bishop as a possible husband. She had certainly been very much in love with him when she was a schoolgirl and he a willowy curate in the early twenties. Belinda had often thought that the reason why Harriet made so much of Mr Donne was because he reminded her of dear Theo Grote. And then Belinda had often heard her say that a bishop needed a wife to help him with certain intimate problems in his diocese, things which a woman could deal with better than a man. It seemed a little hard, Belinda thought, that this new menace should appear, just when she was so relieved at having escaped Mr Mold, but she would just have to leave Harriet to her schemes. Belinda trembled for the unmarried Bishop of Mbàwawa if he did not feel inclined to enter into that blessed state.

'Shall I read aloud to you?' suggested the Archdeacon hopefully. He went over to the bookshelves and invited requests for what anyone would like. But Dr Parnell suddenly got up from his chair and announced that he thought he had better do his packing. It was so tiresome to have a rush at the last minute. Harriet, too, had suddenly remembered that she was to deliver some parish magazines and was already half way out of the door, thanking the Archdeacon for a delightful tea party, and inviting him to drop in at four o'clock any afternoon. She and Dr Parnell hurried out of the room together, the latter remarking that he wondered Henry could spare the time from his parochial duties to listen to the sound of his own voice.

'We should all have time to improve our minds,' said Belinda smiling happily.

The Archdeacon turned towards her with a volume of Spenser in his hand. 'I think it would be pleasant to have something from the *Faerie Queene*,' he declared.

The clock struck half-past five. Belinda settled herself comfortably in her chair. She felt rather drowsy and the *Faerie Queene* was such a soothing poem. It just went on and on.

At six o'clock the Archdeacon suggested a little Wordsworth. Belinda agreed that this would be very nice. She had always been so fond of *The Prelude*.

At half-past six Belinda began to murmur something about being sure that she was disturbing the Archdeacon, who must have a great deal to do.

Well, yes, he supposed that she *was* disturbing him really, but it was very pleasant to be disturbed occasionally, especially when there were so many tiresome things to do.

'Do you know,' he said suddenly, with the air of one who has made an important discovery, 'this reminds me of the old days. I used to read aloud to you then. Does it remind you?'

Belinda was speechless, as she considered this proof of man's oddness. Whatever did he imagine that it reminded her of? 'Oh, yes, it's quite like the old days,' she said at last, and then tried to think of something more intelligent to continue the conversation.

Silences were awkward things, especially when one's mind was only too apt to wander back into the past and remember it so vividly that it became more real than the present. Unless she fixed her attention on something definite, she might find herself saying the wrong thing. Her eyes lighted on a set of Bible commentaries. Well, nobody could expect her to talk about them. She must try again. The mantelpiece is dusty, she thought. Florrie needs keeping up to the mark, and I don't believe she's used the Hoover on this carpet since Agatha went away. Agatha. There was something definite. There was nothing vague or nebulous about an archdeacon's wife, even when she wasn't there. I loved you more than Agatha did, thought Belinda, but all I can do now is to keep silent. I can't even speak to Florrie about the dusty mantelpiece, because it's nothing to do with me. It never was and it never will be.

'Florrie never bothers to dust my study when Agatha's away,' said the Archdeacon, seeing where Belinda was looking.

'No, things always go wrong in a house when there's no woman at the head of things,' agreed Belinda. 'I mean, it's different when Agatha's away.'

The Archdeacon sighed. 'Yes, it is different,' he agreed. 'But there it is. We can't alter things, can we?'

Belinda did not know what to say to this, as she was not quite sure what he meant. She was just wondering what would happen if she led the conversation round to more personal things than dusty mantelpieces, when the door opened and in came Dr Parnell, complaining that he was hungry and asking if they were never going to have anything to eat.

'Why, yes, it must be nearly supper-time,' said Belinda, starting to put on her gloves. 'I must go.'

'Oh, but I insist that you stay,' protested the Archdeacon.

'I really couldn't,' said Belinda mechanically. 'Harriet will be expecting me.'

'Please, dear Belinda,' he said coaxingly. 'You know I asked you to tea the other day and you wouldn't come. The least you can do is to stay now. For the sake of old times,' he added, with uncharacteristic heartiness.

'Really, Henry, I think you might have put it better,' said Dr Parnell. 'I should hardly imagine that poor Belinda can really wish to be reminded of old times.'

But Belinda only smiled. 'All right, I will stay,' she said.

'I shall never understand women,' said Dr Parnell complacently.

CHAPTER FOURTEEN

BELINDA arrived home that evening feeling very happy. It had been so nice having supper at the vicarage without the restraining presence of Agatha, the efficient wife and good philologist. During those few hours Belinda had almost imagined herself back in her youth. As she had listened to the Archdeacon giving a short dissertation on the Beast Fable in the Middle Ages, she had found herself looking at her watch and thinking that she would have to be back at her college by half-past ten if she did not want the Principal to ask any awkward questions. When the Archdeacon had gone on to discuss the sources of his Judgment Day sermon, she had realized regretfully that the Principal of whom she had stood in awe had been in her grave at least ten years.

It was not until she reached her own front door that Belinda began to feel a little uneasy, and wonder if it had been quite the thing for her to spend a whole evening at the vicarage without Agatha or Harriet to chaperone her. For although Dr Parnell had been there, he wasn't quite the same as some respectable middle-aged woman. And yet why should not she be allowed her occasional joys, such very mild ones, which were mostly remembrance of things past?

Sounds of hearty laughter came from the drawing-room. The curate was there. Perhaps he had dropped in after Evensong, as Harriet had so often told him to, and had stayed to supper. Belinda was glad that he was there, as his presence would save her a little from Harriet's ruthless cross-examination, which was bound to come sooner or later.

Belinda went upstairs to take off her hat and coat and then into the middle of the cheerful noise.

Harriet and the curate were sitting on the sofa, deeply engrossed in a book. The curate leaped up and expressed himself delighted to see her. Belinda thought it a little unnecessary of him to welcome her to her own house, but she said nothing.

'I suppose you've had supper?' asked Harriet.

'Yes,' said Belinda, 'I stayed at the vicarage. I hope you didn't wait for me?'

'Oh, no,' said Harriet, 'in fact I didn't expect you back even as soon as *this*.'

Belinda laughed rather uncomfortably. 'What are you reading?' she asked, hoping to change the subject.

'We were reading Catullus. I really don't know how we got on to it,' said Harriet merrily. 'Mr Donne's so good at Latin but of course it's quite thirty years since I read a *word* of it.'

'Oh, come,' said the curate playfully. 'I can't believe that.'

Belinda took up her knitting. She remembered Dr Parnell saying that he thought Catullus rather too indelicate for a young girl to read. If this were so, for Belinda's scanty knowledge of Latin would not enable her to find out for herself, how much more indelicate must the great Roman poet be for a young curate! 'There is a pretty translation of one of his poems by Thomas Campion,' she said vaguely, 'but I suppose it's not like reading the original.'

'No, my friend Olivia Berridge always says that. You remember perhaps, she's Mrs Hoccleve's niece,' explained the curate.

'Oh, yes,' said Harriet, 'she knows Anglo-Saxon and things like that, doesn't she? And of course she made you those socks. I thought the toes were not very well grafted, in that grey pair you showed me. It's quite easy to do, really. You just say knit and slip off, purl and keep on – or it may be the other way round.'

The curate looked mystified. 'She's very clever,' he said. 'I expect she knows that.'

Harriet looked a little annoyed and the conversation flagged. Mr Donne got up to go.

'Perhaps you would like to borrow some books?' suggested

Belinda, seeing that he was looking at the shelves. It was a little difficult to guide his choice, but eventually he went away with some thrillers and the selected poems of the Earl of Rochester, a volume of which Belinda was particularly fond. It had been given to her by Dr Parnell on her twenty-first birthday. Belinda felt that it would not be likely to harm Mr Donne's morals, as it professed to be *a collection of such pieces only, as may be received in a vertuous court, and may not unbecome the Cabinet of the Severest Matron.*

He had hardly gone out of the front door, when Harriet turned eagerly to Belinda and said, 'Now tell me *all* about it.'

Belinda looked up from her knitting rather startled. 'But, Harriet,' she protested, 'there's really nothing to tell. Henry read aloud to me and then we talked a bit and then he persuaded me to stay to supper, which I did. But I don't know whether I ought to have done that,' she added rather unhappily. 'I mean, I shouldn't like Agatha to think . . .'

'No, no, of course not,' said Harriet soothingly. 'Now wouldn't you like a nice cup of Ovaltine?' she said, fussing round Belinda like a motherly hen.

'Well, I don't know, I think I would,' said Belinda. Perhaps a nourishing milky drink was needed to bring her down to earth but it seemed an unromantic end to the evening.

Harriet had already gone into the kitchen and soon returned with the Ovaltine and a selection of biscuits and cakes.

'Now,' she said, as if speaking to an invalid, 'drink it up while it's hot and don't try to talk till you've finished. There'll be plenty of time for you to tell me all about it.'

'But what is there to tell?' protested Belinda, rousing herself. 'I've told you what we did.'

Harriet chose a chocolate biscuit. 'I do believe the Archdeacon has been asking you to elope with him!' she declared triumphantly.

'Oh, Harriet, how dreadful you are!' said Belinda, unable

to help laughing at this monstrous suggestion. 'As if a clergyman, let alone an archdeacon, would do a thing like that.'

'Then he's been telling you that he's very fond of you, and hinting that he wishes he'd married you instead of Agatha,' went on Harriet, gallantly persevering.

'Well, hardly that,' ventured Belinda, growing a little more confidential, for the Ovaltine had loosened her tongue. 'I mean, it's a bit late for anything like that, isn't it? Henry is always loyal to Agatha and feels quite *differently* about her,' she added hastily, in case her sister should take her up wrongly.

Harriet agreed with this ambiguous statement. 'Yes, I'm sure he does,' she said, 'but there's no reason why he shouldn't be fond of you as well. Clergymen are always saying that we should love one another.'

'Oh, *Harriet*,' protested Belinda, rather shocked, 'you know quite well that isn't at all the same kind of thing. But of course Henry and I have always been friends and I hope we always will be.'

Harriet sighed. Poor Belinda was so unworldly, so sentimental.

'Of course he is fond of you,' she declared boldly. 'Anybody can tell that by the way he keeps smiling at you, when he thinks nobody's looking.'

Belinda had always thought that they were smiles of pity rather than of love. But hadn't one of our greater English poets said something about Pity being akin to Love? Or had she made it up herself? A vague recollection of Aristotle's *Poetics* came into her mind. But that was Pity and Fear, rather like her feeling for Miss Prior, not at all the same thing. . . .

'I'm sure everyone knows,' persisted Harriet, nothing daunted by her sister's unwillingness to confide in her and determined to make something interesting out of Belinda's evening at the vicarage.

'Knows what?' asked Belinda, rather startled.

'Why, that you love each other,' beamed Harriet, as if she

were giving her blessing to a young couple, instead of making rather a scandalous suggestion about a married archdeacon and a respectable spinster.

Belinda was now rather agitated and could not think of anything to say.

'Don't deny that he's making the most of Agatha's absence,' Harriet went on, 'and anyway everybody knows that you knew him long before Agatha did.'

'I don't see what that has to do with it,' said Belinda. 'One can hardly claim people on that basis.'

'But didn't he say *anything*? Surely you weren't just reading poetry *all* the time?'

'No, not all the time.' Belinda smiled as she remembered their conversation. 'We talked about the dust on the mantelpiece.'

'Oh, Belinda, surely . . .' Harriet searched vainly in the tin for another chocolate biscuit.

'And I said that of course things did go wrong when there was no woman at the head of things,' Belinda went on. 'I mean, servants neglect their duty and that sort of thing. I think I said, "It's different when Agatha's away", or something like that.'

'Oh, Belinda, wasn't that rather obvious?'

Belinda looked startled. 'Oh, I meant things in the house, naturally. He surely couldn't have taken it any other way?'

'Well, what did he say to that?' went on Harriet relentlessly. 'Do you remember?'

'Oh, yes. I always remember everything Henry says.' She smiled. 'Thirty years of it. It's a pity I don't remember other things so well. He said, "Yes, it is different, but there it is. We can't alter things, can we?" '

Harriet let out a cry of joy. 'Go on,' she said. 'What happened next?'

'Oh, then Nicholas came in and we had supper.' Belinda paused. 'Well, dinner really, because there was soup, though I *think* it was tinned. Still, it was very nice, mushroom or something. It had little bits of things in it.'

'Oh, Belinda, I don't want to hear about the soup,' said Harriet. 'How sickening that Nicholas should have come in just at that moment. Just like him,' she grumbled. 'To think of it, the moment you've been waiting for for thirty years!' She paused dramatically.

'But you know I've never expected anything,' protested Belinda. 'I've no right to.'

'But don't you see what he meant when he said that about not being able to alter things?' said Harriet. 'He meant he'd rather have you than Agatha, only of course he couldn't put it quite as crudely as that.'

'We never mentioned ourselves,' said Belinda hopelessly. 'We were talking about his study not being dusted.'

'Now if only he were a *widower*,' mused Harriet.

'But he isn't,' said Belinda stoutly.

'No, and Agatha's very tough in spite of her rheumatism,' lamented Harriet. 'And soon he won't even be a grass widower because she's coming back.'

'Yes, she's coming back,' said Belinda, even more stoutly. How odd if Henry were a widower, she thought suddenly. How embarrassing, really. It would be like going back thirty years. Or wouldn't it? Belinda soon saw that it wouldn't. For she was now a contented spinster and her love was like a warm, comfortable garment, bedsocks, perhaps, or even woollen combinations; certainly something without glamour or romance. All the same, it was rather nice to think that Henry *might* prefer her to Agatha, although she knew perfectly well that he didn't. It was one of the advantages of being the one he hadn't married that one could be in a position to imagine such things.

Belinda gave a contented sigh. It had been such a lovely evening. Just one evening like that every thirty years or so. It might not seem much to other people, but it was really all one needed to be happy. But Harriet was saying something, so she could not indulge in such thoughts for long.

'I don't like the way Mr Donne keeps mentioning that Olivia Berridge,' she said. 'Although he did say that he was definitely *not* engaged to her, one never knows.'

'He doesn't sound as if he were in love with her,' said Belinda doubtfully. 'But of course Miss Berridge may have made up her mind to marry him. She sounds a bit like Agatha,' she added.

'But Mr Donne is nothing like the Archdeacon,' said Harriet indignantly.

'No, I don't think anybody is quite like the Archdeacon,' said Belinda quietly.

CHAPTER FIFTEEN

DURING THE next week or so the village began to look forward to the homecoming of the Archdeacon's right hand, as many of the church workers called Mrs Hoccleve. They were conventional enough to use this expression, which they had often heard, without troubling to ask themselves whether it could really be applied here. It was a known thing that the wives of clergy often were their right hands, and even if the Hoccleves were sometimes rather snappy with each other there was no doubt that she was the power behind him. The news that she was to be accompanied by the Bishop of Mbawawa had spread rapidly, and little groups of eager Sunday School teachers could be seen talking about it. Some had heard that he was black, a real African bishop, but Harriet soon put them right on this point and achieved a new importance through having known him as a curate. Belinda did not share in this glory, for after so many years she found it difficult to remember which of the many curates her sister had cherished was Theodore Grote.

'He was thin and dark, wasn't he?' she said anxiously. 'But somehow I can't see his face.' There was a blank above the clerical collar, as it were, for so many had been thin and dark.

'Oh, Belinda, you *must* remember him at that Whist Drive,' said Harriet smiling tenderly, for she had no difficulty in recalling him as one of the most sought-after curates in the history of the Church of England. In his heyday there had been quite a procession of doting women towards his lodgings, carrying cooked pheasants and chickens, iced cakes, even jellies in basins . . . Harriet sighed over her reminiscences and then remarked in a regretful tone of voice that she did not think Belinda had really made the most of Agatha's absence.

Belinda could not but agree, for Harriet was perfectly right. And yet, how could one make the most of the absence of an archdeacon's wife. It was a thing no truly respectable spinster could or would do. She pointed this out to Harriet, who refused with characteristic obstinacy to understand and merely remarked that we none of us got any younger.

Ah yes, thought Belinda, as she turned to knitting the dull grey jumper that might have been a pullover for the Archdeacon, that was it. She thought about it so seldom but now she became melancholy at the realization that the fine madness of her youth had gone. She was no longer an original shining like a comet, indeed, it would have been unsuitable if she had been. *Change and decay in all around I see . . . All, all are gone, the old familiar faces . . .* Dear Nicholas was back in the Library, John Akenside was in heaven, while his earthly remains rested in an English cemetery in the Balkans, and if Harriet married Theodore Mbawawa, even she would be gone . . . Who was there apart from the forbidden Archdeacon? One's women friends, of course, people like Edith Liversidge and Connie Aspinall, but they were a cold comfort. Belinda grew even more melancholy, and then she remembered Count Bianco. There was always Ricardo. Perhaps they could read Dante together and find some consolation in the great Italian poet. She did not think she would be equal to reading Tacitus.

In the meantime Belinda had promised to go to the station with the Archdeacon to meet Agatha and the Bishop. On this day she was classed with Agatha's nearest and dearest in a way which seemed to her rather ironical. Who but a man could be so lacking in finer feelings as to think of such a thing? she wondered. But of course she said she would go.

'After all, you both love the Archdeacon,' Harriet had explained, and Belinda supposed that it was true, though one could hardly admit it even to oneself. Possibly, thought Belinda, I love him even more than Agatha does, but my feeling may be the stronger for not having married him.

As they waited on the station, Belinda decided that her sister had been wise to stay at home, for it was bitterly cold. Harriet liked her comfort and had decided that she would appear to better advantage in a less bleak setting.

'The Bishop will surely find our climate very different from that of the tropics,' remarked the curate, as they were stamping their feet on the platform to keep warm.

Belinda thought this remark to be so obvious as not to require an answer, so she turned to the Archdeacon and said that she thought his watch must be fast, as they seemed to have been waiting a long time.

'Oh, no, but the train is late,' he said, with a superior smile. So Milton's Adam must have smiled on Eve. He was not pleased at the prospect of having to entertain the Bishop for an indefinite length of time, but nevertheless he was looking forward to it with a kind of grim relish. He remembered certain minor discomforts about the spare room at the vicarage as he stood there on the cold platform. It was a gloomy room with a northerly aspect and a tall, dark monkey-puzzle growing close to the window, which looked out on to an old potting-shed, full of flower-pots and dried-up roots and bulbs. And in addition, although the Archdeacon had not personally made the bed, he knew that there were sides-to-middle sheets on it, for Florrie had come into his study that morning, very agitated because all the whole sheets were still at the laundry. The Archdeacon was delighted. He seemed to remember also that the mattress was a particularly lumpy one, worn into uncomfortable bumps and hollows by a variety of visiting clergy, and that the bedside lamp did not work. All the same he had taken pleasure in making a suitable selection of books for the bedside table – a volume of Tillotson's sermons, Klaeber's edition of *Beowulf*, the Poems of Mrs Hemans, an old Icelandic grammar, and, as a concession to the Bishop's connection with Africa, a particularly dull anthropological work, which had been included with some other books he had bought at a sale. The Bishop would naturally want thrillers – the clergy always did, he found – but he was keeping his own supply locked up in his study.

Belinda saw him smiling to himself and wondered whether it could be because Agatha was coming home. Naturally it must be, as she knew he was not pleased at the prospect of the Bishop. Prospect of bishops, she thought, liking the phrase, but at that moment the curate espied the train coming round the bend into the station.

'There they are!' he shouted, rushing towards a first-class carriage where Agatha's face had appeared at the window.

'I thought you would be travelling at the rear. I didn't look for you at the front,' said the Archdeacon rather reproachfully.

He kissed his wife, not very affectionately, Belinda thought, but she had kept herself rather in the background, waiting for this reunion of nearest and dearest to be over. There was a forced smile on her face to be used when needed. She looked about her and saw emerging from the railway carriage what she imagined must be the Bishop of Mbawawa. He too was looking as if he did not quite know what to do with himself.

Belinda moved towards him and introduced herself. 'I don't suppose you remember me,' she said, smiling rather awkwardly. Nor did she remember him, if it came to that, for she could have sworn that she had never seen him in all her life. Could a beautiful curate have grown into this tall, stringy-looking man, with a yellow, leathery complexion? His expression reminded Belinda of a sheep more than anything; his face was long, his forehead domed and his head bald. He was even rather toothy, a thing that Harriet abhorred. Could it be the same person? she wondered.

'But I certainly do remember you,' he was saying. 'You knitted me a beautiful scarf when I was a curate.'

Belinda was decidedly taken aback. She had always thought it rather wonderful that she had never done anything of the kind. He must have been thinking of Harriet or another of his many admirers.

'Oh, did I?' she said vaguely, which helped neither of them, and caused the Bishop to be assailed with doubts.

'You did such splendid work with the Guild of St Agnes,' he went on, less certainly.

Belinda, who had never heard of any such guild, felt rather foolish. 'I daresay you remember my sister better,' she ventured, 'Harriet, you know.'

'Ah, *yes*.' His face cleared. 'I shall look forward to renewing my acquaintance with her,' he said politely. 'She was always interested in missions, if I remember rightly.'

'Oh, yes, she was,' said Belinda, thinking that she might as well agree for a change. 'She is looking forward to seeing you so much.'

The Bishop was just saying something about the pleasure of meeting old friends and looked as if he might almost be about to quote some Mbawawa proverb, when Agatha came over to them and Belinda found herself shaking hands cordially and telling her how well she looked.

'You're looking *splendid*,' said Belinda, and indeed Agatha was quite fat in the face and seemed in very good spirits. Belinda was shocked to find herself wondering whether a month's absence from her husband could have anything to do with it.

The curate was now bundling them all into a taxi, saying that he would walk as he had to call and see one of the church wardens. So Belinda found herself sitting by Agatha, while the Bishop and the Archdeacon squatted rather incongruously on the little folding seats.

'I don't think Henry is looking very well,' said Agatha, with something of her old sharpness, so that Belinda felt that it was her fault.

'Oh, I think he's quite well really,' said Belinda quickly. 'A little tired, perhaps, but then he's had so much to do while you've been away.'

The Archdeacon was unable to resist joining in this interesting conversation, so he rather rudely interrupted the Bishop, who was telling him something about the organization of his diocese, to remark that he was really quite exhausted and did not know how he was going to get through the rest of the winter.

'Oh, I expect you'll manage all right,' said Agatha lightly. 'I'm sure Bishop Grote will be only too glad to help with some of the services.'

'Indeed I shall,' said the Bishop, 'and I daresay my own experience in organizing a large diocese will be of use to you. My African priests are dear, good fellows, but they sometimes need a helping hand.'

Belinda did not dare to look at the Archdeacon's face, but she could feel the blackness of his look and she wondered if her own indignation on his account could be seen in her face. To class an English archdeacon with African priests! Surely that was going too far? Not, she hastened to assure herself, because they were Africans: she was certain that, as the Bishop had said, they were dear, good fellows, but she was surprised that he should have so little sense of what was fitting to the occasion.

The remainder of the drive was taken in silence. Fortunately it was not far, but it was long enough for Belinda to realize that the Bishop and the Archdeacon had taken an instant dislike to each other. This was in some ways rather unlucky, as it was essential to the success of Harriet's plans that the Bishop should stay some time, and if the Archdeacon were really rude to him, as he might very well be, there was no knowing what might happen. Of course Harriet might not feel so enthusiastic after she had seen the Bishop. Belinda hoped that this might be so, as she did not think she would like him as a brother-in-law and she certainly did not want her sister to leave her and go to Africa.

They reached the vicarage and Belinda hovered uncertainly by the front door.

'Belinda will stay to tea, of course,' said the Archdeacon quickly.

'Oh, yes, certainly,' said Agatha. 'We want to hear all the parish news.'

'I should like a little moral support,' said the Archdeacon in a low voice. 'I am not sure that tea will be enough.'

Belinda walked quickly into the hall after Agatha. The Bishop followed them, but the Archdeacon stayed behind to supervise the unloading of the luggage.

'I hope it isn't inconvenient,' said Belinda in her usual apologetic manner.

'Not at all,' said Agatha coolly. 'One extra for tea is no trouble at all – I never find that it is.'

'Oh, no, nor do I,' said Belinda, floundering deeper. She was quite grateful to the Bishop for turning the conversation to the Mbawawa hunting customs, by which it appeared that when an animal was killed unlimited hospitality was extended to all neighbouring tribes.

'What a nice custom,' said Belinda inadequately, 'but I imagine they would have to have more than one animal, wouldn't they?'

'Oh, it is a ritual eating,' the Bishop explained. 'The meat is not actually consumed.'

'Well, I hope our tea will be a little more satisfying,' said Agatha, smiling indulgently at the Bishop. 'Where is Harriet, by the way?' she asked Belinda, in a sharper tone.

'She couldn't come to the station,' said Belinda evasively. After all it was none of Agatha's business where Harriet was. She could hardly have told the assembled company that Harriet preferred to wait for some more elegant occasion before renewing her acquaintance with the Bishop. She had visions of herself advancing towards him graciously in her brown velvet or wine crêpe de Chine, and such clothes would hardly have been possible at the station on a cold winter afternoon.

'I hope she is quite well?' said Agatha politely.

'Yes, thank you,' said Belinda. 'She was doing something else, as a matter of fact.'

'With Ricardo, perhaps?' suggested the Archdeacon helpfully.

'Is she married then?' asked the Bishop. 'I did not know.'

'Oh, no,' said Belinda confusedly. 'Ricardo isn't her *husband*. He is an Italian count,' she added quickly, as if that did away with any possibility of a misunderstanding. 'One of our oldest friends here.'

'Of course everybody in the village knows him,' said Agatha. 'He is a charming man, most friendly. I ought not to gossip, I know, but I don't think anybody would be surprised if he were to marry Lady Clara Boulding, the widow of our former Member of Parliament,' she explained for the Bishop's benefit.

'There is no reason why you shouldn't gossip, my dear,' said the Archdeacon, 'but I think a great many people would be surprised if things happened as you suggested. I had an idea that Ricardo's fancy lay in quite another direction.'

At this the Bishop directed a rather coy glance towards Belinda, who began talking quickly about missions and the very interesting preacher they had had one Sunday evening, from the diocese of Ndikpo, or some such name.

'Ah, yes, Ndikpo,' the Bishop shook his head. 'The labourers are indeed few in that field. They have no African priests there.'

'I suppose some parts are more backward than others,' Belinda ventured. 'I mean it takes some time before the natives are ready to be ordained.'

'Ah, yes, yes. Time and Money,' the Bishop nodded again and then asked whether the Archdeacon gave out collecting boxes for Missions to his parishioners.

'No,' replied the Archdeacon shortly. 'We have a collection at Matins every now and then.'

'But surely it would be more lucrative if people took collecting boxes?' suggested the Bishop. 'You would find that the spirit of friendly rivalry would increase the amount considerably. You might publish the results in the parish magazine when the boxes were opened. I have always found that the best way.'

'It wouldn't work here,' said the Archdeacon emphatically.

'I think it's an excellent idea,' said Agatha. 'Miss Smiley does it for the Zenana Mission, you know.'

'Does she?' said the Archdeacon. 'I really could not undertake to do anything about it myself, I am much too busy, as you will realize when you have been here a little longer, my dear Bishop.'

Belinda could only wonder how he was to be made to realize this, but, loyal as ever, she agreed that the Archdeacon was much too busy and, much to her own surprise and dismay, heard herself offering to take on the organization and distribution of the boxes.

'I knew it!' said the Bishop. 'As soon as I saw Miss Bede, I said to myself "Here is one of *us* – that splendid work for the Guild of St Agnes" – do you know, Archdeacon, she even denied that she had been connected with it?'

Belinda was by now covered with confusion and began to wonder whether she had indeed worked splendidly for the Guild of St Agnes; after all, her memory was not always completely reliable. Perhaps she had also knitted the Bishop a beautiful scarf. She felt that it was time to be going.

'Oh, Belinda is a very excellent person altogether,' said the Archdeacon with casual charm. 'I don't know what we should do without her.'

Belinda reflected a little bitterly on these words as she walked home, but the sight of Ricardo and Edith Liversidge, deep in conversation, soon turned her thoughts to other matters. She could guess what they were talking about and was not surprised to hear Ricardo saying that he had hoped the tombstone would be of white marble rather than commonplace grey stone.

'Well, as long as he's dead I don't see that it matters what his tombstone is like,' said Edith very sensibly, but with a lack of feeling regrettable in one who had lost her love so tragically. 'I'm sure John wouldn't mind,' she went on jovially. 'He was never all that particular about appearances.'

'A mind and spirit as great as his needed no outward decoration,' said Ricardo solemnly.

Belinda waited until he had gone before interrupting with an invitation to Edith to come in for a cup of tea.

'I've had mine at the vicarage,' she explained, 'but I expect Harriet will still be having hers.'

'Well, if it isn't a nuisance,' said Edith, with unusual consideration.

'Oh, one extra for tea is no trouble at all,' said Belinda gaily. 'I never find that it is.'

'It might quite easily be,' said Edith. 'If there were only a small piece of cake left, for instance.'

Belinda was confident that the tea table would be well stocked and was quite ready to forget that she had had her own tea at the vicarage. After the little strains and awkwardnesses there she felt that she deserved a second tea and was able to do full justice to the potato cakes and her favourite Belgian buns.

At tea they were all very gay, in the way that happy, unmarried ladies of middle age often are. Naturally they talked about the Bishop. Try as she would, Belinda could not give a flattering description. After several attempts to soften the blow, she burst out, 'Well, Harriet, there's no getting away from it, he reminds me of a *sheep*!'

'But surely a very handsome sheep?' Harriet protested. 'Of course I haven't seen him for many years, but people don't alter all that much, and he was such an exceptionally good-looking curate.'

'Are you sure you're thinking of the same one?' suggested Belinda timidly. 'You've known so *many*. . . .'

But Harriet indignantly denied the possibility of such a mistake. 'And anyway,' she went on stoutly, to justify herself in case of a possible disappointment, 'you can't judge a person by his face.'

'No, of course not,' Belinda agreed. 'I'm sure he's an excellent man,' she said doubtfully. 'Have you ever heard of the Guild of St Agnes, by the way?'

'Oh, I don't think so,' said Harriet. 'There's the Society of St Monica, but that's for widows, I believe.'

'You mean you have to be a widow?' said Belinda. 'I think it could hardly be that.'

'I know,' said Edith suddenly, 'it does work among Fallen Women – Connie's patroness was the President I believe. They used to have teas and sales of work in the house in Belgrave Square.'

'So that's it,' said Belinda, who hardly knew what advice

she could give to a Fallen Woman, let alone what kind of splendid work she could have done. She explained the connection and they all laughed very heartily.

When they had finished tea Edith suddenly began doing a Balkan folk-dance which encouraged Harriet to give a very ludicrous imitation of Mr Mold's proposal. But as Belinda laughed she found herself almost wishing that Harriet were even now Mrs Nathaniel Mold. Then at least there could be no danger of having the Bishop of Mbawawa for a brother-in-law.

CHAPTER SIXTEEN

IT WAS THE morning after the Bishop's arrival and there was a feeling of suppressed excitement in the air. At the Misses Bede's house the morning passed in the usual way until just before luncheon, when the front-door bell rang. Before Belinda and Harriet could begin to guess who it was, Emily had announced the Archdeacon.

It was at once evident that he was in a good temper, which Belinda thought rather surprising, although there was a certain relish in disliking somebody, she supposed; which might account for it.

'I hope the Bishop is well?' she ventured.

'Oh, tolerably well, I think,' said the Archdeacon, rubbing his hands in front of the fire. 'I believe he did not sleep very well, but our spare bed is notoriously uncomfortable.'

'We could easily have him here,' said Harriet, 'our spare bed has a new mattress and is really most comfortable. I have tried it myself.'

'That is kind of you,' said the Archdeacon, 'but the clergy are used to discomfort. They even enjoy it, you know.'

Belinda looked at him doubtfully, but he appeared to be quite serious.

'I hope you are writing to poor Nathaniel Mold,' he said, seeing that Harriet was seated at the writing-desk.

'Oh, no,' said Harriet, thinking it rather interfering of the Archdeacon. 'That is all finished. I was writing to Gorringes' for a new winter dressing-gown.'

'Well, they say that a bird in the hand is worth two in the bush,' declared the Archdeacon.

'I'm not sure that I understand your meaning there,' said Harriet coyly. 'What do you mean by two in the bush?'

'Why, Ricardo and the Bishop,' said the Archdeacon slyly.

Belinda felt inclined to add that poor Ricardo was almost as good as in the hand, but she said nothing as she thought the conversation rather unbecoming. It would have been quite another matter if Edith or Connie had been there instead of the Archdeacon, but for somebody of Harriet's age to discuss her suitors with the vicar of the parish seemed to Belinda hardly the thing.

'But I haven't seen the Bishop for over thirty years,' protested Harriet, enjoying herself very much.

'Then you will see him tonight,' said the Archdeacon.

'*Tonight?*' echoed the sisters incredulously, as if it were the most unlikely thing in the world.

'Yes, I came to see you about it. The Bishop is giving a lantern lecture with slides, and I wanted to know if you would be good enough to work the lantern,' said the Archdeacon, turning to Harriet.

'Why, I should love to,' said Harriet, for she had an unexpected genius for working the lantern and had done it for many years now.

'It should be an unusual experience,' said the Archdeacon, 'to renew your acquaintance with the Bishop over a slide put in upside down.'

Harriet went off into a peal of delighted laughter.

'What's the lecture to be about?' asked Belinda, thinking that somebody ought to show an intelligent interest in it.

'Oh, his natives I believe,' said the Archdeacon rather scornfully. 'Songs and dances and that kind of thing!'

'It should be very interesting,' ventured Belinda.

'And amusing too,' said the Archdeacon. 'The Bishop was practising this morning.'

'The songs or the dances?' asked Harriet.

'Oh, the songs, as far as I could hear. I dare say it will not be possible to demonstrate the dances.'

'I hope *not*,' said Belinda rather indignantly, for from what one heard about these native dances it did not seem as if they were the sort of thing that could properly be performed in a parish hall.

Moved by a sudden impulse of friendliness, Harriet asked the Archdeacon if he would stay to luncheon. 'We're having pheasant,' she added temptingly.

'I'm so sorry,' he said, 'but I'm afraid Agatha will be expecting me. Otherwise nothing could have given me greater pleasure.'

'Yes, that's the worst of having a wife,' said Harriet jovially.

'It is really much wiser for a man to stay single,' said the Archdeacon, 'and then it doesn't matter if he's late for lunch.'

After he had gone Harriet remarked that if he had been single *now*, he might have discovered that there were even greater advantages, but she soon changed the subject, and began asking Belinda's opinion about her hair. Should she leave the back in a neat roll or comb it out into fluffy curls?

Belinda gave some sort of an answer, as she realized that Harriet was determined to have the fluffy curls, and wondered whether she herself should wear her blue marocain or an old wool dress. The parish hall was inclined to be draughty and she had no particular wish to impress the Bishop. On the other hand, the Archdeacon would certainly be there and she did not wish to appear dowdy before him. It was a difficult problem. Harriet had already decided that she would wear her brown velvet, and possibly her fur cape, though working the lantern she would probably be warm enough without it.

Emily was also going to the lecture with the vicarage Florrie, who had given her a most glowing account of the Bishop. He had apparently given her some very pretty African beads and a wooden comb, carved by one of his native converts.

'Putting silly ideas into her head,' Harriet had said to Belinda after hearing this. 'Theo ought to be careful,' she said ominously.

The lecture was to begin at eight o'clock, but Harriet insisted that they should be in good time as she had all sorts of things to do in connection with the lantern, which was inclined to be temperamental.

'And you will want to get a good seat,' she said.

'Oh, not particularly,' said Belinda. 'I don't suppose the hall will be very full and all the chairs are equally hard.'

The problem of where to sit was settled by their meeting Miss Liversidge and Miss Aspinall at the door of the hall.

'Let's go somewhere at the back, where we can have a good laugh,' said Edith.

Belinda agreed that she would also like to sit somewhere at the back, although she did not give any such crude reason for her preference. Poor Miss Aspinall would have liked to sit nearer the front, in case Lady Clara Boulding should be there, but she knew it was no use saying so, and sat meekly on Belinda's other side, glancing hopefully back at the door when anybody came in. Harriet was looking very important, perched up on a table, manipulating the lantern and trying out some specimen slides. Canterbury cathedral, a field with cows, and the head and shoulders of a bearded clergyman followed one another in quick succession: the lantern was obviously working well.

The hall began to fill up until there were very few vacant seats and the Bishop could be seen threading his way among the chairs towards Harriet, carrying a box of lantern slides. Belinda craned forward eagerly, yet as unconcernedly as she could, to witness their reunion after so many years. Edith Liversidge did the same and even went so far as to stand up for a better view.

'How many years did you say it was?' she enquired.

'I can't remember exactly, but I think it must be nearly thirty,' said Belinda in a more subdued tone of voice, for she did not want Miss Beard and Miss Smiley, who were sitting in front of them with a group of fellow teachers, to hear all their conversation. Things half heard were apt to be wickedly exaggerated and Miss Beard, in spite of being an excellent Sunday School teacher, was very much inclined to gossip.

'What a long time!' breathed Connie. 'There is something very wonderful in meeting a friend again after many years.'

'That rather depends,' said Edith brusquely. 'I can think of some I'd much rather not meet.'

'I suppose in that case you would hardly call them friends,' said Belinda. 'Although one doesn't really know what a person is going to be like after thirty years.'

Harriet's position on the table made it necessary for the Bishop to gaze up at her. She bent graciously and extended her hand as if to take his, but received instead the box of lantern slides. Belinda was indignant. How rude and casual of him! she thought. How like a bishop! she went on and then stopped, realizing the injustice of this generalization. For she was certain that Willie Amery or Oliver Opobo and Calabar would not have behaved like this. Theodore Grote was cold, a cold fish as she remembered their dear mother calling him. *Legless, unloving, infamously chaste,* she thought detachedly, remembering Ricardo's goldfish, and was then ashamed of herself for thinking of it. There could be no excuse, for Leigh Hunt was not even one of our greater poets.

Still, there *was* something fishlike about Bishop Grote. Fish and sheep. Was that possible?

'I do wish I knew what they were saying,' said Connie, 'though of course it's the most unpardonable curiosity. Meetings like this ought to be really *sacred*.'

'He's obviously just saying something about the slides,' said Edith. 'Connie is much too romantic. I suppose she thinks he ought to be quoting poetry.'

'Well, he might,' said Belinda, 'if he were that sort of a person, which I doubt. He didn't even shake hands, otherwise he might have quoted that nice line of Cleveland's, where he describes a lady's hand *tender as 'twere a jelly gloved* . . . I always like that, but somehow it doesn't apply to people's hands now.'

Edith looked down complacently at her own fingers, gnarled and stained. 'Not in the country,' she said, 'though Connie's always fussing about hers, rubbing them with lotion and all that sort of nonsense. I always tell her that nobody's likely to want to hold her hand now, so why bother.'

Belinda thought this rather unkind and sympathized with Connie. It wasn't exactly that one hoped to have one's hand held. . . .

'Look, there's the Archdeacon and Father Plowman,' said Connie. 'I suppose it must be going to begin.'

'I imagine one can smoke here?' said Edith, producing a squashed paper packet of Woodbines and offering it to Belinda.

'No, thank you,' said Belinda. She felt that it would be unbecoming for her to smoke, though it seemed right that Edith should do so. Anything that she did seemed to be in character. Her appearance tonight in a homespun skirt with white blouse and Albanian embroidered waistcoat made Belinda feel dowdy and insignificant, one of the many thousand respectable middle-aged spinsters, the backbones or busybodies of countless parishes throughout the country.

The Archdeacon had mounted the platform and was introducing the Bishop in a short and almost gracious speech.

'I, for one, am eagerly looking forward to hearing more about this fascinating country and its people,' he said. 'Many of us will envy Bishop Grote his unique opportunities. It may even be that I too shall feel the urge to labour in a foreign field,' he concluded, with what Belinda could only think was sarcasm, for nothing more unlikely could be imagined.

The audience settled down on the hard chairs. Belinda noticed that Agatha was wearing a becoming new dress, dark green, with little pleated ruffles at the shoulders and neck. From the best houses, she thought, with sad resignation.

'The climate of Mbawawa is temperate and the soil very fertile,' began the Bishop, waving his pointer vaguely in the air.

The first slide appeared. It showed a seascape with some kind of tropical palms in the foreground. Belinda had seen the same type of picture on the covers of dance tunes about the South Sea Islands.

'When I say temperate,' went on the Bishop, 'I dare say many of you might find it rather hot.' He paused and tapped his pointer vigorously on the floor.

There appeared in rapid succession several pictures of handsome natives, dressed in bunches of leaves and garlands of flowers. Some members of the audience were inclined to giggle at these, but the Bishop hastily explained that the pictures were of the natives as they *used* to be.

'We have since introduced a form of European dress which is far more in keeping with Christian ideas of morality,' he said. Another slide followed, showing the natives clad in this way. 'I should like to add here,' he went on, 'that we are often very much in need of garments for our people and should welcome gifts of clothing or material – light cotton materials, of course, nothing elaborate or costly.'

It would be typical of the perfidy of human nature,

thought Belinda indignantly, if the church workers fell so much in love with the Bishop that they forgot about all the other more deserving charities such as the Clothe-Our-Children League and the Society for helping the Poor in Pimlico to which they were accustomed to contribute. She could already notice in the half darkness the beaming looks of approval on their faces, as they nodded and smiled to each other, planning working parties and schemes to raise money. Of course the Mbawawa *were* a deserving cause, she supposed, but were they not happier in their leaves and flowers? Naturally one wished them to have the benefits of Christianity; it was rather difficult to see where one should draw the line. They could hardly appear at a service in a dress of leaves, she reflected, when she herself felt that a short-sleeved dress was unsuitable. But need they wear those shapeless cotton garments? Perhaps the architecture of the church had something to do with it: one's style of dress ought to be somehow in keeping . . . her thoughts wandered on against a background of bleating Bishop's voice. He had somehow got on to the subject of music.

'The language is well suited to singing,' he declared. 'It is soft and pleasing, vowels and liquid sounds predominating. You may be interested to hear that the alphabet contains only eighteen letters,' he went on, 'and I think that if you saw it written you would hardly call it an alphabet at all. Such an odd collection of letters with long tails and squiggles! You see, the Mbawawa had never written their language down until a few years ago, when missionaries attempted it. Then some clever people in London, experts in African languages, made up this alphabet, and I think nobody was more surprised than the Mbawawa themselves!' The Bishop laughed heartily and wiped his brow. 'But I haven't come here tonight to tell you about the alphabet. I think we can safely leave that to the clever people in London,' he added, with what Belinda felt was insufferable patronage, considering the distinction of his audience, which contained at least four University graduates, five, if one counted Father Plowman's failed B.A.

'Their chief musical instrument is the Mhamha, m-h-a-m-h-a,' he spelled the word out and one of the Sunday School teachers could be seen fumbling in her handbag for pencil and paper. There now followed another slide of grinning natives holding musical instruments.

'I dare say some of you would like to hear what the language sounds like,' said the Bishop, 'so I am going to sing a few verses of a song which the Mbawawa adapt to many occasions, birth, marriage, death, all the great events in this mortal life have their own form of it.' He paused, as if wondering which was most suited to a gathering in a parish hall. 'Let me try and give you a gay marriage song,' he said. 'Imagine yourselves taking part in an Mbawawa wedding.'

'I do not feel myself equal to that,' whispered Edith to Belinda. 'Death would have been a better choice, or even birth.'

The voice of the Bishop rang out through the hall in song. Many handkerchiefs were taken out hastily, especially among the younger members of the audience, for the noise which filled the hall was quite unexpected. Even Belinda, who had heard the Bishop sing as a curate, was a little unprepared. And yet perhaps the Mbawawa *did* have voices like that and it was wrong to feel that one wanted to laugh. Belinda glanced at Harriet to see how she was reacting. As far as it was possible to see, she was displaying remarkable self-control, for she was very prone to giggle, and appeared to be gazing at the Bishop with rapt attention. Most of the audience were stirring uneasily. Even Agatha was smiling a little, but she managed to make it look as if she were not really amused, but pleased and approving, which was quite another matter.

At last the noise stopped, and some people relieved their feelings by clapping.

'The song has many more verses,' explained the Bishop.

'Indeed, if the singer is particularly gifted he can go on almost indefinitely; I have known the marriage song go on all night, but I fear I should find the hall empty if I attempted that.'

During the laughter which followed he tapped his pointer on the floor and another slide clicked into place.

'Now this is another characteristic musical instrument. It is called the Hmwoq, spelled h-m-w-o-q.'

Everyone looked with interest at the curiously shaped object which had now appeared on the screen. It was certainly a very peculiar shape and there was more giggling from the back of the hall. It could hardly be what it seemed to be, thought Belinda doubtfully, though one knew that among primitive peoples one might find almost anything. The anthropologist who went among them must go with an open mind. . . .

The Bishop turned towards the screen and prodded it uncertainly. Then he advanced towards the edge of the platform and said in a loud clear voice, 'I think that slide is upside down.'

Everyone turned to look at Harriet, who was not in the least embarrassed at having such attention drawn to her. Indeed, Belinda could not be absolutely sure that her sister had not purposely put the slide in upside down.

'I am *so* sorry, My Lord Bishop,' Harriet's voice rang clearly through the hall. 'How *stupid* of me,' she said, smiling most charmingly into the darkness.

The Bishop responded graciously enough by saying that he feared *he* was too stupid to explain the picture unless it were the right way up, and his explanation was very confused even when the slide was correctly shown. Leaving it rather hurriedly, he produced a large sea shell from an inner pocket and applied it to his lips.

By this time his hearers knew more or less what to expect, so that they were able to bear the strange sounds which came out of the shell with more composure. The noise seemed to be a hollower and more resonant version of the Bishop's own singing voice.

'Wonderful how he does it, isn't it?' whispered Father Plowman to Agatha Hoccleve, who could not but agree that it was indeed most wonderful.

'This instrument is used particularly in agricultural rites,' explained the Bishop, 'where the ceremony of propitiating the earth goddess is carried out.'

'Phallic,' murmured Edith, nodding her head. 'Quite the usual thing.'

Fortunately the Sunday School teachers did not know the word, thought Belinda, or they would most certainly have turned round. It was rather like Edith to show off her smattering of anthropological knowledge, she felt, particularly if it were something rather embarrassing.

After the music came more slides of wedding and funeral scenes, and finally one of the Bishop himself in gaiters and leafy garlands, at which everyone clapped vigorously. It was a relief to be able to let off steam, for much laughter had been bottled up. But the climax came when he turned his back on the audience, fumbled in a suitcase and reappeared facing them in a huge painted wooden mask, with hinged beak, large round eyes and hanging raffia mane, which completely covered his head and shoulders. This brought the house down and there was laughter and clapping from the front seats, stamping and whistling from the back benches.

All that followed was inevitably an anticlimax. The Bishop went on to give a list of rather stray facts which he might have got out of the *Encyclopaedia Britannica*. He mentioned that they tattooed little, that the native chiefs sometimes weighed as much as one hundred and eighty pounds, and that although infanticide was prevalent, cannibalism was almost unknown. They lived chiefly on yams and millet, but rats and mice were also eaten. Beer was brewed from guinea corn; fire was made from a paste of salt, pepper and lizard dung.

'And in conclusion,' he added, 'for the benefit of any anthropologists who may be listening to me, I may as well state that the basic social unit is an exogamous patrilineal kindred or extended family or even clan. I don't think we need worry overmuch about that.'

Hearty laughter greeted these remarks. There was no anthropologist in the audience.

Father Plowman mounted the platform and began to propose a vote of thanks.

'I for one shall never forget this fascinating lecture,' he said. 'I am sure that after tonight there will be many who will be eager to visit this beautiful country and see all these wonders for themselves.'

'Putting ideas into their heads,' muttered Edith, and she was not far wrong, for one of the Sunday School teachers was even at that moment toying with the idea of asking the Bishop whether he could find a place for her in his Mission, and even Miss Aspinall was wondering whether it might not be possible to go out there to teach the gentler arts.

'Truly the wonders of this world are without number. Let us thank God for His goodness to us,' concluded Father Plowman, and everyone agreed that it was a most fitting end to the evening.

It was a little spoilt by the Archdeacon rising to his feet and saying that he was sure everyone would wish him to thank Miss Harriet Bede for her admirable working of the lantern, without which the lecture would not have been half so enjoyable. Of course it was right that she should be thanked, but several people felt that Father Plowman's words should have been the last. Only Belinda was pleased, both because of his acknowledgment of her sister and because no evening was complete for her which did not include a few words from the Archdeacon.

'So like him, that kind thought,' she said to Edith, 'remembering Harriet when the Bishop never said a word, nor

Father Plowman for that matter. I knew the Archdeacon wouldn't forget.'

'Oh, I expect he just wanted to be different,' said Edith, struggling into her mannish navy blue overcoat. 'What happens now?'

'I think we go home,' said Belinda, 'but I dare say Harriet will go and have refreshments at the vicarage with the Bishop. They'll probably have coffee and sandwiches or something light.'

'Oh, I hate standing about balancing a cup and plate and making conversation,' said Edith. 'Come along, Connie,' she called, turning round, 'we're going home.'

But Connie, with a hasty gathering up of bits and pieces and a fluttering of grey draperies, had hurried towards the front of the hall, where she could be seen among the little cluster of people waiting to shake hands with the Bishop.

'Don't make her come away,' pleaded Belinda. 'She would probably like to go to the vicarage with the others.'

'Well, come and take pot luck with me,' said Edith roughly. 'Just coffee and baked beans – you know our kind of supper.'

'That will be lovely,' murmured Belinda.

At the door of Edith's cottage a big, shaggy dog came bounding towards them, his muddy paws scrabbling against their coats and stockings, and inside the living-room, for it could hardly be called a drawing-room, everything was so primitive and comfortless that Belinda felt really sympathetic towards poor Connie. After Belgrave Square too . . . Her harp, shrouded in a holland cover, seemed out of place in the untidy room with its smell of dog and cigarette smoke.

Belinda stood uncertainly on the threshold of the little kitchen, watching Edith cutting bread and scooping the beans out of their tin into a saucepan.

'Hand me that ash tray, will you?' said Edith, but not before Belinda had seen a grey wedge of ash drop into the beans. 'Drat it,' she said. 'Too late. Hope you don't mind?'

'Of course not,' said Belinda nobly, remembering Miss Prior and the caterpillar. Perhaps there was something after all in being a gentlewoman.

CHAPTER SEVENTEEN

WHEN BELINDA awoke next morning, she decided that she did not feel very well. She was not sure whether this was because of the ash in the baked beans, the half-empty bottle of Empire port that Edith had found in the back of a cupboard or the damp walk home, in rather thin shoes. She was inclined to think it must be the last, for what else could have given her such an unromantic, snivelling cold?

'Oh, dear,' said Harriet, sitting down heavily on Belinda's bed, 'the Bishop was coming to tea and I suppose I shall have to put him off if you're going to be ill.'

'Why?' asked Belinda stupidly.

'Well, really, what would people think?'

'They needn't know I'm in bed, and after all, it's only a matter of time,' said Belinda, who was in no mood to humour her sister's coy scruples.

'Yes, perhaps it is,' agreed Harriet, but rather doubtfully. 'He asked particularly if you would be here, though.'

'Did he? Well, we certainly can't have tea in my bedroom,' said Belinda plaintively.

'No, of course not,' Harriet agreed. 'Now are you sure you couldn't fancy a little sausage?' she said brightly. 'Emily will have cooked enough for both of us.'

Belinda did not think she fancied anything at all, but was persuaded to try some weak tea and a piece of toast. And would Harriet be very kind and bring her the *Oxford Book of Victorian Verse*? She might feel like reading later on.

Harriet went downstairs and came back with a tray and the book.

'Isn't it rather heavy to read in bed?' she ventured. 'I've brought you something smaller as well. Here's the Fourth Book of Virgil. I know you like the part about Dido and Aeneas. It's such a nice thin little book.'

'Oh, Harriet, how kind. But it's all in Latin, and you know I can't read it.'

'Never mind, dear,' said Harriet soothingly. 'I shouldn't read at all, if I were you. Just try and rest.'

'I can't think how I caught this cold,' said Belinda.

'I'll go and get you some whisky from the Crownwheel and Pinion,' declared Harriet. 'I shall go as soon as it's open.'

'Oh, Harriet, don't go *there*,' said Belinda, rather concerned. 'I'm sure you could get some at Abbot's, and anyway I don't think I really need it. If I stay in bed and keep warm I'm sure to be better in a day or two. Hot lemon is really a much nicer drink.'

'You never know when you may need whisky,' said Harriet mysteriously. 'It's just as well to have it in the house.'

'I seem to remember a recipe in *Tried Favourites* – a sort of substitute for whisky,' said Belinda. 'I dare say it would be quite easy to make.'

'I think our guests would hardly thank us if we offered them that,' said Harriet.

'Our guests?' Belinda sank back weakly on to her pillows, unable to face the idea of guests who needed to be entertained with whisky. 'I think I'll just rest until lunch-time,' she said. 'I dare say I shan't read after all.'

So Harriet left her and went out to do the shopping. She met several people and told each one about her sister's indisposition, making little or much of it according to the status of her hearer. To the Archdeacon she gave the most exact details, thinking that somehow he ought to be possessed of all the facts.

'She had weak tea and dry toast for breakfast,' said Harriet confidentially, 'and then she asked for the *Oxford Book of Victorian Verse*.'

'She called for madder music and for stronger wine,' said the Archdeacon, but Harriet was not familiar with our great Victorian poets and so the quotation passed over her head.

She pointed out rather sharply that strong wine was the last thing that should be given to an invalid, although a little brandy might be helpful in cases of biliousness.

'But of course Belinda isn't bilious,' she said hastily. 'Nothing like that.'

'Poor Belinda, I am really extremely sorry. Do tell her how very sorry I am. I only wish I could go and see her.'

'Oh, she's not at all seriously ill,' said Harriet. 'Just a little chill. I'm sure it would alarm people if you were seen going to the house. People always think the worst when they see a clergyman.'

'Dear me, I hardly know how to take that,' said the Archdeacon. 'I should have liked to think that we brought comfort to the sick.'

'Oh, well, I suppose you do, in a way,' said Harriet, who was finding it difficult to convey that it all depended on the clergyman.

'I must look out some books for her to read,' said the Archdeacon.

'Thank you very much, but she really has plenty to read.'

'All the same, there might be something she'd like,' persisted the Archdeacon. 'I sometimes wish that I could afford to be ill so that I could read some of the things I normally never have time for.'

Harriet looked contemptuous but said nothing. 'I must be going now,' she said at last. 'I still have quite a lot of shopping to do.'

On her return she found that Belinda had been to sleep and felt a little better.

'I saw the Archdeacon,' said Harriet triumphantly. 'He seemed quite concerned to hear that you were ill and almost suggested coming to see you, but I soon nipped that in the bud.'

Belinda gathered her faded pink bed-jacket more closely round her shoulders. 'Oh, no, I couldn't have him coming to see me,' she said. 'Not without warning, anyway.'

'Well, of course,' said Harriet pompously, 'it is, or should be, customary for a clergyman to visit the sick in his parish. But perhaps that's only for the poor people really, to see if they have all they want and so on.'

'Yes, I suppose I have everything I want,' said Belinda rather sadly.

'Naturally if you were seriously ill or dying it would be another matter,' went on Harriet reassuringly.

'But I'm not,' said Belinda regretfully, thinking of Henry reading *Samson Agonistes* to her on her death-bed.

After lunch she settled down to her own thoughts. Harriet had brought up a light novel from the circulating library and this lay with the *Oxford Book of Victorian Verse* on the eiderdown. But Belinda did not feel like reading. She was quite enjoying her illness now that she felt a little better and could allow her thoughts to wander at random in the past and future without the consciousness that she ought to be more profitably employed. She had no doubt that there would soon be another proposal of marriage in the drawing-room, perhaps even this afternoon, although she judged the Bishop to be a more prudent man than Mr Mold. He had certainly not behaved very cordially to Harriet at the lecture, but Belinda was sure that he would not be able to hold out long against her charms. Nor had Harriet seemed as enthusiastic as might have been expected. Could it be that she had found him less attractive than she anticipated, or was it the very depth of her feeling that kept her from speaking of it? Belinda puzzled over this for some time and then fell to thinking of her own life.

There was very little new to be said or thought about it, she decided. She had loved dear Henry for so many years now that she no longer thought of her love as a hopeless passion. Indeed, Belinda felt that no spinster of her age and respectability could possibly have such a thing for an archdeacon. The fierce flame had died down, but the fire was still glowing brightly.

My very ashes in their urn,
Shall like a hallowed lamp for ever burn. . . .

How much more one appreciated our great literature if one loved, thought Belinda, especially if the love were unrequited! She touched the books affectionately but made no effort to read either of them. As Harriet had said, the *Oxford Book of Victorian Verse* was rather heavy to hold, and many of the poems in it were uncomfortably sentimental for afternoon reading.

Suddenly there was a noise in the hall. Belinda sat up in bed and listened. At first she thought it must be the Bishop arriving rather too early for tea, but then she realized that it was a woman's voice. It sounded almost like Agatha's. She crouched under the bedclothes and began to wonder whether she had a temperature after all and ought not to see people. It was surely not normal to have a sudden longing to hide under the bedclothes when one heard the vicar's wife in the hall, even if one did love her husband better than she did?

Belinda sat up bravely and took out her hand-mirror. She knew that she looked most unattractive and thought what a good thing it was that she was not seriously ill or dying. Her hair was out of curl, her cheeks were pale and her nose needed powdering. She would not have liked Henry to see her like this, even on her death-bed.

Agatha was all too soon in the room, saying, 'Poor Belinda, I was so sorry when Henry told me you were ill. I thought I'd come and see how you were.'

Belinda, who was trying to smuggle the hand-mirror out

of sight, murmured that it was very kind of Agatha and that she was feeling much better.

'And now,' said Agatha, rather too briskly, 'what has been the matter with you?'

'Oh, I think I must have caught a slight chill,' said Belinda vaguely. 'Perhaps I was sitting in a draught at the Bishop's lecture,' she ventured, feeling ashamed of not knowing exactly what was the matter with her and why. 'The lecture was most interesting, wasn't it?'

'Oh, yes, fascinating,' said Agatha. 'The Bishop is such a dear man, so kind and amusing.'

He must be especially pleasant to Agatha, thought Belinda, who had not formed at all that impression of him. Indeed Agatha was quite animated when she spoke of him and even looked a little flushed.

'He asked where you were last night after the lecture,' she went on. 'We had quite a little gathering at the vicarage, you know.'

'I thought you would probably have enough people there without me,' said Belinda weakly, feeling as she so often did with Agatha that she had somehow done the wrong thing. 'I went to supper with Edith Liversidge. I'm surprised that he should have remembered me at all.'

'Well, of course it is a bishop's duty to remember people,' said Agatha. 'My father had a wonderful memory for names and faces.'

'Yes, I suppose they meet so many people,' said Belinda, feeling rather dampened. Not that she wanted the Bishop to remember her particularly, but it was like Agatha to take away any illusions she might have cherished.

'It's some years since you last met, isn't it?' said Agatha conversationally.

'Oh, yes, about thirty years, I think. We none of us grow any younger, do we? *Timor mortis conturbat me*,' murmured Belinda, staring straight in front of her.

Agatha looked at her sharply. Sometimes she wondered whether Belinda was quite all there. She said such odd things.

There was a short pause, but before it had time to become awkward a hearty voice was heard outside the door and Edith Liversidge strode into the room, followed by Connie Aspinall. Their arms were full of books and parcels.

'I must be going now,' said Agatha, who disliked Edith. 'Too many visitors at once will tire you.'

Belinda thanked her for her kindness, but was quite relieved to be left alone with Edith and Connie.

'We've brought you some books,' said Edith. 'And Connie's made you a sponge cake. You know I'm no hand at that kind of thing.'

'Oh, how kind. . . .'

'I thought you might like to see some old copies of *The Gentlewoman*,' said Connie. 'There's a picture of Lady Grudge's daughter in one of them.'

'How interesting, I shall look forward to reading them,' said Belinda. 'You must point her out to me.'

At this moment the front-door bell rang. 'That must be the Bishop arriving,' said Belinda.

'The Bishop?' asked Edith, rather surprised.

'Yes, he is coming to tea today.'

'Does he know you're ill or is he expecting to see both of you?'

'Oh, I'm supposed to be there too, but I suddenly woke up ill,' said Belinda pathetically. 'So Harriet will have to entertain him alone.'

'Alone?' said Edith. 'I don't think he'll like that.'

'Why ever not?' asked Belinda, rather worried. Life was quite difficult enough without Edith making disturbing suggestions. Harriet was going to marry the Bishop and Belinda would be left in her old age to die a lonely death, or with nobody but a paid companion to cheer her last hours. Surely that was enough? She had been trying to prepare herself for the worst and did not wish to be unsettled.

Meanwhile Edith expounded her ideas of what a bishop would think quite proper. 'I don't think Harriet will get him,' she said bluntly.

Belinda had been thinking the same thing not so long ago, but now she was inclined to disagree. After all, dear Edith had had little or no experience of bishops, although poor John had been a very good man in his way.

'I think he has successfully avoided so many women in his life that not even Harriet will be able to catch him,' she went on. 'I know his sort.'

Belinda thought this rather a vulgar way of putting it, though it could hardly be denied that it was what Harriet intended to do.

'I believe women can do almost anything if they are really desperate,' she ventured. 'In one of Lyly's plays, *Endimion*, I think. . . .'

'But I don't think Harriet is really desperate,' Edith interrupted. 'Do you?'

'I really couldn't say,' said Belinda plaintively. 'I think I should like a drink of barley water. It's on the little table.'

'Oh, let me get it for you,' said Connie, coming forward with a glass and a copy of *The Gentlewoman* in her hand. 'This is Lady Joan Grudge,' she said eagerly, indicating a group of people enjoying a joke at a race meeting.

'Yes, she's very pretty, isn't she,' murmured Belinda, and was then informed that she had been looking at the wrong girl, for nobody could call Lady Joan pretty. 'Such a nice expression,' she emended. 'She looks very jolly.'

'Yes, she is a *very* sweet girl. . . .'

Downstairs Harriet had just made the discovery that Bishop Grote never ate anything for his tea.

Now this was exceedingly awkward, for how can any real contact be established between two persons when one is eating and the other merely watching? For some minutes

Harriet did not know what to do. Her recollections of the Bishop as a curate had included cream buns and hot buttered toast, with licking of fingers. Eventually she had to resort to a kind of arch scolding, which was really more suitable for very young curates than for bishops.

'Now, that's *naughty* of you,' she said. 'I expected you to have a really good appetite. I shall be *much* too embarrassed to eat alone,' she added, liberally spreading a piece of buttered toast with strawberry jam.

'I am really very sorry,' said the Bishop complacently, but with no intention of changing his habits even to be polite to his hostess. 'But your sister will be eating something, won't she?' he enquired, looking anxiously towards the door for a sign of the elder Miss Bede.

'Oh, I forgot to tell you,' said Harriet airily, 'poor Belinda is in bed today. She isn't well.'

The Bishop started and half rose from his chair. 'Nothing infectious or contagious, I hope?' he asked, rather too eagerly.

'No, no,' Harriet smiled reassuringly, but at the same time a little dangerously, so that the Bishop knew that there was as yet no possibility of escape. 'Just a slight chill,' she explained, 'but one can't be too careful.'

The Bishop murmured some words of regret but he found it difficult to keep a note of displeasure out of his voice. So might he have rebuked a rebellious African who appeared at Divine Service in his flowery but inadequate native costume. To begin with, he was not sure that he believed this story about Belinda's illness. People didn't suddenly become ill like this, he told himself angrily, and Belinda had seemed quite well at the lecture last night. If she were really indisposed why hadn't Harriet written or sent a message, changing the invitation to another day? She could so easily have done this. That nice maid who had answered the door would have been only too willing to take a message to the vicarage. It was only a few minutes away. Besides, he wanted to see Belinda. He thought her much nicer than Harriet and she had knitted him such a beautiful scarf when he was a curate, however much she might deny it. Harriet must indeed be heartless to leave her sister lying alone and ill upstairs while she entertained guests – the Bishop's indignation had got the better of his accuracy – in the drawing-room.

Harriet interrupted his thoughts by asking if his tea were too strong.

'Oh, no, it is very nice, thank you,' he said quite civilly.

'Perhaps you would like some more sugar in it?' she persisted.

'No, thank you. I never take more than one lump.'

There was a pause while Harriet, who was finding dear Theo not at all as she had imagined, racked her brains for something to say. Surely he had lost some of his charm of manner? she asked herself anxiously. It went without saying that he had once had charm of manner, but what had happened to it now? He did not appear to be enjoying himself at all and was behaving almost as if this visit were a duty rather than a pleasure. She stretched forward and helped herself to another piece of buttered toast. And how extremely irritating this not eating was. It was impolite, too, most impolite.

'I suppose it was in Africa that you got into the habit of not eating any tea?' she asked brightly.

'Oh, no, it was when I was a minor canon,' he replied seriously. 'I found that it interfered with Evensong.'

Harriet burst into a peal of laughter. She thought this very funny and stored it up to tell Belinda. But the Bishop's sheep's face hardly altered its expression.

'A minor canon,' she giggled. 'Now when you were a deacon I seem to remember you eating crumpets for tea,' she said, trying to bring back to him the remembrance that he had once been a typically charming curate with endearing human weaknesses. '*Sic transit gloria mundi*,' she added.

'I beg your pardon?' The Bishop's voice held a note of

surprise. He thought Harriet an extremely silly woman and was wondering how soon he could decently get away. It was in vain that Harriet asked him intelligent questions about the flora and fauna of the Mbawawa country and tried to draw him out on the missionaries' attitude towards polygamy. He seemed disinclined for conversation and at five o'clock got up to go.

As they went out into the hall, Miss Liversidge and Miss Aspinall came down the stairs from Belinda's room.

'Poor Belinda,' said Connie, 'I think she seems rather low. I must say I thought her looking *not at all well*.'

'Rubbish,' said Edith. 'It's only a chill. She'll be up and about in a day or two.'

'I am indeed sorry to hear this,' said the Bishop. 'Will you give her my very kindest regards and good wishes for a speedy recovery? In my diocese we have a special song for such an occasion. It is almost entirely on one note.'

The three ladies looked up expectantly.

'Perhaps I had better not sing it now,' said the Bishop. 'It might disturb Miss Belinda. The African temperament is not quite like ours.'

'Oh, Belinda, he's so stupid and *dull*!' Harriet burst out, when the visitors had gone. 'He sent you his kindest regards. I don't think he really believed you were ill until he saw Edith and Connie.'

'I'm sorry he was such a disappointment,' said Belinda, 'but perhaps he will improve on further acquaintance. He is really quite the opposite to Mr Mold, isn't he? I mean, perhaps he doesn't have all his goods in the shop window.'

Harriet laughed scornfully and became absorbed in looking at *The Gentlewoman*.

'It was kind of Connie to bring these,' said Belinda. 'It makes one feel so secure to look at a paper like this.' She pointed out Lady Joan Grudge, enjoying a joke with friends at a race meeting, a group at a dance held in Eaton Square for somebody's debutante daughter, a party of titled people at a night club and other comforting unrealities. Lulled in security and contentment, they passed the next half-hour very pleasantly until there was a ring at the front door and the sisters started up in agitation.

'Oh, dear, I wonder who that is?' said Harriet, hastily squeezing her feet into the elegant shoes which she had kicked off after the Bishop had gone.

'I really don't think I can do with any more visitors tonight,' said Belinda feebly. 'What is it, Emily?' she asked, as the maid appeared in the doorway.

For answer Emily thrust forward a large bundle, shrouded in many sheets of blue tissue paper. 'Flowers for the invalid, Miss Belinda,' she said brightly, in a nurse's tone.

Harriet rushed forward. Nobody ever sent *Belinda* flowers, but the florist's label was clearly addressed to Miss Belinda Bede. Harriet unwrapped the tissue paper to reveal a dozen beautiful chrysanthemums, bronze and white.

Belinda's heart leapt. They were from Henry. Harriet had seen him that morning, so he knew she was ill, but in any case Agatha would probably have told him.

'There doesn't seem to be a card with them,' said Harriet, fumbling with maddening deliberation. 'Oh, yes, here we are.' She tossed the little envelope over to Belinda, who tore it open eagerly.

When one has reached Belinda's age, and even before, one takes these small disappointments calmly. Of course the flowers were not from the Archdeacon, how could they have been? It would have been most unsuitable, unless, of course, Agatha had joined in the gift, Belinda told herself, as she struggled to decipher the unfamiliar handwriting.

'*With best wishes for a speedy recovery – Theodore Mbawawa.*' she read. 'Oh, Harriet, from the Bishop!' she sank back weakly on to her pillows. 'I really don't think I can bear any more today. Theodore Mbawawa . . . doesn't that sound odd . . . I suppose it's what he calls himself . . .'

CHAPTER EIGHTEEN

BELINDA DID not keep to her bed for very long, and was soon about again. The Bishop stayed on at the vicarage, though it was evident that he and the Archdeacon disliked each other. Agatha, however, seemed to prefer his company to that of her husband, and Belinda could not help noticing the way she beamed at him when beaming was certainly not one of her normal expressions. Perhaps she felt naturally more at ease with bishops, as her father had been one, and it may have been a disappointment to her that her husband was only an archdeacon. Certainly she and Bishop Grote made a very suitable couple, if only because there was something slightly unpleasant about each of them. Belinda began to weave a little fantasy in which they somehow 'came together' and the Archdeacon was left alone and in need of comfort. How this was to come about she did not know, as divorce was against her principles and the Archdeacon's too, she imagined, and she would hardly have wished the Archdeacon to be removed by death and so put beyond the reach of her comfort. It was somehow out of the question, even in a fantasy, that Agatha should die. People like Agatha didn't die. It might of course be discovered that the marriage of Henry and Agatha had not been legal, but that happened only in the novels of Mrs Henry Wood. And supposing Henry were to be left alone and apparently in need of comfort, and did not turn to Belinda? How was that to be borne? It might well be that he would find Agatha's absence comfort enough. When she got to this point, Belinda was firm with herself and set to work helping Emily with the mincemeat and Christmas puddings, for it was already December and it was even rumoured that the Bishop was to spend Christmas at the vicarage.

Soon Christmas cards began to arrive and every post brought something.

'*A Happy, Holy Christmass*,' said Harriet, reading from Father Plowman's card. 'Very nice wording, and such a pretty picture of the Nativity. I think Christ*mass* is rather nice, Belinda. The Archdeacon's card is *very* ordinary, just *A Happy Christmas and a Bright New Year, from Agatha and Henry Hoccleve*, and no picture at all.'

'I expect Agatha had them done,' said Belinda. 'I imagine Henry would have wanted some quotation, but it was probably cheaper without. Of course Christ*mass* is rather High, isn't it, I mean, the use of the word *mass*. It always looks like a misspelling to me.'

'I wonder what Mr Donne's will be like,' said Harriet anxiously. 'I hope he will remember us.'

'Oh, surely,' said Belinda, indignant not so much for herself as for her sister and the many delicacies she had prepared for him. 'He has been here so much.'

'He might even send a calendar,' mused Harriet. 'That's one degree better than a card.'

'Yes, one of those with a quotation from Shakespeare or a Great Thought for every day. I always think it's nice to have one in some convenient place so that you can read it at the beginning of the day. And yet the thoughts they choose are often so depressing, aren't they, as if Great Thinkers were never cheerful.'

'Well, Mr Donne's calendar certainly won't go *there*,' said Harriet, bristling. 'It shall go in the dining-room, where we can read it at breakfast.'

'Yes, dear, that's what I mean.'

But Mr Donne upset their plans by calling round in person with his present, or rather presents, an expensive looking box of chocolates with a coloured picture of Hampton Court on the lid which the sisters felt he could ill afford, and a photograph of himself which he gave to them rather shyly, obviously embarrassed by Harriet's cries of joy.

'Oh, how *lovely*! And how good of you! Belinda, isn't it

good of Mr Donne?' She thrust the photograph at Belinda, who was rather at a loss, as it looked so exactly like any of the other photographs of curates in Harriet's collection upstairs that she could hardly think what to say.

'The lighting is very good,' she ventured, noticing it on his nose and clerical collar. 'So often a photograph is spoiled by bad lighting. You look very serious,' she added, with what was for her a forced note of playfulness. 'Almost as if you were thinking out a sermon.'

'Oh, we shall have you for tomorrow morning, shan't we,' said Harriet, for the Archdeacon, contrary to his normal practice, had been trying out a course of sermons on the evening congregation, sermons written in so-called 'simple language' and full of sentiments to which every bosom might be expected to return an echo, though he had not, of course, mentioned Harriet's Apes of Brazil. Some of his hearers had found the sermons almost too simple and were even beginning to wonder whether the Archdeacon himself were not returning to his second childhood.

'Oh, no, Bishop Grote is to preach on Sunday morning,' said the curate.

'Well, I suppose he must keep his hand in,' said Belinda. 'I expect it will be about Christmas as it's so near.'

'Yes, on Tuesday,' said the curate. 'I can hardly believe it myself, the weather's so mild.'

'They say a green Christmas means a full churchyard,' declared Harriet with satisfaction. 'I dare say some old people will be taken.'

'Taken?' The curate looked puzzled. 'Ah, yes, I see. I suppose we must expect that.'

They were silent for a moment, until Belinda, not liking to see his young face clouded over, said, 'I really can't think of any old people who are likely to die at the moment. Besides, it's the weather *after* Christmas that we have to fear, isn't it?'

'Oh, yes, if it's mild at Christmas it will be cold afterwards,' agreed Harriet. 'It makes one feel very anxious.'

Belinda, looking at Harriet's sturdy figure, could hardly help smiling.

When Sunday came it occurred to Belinda that perhaps the Bishop had his uses after all. For when the Archdeacon came to give out the notices of the Christmas Services it appeared that Bishop Grote and Mr Donne were to take the seven and eight o'clock Celebrations of Holy Communion, while the Archdeacon himself was to preach at Matins and conduct the Celebration afterwards at twelve, for the benefit of the elderly and lazy. He took the opportunity to say a few words of warning to those who intended to go to Midnight Mass at Father Plowman's church, dwelling darkly on the dangers they might meet there and pronouncing the word *Rome* with such horrifying emphasis that many of his hearers were quite alarmed, and those who had thought of doing such a thing began to tell themselves that perhaps the parish church was more convenient after all.

The Bishop's sermon, when it came, was not particularly suited to the season, being very much like his lecture suitably adapted for the pulpit. He had chosen for his text a verse from the psalms, *In them hath he set a tabernacle for the sun, which cometh forth as a bridegroom out of his chamber, and rejoiceth as a giant to run his course.*

Belinda hoped that Harriet would not be upset by the reference to bridegrooms, but she appeared to be quite unmoved and it was evident that she had very sensibly put away any hopes she might once have had. She even whispered to Belinda that he certainly wasn't the preacher he used to be, though he still had that same way of gripping the edge of the pulpit when he wished to emphasize a point.

The text seemed to have little reference to the sermon, although the more intelligent of the congregation saw it as referring to the Bishop himself. He was the giant and his course was the Mission Field. Belinda noticed, however, that when he prayed for his flock he gave the impression that they were so entirely heathen that she began to wonder whether dear Theo had done such wonderful work among them after all. What if the whole of his life had been so taken up with avoiding designing spinsters and widows that no other work had been possible? It was an interesting idea and one which she was able to follow up that evening, when she and Harriet were invited to supper at the vicarage.

Belinda was not sure why they had been asked, but it seemed as if Agatha had decided to dispose of several people to whom she owed invitations, for the company included, besides themselves, the Bishop, Father Plowman, Mr Donne and Miss Aspinall, who had been asked at the last minute instead of Lady Clara Boulding, who had suddenly decided to spend Christmas in Switzerland with her married daughter. Miss Aspinall was radiant, or as near it as she could be, glittering with beads and chains and agreeing rapturously with everything that everybody said. This was rather difficult with four clergymen present, as, with the exception of the curate who hardly ventured an opinion on anything, they tended to disagree with each other wherever they could.

It was such a pity, Belinda reflected, that clergymen were so apt to bring out the worst in each other, especially with the season of Peace and Goodwill so near. As a species they did not *get on*, and being in a small country village made things even more difficult. These embarrassments would not arise in London where the clergy kept themselves to themselves in their own little sets, High, Broad and Low, as it were. It was so odd to hear Father Plowman calling the curate Father Donne, though the curate himself did not appear to think it so. On the contrary, he had that evening preached a most successful sermon in Father Plowman's church on the text *We heard of the same at Ephrata and found it in the wood*, and had been very much impressed by the elaborate service. He would discuss it with Olivia Berridge some time; she was always so sensible and would be sure to give him good advice. He would be seeing her in the New Year as he had been invited to stay for a few days with the chaplain of his old college, in whose rowing he still took a very keen interest. When there was a suitable pause in the conversation, he ventured to mention this visit.

'Oh, if you should see Mr Mold, do give him my very kindest regards,' said Harriet, fingering her long rope of cultured pearls.

'Do you think that is wise?' said the Archdeacon. 'Even kindest regards are a poor substitute for the deeper feelings. I hear that the poor fellow is in quite a bad way as it is.'

The Bishop looked a little alarmed and Agatha, frowning at her husband, hastened to turn the conversation to Olivia, and how glad she would be to see Mr Donne. 'She is generally up during the vacation, you know,' she explained. 'She does a good deal of reading then.'

Mr Donne looked rather embarrassed. 'Oh, yes, it will be jolly to see Olivia again,' he said heartily. 'I expect we shall go for some walks together. She's very keen on walking.'

'Has she made you any more socks?' asked Belinda innocently.

'Yes, indeed, and a pullover too,' said Mr Donne. 'She's really awfully good.'

'Well, I hope she knows how to graft a toe by now,' said Harriet bluntly. 'Belinda could show her.'

'Olivia is a very clever girl,' said Agatha. 'I'm sure she is quite equal to it.'

'I should hardly call her a girl,' said the Archdeacon spitefully. 'But I suppose women like to think of themselves as girls long after they are thirty.'

'Oh, Olivia is only thirty-one or two,' said Agatha impatiently, 'and her work on *The Owl and the Nightingale* has really been a most substantial contribution to Middle English studies.'

'All the same, it is important to know how to graft a toe,'

persisted Harriet. 'What is it, Belinda, knit and slip off, then purl and keep on? I never can remember.'

Just as Belinda was thinking of a tactful answer, the Bishop broke in, saying with a reminiscent sigh, 'Ah, the socks I had knitted for me when I was a curate!'

'I know,' agreed Father Plowman, 'some small, some large, some short, some long, but all acceptable because of the goodwill that inspired the knitters.'

'I should have thought a sock was very little use unless it was the right size,' said the Archdeacon sourly.

When she heard this, Belinda was thankful that she had decided against knitting him a pullover and went cold with horror at the thought of what she had escaped. For there would surely have been something wrong with it. She attended to her soup, straight out of a tin with no subtle additions, she decided. Perhaps only one tin among so many, watered down or with potato water added. It certainly had very little taste.

'What delicious soup, Mrs Hoccleve,' said Miss Aspinall timidly. 'Such a delicate flavour.'

'It reminds me of our native fermented porridge,' said the Bishop. 'The flavour is somewhat similar.'

'Oh, how *interesting*,' said Connie. 'How is it made?'

'My dear Bishop, I hope you will remember that we are at the dinner table and spare us a detailed description,' broke in the Archdeacon.

'Yes, I suppose these natives are very disgusting,' said Harriet complacently. 'It is better not to know too much about them.'

'Many of them will be celebrating the festival of Christmas on Tuesday, just as we shall be doing,' said the Bishop on a faint note of reproach. 'Perhaps it will not be exactly the same in detail, but their feelings will be as ours.'

'I suppose it is because of your work there that they will be able to,' said the curate.

The Bishop smiled and was about to answer when the

Archdeacon gave a short bark of laughter and exclaimed, 'Ah, no, that's where you're wrong. The Romans were there first. Father Vigilio of the Padua Fathers, I believe.'

'Yes, certainly, but I had the honour of starting the first Church of England Mission among the Mbawawa,' said the Bishop, 'though the Roman Catholics *were* there before me.'

'What a shame,' said Harriet indignantly, but Belinda felt that her wrath was directed not so much towards the Church of Rome as the rather dry-looking rissoles, cabbage and boiled potatoes which were now set before them. *Rissoles!* Belinda could imagine her sister's disgusted comments later. At least one would have expected a bird of some kind, especially when there was a bishop present, when indeed all the gentlemen were in Holy Orders.

'I suppose the African's leaning towards ritual would make him a ready convert to Roman Catholicism,' Belinda ventured. 'I mean, one knows their love of bright, gaudy things,' she added rather unfortunately. 'The Church of England might seem rather plain to them.'

'Bright and gaudy?' said Father Plowman, on a pained note. 'Oh, Miss Bede, surely you cannot mean that?'

'I'm sorry,' said Belinda, in confusion, 'naturally I didn't mean to imply . . .'

'Well, Plowman is still with us, you know,' said the Archdeacon almost jovially. 'I don't think he need take your remarks so personally.'

Belinda chewed her stringy cabbage and listened gratefully to dear Henry talking about Frazer and *The Golden Bough*, which he thought remarkably fine.

'At one time I had the idea of giving a course of sermons based on it,' he said, 'but I came to the conclusion, regretfully I must admit, that with a congregation of limited intelligence it would be *too dangerous*.'

Belinda liked the sound of this and could almost have imagined them all back in Victorian days, when a father might forbid a book 'inimical to the faith of the day' to be read in his house.

'How debased anthropology has become since Frazer's day,' sighed the Bishop, 'a mere matter of genealogies, meaningless definitions and jargon, *words*, *words*, *words*, as Hamlet has it; lineage, sib, kindred, extended family, ramage – one doesn't know where one is. Even the good old term *clan* is suspect.'

'What is a sib?' asked Harriet. 'It sounds a nice, friendly kind of thing, or it might be something to eat, a biscuit, perhaps.'

The Bishop shook his head and said nothing, either because he did not deign to be associated with present-day anthropological terminology or because he did not really know what a sib was.

The Archdeacon recalled the Anglo-Saxon meaning of the word, and talked for some minutes about the double meaning of peace and relationship, but Harriet had lost interest and soon they were all in the drawing-room, drinking coffee made with coffee essence. When the gentlemen joined them it was suggested that Harriet should play the piano and she gave a showy performance of Manuel de Falla's *Pantomime*. Then the Bishop sang an unaccompanied Mbawawa Christmas carol, which everyone agreed was very moving. When he had finished, Father Plowman suggested with admirable good manners that the Archdeacon should read aloud to them.

The Archdeacon was so surprised at this that for some minutes he could not even think of anything to read.

'Let it be something that all can understand,' suggested Father Plowman, thinking of an occasion when the Archdeacon had insisted on reading Chaucer's *Canterbury Tales* with an attempt at the original pronunciation.

There was a pause, nobody liking or perhaps wishing to make any suggestion, until Miss Aspinall timidly ventured the observation that Keats had written some very lovely poems.

She was, of course, remembering Lady Grudge's 'evenings' in Belgrave Square, when Canon Kendrick used to read aloud to them.

'Ah, yes, we will have *Hyperion*,' said the Archdeacon. '*Remarkably* fine.'

There was a murmur of assent, during which Harriet could be heard asking the curate if *Hyperion* were a very *long* poem; she had quite forgotten.

Belinda turned to the Bishop and made a chatty remark about always having liked the lines about *Sorrow more beautiful than Beauty's self.*

The Bishop nodded and gave her what Belinda thought was rather an intimate smile. 'I am sure that any poem *you* admire must be very fine,' he said in a low voice.

Belinda was so startled that she wondered whether she could have heard correctly. 'I'm afraid I like what I remember from my student days,' she said. 'I hardly ever read anything new.' *Hyperion* had no memories for her, as the Archdeacon had never read it to her then, so that she was able to listen to it quite dispassionately and join with the polite murmurs that followed his performance.

'And yet I think I prefer the earlier Keats,' she said rather boldly, 'I was always very fond of *Isabella* when I was a young girl.'

The Archdeacon smiled indulgently and Agatha said quite kindly, 'Well, of course, *Isabella* is rather a young girl's poem, isn't it?'

'Oh, yes, completely,' agreed Belinda. 'It is many years since I read it.' It would indeed be an ominous sign if she felt drawn to it at her time of life, she felt.

'What a fine poem Young's *Night Thoughts* is,' said the Bishop. 'I have been reading it every night myself. I have a most interesting collection of books in my room,' he went on. 'There is an Icelandic grammar among them and I have been comparing that language with the Mbawawa.'

'But do you find any similarity?' asked Agatha doubtfully.

'Oh, none whatever,' said the Bishop almost gaily, 'but it is a fascinating study, *fascinating* . . .' his voice trailed off on a bleating note.

'I am surprised and gratified that you find the books interesting,' said the Archdeacon. 'I made the selection myself, but I had no idea of your tastes.'

The evening ended with a song from the curate. Harriet, who accompanied him, was anxious that he should try an Elizabethan love song, and after a rather faltering beginning he sang quite charmingly, Belinda thought, but without much conviction.

Love is a fancie,
Love is a frenzie,
Let not a toy then breed thee such annoy. . . .

Perhaps there was no frenzy in his feeling for Miss Berridge, and love was hardly a *toy*. Surely Count Bianco's affection for Harriet could not be so described, or Belinda's for the Archdeacon? And yet tonight she had the feeling that there might be some truth in what the poet said. It was excellent advice to those of riper years, especially when the imagination became too active. That intimate note in the Bishop's voice, for example, and the way he had seemed to look at her during the reading of the poem. It might just as easily have been Connie Aspinall he was looking at. Belinda had been forced to mention the fact that the chrysanthemums he had sent her were still lasting very well. She almost wished that they might die, and noticed with relief when she got home that some of the foliage was tinged with brown. Suddenly she took them out of their vase and, although it was dark, went out with them to the dustbin. They *were* dead really and one did not like to feel that flowers from the wrong person might be everlasting.

CHAPTER NINETEEN

'I MUST GO and see Ricardo,' declared Belinda, one morning early in the New Year. 'Edith tells me that he has a slight attack of gout which keeps him in the house. It's rather difficult to know what to take him, though.'

'Yes, you have to be very careful with gout,' said Harriet. 'No beef or strawberries or port wine. Do you think I ought to go as well?'

'That would certainly do him more good than anything, but you mustn't come with me. I'm sure he'd prefer to see you *alone*.'

'Yes, I really will go,' said Harriet. 'You may tell him to expect me,' she added graciously.

Now that Harriet's plans about the Bishop were clearly not likely to come to anything, Belinda was determined to bring Count Bianco and her sister together as much as possible. She felt this to be her duty, and although she was not particularly anxious that Harriet should marry and leave her alone, she thought that if a marriage had been arranged in heaven she would prefer Ricardo to be the happy man. He was devoted to Harriet and they had many tastes in common: he came of an ancient Italian family and was very comfortable financially. The only thing that might possibly be against him was that he was not in the Church, but even this was not as great a drawback as might at first appear, for would there not always be tender curates in need of sympathetic attention and perfectly baked cakes?

So Belinda reasoned within herself as she walked up the drive to Ricardo's house. She walked slowly, for she was thinking rather sentimentally of how Ricardo had loved her sister well and faithfully for many years. Surely he deserved some reward for his constancy? She herself had loved the Archdeacon even longer, but naturally there was no hope of any reward for her now, at least not in *this* world, she reflected piously, and we are given to understand that we shall be purged of all earthly passions in that *other* life.

The Count was in and would be delighted to see her. Belinda had been careful to announce herself as Miss *Belinda* Bede, with special emphasis on the Christian name, for she did not want Ricardo to expect Harriet and then be disappointed.

He was in the library, reading a little here and there in his many books. His gouty foot was bound up and rested on a low stool. Beside him on a little table was a pile of letters, which Belinda guessed to be those of his friend, the late John Akenside. There was also a Serbo-Croatian dictionary and the works of Alfred, Lord Tennyson.

The Count greeted Belinda with a sad smile. 'It is indeed kind of you to call,' he said, attempting to get up, but Belinda put her hand on his arm and said how sorry she had been to hear about his gout.

'It is an inconvenience,' he said, 'but I am accustomed to it.'

Touched by his patience and resignation, Belinda wondered how she could show her sympathy. She found it a little difficult to make conversation with Ricardo at the best of times, and could do no more than touch on various matters of general interest. It was inevitable that they should find themselves talking about the Bishop, who showed no signs of moving from the vicarage, where he had now been for nearly two months.

'I hear that he is to be married soon,' said Ricardo, in a calm, patient tone.

'Oh, surely not!' exclaimed Belinda, wondering how it was possible that Ricardo should come out with a piece of news that she and Harriet knew nothing of. 'We haven't heard anything, and I can't really imagine that anybody would want to marry him.'

'I heard that your sister was to marry him,' said Ricardo pathetically.

Belinda now laughed aloud for joy, all the more because it might so nearly have happened. In fact, she told herself soberly, there was still time; but she could at least reassure Ricardo.

'It certainly isn't true at the moment,' she said, 'and I think it most unlikely that it ever will be. Wherever did you hear such a thing?'

Ricardo could not remember exactly; perhaps his manservant had heard it somewhere, or it may have been the Archdeacon who had told him when he called a few days ago. Yes, he was sure now that it must have been the Archdeacon. He had seemed quite certain that he was not misinformed.

The wicked *liar*, thought Belinda angrily. An archdeacon making mischief and spreading false rumours, that was what it amounted to. Although, she told herself hastily, it was possible that Ricardo had misunderstood him, had read too much into a hint or taken a joke too seriously.

'There is no truth in it whatever,' she declared positively, hoping as she did so that the Bishop was not at this moment in their drawing-room asking Harriet to be his wife. 'Harriet does not really care for him at all,' she went on boldly.

Ricardo smiled and looked almost happy, but then his face clouded as he asked if the Bishop were still at the vicarage?

'Yes, he is still there,' said Belinda, 'but I do not think he will stay much longer. He will have to be getting back to his diocese.'

'Then there is still time,' said Ricardo despondently. 'Even now he may be asking her.'

Belinda shifted uneasily in her chair. Of course one never knew for certain what Harriet might be up to, or the Bishop, for that matter. She was grateful when Ricardo's manservant appeared with sherry and biscuits on a silver tray.

'Have you been working on the letters this morning?' she asked, indicating the pile on the table.

'Yes, I have been reading them before you came. How wise he was! He knew what would happen there; no man understood the Balkan mind as he did.'

'No, I'm sure they didn't,' said Belinda inadequately, for she was never quite clear as to what *had* happened there except that poor John had been killed in a riot.

There was a silence, during which Belinda racked her brains for something intelligent to say. But she was too late to stop Ricardo from getting back on to the subject of Harriet.

'It is many days since I have seen your sister,' he said. 'It may be that there is something she does not wish to tell me.'

The warmth of the room and the unaccustomed effect of sherry in the morning were beginning to make Belinda feel a little vague and carefree, in the mood to make rash promises.

'Harriet is coming to see you very soon,' she said. 'I can promise you that.'

'She will never marry me, she does not love me,' said Ricardo as if speaking his thoughts aloud.

'Now, Ricardo, you mustn't lose hope,' said Belinda comfortably. 'I know she is fond of you and even if she will not love you, always remember' – her eyes lighted on the works of Alfred, Lord Tennyson – 'that it is better to have loved and lost than never to have loved at all. I always think those lines are such a great comfort; so many of us have loved and lost.' She frowned: nobody wanted to be one of many, and she did not like this picture of herself, only one of a great crowd of dreary women. Perhaps Tennyson was rather hackneyed after all.

But Ricardo did not appear to think so. 'You are so kind and understanding,' he said. 'I feel that there is a great bond between us.'

Belinda did not quite know what to say, so she merely smiled and said that she was sure that some day everything would be just as Ricardo wished.

'Then I shall ask her again,' he declared, fired with fresh courage and looking as if he were about to quote Dante or

Tacitus at any moment; probably the former, Belinda thought, for it seemed unlikely that there would be anything suitable in Tacitus.

'Yes, Ricardo, do,' she said, 'but not yet. Wait until the spring, when the daffodils are out in your meadow.'

'If I am spared till then,' said Ricardo sadly, looking down at his bandaged foot. He then went on to talk of the fine new bulbs that he had planted in the meadow and to calculate when they would be at their best.

Belinda left the house feeling that she had done good, and with a picture of daffodils and scyllas in her mind. She saw Harriet, the radiant Countess, picking grapes in the conservatory, adorning the head of Ricardo's dinner table, opening a garden fête or bazaar. But all this was in the distant future. For the present Belinda was glad that she had been able to cheer Ricardo and to give him a little hope. What a good thing it was that hope sprang eternal in the human breast! What would she herself have done without hope? Even if nothing came of it, she thought obscurely, for she could not have said exactly what it was that she hoped for *now.* It would be enough if things could return to normal and be as they were before Mr Mold and the Bishop had appeared in the village. They could get on very well without them.

Belinda took out her shopping list and stopped for a moment, deep in contemplation of it. Coffee, rice, steel wool, kitchen soap, written in her own hand and then, in Harriet's, tinned peaches, sponge cakes, sherry (*not* cooking), set of no. 14 knitting needles (*steel*) . . . Belinda frowned. They had plenty of knitting needles of all sizes and did they really *need* sherry or peaches or sponge cakes? Perhaps Mr Donne was coming to supper again.

'Good morning!' said a bright, cheerful voice, which Belinda did not at first recognize as Agatha's, calling to her from the other side of the narrow street.

'Good morning,' Belinda called back, and was just moving

on when she saw that Agatha was hurrying across to speak to her.

'Isn't it a lovely morning?' she said, beaming with such unusual good humour that Belinda stared at her quite curiously, wondering what could have happened to bring about this change.

'Yes, isn't it. Really quite mild,' murmured Belinda expectantly.

'I have some great news for you,' said Agatha, smiling.

'News? For me?' All kinds of wild ideas rushed through Belinda's head, most of which she rejected hastily. Henry had been made a dean or a bishop, that was it. It seemed unlikely, in a way, and yet what else could it be?

'I had a letter from my niece Olivia this morning,' went on Agatha. 'She and Edgar are to be married – quite soon.' She paused and peered so intently and beamingly at Belinda that the latter drew back, a little embarrassed.

'Edgar?' said Belinda stupidly. 'Do I know him?'

'Why, of course you do! Our curate, Mr Donne,' said Agatha with some of her usual impatience which made Belinda feel more at home. 'Such a suitable thing altogether, I've been hoping all along that it would happen like this.'

'But isn't she a lot older than he is,' said Belinda tactlessly.

'Oh, well, a year or two, but Mr Donne needs an older woman. Besides, he's rather shy and an older woman can often help things along, you know.'

'How do you mean?' asked Belinda. 'I suppose if young people want to marry, they will. I mean if they both do.'

'Ah, yes,' said Agatha, 'but there is often a natural hesitation on the part of the man, especially if he feels, as I know Edgar does, that a woman is far superior to him intellectually.'

And older too, thought Belinda perversely. 'Yes, I suppose a young man might well hesitate in those circumstances,' she said aloud.

'He who hesitates is lost,' said Agatha briskly. 'I told Edgar that and I dropped a hint to Olivia.'

'Oh, did *she* propose to *him*?' asked Belinda in a loud, interested tone. 'I've often wondered if it was done very much. I suppose it must be done a good deal more than one realizes.'

'Oh, yes,' said Agatha casually, 'it is not at all unusual. Men are understandably shy about offering what seems to them very little and when a woman realizes this she is perfectly justified in helping him on a bit, as it were.'

At this moment an idea came into Belinda's head. At first it seemed fantastic, then quite likely, and finally almost a certainty. Agatha had proposed to Henry. Why had this never occurred to her before? And now that it had, what was the use of it? Belinda could not answer this, but she knew that she could put it away in her mind and take it out again when she was feeling in need of comfort.

'Yes, I suppose it can happen like that,' she agreed calmly. 'There is no reason why it shouldn't. And yet,' she ventured, 'I don't think I should ever feel certain enough to take on that responsibility myself. I know men have to take it, but supposing one met somebody else afterwards . . .' she stopped in confusion.

'Ah, yes,' Agatha's face seemed to soften for a moment, 'that can happen too. One wonders how often it *does* happen when one knows that it *can*.'

Belinda hurried home in a great turmoil. So many exciting things to tell Harriet and somehow the curate's engagement seemed to be the least exciting of them all. Nevertheless, she could not help wondering how her sister would take the news. Not that one could say it had really been a 'disappointment' to Harriet in the usual sense, but what would she do without a curate to dote upon? It was unlikely that Miss Berridge – perhaps they would soon be calling her Olivia – would approve of anybody else doting on her husband, for

Harriet would not like it to be suggested that she was too old and unattractive for there to be any danger, which led Belinda to speculate upon the age at which a single woman could safely have a curate to live with her without fear of scandal. She feared that whatever the age might be, seventy-five or even eighty, it would be many years before Harriet would attain it. What a solution it would be! Belinda sighed as she walked through the gate, fearful of what might happen.

But Harriet had already heard the news and although it was obvious that she was rather upset, her attitude was rather one of indignation and pity for Mr Donne.

'*Poor* young man,' she said, 'I could hardly believe it when I heard the news. Of course it's obvious that she's been after him for a long time. I expect *she* proposed to *him*.'

'Why, yes,' said Belinda eagerly, 'Agatha as good as told me so. And I think *she* proposed to Henry, and now she finds that she prefers the Bishop. At least,' she added, feeling that she had gone rather too far, 'she might not necessarily have meant that, but she did hint at it.'

'I can quite imagine it,' said Harriet. 'If only *you* could have thought of proposing, Belinda.'

'It wouldn't have occurred to me, I'm afraid. And think how dreadful it would be to be refused. I sometimes wonder how men can bear it, though they usually go off and ask somebody else, don't they, all except Ricardo, that is. But I think it's much better not to have asked, not to know definitely that one wasn't wanted,' said Belinda hastily. 'I always feel that a man should do his own proposing.'

'Yes, and then he can be blamed for the results,' said Harriet stoutly.

'Perhaps clergymen feel that they ought not to ask people to marry them,' said Belinda. 'The celibacy of the clergy, you know,' she added vaguely.

'It's much better for a curate not to marry. Just imagine, a *married* curate,' said Harriet in disgust.

'Ricardo has given me the recipe for ravioli,' said Belinda. 'He seemed rather low, I thought, and I promised that you would go up and see him.'

'Oh, yes, I really ought to go,' said Harriet, 'perhaps this afternoon,' she added, brightening up a little, as if the thought of the Count's admiration would do something to make up for the prospect of a married curate. 'No, this afternoon won't do. I shall go tomorrow after I've had my hair done.'

'All right, but let it be soon,' said Belinda. 'It would cheer him up so much. I think I shall make some ravioli for supper; it seems quite easy.'

'Yes, that would be nice. We have some cold meat, haven't we, for the filling?' Harriet suddenly chuckled. 'I wonder if Agatha *does* prefer the Bishop to Henry,' she said. 'How ironical life is; he sent you those flowers and you weren't at all pleased.'

Belinda looked startled, almost as if she expected to see the chrysanthemums still there. But the place where they had stood was reassuringly filled with dried Cape gooseberries and honesty.

CHAPTER TWENTY

BELINDA ALWAYS liked working in the kitchen when Emily was not there and was glad that she had decided to make the ravioli on her afternoon out. Emily always seemed so critical, though generally in a silent way which was far more unnerving than if she had put it into words. Belinda could feel her scornful, pitying glances as she creamed butter and sugar or rubbed fat into flour. For this reason she usually chose some foreign dish of which Emily would be unlikely to have knowledge.

This afternoon she felt a great sense of freedom and spread the things around her in a most wanton manner, though the recipe did not need complicated ingredients. The secret seemed to lie in the kneading or rolling, which was to be carried out for a full half-hour or until the paste was quite smooth and 'of the consistency of the finest chamois leather', as the Count's translation of the Italian read.

When Belinda had been kneading and rolling for about ten minutes she felt she must rest. It was exhausting work, and the paste was nowhere near the desired consistency yet. It was sticky, full of little lumps and greyish looking – not at all like any kind of chamois leather.

Harriet was bustling in and out of the kitchen as she was expecting a visit from Mrs Ramage, the wardrobe woman. She had spread practically the whole of Belinda's wardrobe out on the floor, and was quite ruthless in brushing aside Belinda's feeble protest on seeing a nearly new green crêpe afternoon frock among the things to be sold.

'Oh, but Harriet, I rather like that dress,' said Belinda, 'and there's still a lot of wear in it. I'm sure Miss Prior could bring it up to date in some way, if it needs it. Perhaps a little lace collar or a contrasting jabot,' she suggested uncertainly.

'Neither lace collars nor jabots are being worn at the moment,' said Harriet firmly, 'and I've always thought it rather a trying shade of green. It makes you look yellow.'

Belinda paused in her kneading, remembering the many times she had worn the dress. Had she always looked yellow in it? It was a disturbing thought. 'I suppose that old tweed coat *is* past wearing,' she went on sadly, 'but I've always liked it so much.'

'It's no use being sentimental about things,' said Harriet. 'You shouldn't keep a clutter of clothes you never wear just because you once liked them.'

Belinda made no comment on this, for she was thinking that Harriet's words might be applied to more serious things than clothes. If only one could clear out one's mind and heart as ruthlessly as one did one's wardrobe. . . .

'I shall see Mrs Ramage in the dining-room,' declared Harriet. 'I shall not take more than two or three things in at once. I shall start by asking £5 for your green dress.'

'But I believe it hardly cost that when it was new,' protested Belinda. 'What a good thing *you* are seeing her,' she added, thinking also that it was just as well that Harriet had something to take her mind off Mr Donne's engagement. 'I'm afraid I never have the courage to ask a big price but just agree to what she offers.'

Harriet snorted. 'She'd probably offer a pound for the lot if you asked her.' The front-door bell rang. 'There, that must be her now.' Harriet strode out with a purposeful step, carrying Belinda's old tweed coat and an old jumper suit of her own over her arm. She would lead up to the green crêpe dress artistically and not bring it out until the last moment.

Belinda returned to her kneading and rolling. The paste still did not seem quite right. Perhaps it was too sticky. She sprinkled more flour on the board and on her hands and went on rather grimly. Her back was aching a little now and she was startled when the front-door bell rang again, and stood for a moment undecided what to do. It was no use expecting Harriet to answer it and she herself with her floury hands and generally dishevelled appearance was really in no fit state to go. But of course it probably wouldn't be anybody who mattered. It certainly wouldn't be the Archdeacon at ten to three in the afternoon.

The bell rang again, a long ring, as if it had been firmly pressed. Belinda wiped her floury hands on her apron and hurried into the hall.

A man's figure showed through the frosted glass panel of the front door. A tall figure, but definitely not the Archdeacon's. It was probably a man selling something. A suitcase would be opened on the doorstep, full of combs, cards of safety pins and darning wool, packets of needles . . . Still, such things were useful, one could always do with them, thought Belinda opening the door, for she felt much too sorry for the men not to buy something.

'Ah, Miss Bede, good afternoon.' It was an unctuous voice, a clergyman's voice, a Bishop's voice. Why was it that they were so unmistakable? Only the Archdeacon's was different.

'Oh, dear, Bishop Grote.' Theodore Mbawawa. Belinda rubbed her hands vigorously on her grey tweed skirt – for her apron was already too floury to be of much use – and backed into the hall. 'I'm afraid I'm hardly in a fit state to receive visitors, but do come in.' She edged towards the drawing-room door and put out a still floury hand to open it.

But the Bishop was almost too quick for her. His hand reached the knob simultaneously with hers. For one panic-stricken moment she even imagined that it lingered for a fraction of a second, but then dismissed the unworthy thought almost before it had time to register in her mind. She was in an agitated state, and she had read somewhere that in any case middle-aged spinsters were apt to imagine things of this kind. . . .

Inside the drawing-room Belinda stood uncertainly, while the Bishop advanced towards the fireplace, where a fire was laid but not yet lit. He made a remark about the weather, observing that it was a raw and chilly afternoon. In his diocese, he added, they would be enjoying some of the hottest weather now.

'It must be a lovely climate,' said Belinda, fumbling in the Toby jug on the mantelpiece for a box of matches. 'I'm so sorry about there being no fire. We usually light it just before tea.' She wondered if she could perhaps offer him a cup now. It was certainly a little early, but it would at least fill in the time until Harriet had finished with Mrs Ramage and would also give Belinda an opportunity to slip away and make herself more presentable. 'I will go and tell my sister that you are here,' she said crouching over the fire and setting a match to a corner of the *Church Times*. 'She will be so pleased to see you.'

The Bishop held up his hand. 'No, please, Miss Bede. It is *you* I have come to see.'

Belinda stood up. 'Oh?' Whatever could he want? '*Me?* Please sit down, won't you? I must apologize again for my untidiness, but I was doing something in the kitchen.'

The Bishop smiled. 'And doing it admirably, I'm sure.'

Belinda smiled uneasily. She began to wonder whether she had thanked him enough for the flowers, though that was some weeks ago now, and was just going to make a remark about them when he began to speak in a hurrying way, as if he were not quite sure of himself.

'Miss Bede, I am sure you must have realized – have noticed, that is – my preference for you above all the other ladies of the village,' he said, and peered at her so intently that Belinda – they were sitting together on the sofa – drew back, considerably alarmed.

'No, I don't think I have,' she said anxiously. 'In any case you can hardly know me very well or you would realize that there is nothing very special about me.'

'Ah, well, one hardly looks for beauty at our time of life,' he said, with a return of some of his usual complacency. '*She is not fair to outward view* . . . how does Wordsworth put it?'

'Not *Wordsworth*,' said Belinda automatically. 'Coleridge, Hartley Coleridge, I think.' She felt rather annoyed. Not even a middle-aged spinster likes to be told in so many words that she is not fair to outward view. Besides, she felt that the Bishop had taken an unfair advantage of her, calling on Emily's afternoon off, when she had had no opportunity to tidy herself. 'Although I am not beautiful myself and never have been,' she went on, 'I must confess that I like to see beauty in other people.'

'You mean beauty of character, ah, yes. That is something we all like to see.'

'No, I mean beauty of person,' said Belinda obstinately.

The Bishop smiled. 'Then perhaps you will not be so ready to accept what I have to offer,' he said, though it was obvious that he really thought quite otherwise.

'Offer?' said Belinda in a startled tone. 'I don't think I understand.' The man on the doorstep opening his suitcase was simpler and less alarming than this. She hardly dared to let herself guess what the Bishop meant; it was too fantastic and terrible to be thought of.

'Perhaps you are not accustomed to receiving such offers?' he went on. 'Or perhaps it is some time since you last had one? After all, this is a quiet country village; it is unlikely that you would meet many strangers.'

'That may be,' said Belinda feeling very angry, 'but I think I can say that I have had my share, in the past, that is. Naturally not lately,' she fumbled, her natural honesty getting the better of her.

'I think I had better speak more plainly,' the Bishop went on. 'I am asking you to marry me.'

There was a short but awkward silence, and then Belinda heard herself stammering out the first words that came into her head, 'Oh, but I *couldn't* . . .'

'My dear, you are equal to being the wife of a bishop,' he said kindly, making a movement towards her. 'You need have no fears on that account. When I was a younger man I held views about the celibacy of the clergy, young curates often do, you know,' he smiled indulgently, 'it is a kind of protection, if you see what I mean. But a man does need a helpmeet, you remember in *Paradise Lost*. . . .'

Belinda interrupted him with a startled exclamation. '*Paradise Lost*!' she echoed in horror. '*Milton*. . . .'

'I think when one has reached er – riper years,' the Bishop continued, 'things are different, aren't they?'

A man needs a woman to help him into his grave, thought Belinda, remembering a remark Dr Parnell had made. Well, there would be plenty who would be willing to do that.

'I'm afraid I can't marry you,' she said, looking down at her floury hands. 'I don't love you.'

'But you respect and like me,' said the Bishop, as if that went without saying. 'We need not speak of love – one would hardly expect that now.'

'No,' said Belinda miserably, 'I suppose one would not *expect* it. But you see,' she went on, 'I did love somebody once and perhaps I still do.'

'Ah . . .' the Bishop shook his head, 'he died, perhaps? A very sad thing.'

They were both silent. He died, yes, it was better that the Bishop should think that, it sounded more suitable; there was even something a little noble about it. *She never married* . . . Belinda began to see herself as a romantically tragic figure.

'Of course, as Lord Byron says,' began the Bishop, and then paused.

Could Lord Byron have said anything at all suitable? Belinda wondered. *When we two parted in silence and tears?* Possibly, though the poem was not really applicable. 'Do tell me,' she said, her literary curiosity driving other thoughts from her mind. 'What *did* Lord Byron say?'

But the Bishop was standing up now and saying that he did not think he would be able to stay for tea, although Belinda was not conscious of having offered it. 'I think it is perhaps a little early for tea, Miss Bede, and I have still another call to make.'

'Oh, I expect you will get tea there,' said Belinda in a full, relieved tone. 'Now that I come to think of it, we have only very little cake, just a small piece of gingerbread, I believe. When one has guests one likes to have rather more than that to offer them.' She frowned, wishing she had not used the word 'offer', but the Bishop did not seem to be at all upset, or even, indeed, to have noticed. 'I'm so sorry,' said Belinda ambiguously. 'I am really most honoured that you should have felt . . . but I'm sure you will understand how it is.'

'Do not give it another thought, Miss Bede,' he said briskly, 'I assure you that *I* shall not. After all, we must remember that *God moves in a mysterious way, His wonders to perform*.'

'Yes, certainly,' agreed Belinda, feeling a little annoyed that he should quote her favourite hymn. But perhaps it was presumptuous to suppose that God would be more likely to reveal His ways to her than to the Bishop. She did not quite see how the lines applied here, no doubt he had something else in mind. Perhaps he would come another day and ask Harriet? At all events he was not going to give her refusal another thought, so he could not care very much. It was not very flattering to her, though she supposed that as she was not fair to outward view she could hardly expect anything else.

It was not until they were in the hall that she realized that she had been offered and refused something that Agatha wanted, or that she may have wanted, for the hint she had given had been very slight. She wondered if the Bishop had any idea of it.

'It is nice that you have been able to stay so long here,' she said, with unaccustomed guile. 'I expect the Archdeacon and Mrs Hoccleve will miss you when you go back.'

'Yes, I think I can say that they will.' The Bishop smiled to himself. 'I have been able to give the Archdeacon a few tips, although a small country parish hardly presents the same problems as a large African diocese.'

'No, of course not,' said Belinda. 'Nobody would imagine that it did.'

'Mrs Hoccleve has been most kind in helping me to buy various things that I need to take back to Africa with me. She has also knitted me some socks.'

'Oh, how kind!' exclaimed Belinda. 'There is nothing like hand-knitted socks.'

'No, indeed, there isn't. Particularly when they are not

quite long enough in the foot.' The Bishop laughed with a silly, bleating noise. 'Quite between ourselves, of course,' he added.

'Of course,' repeated Belinda, closing the front door behind him. She felt that she could almost love Agatha as a sister now. The pullover that she might have made for the Archdeacon would surely have been wrong somewhere, but as it had never even been started, it lacked the pathos of the socks not quite long enough in the foot. To think of Agatha as pathetic was something so new that Belinda had to sit down on a chair in the hall, quite overcome by the sensation. She began to find ways of making things better and more bearable. Agatha couldn't really have meant that she cared for the Bishop; nobody could love a man like that. She almost longed to see Agatha and to be crushed by one of her sharp retorts, to know that she was still the same.

At last she remembered the ravioli, and was almost glad of an excuse to stop thinking about these disturbing matters. She paused for a moment by the looking-glass and studied her wispy hair, flushed face smeared with flour and faded blue overall. Looking like that one could not feel even a romantic figure whose lover had died.

The sound of raised, almost angry, voices came from behind the closed door of the dining-room. It was a clash of wills between Harriet and Mrs Ramage, but Harriet would win in the end. It was known that the Misses Bede had 'good' things – though hardly of the same standard as Mrs Hoccleve – and Mrs Ramage would be unwilling to leave without buying them.

Belinda went quietly back to the kitchen and sat down. She wished Harriet would come, so that she could tell her all about it. After all, she supposed, it was something to have been considered worthy to be the wife of a bishop, even if only a colonial one. There was something rather sad about the kitchen now. It was beginning to get dark, and the greyish mass of dough on the table reminded Belinda of the unfinished ravioli. Twenty minutes more kneading, and perhaps it would be of the consistency of the finest chamois leather.

The trivial round, the common task – did it furnish *quite* all we needed to ask? Had Keble *really* understood? Sometimes one almost doubted it. Belinda imagined him writing the lines in a Gothic study, panelled in pitch-pine and well dusted that morning by an efficient servant. Not at all the same thing as standing at the sink with aching back and hands plunged into the washing-up water.

'Three pounds, fifteen and six!' Harriet came triumphant into the kitchen, waving the notes in her hand. 'She was pleased with your green dress, but she wondered how you could ever have worn it. "Not at all Miss Bede's colour", she said.'

'No, I begin to wonder now myself how I could ever have worn it,' said Belinda. 'Perhaps it is hardly surprising that Bishop Grote does not think me fair to outward view, though I think I was wearing my blue marocain that evening at the vicarage, and I always think I look quite nice in that.'

'Oh, was it Theo who called just now?' asked Harriet. 'What did he want?'

'He wanted me to be his wife,' said Belinda, enjoying the dramatic simplicity of her announcement.

'*No!*' Harriet's surprise was a little uncomplimentary, but her joy and relief at having her sister spared to her more than made up for it. 'What a pity you and Agatha can't change, though,' she lamented. 'But of course he can't really care for her very much or he wouldn't have asked you, would he?'

'I don't know,' said Belinda, who was beginning to think that she did not understand anything any more. 'Anyway I don't suppose Agatha really cares for him. I ought not to have told you what she said.' She felt that she could not tell even Harriet about the socks and was glad when she left the subject and came out with a piece of news of her own. Mrs

Ramage, in the intervals of bargaining, had told her that she had heard that Mr Donne had been offered a 'post' at his old University – chaplain in the college or something like that.

'How suitable,' said Belinda, 'but of course it will mean him leaving here, won't it?'

'Oh, yes, of course,' said Harriet casually. 'But don't you see, we shall get a new curate? The Archdeacon will never be able to manage by himself.'

'No, of course not,' agreed Belinda fervently, 'he couldn't possibly manage by himself. He will certainly have to get a new curate.'

'This is really a place for a young man,' said Harriet.

'Well, I don't know. A young man might want more scope, a more active parish with young people. Something in the East End of London, perhaps,' Belinda suggested. 'I should think this curacy might very well suit an older man.'

'Oh, I can't imagine that,' said Harriet in disgust. 'And anyway, curates are nearly always young.'

'Not necessarily,' said Belinda, feeling that she ought to help her sister to face up to the problem from every possible angle. 'Sometimes a man in middle life suddenly feels called upon to take Holy Orders. I always feel it must be so awkward and upsetting for his family.'

'Oh, dear,' Harriet's face clouded. 'I do hope it won't be anyone like that.'

'I'm not saying it will be, but it *could* be,' said Belinda. 'I think the Archdeacon would prefer a young man, though.'

'Yes, working with the Archdeacon must be a great experience,' said Harriet obscurely. 'A young man of good family, just ordained, that's what we really want. Do you suppose the Archdeacon will advertise in the *Church Times*?'

'He could hardly advertise for somebody of good family,' said Belinda smiling.

'They sometimes say "genuine Catholic" or "prayer-book Catholic",' mused Harriet, 'but of course we should hardly want that here.'

'Oh, Harriet, *look*!' Belinda held up the sheet of ravioli she had been rolling.

'But, Belinda, it's just like a piece of leather. I'm sure that can't be right,' protested Harriet.

'It is,' said Belinda joyfully, 'it's even finer than the finest chamois leather.'

CHAPTER TWENTY-ONE

THE NEXT few weeks were entirely taken up with preparations for the curate's wedding. It may be said without exaggeration that it was the only topic of conversation in the village at this time, and many a church worker's dingy life had been brightened by the silver and white invitation card, which was prominently displayed on many mantelpieces. The marriage of their dear Mr Donne was something in which all could share, for had he not at some time or another been to meals at all their houses? Many were the chickens which had been stuffed and roasted or boiled and smothered in white sauce in his honour.

One afternoon, a few days before the wedding, there was a gathering at the parish hall, the object of which was to make a presentation to Mr Donne and his fiancée. Miss Berridge was to stay at the vicarage and be married from there, as her parents were dead and Mrs Hoccleve, perhaps because of her niece's substantial contribution to Middle English studies, had always been particularly fond of her.

There was great excitement in the hall for nobody had yet seen Miss Berridge, though Edith Liversidge had caught a glimpse of her coming from the station the previous evening. As it had been a very dark night she had not been able to give a satisfactory description, except to say that she had been wearing a fur coat, a dark, rather bushy fur, musquash, she thought, and that she was very tall, perhaps taller than Mr Donne, who was only of middle height for a man.

'Taller than he is,' said Harriet in a disgusted tone, as they sat waiting for the proceedings to begin. 'What a pity! I always think it looks so bad.'

'Yes,' agreed Belinda, 'but of course it can't be helped. I mean, there are other things more important.'

'Tall women always droop,' said Edith sharply. 'I'm always telling Connie to hold herself up. It never had any effect until Bishop Grote said something about liking tall women – she's been better since then.'

'Did he say that?' asked Belinda, interested. 'I didn't think he really minded what people looked like – or expected much from people of our age, anyway.'

'Bishops ought not to mind or expect,' said Edith, 'but I suppose they're human. Besides, don't forget all those native women . . .' she paused darkly. 'He was describing their costume or lack of it when he came to tea with us the other day. Poor Connie was quite embarrassed.'

'Well, he's gone now,' said Belinda comfortably, 'and he'll probably be quite glad to be back among those dear, good fellows.'

'Agatha was sorry to see him go,' said Harriet. 'That was obvious. *Ah, quotiens illum doluit properare Calypso* – Ah, how many times did Calypso grieve at his hastening.'

'Connie was sorry too,' said Edith. 'If it hadn't been that she was due for her annual visit to Belgrave Square she would have been very low.'

'I do hope she will be back in time for Mr Donne's presentation,' said Harriet, 'she wouldn't want to miss his speech, I'm sure.'

'Her train is due in at a quarter to three, so I suppose she should be here for most of it – in at the death, you know.'

'Poor Mr Donne,' sighed Harriet, 'one almost feels that it *is* a death.'

At this moment there was a stir among the rows of waiting women, and the door on to the platform opened. Agatha Hoccleve, in a black tailored costume of good cut, came in, followed by a tall, pleasant-looking woman in the early or middle thirties, in a blue tweed costume of rather less good cut. She had a pale, rather long face and wore spectacles. Her hair was neatly arranged at the back of her head, though this was rather difficult to see as her navy felt hat was pulled down at a sensible angle.

Long, English gentlewoman's feet, thought Belinda, noticing her shoes and good, heavy silk stockings.

Miss Berridge was followed by Mr Donne, looking rather sheepish, Father Plowman, whose parish had wished to join in the presentation, and, finally, the Archdeacon, smiling sardonically and bearing in his arms a large square object shrouded in a cloth which he placed on a small table at one side of the platform.

'She *is* taller than he is,' whispered Harriet, 'and she looks much older. What a pity! She's rather plain, too, isn't she? Why doesn't she use lipstick?'

'Ladies and Gentlemen . . .' Agatha Hoccleve's clear voice rang out. She was a confident public speaker and this afternoon's audience of parish women with a few churchwardens and choirmen held no terrors for her. 'It gives me great pleasure to introduce my niece, Miss Berridge, soon to be Mrs Donne, to you all. I only wish she were going to stay longer with us, but we must not – I am sure we do not – grudge her to Mr Donne, and I am equally sure that he' – she gave a sideways glance to where the curate was sitting looking down at his shoes – 'will not grudge *us* the opportunity of getting to know her while she is here. Of course *I* know her already,' she added with a little laugh, and sat down amid the mild clapping which followed.

By this time the Archdeacon had got up and moved over to the side of the platform where the shrouded object stood and seemed about to uncover it, but he was prevented by an agitated gesture from Father Plowman. The situation was saved by Agatha stepping forward and saying in a loud voice, 'Before the Archdeacon makes the presentation, I think Mr Plowman has something to say.'

'*Father* Plowman,' giggled Harriet.

'Yes, indeed, I have,' said that clergyman, with a grateful glance at Agatha and a rather baleful one at the Archdeacon. 'My parishioners and I felt that we could not let this opportunity pass without adding our good wishes and our widow's mite, as it were, towards this gift. I think we shall not soon forget Father Donne's gifts to *us*. I mean,' he added, sensing a faint bewilderment among his hearers, 'his Sunday evening sermons. I can see him now, walking across the fields in the evening sunshine, his cassock and surplice over his arm . . .' Mr Donne himself now looked a little startled as Father Plowman's church was some seven or eight miles away and he had always gone over on his bicycle . . . 'pausing perhaps to drink in the beauty of our old church seen in that gracious evening light, pondering his message to us that evening, the *gift* he was bringing us.' Father Plowman paused, a little overcome by his eloquence. 'May he, with the help of Miss Berridge, go on from strength to strength, as I am sure he will. *From glory to glory advancing, we praise Thee, O Lord.*' He bowed his head. 'And now a prayer, *Prevent us O Lord in all our doings . . .*'

The obvious prayer, of course, thought Belinda, who had noted with anxiety the expression of irritation on the Archdeacon's face. Perhaps Father Plowman ought not to have said a prayer at all – it should have been left to the last speaker – the Archdeacon – who was now advancing once more towards the shrouded object.

As if in deliberate contrast, he adopted a more ominous tone, and dwelt, not so much on the parish's loss, though he did mention that Mr Donne's going would mean a great deal of extra work for *him*, as on the difficulties that Mr Donne might be expected to encounter in his new life. 'The University is a stony and barren soil,' he declared in a warning tone, 'one might almost say that the labourers are too many for the scanty harvest that is to be reaped there. The undergraduates are as in Anthony à Wood's day, much given over to drinking and gaming and vain brutish pleasures.' He looked as if he were warming to his subject, and Belinda began to fear that he might quote other and more unsuitable passages from that crabbed antiquary, but after a short pause he left the subject and went on. 'It is to be hoped that Mr Donne may succeed where others have failed. Indeed, with the help of Miss Berridge' – he gave her a most charming smile – 'one feels that he may. I am certain too that with her considerable linguistic gifts she will be a great help to him if ever he feels called upon to labour in the Mission Field.'

There was a visible stir in the audience at these words and some indignant whispering.

From Greenland's icy mountains
From India's coral strand. . . .

'It is not so very long since we were singing Bishop Heber's fine hymn in *our* fine old church.' The Archdeacon paused as if to let the significance of his words sink in and then began to fumble with the cloth which shrouded the square object.

'Isn't it the tablecloth out of the morning-room at the vicarage?' whispered Harriet. 'How unsuitable!'

We take no note of time but from its loss.
To give it then a tongue is wise in man. . . .

The Archdeacon paused – 'Edward Young, the eighteenth-century poet and divine wrote those words nearly two hundred years ago. Not a *great* poet, you may say, no, one would hardly call him that, but I think his words are still true today. That is why we are giving this chiming clock to Mr

Donne and Miss Berridge as a wedding present.' He flung aside the cloth with a dramatic gesture that Belinda thought very fine, if a little too theatrical for the occasion. 'May it do something to ease the burdens they will be called upon to bear in their new life.'

'I should think Mr Donne's burdens will be infinitely lighter in his new life than they have been here,' murmured Edith, 'but I suppose the Archdeacon cannot bear to think of anybody without some kind of burden.'

'Well, we know that life is never without them,' said Belinda loyally. 'It is perhaps just as well to remember that. And even if we appear to have none we really *ought* to have . . .' her voice trailed off obscurely, for Miss Berridge had come forward and was making a speech of thanks. Her voice was clear and ringing, as if she were used to giving lectures or addressing meetings. What an excellent clergyman's wife she would make with this splendid gift!

'Edgar and I are simply delighted . . .' there was comfort in the words, as if she were protecting Mr Donne in a sensible tweed coat or even woollen underwear. It was obvious that she would take care of him, not letting him cast a clout too soon. She would probably help with his sermons too, and embellish them with quotations rarer than her husband, with his Third Class in Theology, could be expected to know. A helpmeet indeed.

'Rather *toothy* when she smiles, isn't she,' whispered Harriet. 'I wonder what *he* will say.'

Mr Donne's speech was very short. 'Olivia has said exactly what I would have said,' he began. Here again the use of Christian names gave a cosy, intimate feeling. Agatha and Father Plowman were smiling and even the Archdeacon was looking benevolent.

Mr Donne concluded on a serious note. 'I think we shall both remember what the Archdeacon has said about the burdens we may have to bear in our new life. I hope we may not be found wanting at the testing time. And now, let us pray. . . .'

Belinda wondered whether he would be able to think of another suitable prayer when Father Plowman had rather unfairly used the obvious one already. But she had to admit that his choice was an admirable one. *Lord, we pray Thee that Thy grace may always prevent and follow us, and make us continually to be given to all good works*. . . . She bowed her head and could see out of the corner of her eye Miss Prior and Miss Jenner, creeping in through a side door carrying a tea-urn. When they realized that a prayer was being said, they stood stiffly with the urn, like children playing a game of 'statues'.

The prayer ended, and after a decent pause Miss Berridge and Mr Donne – or Olivia and Edgar as they had now become in the minds of their hearers – came down from the platform and moved among the audience, shaking hands and chatting.

Belinda found herself talking to Miss Berridge and offering her a cake from a plate which seemed to have got into her hand. She felt a glow of warm friendliness towards her, perhaps because of her rather plain, good-humoured face, her sensible felt hat, her not particularly well-cut tweed suit and her low-heeled shoes. Nothing from the 'best houses' here – all was as it should be in a clergyman's wife.

'Where will you live?' Belinda asked. 'I suppose suitable accommodation is provided for married chaplains even in a place that is in other ways as old-fashioned as our University.'

'Oh, we've already taken a very nice house, rather Gothic in style, but I think it will be comfortable and it has a large garden,' said Olivia. 'And Edgar will have rooms in college as well, of course. I hope you and your sister will come and see us when we are settled in. Edgar tells me you have been so good to him.'

Belinda managed to stop herself saying, 'Oh, it was really Harriet, my sister, she dotes on curates,' and asked instead whether it was decided who should come in place of Mr Donne. 'Will he be a young man or an older one who needs the quiet and country air of a little place like this?' she asked.

'Both, in a way,' said Olivia. 'He *is* young, but he has recently been ill – I think you'll like him very much. I believe he's a Balliol man and he's certainly very handsome, dark and rather Italian-looking, really. Edgar looks quite plain beside him.' She laughed affectionately. 'Anyway, you'll see him at our wedding.'

'How splendid! My sister will be delighted,' said Belinda with unguarded enthusiasm. 'She has such a respect for Balliol men,' she added hastily.

'Yes, it still maintains its great tradition of scholarship,' agreed Olivia. 'I had an idea that Archdeacon Hoccleve was a Balliol man.'

'No, he isn't, as a matter of fact,' said Belinda, 'but he is a very fine preacher. His knowledge of English literature is quite remarkable for a clergyman.'

'His sermons are full of quotations,' said Harriet bluntly. 'I consider Mr Donne a *much* better preacher.'

'I think that English Literature and Theology can be very happily combined,' said Olivia gracefully. 'I dare say I shall find myself encouraging Edgar to write more literary sermons.'

'Ah, yes,' said her fiancé, 'I expect Olivia will help me to outdo even the Archdeacon with obscure quotations from the *Ormulum*.'

'Whatever is that?' asked Harriet. 'It sounds very learned.'

'A kind of moral treatise, I believe.'

'Oh, well, I hope you won't listen to her,' said Harriet. 'I suppose people liked things like that in the old days.'

'And I hope that we in these days may still be said to like "things like that",' said Father Plowman, smiling indulgently at Harriet, as if she were a naughty child.

'Perhaps we would like them better if we could understand

them,' said Belinda. 'I mean the language, of course.' She spoke rather hastily as she could see the Archdeacon approaching and thought it might be as well to change the subject before he came. 'I wish somebody would have another cake,' she said, offering the plate which she was still holding. Harriet took it from her and began to encourage Mr Donne to eat a cake with pink icing, much to the amusement of Olivia, who did not appear to mind Harriet's proprietary attitude in the very least.

Belinda, feeling that she had monopolized the young couple for quite long enough, withdrew quietly and found herself near the tea-urn over which Miss Prior and Miss Jenner were presiding.

'Would you like another cup, Miss Bede?' asked Miss Prior. 'I know you're one for tea, like I am.'

'Yes, please, I would,' said Belinda, feeling this to be a comfortable classification. 'I'm sure we need plenty of tea after all this excitement.'

'We certainly do,' agreed Miss Prior. 'Miss Aspinall, too! *That* news was a surprise, I can tell you. A shock, you might almost say.'

'Oh, I always thought he had his eye on her,' said Miss Jenner in her shrill, arch voice. 'I said to mother only the other day that something would come of it.'

'Come of it?' asked Belinda, looking over to where, as she now realized, Connie Aspinall, fresh from Belgravia, was standing in the centre of a little crowd. She looked almost happy and was talking with unusual animation. Even Belgrave Square could hardly have made such a change in her. 'I don't quite understand,' Belinda went on, 'has something happened to Miss Aspinall? Is *she* getting married as well?'

'Didn't you know?' Miss Jenner almost shrieked. 'Miss Aspinall's got engaged to Bishop Grote. You remember, Miss Bede, he was staying at the vicarage not so long ago.'

Belinda had taken a large gulp of tea and narrowly escaped choking, but she was able to indicate that she did remember Bishop Grote. 'But this is amazing, wonderful,' she emended, 'news. I must go and congratulate her immediately.' She put down her cup and made her way over to Miss Aspinall's corner.

'My *dear* Connie,' she said. 'I've just heard your wonderful news. I *am* glad.'

'Yes, I'm so happy,' said Connie. 'Theodore told me that as soon as he came here he felt that he was destined to find happiness, and that when he saw me he knew *it was to be*.' She gave a mysterious emphasis to these last words.

Belinda was silent for a moment in thankfulness and wonder. She did not now resent the Bishop's quoting of her favourite hymn *God moves in a mysterious way*. It was manifest that He did.

'But how did you come to meet again?' she asked, curiosity taking the place of wonder. 'Did he visit you in Belgrave Square?'

'No, we met one afternoon in the Army and Navy Stores,' said Connie. 'That was the wonderful part of it. I had gone into the garden-furniture department to buy a trowel and I was standing looking at a sweet little bird bath – you know they have such pretty carved stone ones – when I heard footsteps behind me – the place was *quite* deserted – I happened to look round and there was Theodore.'

'How extraordinary!' said Belinda, imagining the shock she herself would have felt.

'Yes, it seemed he had lost his way. He wanted to buy a new tin trunk to take back to Africa and found himself in the garden-furniture department by mistake. The man he asked had misdirected him or the department had been moved, I believe.'

'How extraordinary life is,' Belinda interposed. 'To think that the moving of a department, if it *had* been moved. . . .'

'And so then he asked me to go and have tea with him and luckily there was a Fuller's teashop quite near and he proposed to me over tea.'

'Did you have that lovely walnut cake?' asked Harriet, who had now joined them.

'I don't suppose Connie noticed what she was eating,' said Belinda. 'My dear, I'm so glad for you. I hope you will be very happy. I'm *sure* you will,' she added, feeling that she may have sounded doubtful.

'Well, I think we shall be,' said Connie. 'At first I naturally felt rather nervous – the importance of the position, you see – but Theodore assured me that I was quite equal to being a bishop's wife.'

'Yes, I am *sure* he did,' said Belinda, remembering. 'Are you to be married here or in London?'

'Oh, from Belgrave Square. Lady Grudge insisted on it. She's been so *very* kind and is most interested in the splendid work Theodore's been doing.'

'I feel that Connie's cup is almost too full,' said Belinda, as she and Harriet walked home together, 'but I'm very glad she's so happy. Perhaps they really do love each other, though he may have told her not to expect that. But perhaps it was only *I* who was not to expect love,' she added rather sadly.

'And being married from Belgrave Square!' said Harriet, who was in high spirits. 'One feels that is almost the best thing about it. *Hymen Io!*' she chanted, producing a most appropriate left-over fragment of her classical education. 'That is suitable for weddings isn't it?'

'I suppose so,' said Belinda, who had not had the same advantages. 'Of course there are many beautiful Epithalamia in the English language, but one feels somehow that they are more for *young* people.'

But Harriet had lost interest in Connie and the Bishop. She was remembering Olivia Berridge's description of the new curate. 'Balliol and rather Italian-looking,' she breathed, 'and just recovered from an illness. Oh, Belinda, he will need such special care!' Later that evening she could be seen studying a book of Invalid Cookery, and was quite annoyed when Belinda pointed out that he would probably be eating with a normal appetite by the time he came to them.

CHAPTER TWENTY-TWO

FORTUNATELY the wedding day was fine, one of those unexpected spring days that come too soon and deceive one into thinking that the winter is over. Belinda had great difficulty in restraining Harriet from casting off her woollen vest, and was only successful after she had pointed out, with great seriousness, that the curate would surely not be so foolish as to leave off his winter combinations in February.

'Oh, I suppose Miss Berridge would see to that,' said Harriet sulkily. 'It's quite obvious that she's going to fuss over him and turn him into a molly-coddle.'

Belinda could think of no answer to make to this, but could only wonder at the shortness of Harriet's memory. It seemed such a little time since she had thought of nothing but knitting and cooking special dishes for Mr Donne.

By many deeds of shame
We learn that love grows cold,

thought Belinda. Did the author of that fine hymn realize how often his lines had been frivolously applied? She turned to her prayer-book and saw that he had died in 1905: so he was beyond the realization. No doubt we are more frivolous now than we were then, she thought, feeling in her jewel-box for her little seed-pearl brooch. The neck of her new dress – a soft shade of blue that could not possibly make her look yellow – needed something to relieve its severity. Miss Prior had really made it very well; it even fitted quite closely as a result of Belinda's timid and carefully phrased request for something a little less shapeless than usual. Harriet had ordered a creation from Gorringe's which Belinda considered an unnecessary expense. She had not, however, mentioned this to her sister as she realized that the loss of a dear curate was something of an occasion and this was, as far as she could remember, the first time one had been lost by marriage. Usually it was the Mission Field or the East End of London that claimed them, or, more rarely, a comfortable living in the gift of a distant relative. . . .

'Belinda! Are you ready?' Harriet stood in the room, magnificent in furs and veiled hat.

'Oh, yes, I just have to put on my hat and coat. There! You *do* look nice, Harriet. I wonder if a veil would suit me? One feels that it's *kinder* somehow – not that your complexion needs to be hidden, of course, but I sometimes think that for *me* . . . and yet, I don't know . . .' she broke off, wondering whether it would really make any difference now if she were to appear with her face softened by clouds of veiling. Henry knew the face underneath and would not be deceived and that was all that really mattered.

'Yes, I think it's one of my most successful hats,' said Harriet. 'Yours is nice too,' she added kindly. 'I think I should wear it just a *little* further back, though.'

Belinda adjusted it without looking in the mirror and they went downstairs.

'It's really a perfect day,' said Harriet, 'amazingly mild.'

'But I'm glad you kept on your vest,' said Belinda, 'it would have been most unwise to leave it off. It's certainly mild compared with what it has been, but it may be colder tonight.'

As they passed the vicarage she drew Harriet's attention to an almond tree in full blossom.

'Look, the almond tree's out,' she said. 'I always feel it looks lovelier every year, so beautiful that one can hardly bear it.'

Harriet looked at her sister apprehensively. She hoped Belinda wasn't going to cry too much at the wedding. They did not have many weddings in the village and it would hardly be surprising if Belinda began to distress herself by remembering that if Fate had willed otherwise she herself might have married the Archdeacon thirty years ago. She was relieved when Belinda went on to talk about ordinary things, whether it would be wise to take more than one glass of champagne at the reception, always assuming it were offered, what Agatha would be wearing and whether the new curate would be at the church.

The sisters arrived in good time so that they could choose their place carefully. Harriet looked round quite unashamedly to watch people coming into the church. Belinda occasionally turned her head, but most of the time she sat quietly with her hands folded in her lap, though she could not help showing her interest and even whispering to Harriet when Agatha came in, very elegant in dark red, with a fur coat and wide-brimmed hat. A group of nondescript-looking women – possibly relatives or friends of the bride, fellow-workers in the field of Middle English studies – came behind Agatha and they sat together in one of the front pews.

Dr Nicholas Parnell had unfortunately not been able to come down for the wedding as he had to welcome to the Library some distinguished Russian visitors who were bringing with them a number of interesting relics. Mr Mold had recently left for China, where he was to make a tour of libraries and a special study of the heating systems employed in them. There was, however, to be one distinguished visitor, the University Professor of Middle English, who was to give the bride away.

'Perhaps he wanted Miss Berridge too,' Harriet had suggested, 'but hadn't the courage to speak.'

'Oh, surely not,' said Belinda, 'or how could he bear to come to the wedding?' She could certainly not have attended Agatha and Henry's.

In the meantime the church was filling up. Count Bianco, whose gout was well enough now to allow him to go out, had chosen his seat carefully so that he could have a good view of Harriet. Edith Liversidge came in alone, for Connie Aspinall was in Belgravia, preparing for her own wedding in a few weeks' time. Edith had honoured the occasion by wearing her best purple dress, and a kind of toque on her head, a little like a tea-cosy but dignified for all that. How dear John would have loved to see her, thought Belinda sadly. Being in church often made her think of John and his tragic death in Prague. They said it was a golden city, but how much more golden must it be from its associations with him.

She began to study the white and silver leaflet, announcing the marriage of Olivia Mary Berridge with Edgar Bernard Amberley Donne. The young couple had not chosen *God moves in a mysterious way* among the hymns, indeed, Belinda had hardly hoped for that. Their selection, except for a Middle English lyric to a setting by a relative of the bride's, was conventional. *Gracious Spirit, Holy Ghost* and *The voice that breathed o'er Eden* were very suitable. It was true that the latter was often sung to the tune of *Brief life is here our portion*, but it did no harm to be reminded of that. Brief life *was* here our portion . . . Belinda's eyes strayed to the rows of memorial tablets to past vicars. She could hardly bear to think that one day Henry's would be among them and that she might be there to see it.

At this moment there was a stir of excitement as the curate appeared with his best man, a stocky, red-haired young clergyman, a typical rowing man, as Harriet whispered to Belinda.

Shortly afterwards the bride entered on the arm of the Professor of Middle English, a tall, thin man, ill at ease in his formal clothes. Belinda wondered whether Henry and

Agatha were remembering their own wedding day. She had heard that people did on these occasions unless they were in a position to look forward rather than back. Count Bianco might be looking forward, but more quietly and with less rapture than a younger man. Was there anybody in the church without some romantic thought? Possibly Miss Prior, sitting with her old mother, was more interested in the bride's dress which, Belinda noticed with approval, was not white but sapphire-blue velvet, the kind of thing that would 'come in' afterwards and could if necessary be dyed and worn for years. She really looked very nice, almost pretty and not as tall as she had seemed to be at the presentation.

'If I'm ever married I shall certainly have a *fully* choral ceremony,' said Harriet enthusiastically as they filed out of the church. 'Or is there a special one for those of riper years?'

Belinda said nothing because she had been crying a little and could not trust herself to speak yet.

'No, that's only baptism,' said Edith cheerfully. 'I believe Connie and the Bishop are having quite an elaborate affair. You will be getting your invitations soon. She's having a dress made at Marshall's – embossed chenille velvet – though goodness knows what use that will be in the tropics,' she snorted.

'No, it doesn't seem as if it would be much use,' Belinda agreed. 'But of course he won't be Bishop of Mbawawa all his life. I suppose he may retire and write a book about his experiences. They often do, don't they?'

'With cassock and surplice in Mbawawa-land,' retorted Edith. 'Yes, one knows the kind of thing only too well.'

'What a beautiful day,' said a gentle voice behind them. 'It is quite like Naples.'

'My dear Ricardo,' said Edith, looking round, 'where in Naples would you see such a very odd-looking crowd of people as are now coming out of this church?'

'I don't see the new curate among them,' said Harriet, looking worried. 'It can't be the best man, can it? Nobody would call him Italian-looking. Ricardo, Italians don't ever have red hair, do they?'

The Count considered the question seriously. 'Red hair is certainly not unknown in Italy,' he pronounced at length, 'but I do not think you would say that it is characteristic of the Italians. In the north of course it is sometimes found, but,' he paused impressively, 'I do not remember that I ever saw a red-haired man in Naples.'

'Oh, that's good,' said Harriet perfunctorily, 'it can't be him, then. But I did hope he was going to be at the wedding.'

'I dare say there was some difficulty about the trains,' suggested Belinda. 'We shall probably find that he is at the reception.'

This was to be held at the parish hall. The curate had invited all the village, so that the vicarage drawing-room would hardly have contained them. The bride and bridegroom were in the doorway to shake hands with the guests as they filed in.

Belinda murmured what she hoped was a suitable greeting and passed on but she heard Harriet laughing loudly with Mr Donne, so that she wondered rather fearfully what her sister could have said. She found herself standing by Agatha and confronted by a tray of glasses of champagne which one of the hired waiters was holding in front of her.

'I must just have a sip, to drink their health, you know,' she said apologetically, feeling Agatha's eyes on her.

'Oh, certainly,' said Agatha. 'It is quite the thing.'

'I'm not really very used to drinking champagne,' Belinda admitted.

'Aren't you?' Agatha gave a little social laugh, which would normally have crushed Belinda and made her feel very gauche and inferior. But today she did not mind. She was almost glad to be able to see Agatha as her old self again. The socks not quite long enough in the foot, which the Bishop had so unkindly mentioned, had been worrying Belinda. She had suddenly seen Agatha as pathetic and the picture was disturbing. Now she knew that there could never be anything pathetic about Agatha. Poised and well-dressed, used to drinking champagne, the daughter of a bishop and the wife of an archdeacon – that was Agatha Hoccleve. It was Belinda Bede who was the pathetic one and it was so much easier to bear the burden of one's own pathos than that of somebody else. Indeed, perhaps the very recognition of it in oneself meant that it didn't really exist. Belinda took a rather large sip of champagne and looked round the hall with renewed courage.

Most of the guests were known to her, although some people from neighbouring villages had been invited. She noticed Father Plowman, near the food and with a well-filled glass, Lady Clara Boulding, putting a small *vol-au-vent* whole into her mouth, and a group of Sunday School teachers, Miss Beard, Miss Smiley and Miss Jenner, standing in a corner by themselves and looking suspiciously into their glasses. Agatha had left her now and was greeting some of the guests, so Belinda moved over to where Miss Prior and her mother were standing.

'Very nice, isn't it?' she said inadequately, nodding and smiling in their direction.

'Oh, yes, it's quite nice,' said Mrs Prior. 'It's nice to see everyone enjoying themselves. I like to see that.'

'Mother was saying she wished there was a cup of tea,' said Miss Prior in a low voice, 'but we'll have one when we get home. You see, Miss Bede, we're not really used to drinking champagne. It's different for you of course.'

'Well, I don't often have it,' Belinda admitted, feeling that she must stand midway between Agatha and the Priors in this matter, 'but of course we all want to drink the health of the bride and bridegroom in it.'

'Yes, of course,' Miss Prior agreed. 'She looks very sweet, doesn't she? That *Vogue* pattern makes up well in velvet, it was in the December book. Your dress has turned out quite nicely, too, Miss Bede. I had such trouble with the sleeves, you wouldn't believe it. I found I'd put them in the wrong way round!' Miss Prior laughed rather shrilly and took a gulp of champagne.

'Are they the right way round now?' asked Belinda.

'Oh, of course, Miss Bede. I took them out again. I couldn't let you wear a dress with the sleeves in the wrong way round.'

'No,' said Belinda, feeling all the same that this kind of thing might very well happen to her. 'Mrs Hoccleve's dress is very smart, isn't it?' she ventured, feeling that it was not at all the thing to discuss the guests' clothes with Miss Prior but being unable to resist the temptation. Perhaps, she thought, Miss Prior's profession will excuse me.

'Smart, yes, that's what I would call it too,' said Miss Prior. 'But red's not her colour. The material's good, I can see that, but you take a look at the seams inside – you won't find them finished off like mine are.'

'No, I dare say not,' said Belinda, realizing that she would certainly never have the opportunity of examining the dress so minutely, but feeling, none the less, that Agatha's splendour was considerably diminished.

'Oh, look, the Archdeacon's going to make a speech,' said Miss Prior. 'Pray silence for the Venerable Hoccleve,' she giggled.

The champagne was having a different effect on Belinda, who was now gazing very sentimentally at the Archdeacon, thinking how nice he looked and what a clever speech he was making, not at all obvious or vulgar as wedding speeches so often were. She had really no idea what he was talking about, but there were a great many quotations in it, including one from Spenser which really seemed to be quite appropriate, something about love being a celestial harmony of likely hearts

> *Which join together in sweet sympathy,*
> *To work each others' joy and true content. . . .*

He was not saying anything about Burdens or sudden calls to the Mission Field.

The curate replied very nicely after the health had been drunk and was followed by the Professor of Middle English, who made an unintelligible but obviously clever little speech about *The Owl and the Nightingale,* embellished with quotations from that poem. Agatha and Olivia were smiling knowledgeably at each other, and Belinda turned away to meet Harriet, who was moving towards her through the crowd. Her face radiated joy and happiness. How nice it is that Harriet is entering so wholeheartedly into their feelings, thought Belinda, for she had been so afraid that her sister might be made unhappy by the curate's marriage and departure.

'The third from the left,' whispered Harriet eagerly.

Belinda looked about her, rather puzzled. Then she saw what her sister meant, for in a corner she saw five curates, all young and all pale and thin, with the exception of one, who was tall and muscular and a former Rugby Blue, as she afterwards learned.

The third from the left. How convenient of the curates to arrange themselves so that Belinda could so easily pick out Harriet's choice. He was dark and rather Italian-looking, paler and more hollow-cheeked than the others. Now Belinda understood her sister's joy and suddenly she realized that she too was happier than she had been for a long time.

For now everything would be as it had been before those two disturbing characters Mr Mold and Bishop Grote appeared in the village. In the future Belinda would continue to find such consolation as she needed in our greater English poets, when she was not gardening or making vests for the poor in Pimlico.

Harriet would accept the attentions of Count Bianco and listen patiently and kindly to his regular proposals of marriage. Belinda did not go any further than this in her plans for the future: she could only be grateful that their lives were to be so little changed. It was true that the curate on whom Harriet had lavished so much care and affection was now a married man and lost to them, but another had come in his place, so like, that they would hardly realize the difference, except that he was rather Italian-looking and had had a nervous breakdown.

Then she fretted, ah she fretted,
But ere six months had gone past,
She had got another poodle dog
Exactly like the last. . . .

thought Belinda frivolously, but the old song had come into her head and seemed appropriate. Some tame gazelle or some gentle dove or even a poodle dog – something to *love*, that was the point.

'I think I'll ask him after the reception, although it's rather soon. But we do want to make him welcome *at once*, don't we?' Harriet was speaking eagerly to her sister.

Belinda smiled. 'Of course, dear.' Asking the new curate to supper seemed a particularly happy thought.

'I knew you would agree,' said Harriet, making boldly for the curates' corner.

Belinda was looking round the room to see if she could find some sympathetic person to whom she could say that Dr Johnson had been so right when he had said that all change is of itself an evil, when she saw Harriet approaching with the new curate.

She smiled and shook hands with him, but before either of them could utter a suitable platitude, Harriet had burst in with the news that the young man was coming to supper with them on his first Sunday evening in the village, which would be in about a fortnight's time.

'He says he is fond of boiled chicken,' she added.

Belinda laughed awkwardly and hoped that the new curate would not be embarrassed by Harriet's behaviour.

But he seemed completely at ease as Harriet confided to him that she always liked to eat chicken bones in her fingers.

'Like dear Queen Victoria used to,' she sighed.

'Now, I'm sure *you* don't remember Queen Victoria,' he said gallantly.

'We older people remember a great deal more than you think,' said Harriet coyly.

'Oh, *come*, now,' laughed the curate, and although his voice was rather weak as a result of his long illness, Belinda was overjoyed to hear that it had the authentic ring.

Excellent Women

To my sister

CHAPTER ONE

'AH, YOU LADIES! Always on the spot when there's something happening!' The voice belonged to Mr Mallett, one of our churchwardens, and its roguish tone made me start guiltily, almost as if I had no right to be discovered outside my own front door.

'New people moving in? The presence of a funiture van would seem to suggest it,' he went on pompously. 'I expect *you* know about it.'

'Well, yes, one usually does,' I said, feeling rather annoyed at his presumption. 'It is rather difficult not to know such things.'

I suppose an unmarried woman just over thirty, who lives alone and has no apparent ties, must expect to find herself involved or interested in other people's business, and if she is also a clergyman's daughter then one might really say that there is no hope for her.

'Well, well, *tempus fugit*, as the poet says,' called out Mr Mallett as he hurried on.

I had to agree that it did, but I dawdled long enough to see the furniture men set down a couple of chairs on the pavement, and as I walked up the stairs to my flat I heard the footsteps of a person in the empty rooms below me, pacing about on the bare boards, deciding where each piece should go.

Mrs Napier, I thought, for I had noticed a letter addressed to somebody of that name, marked 'To Await Arrival'. But now that she had materialized I felt, perversely, that I did not want to see her, so I hurried into my own rooms and began tidying out my kitchen.

I met her for the first time by the dustbins, later that afternoon. The dustbins were in the basement and everybody in the house shared them. There were offices on the ground floor and above them the two flats, not properly self-contained and without every convenience. 'I have to share a bathroom,' I had so often murmured, almost with shame, as if I personally had been found unworthy of a bathroom of my own.

I bent low over the bin and scrabbled a few tea leaves and potato peelings out of the bottom of my bucket. I was embarrassed that we should meet like this. I had meant to ask Mrs Napier to coffee one evening. It was to have been a gracious, civilized occasion, with my best coffee cups and biscuits on little silver dishes. And now here I was standing awkwardly in my oldest clothes, carrying a bucket and a waste-paper-basket.

Mrs Napier spoke first.

'You must be Miss Lathbury,' she said abruptly. 'I've seen your name by one of the door-bells.'

'Yes, I live in the flat above yours. I do hope you're getting comfortably settled in. Moving is such a business, isn't it? It seems to take so long to get everything straight. Some essential thing like a teapot or a frying-pan is always lost . . .' Platitudes flowed easily from me, perhaps because, with my parochial experience, I know myself to be capable of dealing with most of the stock situations or even the great moments of life – birth, marriage, death, the successful jumble sale, the garden fête spoilt by bad weather . . . 'Mildred is such a help to her father,' people used to say after my mother died.

'It will be nice to have somebody else in the house,' I ventured, for during the last year of the war my friend Dora Caldicote and I had been the only occupants, and I had been quite alone for the past month since Dora had left to take up a teaching post in the country.

'Oh, well, I don't suppose I shall be in very much,' said Mrs Napier quickly.

'Oh, no,' I said, drawing back; 'neither shall I.' In fact, I was very often in, but I understood her reluctance to pledge herself to anything that might become a nuisance or a tie. We were, superficially at any rate, a very unlikely pair to become friendly. She was fair-haired and pretty, gaily dressed in corduroy trousers and a bright jersey, while I, mousy and rather plain anyway, drew attention to these qualities with my shapeless overall and old fawn skirt. Let me hasten to add that I am not at all like Jane Eyre, who must have given hope to so many plain women who tell their stories in the first person, nor have I ever thought of myself as being like her.

'My husband will be coming out of the Navy soon,' said Mrs Napier, almost in a warning tone. 'I'm just getting the place ready.'

'Oh, I see.' I began to wonder what could have brought a naval officer and his wife to this shabby part of London, so very much the 'wrong' side of Victoria Station, so definitely *not* Belgravia, for which I had a sentimental affection, but which did not usually attract people who looked like Mrs Napier. 'I suppose it's still very difficult to find a flat,' I went on, driven by curiosity. 'I've been here two years and it was much easier then.'

'Yes, I've had an awful time and this isn't really what we wanted. I don't at all like the idea of sharing a bathroom,' she said bluntly, 'and I don't know what Rockingham will say.'

Rockingham! I snatched at the name as if it had been a precious jewel in the dustbin. Mr Napier was called Rockingham! How the bearer of such a name would hate sharing a bathroom! I hastened to excuse myself. 'I'm always *very* quick in the mornings, and on Sundays I usually get up early to go to church,' I said.

She smiled at this, and then seemed to feel bound to add that of course she had no use for church-going.

We walked upstairs in silence with our buckets and waste-paper-baskets. The opportunity for 'saying a word', which was what our vicar always urged us to do, came and went. We had reached her flat, and much to my surprise she was asking me if I would like to have a cup of tea with her.

I don't know whether spinsters are really more inquisitive than married women, though I believe they are thought to be because of the emptiness of their lives, but I could hardly admit to Mrs Napier that at one point during the afternoon I had arranged to be brushing my flight of stairs so that I could peer through the banisters and watch her furniture being brought in. I had noticed then that she had some good things – a walnut bureau, a carved oak chest and a set of Chippendale chairs, and when I followed her into her sitting-room I realized that she also possessed some interesting small objects, Victorian paperweights and snowstorms, very much like those I had on my own mantelpiece upstairs.

'Those are Rockingham's,' she said, when I admired them. 'He collects Victoriana.'

'I have hardly needed to collect them,' I said. 'My old home was a rectory and full of such objects. It was quite difficult to know what to keep and what to sell.'

'I suppose it was a large, inconvenient country rectory with stone passages, oil lamps and far too many rooms,' she said suddenly. 'One has a nostalgia for that kind of thing sometimes. But how I'd hate to live in it.'

'Yes, it was like that,' I said, 'but it was very pleasant. I sometimes feel rather cramped here.'

'But surely you have more rooms than we have?'

'Yes, I've got an attic, too, but the rooms are rather small.'

'And there's the shared bathroom,' she murmured.

'The early Christians had all things in common,' I reminded her. 'Be thankful that we have our own kitchens.'

'Oh, God, yes! You'd hate sharing a kitchen with me. I'm such a slut,' she said, almost proudly.

While she made the tea I occupied myself by looking at her books, which were lying in stacks on the floor. Many of them seemed to be of an obscure scientific nature, and there was a pile of journals with green covers which bore the rather stark and surprising title of *Man*. I wondered what they could be about.

'I hope you don't mind tea in mugs,' she said, coming in with a tray. 'I told you I was a slut.'

'No, of course not,' I said in the way that one does, thinking that Rockingham would probably dislike it very much.

'Rockingham does most of the cooking when we're together,' she said. 'I'm really too busy to do much.'

Surely wives shouldn't be too busy to cook for their husbands? I thought in astonishment, taking a thick piece of bread and jam from the plate offered to me. But perhaps Rockingham with his love of Victoriana also enjoyed cooking, for I had observed that men did not usually do things unless they liked doing them. 'I suppose the Navy has taught him that?' I suggested.

'Oh, no, he's always been a good cook. The Navy hasn't taught him anything, really.' She sighed. 'He's been Flag Lieutenant to an Admiral in Italy and lived in a luxurious villa overlooking the Mediterranean for the past eighteen months, while I've been trailing round Africa.'

'*Africa?*' I echoed in amazement. Could she be a missionary, then? It seemed very unlikely and I suddenly remembered that she had said she never went to church.

'Yes, I'm an anthropologist,' she explained.

'Oh.' I was silent with wonder, and also because I was not at all sure what an anthropologist was and could think of no intelligent comment to make.

'Rockingham hasn't had to do anything much but be charming to a lot of dreary Wren officers in ill-fitting white uniforms, as far as I can make out.'

'Oh, surely . . .' I began to protest, but then decided that this, was, after all, a work well worth doing. Clergymen were often good at it; indeed, so many of their flock wore drab, ill-fitting clothes that it came as second nature to them. I had not realized that it might also be among the accomplishments of naval officers.

'I've got to write up my field notes now,' Mrs Napier went on.

'Oh, yes, of course. How interesting . . .'

'Well, well . . .' she stood up and put her mug down on the tray. I felt that I was being dismissed.

'Thank you for the tea,' I said. 'You must come and see me when you get settled. Do let me know if there's anything I can do to help.'

'Not at the moment, thank you,' she said, 'but there may be.'

I thought nothing of her words at the time. It did not seem then as if our lives could ever touch at any point beyond a casual meeting on the stairs and of course the sharing of a bathroom.

This last idea may have occurred to her too, for when I was halfway up the stairs to my own flat she called out, 'I think I must have been using your toilet paper. I'll try and remember to get some when it's finished.'

'Oh, that's quite all right,' I called back, rather embarrassed. I come from a circle that does not shout aloud about such things, but I nevertheless hoped that she would remember. The burden of keeping three people in toilet paper seemed to me rather a heavy one.

When I got into my sitting-room I found to my surprise that it was nearly six o'clock. We must have talked for over an hour. I decided that I did not like Mrs Napier very much, and then began to reproach myself for lack of Christian charity. But must we always like everybody? I asked myself. Perhaps not, but we must not pass judgment on them until we have known them a little longer than one hour. In fact, it was not our business to judge at all. I could hear Father Malory saying something of the kind in a sermon, and at that moment St Mary's church began to strike six.

I could just see the church spire through the trees in the square. Now, when they were leafless, it looked beautiful, springing up among the peeling stucco fronts of the houses, prickly, Victorian-gothic, hideous inside, I suppose, but very dear to me.

There were two churches in the district, but I had chosen St Mary's rather than All Souls', not only because it was nearer, but because it was 'High'. I am afraid my poor father and mother would not have approved at all and I could imagine my mother, her lips pursed, shaking her head and breathing in a frightened whisper, '*Incense.*' But perhaps it was only natural that I should want to rebel against my upbringing, even if only in such a harmless way. I gave All Souls' a trial; indeed I went there for two Sundays, but when I returned to St Mary's, Father Malory stopped me after Mass one morning and said how glad he was to see me again. He and his sister had been quite worried; they feared I might have been ill. After that I had not left St Mary's again, and Julian Malory and his sister Winifred had become my friends.

I sometimes thought how strange it was that I should have managed to make a life for myself in London so very much like the life I had lived in a country rectory when my parents were alive. But then so many parts of London have a peculiarly village or parochial atmosphere that perhaps it is only a question of choosing one's parish and fitting into it. When my parents had died, within two years of each other, I was left with a small income of my own, an assortment of furniture, but no home. It was then that I had joined forces with my old school friend Dora Caldicote, and while she was teaching I worked in the Censorship, for which, very fortunately, no high qualifications appeared to be necessary, apart from patience, discretion and a slight tendency towards eccentricity. Now that Dora had gone I looked forward to being alone once more, to living a civilized life with a bedroom and a sitting-room and a spare room for friends. I have not Dora's temperament which makes her enjoy sleeping on a camp bed and eating off plastic plates. I felt that I was now old enough to become fussy and spinsterish if I wanted to. I did part-time work at an organization which helped impoverished gentlewomen, a cause very near to my own heart, as I felt that I was just the kind of person who might one day become one. Mrs Napier, with her gay trousers and her anthropology, obviously never would.

I was thinking about her as I changed to go out to supper at the vicarage, and was glad that I was wearing respectable clothes when I met her on the stairs with a tall, fair man.

'You'll have to drink gin out of a mug,' I heard her say. 'The glasses aren't unpacked.'

'It doesn't matter,' he answered rather stiffly as if it mattered a great deal. 'I suppose you haven't got things straight yet.'

Not Rockingham, I felt; no, it could hardly be when he was in Italy being charming to Wren officers. Perhaps a fellow anthropologist? The bell of St Mary's began to ring for Evensong and I realized that it was none of my business who he was. It was too early to go to the vicarage, so I hurried into church and took my place with the half-dozen middle-aged and elderly women who made up the weekday evening congregation. Winifred Malory, late as always, came and sat by me and whispered that somebody had sent quite a large donation, most generous, towards the cost of repairing the west window which had been damaged by a bomb. An *anonymous* donation – wasn't it exciting? Julian would tell me about it at supper.

CHAPTER TWO

JULIAN MALORY was about forty, a few years younger than his sister. Both were tall, thin and angular, but while this gave to Julian a suitable ascetic distinction, it only seemed to make Winifred, with her eager face and untidy grey hair, more awkward and gaunt. She was dressed, as usual, in an odd assortment of clothes, most of which had belonged to other people. It was well known that Winifred got most of her wardrobe from the garments sent to the parish jumble sales, for such money as she had was never spent on herself but on Good – one could almost say Lost – Causes, in which she was an unselfish and tireless worker. The time left over from these good works was given to 'making a home' for her brother, whom she adored, though she was completely undomesticated and went about it with more enthusiasm than skill.

'If only I could paint the front door!' she said, as the three of us went into the vicarage after Evensong. 'It looks so dark and drab. A vicarage ought to be a welcoming sort of place with a bright entrance.'

Julian was hanging up his biretta on a peg in the narrow hall. Next to it hung a rather new-looking panama hat. I had never seen him wearing it and it occurred to me that perhaps he had bought it to keep until its ribbon became rusty with age and the straw itself a greyish yellow. My father had worn just such a hat and it always seemed to me to epitomize the wisdom of an old country clergyman, wisdom which Julian could not hope to attain for another twenty or thirty years.

'A welcoming sort of place with a bright entrance,' Julian repeated. 'Well, I hope people do get a welcome even if our front door is dark and I hope Mrs Jubb has got some supper for us.'

I sat down at the table without any very high hopes, for both Julian and Winifred, as is often the way with good, unworldly people, hardly noticed what they ate or drank, so that a meal with them was a doubtful pleasure. Mrs Jubb, who might have been quite a good cook with any encouragement, must have lost heart long ago. Tonight she set before us a pale macaroni cheese and a dish of boiled potatoes, and I noticed a blancmange or 'shape', also of an indeterminate colour, in a glass dish on the sideboard.

Not enough salt, or perhaps *no* salt, I thought, as I ate the macaroni. And not really enough cheese.

'Do tell me about this anonymous donation,' I asked. 'It sounds splendid.'

'Yes, it's really most encouraging. Somebody has sent me ten pounds. I wonder who it can be!' When Julian smiled the bleakness of his face was softened and he became almost good-looking. There was usually something rather forbidding about his manner so that women did not tend to fuss over him as they might otherwise have done. I am not even sure whether anyone had ever knitted him a scarf or pullover. I suppose he was neither so handsome nor so conceited as to pretend a belief in celibacy as a protection, and I did not really know his views on the matter. It seemed a comfortable arrangement for the brother and sister to live together, and perhaps it is more suitable that a High Church clergyman should remain unmarried, that there should be a biretta in the hall rather than a perambulator.

'I always think an anonymous donation is so exciting,' said Winifred with adolescent eagerness. 'I'm longing to find out who it is. Mildred, it isn't you, is it? Or anyone you know?'

I denied all knowledge of it.

Julian smiled tolerantly at his sister's enthusiasm. 'Ah, well, I expect we shall know soon enough who has sent it. Probably one of our good ladies in Colchester or Grantchester Square.' He named the two most respectable squares in our district, where a few houses of the old type, occupied by one family or even one person and not yet cut up into flats, were to be found. My flat was in neither of these squares, but in a street on the fringe and at what I liked to think was the 'best' end.

'It doesn't seem like them, somehow,' I said. 'They don't usually do good by stealth.'

'No,' Julian agreed, 'their left hand usually knows perfectly well what their right hand is doing.'

'Of course,' said Winifred, 'a lot of new people have moved here since the war ended. I've noticed one or two strangers at church lately. It may be one of them.'

'Yes, it probably is,' I agreed. 'The new people moved into my house today and I met Mrs Napier for the first time this afternoon. By the dustbins, too.'

Julian laughed. 'I hope that isn't an omen, meeting by the dustbins.'

'She seemed very pleasant,' I said rather insincerely. 'A bit younger than I am, I should think. Her husband is in the Navy and is coming home soon. He has been in Italy.'

'Italy, how lovely!' said Winifred. 'We must ask them in. Don't you remember, dear,' she turned to her brother, 'Fanny Ogilvy used to teach English in Naples? I wonder if he met her.'

'I should think it very unlikely,' said Julian. 'Naval officers don't usually meet impoverished English gentlewomen abroad.'

'Oh, but his wife told me that he spent his time being charming to dull Wren officers,' I said, 'so he sounds rather a nice person. She is an anthropologist, Mrs Napier. I'm not quite sure what that is.'

'Really? It sounds a little incongruous – a naval officer and an anthropologist,' said Julian.

'It sounds very exciting,' said Winifred. 'Is it something to do with apes?'

Julian began to explain to us what an anthropologist was, or I suppose he did, but as it is unlikely that any anthropologist will read this, I can perhaps say that it appeared to be something to do with the study of man and his behaviour in society – particularly among 'primitive communities', Julian said.

Winifred giggled. 'I hope she isn't going to study *us*.'

'I'm very much afraid that we shan't see her at St Mary's,' said Julian gravely.

'No, I'm afraid not. She told me that she never went to church.'

'I hope you were able to say a word, Mildred,' said Julian, fixing me with what I privately called his 'burning' look. 'We shall rely on you to do something there.'

'Oh, I don't suppose I shall see anything of her except at the dustbins,' I said lightly. 'Perhaps her husband will come to church. Naval officers are often religious, I believe.'

'*They that go down to the sea in ships: and occupy their business in great waters; These men see the works of the Lord: and His wonders in the deep*,' Julian said, half to himself.

I did not like to spoil the beauty of the words by pointing out that as far as we knew Rockingham Napier had spent most of his service arranging the Admiral's social life. Of course he might very well have seen the works of the Lord and His wonders in the deep.

We got up from the table and Julian went out of the room. There was to be some kind of a meeting at half-past seven and I could already hear the voices of some of the 'lads' in the hall.

'Let's go into the den,' said Winifred, 'and I'll make some coffee on the gas ring.'

The den was a small room, untidily cosy, looking out on to the narrow strip of garden. Julian's study was in the front on the same side, the drawing-room and dining-room on the other side. Upstairs there were several bedrooms and attics and a large cold bathroom. The kitchen was in the basement. It was really a very large house for two people, but Father

Greatorex, the curate, a middle-aged man who had been ordained late in life, had his own flat in Grantchester Square.

'We really ought to do something about letting off the top floor as a flat,' said Winifred, pouring coffee that looked like weak tea. 'It seems so selfish, *wrong*, really, just the two of us living here when there must be so many people wanting rooms now. I do hope this coffee is all right, Mildred? You always make it so well.'

'Delicious, thank you,' I murmured. 'I'm sure you'd have no difficulty in getting a nice tenant. Of course you'd want somebody congenial. You might advertise in the *Church Times*.' At this idea a crowd of suitable applicants seemed to rise up before me – canons' widows, clergymen's sons, Anglo-Catholic gentlewomen (non-smokers), church people (regular communicants) . . . all so worthy that they sounded almost unpleasant.

'Oh, yes, we might do that. But I suppose you wouldn't think of coming here yourself, Mildred?' Her eyes shone, eager and pleading like a dog's. 'You could name your own rent, dear. I know Julian would like to have you here as much as I should.'

'That's very kind of you,' I said, speaking slowly to gain time, for fond as I was of Winifred I valued my independence very dearly, 'but I think I'd better stay where I am. I should be only one person and you'd really have room for two, wouldn't you?'

'A couple, you mean?'

'Yes, or two friends. Something like Dora and me, or younger people, students, perhaps.'

Winifred's face brightened. 'Oh, that would be lovely.'

'Or a married curate,' I suggested, full of ideas. 'That would be very suitable. If Father Greatorex does get somewhere in the country, as I believe he wants to, Julian will be wanting another curate and he may very well be married.'

'Yes, of course, they don't all feel as Julian does.'

'Does he?' I asked, interested. 'I didn't realize he had any definite views about it.'

'Well, he's never actually said anything,' said Winifred vaguely. 'But it's so much nicer that he hasn't married, nicer for me, that is, although I should have liked some nephews and nieces. And now,' she leapt up with one of her awkward impulsive movements, 'I must show you what Lady Farmer's sent for the jumble sale. Such *good* things. I shall be quite set up for the spring.'

Lady Farmer was one of the few wealthy members of our congregation, but as she was over seventy I was doubtful whether her clothes would really be suitable for Winifred, who was much thinner and hadn't her air of comfortably upholstered elegance.

'Look,' she shook out the folds of a maroon embossed chenille velvet afternoon dress and held it up against her, 'what do you think of this?'

I had to agree that it was lovely material, but the dress was so completely Lady Farmer that I should have hated to wear it myself and swamp whatever individuality I possess.

'Miss Enders can take it in where it's too big,' said Winifred. 'It will do if people come to supper, you know, the Bishop or anybody like that.'

We were both silent for a moment, as if wondering whether such an occasion could possibly arise.

'There's always the parish party at Christmas,' I suggested.

'Oh, of course. It will do for that.' Winifred sounded relieved and bundled the dress away again. 'There's a good jumper suit, too, just the thing to wear in the mornings. How much ought I to give for them?' she asked anxiously. 'Lady Farmer said that I could have anything I wanted for myself, but I must pay a fair price, otherwise the sale won't make anything.'

We discussed the matter gravely for some time and then I got up to go.

There were lights in Mrs Napier's windows as I approached the house, and from her room came the sound of voices raised in what sounded like an argument.

I went into my little kitchen and laid my breakfast. I usually left the house at a quarter to nine in the morning and worked for my gentlewomen until lunchtime. After that I was free, but I always seemed to find plenty to do. As I moved about the kitchen getting out china and cutlery, I thought, not for the first time, how pleasant it was to be living alone. The jingle of the little beaded cover against the milk jug reminded me of Dora and her giggles, her dogmatic opinions and the way she took offence so easily. The little cover, which had been her idea, seemed to symbolize all the little irritations of her company, dear kind friend though she was. 'It keeps out flies and dust,' she would say, and of course she was perfectly right, it was only my perverseness that made me sometimes want to fling it away with a grand gesture.

Later, as I lay in bed, I found myself thinking about Mrs Napier and the man I had seen with her. Was he perhaps a fellow anthropologist? I could still hear their voices in the room underneath me, raised almost as if they were quarrelling. I began to wonder about Rockingham Napier, when he would come and what he would be like. Cooking, Victorian glass paperweights, charm . . . and then there was the naval element. He might arrive with a parrot in a cage. I supposed that, apart from encounters on the stairs, we should probably see very little of each other. Of course there might be some embarrassment about the sharing of the bathroom, but I must try to conquer it. I should certainly have my bath *early* so as to avoid clashing. I might perhaps buy myself a new and more becoming dressing-gown, one that I wouldn't mind being seen in, something long and warm in a rich colour . . . I must have dropped off to sleep at this point, for the next thing I knew was that I had been woken up by the sound of the front door banging. I switched on the light and saw that it was ten minutes to one. I hoped the Napiers were not going to keep late hours and have noisy parties. Perhaps I was getting spinsterish and 'set' in my ways, but I was irritated at having been woken. I stretched out my hand towards the little bookshelf where I kept cookery and devotional books, the most comforting bedside reading. My hand might have chosen *Religio Medici*, but I was rather glad that it had picked out *Chinese Cookery* and I was soon soothed into drowsiness.

CHAPTER THREE

IT WAS SEVERAL days before I saw Mrs Napier again, although I heard her going in and out and there seemed to be voices coming from her room every evening. I had an idea that I might ask her in to coffee sometime but hesitated about it because I did not quite know how to convey the impression that it was not, of course, to become a regular thing. I wanted to appear civil rather than friendly. One day a new roll of toilet paper of a rather inferior brand appeared in the lavatory, and I also noticed that an attempt had been made to clean the bath. It was not as well done as I should have liked to see it; people do not always realize that cleaning a bath properly can be quite hard work.

'I suppose *she* did it,' said Mrs Morris, my 'woman', who came twice a week. 'She doesn't look as if she could clean anything.'

Mrs Morris was a Welshwoman who had come to London as a girl but still retained her native accent. I marvelled as always at her secret knowledge, when, as far as I knew, she had not yet set eyes on Mrs Napier.

'Kettle's boiling, miss,' she said, and I knew that it must be eleven o'clock, for she made this remark so regularly that I should have thought something was wrong if she had forgotten.

'Oh, good, then let's have our tea,' I said, making the response expected of me. I waited for Mrs Morris to say, 'There's a drop of milk in this jug,' as she always did on discovering the remains of yesterday's milk, and then we were ready for our tea.

'I was cleaning at the vicarage yesterday, those rooms they're going to let,' said Mrs Morris. 'Miss Malory was saying how she wanted you to go there.'

'Yes, I know, but I think it's really better for me to stay here,' I said.

'Yes, indeed, Miss Lathbury. It wouldn't be right at all for you to live at the vicarage.'

'Well, Father Malory and Miss Malory are my friends.'

'Yes, but it wouldn't be right. If Miss Malory was to go away now . . .'

'You think it wouldn't be quite respectable?' I asked.

'Respectable?' Mrs Morris stiffened, and straightened the dark felt hat she always wore. 'That isn't for me to say, Miss Lathbury. But it isn't natural for a man not to be married.'

'Clergymen don't always want to,' I explained, 'or they think it better they shouldn't.'

'Strong passions, isn't it,' she muttered obscurely. 'Eating meat, you know, it says that in the Bible. Not that we get much of it now. If he was a *real* Father like Father Bogart,' she went on, naming the priest of the Roman Catholic Church in our district, 'you could understand it.'

'But Mrs Morris, you're a regular churchwoman. I thought you liked Father Malory.'

'Oh, yes, I've nothing against him really, but it isn't right.' She finished her tea and went over to the sink. 'I'll just wash up these things.'

I watched her stiff uncompromising back which hardly seemed to bend even though the sink was a low one.

'Has something upset you?' I asked. 'Something about Father Malory?'

'Oh, miss,' she turned to face me, her hands red and dripping from the hot water. 'It's that old black thing he wears on his head in church.'

'You mean his biretta?' I asked, puzzled.

'I don't know what he calls it. Like a little hat, it is.'

'But you've been going to St Mary's for years,' I said. 'You must have got used to it by now.'

'Well, it was my sister Gladys and her husband, been staying with us they have. I took them to church Sunday evening and they didn't like it at all, nor the incense, said it was Roman Catholic or something and we'd all be kissing the Pope's toe before you could say knife.'

She sat down with the drying-cloth in her hands. She looked so worried that I had to stop myself smiling.

'Of course,' she went on, 'Evan and I have always been to St Mary's because it's near, but it isn't like the church I went to as a girl, where Mr Lewis was vicar. He didn't have incense or wear that old black hat.'

'No, I don't suppose he did,' I agreed, for I knew the seaside town she came from and I remembered the 'English' church, unusual among so many chapels, with the Ten Commandments in Welsh and in English on either side of the altar and a special service on Sunday morning for the visitors. I did not remember that they had expected or received 'Catholic privileges'.

'I was always church,' said Mrs Morris proudly. 'Never been in the chapel, though I did once go to the Ebenezer social, but I don't want to have anything to do with some old Pope. Kissing his toe, indeed!' She looked up at me, half laughing, not quite sure if Gladys and her husband had been joking when they said it.

'There's a statue in St Peter's Church in Rome,' I explained, 'and people do kiss the toe. But that's only *Roman*

Catholics,' I said in a loud clear voice. 'Don't you remember Father Malory explaining about the Pope in his Sunday morning sermons last year?'

'Oh, Sunday morning, was it?' she laughed derisively. 'That's all very fine, standing up and talking about the Pope. A lot of us could do that. But who's going to cook the Sunday dinner?'

No answer seemed to be needed or expected to this question, and we laughed together, a couple of women against the whole race of men. Mrs Morris dried her hands, fumbled in the pocket of her apron and took out a squashed packet of cigarettes. 'Let's have a fag, any road,' she said cheerfully. 'I'll just tell Gladys what you said, Miss Lathbury, about it being some old statue.'

I did not feel that I had done as well as I might have in my attempt to instruct Mrs Morris in the differences between the Roman Church and ours, but I did not think that Julian Malory could have done much better.

After she had gone I boiled myself a foreign egg for lunch and was just making some coffee when there was a knock on the kitchen door.

It was Mrs Napier.

'I've come to ask something rather awkward,' she said, smiling.

'Well, come in and have a cup of coffee with me. I was just making some.'

'Thank you, that would be nice.'

We went into the sitting-room and I switched on the fire. She looked around her with frank interest and curiosity.

'Rather nice,' she said. 'I suppose this is the best from the country rectory?'

'Most of it,' I said, 'and I've bought a few things from time to time.'

'Look,' she said abruptly, 'I was wondering if your woman, the one who's been here this morning, could possibly do for me at all? Perhaps on the mornings when you're not here?'

'I dare say she would be glad to have some more work,' I said, 'and she's quite good. She does go to the vicarage occasionally.'

'Oh, the vicarage.' Mrs Napier made a face. 'Will the vicar call?'

'I can ask him to, if you like,' I said seriously. 'He and his sister are friends of mine.'

'He isn't married then? One of *those* . . . I mean,' she added apologetically as if she had said something that might offend me, 'one of the kind who don't marry?'

'Well, he isn't married and as he's about forty I dare say he won't now.' I seemed to have spent so much time lately in talking about the celibacy of the clergy in general and Julian Malory in particular that I was a little tired of the subject.

'That's just when they break out,' laughed Mrs Napier. 'I always imagine that clergymen need wives to help them with their parish work, but I suppose most of his congregation are devout elderly women with nothing much to do, so that's all right. Holy fowl, you know.'

I felt that I did not like Mrs Napier any more than I had at our first meeting, and she was dropping ash all over my newly brushed carpet.

'Will your husband be coming back soon?' I asked, to break the rather awkward silence that had developed.

'Oh, soon enough,' she said casually. She stubbed out her cigarette in a little dish that wasn't meant to be an ashtray and began walking about the room. 'I know it sounds awful,' she said, standing by the window, 'but I'm not really looking forward to his coming very much.'

'Oh, that's probably because you haven't seen him for some time,' I said, in a bright sensible tone.

'That doesn't really make any difference. There's more to it than that.'

'But surely it will be all right once he is here and you've

had a little time together?' I said, beginning to feel the inadequacy that an unmarried and inexperienced woman must always feel when discussing such things.

'Perhaps it will. But we're so different. We met at a party during the war and fell in love in the silly romantic way people did then. You know . . .'

'Yes, I suppose people did.' In my Censorship days I had read that they did and I had sometimes wanted to intervene and tell them to wait a little longer, until they were quite sure.

'Rockingham is rather good-looking, of course, and everyone thinks him charming and amusing. He has some money of his own and likes to dabble in painting. But you see,' she turned to me very seriously, 'he knows nothing about anthropology and cares less.'

I listened in bewildered silence. 'Why, ought he to?' I asked stupidly.

'Well, I did this field trip in Africa when he was away and I met Everard Bone, who was in the Army out there. He's an anthropologist too. You may have seen him on the stairs.'

'Oh, yes, I think I have. A tall man with fair hair.'

'We've done a lot of work together, and it does give one a special link with a person, to have done any academic work with him. Rockingham and I just haven't got that.'

Did she always call him Rockingham? I wondered irrelevantly. It sounded so formal, and yet it was difficult to know how to abbreviate it unless one called him Rocky or used some other name.

'Surely you and your husband have other things in common, though, perhaps deeper and more lasting than this work?' I asked, feeling that I must try to take my part in this difficult conversation. I hardly liked to think that she might also have these other things with Everard Bone. Indeed, I did not think that I liked Everard Bone at all, if he was the person I had seen on the stairs. His name, his pointed nose, and the air of priggishness which fair men sometimes have, had set me against him. Also, and here I was ready to admit that I was old-fashioned and knew nothing of the ways of anthropologists, I did not think it quite proper that they should have worked together while Rockingham Napier was serving his country. Here the picture of the Wren officers in their ill-fitting white uniforms obtruded itself, but I resolutely pushed it back. Whatever he may have had to do, he had been serving his country.

'Of course,' Mrs Napier went on, 'when you're first in love, everything about the other person seems delightful, especially if it shows the difference between you. Rocky's very tidy and I'm not.'

So he could be called Rocky now. Somehow it made him seem more human.

'You should see my bedside table, such a clutter of objects, cigarettes, cosmetics, aspirins, glasses of water, *The Golden Bough*, a detective story, any object that happens to take my fancy. Rocky used to think that so sweet, but after a while it maddened him, it was just a mess.'

'I suppose it does get like that,' I said. 'One ought to be careful of one's little ways.' Dora's beaded cover on the milk jug, her love of bakelite plates, and all the irritating things I did myself and didn't know about . . . perhaps even my cookery books by my bed might drive somebody mad. 'But surely that's only a detail,' I said, 'and it ought not to affect the deeper relationship.'

'Of course you've never been married,' she said, putting me in my place among the rows of excellent women. 'Oh, well . . .' she moved towards the door. 'I suppose we shall go our own ways. That's how most marriages turn out and it could be worse.'

'Oh, but you mustn't say that,' I burst out, having all the romantic ideals of the unmarried. 'I'm sure everything will be all right really.'

She shrugged her shoulders. 'Thank you for the coffee,

anyway, and a sympathetic hearing. I really ought to apologize for talking to you like this, but confession is supposed to be good for the soul.'

I murmured something, but I did not think I had been particularly sympathetic and I certainly had not felt it, for people like the Napiers had not so far come within my range of experience. I was much more at home with Winifred and Julian Malory, Dora Caldicote, and the worthy but uninteresting people whom I met at my work or in connection with the church. Such married couples as I knew appeared to be quite contented, or if they were not they did not talk about their difficulties to comparative strangers. There was certainly no mention of them 'going their own ways', and yet how did I really know that they didn't? This idea raised disquieting thoughts and doubts, so I turned on the wireless to distract me. But it was a woman's programme and they all sounded so married and splendid, their lives so full and yet so well organized, that I felt more than usually spinsterish and useless. Mrs Napier must be hard up for friends if she could find nobody better than me to confide in, I thought. At last I went downstairs to see if there were any letters. There was nothing for me, but two for Mrs Napier, from one of which I learned that her Christian name was Helena. It sounded rather old-fashioned and dignified, not at all the kind of name I should have imagined for her. Perhaps it was a good omen for the future that she should have such a name.

CHAPTER FOUR

IT WAS CERTAINLY unfortunate that Helena Napier should be out when the telegram came. Wives ought to be waiting for their husbands to come back from the wars, I felt, though perhaps unreasonably, when a few hours by aeroplane can transport a husband from Italy to England.

I heard her bell being rung and then mine, and when I opened the door and saw the boy standing there with the telegram I knew at once as if by instinct what its news must be. The question was, when would he arrive? It sounded as if it might be that very evening and I had heard Mrs Napier go out about six o'clock. She was probably meeting Everard Bone somewhere. Ought I to try to find out where she was and let her know? I felt that I ought to make an attempt and began searching through the telephone directory to see if I could find his number. If I couldn't, so much the better – I should be saved from interfering in something which didn't really concern me. But there it was, a Chelsea address – there could hardly be two Everard Bones. I dialled the number fearfully and heard it ring. 'Hello, hello, who is that?' a querulous elderly woman's voice answered. I was completely taken aback, but before I could speak the voice went on. 'If it's Miss Jessop I can only hope you are ringing up to apologize.' I stammered out an explanation. I was not Miss Jessop. Was Mr Everard Bone there? 'My son is at a meeting of the Prehistoric Society,' said the voice. 'Oh, I see. I'm so sorry to have bothered you,' I said. 'People are always bothering me – I never wanted to have the telephone put in at all.'

After a further apology I hung up the receiver, shaken and mystified but at the same time relieved. Everard Bone was at a meeting of the Prehistoric Society. It sounded like a joke. I could hardly be expected to pursue my enquiries any further, so I decided that I was an interfering busybody and went upstairs to get my supper. I opened a tin of baked beans, thinking that it would be easy and quick, for I could not rid myself of the feeling that Rockingham Napier might arrive at any moment and that I might have to go down and open the door. He would certainly have no latch-key and he might not have had supper. I now began to feel almost agitated; I hurried about the kitchen, eating the baked beans in ten minutes or less, quite without dignity, and then washing up. I had made a cup of coffee and taken it into the sitting-room when I heard a taxi draw up and then Mrs Napier's bell ringing.

I hesitated at the top of the stairs, feeling nervous and stupid, for this was a situation I had not experienced before, and my training did not seem to be quite equal to it. Also, I suddenly thought of the parrot in a cage and that was distracting.

I opened the door rather timidly, hoping that he would not be too disappointed when he saw that I was not his wife.

'I'm afraid Mrs Napier is out,' I said, 'but I heard the bell and came down.'

It was a good thing he began talking, for I am not used to meeting handsome men and I am afraid that I must have been staring at him rather rudely. And yet it was his manner that charmed me rather than his looks, though he was dark and elegant and had all those attributes that are usually considered to make a man handsome.

'How very nice of you to come down,' he said, and I could see, though it is impossible to put it into words, exactly what Helena had meant when she talked about him putting the awkward Wren officers at their ease. 'It's lucky for me you were in. I think you must be Miss Lathbury.'

'Yes, I am,' I said, surprised. 'But how did you know?'

'Helena mentioned you in a letter.'

I could not help wondering how she had described me. 'Yes, we have met once or twice,' I said, 'I live in the flat above you.'

We were going upstairs now, I leading the way and he following with his suitcases. Fortunately the doors of their flat were unlocked and I showed him into the sitting-room.

'Oh, my things, how good it is to be with them again!' he exclaimed, going over to the bookcase and picking up one of the paperweights which were arranged on the top. 'And my chairs, too. Don't you think they're beautiful?'

'Yes, they are lovely,' I said, hovering in the doorway. 'Do let me know if there's anything I can do, won't you?'

'Oh, please, don't go, unless you have to, that is . . .?' He turned his charming smile full on me and I felt a little dazed.

'Have you had anything to eat?' I asked.

'Yes, thank you. I had dinner on the train. It isn't wise to drop in on Helena and expect to find a meal ready or even anything in the larder. I'm afraid we don't always agree about the importance of civilized eating.' He looked round the room. 'Quite pleasing, isn't it? I rather feared the worst when Helena told me where we were going to live.'

'I'm afraid it isn't one of the best parts of London,' I said, 'but I'm fond of it.'

'Yes, I believe it may have a certain *Stimmung*. If you live in an unfashionable district you have to find at least that to make it tolerable.'

I was not quite sure what he meant. 'I like to think of it when it was a marsh and wild boars roamed over it,' I ventured, remembering something I had read in the local weekly paper. 'And Aubrey Beardsley lived here once, you know. There is a plaque marking his house.'

'Oh, perfect!' He seemed pleased. 'That does make things rather better. Those exquisite drawings.'

Personally I thought them disgusting, but I made a non-committal reply.

'It's going to be very cold after Italy, though.' He shivered and rubbed his hands together.

'I don't know whether you would like to come up to my

flat for a while?' I suggested. 'I have a fire and was just going to make some coffee. But perhaps you'd rather unpack?'

'No, I should love some coffee.'

'What a charming room,' he said when we were in it. 'You are obviously a person of taste.'

I could not help being pleased at the implied compliment but felt bound to explain that most of the furniture had come from my old home.

'Ah, yes,' he paused, as if remembering something, 'from the old rectory. Helena told me that, too.'

I went into the kitchen and busied myself making more coffee.

'I hope you've had your meal?' he said, coming in and watching me. 'I've arrived at rather an awkward time.'

I explained that I had just finished supper and added that I found it rather a bother cooking just for myself. 'I like food,' I said, 'but I suppose on the whole women don't make such a business of living as men do.' I thought of my half-used tin of baked beans; no doubt I should be seeing that again tomorrow.

'No, and women don't really appreciate wine either. I suppose you wouldn't dream of drinking a bottle of wine by yourself, would you?'

'Of course not,' I said, rather primly, I am afraid.

'That's what's so wonderful about living out of England,' he said, pacing round the small kitchen, 'such a glorious feeling of well-being, sitting at a table in the sun with a bottle of whatever it happens to be – there's nothing to equal that, is there?'

'Yes, I like sitting at a table in the sun,' I agreed, 'but I'm afraid I'm one of those typical English tourists who always wants a cup of tea.'

'And when it comes, it's a pale straw-coloured liquid . . .'

'And the tea's in a funny little bag . . .'

'And they may even bring *hot* milk with it . . .'

We both began laughing.

'But even that has its own kind of charm,' I said stubbornly; 'it's all part of the foreign atmosphere.'

'The English tourists certainly are,' he said, 'though there weren't any in Italy, of course. I think that was what was lacking, what made life so unnatural. The sightseers were all in uniform, there were no English gentlewomen with Baedekers and large straw hats. I missed that.'

We went on talking about Italy and then somehow I was telling him about the neighbourhood, Julian Malory and his sister and the church.

'High Mass – with music and incense? Oh, I should like that,' he said. 'I hope it is the *best* quality incense? I believe it varies.'

'Yes, I've seen advertisements,' I admitted, 'and they have different names. Lambeth is *very* expensive, but Pax is quite cheap. It seems as if it ought to be the other way round.'

'And have you dozens of glamorous acolytes?'

'Well . . .' I hesitated, remembering Teddy Lemon, our Master of Ceremonies, with his rough curly hair and anxious face, and his troop of well-drilled, tough-looking little boys, 'they are very nice good boys, but perhaps you should go to a Kensington church if you want to see glamorous acolytes. I hope you will come to our church sometimes,' I added more seriously, for I felt that Julian would expect me to 'say a word' here.

'Oh, yes, I shall look in. I'm very fond of going to church, but I don't like doing anything before breakfast, you know. That's always seemed to me to be the great snag about religion, don't you agree?'

'Well, one feels that a thing is more worth doing if it's something of an effort,' I attempted.

'You mean virtue goes out of you? Ah, yes, how it does, or rather how it would if there was any to go out of me,' he sighed. 'I'm sure you have so much.'

I did not altogether like his frivolous attitude, but I could not help liking him. He was so easy to talk to and I could see him at any social gathering, using his charm to make people feel at home, or rather not consciously using it, for the exercise of it seemed natural to him as if he could not help being charming.

We were still talking about churches when we heard voices on the stairs.

'Do excuse me,' he said, 'that must be Helena. Thank you so much for being so kind to me. I hope we shall be meeting often.' He ran out on to the landing and down the stairs.

I put the coffee cups on to a tray and took them into the kitchen. It was a pity, I felt, that Everard Bone should intrude on the Napiers' reunion. Still, Helena would no doubt be capable of managing the two of them and it was to be hoped that Everard Bone would have the tact to go away quickly and leave them alone. I was just starting to wash the cups when there was a knock at the door. Rockingham stood there with a straw-covered flask of wine in his hand.

'We feel this is an occasion,' he said, 'and should like you to join us. That is, if you approve of drinking wine at this hour.'

'Oh, but surely you'd rather be by yourselves . . .'

'Well, the anthropologist is with us, so it seemed a good idea to make it a party,' he explained.

I began taking off my apron and tidying my hair, apologizing as I did so, in what I felt was a stupid, fussy way, for my appearance. As if anyone would care how I looked or even notice me, I told myself scornfully.

'You look very nice,' said Rockingham, smiling in such a way that he could almost have meant it.

Helena and Everard Bone were in the sitting-room, she putting glasses out and he standing over by the window. I was able to study his profile with its sharp-pointed nose and decide that I disliked it, until he turned towards me and stared with what seemed to be disapproval.

'Good evening,' I said, feeling very silly.

'You do know each other, don't you?' said Helena.

'Yes, at least I've seen Mr Bone on the stairs,' I explained.

'Oh, yes, I do remember meeting somebody on the stairs once or twice,' he said indifferently. 'Was it you?'

'Yes.'

'How marvellous that you were here when Rocky arrived,' said Helena in a quick nervous tone, 'too awful for him, coming home to an empty house, but he said you were marvellous and I don't believe he's missed me at all, have you, darling?'

She did not wait for him to answer but ran back into the kitchen to fetch something. Rockingham was pouring the wine, so that I was left standing awkwardly with Everard.

'I believe you're an anthropologist,' I said, making what I felt was a brave attempt at conversation. 'But I'm afraid I don't know anything about anthropology.'

'Why should you?' he asked, half smiling.

'It must be fun,' I floundered, 'I mean, going round Africa and doing all that.'

' "Fun" is hardly the word,' he said. 'It's very hard work, learning an impossibly difficult language, then endless questionings and statistics, writing up notes and all the rest of it.'

'No, I suppose it isn't,' I said soberly, for he had certainly not made it sound fun. 'But there must be something satisfying in having done it, a sort of feeling of achievement?'

'Achievement?' He shrugged his shoulders. 'But what *has* one done really? I sometimes wonder if it isn't all a waste of time.'

'It depends what you set out to do,' I said rather crossly, feeling like Alice in Wonderland. I was doing very badly here and was grateful when Rockingham came to the rescue.

'Oh, they hate you to think they get any enjoyment out of it,' he said rather spitefully.

'But I do enjoy it,' said Helena; 'we aren't all as dreary as

Everard. I simply loved it. And now we've got to do all the writing up; that's what we've been discussing this evening. We're to give a paper before one of the learned societies. Miss Lathbury,' she turned to me with unnatural animation, 'you simply must come and hear it.'

'Yes, Miss Lathbury, you and I will sit at the back and observe the anthropologists,' said Rockingham. 'They study mankind and we will study them.'

'Well, the society is in many ways a primitive community,' said Everard, 'and offers the same opportunities for fieldwork.'

'When is it to be?' I asked.

'Oh, quite soon, next month even,' said Helena.

'We must *get on*,' said Everard in an irritable tone. 'The thing will never be ready if we don't hurry.'

'It must take a lot of work putting it all together,' I said. 'I should be very nervous at the thought of it.'

'Oh, well, it isn't that. Our stuff is quite new but one wants it to be good.'

'Oh, certainly,' I agreed.

'Well, darling . . .' Helena looked at her husband and raised her glass. 'Isn't it lovely to have him back again?' she said to nobody in particular.

Everard said nothing but raised his glass politely, so I did the same.

'More to drink!' said Rockingham with rather forced gaiety. He came towards me with the straw-covered flask and I let him refill my glass, although it was by no means empty. I began to see how people could need drink to cover up embarrassments, and I remembered many sticky church functions which might have been improved if somebody had happened to open a bottle of wine. But people like us had to rely on the tea-urn and I felt that some credit was due to us for doing as well as we did on that harmless stimulant. This party, if such it could be called, was not going well and I did not feel socially equal to the situation. My experience, which had admittedly been a little narrow, had not so far included anything in the least like it. I wished that Everard Bone would go, but he was talking seriously to Helena about some aspect of their paper, ignoring or not noticing the awkwardness. At last, however, he said he must be going, and said good night quite pleasantly to Rockingham and me and rather more coldly to Helena, mentioning that he would be ringing her up within the next few days about the kinship diagrams.

'We must *get on*,' he repeated.

'I shall look forward to hearing your paper,' I said, feeling that some effort was required and that it was up to me to make it.

'Oh, you will find it deadly dull,' he said. 'You mustn't expect too much.'

I forebore to remark that women like me really expected very little – nothing, almost.

'Well, well,' said Rockingham as we heard the front door close, 'so that is the great Everard Bone.'

'Great?' said Helena, surprised. 'I'm afraid he was at his worst tonight. Don't you think he's intolerably pompous and boring, Miss Lathbury?' She turned to me, her eyes shining.

'He seems very nice and he's certainly rather good-looking.'

'Oh, do you think so? I don't find fair men at all attractive.'

It seemed pointless to follow up that line, so I admitted that I had found him difficult to talk to, but that that was not surprising since I was not used to meeting intellectuals.

'Oh, he's impossible!' she burst out.

'Never mind, wait till you see what I've brought for you,' said Rockingham in a soothing tone as if speaking to a child. 'I've got some majolica and a pottery breakfast set packed up with my other luggage, and the usual trifles here.' He opened one of his suitcases and took out a bottle of perfume, several pairs of silk stockings and some small pottery objects. 'And you mustn't go yet, Miss Lathbury,' he called, seeing me moving uncertainly towards the door. 'I should like you to have something.'

He put a little china goat into my hand. 'There, let it go among the bearded archdeacons and suchlike.'

'Oh, it's charming – thank you so much . . .'

I went upstairs and put it on the table by my bed. Had he been a little drunk? I wondered. I believed the wine had made me feel a little unsteady too, but then I was not used to it and the whole evening had a fantastic air about it, as if it couldn't really have happened.

I lay awake feeling thirsty and obscurely worried about something. Well, there was really no need for me to see very much of the Napiers. Circumstances had thrown us together this evening but tomorrow we should all be keeping to ourselves. I did not suppose that Helena would remember her invitation to me to hear their paper at the learned society, so I would not expect it. I would ask Dora to stay in the Easter holidays. I couldn't see her getting on very well with Rockingham, or Rocky as I now thought of him. He was not at all the sort of person either of us had been used to meeting, yet I seemed to have found it quite easy to talk to him, I thought smugly. But then I remembered the Wren officers and I knew what it was that was worrying me. It was part of his charm that he could make people like that feel at ease. He must be rather a shallow sort of person really. Not nearly so worthwhile as Julian Malory, or Mr Mallett and Mr Conybeare our churchwardens, or even Teddy Lemon, who had no social graces . . . as I dozed off I remembered that I had forgotten to say my prayers. There came into my mind a picture of Mr Mallett, with raised finger and roguish voice, saying, 'Tut, tut, Miss Lathbury . . .'

CHAPTER FIVE

THE NEXT afternoon I was helping Winifred to sort out things for the jumble sale.

'Oh, I think it's *dreadful* when people send their relations to jumble sales,' she said. 'How *can* they do it?' She held up a tarnished silver frame from which the head and shoulders of a woman dressed in Edwardian style looked out. 'And here's another, a clergyman, too.'

'A very young curate, just out of the egg, I should think,' I said, looking over her shoulder at the smooth beardless face above the high collar.

'It might almost be somebody we know,' lamented Winifred. 'Imagine if it were and one saw it lying on the stall! What a shock it would be! I really think I must take the photographs out – it's the frames people will want to buy.'

'I don't suppose their own relatives send them,' I said comfortingly. 'I expect the photographs have been in the box-room for years and nobody knows who they are now.'

'Yes, I suppose that's it. But it's the idea of being unwanted, it's like sending a *person* to a jumble sale – do you see? You feel it more as you get older, of course. Young people would only laugh and think what a silly idea.'

I could see very well what she meant, for unmarried women with no ties could very well become unwanted. I should feel it even more than Winifred, for who was there really to grieve for me when I was gone? Dora, the Malorys, one or two people in my old village might be sorry, but I was not really first in anybody's life. I could so very easily be replaced . . . I thought it better not to go into this too deeply with Winifred, for she was of a romantic, melancholy nature, apt to imagine herself in situations. She kept by her bed a volume of Christina Rossetti's poems bound in limp green suede, though she had not, as far as I knew, had the experience to make those much-quoted poems appropriate. I feel sure that she would have told me if there had been someone of whom she could think when she read

Better by far you should forget and smile,
Than that you should remember and be sad . . .

'Well, you'll never be unwanted,' I said cheerfully. 'Goodness knows what Julian would do without you.'

'Oh, my goodness!' She laughed as if she had suddenly remembered something. 'You should just see him now! He had the idea that he'd distemper the rooms we're going to let and he's got into such a mess. I started to help, but then I remembered I had to do these things, so Miss Statham and Miss Enders and Sister Blatt are up there giving helpful advice.'

'Oh, dear, I should think he needs more practical help than that,' I said. 'May I go up and see?'

'Yes, do. I'll go on sorting out these things. You know, I think I shall buy this skirt for myself,' I heard her murmuring; 'there's a *lot* of wear in it yet.'

The sound of women's voices raised in what seemed to be a lamentation led me to a large room on the top floor, where I found Julian Malory sitting on top of a stepladder, holding a brush and wearing an old cassock streaked with yellow distemper. Standing round him were Miss Statham and Miss Enders, two birdlike little women whom I tended to confuse, and Sister Blatt, stout and rosy in her grey uniform, with a blunt no-nonsense manner.

They were all staring at a wall which Julian had apparently just finished.

'Well, I hope it's going to dry a different colour,' said Sister Blatt; 'the one it is now would drive anyone mad.'

'It said Old Gold on the tin,' said Julian unhappily. 'Perhaps I mixed it too thickly.'

'Of the consistency of thin cream,' said Miss Enders, reading from the tin. 'That's how it should be.'

'Of course it's difficult to remember what cream was like,' said Miss Statham. 'I suppose *thin* cream might be like the top of the milk.'

'Oh, Mildred,' Julian waved his brush towards me in a despairing gesture, showering everybody with drops of distemper, 'do come to the rescue!'

'What can I do?'

'Nothing,' said Sister Blatt, almost with satisfaction. 'I'm afraid Father Malory has done the wall the wrong colour. The only thing will be to wait till it's dry and then do it over again with a lighter shade. And it looks so streaky, too,' she bent down and peered closely at the wall. 'Oh dear, oh dear, I'm afraid *I* shouldn't care to live with walls that colour.'

'I believe it *does* dry lighter,' I said hopefully.

'I wish I'd got the boys' club to do it,' said Julian. 'I'm afraid I'm no good at practical things. I always think it must be such a satisfying feeling, to do good work with one's hands. I'm sure I've preached about it often enough.'

'Ah, well, we aren't meant to be satisfied in this world,' said Sister Blatt; 'perhaps that's what it is.'

Julian smiled. 'It seems a little hard that I shouldn't be allowed even this small satisfaction, but I've certainly learnt humility this afternoon, so the exercise will have served some purpose. It looked so easy, too,' he added sadly.

'Oh, well, things are never as easy as they seem to be,' said Miss Statham complacently.

'No, they certainly are not,' agreed Miss Enders, who was a dressmaker. 'People often say to me that they're just going to run up a cotton dress or a straight skirt, but then they find it isn't as easy as it looks and they come running to me to put it right.'

'I wish you could put this right, Miss Enders,' said Julian, drooping on the top of his ladder.

'Look,' I called out, 'it *is* drying lighter, and quite evenly too. I suppose it would naturally be darker when it was wet.'

'Why, so it is,' said Sister Blatt. 'It's quite a nice colour now.'

'Mildred, how clever of you,' said Julian gratefully. 'I knew you would help.'

'Well, well, now that we've seen you on your way we may as well be going on ours,' said Sister Blatt good-humouredly.

'Thank you for your help and advice,' said Julian with a touch of irony.

'Is Father Malory going to attempt the ceiling?' asked Miss Statham in a low voice.

'That's the most difficult part,' said Miss Enders.

'Oh, well, as a clergyman he will naturally wish to make the attempt,' said Sister Blatt, with a jolly laugh. 'Perhaps Miss Lathbury will help him. I'm afraid the ladder would hardly bear my weight,' she added comfortably, looking down at her grey-clad bulk. 'In any case, I believe the ceiling should have been done *before* the walls. If you do the ceiling now, Father, the walls will get splashed with white.'

'So they will,' said Julian patiently. 'Excellent women,' he sighed, when they had gone. 'I think we will knock off for tea now, don't you?'

'You could ask for volunteers from the choir or the boys' club to finish it,' I suggested. 'I'm sure Teddy Lemon would be good at that kind of thing. Men love messing about with paint and distemper.'

'I suppose I am not to be considered as a normal man,' said Julian, taking off his yellow-streaked cassock and draping it over the step ladder, 'and yet I do have these manly feelings.'

We found Winifred in the hall with a case of stuffed birds.

'Look,' she said, 'from Mrs Noad – the usual.'

'The house must be quite bare of birds considering that she sends some to every sale,' I remarked.

'Oh, there are plenty more,' said Julian. 'I believe these come from the lumber-room. There are even finer specimens in the hall, some quite menacing with raised wings. These are *very* small ones, almost like sparrows.'

'Oh, they'll go like hot cakes,' said Winifred; 'there's always competition to buy them. Let's go and have tea.'

Tea at the vicarage was a safer meal than most and today there was even a rather plain-looking cake.

'I must ask the Napiers if they have any jumble,' I said. 'He may have some old civilian suit that he doesn't want or even a uniform with the buttons and braid removed.'

'One hears that so many husbands coming back from the war find that their civilian clothes have been devoured by *moth*,' said Winifred seriously. 'That must be a dreadful shock.'

'Oh, the women should look after that sort of thing,' said Julian. 'Mothballs, camphor and so on,' he added vaguely. 'I believe it's perfectly possible to keep the moth at bay. Do you think Mrs Napier has done her duty in that respect?'

'I don't know,' I said slowly, for it occurred to me that perhaps she had not. I could not imagine her doing these methodical wifely things.

'Have you met *him* yet?' Winifred asked.

'Oh, yes, he's charming. Good-looking, amusing and so easy to talk to. I'm very much taken with him.'

'It sounds almost as if you have fallen in love with him,' said Julian teasingly, 'if he has made such a favourable first impression.'

'Oh, that's ridiculous!' I protested. 'I've only met him once and he's probably younger than I am. Besides, he's a married man.'

'I'm very glad to hear you say that, Mildred,' said Julian more seriously. 'So many people nowadays seem to forget that it should be a barrier.'

'Now, Julian, we don't want a sermon,' said Winifred. 'You know Mildred would never do anything wrong or foolish.'

I reflected a little sadly that this was only too true and hoped I did not appear too much that kind of person to others. Virtue is an excellent thing and we should all strive after it, but it can sometimes be a little depressing.

'Pass Mildred something to eat,' said Winifred.

'I hope she knows us well enough to help herself without being asked,' said Julian, 'otherwise I'm afraid she would get very little.'

I took another piece of cake and there was a short lull in the conversation, during which I considered Julian's suggestion that I might have fallen in love with Rockingham Napier. It was of course quite impossible, but I certainly felt the power of his charm, and I should often have to remind myself of the awkward Wren officers and how he had made them feel at ease in the Admiral's villa. But I have never been very much given to falling in love and have often felt sorry that I have so far missed not only the experience of marriage, but the perhaps even greater and more ennobling one of having loved and lost. Of course there had been a curate or two in my schooldays and later a bank-clerk who read the lessons, but none of these passions had gone very deep.

'And now,' said Julian, taking advantage of the silence, '*I* have an announcement to make.'

'Oh, what is it?' we both exclaimed.

'I believe I have found a tenant for our flat.'

'Oh, Julian, how exciting!' Winifred waved her hands in an impulsive movement and knocked over the hot-water jug. '*Do* tell us who it is!'

'Is it somebody really suitable?' I asked.

'Most suitable, I think,' said Julian. 'She is a Mrs Gray, a widow.'

'That sounds excellent. A Mrs Gray, a widow,' I repeated. 'I can just imagine her.'

'Oh, so can I!' said Winifred enthusiastically. 'A neat little person of about sixty, rather nicely dressed.'

'Well, I'm afraid you're quite wrong,' said Julian. 'I should think she is very little older than Mildred. And she is tall, but nicely dressed, I dare say; you know I don't really notice such things.'

'But where did you find her?' I asked. 'Did you advertise in the *Church Times*?'

'No, that was not necessary. She is actually living in this parish, in furnished rooms at the moment. You may have seen her in church, though she told me she always sat at the back.'

'Oh, really? I wonder . . .' Winifred began to enumerate all the strangers she had noticed lately, but somehow we did not seem to be able to identify Mrs Gray. Julian's description was vague enough to fit any of two or three women we could remember having noticed as strangers.

'How did she know about the flat?' I asked.

'She went to Miss Enders to have a dress altered and I suppose they got talking. Then she mentioned the matter to Father Greatorex and he told me. She felt she did not like to approach me directly. She is a clergyman's widow, you see,' Julian added, as if this would explain a delicacy not usually displayed by people engaged in the desperate business of flat-hunting.

'Oh, *good*,' I exclaimed involuntarily, for I had an inexplicable distrust of widows, who seem to be of two distinct kinds, one of which may be dangerous. I felt that Mrs Gray sounded very definitely of the safer kind.

'I gather that she hasn't much money,' said Julian, 'so I hardly know what would be a fair rent to ask. I found I couldn't bring myself to mention it, and neither, apparently, could she.'

'Well, really, I should have thought that would have been her first question,' I said, thinking what a remarkably delicate conversation they must have had. 'She can hardly expect to get three rooms for nothing. You must be careful she doesn't try to do you down.'

'Oh, Mildred,' Julian looked grieved, 'you wouldn't say that if you had seen her. She has such sad eyes.'

'No; I'm sorry,' I mumbled, for I had been forgetting that she was a clergyman's widow.

'Of course we don't want to make any profit out of it,'

said Winifred, 'so I'm sure we can come to some friendly arrangement. Perhaps *I* could discuss it with her; it might be less embarrassing with a woman.'

Julian looked at his sister doubtfully and then at me. 'Of course Mildred would be the ideal person,' he said.

'You mean because I'm used to dealing with impoverished gentlewomen?' I asked. 'But I'm afraid it's made me develop a rather suspicious attitude. You see, we sometimes get people who aren't genuine and every case has to be carefully investigated.'

'Really, how distressing! I had no idea people would try that sort of thing.'

'How terrible!' said Winifred. 'It always saddens me when I hear of wickedness like that. Especially among gentlewomen.'

'Yes, perhaps one does expect rather more of them,' I agreed, 'but I can assure you it does sometimes happen.' The Malorys often gave me a feeling that I knew more of the wickedness of the world than they did, especially as I had learned much of the weakness of human nature in my Censorship work, but so much of my knowledge was at second hand that I doubted whether there was much to choose between us in worldly wisdom. But I did feel that they were simpler and more trusting by nature than I was.

'Oh, I expect I shall be able to manage it quite satisfactorily,' said Julian. 'It would hardly be fair to expect Mildred to deal with something that doesn't concern her at all.'

'I will if you like,' I said doubtfully, 'but of course it's not really my business.' I did not then know to the extent I do now that practically anything may be the business of an unattached woman with no troubles of her own, who takes a kindly interest in those of her friends.

'We must look out for Mrs Gray in church,' said Winifred. 'I *think* I know who she is. I believe she sometimes wears a silver fox fur.'

'I thought Julian said she hadn't much money,' I said,

'though of course the fur might have been left over from more prosperous days.'

'It's a rather *bushy* fur,' said Winifred. 'Perhaps it isn't silver fox at all. I don't know much about these things.'

'I don't think she was wearing a fur when I saw her,' said Julian, 'but she did appear to be nicely dressed.'

'I hope she won't distract you from writing your sermons, Julian,' I said jokingly. 'We shall probably notice a marked falling off in your preaching when Mrs Gray moves in.'

Julian laughed and got up from the table. 'I must go back to my distempering,' he said, 'or the place won't be habitable. I shall enjoy it now that I know the colour dries lighter. I have certainly learnt something this afternoon.'

Winifred smiled affectionately after him as he left the room. 'Men are just children, really, aren't they. He's as happy as a sandboy when he's doing something messy. Now, Mildred, perhaps we could get on with pricing these things for the sale?'

We spent a contented half hour going through the jumble and speculating about Mrs Gray.

'Julian didn't *really* tell us what she was like,' lamented Winifred.

'No, but I suppose women of my sort and age are difficult to describe, unless they're strikingly beautiful, of course.'

'Oh, wouldn't that be lovely,' Winifred pushed back her untidy grey hair, 'if she were strikingly beautiful!'

'Oh, I don't know,' I said. 'Perhaps it would if she could be nice as well, but one feels that beautiful people aren't always.'

'But she's a clergyman's widow . . .'

'Oh, dear,' I laughed. 'I'd forgotten that.' It seemed like a kind of magic formula. 'So she's to be beautiful as well as good. That sounded almost *too* much. We don't know how her husband died, do we? She may have driven him to his grave.'

Winifred looked rather shocked, so I stopped my foolish imaginings and went on pricing the worn garments, stuffed birds, old shoes, golf clubs, theological books, popular dance tunes of the thirties, fenders and photograph frames – jumble in all its glory.

'I wonder . . .' said Winifred thoughtfully. 'I wonder what her *Christian* name is?'

CHAPTER SIX

LENT BEGAN in February that year and it was very cold, with sleet and bitter winds. The office where I dealt with my impoverished gentlewomen was in Belgravia, and it was my custom to attend the lunchtime services held at St Ermin's on Wednesdays.

The church had been badly bombed and only one aisle could be used, so that it always appeared to be very full with what would normally have been an average congregation crowded into the undamaged aisle. This gave us a feeling of intimacy with each other and separateness from the rest of the world, so that I always thought of us as being rather like the early Christians, surrounded not by lions, admittedly, but by all the traffic and bustle of a weekday lunch-hour.

On Ash Wednesday I went to the church as usual with Mrs Bonner, one of my fellow-workers, who was drawn more by the name of the preacher than by anything else, for, as she confessed to me, she loved a good sermon. We had hurried over our lunch – a tasteless mess of spaghetti followed by a heavy steamed pudding, excellent Lenten fare, I felt – and were in our seats in good time before the service was due to begin. We had made our way through the ruins, where torn-down wall tablets and an occasional urn or cherub's head were stacked in heaps, and where, incongruous in the middle of so much desolation, we had come upon a little grey woman heating a saucepan of coffee on a Primus stove.

Mrs Bonner settled herself down comfortably with the anticipation of enjoyment and peered round at the people coming in, as if she were at a fashionable wedding. I am afraid that she cannot have found them very interesting, for they were a mixed collection of office-workers and passers-by, together with the elderly ladies and dim spinsters who form a proportion of church congregations everywhere. The vicar stood at the door, a gaunt figure in his rusty black cassock, while his wife fussed over the new arrivals, trying to prevent them from following their natural inclination to crowd into the back of the church, leaving no room for latecomers.

I sat quietly, sometimes turning my head, and it was on one of these occasions that, to my surprise and dismay, I found myself looking straight at Everard Bone, who was coming in at that moment. He looked back at me but without any sign of recognition. I suppose I was indistinguishable from many another woman in a neutral winter coat and plain hat and I was thankful for my anonymity. But he was unmistakable. His tall figure, his well-cut overcoat, his long nose and his fair hair were outstanding in this gathering of mediocrity. I felt that I could almost understand the attraction he might have for the kind of person who is drawn to the difficult, the unusual, even the unpleasant.

'What a handsome man – though his nose is a shade too long,' said Mrs Bonner in a loud whisper, as Everard took his seat a few rows in front of us.

I did not answer but I found that I could not help thinking about him. He was certainly the last person I should have expected to see here. I suppose I was ignorant enough to imagine that all anthropologists must be unbelievers, but the appearance of Everard Bone had shaken my complacency considerably. And yet, of course, it might be that he was here in a professional capacity, observing our behaviour with a view to contributing a note on it to some learned journal. I should have to ask Helena about it the next time I saw her.

A grey little woman – perhaps the same one who had been brewing coffee in the ruins – took her seat at the harmonium and played the first line of a Lenten hymn. The singing was hearty, if a little ragged, and as I sang I began to feel humble and ashamed of myself for my unkind thoughts about Everard Bone. He was certain to be a much nicer person and a better Christian than I was, which would not be difficult. Besides, what reason had I for disliking him? His pointed nose and the fact that I had found him difficult to talk to? His friendship or whatever it was with Helena Napier? The last, certainly, was none of my business.

The preacher was forceful and interesting. His words seemed to knit us together, so that we really were like the early Christians, having all things in common. I tried to banish the feeling that I should prefer not to have all things in common with Everard Bone but it would keep coming back, almost as if he was to be in some way my Lenten penance, and I was quite upset to find myself near him as we crowded out of the church.

'Oh dear, oh *dear*,' whispered Mrs Bonner loudly, 'a very interesting sermon, but what a lot of talk about *sin*. I suppose it's only to be expected at the beginning of Lent, but it's all *miserable*, don't you think?'

I could think of no suitable comment and her loud whispering embarrassed me, for I was afraid that Everard Bone's attention would be attracted and that he might recognize me. But I need not have feared for, after standing uncertainly outside the church for a second or two, he walked quickly away in the opposite direction from the one we were taking.

'I can understand that man packing the churches,' went on Mrs Bonner. 'He certainly has a forceful personality, and yet I can't believe we're really so wicked.'

'No, but we have to be made to realize it,' I said unconvincingly, for we certainly seemed harmless enough, elderly and middle-aged people with one or two mild-looking younger men and women. Indeed, Everard Bone had been the only person one would have looked at twice.

'Of course a lot of very *good* people aren't religious in the sense of being churchgoers,' persisted Mrs Bonner.

'No, I know they aren't,' I agreed, feeling that at any moment she would begin talking about it being just as easy to worship God in a beech wood or on the golf links on a fine Sunday morning.

'I must admit I always feel the presence of God much more when I'm in a garden or on a mountain,' she continued.

'I'm afraid I haven't got a garden and am really never on a mountain,' I said. Was it perhaps likely though, that one might feel the presence of God more in Whitehall or Belgrave Square, than, say, Vauxhall Bridge Road or Oxford Street? No doubt there was something in it.

'*A garden is a lovesome thing, God wot,*' said Mrs Bonner rather half-heartedly. 'Well, we must certainly go next week. It's interesting having a different preacher every time – one never knows what will turn up.'

When I got home it occurred to me that I might ask the Napiers whether they had anything suitable for the jumble sale, which was to be held the next Saturday. It also occurred to me that I might find out something about Everard Bone and why he had been at the service. Of course it was nothing to do with me but I was curious to know. Perhaps if I did know I should understand and like him better.

As I walked upstairs past the Napiers' flat I could hear that they were in, for they always seemed to keep their doors half open. Now their voices were raised in what seemed to be an argument.

'Darling, you are *filthy*,' I heard Rocky say, 'putting down a hot greasy frying-pan on the linoleum!'

'Oh, don't fuss so!' came her voice from the sitting-room.

I was just creeping slowly and guiltily past, feeling as if I had been eavesdropping, when Rocky came out of the kitchen with a cloth in his hand and invited me in to have some coffee with them.

I went into the sitting-room where Helena was sitting writing at a desk. Pieces of paper covered with diagrams of little circles and triangles were spread around her.

'That looks very learned,' I said, in the feeble way that one does.

'Oh, it's just kinship diagrams,' she said rather shortly.

Rocky laughed and poured out the coffee. I had the impression that Helena was annoyed with him for having invited me in.

'You mustn't mind if I get on with this,' she said. 'Our paper is due to be read soon and there's a lot to do.'

'I expect you'll be quite relieved when it's over,' I said.

'*I* shall be,' said Rocky. 'At the moment I have to do all the cooking and washing-up. I'm worn out.'

'Well, you're not in the Admiral's villa now, and anyway it won't be long. I thought you *liked* cooking, darling,' said Helena in an edgy voice.

I felt rather uncomfortable. I suppose married people get so used to calling each other 'darling' that they never realize how false it sounds when said in an annoyed or irritable tone.

'I wonder if you could let me have anything for the jumble sale on Saturday?' I asked quickly. 'Old clothes, shoes or anything?'

'Oh, I've always got lots of junk. It will be a good chance to get rid of it,' said Helena without looking up from her writing. 'I'll look out some things this evening.'

'I've got a pair of shoes and a suit that the moth got,' said Rocky, with a glance at his wife. 'I'll bring them to you tonight. Everard Bone is coming to talk to Helena about the paper.'

'Oh, I saw him today,' I said in what I hoped was a casual tone.

'*Did* you?' Helena turned round from her desk, her face animated.

'Yes, I've been to the Lent service at St Ermin's and I saw him there. I was quite surprised. I mean,' I added, not wanting to sound smug, 'I was surprised because one doesn't usually see anyone one knows there.'

'You mean you don't expect anthropologists to go to church, Miss Lathbury,' said Helena. 'But Everard is a convert, quite ardent, you know.'

'I thought converts always were ardent,' said Rocky. 'Surely that's the point about them? The whole set-up is new and interesting to them. Did he get converted in Africa, seeing the missionaries going about their work? One would have thought it might have the opposite effect.'

'Oh, *no*,' I protested, 'they do such splendid work.'

'Splendid work,' Rocky repeated, savouring the words, 'how I love that expression! It has such a very noble sound. Perhaps Miss Lathbury is right – it may have been the sight of his fellow anthropologists that sent him over to the other side.'

'Well, it wasn't in Africa,' said Helena, not sounding amused. 'I think it happened when he was at Cambridge, though he never talks about it.'

'Perhaps it is rather an awkward thing,' said Rocky. 'In many ways life is easier without that.'

'Of course it is more of an intellectual thing with him,' said Helena. 'He knows all the answers.'

'We certainly want people like that,' I said. 'The Church needs intelligent people.'

'I should think so,' said Helena scornfully. 'All those old women swooning over a good-looking curate won't get it anywhere.'

'But our curate isn't good-looking,' I said indignantly, visualizing Father Greatorex's short stocky figure in its untidy clothes. 'He isn't even young.'

'And anyway, why should the Church want to get anywhere?' said Rocky. 'I think it's much more comforting to think of it staying just where it is.'

'Wherever that may be,' Helena added.

I made a faint murmur of protest, but it *was* rather faint, for between the two of them I hardly knew where I was, though Rocky's attitude seemed the more sympathetic. 'I'm afraid we aren't all very intelligent about our religion,' I said, slightly on the defensive, 'we probably don't know many of the answers and can't argue cleverly. And yet I suppose there's room for the stupid as well,' I added, for I was thinking of the lines in Bishop Heber's hymn,

Richer by far is the heart's adoration,
Dearer to God are the prayers of the poor.

Though obviously He must be very pleased to have somebody as clever as Everard Bone.

'Did he speak to you?' Helena asked.

'Oh, no, I don't think he saw me, or if he did he didn't recognize me. People don't, you know. I suppose there's really nothing outstanding about me.'

'*Dear* Miss Lathbury,' Rocky smiled, 'how completely untrue!'

Once more I was transported to the terrace of the Admiral's villa and took my place among the little group of Wren officers. Naturally, I did not know what to say.

'Why shouldn't we call you Mildred?' said Rocky suddenly. 'After all, we shall probably be seeing a lot of each other and I think we're going to be friends.'

I felt a little embarrassed but could hardly refuse him.

'And you must call us Helena and Rocky. Could you do that?'

'Yes, I think so,' I said, wondering when I should begin.

'And you can call Everard Bone Everard,' said Helena, suddenly laughing.

'Oh, no,' I protested; 'I can't imagine that ever happening.'

'You should have spoken to him after the service,' she said, 'made some comment on the sermon or something. He's very critical.'

'He hurried away,' I explained, 'so I had no chance to, even if he had recognized me.'

'Oh, it is nice having you living above us,' said Helena surprisingly. 'Just think who we might have had, some dreary couple, or "business women" or a family with children, too awful.'

I hurried upstairs feeling lighthearted and pleased. I was a little amused to think that my having seen Everard Bone at the Lent service should have made me into a nice person to have living above them. For Helena's sake, if not for my own, I ought perhaps to make some friendly overture if he were there next week. I could make it a Lent resolution to try to like him. I began imagining the process, what I should say and how he would respond. Some comment on the preacher or the weather, or a friendly enquiry about the progress of his work would be an obvious beginning.

I stood by the window, leaning on my desk, staring absent-mindedly at my favourite view of the church through the bare trees. The sight of Sister Blatt, splendid on her high old-fashioned bicycle like a ship in full sail, filled me with pleasure. Then Julian Malory came along in his black cloak, talking and laughing with a woman I had not seen before. She was tall and rather nicely dressed but I could not see her face. It suddenly occurred to me that she must be Mrs Gray, who was coming to live in the flat at the vicarage. I watched them out of sight and then went into the kitchen and started to wash some stockings. I had a feeling, although I could not have said why, that she was not quite what we had expected. A clergyman's widow . . . she has such sad eyes . . . Perhaps we had not imagined her *laughing* with Julian, I could not put it more definitely than that.

CHAPTER SEVEN

I WAS FORMALLY introduced to Mrs Gray at the jumble sale on the following Saturday afternoon. She was behind one of the stalls with Winifred, who was looking very pleased and animated, rather reminding me of a child who has asked 'Will you be friends with me?' and has been accepted.

Mrs Gray was, as I had supposed from my first brief glimpse of her, good-looking and nicely dressed, rather *too* nicely dressed for a clergyman's widow, I felt, remembering many such whom I had met before. Her quiet manner suggested self-sufficiency rather than shyness and there was something secret about her smile, as if she saw and thought more than she would ever reveal.

'You will have to tell me what to do,' she said, addressing Winifred and me, 'though I suppose jumble sales are the same the world over.'

'Oh, we get a tough crowd,' said Winifred gaily. 'This isn't a very *nice* part, you know, not like Belgravia. I'm afraid a lot of the people who come to our sales never put their noses inside the church.'

'Do you think they have jumble sales in Belgravia?' asked Mrs Gray; 'that hadn't occurred to me.'

'I believe St Ermin's has one occasionally,' I said.

'One likes to think of Cabinet Ministers' wives attending them,' said Mrs Gray, with what seemed to me a rather affected little laugh.

Winifred laughed immoderately and began rearranging the things on the stall. She and Mrs Gray were in charge of the odds-and-ends or white elephant stall. The stuffed birds made a magnificent centre-piece, surrounded by books, china ornaments, pictures and photograph frames, some with the photographs still in them. Winifred had removed the Edwardian lady and the young clergyman, but others had escaped her and now seemed to stare out almost with indignation from their elaborate tarnished settings, an ugly woman with a strained expression – perhaps a governess – a group of bearded gentlemen in cricket clothes, a wayward-looking child with cropped hair.

'Oh, look,' I heard Winifred exclaming, 'those poor things! I thought I'd taken them all out.'

'Never mind,' Mrs Gray said in a soothing tone as if she were speaking to a child, 'I think the people who buy the frames don't really notice the photographs in them. I remember in my husband's parish . . .'

So her husband had had a parish, I thought. Somehow I had imagined him an Army chaplain killed in the war. Perhaps he had been elderly, then? After this I could hear no more, for Mrs Gray's voice was quiet and Sister Blatt was upon me. I was glad that I should have her help at the clothing stall, always the most popular. Each garment had been carefully priced, but even so there would be arguments and struggles among the buyers and the usual appeals for one of us to arbitrate.

The sale was being held in the parish hall, a bare room with green painted walls, from which an oil painting of Father Busby, the first vicar, looked down to bless our activities. At least, we liked to think of him as doing that, though if one examined the portrait carefully it appeared rather as if he were admiring his long bushy beard which one hand seemed to be stroking. A billiard table, a dartboard and the other harmless amusements of the boys' club stood at one end of the hall. Behind the hatch near the door Miss Enders, Miss Statham and my Mrs Morris, apparently no longer troubled about birettas and Popes' toes, were busy with the tea urns. Julian Malory, in flannels and sports jacket, supported by Teddy Lemon and a few strong 'lads' waited near the doors to stem the rush when they should be opened. Father Greatorex, wearing a cassock and an old navy blue overcoat of the kind worn by Civil Defence workers during the war, stood uncertainly in the middle of the room.

Sister Blatt looked at me and clicked her teeth with irritation. 'Oh, that man! How he gets on my nerves!'

'He certainly is rather useless at jumble sales,' I agreed, 'but then he's so good, saintly almost,' I faltered, for I really had no evidence to support my statement apart from the fact that his habitual dress of cassock and old overcoat seemed to indicate a disregard for the conventions of this world which implied a preoccupation with higher things.

'Saintly!' snorted Sister Blatt. 'I don't know what's given you that idea. Just because a man takes Orders in middle age and goes about looking like an old tramp! He was no good in business so he went into the Church – that's not what we want.'

'Oh, come now,' I protested, 'surely you're being rather hard? After all, he *is* a good man . . .'

'And Mr Mallett and Mr Conybeare, just look at them,' she went on in a voice loud enough for our two churchwardens to hear. 'It wouldn't do them any harm to soil their hands with a little honest toil. Teddy Lemon and the boys put up all the trestles and carried the urns.'

'Yes, Sister, we found everything had been done when we put in an appearance,' said Mr Mallett, a round jolly little man. 'It was quite a blow, I can tell you. We had hoped to be able to help you ladies. But they also serve who only stand and wait, as the poet says.'

'You certainly came early enough,' said Sister Blatt with heavy sarcasm.

'The early bird catches the worm,' said Mr Conybeare, a tall stringy man with pince-nez.

'Now, Mr Conybeare, I hope you're not suggesting that there are any worms here,' giggled Miss Statham from behind the hatch. 'You'll catch something else if you don't get out of the way. And don't think I'm going to give you a cup of tea till you've earned it . . .'

But at that moment, Julian, watch in hand, ordered the

doors to be opened. The surging crowd outside was kept in check by Teddy Lemon and his supporters, while Julian took the three pences for admission; but once past him they rushed for the stalls.

'Talk about landing on the Normandy beaches,' said Sister Blatt, 'some of our jumble sale crowd would make splendid Commandos.'

The next few minutes needed great concentration and firmness. I collected money, gave change and tried at the same time to rearrange the tumbled garments, settle arguments and prevent the elderly from being injured in the crush.

Sister Blatt was free with advice and criticism. 'You'll never get into that, Mrs Ryan,' she called out derisively to a stout Irishwoman, a Roman Catholic incidentally, who was always in the front of the queue for our sales.

Mrs Ryan laughed good-humouredly and clutched the flowered artificial silk dress she had picked up. Her soft brogue beguiled me, as always, so that I listened, fascinated, not knowing what she said. I just caught the words 'a lovely man' as she went off with her dress.

Sister Blatt was laughing in spite of herself. 'Well, really, that woman has a nerve, inviting me over to *their* jumble sale next week and telling me that their new priest, Father Bogart, is a lovely man! As if that would attract me!'

'Oh, but think how it does and how it has done, that kind of thing. Where would the Church be if it hadn't been for a "lovely man" here and there? It's rather nice to think of churches being united through jumble sales,' I suggested. 'I wonder if the Methodists are having one too?'

'Churches united through jumble sales?' said Julian, coming up to our stall. 'Well, we might do worse.' He glanced round at the crowd, less struggling than it had been half an hour ago, with satisfaction. 'You didn't persuade your friends the Napiers to come?' he asked me.

'I'm afraid I didn't try,' I admitted. 'They sent some things but somehow I just couldn't imagine them here. It wouldn't be the right kind of setting for them.'

Julian glanced round at the dingy green walls. 'Well, I suppose we all of us think that we're worth a better one.'

'Except for Father Greatorex,' said Sister Blatt spitefully. 'He's quite in his place here. He hasn't done a thing all afternoon. And why doesn't he take his coat off? He must be boiled.'

'Oh, look,' I said, 'he's taking tea to Miss Malory and Mrs Gray.'

'Well, that's completely out of character,' said Sister Blatt.

'You can hardly blame him for wanting to do it,' said Julian, watching the little group with interest. 'I wonder if they have cakes? He would hardly be able to carry everything at once. I think I had better go and help.'

I saw him go to the hatch, come away with a plate of brightly-coloured iced cakes and then offer one to Mrs Gray.

Sister Blatt and I looked at each other.

'Well,' I began rather doubtfully, 'the vicar is always charming to new parishioners, or he ought to be. That's a known thing.'

'But *we* hadn't got any tea,' she pointed out indignantly. 'I think it was extremely rude of him to ignore us like that. All because of a new face.

Make new friends but keep the old,
One is silver, the other gold . . .'

she recited. 'Perhaps we shouldn't value ourselves as highly as that, but all the same . . .'

'Yes, I think he did rather forget his manners,' I agreed. 'Of course, Mrs Gray is going to live in his house, you know, so perhaps he feels that the relationship between them should be especially cordial.'

'Oh, rubbish! I never heard such far-fetched excuses.'

'Oh-ho, jealous are you, Sister?' said Mr Mallett roguishly. 'You'd better go and get your tea before all the cakes go.'

'You mean before you and Mr Conybeare eat them all,' said Sister Blatt. 'I expect you've been tucking in for hours.'

'Now you ladies, run along. I'll look after the stall,' said Mr Mallett, picking up a dress and holding it up against himself in a comic manner. 'I'll guarantee that business will look up now that I'm in charge.'

'Yes, I think we can safely leave the stall now,' I said, with a backward glance at the tumbled garments lying on the bare boards of the table. An old velvet coat trimmed with moth-eaten white rabbit, a soiled pink georgette evening dress of the nineteen-twenties trimmed with bead embroidery, a mangy fur with mad staring eyes priced at sixpence – these things were 'regulars' and nobody ever bought them.

At the tea hatch, too, trade had slackened and we were able to talk as we ate and drank. Mrs Morris's sing-song voice could be heard above the others: 'Lovely *antique* pieces they've got. I said what about giving them a bit of a polish and *he* said oh yes a good idea, but *she* said not to bother, it was the washing-up and cleaning that was the main thing.'

I knew that she was talking about the Napiers, but though my natural curiosity would have liked to hear more, I felt I could hardly encourage her. Is it a kind of natural delicacy that some of us have, or do we just lack the courage to follow our inclinations?

'Of course he's been in the Navy,' said Mrs Morris.

'Yes, Lieutenant-Commander Napier was in Italy,' I said in a rather loud clear voice, as if trying to raise the conversation to a higher level.

'How nice,' said Miss Enders. 'My sister once went there on a tour, my married sister, that is, the one who lives at Raynes Park.'

'Such a nice young man, he is, Mr Napier,' said Mrs Morris. 'Too good for her, I shouldn't wonder.'

My efforts had obviously not been very successful but I did not feel I could try again.

'The Italians are very forward with women,' declared Miss Statham. 'Of course it's unwise to walk about after dark in a foreign town anywhere when you're alone.'

'Pinch your bottom they would before you could say knife,' burst out Mrs Morris, but the short silence that followed told her that she had gone too far. Strictly speaking, she was socially inferior to Miss Enders and Miss Statham; it was only her participation in parish activities that gave her a temporary equality.

'Of course my sister had her husband with her,' said Miss Enders stiffly, 'so there couldn't be anything like that.'

Sister Blatt let out a snort of laughter.

'Excuse me . . .' Julian came up behind us with some empty cups and saucers which he put down on the hatch.

'Did you get some of my home-made sandwich cake, Father?' asked Miss Statham anxiously. 'I particularly wanted you to try it.'

'Yes, thank you, delicious,' he murmured absently.

'I don't think he did, you know,' said Miss Enders to me in a low tone. 'He only took a plate of fairies and iced buns.'

'Perhaps Father Greatorex did,' I suggested.

'If you ask me, I think Mr Mallett and Mr Conybeare had most of it. They were the first to have their tea. And I did see Teddy Lemon take a piece.'

'I'm sure he deserved a good tea,' I said. 'He worked very hard.'

'Oh, yes, Mr Mallett and Mr Conybeare didn't do a hand's turn. Just got in everybody's way as usual.'

The group started to break up and we went back to the stalls to tidy them. Another jumble sale was over.

Winifred came up to me, her eyes shining. 'Oh, Mildred,' she breathed, '*what* do you think her name is?'

I said I had no idea.

'Allegra!' she told me. 'Isn't that lovely? Allegra Gray.'

I found myself wondering if it was really Mrs Gray's name, or if she had perhaps adopted it instead of a more conventional and uninteresting one. 'Wasn't Allegra the name of Byron's natural daughter?' I asked.

'Byron! How splendid!' Winifred clasped her hands in rapture.

'I'm not sure that it was splendid,' I persisted.

'Oh, but Byron was such a splendid romantic person,' said Winifred, 'and that's the main thing, isn't it?'

'Is it really?' I asked, still determined that I would not be forced to admire Mrs Gray. 'Doesn't one look for other qualities in people?'

'Oh, Mildred, you're so practical,' laughed Winifred. 'Of course I've always been silly and romantic – it's just how you're made.'

I thought of the Christina Rossetti in its limp green suede cover. *When I am dead, my dearest* . . . when there had perhaps never been a dearest. Weren't we all a little like that? I began to consider the people I knew in terms of splendour and romance. I had certainly known very few who could be described as splendid and romantic. Clergymen could and should be left out of it straight away, I felt, and that didn't leave many others. Only Rocky Napier and Everard Bone, perhaps, who were both good-looking in their different styles. Rocky had charm, too, and must have seemed a splendidly romantic person to a great many women.

I crept quietly up to my flat and began to prepare supper. The house seemed to be empty. Saturday night . . . perhaps it was right that it should be and I sitting alone eating a very small chop. After I had washed-up I would listen to Saturday Night Theatre and do my knitting. I wondered where the Napiers were, if they were out together, or if Helena was with Everard Bone. *My son is at a meeting of the Prehistoric Society* . . . I began to laugh, bending over the frying-pan.

There was certainly nothing romantic about *him*, but was he perhaps just a little splendid?

CHAPTER EIGHT

DURING THE next few weeks the weather improved and suddenly it was almost spring. The time came round for my annual luncheon with William Caldicote, the brother of my friend Dora. This was always something of a ceremonial occasion and dated from the days when Dora, and perhaps even William himself, had hoped that 'something might come of it'. But as the years had passed our relationship had settled down into a comfortable dull thing. I do not remember when it was that I first began to realize that William was not the kind of man to marry, and that I myself did not mind in the very least. It now seemed so natural that if we were in a taxi together he should express the emotion that it was a relief to sit down rather than that it was pleasant to be alone with me. His care for his food and drink, too, was something I accepted and even found rather endearing, especially as I benefited from it myself. I could always be sure of a good meal with William.

He worked in a Ministry somewhere near Whitehall and was now a rather grey-looking man in the late thirties, with surprisingly bright beady eyes. We always met in the restaurant, one in Soho where he was known, and as I hurried towards it – for I was a little late – I began thinking that William wasn't really the most suitable person to be having luncheon with on this fresh spring day. Surely a splendid romantic person was the obvious companion? The blue sky full of billowing white clouds, the thrilling little breezes, the gay hats of some of the women I met, the mimosa on the barrows – all made me feel disinclined for William's company, his preoccupation with his health and his food and his spiteful old-maidish delight in gossip.

He was in a fussy mood today, I could see, as he went rather petulantly through the menu. The liver would probably be overdone, the duck not enough done, the weather had been too mild for the celery to be good – it seemed as if there was really nothing we could eat. I sat patiently while William and the waiter consulted in angry whispers. A bottle of wine was brought. William took it up and studied the label suspiciously. I watched apprehensively as he tasted it, for he was one of those men to whom the formality really meant something and he was quite likely to send the bottle back and demand another. But as he tasted, he relaxed. It was all right, or perhaps not that, but it would do.

'A tolerable wine, Mildred,' he said, 'unpretentious, but I think you will like it.'

'Unpretentious, just like me,' I said stupidly, touching the feather in my brown hat.

'We really should have a tolerable wine today. Spring seems to be almost with us,' he observed in a dry tone.

'Nuits St Georges,' I read from the label. 'How exciting that sounds! Does it mean the Nights of St George? It conjures up the most wonderful pictures, armour and white horses and dragons, flames too, perhaps a great procession by torchlight.'

He looked at me doubtfully for a moment and then, seeing that I had not yet tasted my wine, began to explain that Nuits St Georges was a place where there were vineyards, but that not every bottle bearing the name on its label was to be taken as being of the first quality. 'It might,' he said seriously, 'be an *ordinaire*. Always remember that. *A little learning is a dangerous thing*, Mildred.'

'*Drink deep, or taste not the Pierian spring*,' I went on, pleased at being able to finish the quotation. 'But I'm afraid I shall never have the chance to drink deep so I must remain ignorant.'

'Ah, Pope at Twickenham,' sighed William. 'And now Popesgrove is a telephone exchange. It makes one feel very sad.' He paused for a moment and then began to eat with great enjoyment.

It was certainly an excellent luncheon and what we were having did not appear to be on the menu. After we had been eating for some time and had satisfied our first brutish hunger, he began to ask me about myself, what I had been doing since the last time we met, whether there had been any interesting cases before my committee.

'How I should love to do work of that kind,' he said, 'I feel that I almost have a natural gift for it. You see, I would understand so well what these unfortunate gentlepeople had lost. The great house in Belgrave Square with the servants bringing up trays from the basement, the Edwardian country house parties with visiting foreign royalties, the villa at Nice or Bordighera for the winter months . . .'

'Oh, but the people we have to deal with aren't usually as grand as that,' I said, marvelling at William's understanding, when he and Dora, the children of a doctor, had been brought up in a Birmingham suburb. 'They are gentlepeople, of course, but more like us, daughters of clergymen or professional people, who may have been comfortably off but never really wealthy.'

'A pity, I mean that you don't get the grander kind, because the greater the fall the more poignant the tragedy.'

'Yes, I suppose so.' I remembered reading something of the kind at school when we had been studying Shakespeare's tragedies. 'But we do have some very tragic cases,' I said, 'and I'm afraid there is nothing at all dramatic about them, poor souls.'

'Ah, yes.' He became serious, but then seemed to brighten up. 'Tell me about the new people who have come to live in your house.'

I began to describe the Napiers, rather hesitantly, for I did not want to make too much of their disagreements as I knew that William with his love of gossip and scandal would seize eagerly on any scrap. Not that it really mattered, I supposed, and as I went on talking I must have become less cautious for I found myself, rather to my dismay, insisting that *he* was much too nice for *her*.

'But, my dear, that's so often the way,' said William, 'one should never be surprised at it. All these delightful men married to such monsters, such fiends.'

'Oh, Mrs Napier isn't like that,' I protested, 'it's just that he is exceptionally nice.'

I suppose it must have been the Nuits St Georges or the spring day or the intimate atmosphere of the restaurant, but I heard myself, to my horror, murmuring something about Rocky Napier being just the kind of person I should have liked for myself.

There was a marked silence after I had said this, during which I looked round the restaurant with detachment, noticing a waiter concocting some dish over a flame at a side table, a man leaning across to touch the hand of the girl sitting opposite him, and I suddenly felt irritated with William for being so grey and fussy and Dora's brother whom I had known for years.

'But my dear Mildred, *you* mustn't marry,' he was saying indignantly. 'Life is disturbing enough as it is without these alarming suggestions. I always think of you as being so very balanced and sensible, such an excellent woman. I do hope you're *not* thinking of getting married?'

He stared across the table at me, his eyes and mouth round and serious with alarm. I began to laugh to break the unnatural tension which had arisen, and also at Dora's idea, which I believe she still cherished, that William and I might marry one day.

'Oh, no, of course not!' I said. 'I'm so sorry if I alarmed you. Why, I don't know anyone suitable, to begin with.'

'What about the vicar?' asked William suspiciously.

'Father Malory? Oh, he doesn't believe in marriage for the clergy, and in any case he isn't really the kind of person I should want to marry,' I reassured him.

'Well, that's a relief,' said William. 'We, my dear Mildred, are the observers of life. Let other people get married by all means, the more the merrier.' He lifted the bottle, judged the amount left in it and refilled his own glass but not mine. 'Let Dora marry if she likes. She hasn't your talent for observation.'

I suppose I should have felt pleased at this little compliment but I was somehow irritated. In any case, it was not much of a compliment, making me out to be an unpleasant inhuman sort of person. Was that how I appeared to others? I wondered.

'What news have you of Dora?' I asked, to change the subject. 'I'm afraid I owe her a letter.'

'Oh, a lot of news.' He spread out his hands with an expansive gesture and leaned back in his chair. 'Much seems to happen in that little world. And yet I suppose a girls' school has as much happening in it as most worlds and the undercurrents are more deadly.'

'Oh? Anything in particular?'

William leaned forward and his small beady eyes gleamed with delight. '*Unpleasantness*,' he whispered dramatically.

'Oh, dear, what about?' I asked, but I was not surprised, for there seemed to be so much of it at Dora's schools. I had at times found myself wondering disloyally whether she did not perhaps invite it.

'Something about the girls wearing hats in chapel, or not wearing hats – it doesn't really matter which. Oh, the infinite variety and complication of that little world! The greater things, birth, death and copulation are just passed by as if they were nothing.'

'Well, they don't really have things like that in a girls' school, at least not often,' I said, my thoughts going back to an occasion in my own schooldays when a mistress had died and her coffin had been placed in the chapel, 'and then only death.'

'Oh, not the other things!' said William, now in high good humour. 'But supposing they did!'

I stirred my coffee, feeling embarrassed, particularly as his voice had a penetrating quality.

'Of course Miss Protheroe is rather difficult to get on with,' I ventured. 'I've only met her once, but she seemed to me the kind of person I shouldn't like to have to work with myself.'

'But poor Dora is so irritating, too,' said William. 'I can never bear her for more than a week-end.'

We were standing outside on the pavement. After the warm rosy gloom of the restaurant, the fresh spring air was like another bottle of wine. There was a barrow full of spring flowers just opposite.

'Oh, look, mimosa!' I exclaimed, though not with any hope that William would buy me any. 'I must have some.'

'It always reminds me of cafés in seaside towns, all dried-up and rattling with the bottles of sauces on the table,' said William, standing by while I bought a bunch.

'Yes, I know the fluffiness doesn't last long, but it's so lovely while it does.'

'You seem unlike yourself today,' he said disapprovingly. 'I hope it wasn't the Nuits St Georges.'

'You know I'm not used to wine, particularly in the middle of the day,' I said, 'but it's rather pleasant to be unlike oneself occasionally.'

'I don't agree. They've moved me to a new office and I don't like it at all. Different pigeons come to the windows.'

'I've never been in your office,' I said boldly, 'may I come back with you and see it?'

'Oh, the prison, you mean, with its stone walls and iron bars, which the poet tells us do *not* a prison make. Yes, you may come if you like.'

We walked into Trafalgar Square and then into an anonymous-looking entrance in a back street somewhere beyond it. Grey-looking men like William, some even greyer, were hurrying in. He greeted one or two of them; they seemed to have double-barrelled names like Calverley-Hibbert and Radcliffe-Forde, but they did not look any the less grey for all that.

'Here we are!' William flung open a door with his name on it and I went in. Two elderly grey men were sitting at a table, one with a bag of sweets which he hastily put away into a drawer, the other with a card-index which he naturally did not attempt to conceal. William did not acknowledge them in any way nor did they take any notice of him. He sat down at an enormous desk in the centre of the room, which had two telephones on it and a line of wire baskets, importantly labelled and stacked with files. I had no very clear idea of what it was that he did.

'This is a nice room,' I said, going to the window, 'and what a lovely desk you have.' I felt embarrassed at the presence of the grey men and did not quite know what to say. But suddenly a rattling sound, as if a trolley was being wheeled along the corridor, was heard and the two men leaped up, each carrying a china mug.

'Oh, excuse me,' said William, leaping up too and taking a china mug from a drawer in his desk, 'I think I hear the tea.'

He did not offer to get me any, nor did I feel I really wanted any as it was barely three o'clock. I wondered why the grey men, who were obviously of a lower grade or status than William, had not fetched his tea for him, but perhaps there was a rigid etiquette in these matters. Also, knowing William's fussiness, it was quite likely that he would insist on fetching his own tea. I began to wonder whether important-sounding people like Calverley-Hibbert and Radcliffe-Forde were also at this moment hurrying along corridors with mugs. Perhaps even the Minister himself was joining in the general scramble. I went on standing by the window and looked out at the view which was of another office building, perhaps the same Ministry, where there were rows of uncurtained windows and the activities of the rooms were exposed as if it was a doll's house. Grey men sat at desks, their hands moving among files; some sipped tea, one read a newspaper, another manipulated a typewriter with the uncertain touch of two fingers. A girl leaned from a window, another combed her hair, a third typed with expert speed. A young man embraced a girl in a rough playful way and she pulled his hair while the other occupants of the room looked on encouragingly . . . I watched, fascinated, and was deep in contemplation when William and his underlings came back with their steaming mugs.

'Is that another Ministry across there?' I asked.

'Ah, yes, the Ministry of Desire,' said William solemnly.

I protested, laughing.

'They always look so far away, so not-of-this-world, those wonderful people,' he explained. 'But perhaps we seem like that to them. They may call *us* the Ministry of Desire.'

At that moment a clock struck a quarter past three. William jumped up, and picking up a paper bag from one of the wire trays, walked over to the window and flung it open. There was a whirring of wings and a crowd of pigeons swooped down on to the flat piece of roof outside the window. Some hopped up on to the sill and one even came into the room and perched on William's shoulder. He took two rolls from the paper bag and began to crumble them and throw the pieces among the birds.

One of the grey men looked up from his card-index and gave me a faint, as it were pitying, smile.

'Does this happen every afternoon?' I asked William.

'Oh, yes, and every morning too. I couldn't get through the day without my pigeons. I feel like one of those rather dreadful pictures of St Francis – I'm sure you and Dora had one at school – but it's a good feeling and one does so like to have that.'

I could not help smiling at the association of St Francis with a civil servant, but I had not known about William's fondness for pigeons and there was something unexpected and endearing about it. He seemed so completely absorbed in them, calling them by names, encouraging this one to come forward and telling that one not to be greedy, that I decided that he had forgotten all about me and it was time to go home.

'I really ought to be going now,' I said. 'I must be keeping you from your work,' I added, with no thought of irony until after I had said it.

William returned to his desk and opened a file. 'You must come and see my new flat,' he said, mentioning an address in Chelsea which seemed familiar.

I thanked him for my luncheon and walked away, carrying my bunch of mimosa down the bare corridors. Of course, I remembered as I waited for a bus, Everard Bone and his mother lived in that street, that was why the address had seemed familiar. What a good thing I had not said anything to William about Helena Napier and Everard Bone, though it was unlikely that he would know them. *My son is at a meeting of the Prehistoric Society* . . . I heard again Mrs Bone's querulous voice and smiled to myself.

When I reached the front door of my house I saw Rocky Napier approaching from the other side of the street.

'*Mimosa!*' he exclaimed. 'Why didn't *I* think of that?'

'I couldn't resist it,' I said. 'It makes one think . . .'

'Of Italy and the Riviera, of course.'

'I've never been there,' I reminded him; 'it's just that it seemed such a lovely day and I felt I wanted it.'

'Yes, that's a better reason.'

We walked upstairs together. As we came to his door some impulse made me unwrap the flowers. I saw that the bunch divided easily into two branches. 'Do have a piece,' I said, 'I should like you to.'

'How sweet of you and how like you,' he said easily. 'Have you got anything nice for tea? I haven't.'

'I don't think I have particularly,' I said, my thoughts going inside my cake tin with a harlequin on the lid and remembering only a small wedge of sandwich cake there.

'I know, let's be daring and go *out* to tea.'

I stood holding the mimosa. 'We must put this in water first.'

'Yes, put it in our kitchen.' He took it from me, filled a jug with water and put it on the draining-board.

We went out again to a café he knew, a place I had never discovered, where they had good cakes. But it hardly seemed to matter about the cakes. Perhaps it was because I had had a large and rather late luncheon, but I didn't feel very hungry. He was so gay and amusing and he made me feel that I was gay and amusing too and some of the things I said were really quite witty.

It wasn't till afterwards that I remembered the Wren officers. By that time it was evening and I was back in my own kitchen, wondering what to have for supper. I suddenly realized, too, that we had left all the mimosa in the Napiers' kitchen. I could hardly go and ask him to give me back my half of it. Anyway, Helena had come in and I could hear them laughing together. I shouldn't have gossiped to William in that naughty way, and in Lent, too. It served me right that I should have no mimosa to remind me of the spring day, but only a disturbed feeling which was most unlike me. There was a vase of catkins and twigs on the table in my sitting-room. 'Oh, the kind of women who bring dry twigs into the house and expect leaves to come on them!' Hadn't Rocky said something like that at tea?

CHAPTER NINE

ROCKY RETURNED my half of the mimosa next morning, when I was hurrying to go out to my work. It had lost its first fluffiness and looked like the café table decoration that William disliked. The spring weather had also gone and Rocky himself appeared in a dressing-gown with his hair ruffled. I felt too embarrassed to look at him and put my hand out through the half open kitchen door and took the mimosa quickly, putting it in the vase with the twigs and catkins.

On the bus I began thinking that William had been right and I was annoyed to have to admit it. Mimosa did lose its first freshness too quickly to be worth buying and I must not allow myself to have feelings, but must only observe the effects of other people's.

I sat down at my table and began going grimly through a card-index of names and addresses. Edith Bankes-Tolliver, 118 Montgomery Square . . . that was quite near me. I wondered if she came to our church. Perhaps Julian would know her . . . I really ought to make a list of the distressed gentlewomen in our district and try to visit them. Most of them lived alone and it was quite likely that I might be able to do some shopping for them or read to them or even just sit and let them talk . . . I was deep in thoughts of the good works I was going to immerse myself in, when Mrs Bonner came into the room and reminded me that it was Wednesday and that we had arranged to go to the lunchtime service at St Ermin's. This meant that we had to hurry over our lunch – unlike yesterday's meal, it could not, I felt, be called luncheon – which we had at a self-service cafeteria near the church. Our trays rattled along on a moving belt at a terrifying speed, so that at the end of it all I found myself, bewildered and resentful, holding a tray full of things I would never have chosen had I had time to think about it, and without a saucer for my coffee. Mrs Bonner, who always came to such places, had done much better and began explaining to me where I had gone wrong.

'You get the saucer *after* you've taken a roll, if you have one. I generally don't as we are told not to waste bread, and *before* you get the hot dish,' she said, as we stood with our trays looking for two vacant places.

'Oh, that must be where I went wrong,' I said, looking down at the bullet-hard roll which I was sure I was going to waste. 'I think one ought to be allowed a trial run-through first, a sort of dress rehearsal.'

Mrs Bonner laughed heartily at the idea and at that moment saw two places at a table with two Indian gentlemen. 'I shouldn't go here if I were *alone*,' she whispered before we sat down, 'you never know, do you, but I think it's all right if you have somebody with you.'

Our companions certainly looked harmless enough and were evidently students of some kind, as they appeared to be discussing examination results. I listened fascinated to their staccato voices and the way they kept calling each other 'old boy'. They took no notice of us whatsoever and I do not think Mrs Bonner need have feared even if she had been alone.

We settled ourselves and our food at the table and I paused for a moment to draw breath before eating. The room was enormous, like something in a nightmare, one could hardly see from one end of it to the other, and as far as the eye could see was dotted with tables which were all full. In addition, a file of people moved in through a door at one end and formed a long line, fenced off from the main part of the room by a brass rail.

'*Time like an ever-rolling stream*
Bears all its sons away . . .'

I said, more to myself than to Mrs Bonner. 'This place gives me a hopeless kind of feeling.'

'Oh, it's quite cheap and the food isn't bad if you don't come here too often,' she said, cheerfully down-to-earth as always. 'It's useful if you're in a hurry.'

'One wouldn't believe there could be so many people,' I said, 'and one must love them all.' These are our neighbours, I thought, looking round at the clerks and students and typists and elderly eccentrics, bent over their dishes and newspapers.

'Hurry up, dear,' said Mrs Bonner briskly, 'it's twenty past already.'

The Indians had left us by now so I ventured to tell her what I had been thinking.

She looked up from her chocolate trifle, rather shocked. 'Oh, I don't think the Commandment is meant to be taken as literally as that,' she said sensibly. 'We really ought to be going, you know, or we shan't get a good seat. You know how crowded the church gets.'

We managed to find places rather near the back and Mrs Bonner expressed doubts as to whether we should be able to hear – the man last week had mumbled rather. Today the preacher was to be Archdeacon Hoccleve, a name that was unknown to me, and I guessed that he would be some old country clergyman who would certainly mumble. But I was completely wrong. He was an elderly man, certainly, but of a handsome and dignified appearance and his voice was strong and dramatic. His sermon too was equally unexpected. Hitherto the Lenten series had followed a more or less discernible course, but Archdeacon Hoccleve departed completely from the pattern by preaching about the Judgment Day. It was altogether a most peculiar sermon, full of long quotations from the more obscure English poets, and although the subject may in itself have been a suitable one for Lent, its matter and the manner of its delivery occasioned dismay and bewilderment rather than any more suitable feelings. It was also much longer than the sermons usually were, so that some of the office workers, who no doubt had stringent lunch hours, could be seen creeping out before it was finished.

Mrs Bonner was disgusted. 'That talk about the *Dies Irae*,' she said, 'that's Roman Catholic, you know. It ought not to be allowed here. Not that he seemed very High in other ways, though. I couldn't make him out at all. Some of the things he said were really quite abusive.'

We were by now at the church door, moving slowly out. I had been so absorbed and astonished by the sermon that I had forgotten to look for Everard Bone and I now saw that he was standing almost beside me. I remembered my resolution to try to think well of him and to make some friendly advance if the opportunity should arise. I felt that there could never be a better one than the extraordinary sermon we had just heard.

'Good afternoon,' I said quietly; 'what did you think of the sermon?'

He looked down at me with a puzzled expression and then his rather austere features softened into a smile. 'Good afternoon,' he said. 'I'm afraid I was so busy trying to keep myself from laughing that I was hardly able to take it in. I had always thought that grown-up people should have no difficulty in keeping their composure, but I know differently now.'

We were standing by ourselves, for Mrs Bonner, seeing that I was talking to a man, had slipped tactfully away. But I knew that I should have to face her questionings, unspoken though they might be, at the office next day. For she was both inquisitive and romantic and could not bear that anyone under forty should remain unmarried.

'Yes, it was certainly most unexpected,' I said, liking him better for admitting to a human failing. 'How is your paper getting on?' I asked, trying to put an interested note into my voice.

'Oh, we are giving it in two or three weeks' time. I believe you wanted to come and hear it, but I shouldn't advise you to. It will be frightfully dull.'

'Oh, but I should like to hear it,' I said, remembering that Rocky and I had been going to observe the anthropologists.

'Well, Helena can get you an invitation,' he said. 'And now, if you'll excuse me, I really must hurry off. Perhaps I shall see you there.'

I felt that I had made a slight advance, that an infinitesimal amount of virtue had gone out of me, and although I did not really like him I did not feel so actively hostile to him as I had before. But how was it possible to compare him with Rocky? All the same, I told myself sternly, it would not do to go thinking about Rocky like this. Yesterday, with the unexpected spring weather and the wine at luncheon there had perhaps been some excuse; today there was none. The grey March day, the hurried unappetizing meal and the alarming sermon made it more suitable that I should think of the stream of unattractive humanity in the cafeteria, the Judgment Day, even Everard Bone.

I decided to call in at the vicarage on my way home to see Winifred. It seemed a long time since I had had a talk with her and she would be interested to hear about the sermon.

I rang the bell and Mrs Jubb came to the door. Miss Malory was upstairs with Mrs Gray, helping her to get settled in. Perhaps I would like to go up to them?

I walked slowly upstairs, pausing on the first landing by the picture of the infant Samuel which hung in a dark corner and wondering if I should not turn back after all, for a talk with Winifred and Mrs Gray was not quite the same as the talk with Winifred which I had intended. But I decided that as Mrs Gray was coming to live at the vicarage I might just as well get to know her, so I went on and knocked at the door from behind which I heard voices.

'Oh, it's Miss Lathbury; how nice!' Mrs Gray herself opened the door. I looked beyond her into the room which Julian had been distempering not many weeks earlier. It was now attractively furnished and there was a coal fire burning in the grate. Winifred was crouching on the hearth-rug, tacking up the hem of a curtain.

'Hasn't Allegra made this room nice, Mildred?' she said as I came in. 'You'd never recognize it as being the same place.'

'Well, Winifred has helped me so much,' said Mrs Gray. 'You know what a lot there is to do when you move.'

I agreed, noting to myself that they were now 'Allegra' and 'Winifred' to each other, and being surprised and, I was forced to admit, a little irritated. 'Moving is certainly a business,' I observed tritely, 'but you seem to have everything beautifully arranged.' I remembered that I had not helped Helena Napier with the hems of her curtains when she moved in. I had merely peered through the banisters at her furniture being taken in and had only offered to help when it seemed almost certain that there would be nothing for me to do. What a much nicer character Winifred was than I! And yet perhaps the circumstances were a little different. One could hardly offer to help complete strangers, especially when they were as independent as Helena Napier. 'Can't I help with the curtains?' I asked.

'Well, that would be most kind.' The words hardly seemed to be out of my mouth before Mrs Gray had picked up another pile of curtains which were to be shortened along the line of the pins. I was a little dismayed, as we often are when our offers of help are taken at their face value, and I set to work rather grimly, especially as Mrs Gray herself was not doing anything at all. She was sitting gracefully in an armchair, stroking back her hair which was arranged at the back of her head in a kind of Grecian knot. This style, together with her pale oval face and rather vague graceful air, made her appear like a heroine in an Edwardian novel. There was something slightly unreal about her.

'I'm afraid I'm not very good at sewing,' she said, as if in explanation of her idleness, 'but I can at least be making a cup of tea. I do hope you can stay, Miss Lathbury?'

'Thank you, I should like to.'

She went out of the room and I could hear her filling a kettle and collecting china. I also heard a step on the stairs and Julian's voice saying 'May I come up? I can hear the attractive rattle of tea things. I hope I'm not too late?'

He did not come straight into the room where we were, but stayed to talk to Mrs Gray in the kitchen. Winifred and I sat with our curtains, not speaking. I could feel that we were both wanting to talk about Mrs Gray, but that was naturally quite impossible at that moment.

'One of these curtains seems a little longer than the other I remarked in a loud, stilted tone. 'I wonder if they were hung up or just measured with a tape? You often find when you come to hang them that there's some inequality in the length.'

Julian came into the room carrying a tray with crockery, bread-and-butter, jam and a cake. Mrs Gray followed with the tea.

'Isn't it fun, just like a picnic,' said Winifred from her seat on the hearthrug.

'I really ought not to be eating your jam, Mrs Gray,' I protested in the way one did in those days. 'I like plain bread-and-butter just as well, really I do.'

'Oh, please have some of this,' she said. 'It isn't really my ration, it was a present from Father Greatorex.'

'What, does Greatorex make jam?' asked Julian. 'I never knew he had such accomplishments.'

'Oh, no,' Mrs Gray laughed; 'just imagine it, the poor old thing! This was made by his sister who lives in the country. It's really delicious.'

'How nice of him to give it to you,' I said, 'it's certainly lovely jam.'

'Oh, Allegra's the sort of person people *want* to give things to,' said Winifred enthusiastically. 'Mildred, doesn't this hearthrug look familiar to you?'

I glanced at it and then realized to my surprise that I had

seen it somewhere before. In the vicarage, surely, perhaps in Julian's study?

'Yes, it's the one out of Julian's study,' said Winifred.

'Terribly kind of him, wasn't it?' said Mrs Gray. 'I hadn't got one suitable for this room and I just happened to be admiring it in Father Malory's study, quite *innocently* of course, when he gave it to me!'

'It looks much nicer in Mrs Gray's room than it did in my study,' said Julian, 'and anyway a rug isn't really necessary in a study.'

I noted with interest that they were still 'Mrs Gray' and 'Father Malory' to each other. 'It certainly matches this carpet very well,' I ventured.

'Yes, but it matched Father Malory's carpet too,' said Mrs Gray. 'It was really very self-sacrificing of him to give it to me.'

Julian murmured a little in embarrassment.

'Of course,' went on Mrs Gray in a clear voice as if she were making a speech, 'I always feel that one *ought* to give men the opportunity for self-sacrifice; their natures are so much less noble than ours.'

'Oh, do you think so?' asked Winifred seriously. 'I have known some very fine men.'

Julian smiled indulgently, but said nothing. I felt it was not a very suitable remark for a clergyman's widow to have made, though it was certainly amusing in a rather cheap way.

'I really must be going now,' I said in a voice that may have sounded a little chilly.

'Oh, Mildred, you haven't finished your curtains,' said Winifred.

'No I'm sorry, I'm afraid I haven't.'

'I know, why don't you come to tea on Friday and finish them then?' suggested Mrs Gray, smiling rather sweetly.

'Thank you, that would be nice,' I said, very much taken aback. I had not really imagined that she would expect me to finish the curtains.

'Then you can see the rest of my little flat,' said Mrs Gray. 'It isn't really on show yet, but I hope to have got it tidy by then.'

'Shall I come down with you?' asked Julian.

'Oh, please don't bother. I'll let myself out,' I said. I hurried down the stairs, feeling that I had made an ungraceful exit. The three upstairs seemed so self-sufficient, as if they did not want me there. Was I annoyed because Mrs Gray seemed to be getting on so well with the Malorys? I asked myself. It surely could not be that I was jealous? No, I dismissed that disturbing thought from my mind as quickly as it came in. Today was obviously not a good day, that was it. It had not started well and it would not end well. But I could at least save something of it by going home and doing some washing.

'Hullo! You look like a wet week at Blackpool,' Sister Blatt's jolly voice boomed out of the dusk.

'Do I?' I said, forced to smile in spite of everything.

'Been to the vicarage?'

'Yes.'

'Oh, they're always with Mrs Gray now, those two,' said Sister Blatt bluntly. 'I wanted to see Father Malory about the Confirmation classes but he was helping her to put up curtain rods.'

'Well, the Malorys are such friendly, helpful sort of people,' I said.

She snorted and I watched her hoist herself slowly on to her bicycle and move off to perform some good work. Then I went back to my flat and collected a great deal of washing to do. It was depressing the way the same old things turned up every week. Just the kind of underclothes a person like me might wear, I thought dejectedly, so there is no need to describe them.

CHAPTER TEN

AT LAST THE day came when Helena and Everard were to read their paper before the Learned Society. I had been afraid that she would forget her promise to invite me, but she came up to my flat the evening before and we arranged what time we should go. There was a tea party first to which guests could be taken.

'The new President will be in the Chair,' said Helena rather formally. 'He is such an old man that it's a wonder he hasn't been President before, but then there are a lot of the old ones. It will be our turn soon.'

I was a little preoccupied with what I should wear. I did not think it likely that a meeting of a Learned Society would be in any sense a fashionable gathering, but I was anxious not to disgrace the Napiers and had taken the bold step of buying a new hat to go with my brown winter coat even before I knew definitely that I was to go. Helena was very elegant in black. 'One mustn't *look* like a female anthropologist,' she explained.

'It wouldn't matter if you looked like some of those American girls,' said Rocky. 'They know how to dress.'

'Trust you to notice that,' she said rather sourly.

'I notice everything. Especially Mildred's charming new hat.'

I accepted the compliment as gracefully as I could, but I was sufficiently unused to having anybody make any comment on my appearance to find it embarrassing to have attention drawn to me in any way.

'Nothing is more becoming than a velvet hat,' Rocky went on, 'and the brown brings out the colour of your eyes which look like a good dark sherry.'

'Everard will meet us there,' said Helena rather impatiently. 'We shall have a few last-minute things to discuss, so perhaps you would look after Mildred?' she added, turning to her husband. 'I think we had better take a taxi.'

The premises of the Learned Society were not very far from St Ermin's and I pointed it out to Helena on the way.

'Why, isn't it a ruin?' she asked. 'Fancy having services in a ruin! I should feel there was something particularly holy about that.'

I explained that one aisle was undamaged and that we had the services there, but I suppose she must have been nervous at the idea of the paper, for she did not seem to be listening and a minute or two afterwards the taxi drew up outside a good solid-looking Victorian house, with the brass plate of the Learned Society on its door.

In the hall Helena signed a book for us and we went upstairs to the library where the tea party was to be held. Everard Bone, looking elegant and rather cross, was standing by the door.

'I thought you were never coming,' he said to Helena, and then nodded 'good afternoon' to Rocky and me in a cursory way.

'I think we had better retire to a corner and observe the Learned Society,' said Rocky, guiding me over to where a table was spread with cups and saucers and plates of food.

'What a lot of strange-looking people,' I whispered.

'Nobody seems to be eating yet,' Rocky observed, 'but I think we had better station ourselves near the food. I dare say these types are little better than primitive people when it comes to eating.'

'My dear sir, I fear we are even worse,' said an elderly man with a large head, who was standing near us. 'The so-called primitive peoples have an elaborate order and precedence in eating but I'm afraid that when we get started it's every man for himself.'

'The survival of the fittest?' Rocky suggested.

'Yes, perhaps that is it. I hope we shall remember our

manners sufficiently to offer refreshment to the ladies first,' continued the old man, with a little bow in my direction. 'Ah, here is our excellent Miss Clovis with the teapot.' He turned away and busied himself with cups and saucers.

'Do you think he is going to bring some to us?' I asked Rocky.

'Well, after what he has just said I should think he will surely bring you a cup of tea.'

But we were wrong, for he quickly helped himself to tea, collected an assortment of sandwiches and cakes on a plate and retired to the opposite corner of the room. We watched other elderly and middle-aged men doing the same, though one was held back by an imperious woman's voice calling 'Now, Herbert, no milk for Miss Jellink, remember!'

Rocky and I joined in a general scramble and took our spoils to a convenient bookcase where we could put our cups down on a shelf.

'These are quite obviously the books that nobody reads,' said Rocky, studying their titles. 'But it's a comfort to know that they are here if you ever should want to read them. I'm sure I should find them more entertaining than the more up-to-date ones. *Wild Beasts and their Ways; Five Years with the Congo Cannibals; With Camera and Pen in Northern Nigeria; Sunshine and Storm in Rhodesia*. I wish people still wrote books with titles like that. Nowadays I believe it simply isn't done to show a photograph of "The Author with his Pygmy Friends" – we have become too depressingly scientific.'

'You might write a book about your adventures in Italy,' I suggested. 'It might well have such a title.'

We amused ourselves by discussing the variations on this theme and while we were in the middle of our fantasies Everard and Helena came up to us and began to point out some of the more eminent persons present. The President was a tall mild-looking old man with a white wispy beard, in which some crumbly fragments of meringue had lodged themselves. In his younger days he had apparently written some rather startling pamphlets about the nature of the universe.

'I believe his father turned him out of the house,' said Everard. 'You see, he was a Methodist Minister and when he found out that his son was a militant atheist I suppose it became awkward.'

'That old man an atheist!' I exclaimed, unable to believe that anyone who looked so mild and benevolent should be what always sounded such a very wicked and startling thing. 'But he looks so unlike that. More like a bishop, really.'

'Or an old-fashioned picture of God,' suggested Rocky. 'I like to imagine the scene in the Victorian household, the father's wrath and the mother's tears, those dreadful scenes at the breakfast table. And yet, what does it all matter now? In a few years' time they will all be together in Heaven.'

'Oh, *darling*,' said Helena impatiently, 'how ridiculous you are. Afterwards I'll introduce you to some of the really worth-while people here. Apfelbaum, Tyrell Todd, and Steinartz from Yale – the new generation.'

'They sound delightful,' said Rocky gravely.

'I think we should be going in,' said Everard. 'The President seems to be moving.'

We now followed them into a room adjoining the library where a number of people were already sitting. I noticed that the front rows were basket chairs and that one or two elderly men and women had settled themselves comfortably. One old man wore a purple muffler wound round his neck; an old woman took a piece of multi-coloured knitting from a raffia bag and began to work on it.

Rocky and I took our seats somewhere in the middle of the room on the harder chairs. The younger people sat here, girls with flowing hair and scarlet nails and youths with hair almost as flowing and corduroy trousers. I noticed one or two Americans, serious-looking young men with rimless glasses and open notebooks, and a group of Africans, talking in a strange language. There was a buzz of unintelligible conversation all around us.

'What an interesting-looking lot of people,' I said, 'quite unlike anything I'm used to.'

'You can understand people saying that it takes all sorts to make a world,' said Rocky. 'One wonders if quite so many sorts are necessary.'

'It must be wonderful to have an interest in some learned subject,' I said. 'This seems to be a thing that old and young can enjoy equally.'

Rocky laughed. 'I don't think Helena or Everard would approve of that attitude. You make it sound like a game of golf. And remember, we aren't here to enjoy ourselves. The paper will be long and the chairs hard. I think our ordeal is about to begin.'

The President had now risen to his feet and was introducing Helena and Everard in a vague little speech. It almost sounded as if he thought they were husband and wife, but he smiled so nicely through his wispy beard that nobody could possibly have taken offence. Everard and Helena sat to one side of him, while a stocky red-haired young man, who had been pointed out to us as the Secretary, took notes.

'And now I will leave our young friends to tell their own tale,' said the President. 'Their paper is entitled . . .' he fumbled with a pair of gold-rimmed spectacles and then read in a clear deliberate voice some words which conveyed so little to me at the time that I am afraid I have now forgotten them. Doubtless the title is recorded somewhere in the archives or minutes of the Learned Society.

I looked hopefully towards the lantern which stood at the back of the room, but it did not seem as if there were going to be any slides. The Americans' pencils were poised over their notebooks, the elderly lady put down her knitting for a moment. Helena Napier stood up and began to speak. I can only say that she 'began to speak' for I very soon lost the thread of what she was saying and found myself looking round the room, studying my surroundings and companions.

The room was very high with a lincrusta ceiling and an elaborate mantelpiece of brawn-like marble. Long windows opened on to a balcony and through them I could just see the tender green of a newly unfolded tree in the square gardens. It seemed strange that we should all be sitting indoors on such a lovely day. But I must not look out of the window; this was a great occasion and I was a privileged person. It was certainly a pity that my lack of higher education made it impossible for me to concentrate on anything more difficult than a fairly straightforward sermon or committee meeting. Helena's voice sounded so clear and competent that I was sure that what she was saying was of great value. Rocky must be very proud of her. I noticed the Americans writing furiously in their books. It was a pity I had not thought of reading up on the subject a little; that would have been far more to the point than buying a new hat. It was humiliating to realize that everybody in the room but me understood and was able to take an intelligent interest in what Helena was saying. I fixed my eyes on her with a fresh determination to concentrate, but then my attention was distracted by the old lady with her knitting. I saw that the knitting drooped slackly from her hands and that her head was bowed forward on her breast. Then I saw it suddenly jerk up. She had been asleep. This revelation gave me some comfort and I began looking round the room again, this time at the gold-lettered boards with the names of those who had won a particular medal or had been benefactors of the society in some way. I read down the list, fascinated. 1904 – Herbert Franklin Crisp, 1905 – Egfried Stummelbaum, 1906 – Edward Ellis Darwin Rumble, 1907 – Ethel Victoria Thorneycroft-Nollard . . . A woman in 1907! What had she done to win this medal? What must she have been like? I imagined her in a long skirt, striding through the jungle, fearlessly questioning natives who had never before seen a white woman. A kind of Mary Kingsley, but perhaps even more remarkable in that she was an anthropologist, the kind of thing a woman would not naturally be, especially in 1907. Perhaps she was among the elderly people in the basket chairs, she might even be the one knitting and dozing . . . I was so absorbed in my speculations that I did not notice that Helena had stopped speaking, until I was aware of Everard Bone standing up in her place and saying, as far as I could judge, very much the same sort of thing that Helena had already said. He spoke exceptionally well, hardly consulting his notes at all, and once or twice a ripple of laughter ran through the audience as if he had made a joke. I took this opportunity of studying him dispassionately, wondering what it was that made Helena's eyes sparkle when his name was mentioned. He was certainly very clever and handsome, too, in his own way, but there was no warmth or charm about his personality. I began imagining him as a clergyman and decided that he would make a good one. His rather forbidding manner would be useful to him. I realized that one might love him secretly with no hope of encouragement, which can be very enjoyable for the young or inexperienced.

When Everard had finished, the President, who looked as if he too had been dozing, got up and made a kindly speech. 'And now, I am sure there are many points you are eager to discuss,' he went on, 'who is – ah – going to start the ball rolling?'

There was the usual embarrassed silence, nobody liking to be first. Some chairs scraped on the floor and a woman sitting along our row pushed past us and went out. She was carrying a string-bag, containing a newspaper-wrapped bundle from which a fish's tail protruded. Helena smiled nervously. Everard took off his horn-rimmed spectacles and covered his eyes with his hand.

'Ah, Dr Apfelbaum – first in the field,' said the President in a relieved voice and everybody sat back in their chairs and looked up expectantly. How dreadful it would have been, I thought, if *nobody* had wanted to ask a question.

Dr Apfelbaum was a stocky man of Teutonic appearance. What he said was quite unintelligible to me, both from its content and because of his very marked foreign accent, but Everard dealt with him very competently. Now that the ball was rolling, other speakers followed in quick succession. In fact, they were jumping up and down like Jacks-in-the-boxes, hardly waiting for each other to finish. It seemed that they had all 'done' some particular tribe or area and could furnish parallels or contradictions from their own experience.

'I shall just let it *flow* over me,' said Rocky, but this was not always possible. There was, at one point, a sharp exchange between Dr Apfelbaum and a stout dark-haired woman, and an apparently irrelevant question from the old man in the purple muffler provoked hearty laughter.

'*No* ceremonial devouring of human flesh?' he repeated in a disappointed tone, and sat down, shaking his head and muttering.

At last the meeting appeared to be at an end. Helena took Rocky away and began to introduce him to various people. I stood rather awkwardly by the door, wondering whether I ought to go home now or whether it would seem discourteous not to thank Helena and Everard for inviting me. The people round me seemed to have settled down into little groups, many of which were carrying on learned discussions.

'Well, what did you think of it? I'm afraid you must have been very bored?'

Everard Bone had broken away from a group of Americans and was standing by my side. I was grateful to him for rescuing me though I could think of no conversation beyond a polite murmur and was quite sure that he was wanting to get back to discussing his paper with people who were able to.

'I think I must be going home now,' I said. 'Thank you very much for asking me.'

'Oh, I expect we shall be going somewhere for dinner,' he said vaguely. 'You may as well come too.'

'Well, I haven't really anything to eat at home,' I began, but then stopped as I realized that a dreary revelation of the state of one's larder was hardly the way to respond to an invitation to dinner. 'I should like to join you if I may.'

'I wish they'd hurry up,' said Everard, looking over to where Helena and Rocky were talking to a group of people.

'They are just like everybody else, really,' I said, half to myself. 'That old woman knitting, she went to sleep.'

'That was the President's wife,' said Everard, 'she always does.'

'Did she work with him in the field?' I asked.

'Good Heavens, no! She knows nothing at all about anthropology.'

'Didn't she even do the index or the proof-reading for one of his books? You know what it often says in a preface or dedication – "To my wife, who undertook the arduous duty of proof-reading" or making the index.'

'She may have done that. After all, it's what wives are for.' He suddenly smiled and I remembered my Lenten resolution to try to like him. It was getting a little easier but I felt that at any moment I might have a setback.

'God, how I want a drink!' said Helena in her characteristic way. She and Rocky had now joined us.

'I hope God is listening,' said Rocky, 'because I do too. I was very much afraid that those people were going to join us for dinner.'

'I think you were rude to them,' said Helena crossly, 'otherwise they might have done and we could have had some interesting conversation for a change.'

'Are there any of the conveniences of civilization in this place?' asked Rocky.

'Yes, of course there are. Everard will show you. Perhaps you would like to come with me, Mildred?' said Helena.

I followed her upstairs and into a room which had 'Ladies' printed on a card on the door. The first thing that caught my eye inside was a rolled-up Union Jack. This seemed a little out of place, as did the portraits of native chiefs which were stacked against the walls under the wash-basins.

'There isn't nearly enough storage space here, as you may have gathered,' explained Helena. 'This room is the repository for any junk that can't go anywhere else.'

'It seems in character with the rest of the place,' I remarked.

'So does the fact that there is neither soap nor towel,' said Helena. 'We are at our most primitive here, but after all it is only the basic needs that have to be supplied.'

'Well, that's the main thing,' I said feebly.

'At least we don't have a brooding old woman who expects you to drop sixpence into a saucer,' said Helena. 'I always think those women must see real drama, when you realize what scenes are enacted in ladies' cloakrooms.'

'Yes, I suppose things do go on there,' I agreed. I remembered girlhood dances where one had stayed there too long, though never long enough to last out the dance for which one hadn't a partner. I didn't suppose Helena had ever known that, and yet it was in its way quite a deep experience.

'It used to be worse, somehow, during the war,' said Helena. 'I remember once – oh, it was so depressing – there was just a dim blue bulb that made everything look ghastly and I was never going to see him any more. When I came out he was going to tell me that it was all over – you know the kind of thing, tears and whisky and then going out into that awful darkness.'

As I did not know I could only go on tidying my hair in a sympathetic silence. Helena came to the mirror and began doing something to her eyelashes with a little brush. 'Everard seems to like you,' she remarked carelessly.

'Oh, I'm sure he doesn't. I can never think of anything to say to him.'

'You think Rocky is much more attractive, don't you?'

'Well, yes, I do think he is nicer,' I said confusedly, for I was not used to discussing people in such terms. And yet I supposed that if I was honest with myself I should have to admit that 'attractive' was a better word than 'nice', and expressed my feeling about Rocky more accurately. But it was wrong to talk like this, and I wished Helena would stop or that I had gone home and left the three of them to have dinner together. 'I suppose we'd better not keep them waiting too long,' I said, in an attempt to stop the conversation from going any further.

'Oh, it won't do them any harm, but I could certainly do with a drink,' said Helena. 'Come along.'

I followed her downstairs, feeling like a dog or some inferior class of person.

The men were standing waiting for us in the hall. Whatever conversation they may have been having appeared to be at an end now, and they hurried us out rather unceremoniously leaving us to walk a little way behind them. I suppose they were too hungry and tired of waiting to think anything of it, but it did not seem a very good beginning to the evening.

Eventually we reached a restaurant and were shown to a table. Some drinks were ordered and one was handed to me. It was something very strong, made with gin, I think. I sipped cautiously while Rocky and Everard argued over the wine list. They were nearly as fussy as William, though in a different way, and I began to think that it would really be much easier if we just had water, though I lacked the courage to suggest it.

When the first course came, it turned out to be spaghetti of a particularly long and rubbery kind. Rocky showed me how to twist it round my fork but I found it very difficult to manage and it made conversation quite impossible. Perhaps long spaghetti is the kind of thing that ought to be eaten quite alone with nobody to watch one's struggles. Surely many a romance must have been nipped in the bud by sitting opposite somebody eating spaghetti?

After that ordeal some meat was brought and the wine with it, and conversation started again. Rocky began to ask frivolous questions about the paper.

'What was that about a man being expected to sleep with an unmarried sister-in-law who is visiting his house?' he asked.

'That's called a joking relationship,' said Everard precisely.

'Not exactly what one would call a joke,' said Rocky, 'though it could be fun. It would depend on the sister-in-law, of course. Does he *have* to sleep with her?'

'Oh, Rocky, you don't understand,' said Helena impatiently. It was obvious that she and Everard did not appreciate jokes about their subject.

'I wonder if the study of societies where polygamy is a commonplace encourages immorality?' asked Rocky seriously, turning to Everard. 'Would you say that it did?'

'There is no reason why it should,' said Everard.

'Do anthropologists tend to have many wives at the same time?' he went on. 'Have you found that?'

'They would naturally tend to conceal such things,' said Everard with a half smile, 'and one could hardly ask them.'

'Oh, they are drearily monogamous,' said Helena, 'and very virtuous in other ways too. Much better than many of these so-called good people who go to church.' She turned a half-amused, half-spiteful glance towards me.

'Well, Mildred, what do you say to that?' asked Rocky.

'Churchgoers are used to being accused of things,' I said. 'I have never found out what exactly it is that we do or are supposed to do.'

'We are whited sepulchres,' said Everard. 'We don't practise what we preach. Isn't that it, Helena?'

'One expects you to behave better than other people,' said Helena, 'and of course you don't.'

'Why should we? We are only human, aren't we, Miss Lathbury?'

It seemed now as if we had changed sides. Before, Helena and Everard had been ranged against Rocky and me – now Everard was my partner. I have never been very good at games; people never chose me at school when it came to picking sides. But Everard had no choice. This state of affairs continued through dinner and afterwards when we went out into the street. Everard and I walked together, almost as if he had arranged it that way, but it cannot have been for the pleasure of my company, as our conversation was very poor.

'Do you live near here?' I asked, knowing that he did not.

'No, I live in Chelsea. I suppose one would hardly call it near.'

'No, but it isn't as far away as if you lived in Hendon or Putney.'

'That would be further, certainly.'

We walked a few steps in silence. I could hear Rocky and Helena having an argument in low angry tones.

'Do you live in a house or a flat?' I asked in a loud desperate voice.

'I did live in my mother's house after I came out of the Army, but I've just moved into a flat of my own, quite near.'

'You were lucky to find one.'

'Yes, I know the person who owns the house and one of the tenants happened to be leaving.' He stood by a bus-stop. 'I think I can get a bus from here.'

Helena and Rocky had caught us up and we stood in a little group by the bus-stop. Good nights and thanks were exchanged.

'Will you ring me up?' said Helena to Everard.

'I shall probably be away for a few days,' he said vaguely.

At a meeting of the Prehistoric Society? I wondered.

'Aren't you coming to the next meeting?' Helena persisted. 'Tyrell Todd is reading a paper on pygmies.'

'Oh, pygmies – well, I don't know.'

At that moment Everard's bus came and he got on to it without looking back.

Rocky found a taxi and we drove most of the way in silence, or rather Helena was silent while Rocky and I discussed the evening or as much of it as could be discussed.

'You and Everard seemed to be having an interesting conversation,' said Helena at last. 'Was he declaring himself or something?' Her tone was rather light and cruel as if it were the most impossible thing in the world.

'He was telling me about his new flat,' I said lamely.

'Actually he might do very well for Mildred,' said Rocky. 'Had we thought of that? Obviously, we must find her a good husband.'

'The driver seems to be going past our house,' I said. 'Did you tell him the number?'

'Oh, this will do.' Rocky tapped on the glass and we got out. We were rather far from our own door, and just as we were walking past the parish hall, Teddy Lemon and a group of lads came out, laughing and talking in their rough voices. My heart warmed towards them, so good and simple with their uncomplicated lives. If only I had come straight home after the paper. This was Julian's boys' club night and I could have been there serving in the canteen – much more in my line than the sort of evening I had just spent.

CHAPTER ELEVEN

LOVE WAS rather a terrible thing, I decided next morning, remembering the undercurrents of the evening before. Not perhaps my cup of tea. It would be best not to see too much of the Napiers and their disturbing kind of life, but to meet only people like Julian and Winifred Malory and Dora Caldicote, from whom I had had a letter that morning. She hinted vaguely at 'unpleasantness' at school, perhaps the affair William had told me about, and asked if she might come and stay with me for a part of her Easter holiday. So I busied myself getting the little spare-room ready, arranging daffodils in a bowl on the mantelpiece and putting out the rather useless little embroidered guest towels. The room looked pretty and comfortable, like an illustration in one of the women's magazines. I knew it would not look like that for long after Dora's arrival and was a little sad when I went to talk to her over her unpacking and saw the familiar bulging canvas bag and her hair-net lying on the mantelpiece.

'Why, Mildred,' she exclaimed, 'what have you done to yourself? You look different.'

No compliments, of course; Dora was too old and honest a friend ever to flatter me, but she had the power of making me feel rather foolish, especially as I had not realized that she might find any difference in my appearance since the last time we met. I suppose I had taken to using a little more make-up, my hair was more carefully arranged, my clothes a little less drab. I was hardly honest enough to admit even to myself that meeting the Napiers had made this difference and I certainly did not admit it to Dora.

'You must be trying to bring William up to scratch,' she said, 'is that it?'

I laughed gratefully.

'There's not much you can do when you're over thirty,' she

went on complacently. 'You get too set in your ways, really. Besides, marriage isn't everything.'

'No, it certainly isn't,' I agreed, 'and there's nobody I want to marry that I can think of. Not even William.'

'I don't know anyone either, at the moment,' said Dora.

We lapsed into a comfortable silence. It was a kind of fiction that we had always kept up, this not knowing anyone at the moment that we wanted to marry, as if there had been in the past and would be in the future.

'How's school?' I asked.

'Oh, Protheroe and I aren't on speaking terms,' said Dora vigorously. She was a small, stocky person with red hair, not at all like her brother, and could look very fierce at times.

'I'm sorry to hear that,' I said. 'But I should imagine Miss Protheroe is rather difficult to get on with.'

'Difficult! It's a wonder that woman keeps any of her staff.'

'What happened?'

'Oh, well, I let my form go into chapel without hats one morning, and you know how she is about that sort of thing. Of course I've no use for any of this nonsense . . .' I let Dora go on but did not really listen, for I knew her views on Miss Protheroe and on organized religion of any kind. We had often argued about it in the past. I wondered that she should waste so much energy fighting over a little matter like wearing hats in chapel, but then I told myself that, after all, life was like that for most of us – the small unpleasantnesses rather than the great tragedies; the little useless longings rather than the great renunciations and dramatic love affairs of history or fiction.

'What would you like to do this afternoon?' I asked. 'Shall we go shopping?'

Dora's face brightened. 'Oh, yes, that would be nice.'

Later, as we were trying on dresses in the inexpensive department of a large store, I forgot all about the Napiers and the complications of knowing them. I was back in those happier days when the company of women friends had seemed enough.

'Oh, dear, this is too tight on the hips,' said Dora, her ruffled head and flushed face emerging through the neck of a brown woollen dress.

'I'm not sure that it's your colour,' I said doubtfully. 'I've come to the conclusion that we should avoid brown. It does the wrong kind of things to people over thirty, unless they're *very* smart. When my brown coat is worn out I shall get a black or a navy one.'

'Now you're talking like a fashion magazine,' said Dora, struggling with the zip-fastener. 'I've always had a brown wool dress for everyday.'

Yes, and look at you, I thought, with one of those sudden flashes of unkindness that attack us all sometimes. 'Why not try this green?' I suggested. 'It would suit you.'

'Good Heavens, whatever would people at school say if I appeared in a dress that colour?' Dora exclaimed. 'I shouldn't know myself. No, I'll just ask for the brown in a larger size. It's just what I want.'

They had the dress in a larger size which was now a little too large, but Dora seemed perfectly satisfied and bought it. 'I don't know what's the matter with you, Mildred,' she complained. 'You never used to bother much about clothes.'

'Where shall we have tea?' I asked, changing the subject because I felt myself unable to give a satisfactory explanation.

'Oh, the Corner House!' said Dora enthusiastically. 'You know how I enjoy that.'

We made our way to one of these great institutions and found ourselves in an almost noble room with marble pillars and white and gold decorations. The orchestra was playing *Si mes vers avaient des ailes* and I was back in imagination in some Edwardian drawing-room. How had they been able to bear those songs? I wondered. Sometimes we could hardly bear them now, although we might laugh at them, the nostalgia was too much. I felt suddenly desolate in Dora's company.

She was studying the menu with a satisfied expression on her face. 'Scrambled eggs,' she read, 'but of course they wouldn't be real. Curried whale, goodness, you wouldn't feel like having that for tea, would you? I had an argument about it the other day with Protheroe – you know how strictly she keeps Lent and all that sort of nonsense – well, there she was eating whale meat thinking it was fish!'

'Well, isn't it?'

'No, of course it isn't. The whale is a *mammal*,' said Dora in a loud truculent tone. 'So you see it can hardly count as fish.'

The waitress was standing over us to take our order. 'Just tea and a cake for me,' I murmured quickly, but Dora took her time and ordered various sandwiches.

'Was there unpleasantness about the whale?' I asked unkindly.

'Oh, no. I think Protheroe was rather upset though. I couldn't help feeling it was one up to me – paid her back for all that fuss about wearing hats in chapel.'

The orchestra started to play a rumba and I to pour out the tea. Dora opened a sandwich and looked inside. 'Paste,' she declared. 'I tell you what, Mildred, how would it be if we went down to the Old Girls' Reunion on Saturday? You know they're dedicating the window in memory of Miss Ridout? Had you thought of going?'

'Oh, is it this Saturday? I had a notice about it, of course, but hadn't realized it was so soon. It would be a nice expedition,' I ventured. 'The spring flowers would be out.'

We discussed the expedition further as we rode along Piccadilly on the top of a bus. The sun was out and there were still people sitting on chairs in the park.

'It looks odd to see a clergyman holding somebody's hand in public,' said Dora chattily. 'I don't know why, but it does.'

'Where?' I asked.

'Look – there,' she said, pointing out a couple lolling in deckchairs.

'Oh, but it *can't* be!' I exclaimed, but there was no doubt that the clergyman was Julian Malory and that the hand he was holding was Allegra Gray's.

'How do you mean it can't be?' said Dora looking again. 'He certainly was holding her hand. Why, isn't it Julian Malory? What a joke! Who's he with?'

'She's a widow, a Mrs Gray, who's come to live in the flat at the vicarage.'

'Oh, I see. Well, I suppose there's nothing wrong in that?'

'No, of course there isn't,' I said rather sharply. It was just thoroughly unsuitable, sitting there for everyone to see, not even on the hard iron chairs but lolling in deckchairs. 'Fancy going into the park to hold hands, though, it seems rather an odd thing to do.'

'Well, I don't suppose they went there expressly for that purpose,' said Dora stubbornly. 'They probably went for a walk and decided to sit down and then somehow it came about. After all, holding hands is quite a natural affectionate gesture.'

'How do *you* know?' I heard myself say.

'Mildred! What *is* the matter with you? Are *you* in love with the vicar or what?' she said, so loudly that the people in front of us nudged each other and sniggered.

'No, of course not,' I said in a low angry tone, 'but it seems so unsuitable, the whole thing. Winifred and everything, oh, I can't explain now.'

'Well, I don't see what you're making such a fuss about,' said Dora, maddeningly calm. 'It's a lovely day and she's very attractive and a widow and he's not married, so it's all right. I see quite a little romance blowing up.'

By the time we had got off the bus we were arguing quite openly. It was foolish and pointless but somehow we could not stop. I saw us in twenty or thirty years' time, perhaps living together, bickering about silly trifles. It was a depressing picture.

'After all a clergyman is a man and entitled to human feelings,' Dora went on.

It was obvious to me now that she was in the kind of mood to disagree automatically with everything I said, for usually she maintained that clergymen didn't count as men and therefore couldn't be expected to have human feelings.

'Julian isn't the marrying sort,' I persisted. 'Anyway, Mrs Gray wouldn't be at all suitable for him.'

'Oh, I think you've had your eye on him for yourself all this time,' said Dora in an irritating jocular tone. '*That's* why you've been smartening yourself up.'

It was useless to deny it, once she had got the idea into her head. I was grateful to see the grey bulk of Sister Blatt looming before us as we reached the church.

'Hullo,' she said as we came up to her. 'What on earth's happened to Father Malory?' she asked. 'Evensong's in five minutes and there's no sign of him. Miss Malory said he was going to a meeting at S.P.G. House this afternoon. It must have been a very long one.' She laughed. 'You don't think he's had a sudden call to the Mission Field, do you?'

'Surely he would have come back here first and let us know?' I said.

'Oh, well, I dare say Father Greatorex will turn up,' said Sister Blatt cheerfully and went into church.

Dora giggled. '*We* could tell her where Father Malory is, couldn't we, Mildred? I think we should blackmail him.'

We went into the house. Dora decided to do some washing before supper and within half an hour the kitchen was festooned with lines of depressing-looking underwear – fawn lock-knit knickers and petticoats of the same material. It was even drearier than mine.

At supper we talked about our old school, William, and matters of general interest. Julian Malory was not mentioned again. I was in the kitchen making some tea when there was a knock at the door and Rocky's head peeped round.

'Helena has gone to hear a paper about pygmies,' he said, 'and I'm all alone. May I come in?'

'Yes, do,' I said, in a confused way, embarrassed by the washing hanging up.

'My friend Dora Caldicote is here,' I said, as he threaded his way through the lines of dripping garments.

'Oh, what fun!' he said lightly. 'Are you going to give me some coffee?'

'Well, we were having tea,' I said, feeling a little ashamed, both of the tea and of myself for feeling ashamed of it, 'but I can easily make you some coffee.'

'No, indeed you won't. I love tea.'

'You are Mildred's old school chum,' he said to Dora in a teasing way. 'I've heard all about you.'

Dora flushed and smiled. Oh, the awkward Wren officers, I thought, seeing them standing on the balcony at the Admiral's villa. How they must have blossomed under that charm!

Rocky was standing by the window. 'There's your vicar,' he said. 'Would there be a service now?'

'Is he alone?' asked Dora.

'Yes, very much so, and wearing rather a becoming cloak. I always think I should look rather well in one of those.'

'We saw him holding somebody's hand in the park this afternoon and Mildred was rather upset,' said Dora gaily. 'Poor man, *I* didn't see why he shouldn't.'

'Oh, but we can't have that,' said Rocky. 'I always look on him as Mildred's property. But never mind,' he turned towards me, 'I don't suppose his hand would be very pleasant to hold. We'll find somebody better for you.'

'He was supposed to be in church taking Evensong,' said Dora, who would not leave the subject.

'Oh, the poor man, I can imagine nothing more depressing on a fine weekday evening. Wondering if anybody will come or getting tired of seeing just the same faithful few. Why don't we go out and have a drink?' he asked in a bored way.

'Not after drinking tea, thank you. I don't think I should feel like it,' I said.

'Dear Mildred, you must learn to feel like drinking at *any* time. I shall make myself responsible for your education.'

So of course we did go. Dora had cider and got rather giggly with Rocky, telling him stories about our schooldays which I found embarrassing. I, in my wish to be different and not to be thought a school-marm, had said I would have beer, which turned out to be flat and bitter, with a taste such as I imagine washing-up water might have.

'Mildred is sad about her vicar,' said Rocky. 'We'll find her an anthropologist.'

'I don't want anyone,' I said, afraid that I was sounding childish and sulky but quite unable to do anything about it.

'If Everard Bone were here we might persuade him to hold your hand,' he went on teasingly. 'How would you like that?'

For a moment I almost did wish that Everard Bone could be with us. He was quiet and sensible and a churchgoer. We should make dull stilted conversation with no hidden meanings to it. He would accept the story of Julian and Mrs Gray in the park without teasing me about it; he might even understand that it was a worrying business altogether. For it was. If Julian were to marry Mrs Gray what was to happen to Winifred? I was quite sure now that he did intend to marry her and could not imagine why I had not seen it all along. Clergymen did not go holding people's hands in public places unless their intentions were honourable, I told myself, hoping that I might perhaps be wrong, for clergymen were, as Dora had pointed out, human beings, and might be supposed to share the weaknesses of normal men. I worried over the problem in bed that night and wondered if I ought to do anything. I suddenly remembered some of the 'Answers to Correspondents' in the *Church Times*, which were so obscure that they might very well have dealt with a problem like this. 'I saw our vicar holding the hand of a widow in the park – what should I do?' The question sounded almost frivolous put like that; what kind of an answer could I expect? 'Consult your Bishop immediately'? Or, 'We feel this is none of your business'?

CHAPTER TWELVE

BY THE TIME Saturday came things seemed better. It was a sunny day and Dora and I were to go to our old school for the dedication of the window in memory of Miss Ridout, who had been headmistress in our time. In the train we read the school magazine, taking a secret pleasure in belittling those of the Old Girls who had done well and rejoicing over those who had failed to fulfil their early promise.

' "Evelyn Brandon is still teaching Classics at St Mark's, Felixstowe," ' Dora read in a satisfied tone. 'And she was so *brilliant*. All those prizes she won at Girton – everyone thought she would go far.'

'Yes,' I agreed, 'and yet in a sense we all go far, don't we? I mean far from those days when we were considered brilliant or otherwise.'

'Oh, I don't think you and I have altered much.'

'Well, we haven't got shingled hair and waists round the behind still. Isn't it depressing, really, to think that we remember those fashions? It seems very unromantic to have been young then.'

'But, Mildred, we were only twelve or thirteen then. Look, here's a bit about you – "M. Lathbury is still working part-time at the Society for the Care of Aged Gentlewomen",' she read. 'That doesn't sound much better than Evelyn Brandon.'

'Yes, of course, that is what I do,' I agreed, but somehow it seemed so inadequate; it described such a very little part of my life. 'Of course,' I went on, 'some people do write more details about themselves, don't they, so that one gets more of a picture of their lives.'

'Oh, yes. Here's a bit about Maisie Winterbotham: do you remember her, red hair and glasses? She married a missionary or something. "M. Arrowsmith (Winterbotham) writes from Calabar, Nigeria, that her husband is opening a new mission station on the Imo River. 'My third child (Jeremy Paul) was born out here, so that what with Christopher and Fiona still at the toddling stage I really have my hands full. Luckily I have a wonderful African nurse for them. I ran into Miss Caunce in Lagos, but came on here immediately.' " ' Dora giggled. 'The Caunce would be enough to make anyone leave a place immediately. Oh, look, we're nearly there!'

My heart sank as I recognized familiar landmarks. I could almost imagine myself a schoolgirl again, arriving at the station on a wet September evening for the autumn term and smelling the antiseptic smell of the newly scrubbed cloakrooms.

'Oh, look, there's Helen Eggleton and Mavis Bush . . .' Dora was leaning out of the window as the train drew into the platform. It seemed as if most of the Old Girls had chosen the same train for there was quite a crowd of us getting out of it. Now the printed news in the magazine seemed to come alive. 'M. Bush is doing Moral Welfare work in Pimlico . . . H. B. Eggleton is senior Domestic Science mistress at St Monica's, Herne Hill . . .' Now one saw them and they were very much as one had remembered them. There were older women too, some of whom might have been grandmothers, and younger ones whose rather too smart clothes indicated that they had left school only very recently. The staff were comfortingly the same. Miss Lightfoot, Miss Gregg, Miss Davis . . . it seemed that they had not aged at all, but there were one or two new mistresses, younger than we were, mere girls.

Tea was served in the hall before the dedication service and there was an opportunity for conversation, or rather exchange of news, for it could hardly be called conversation, consisting as it did of phrases like 'What's so-and-so doing now? Are you still teaching? Fancy old Hurst getting married!'

After tea we moved rather soberly in the direction of the chapel to inspect the new window before the ceremony. The chapel had been built in 1925 and was in a rather cold modern style with white walls, uncomfortable light oak chairs and rather a lot of saxe blue in carpets and hangings. Here Dora and I had been confirmed at the age of fifteen and here we had knelt, uncomfortably, expecting something that never quite came. Certainly I myself had no very inspiring memories of school religion. Only agonized gigglings over certain lines in hymns and psalms and later a watchfulness to reprove those same gigglings in the younger girls. I supposed that Dora and I, who had both been fat as schoolgirls, could now stand side by side singing

Frail children of dust,
And feeble as frail,

without a tremor or the ghost of a smile. It was rather sad, really.

The window to be dedicated was by a modern stained-glass artist and in keeping with the rest of the chapel. It showed the figure of a saint with the name OLIVE STURGIS RIDOUT in Gothic lettering, her dates and a Latin inscription. We stood in front of it in a reverent silence, which was unbroken save for an occasional admiring comment. After a few minutes we took our places for the service which was to be conducted by the school chaplain. In our day he had been a tall good-looking middle-aged man, a canon of the town's cathedral, with whom all of us were more or less secretly or openly in love. Then his visits had been eagerly looked forward to, but now, perhaps wisely, things appeared to be different, for the chaplain was a fussy little man, bald and wearing pince-nez. He conducted a suitable form of service and gave a short address, extolling the virtues of Miss Ridout, the Sturge, we had called her, after her middle name. Suddenly I was moved and felt the tears pricking at the back of my eyes. The Sturge had been a good woman and very kind to me; she had had a keen sense of the ridiculous too, which I had not appreciated until I had grown up. I imagined her now smiling down on us from some kind of Heaven, perhaps a little sardonically.

Going back in the train Dora and I were both in an elegiac mood and started reminiscing. We no longer belittled our successful contemporaries or rejoiced over our unsuccessful ones. For after all, what had *we* done? We had not made particularly brilliant careers for ourselves, and, most important of all, we had neither of us married. That was really it. It was the ring on the left hand that people at the Old Girls' Reunion looked for. Often, in fact nearly always, it was an uninteresting ring, sometimes no more than the plain gold band or the very smallest and dimmest of diamonds. Perhaps the husband was also of this variety, but as he was not seen at this female gathering he could only be imagined, and somehow I do not think we ever imagined the husbands to be quite so uninteresting as they probably were.

'Fancy anyone marrying old Hurst!' said Dora, as if reading my thoughts. 'I wonder what on earth her husband can be like?'

'How can we ever know? A little dim man going bald but very kind and good-tempered? An elderly clergyman, perhaps a widower? Or even somebody distinguished and handsome? It might be any of those.'

We fell into a melancholy silence. It was dark now and the train went slowly. Every time I looked out of the window we seemed to be passing a churchyard.

Within the churchyard side by side
Are many long low graves,

I thought, but once we passed a large cemetery and there was something less comfortable about the acres of tombstones, relieved occasionally by a white marble figure whose outstretched arms or wings looked almost menacing in the dim light.

I turned the pages of the school magazine and found something sympathetic to my mood, an obituary notice of an Old Girl who had been at the school from 1896 to 1901. Dorothy Gertrude Pybus. 'D.G. or Pye to her friends', with her eager face, her love of practical jokes, her splendid work at St Crispin's, and then the poem of an embarrassing badness, a confused thing about mists and mountain tops rather in the style of 'Excelsior' . . . all these details and obscure personal references moved me deeply so that I hardly knew whether to laugh or cry. Dora and I were obviously not old enough yet, but there might come a time when one of us might write an obituary for the other, though I hoped that neither of us would be rash enough to attempt a poem.

There was a young woman in the carriage with us, but we did not realize she had come from the school until Dora drifted into conversation with her. She told us that she had left school at the beginning of the war and had afterwards served in the Wrens.

'I was awfully lucky and got sent to Italy,' she babbled. 'Marvellous luck – I was there over a year.'

'Did you know Rockingham Napier?' I asked idly. 'He

was in an Admiral's villa somewhere, I believe.'

'Did I know Rocky – the most glamorous Flags in the Med.? Why, *everyone* knew him!'

I looked at her with a new interest. She had not seemed to be the kind of person who could have had any interesting experiences, one wouldn't have given her a second glance, but now I saw her on the terrace of the Admiral's villa in that little group.

'You had white uniforms,' I ventured.

'Oh, goodness, yes! And they never fitted properly until they had shrunk with washing or been altered. Mine were like sacks on me at first. We were invited to cocktails at the Admiral's villa the day after we arrived and Rocky Napier was awfully kind to us. You see, it was his job to arrange the Admiral's social life and be nice to people.'

'I'm sure he did it well,' I murmured.

'Oh, yes,' she said gaily. 'People used to fall in love with him but it only lasted about a month or two, usually. After that one saw what a shallow kind of person he really was. He used to take people up for a week or two and then drop them. We Wren officers used to call ourselves the Playthings – sometimes we were taken off our shelf and dusted and looked at, but then we were always put back again. Of course, he had an Italian girl friend, so you see . . .'

'Yes, of course . . .' An Italian girl friend, yes, that was to be expected. I wondered if Helena had known or minded, and then decided that it was probably naïve of me to look at it like that.

'Men are very strange,' said Dora complacently. 'You never know what they'll be up to.'

'No,' I agreed, for that seemed a comfortable way of putting it. 'Of course all men aren't like that,' said the Wren officer. 'There were some very nice Army officers out there too.'

'And didn't they have Italian girl friends?'

'Oh, no. They used to show you photographs of their wives and children.'

I looked at her suspiciously but she appeared to be quite serious.

The train drew into the station and we prepared to get out.

'By the way, I hope Rocky Napier isn't a bosom friend of yours or a relation? Perhaps I ought not to have said what I did.'

'Oh, not a bosom friend,' I said. 'He and his wife live in the same house as I do and he always seems very pleasant.' After all, what did it matter what this depressing woman thought of him? She had only seen him in falsely glamorous surroundings.

The train drew up at a platform and we went our separate ways.

'Well, there you are,' said Dora in a satisfied tone. 'I thought as much. I wasn't a bit surprised to hear that about him. We've had a lucky escape, if you ask me.'

A lucky escape? I thought sadly. But would we have escaped, any of us, if we had been given the opportunity to do otherwise?

'Perhaps it's better to be unhappy than not to feel anything at all,' I said.

'*Oh Love they wrong thee much*
That say thy sweet is bitter . . .'

Dora looked at me in astonishment. 'I think I'd just like to go in to the Ladies,' she said, 'before we get the bus home.'

I followed her meekly although I did not really want to go myself. It was a sobering kind of place to be in and a glance at my face in the dusty ill-lit mirror was enough to discourage anybody's romantic thoughts.

CHAPTER THIRTEEN

THE NEXT FEW weeks passed uneventfully. Rocky was as charming as ever, but I was careful to say to myself 'Italian girl friend' or 'rather a shallow sort of person' whenever I saw him, so that I might stop myself from thinking too well of him. He and Helena had managed to acquire some kind of a country cottage and were now spending quite a lot of time there. He told me that he had started to paint again but I could not make anything of the specimens of his work that he showed me. I did not see Everard Bone at all and soon forgot all about him and my efforts to like him. Dora went back to school with her brown woollen dress and I settled down to my gentlewomen in the mornings and the routine of home and church for the rest of the day. It seemed that the spring had unsettled us all but now that summer had come we were our more sober selves again. I did not see Julian Malory and Allegra Gray holding hands anywhere, although it was obvious that she was very friendly with both Julian and Winifred, and Winifred continued to be enthusiastic about her.

'Allegra's going to help me about my summer clothes,' she said. 'She has such good taste. Don't you think so, Mildred?'

I agreed that she always looked very nice.

'Yes, and she's even smartening Julian up. Haven't you noticed? She'll probably start on Father Greatorex next.'

'Are you all getting on well together in the house?' I asked. 'You don't find that you have lost any of your independence having somebody living above you?'

'Oh, no, it's really like having Allegra living with us. We're in and out of each other's rooms all the time.'

It was Saturday morning and we had assembled in the choir vestry before decorating the church for Whit Sunday. It was the usual gathering, Winifred, Sister Blatt, Miss Enders, Miss Statham and one or two others. The only man present, apart from the clergy, was Jim Storry, a feeble-minded youth who made himself useful in harmless little ways and would sometimes arrange the wire frames on the window-sills for us or fill jam jars with water.

The vestry was a gloomy untidy place, containing two rows of chairs, a grand piano and a cupboard full of discarded copies of *Hymns Ancient and Modern* – we used the *English Hymnal*, of course – vases, bowls and brasses in need of cleaning.

'Well, well, here we all are,' said Julian in a rather more clerical tone than usual. 'It's very good of you all to come along and help and I'm especially grateful to all those who have brought flowers. Lady Farmer,' he mentioned the only titled member remaining in our congregation, 'has most kindly sent these magnificent lilies from her country home.'

There was a pause.

'Is he going to say a prayer?' whispered Sister Blatt to me, and as nobody broke the silence I bent my head suitably and waited. But the words Julian spoke were not a prayer but a gay greeting to Allegra Gray, who came in through the door at that moment.

'Ah, here you are, now we can start.'

'Well, really, were we just waiting for *her*?' mumbled Sister Blatt. 'We've been decorating for years – long before Mrs Gray came.'

'Well, she is a newcomer, perhaps Father Malory thought it more polite to wait for her. I dare say he will help her.'

'Father Malory help with the decorating! Those men never do anything. I expect they'll slink off and have a cup of coffee once the work starts.'

We went into the church and began sorting out the flowers and deciding what should be used where. Winifred, as the vicar's sister, had usurped the privilege of a wife and always did the altar, but I must confess that it was not always very well done. I had graduated from a very humble window that nobody ever noticed to helping Sister Blatt with the screen, and we began laboriously fixing old potted-meat jars into place with wires so that they could be filled with flowers. Lady Farmer's lilies were of course to go on the altar. There was a good deal of chatter, and I was reminded of Trollope's description of Lily Dale and Grace Crawley, who were both accustomed to churches and 'almost as irreverent as though they were two curates'. For a time all went peacefully, each helper was busy with her particular corner, while Julian and Father Greatorex wandered round giving encouragement, though no practical help, to all.

'That's it!' said Julian as I placed a cluster of pinks into one of the potted-meat jars. 'Splendid!'

I did not feel that there was anything particularly splendid about what I was doing and Sister Blatt and I exchanged smiles as he passed on to Miss Statham and Miss Enders at the pulpit. It was at this point that I heard Winifred and Mrs Gray, who were both doing the altar, having what sounded like an argument.

'But we always have lilies on the altar,' I heard Winifred say.

'Oh, Winifred, why are you always so conventional!' came Mrs Gray's voice rather sharply. 'Just because you've always had lilies on the altar it doesn't mean that you can never have anything else. I think these peonies and delphiniums would look much more striking. Then we can have the lilies in a great jar on the floor, at the side here. Don't you think that would look splendid?'

I could not hear Winifred's reply but it was obvious that the flowers were going to be arranged in the way Mrs Gray had suggested.

'Of course she's been a vicar's wife,' said Sister Blatt, 'so I suppose she's used to ordering people about and having her own way with the decorations.'

'I suppose it's really a question of whether a vicar's sister should take precedence over a vicar's widow,' I said. 'I don't imagine that books of etiquette deal with such refinements. But I didn't realize Mrs Gray's husband had been a vicar – I thought he was just a curate and then an Army chaplain.'

'Oh, yes, he had a parish before he became a chaplain. They say he was a very good preacher, too, very slangy and modern. But I *have* heard,' Sister Blatt lowered her voice as if about to tell me something disgraceful, 'that he had *leanings* . . .'

'Leanings?' I echoed.

'Yes, the Oxford Group movement. He had tendencies that way, I believe.'

'Oh, dear, then perhaps . . .'

'You mean that it was just as well that he was taken, poor man?' said Sister Blatt, finishing my sentence for me.

'Do you think Mrs Gray will marry again?' I asked craftily, wondering if Sister Blatt had seen or heard anything.

'Well, who, that's the point, isn't it? She's an attractive woman, I suppose, but there aren't any eligible men round here, are there?'

'What about the clergy?'

'You mean Father Greatorex?' asked Sister Blatt in astonishment.

'He did give her a pot of jam.'

'Well, well, that's certainly news to me.'

'And Father Malory gave her a hearthrug,' I went on, unable to stop myself.

'Oh, that moth-eaten old thing out of his study? I shouldn't think that means anything. Besides, Father Malory wouldn't marry,' said Sister Blatt positively.

'I don't know. We have no reason for thinking that he wouldn't. Anyway, widows nearly always do marry again.'

'Oh, they have the knack of catching a man. Having done it once I suppose they can do it again. I suppose there's nothing in it when you know how.'

'Like mending a fuse,' I suggested, though I had not previously taken this simple view of seeking and finding a life partner.

It was just as well that we were interrupted here by Miss Statham, asking if we had any greenery to spare, for our conversation had not been at all suitable for church and I really felt a little ashamed.

The church looked as beautiful as its Victorian interior would allow when we had finished decorating. The altar was striking and unusual and the lilies stood out very well, so that even if Lady Farmer had been present, which she was not, she would not have thought that they had been overlooked.

The next morning we were all singing *Hail Thee Festival Day,* as the procession wound round the church, and the smell of incense and flowers mingled pleasantly with the sunshine and birdsong outside. The Napiers were away and I was feeling peaceful and happy, as I had felt before they came and disturbed my life. As I walked out of the church Mrs Gray came up to me. We were both wearing new hats for Whitsuntide, but I felt that hers with its trimming of fruit was smarter and more unusual than mine with its conventional posy of flowers.

'Oh, dear, that *is* a difficult hymn,' she said, 'the one we had for the procession.'

'But so beautiful,' I said, 'and well worth singing even if one falters a little in the verse part sometimes.'

'I was wondering if you'd have lunch with me one day,' said Mrs Gray suddenly and surprisingly.

'Lunch?' I asked as if I had never heard of the meal, for I was wondering whatever could have induced her to want to have lunch with me. 'Thank you, I should like to very much.'

'Of course tomorrow is Whit Monday, so perhaps we had better say Tuesday or Wednesday – if you're free, that is?'

'Oh, I'm always free,' I said unguardedly. 'Tuesday would suit me very well. Where shall I meet you?'

She named a restaurant in Soho which I had often seen

from the outside. 'Would that be convenient for you? At one-fifteen, say?'

I went back to my flat puzzling a little about this friendly overture. I was sure that she did not really like me, or at best thought of me as a dim sort of person whom one neither liked nor disliked, and I did not feel that I really cared for her very much either. Still, this was no doubt an interesting basis for social intercourse and we might even become friends. The people I was going to become friendly with! It made me laugh to think of them and I began playing with the idea of bringing them together. Everard Bone and Allegra Gray – perhaps they might marry? It would at least take her away from Julian, unless he was really determined to have her. Did the clergy display the same determination in these matters as other men? I wondered. I supposed that they did. And who would win if it came to a fight – Julian or Everard Bone?

On Whit Monday I decided to tidy out some drawers and cupboards and possibly begin making a summer dress. I always did these tidyings on Easter and Whit Mondays, but somehow not at any other time. It seemed to be connected with fine weather rather than the great Festivals of the Church – a pagan rather than a Christian rite.

I started with the pigeon-holes of my desk, but I did not get very far because I came upon a bundle of old letters and photographs which set me dreaming and remembering. My mother in a large hat, sitting under the cedar tree on the rectory lawn – I would be too young to remember the exact occasion but I knew the life, even to the shadowy curate who could be seen hovering in the background, his features a little blurred. Then there was one of Dora and me at Oxford, on the river with William and a friend. Presumably the friend, a willowy young man of a type that does not look as if it would marry, had been intended for Dora, as William was regarded as my property. But what had happened that afternoon? I could not even remember the occasion now.

I opened a drawer and came upon a large and solemn-looking studio portrait (in sepia) of the young man with whom I had once imagined myself to be in love, Bernard Hatherley, a bank clerk who occasionally read the lessons and who used to be included with the curates in Sunday evening supper parties. The face reminded me a little of Everard Bone, except that the features were less striking. It seemed incredible to remember now how often at nineteen I had pressed my cheek against the cold glass, and I found the recollection embarrassing, turning from it quickly and from the remembrance of myself hurrying past his lodgings in the dusk, hoping yet fearing that I might see his face at the window, his hand drawing aside the lace curtain of his first floor sitting-room. 'Loch Lomond', Victoria Parade . . . I could still remember the name of the house and street. He had given me the photograph one Christmas and I had given him an anthology of poetry, which seemed an unfair exchange, my gift being so much more revealing than his. It had all seemed rather romantic, hearing him read the lessons at Evensong, seeing him by chance in the town or through the open door of the bank, and then the long country walks on Saturday afternoons and the talks about life and about himself. I did not remember that we had ever talked about me. Eventually he had gone off on a holiday to Torquay and things were not the same after that. I had suffered, or I supposed that I had, for he had not broken the news of another attachment very gracefully. Perhaps high-principled young men were more cruel in these matters because less experienced. I am sure that Rocky would have done it much more kindly.

I got up stiffly, for I had been crouching uncomfortably on the floor. I bundled the letters and photographs back and decided that it would be more profitable to make tea and cut out my dress. Tidying was over now until next Easter or Whitsuntide.

CHAPTER FOURTEEN

I DRESSED rather carefully in preparation for my lunch with Mrs Gray and my appearance called forth comments from Mrs Bonner, who assumed that I was going to have lunch with 'that good-looking man you spoke to after one of the Lent services'. She was disappointed when I was honest enough to admit that my companion was to be nobody more exciting than another woman.

'I did hope it was that young man,' she said. 'I took a liking to him – what I saw, that is.'

'Oh, he's not at all the kind of person I like,' I said quickly. 'And he doesn't like me either, which does make a difference, you know.'

Mrs Bonner nodded mysteriously over her card-index. She was a great reader of fiction and I could imagine what she was thinking.

I was punctual at the restaurant and I had been waiting nearly ten minutes before Mrs Gray arrived.

'I'm so sorry,' she smiled, and I heard myself murmuring politely that I had arrived too early, as if it were really my fault that she was late.

'Where do you usually have lunch?' she asked. 'Or perhaps you go home to lunch as you only work in the mornings?'

'Yes, I do sometimes – otherwise I go to Lyons or somewhere like that.'

'Oh, dear, Lyons – I don't think I could! *Far* too many people.' She shuddered and began looking at the menu. 'I think we should like a drink, don't you? Shall we have some sherry?'

We drank our sherry and made rather stilted conversation about parish matters. When the food came Mrs Gray ate very little, pushing it round her plate with her fork and then leaving it, which made me feel brutish, for I was hungry and had eaten everything.

'I'm like the young ladies in *Crome Yellow*,' she said, 'although it isn't so easy nowadays to go home and eat an enormous meal secretly. What was it they had? A huge ham, I know, but I don't remember the other things.'

I did not really know what she was talking about and could only ask if she would like to order something else.

'Oh, no, I'm afraid I have a very small appetite naturally. And then things haven't been too easy, you know.' She looked at me with a penetrating gaze that seemed to invite confidences.

It made me feel stiff and awkward as if I wanted to withdraw into my shell. But I felt that I had to say something, though I could produce nothing better than 'No, I suppose they haven't.'

At that moment the waiter came with some fruit salad.

'I don't suppose you have had an altogether easy life, either,' Mrs Gray continued.

'Oh, well,' I found myself saying in a brisk robust tone, 'who has, if it comes to that?' It began to seem a little absurd, two women in their early thirties, eating a good meal on a fine summer day and discussing the easiness or otherwise of their lives.

'I haven't been married, so perhaps that's one source of happiness or unhappiness removed straight away.'

Mrs Gray smiled. 'Ah, yes, it isn't always an unmixed blessing.'

'One sees so many broken marriages,' I began and then had to be honest with myself and add up the number of which I had a personal knowledge. I could not think of a single one, unless I counted the Napiers' rather unstable arrangement, and I hoped that Mrs Gray would not take me up on the point.

'Yes, I suppose you would see a good deal of that sort of thing in your work,' she agreed.

'In my work?' I asked, puzzled. 'But I work for the Care of Aged Gentlewomen.'

'Oh,' she smiled, 'I had an idea it was fallen women or something like that, though I suppose even a gentlewoman can fall. But now I come to think of it, Julian did tell me where you worked.'

She said the name casually but it was obvious that she had been waiting to bring it into the conversation. I imagined them talking about me and wondered what they had said.

'Julian has asked me to marry him,' she went on quickly. 'I wanted you to be the first to know.'

'Oh, but I think I *did* know, I mean I guessed,' I said rather quickly and brightly. 'I'm so glad.'

'You're glad? Oh, what a relief!' She laughed and lit another cigarette.

'Well, it seems a very good thing for both of you and I wish you every happiness,' I mumbled, not feeling capable of explaining any further a gladness I did not really feel.

'That really is sweet of you. I was so afraid . . . oh, but I know you're not that kind of person.'

'What were you afraid of?' I asked.

'Oh, that you'd disapprove . . .'

'A clergyman's widow?' I smiled. 'How could I possibly disapprove?'

She smiled too. It seemed wrong that we should be smiling about her being a clergyman's widow.

'You and Julian will be admirably suited to each other,' I said more seriously.

'I think you're marvellous,' she said. 'And you really don't mind?'

'Mind?' I said, laughing, but then I stopped laughing because I suddenly realized what it was that she was trying to say. She was trying to tell me how glad and relieved she was that I didn't mind too much when I must surely have wanted to marry Julian myself.

'Oh, no, of course I don't mind,' I said. 'We have always been good friends, but there's never been any question of anything else, anything more than friendship.'

'Julian thought perhaps . . .' She hesitated.

'He thought that I loved him?' I exclaimed, in rather too loud a voice, I am afraid, for I noticed a woman at a nearby table making an amused comment to her companion. 'But what made him think that?'

'Oh, well, I suppose there would have been nothing extraordinary in it if you had,' said Mrs Gray slightly on the defensive.

'You mean it would be quite the usual thing? Yes, I suppose it might very well have been.'

How stupid I had been not to see it like that, for it had not occurred to me that anyone might think I was in love with Julian. But there it was, the old obvious situation, presentable unmarried clergyman and woman interested in good works – had everyone seen it like that? Julian himself? Winifred? Sister Blatt? Mr Mallett and Mr Conybeare? Of course, I thought, trying to be completely honest with myself, there had been a time when I first met him when I had wondered whether there might ever be anything between us, but I had so soon realized that it was impossible that I had never given it another thought.

'Oh, I hope you weren't worrying about that,' I said in a hearty sort of way to cover my confusion.

'No, not *worrying* exactly. I'm afraid people in love are rather selfish and perhaps don't consider other people's feelings as much as they ought.'

'Certainly not when they fall in love with other people's husbands and wives,' I said.

Mrs Gray laughed. 'There you are,' she said, 'one *does* see these broken marriages.'

'Winifred will be delighted at your news,' I said.

'Oh, yes, dear Winifred,' Mrs Gray sighed. 'There's a bit of a problem there.'

'A problem? How?'

'Well, where is she going to live when we're married, poor soul?'

'Oh, I'm sure Julian would want her to stay at the vicarage. They are devoted to each other. She could have the flat you've been living in,' I suggested, becoming practical.

'Poor dear, she *is* rather irritating, though. But I know you're very fond of her.'

Fond of her? Yes, of course I was, but I could see only too well that she might be a very irritating person to live with.

'That's why I was wondering,' Mrs Gray began and then hesitated. 'No, perhaps I couldn't ask it, really.'

'You mean you think that she might live with me?' I blurted out.

'Yes, don't you think it would be a splendid idea? You get on well, and she's so fond of you. Besides, you haven't any other ties, have you?'

The room seemed suddenly very hot and I saw Mrs Gray's face rather too close to mine, her eyes wide open and penetrating, her teeth small and pointed, her skin a smooth apricot colour.

'I don't think I could do that,' I said, gathering up my bag and gloves, for I felt trapped and longed to get away.

'Oh, do think about it, Mildred. There's a dear. I know you are one.'

'No, I'm not,' I said ungraciously, for nobody really likes to be called a dear. There is something so very faint and dull about it.

The waiter was hovering near us with a bill, which Mrs Gray picked up quickly from the table. I fumbled in my purse and handed her some silver, but she closed my hand firmly on it and I was forced to put it back.

'The very least I can do is to pay for your lunch,' she said.

'Does Julian know this? About Winifred, I mean?' I asked.

'Heavens, no. I think it's much better to keep men in the dark about one's plans, don't you?'

'Yes, I suppose it is,' I said uncertainly, feeling myself at a disadvantage in never having been in the position to keep a man in the dark about anything.

'I'm sure you and Winifred would get on *frightfully* well together,' said Mrs Gray persuasively.

'She could live with Father Greatorex,' I suggested frivolously.

'Poor dears; I can just imagine them together. I wonder if there *could* be anything in that, or would it be quite impossible? What do women *do* if they don't marry,' she mused, as if she had no idea what it could be, having been married once herself and being about to marry again.

'Oh, they stay at home with an aged parent and do the flowers, or they used to, but now perhaps they have jobs and careers and live in bed-sitting-rooms or hostels. And then of course they become indispensable in the parish and some of them even go into religious communities.'

'Oh, dear, you make it sound rather dreary.' Mrs Gray looked almost guilty. 'I suppose you have to get back to your work now?' she suggested, as if there were some connection, as indeed there may well have been, between me and dreariness.

'Yes,' I lied, 'I have to go back there for a while. Thank you very much for my lunch.'

'Oh, it was a pleasure. We must do it again some time.'

I walked away in the direction of my office and, when I had seen Mrs Gray get on to a bus, went into a shop. I had a feeling that I must escape and longed to be lost in a crowd of busy women shopping, which was why I followed blindly the crowd that surged in through the swinging doors of a large store. Some were hurrying, making for this or that department or counter, but others like myself seemed bewildered and aimless, pushed and buffeted as we stood not knowing which way to turn.

I strolled through a grove of dress materials and found myself at a counter piled high with jars of face-cream and lipsticks. I suddenly remembered Allegra Gray's smooth apricot-coloured face rather too close to mine and wondered what it was that she used to get such a striking effect. There was a mirror on the counter and I caught sight of my own face, colourless and worried-looking, the eyes large and rather frightened, the lips too pale. I did not feel that I could ever acquire a smooth apricot complexion but I could at least buy a new lipstick, I thought, consulting the shade-card. The colours had such peculiar names but at last I chose one that seemed right and began to turn over a pile of lipsticks in a bowl in an effort to find it. But the colour I had chosen was either very elusive or not there at all, and the girl behind the counter, who had been watching my scrabblings in a disinterested way, said at last, 'What shade was it you wanted, dear?'

I was a little annoyed at being called 'dear', though it was perhaps more friendly than 'madam', suggesting as it did that I lacked the years and poise to merit the more dignified title.

'It's called Hawaiian Fire,' I mumbled, feeling rather foolish, for it had not occurred to me that I should have to say it out loud.

'Oh, Hawaiian Fire. It's rather an orange red, dear,' she said doubtfully, scrutinizing my face. 'I shouldn't have thought it was quite your colour. Still, I think I've got one here.' She took a box from behind the counter and began to look in it.

'Oh, it doesn't matter really,' I said quickly. 'Perhaps another colour would be better. What would you recommend?'

'Well, dear, I don't know really.' She looked at me blankly, as if no shade could really do anything for me. 'Jungle Red is very popular – or Sea Coral, that's a pretty shade, quite pale, you know.'

'Thank you, but I think I will have Hawaiian Fire,' I said obstinately, savouring the ludicrous words and the full depths of my shame.

I hurried away and found myself on an escalator. Hawaiian Fire, indeed! Nothing more unsuitable could possibly be imagined. I began to smile and only just stopped myself from laughing out loud by suddenly remembering Mrs Gray and the engagement and the worry about poor Winifred. This made me proceed very soberly, floor by floor, stepping on and off the escalators until I reached the top floor where the Ladies' Room was.

Inside it was a sobering sight indeed and one to put us all in mind of the futility of material things and of our own mortality. *All flesh is but as grass* . . . I thought, watching the women working at their faces with savage concentration, opening their mouths wide, biting and licking their lips, stabbing at their noses and chins with powder-puffs. Some, who had abandoned the struggle to keep up, sat in chairs, their bodies slumped down, their hands resting on their parcels. One woman lay on a couch, her hat and shoes off, her eyes closed. I tiptoed past her with my penny in my hand.

Later I went into the restaurant to have tea, where the women, with an occasional man looking strangely out of place, seemed braced up, their faces newly done, their spirits revived by tea. Many had the satisfaction of having done a good day's shopping and would have something to gloat over when they got home. I had only my Hawaiian Fire and something not very interesting for supper.

CHAPTER FIFTEEN

On my way home, I was just passing the vicarage when Julian Malory came out.

'Congratulations,' I said. 'I've just heard your news.'

'Thank you, Mildred, I wanted you to be among the first to know.'

I felt that the 'among' spoilt it a little and imagined a crowd of us, all excellent women connected with the church, hearing the news.

'I had lunch with Mrs Gray,' I explained.

'Ah, yes.' He paused and then said, 'I thought it would be better, easier, more suitable, that is, if you heard the news from her.'

'Oh, why?'

'Well, for one thing I thought it would be nice if you got to know each other better, became friends, you know.'

'Yes, men do seem to like the women they know to become friends,' I remarked, but then it occurred to me that of course it is usually their old and new loves whom they wish to force into friendship. I even remembered Bernard Hatherley, the lay-reader bank clerk, saying about the girl he had met on holiday in Torquay, 'You would like her so much – I hope you'll become friends.' But as I had been at home in my village and she had been in Torquay the acquaintance had never prospered.

'Well, yes, naturally one likes everybody one is fond of to like each other,' said Julian rather feebly.

'Yes, of course,' I agreed feeling that I could hardly do otherwise. 'I expect Winifred is very pleased, isn't she?'

'Oh, yes, although she did once say that she hoped – I wonder if I can say what she hoped?' Julian looked embarrassed, as if he had said more than he meant to.

'You mean . . .' I did not quite like to go any further.

'Ah, Mildred, you understand. Dear Mildred, it would have been a fine thing if it could have been.'

I pondered on the obscurity of this sentence and gazed into my basket, which contained a packet of soap powder, a piece of cod, a pound of peas, a small wholemeal loaf and the Hawaiian Fire lipstick.

'It's so splendid of you to understand like this. I know it must have been a shock to you, though I dare say you weren't entirely unprepared. Still, it must have been a shock, a blow almost, I might say,' he laboured on, heavy and humourless, not at all like his usual self. Did love always make men like this? I wondered.

'I was never in love with you, if that's what you mean,' I said, thinking it was time to be blunt. 'I never expected that you would marry *me*.'

'Dear Mildred,' he smiled, 'you are not the kind of person to expect things as your right even though they may be.'

The bell began to ring for Evensong. I saw Miss Enders and Miss Statham hurrying into church.

'I'm sure you'll be very happy,' I said, my consciousness of the urgent bell and hurrying figures making me feel that the conversation should come to an end.

But Julian did not appear to be in any hurry to go.

'Thank you, Mildred, it means a great deal to me, your good wishes, I should say. Allegra is a very sweet person and she has had a hard life.'

I murmured that yes, I supposed she had.

'The fatherless and widow,' said Julian in what seemed a rather fatuous way.

'Is she fatherless too?'

'Yes, she is an orphan,' he said solemnly.

'Well, of course, a lot of people over thirty are orphans. I am myself,' I said briskly. 'In fact I was an orphan in my twenties. But I hope I shan't ever be a widow. I'd better hurry up if I'm going to be even that.'

'And I had better hurry into Evensong,' said Julian, for the bell had now stopped. 'Are you coming or do you feel it would upset you?'

'Upset me?' I saw that it was no use trying to convince Julian that I was not heartbroken at the news of his engagement. 'No, I don't think it will upset me.' Perhaps the consciousness that I was already an orphan and not likely to be a widow was enough cause for melancholy, I thought, as I put my basket down on the pew beside me.

We were the usual little weekday congregation, though Mrs Gray was not with us. It seemed almost as if the service might be a kind of consolation for the rejected ones, although I did not imagine that Miss Enders or Miss Statham or Sister Blatt had ever been in the running.

After the service I went home and cooked my fish. Cod seemed a suitable dish for a rejected one and I ate it humbly without any kind of sauce or relish. I began trying to imagine what it would have been like if Julian had wanted to marry me and was absorbed in these speculations when there was a knock at the door and Rocky came in.

'I'm all alone,' he said, 'and hoping that you will offer me some coffee.'

'Yes, of course,' I said, 'do come in and talk to me.'

'Helena has gone to a memorial service, or rather, the equivalent of one.'

'Can there be such a thing?'

'I gather so. You remember the President of the Learned Society where they read their paper? Well, he died suddenly last week and this is in commemoration of him.'

'Oh, dear, how sad.' I was really sorry to think that the benevolent-looking old man with crumbs in his beard was no more.

'He dropped down dead in the library – the kind of way everybody says they'd like to go.'

'But so suddenly, with no time for amendment of life . . .' I said. 'What form will the service take?'

'Oh, I gather it's a sort of solemn meeting. Fellow anthropologists and others will read out tributes to him. One feels that they ought to sing Rationalist hymns as he was so strong in the movement.'

'But do they have hymns?'

'I think they may very well have done in the early days. Most of them had a conventional Victorian childhood and probably felt the need for something to replace the Sunday services they were rejecting.'

'Poor old man,' I murmured. And of course the old lady knitting and dozing in the basket chair would now be a widow, I thought, which led me on to remember Julian's engagement. 'I've heard a piece of news today,' I said. 'Julian Malory is to marry Mrs Gray.'

'The fascinating widow whose hand he was holding in the park?' asked Rocky. 'Poor Mildred, this is a sad day for you.'

'Oh, don't be ridiculous!' I said indignantly. 'I didn't care for him at all in that way. I never expected that he would marry me.'

'But you may have hoped?' said Rocky looking at me. 'It would be a very natural thing, after all, and I should think you would make him a much better wife than that widow.'

'She is a clergyman's widow,' I reminded him.

'Oh, then she is used to loving and losing clergymen,' said Rocky lightly.

'Widows always do marry again,' I said thoughtfully, 'or they very often do. It must be strange to replace somebody like that, though I suppose one doesn't actually replace them, I mean, not in the way you buy a new teapot when the old one is broken.'

'No, my dear, hardly in that way.'

'It must be a different kind of love, neither weaker nor stronger than the first, perhaps not to be compared at all.'

'Mildred, the coffee has loosened your tongue,' said Rocky. 'I've never heard you talk so profoundly. But surely you've been in love more than once, haven't you?'

'I don't know,' I said, conscious of my lack of experience and ashamed to bring out the feeble memory of Bernard Hatherley reading the lessons at Evensong and myself hurrying past his lodgings in the twilight.

'Once you get into the habit of falling in love you will find that it happens quite often and means less and less,' said Rocky lightly. He went over to my bookcase and took out a volume of Matthew Arnold which had belonged to my father.

> 'Yes! In the sea of life enisled,
> With echoing straits between us thrown,
> Dotting the shoreless watery wild,
> We mortal millions live *alone*,'

he read. 'How I hate his habit of emphasizing words with italics! Anyway, there it is.'

'What a sad poem,' I said. 'I don't know it.'

'Oh, there's a lot more.'

'Father used to be so fond of Matthew Arnold,' I said, rather hoping that Rocky would not read aloud any more; I found it embarrassing, not quite knowing where to look, 'and I love *Thyris* and *The Scholar Gipsy*.'

'Ah, yes.' Rocky shut the book and flung it down on the floor. 'Long tramps over the warm green-muffled Cumnor hills. How one longs for that world. I can imagine your father striding along with a friend. But I don't think they'd have taken much notice of the poem I read to you. Healthy undergraduates would have no time for such morbid nonsense.'

'No, perhaps not. And then, of course, my father was a theological student.'

Rocky sighed and began pacing round the room. I suppose it was a compliment to me that he made no effort to hide his moods, but I did not really know how to deal with him.

'The other day I met somebody who knew you,' I said brightly, 'or rather who had known you in Italy. She was a Wren officer.'

'What was her name?' he asked with a faint show of interest.

'Oh, I don't know. She was tall with greyish eyes and

brown hair, not pretty but quite a pleasant face.'

'Oh, Mildred,' he looked at me seriously, 'there were so *many*. I couldn't possibly recognize her from that description – "not pretty but quite a pleasant face" – most Englishwomen look like that, you know.'

I realized that it was probably how I looked myself and was sad to think that after a year or two he might not remember me either.

'I think she rather liked you,' I said tentatively. 'She may even have been a little in love with you.'

'But, Mildred, there again,' said Rocky gently, 'there were so *many*. I know I can be honest with you.'

'Poor things,' I said lightly. 'Did you throw them any scraps of comfort? They may have been unhappy.'

'Oh, I'm sure they were,' he said earnestly, 'but that was hardly my fault. I was nice to them at the Admiral's cocktail parties, naturally, that was part of my duty. I'm afraid women take their pleasures very sadly. Few of them know how to run light-hearted flirtations – the nice ones, that is. They cling on to these little bits of romance that may have happened years ago. *Semper Fidelis*, you know.'

I burst out laughing. 'Why, that's our old school motto! Dora and I used to have it embroidered on our blazers.'

'How charming! But of course it has a kind of school flavour about it. Or it might be the title of a Victorian painting of a huge dog of the Landseer variety. But it's very suitable for a girls' school when you consider how faithful nice women tend to be. I can just see you all, running out on to the asphalt playground at break after hot milk or cocoa in the winter or lemonade in the summer.'

'We didn't have an asphalt playground. Still, I suppose *Semper Fidelis* would remind one of that rather than of a past love,' I said. 'I suppose it was too much to expect that you would remember that girl.'

The conversation seemed to come to an end here. Rocky

stood by the door and thanked me for the coffee. 'And your company too,' he added. 'You really must come and see our cottage now that the weather is nice. It needs a woman's hand there and Helena isn't really interested. Perhaps I should never have married her.'

I stood awkwardly, not knowing what to say, I, who had always prided myself on being able to make suitable conversation on all occasions. Somehow no platitude came, the moment passed and Rocky went down to his own flat.

CHAPTER SIXTEEN

ONE EVENING a few days later I was coming out of my office at six o'clock when I noticed Everard Bone, standing and looking in a nearby shop window. I was thinking of hurrying past him as I was not very well dressed that day – I had had a 'lapse' and was hatless and stockingless in an old cotton dress and a cardigan. Mrs Bonner would have been horrified at the idea of meeting a man in such an outfit. One should always start the day suitably dressed for anything, she had often told me. Any emergency might arise. Somebody – by which she meant a man – might suddenly ring up and ask you out to lunch. Although I agreed with her in theory I found it difficult to remember this every morning as I dressed, especially in the summer.

'Mildred – at last!' He turned round and faced me, but his voice betrayed the irritation of one who has been waiting for a long time rather than any pleasure at the sight of me. 'I thought you were never coming out. Don't people usually work till five?'

'I don't usually work in the afternoons at all,' I said, 'but some of our staff are away on holiday and I'm helping out. I hope you haven't been waiting here on other evenings?'

'No; I found out that you were working this afternoon.'

'Really? But how?'

'Oh, there are ways of finding out things,' he answered shortly.

'But you could have telephoned me and saved yourself this trouble,' I said, wondering why he should want to see me and whether I ought to feel flattered.

'Let's go and have a drink, shall we?' he asked.

I looked down at myself doubtfully, but he seemed impatient to be off, so I followed a step behind him, my string bag with its loaf of bread and biography of Cardinal Newman dangling at my side. I had certainly not expected to have any engagement that evening. We passed ruined St Ermin's and I saw the grey-haired lady who played the harmonium hurrying out, also with a string bag. I wondered if she too had a biography of Cardinal Newman – I could see that she had a loaf and a large book that might well have been a biography.

'Omar Khayyam,' I murmured to myself, 'only it was a book of verse, wasn't it?' And Everard Bone wasn't very suitable for the 'Thou' and although we were going to have a drink it probably wouldn't be wine. So it was not really like Omar Khayyam at all.

'Let's go in here, shall we?' he said, stopping at a public house near St Ermin's, but he was already opening the door before I could say whether I wanted to or not.

I am not used to going into public houses, so I entered rather timidly, expecting a noisy, smoky atmosphere and a great gust of laughter. But either it was too early or the house was too near the church, for all that I saw and heard was two elderly women sitting in a corner together talking in low voices and drinking stout, and a young man, whom I recognized as the curate of St Ermin's without his clerical collar, having what seemed to be an earnest conversation with the woman behind the bar. I could not call her a barmaid, for she was elderly and of a prim appearance. I felt that she probably cleaned the brasses in St Ermin's when she wasn't polishing the handles of the beer pumps.

'Good Heavens,' murmured Everard, 'isn't it quiet? I suppose it's early.'

'Yes, I expect most people hurry away from this district at this time.'

'Well, we needn't stay long. What would you like to drink?'

'Beer,' I said uncertainly.

'What kind of beer?'

'Oh, bitter, I think,' I said, hoping that it wasn't the kind that tasted like washing-up water, but not being certain.

When it came I found that it was and I was a little annoyed to see that Everard himself had a small glowing drink that looked much more attractive than mine. He shouldn't have asked me what I wanted just like that, I thought resentfully; he should have suggested various things, as Rocky would certainly have done.

I took a sip of my bitter drink and looked round the room. Being so near St Ermin's gave it an almost ecclesiastical air, especially as there was much mahogany, and I was fanciful enough to imagine that I even detected a faint smell of incense. A few more people had come in now and were drinking very quietly and soberly, almost sadly, sitting on a black horsehair bench or at one of the little tables. I stared into the fireless grate, filled now with teazles and pampas grass, and wondered why I should be sitting here with Everard Bone. He was silent too, which did not help matters, and the other people in the bar were so quiet that it was difficult to think of having a private conversation, assuming that we had anything private to talk about, which seemed unlikely.

'I'm reading a biography of Cardinal Newman,' I began, feeling that I could hardly have chosen a more unsuitable topic of conversation for a convivial evening's drinking.

'That must be very interesting,' he said, finishing his drink.

'Yes, it is really,' I faltered. 'One has great sympathy for him, I think.'

'Rome, yes, I suppose so. One can see its attraction.'

'Oh, that wasn't what I really meant,' I said, with really very little idea of what I had meant. 'More as a person . . .' my sentence trailed off miserably and there was now complete silence in the room.

Everard stood up holding his glass. 'You don't seem to like that drink,' he said, suddenly becoming less withdrawn. 'What do you really like?'

'What you had looked nice.'

'I rather doubt if you would like it. I'll get you something like gin and orange or lime – they're quite harmless.'

I felt somewhat humiliated but was glad when he came back from the bar with a gin and orange for me, and after I had taken a sip or two I felt quite cheerful.

'Why did you say you wanted bitter when you obviously don't like it?' Everard asked.

'I don't know, really, I thought it was the kind of thing people did drink. I'm not really used to drinking much myself.'

'Well, you stay as you are. It isn't the kind of thing one wants to get used to,' he said, in what I thought was rather a priggish way. 'You're better off reading about Cardinal Newman.'

I laughed. 'When I was at school we were sometimes allowed to choose hymns, but Miss Ridout would never let us have *Lead, kindly light* – she thought it was morbid and unsuitable for schoolgirls. Of course we loved it.'

'Yes, I can imagine that. Women are quite impossible to understand sometimes.'

I pondered over this remark for a while, asking myself what it could be going to lead up to, and then wondered why I had been so stupid as not to realize that he wanted to say something about Helena Napier. It was not for the pleasure of my company that Everard Bone had asked me out this evening – or rather not even asked me and given me the chance of appearing better dressed and without my string bag, but had waylaid me in the street.

'I suppose each sex finds the other difficult to understand,' I said, doing the best I could. 'But perhaps one shouldn't expect to know too much about other people.'

'One can't always help knowing,' said Everard. 'Some things are so obvious and stand out even to the most imperceptive.'

I reflected that we could not go on indefinitely in this cryptic way, it was altogether too much of a strain. I took a rather large sip of my drink and said boldly, 'I feel perhaps that women show their feelings for men without realizing it sometimes.'

'Have you noticed that too?'

'Why, yes,' I said, rather at a loss. 'It's often a difficult thing to conceal.'

'But it ought to be concealed,' he said irritably, 'especially when the whole thing is quite impossible and the feeling isn't returned in the same way. If they are really going to separate, the whole thing may become most awkward and unpleasant.'

'What *are* you talking about?' I asked, startled.

'Oh, you must know that I mean the Napiers. Helena has been behaving in a most foolish and indiscreet way.'

'I'm afraid I haven't seen much of her lately,' I said, as if I could somehow have prevented her.

'She came to my flat the other night after ten o'clock, *alone*, and stayed for nearly three hours talking, although I did everything I could to get her to go.'

I felt I could hardly ask what methods he had employed.

'Of course I had to go out with her eventually to find her a taxi – you will agree that I could hardly have done less than that,' Everard continued. 'By that time it was nearly one o'clock and naturally I didn't expect to see many people about, let alone anyone who knew both of us.'

'And did you?' I asked, feeling that the story was really getting quite exciting.

'Yes, it could hardly have been more unfortunate. We were just coming out of the house when who should walk by but Apfelbaum and Tyrell Todd – the last two people I should have expected or chosen to see.'

'Oh, Tyrell Todd's the man who gave the paper on pygmies, isn't he?' I asked, in an honest effort to place him. 'And Apfelbaum kept asking questions after your paper.'

Everard looked annoyed at this irrelevant interruption, so I said soothingly, 'I don't see why you should worry about seeing them. I am sure they would think nothing of it. Anthropologists must see such very odd behaviour in primitive societies that they probably think anything we do here is very tame.'

'Don't you believe it. Tyrell Todd revels in petty gossip.'

I stopped myself from making the facetious observation that possibly it was his work among the pygmies that had made him small-minded and petty, and went on to ask reassuring questions.

'But what were *they* doing together so late? It may well have been something disgraceful. Did they speak to you?'

'No, they just said "Good evening" or words to that effect. I think we were all a little surprised.'

'Four anthropologists meeting unexpectedly in a London square at one o'clock in the morning,' I said. 'There does seem to be something a little surprising about that.'

'You make everything into a joke,' said Everard resentfully, but with the suspicion of a smile.

'Well, I think the whole thing sounds slightly ridiculous. If you can see it like that perhaps you won't worry about it.'

'But Helena is so indiscreet and from what I've seen of

Rockingham I shouldn't imagine he would be likely to behave in a very sensible way, either.'

'No,' I murmured, 'I don't think you would exactly call him sensible.'

'On the other hand, it is unlikely that he would want a divorce,' said Everard thoughtfully.

'Oh, *no*,' I exclaimed, shocked out of the pleasant haze into which the drink had lulled me, 'and I suppose you would not want to marry Helena even if she were free. I mean, divorce would be against your principles.'

'Naturally,' he said stiffly. 'And I don't love her, anyway.'

'Oh, poor Helena. I think she may love you,' I said rashly.

'I'm sure she does,' said Everard in what seemed to be a satisfied tone. 'She has told me so.'

'Oh, no! Not without encouragement! Do women declare themselves like that?'

'Oh, yes. It is not so very unusual.'

'But what did you tell her?'

'I told her that it was quite impossible that I should love her.'

'You must have been rather startled,' I said. 'Unless you had expected it, and perhaps you had if it can happen. But it must have been like having something like a large white rabbit thrust into your arms and not knowing what to do with it.'

'A white rabbit? What do you mean?'

'Oh, if you don't see I can't explain,' I said. I gathered my string bag to me. 'I think I had better be going home now.'

'Oh, please don't go,' said Everard. 'I feel you are the only person who can help. You could perhaps say something to Helena.'

'*I* say something? But she wouldn't listen to *me*.'

We stood up and went out together.

'I'm sorry,' said Everard. 'Why should you be brought into it, really? I just thought you might be able to drop a hint.'

'But men ought to be able to manage their own affairs,' I

said. 'After all most of them don't seem to mind speaking frankly and making people unhappy. I don't see why you should.'

We walked on in silence.

'I should be very distressed if I thought I had purposely made anybody unhappy,' said Everard at last.

There seemed to be nothing more to say. I was to tell Helena that Everard Bone did not love her. I might just as well go home and do it straight away.

We came to St Ermin's. 'I wonder if anybody is making coffee on a Primus in the ruins?' I asked idly.

'Do people do that?'

'Oh, yes, that little woman who plays the harmonium.'

'Yes, she looks as if she might.'

We had suddenly forgotten about Helena Napier and were talking quite easily about other things.

'I promised to go and have dinner with my mother tonight,' said Everard. 'Perhaps you would like to come too?'

I decided that I might as well put off telling Helena that Everard did not love her for an hour or two at least, so we got into a taxi and drove to a dark red forbidding-looking house in a street of similar houses.

'My mother is a little eccentric,' he said as we got out of the taxi. 'I just thought I should warn you.'

'I don't suppose I shall find her any more odd than many people I have met,' I said, feeling that it was not perhaps a good beginning to the evening. 'I'm sorry I'm not more suitably dressed. If I had known . . . only, things do seem to happen so unexpectedly.'

'You seem to be very nicely dressed,' said Everard without looking. 'And my mother never notices what anybody is wearing.'

An old bent maidservant opened the door and we went in. There was a good deal of dark furniture in the hall and a faintly exotic smell, almost like incense. The walls were covered with animals' heads and their sad or fierce eyes looked down on us.

'Perhaps you would care to wash your hands, miss?' said the maid in a hushed voice. She led me upstairs and into a bathroom, with much marble and mahogany and a stained-glass window. I began to think that it was perhaps suitable that I was carrying a biography of Cardinal Newman in my string bag, and as I washed my hands and tidied my hair I found myself thinking about the Oxford Movement and the architecture associated with it. But then I was seized with a feeling of alarm, waiting outside the bathroom door on a dark landing, then creeping down the stairs and wondering where I should go when I got to the bottom. I was surprised to see that Everard was standing in the hall waiting for me, turning over a heap of old visiting cards that lay in a brass bowl on an antique chest.

'Mother will be in the drawing-room,' he said, opening a door.

I found myself in a room with two women, one of whom was standing by the fireplace while the other was sitting on the edge of a chair with her hands folded in her lap.

'This is my mother,' said Everard, leading me towards the standing woman, who was tall with a long nose like his own, 'and this is – er . . .' he glanced at the nondescript woman sitting on the edge of her chair who might really have been anybody or nobody, and then back to his mother.

'It's Miss Jessop, dear,' she said.

'Oh, yes, of course.'

Miss Jessop! I remembered my telephone conversation with Mrs Bone and looked at the nondescript woman with new interest. *If it's Miss Jessop, I can only hope you're ringing up to apologize . . .* She did not look the kind of person who could possibly do anything for which an apology might be demanded. What *had* she done? I supposed I should never know. Presumably all was now well between her and Mrs Bone.

We all murmured politely to each other and Mrs Bone did not seem to be at all eccentric. I was beginning to think that Everard had misjudged his mother when she suddenly said in a clear voice, 'Miss Jessop and I are very much interested in the suppression of woodworm in furniture.'

'I should think it's very important,' I said. 'I know a lot of our furniture at home got the worm in it. There didn't seem to be anything we could do about it.'

'Oh, but there is a preparation on the market now which is very effective,' said Mrs Bone, clasping her hands together almost in rapture. 'It has been used with excellent results in many famous buildings.' She began to enumerate various Oxford and Cambridge colleges and well-known churches and cathedrals. 'It has even been used in Westminster Cathedral,' she declared.

'Not Westminster Cathedral, surely, Mother,' said Everard. 'The wood isn't old enough.'

'Westminster Abbey, perhaps?' I suggested.

'Oh, well, it was something to do with Westminster,' said Mrs Bone. 'Wasn't it, Miss Jessop?' She turned towards her with a rather menacing look.

Miss Jessop seemed to agree.

'I think we had better have some sherry,' said Everard, going out of the room.

I thought I had better revive the conversation which had lapsed, so I commented on the animals' heads in the hall, saying what fine specimens they were.

'My husband shot them in India and Africa,' said Mrs Bone, 'but however many you shoot there still seem to be more.'

'Oh, yes, it would be a terrible thing if they became extinct,' I said. 'I suppose they keep the rarer animals in game reserves now.'

'It's not the animals so much as the birds,' said Mrs Bone fiercely. 'You will hardly believe this, Miss – er – but I was sitting in the window this afternoon and as it was a fine day I had it open at the bottom, when I felt something drop into my lap. And do you know what it was?' She turned and peered at me intently.

I said that I had no idea.

'Unpleasantness,' she said, almost triumphantly so that I was reminded of William Caldicote. Then lowering her voice she explained, 'From a bird, you see. It had *done* something when I was actually sitting in my own drawing-room.'

'How annoying,' I said, feeling mesmerized and unable even to laugh.

'And that's not the worst,' she went on, rummaging in a small desk which stood open and seemed to be full of old newspapers. 'Read this.' She handed me a cutting headed OWL BITES WOMAN, from which I read that an owl had flown in through a cottage window one evening and bitten a woman on the chin. 'And this,' she went on, handing me another cutting which told how a swan had knocked a girl off her bicycle. 'What do you think of *that*?'

'Oh, I suppose they were just accidents,' I said.

'*Accidents!* Even Miss Jessop agrees that they are rather more than *accidents*, don't you, Miss Jessop?'

Miss Jessop made a quavering sound which might have been 'Yes' or 'No' but it was not allowed to develop into speech, for Mrs Bone broke in by telling Everard that Miss Jessop wouldn't want any sherry.

'The Dominion of the Birds,' she went on. 'I very much fear it may come to that.'

Everard looked at me a little anxiously but I managed to keep up the conversation until Mrs Bone declared that it was dinner time. 'You had better be going home, now, Miss Jessop,' she said. 'We are going to have our dinner.'

Miss Jessop stood up and put on her gloves. Then, with a little nod which seemed to include all of us, she went quietly out of the room.

'I eat as many birds as possible,' said Mrs Bone when we

were sitting down to roast chicken. 'I have them sent from Harrods or Fortnum's, and sometimes I go and look at them in the cold meats department. They do them up very prettily with aspic jelly and decorations. At least we can eat our enemies. Everard, dear, which was that tribe in Africa which were cannibals?'

'There are several thousand tribes in Africa, Mother,' said Everard patiently, 'and many of them have been and probably still are cannibals.'

'But surely the British Administration have stamped it out?' I asked.

'Certainly they have attempted to,' said Everard. 'And the missionaries have also done a lot to educate the people.'

'Yes, I suppose that would make them see that it was wrong,' I said feebly, wondering whether anthropologists really approved of these old customs being stamped out.

'Missionaries have done a lot of harm,' said Mrs Bone firmly. 'The natives have their own religions which are very ancient, much more ancient than ours. We have no business to try to make them change.'

'My mother is not a Christian,' said Everard, perhaps unnecessarily.

'The Jesuits got at my son, you know, Miss – er – ' said Mrs Bone, turning to me. 'They will stop at nothing, those Jesuits. You would hardly believe the things that go on in their seminaries. I can lend you some very informative pamphlets if you are interested.'

I was by now in a state of considerable confusion and wished that Everard would make some attempt to lead the conversation into normal channels, though I realized that this would probably be quite impossible. It occurred to me that I had been bearing the full burden of the evening, and at half-past nine I began to feel both tired and resentful and decided that I would go home.

'You seem to have made a favourable impression,' he said,

as I stuffed some pamphlets about woodworms and Jesuits into my string bag with Cardinal Newman and the loaf. 'Most people are quite incapable of carrying on a conversation with my mother. I admired the way you did it.'

'Oh, but I'm used to coping with people,' I said. 'Being a clergyman's daughter is a good training.' It was only people like the Napiers who were beyond my experience. 'It is splendid that your mother should have so many interests in her life,' I said. 'So often elderly people think only of themselves and their illnesses.' Birds, worms and Jesuits . . . it might almost have been a poem, but I could not remember that anybody had ever written it.

'Yes, her life is quite busy, I suppose, but she is getting rather difficult now.'

'Who is Miss Jessop?' I asked.

'Oh, I don't know; just some woman who comes to see my mother sometimes,' said Everard vaguely. 'She is quite often there.'

'But does she never speak?'

'Oh, I don't know. It would be such a help if you could say something to Helena. You remember what we were talking about earlier in the evening.'

It seemed to have been a very long evening, but I did remember and the memory depressed me.

'A sensible person, with no axe to grind,' Everard was saying, almost to himself.

I accepted this description of myself without comment. 'But what could I say?' I protested. 'The occasion may not arise and even if it did I still shouldn't know.'

'Oh, surely, words would come,' said Everard impatiently. 'You said you were used to coping with people.'

I did not attempt to explain that my training had not fitted me for this kind of situation. But I saw myself, having no axe to grind, calling in on the Napiers as I went up to my flat and making the attempt. But Rocky would be there, so of course it wouldn't do. And when I passed their door their voices seemed to be raised as if they were having an argument. I am afraid it was impossible not to hear some of the things they were saying, but I cannot bring myself to record them here. I think I hurried up to my kitchen and made a cup of tea and then went to bed trying to take my mind off the situation by thinking about Miss Jessop and her curious relationship with Mrs Bone. I wondered if I should ever hear her speak or know why an apology had been demanded from her.

CHAPTER SEVENTEEN

THE NEXT DAY I worked until lunchtime and came home at about half-past one. This was the only time when the offices on the ground floor of the house where I lived seemed to show any signs of life. Typewriters were clacking, telephones ringing, and a man was dictating a letter, weighing each word, or so it appeared, though the words that came to my ears through the open door seemed hardly worth such ponderous consideration.

Above this it was very quiet, so I guessed that the Napiers must be out, but when I passed their kitchen I could hear the gas hissing and there was a smell of something burning. I knocked on the half-open door but there was no answer, so I went in. I found one of the gas rings full on and on it a saucepan of potatoes which had boiled dry and were now sticking to the bottom in a brownish mass. I dealt with them quickly but the saucepan was in a very bad state. I ran some water into it so that it could soak. I noticed with distaste and disapproval that the breakfast things and what appeared to be dishes and glasses from an even earlier date were not washed up. The table by the window was also crowded; there were two bottles of milk, each half-full, an empty gin bottle, a dish of butter melting in the sun, and a plate full of cigarette stubs. I felt very spinsterish indeed as I stood there, holding the burnt saucepan in my hand.

'The potatoes – I forgot them.' Rocky was standing behind me in the doorway.

'Yes, you did,' I said rather sharply. 'The gas was full on and they boiled dry. I'm afraid the saucepan's ruined.'

'Oh, the saucepan,' Rocky said, passing his hand over his brow with a gesture of weariness that seemed to me rather theatrical. 'There have been other things to think about besides saucepans.'

'Oh. Is anything the matter?' I asked, moving towards him, still holding the saucepan in my hand.

'Yes, I suppose so. Helena has left me.' He went into the sitting-room and sank into an armchair. I stood helplessly by him, trying to think of something to say or do, but he took no notice of my faltering words of sympathy. I looked round the room and saw that another saucepan had evidently been put down on a polished walnut table, where it had burnt an unsightly mark.

'That was the last straw, the table,' he said. 'She put a hot saucepan down on the table. Such a trivial thing, I suppose you might think, but typical of her lack of consideration. And all the washing-up left for days sometimes until Mrs Morris came . . .' He rambled on, cataloguing her faults while I sat by him not liking to interrupt. At last I was conscious of a feeling something like hunger stirring in me, for it was now about two o'clock, and I began to wonder whether Rocky had had any lunch.

'Lunch? I haven't thought about it,' he said. 'Perhaps one doesn't on these occasions.'

'I'm sure you should eat something,' I said. 'Why don't you come up to my flat, which is tidier than this, and I will clear up these things afterwards.'

He followed me apathetically and began to tell me what had happened. It appeared that they had had a quarrel when he was setting lunch and that Helena had run out of the house, saying that she was never coming back.

'I went after her,' Rocky said, 'but she must have got into a taxi, because there was no sign of her. So eventually I just came here.'

'But surely she will have to come back? Did she take anything with her, any luggage?'

'I don't know. I shouldn't think so.'

'But where could she have gone?' I persisted, feeling that somebody ought to be practical.

'To Everard Bone, I suppose,' said Rocky indifferently.

'No, surely not!' I exclaimed. That must not happen. The irrelevant and unworthy thought crossed my mind that he would think I had failed in my duty and I should be blamed. But I had really had very little time in which to tell Helena that Everard did not love her; I had been meaning to say something at the first opportunity. And yet, in a way, I could not help feeling that it would serve him right if she did arrive on his doorstep and cause him embarrassment. 'If she *has* gone to him,' I said, 'she will have arrived by now. I will ring up his flat and find out.'

I was a little taken aback when Everard himself answered me, though I don't know who else I had expected, and could only stammer out the news and ask if Helena had come to him.

'No, she certainly has not,' he said, his voice full of alarm. 'In any case, I am leaving for Derbyshire immediately.'

'Derbyshire?' I repeated stupidly. It seemed such an unlikely place.

'Yes, the Prehistoric Society is holding a conference there,' he said quickly.

'You will be able to hide in a cave,' I said, giggling in the nervous way one does sometimes at a moment of crisis. I composed myself before going back to Rocky, who was still reclining in a chair.

'She isn't with Everard Bone,' I said, 'so perhaps she will be back soon, unless there are any friends of hers I could ring up for you?'

'Oh, no, don't bother. One can't go ringing up people all over London.'

'Well, I may as well get lunch,' I said. 'I'm afraid it will be something very simple, but you must eat.'

Rocky followed me into my kitchen and stood under the line of washing, which I noticed with irritation had become too dry to be ironed comfortably. He began pulling down the garments and making jokes about them, but I felt that this was not the time for coyness or embarrassment, so I took no notice of him.

I washed a lettuce and dressed it with a little of my hoarded olive oil and some salt. I also had a Camembert cheese, a fresh loaf and a bowl of greengages for dessert. It seemed an idyllic sort of meal that ought to have been eaten in the open air, with a bottle of wine and what is known as 'good' conversation. I thought it unlikely that I should be able to provide either the conversation or the wine, but I remembered that I had a bottle of brandy which I kept, according to old-fashioned custom, for 'emergencies' and I decided to bring it in with the coffee. I could see my mother, her lips slightly pursed, saying, 'For medicinal purposes only, of course . . .' But now respectable elderly women do not need to excuse themselves for buying brandy or even gin, though it is quite likely that some still do and perhaps one may hope that they always will.

Rocky began to eat with a show of appetite, but the conversation he made was not 'good' conversation.

'She couldn't even *wash* a lettuce properly,' he said, 'let alone prepare a salad like this.'

I did not know what answer to make and we continued to

eat in silence on my part. The brandy seemed to rouse him a little further, though to no great heights, but what he said was pleasing to me personally.

'Mildred, you are really the most wonderful person,' he said, turning his gaze on me. 'I don't know *what* I should do without you.'

You do very well without me, I thought, with a flash of impatience, and will continue to do well.

'To think that you should have come in just at this moment, this awful crisis, and given me a delicious lunch.' He closed his eyes and lay back in his chair. 'I really couldn't have borne to have got lunch myself.'

'Oh, it was nothing,' I said, feeling that no other answer could be given. 'Anybody else would have done the same.' And perhaps even a less attractive man than Rocky would have a devoted woman to prepare a meal for him on the day his wife left him. A mother, a sister, an aunt, even . . . I remembered an advertisement I had once seen in the *Church Times* – 'Organist and aunt require unfurnished accommodation; East Sheen or Barnes preferred'. Rather fishy, I had thought it, probably not his aunt at all, though surely the kind of people who expressed a preference for East Sheen or Barnes could hardly be anything but highly respectable?

'What are you smiling at?'

I started guiltily, for I had temporarily forgotten the dreadful thing that had happened. 'I'm sorry,' I said. 'I didn't realize I was smiling.'

'You are almost cheering me up,' said Rocky resentfully. 'I suppose everyone must have a friend to comfort them at times like this.'

'Not everybody,' I said, thinking of the many rejected ones who lived in lonely bed-sitting-rooms with nobody to talk to them or prepare meals for them. I told Rocky of my thought.

'They could always wash stockings or something,' he said callously. 'Assuming of course, that they are women, and it's usually women who live in bed-sitting-rooms.'

'And are rejected,' I added.

'Well, yes, it all hangs together somehow, doesn't it? Of course my position is hardly the same. You mustn't think that *I* have been rejected.'

We sat there almost bickering until the church clock struck a quarter to four.

'Tea,' said Rocky, 'I think I should like some tea now.'

'Yes, of course,' I said, going meekly to the kitchen. I was just filling the kettle when my bell rang. 'Oh, dear, who can that be?' I asked.

'Perhaps Helena has also come to you for comfort,' said Rocky. 'I think it would be more suitable if you answered the door, just in case, you know.'

He continued to loll in the armchair, so there was nothing for me to do but hurry downstairs, feeling rather flustered and irritated. I'm afraid my dismay must have shown in my face when I opened the front door and found Julian Malory standing there, for his expression altered and he hesitated before coming in.

'I was just going to make some tea,' I said, as we walked upstairs, 'so you're just in time.'

'Ah, tea,' he said. 'I had hoped to be in time for that.'

I did not tell him that Rocky Napier was with me and the expressions of the two men when they saw each other was something that made me smile, Rocky frowning and sulky and Julian puzzled and dismayed. Rocky rose rather ungraciously and offered Julian his armchair, though in a half-hearted manner. Julian accepted it. Rocky then flung himself down on the sofa. At this point I hurried out to see if the kettle was boiling and by the time I had come back with the tea the two men were engaged in some sort of conversation about Italy. Julian was asking about the church of Santa Chiara in Naples and quoting a poem about Palm Sunday, but Rocky said that the church had been destroyed by bombs and the poem always depressed him anyway.

I began to pour out tea. As so often happens at a moment of crisis, there was something wrong with it. It seemed much too weak and flowed in what a poet might call an amber stream from the imperfectly cleaned spout of the silver teapot. Mrs Morris had been neglecting her duty and I should have to 'speak' to her.

'Ah, what a treat, China tea!' Julian exclaimed.

I have often wondered whether it is really a good thing to be honest by nature and upbringing; certainly it is not a good thing socially, for I feel sure that the tea-party would have been more successful had I not explained that the tea was really Indian which I had unfortunately made too weak. Thus, instead of feeling that I had provided a treat for them the two men seemed resentful and embarrassed, almost as if I had done it on purpose. I stirred the pot despairingly and offered to go and make some more, but neither of them would hear of it. Rocky was polite but impatient and Julian polite but disappointed, almost grieved.

It seemed to me that both men appeared at their worst that afternoon, as if they had the effect of bringing out the worst in each other, unless it was that I had never before had the opportunity of observing each of them dispassionately. Rocky seemed shallow and charming in an obvious and false way, and his sprawling on the sofa seemed to me both affected and impolite. Julian, on the other hand, appeared to have no charm at all, not even of an obvious kind. By the side of Rocky he seemed pompous and clerical, almost like a stage clergyman, his voice taking on an unctuous quality which it did not usually possess. 'She worships at St Mary's . . . The other morning, after I had said Mass . . .' even his conversation seemed stilted and unnatural. This had the effect of making Rocky flippant, so that although Julian made an effort to respond to his little jokes about the best quality incense and glamorous acolytes, there was a kind of hostility between them, and I felt almost as if I were the cause of it. It was unusual, certainly, for me to be alone with two men even when each of them was the property of some other woman, but I could not make anything of the opportunity.

I fussed over the weak tea, regretted that I had not bought another cake or some tomatoes or a cucumber to make sandwiches, wished passionately that I had been a more brilliant conversationalist. As it was, Rocky had now lapsed into silence and Julian was looking around him with frightened, suspicious glances. What was the matter with him? I wondered. There was surely nothing compromising or embarrassing about the situation? And then I saw what it was that was upsetting him – the brandy bottle was still on the mantelpiece, looking very large and shocking among my small ornaments and the picture postcards of Exmoor and North Wales, where Mrs Bonner and another woman from my office respectively were spending their holidays. I supposed that on all the occasions when Julian had visited me before he had never seen a brandy bottle on the mantelpiece.

'Have you made any plans for your wedding?' I asked, anxious to make light conversation.

'Oh, yes, we are hoping to be married quite soon,' said Julian gratefully. 'And we do want all the congregation of St Mary's and all our friends to come to the wedding.'

'I suppose you mean what are known as "regular communicants"?' asked Rocky. 'Mildred may have told you that I can't do with religion before breakfast. Would those who have just been to Evensong be eligible? They might surely count as friends?'

'Oh, anybody, really, all well-wishers, of course,' said Julian in an embarrassed but jocular manner. 'We want everybody to rejoice with us.'

'I should certainly like to do that,' said Rocky. 'You see, I *do* wish you well, and as my wife has just left me the very least I can do is to hope that yours will not do the same.'

Julian dropped half of the slice of cake he was holding on to the floor and stooped quickly to pick up the fragments.

I took off the lid of the teapot and peered into its depths, but without hope. I supposed that the shock he had suffered should be enough to excuse Rocky's curious behaviour but it made me feel rather uneasy.

'My dear fellow,' Julian began in a confused way, 'I really am most awfully distressed . . . but surely you must be mistaken? Some misunderstanding, perhaps, or a quarrel . . . Why, I saw Mrs Napier only this morning.'

'Oh, these things happen quickly when they do happen,' said Rocky, who now seemed to be almost enjoying himself. 'After all, somebody must have seen her for the last time – perhaps it was you.'

'This is *most* distressing news – there must be something we can do.' Julian was now pacing about the room, frowning.

I began piling cups and saucers on to a tray. I suppose it was cowardly of me, but I felt that I wanted to be alone, and what better place to choose than the sink, where neither of the men would follow me?

I started in my own kitchen where the lunch and tea things were quickly washed and dried, but then I moved down to the Napiers' with the idea of making some order out of the confusion there. No sink has ever been built high enough for a reasonably tall person and my back was soon aching with the effort of washing-up, especially as yesterday's greasy dishes needed a lot of scrubbing to get them clean. My thoughts went round and round and it occurred to me that if I ever wrote a novel it would be of the 'stream of consciousness' type and deal with an hour in the life of a woman at the sink. I felt resentful and bitter towards Helena and Rocky and even towards Julian, though I had to admit that nobody had compelled me to wash these dishes or to tidy this kitchen. It was the fussy spinster in me, the Martha, who could not comfortably sit and make conversation when she knew that yesterday's unwashed dishes were still in the sink. Martha's back must have ached too, I thought grimly, noticing that the plate rack needed scrubbing and the tea-cloths boiling.

At last everything was done except for the saucepan with the burnt potatoes. I looked hopelessly around for something to scrape it with.

'Clean glasses?' came Rocky's voice from outside the door. 'Are there any?'

'Yes, in the cupboard,' I said. 'I've just washed them.'

'There *was* some gin,' said Rocky, delving among a cluster of bottles in a corner. 'I suppose we could drink your brandy?'

'Oh, yes, do.'

'Ah, this is better.' He held up a straw-covered flask of wine. 'The vicar and I are really getting on rather well. I like him. It's a pity you didn't marry him, Mildred, you'd have made a pleasant pair. Come and have a drink with us when you've finished that saucepan. We're upstairs in your room.'

I sat down on a chair in the Napiers' kitchen, ready to feel tired and resentful, but suddenly something came to the rescue and I began to see the funny side of it. Then the telephone rang. It was Helena.

'Oh, thank goodness, it's you, Mildred,' she said. 'I couldn't bear it to be Rocky after all the things he said. Listen, I'm staying with Miss Clovis.'

'Miss Who?'

'Miss Clovis – you remember her, surely? She works at the Learned Society.'

'Oh, of course.' Our excellent Miss Clovis with the tea. Did she also give sanctuary to runaway wives?

'She has offered to collect some of my things. I was wondering if you could pack a suitcase for me and meet her at Victoria Station under the clock?'

I agreed to do this, mainly because it seemed simpler to agree. I was to pack a few necessities and slip out of the house without letting Rocky know what I was doing, though I could tell him later that Helena was with Miss Clovis.

It was not very easy to find the things Helena had asked for, all the drawers in the bedroom were so untidy that it was difficult to know what was supposed to be where, but at last I had packed the case and was waiting at the appointed place at Victoria, feeling rather foolish, as if I were about to elope with somebody myself.

It was the rush hour and droves of people hurried by me to catch their trains. Men in bowler hats, with dispatch cases so flat and neat it seemed impossible that they could contain anything at all, and neatly rolled umbrellas, ran with undignified haste and jostled against me. Some carried little bundles or parcels, offerings to their wives perhaps or a surprise for supper. I imagined them piling into the green trains, opening their evening papers, doing the crossword, not speaking to each other . . .

'Miss Lathbury?' A crisp voice interrupted my fantasies and the stocky figure of Miss Clovis was standing at my side.

'Yes. I've brought the things Mrs Napier asked for.'

'Splendid!' She took the case from me with a firm gesture.

'I hope she's all right?' I asked.

'Oh, perfectly – now that she's got away from that brute of a husband.'

I wanted to protest but hardly knew what to say. I was surprised that such a person as Miss Clovis appeared to be should express herself so conventionally.

'She will be quite safe with me,' she went on chattily. 'I have a cosy little flat on top of the Society's premises, you know.'

Pictures of savage chiefs and a rolled-up flag in the lavatory, I thought, but perhaps she would have a bathroom of her own.

'I do hope that Mrs Napier will soon return to her husband,' I said firmly. 'He is very upset.'

'You think the separation may be only temporary?' said Miss Clovis, looking disappointed. '*I* hadn't gathered that at all. He will go to the country where I believe he has a cottage and she will return to the flat. That's what I understood.'

'Oh, I see. Well, I hope they will meet again and talk it over before doing anything so drastic.' I could not admit to Miss Clovis that apart from anything else I did not want Rocky to go away.

'Well, I must be going,' said Miss Clovis. 'Thank you for bringing the things. I will let you know if there are any developments. I believe Mr Bone is in Derbyshire?'

'Oh, surely this has nothing to do with him?' I exclaimed in alarm. 'I'm certain he wouldn't want to be concerned in it.'

'For the sake of anthropology,' declared Miss Clovis, grasping her umbrella and brandishing it as if it were a weapon or a banner. 'There is a great bond between those who have worked together *in the field* – their work on matrilineal groupings, most valuable, a real contribution . . .' She lowered her voice confidentially. 'There was that affair of Dr Medlicott and Miss Etty – I don't know if you heard about it – I always feel that I brought them together. His wife didn't like it at first. Still, there you are.' She nodded briskly and was off.

I stood for a moment in a kind of daze and then made my way slowly home. I was just approaching Grantchester Square when I saw two men going into the public-house at the end of it. They were Rocky Napier and Julian Malory. Well, let them go, I thought. It was somehow a comfort to know that they had made friends over a glass of wine. A comfort for them, though not for me, I decided, unable to face the thought of returning to the flat to wash their empty glasses which they had no doubt left in my sitting-room. It would be better to call in at the vicarage and see Winifred.

I had just rung the bell when it occurred to me that Allegra Gray would probably be there and I should have turned back had not Winifred herself opened the door almost immediately.

'Oh, Mildred, how nice! You hardly ever come to see us now,' she complained. 'Since Allegra and Julian became engaged, things haven't been the same, somehow. But she's gone to supper with a friend in Kensington tonight and Julian's out somewhere, so I'm all alone. You look upset, dear. Has anything happened?'

'I almost wish the Napiers hadn't come to live in my house,' I said. 'Things were much simpler before they came.'

Winifred did not ask questions but under the influence of a cup of tea her tongue was loosened. We began talking about 'old times' as they now seemed to be. 'Oh, Mildred,' she blurted out, 'sometimes I wish Allegra hadn't come to live here, either!'

CHAPTER EIGHTEEN

ROCKY BEHAVED rather dramatically the next day, packing suitcases and going round his flat marking various articles of furniture and small objects which were to be sent after him to his cottage in the country. When I came home after lunch I found him almost ready to go.

He came up to me with a list in his hand.

'We may as well get it quite clear,' he said. 'I shall want to have my own things with me and you can hardly be expected to know exactly which they are.'

'*I?*' I exclaimed in surprise.

'Oh, yes, I imagine you will be here, won't you? I have asked the remover's men to come on Saturday morning so that you will be able to supervise them.'

'Yes, of course,' I said weakly. 'I suppose they couldn't be expected to do it alone. About what time will they be coming?'

'Oh, I told them to come really early, about eight o'clock.

Then Helena can come back on Sunday or Monday if she wants to. You might ring up Miss Clovis and tell her so' – I had of course told him where Helena was – 'and then everything will be as it was.'

I wanted to protest, not so much about the furniture-removing and the part I was to play in it, as about his idea that everything could then be as it had been before. But no words came. I wondered if he would suggest that we had tea together before he went, but he did not say anything and somehow I did not feel inclined to offer to make any. I suppose I did not want him to remember me as the kind of person who was always making cups of tea at moments of crisis.

'Goodbye, Mildred; we'll meet again, of course,' he said casually. 'You must come and stay at my cottage one week-end.'

'I should like to,' I began, wondering even as I said it if it would be quite proper. But obviously no such thought had occurred or would ever occur to Rocky. 'You *will* remember which pieces of furniture are to come, won't you?' were his last words to me.

After he had gone I stood looking out of the window until his taxi was out of sight.

The effects of shock and grief are too well known to need description and I stood at the window for a long time. At last I did make a cup of tea but I could not eat anything. There seemed to be a great weight inside me and after sitting down for a while I thought I would go into the church and try to find a little consolation there.

I opened the door rather timidly and went in. I was relieved to see that there was nobody else there and I sat down hopelessly and waited, I did not know for what. I did not feel that I could organize my thoughts but I hoped that if I sat there quietly I might draw some comfort from the atmosphere. Centuries of devotion leave their mark in a place, I knew, but then I remembered that it was barely seventy years since St Mary's had been built; it seemed so bright and new and there were no canopied tombs of great families, no weeping cherubs, no urns, no worn inscriptions on the floor. Instead I could only read the brass tablets to past vicars and benefactors or contemplate the ugly stained glass of the east window. And yet, I thought after a while, wasn't the atmosphere of good Victorian piety as comforting as any other? Ought I not to be as much consoled by the thought of our first vicar, Father Busby – Henry Bertram Busby and Maud Elizabeth, his wife – as by any seventeenth-century divine? I was half unconscious of my surroundings now and started when I heard a voice calling my name.

'Miss Lathbury! Miss Lathbury!'

I looked up almost guiltily as if I had been doing something disgraceful and saw Miss Statham creeping towards me. She held a polishing-cloth and a tin of Brasso in her hand.

'You were sitting so still, I thought perhaps you'd had a turn.'

'A turn?' I repeated stupidly.

'Yes, been taken ill, you know. I said to myself as I came out of the vestry, "Why, there's Miss Lathbury sitting there. I wonder what *she's* doing? It isn't her week for the brasses and it's too early for Evensong." Then I thought you must be ill.'

'No, I'm all right, thank you,' I said, smiling at Miss Statham's reasons for my presence in church. 'I was just thinking something over.'

'Thinking something over? Oh, dear . . .' she let out a stifled giggle and then clapped her hand over her mouth fearfully. 'I'm sorry, Miss Lathbury, I didn't mean to laugh really. Only it seemed a bit funny to be sitting here on such a nice afternoon thinking things over. Wouldn't you like to come home with me and have a cup of tea?'

I refused as graciously as I could and Miss Statham went off to do her brasses. My little meditation in the church was at an end; obviously I could not go on with it now. Had the church been older and darker and smaller, had it perhaps been a *Roman* Catholic church, I thought wickedly . . . But it was no use regretting it; the fault lay in myself. Nevertheless, I did feel a little calmer and better able to face furniture removals and whatever else might be in store for me.

When I got home Mrs Morris was cleaning my sitting-room. It was really her day for the Napiers, but she had finished their work sooner than usual and expressed surprise at the tidiness of the kitchen.

'Only the breakfast washing-up to do and a few odd plates,' she said. 'Usually it's all the meals from the day before and *glasses* – you'd think they lived on wine.'

I explained that I had done some washing-up the previous afternoon. 'Mrs Napier is away,' I said delicately, 'so she wasn't able to do it.'

'And she wouldn't do it even if she was here,' said Mrs Morris emphatically. '*He's* always the one to do things in the house. The next thing is we'll have the vicar washing-up. Just wait till he's married and you'll soon see.'

'You don't think that men should help with the house-work?' I asked.

She gave me a look but said nothing for a moment. 'Not a clergyman, Miss Lathbury,' she said at last, shaking her head.

'You think they have enough burdens to bear without that?'

'I don't know about *burdens*,' she said doubtfully, 'but that Mrs Gray will lead him a dance, I don't mind telling you. A widow! What happened to her first? That's what *I'd* like to know!' She opened the window and shook the mop vigorously out of it.

'Oh, I think he was killed in the war,' I said.

Mrs Morris shook her head again.

'You told me, Miss Lathbury, that the vicar wasn't a marrying man,' she said accusingly.

'Well, I had always thought he wasn't,' I admitted. 'But we're sometimes mistaken, aren't we?'

'A pretty face,' said Mrs Morris; 'well, she has got that. But what's his poor sister going to do? What about poor Miss Winifred? Hasn't she made a home for him for all these years? Given up the best years of her life to making him comfortable?'

I could think of no ready answers to her challenging questions, especially when I remembered with some uneasiness what Winifred had hinted at the other evening. Not that she had exactly *said* anything against Allegra Gray, but she seemed less enthusiastic than she had been.

'I wouldn't put it quite like that, Mrs Morris,' I said at last. 'I think Miss Malory has liked to make a home for her brother. After all, it was the natural thing for her to do, as I suppose it would be for most women.'

'*You* haven't made a home for a man, Miss Lathbury,' Mrs Morris went on, her tone full of reproach so that I felt as if I had in some way failed in my duty.

'Well, no,' I admitted, 'though after my mother died I kept house for my father for a short time. But then he died too and I've been by myself ever since, except when Miss Caldicote was here.'

'It's not natural for a woman to live alone, without a husband.'

'No, perhaps not, but many women do and some have no choice in the matter.'

'No choice!' Mrs Morris's scornful laugh rang out. 'You want to think of yourself a bit more, Miss Lathbury, if you don't mind me saying so. You've done too much for Father Malory and so has Miss Winifred and in the end you both get left, if you'll excuse me putting it plainly.'

'Yes, I suppose you're right,' I said, smiling, for really she *was* right. It was not the excellent women who got married but people like Allegra Gray, who was not good at sewing, and Helena Napier, who left all the washing-up. 'I can't change now. I'm afraid it's too late.' I felt it would not sound very convincing if I said that I hadn't really wanted to marry Julian Malory. I was obviously regarded in the parish as the chief of the rejected ones and I must fill the position with as much dignity as I could.

'You're not bad-looking,' said Mrs Morris quickly and then looked shocked, as if she had gone too far. She bent down, unhooked the bag from the Hoover and shook out a great mound of dust on to a newspaper. 'Things happen, even at the last minute,' she said mysteriously. 'Not that you'd want to marry a man who'd been divorced. Too much of this old divorce, there is,' she muttered, going out into the kitchen with the bundle of dust. I heard her say that there was a drop of milk in the jug that would do for my tea.

She left me feeling a little shaken, almost as if I really had failed in some kind of duty and must take immediate action to make up for it. I must go to Julian and not do things for him and then he might reject Allegra and marry me. As for Rocky, in his cottage surrounded by nettles, perhaps it did not matter how much I did for him since he could never be regarded as a possible husband. Too much of this old divorce. But then I smiled at myself for the heavy seriousness of my thoughts. Had the Wren officers had their dreams too? I wondered. Had they imagined Rocky wifeless and turning to them for comfort or had they always known they were just playthings, taken down from their shelves only when he wanted an evening's diversion? I could not flatter myself that I had done even that for him.

I also had a limp suede-bound volume of Christina Rossetti's poems among my bedside books.

Better by far you should forget and smile,
Than that you should remember and be sad . . .

It was easy enough to read those lines and to be glad at his smiling but harder to tell myself that there would never be any question of anything else. It would simply not occur to him to be sad.

It must not be poetry that I read that night, but a devotional or even a cookery book. Perhaps the last was best for my mood, and I chose an old one of recipes and miscellaneous household hints. I read about the care of aspidistras and how to wash lace and black woollen stockings, and I learned that a package or envelope sealed with white of egg cannot be steamed open. Though what use that knowledge would ever be to me I could not imagine.

CHAPTER NINETEEN

IT SEEMED ODD to be able to enter the Napiers' flat freely and to treat their possessions almost as if they had been my own. Rocky's list made it quite clear what was to be moved – the big desk, the Chippendale chairs, the gate-legged table and then the smaller objects, paper-weights and snow-storms and some china. Even the books were to be sorted out, leaving only Helena's forbidding-looking anthropological works and a few paper-backed novels. The rooms would be bare and characterless when these things were gone, but even now they looked impersonal and depressing. I wondered if I ought to attempt to tidy the desk, whose pigeon-holes were stuffed with papers, and I did make an effort, conscious all the time that I might come across something which was none of my business. I dare say I hoped that I might but my curiosity was not gratified. There were no love-letters, no diaries, no photographs, even. The pigeon-holes contained only bills and Helena's anthropological notes. The love-letters from the Wren officers had no doubt been crumpled up and thrown into the waste-paper basket after a perfunctory reading. But perhaps they had been wise enough not to tell their love. It seemed to me that the natural inclination of women to assume a Patience-on-a-monument attitude was a kind of strength, though judging by what Everard Bone had told me they sometimes gave away their advantage by declaring themselves.

I took care to be up before eight o'clock on the Saturday morning, but it was after half-past nine when the remover's men arrived. There were three of them, two cheerful and strong-looking, and the third, perhaps as befitted his position as foreman, wizened and melancholy and apparently incapable of carrying anything at all.

He shook his head when he saw the big desk.

'We'll never get that round the corner of the stairs,' he declared.

I pointed out that it could be taken to pieces, but he had his moment of triumph when the bottom half of the desk was pulled away from the wall and a fine powdering of sawdust was revealed on the carpet.

'Worm,' he said. 'I knew it as soon as I set eyes on it.'

'Oh, dear,' I said feebly feeling that it might almost be my fault. 'I wonder if Mr Napier knows about that.'

'I shouldn't think he does. You never know what goes on at the back, unless you're an expert. I've been handling furniture for over forty years, of course.'

'I suppose there's nothing we can do about it now?' I asked, thinking of Everard Bone's mother but feeling that it would hardly be any use to telephone her now. I should have to mention it to Rocky in a letter.

'Hundreds of them,' said the foreman, tapping the little holes with his finger and watching the fine dust pour out. 'We shall be lucky if it doesn't fall to pieces. It rots the whole piece, madam. It's probably riddled with them.'

'Amazing how those little insects get in, boring all those neat little holes,' I commented fatuously.

'Ah,' he smiled for the first time, 'that's just what they *don't* do, madam. It's surprising the number of people that think that. The holes are made when the beetles come *out* – that's what it is.'

'Oh, really? That's interesting,' I murmured.

'Slowly, now,' he called, as two strong men lifted the base of the desk as easily as if it had been made of cardboard. I was relieved to see that it did not fall to pieces, but the episode had disturbed me. It was disconcerting to think that worms or beetles could eat their way secretly through one's furniture. *Something is rotten in the state of Denmark . . . Men have died and worms have eaten them, but not for love . . .* 'Perhaps you would like a cup of tea?' I suggested.

This proved to be a good idea and the rest of the things were taken away smoothly and without incident. The foreman was able to carry a cushion downstairs but otherwise took little part in the proceedings. After I had seen the van go away I went upstairs to my flat to eat a melancholy lunch. A dried-up scrap of cheese, a few lettuce leaves for which I could not be bothered to make any dressing, a tomato and a piece of bread-and-butter, followed by a cup of coffee made with coffee essence. A real *woman's* meal, I thought, with no suggestion of brandy afterwards, even though there was still a drop left in the bottle. Alcohol would have made it even more of a mockery.

I had just finished when the telephone bell rang. It was Miss Clovis, asking if I would care to take tea with her and Mrs Napier.

'No doubt you will have something to report?' she asked eagerly.

'Oh, yes, the furniture has just gone.'

'What, all of it?' she asked in alarm.

'Oh, no, just Mr Napier's own things. The flat is quite habitable now for Mrs Napier whenever she likes to come back.'

A snorting noise came down the telephone.

'That man! I think it's the limit. Anyway, Miss Lathbury, I shall expect you about four o'clock.'

I was a little apprehensive at entering the premises of the Learned Society alone and felt quite nervous as I pushed open the heavy door, whose dark carvings might have been the work of some primitive sculptor. On the stairs I met an old bearded man, and I thought for a moment that it was the old President, until I remembered that he was dead. He stood aside courteously for me to pass and said, beaming and nodding, 'Ah, miss, er – hard at work, I see.'

'Oh, yes,' I beamed and nodded back at him.

'It would be pretty hot in New Guinea now, eh?' he chuckled as I mounted the flight of stairs above him.

'Yes, it certainly would be,' I called out, confident that this was a safe answer to make.

'Oh, good. I was just going to make tea.' Miss Clovis emerged from a door with a kettle in her hand. 'Do go on into the sitting-room – it's the door in front of you.'

I went into the room indicated, but then drew back, thinking that I had entered a library or store-room by mistake, for the floor was littered with books which seemed to have overflowed from the tall shelves which lined three of the walls. There were also several dark wooden images, some with fierce and alarming expressions. In the middle of the books and images sat Helena Napier, wearing a crumpled cotton dress and apparently busy sorting out a mass of notes in typescript and sprawling handwriting.

We greeted each other stiffly, for I could not help feeling self-conscious at being, as it were, the last person to see her husband, and she may have had something of the same feeling.

'You look busy,' I began.

'Has he taken the furniture?' she asked bluntly.

'Oh, yes; it went this morning.'

Miss Clovis came in with a teapot which she put down on a low table on which a rough attempt at laying tea had been made, with three odd cups and saucers, a loaf of bread, a pot of jam and a slab of margarine still in its paper. Helena must feel quite at home here, I thought spitefully.

'Dig in,' said Miss Clovis. 'I've got a cake somewhere, left over from the Society's last tea party.' She produced a tin from behind one of the images. I wondered whether there had been a tea-party since the one I had been to in the spring, for the cake, when it was put out, looked weeks or even months old. Fortunately, however, it was a shop cake made of substitute ingredients and I had learned from my own experience that such cakes would keep almost indefinitely.

'I met such a nice old man on the stairs,' I said. 'He had a grey beard and looked very much like the old President, the one who died.'

'Oh, that would be old Hornibrook – New Guinea, 1905,' said Helena shortly.

'How sad that was, the old President dying,' I said.

'Oh, well, in the midst of life we are in death,' said Miss Clovis casually, cutting a thick slab of bread.

'Yes, of course, he went so suddenly.'

'Suddenly with meat in his mouth,' said Miss Clovis.

'Oh, surely . . .'

'Ah, I can see you aren't an antiquarian, Miss Lathbury,' said Miss Clovis triumphantly, 'or you would know your Anthony à Wood better. *In the beginning of this month I was told that Henry Marten died last summer, suddenly with meat in his mouth, at Chepstow in Monmouthshire*,' she quoted. 'But that's the way they go. The President was standing in the library and was just reaching up to take *Dynamics of Clanship among the Tallensi* out of a shelf, when he fell.'

'What a splendid title for a book,' I remarked. 'Perhaps not a book for an *old* man to read, though. Who is to be the new President?'

'Tyrell Todd,' said Helena. 'You may remember him at our do.'

'Oh, yes, he talked about pygmies.'

'He is a young man,' said Miss Clovis. 'New brooms sweep clean, or so they say.'

The conversation now turned into an exchange of views about various personalities whose names meant nothing to me. I am afraid Miss Clovis brought out little tit-bits of scandal about them and she and Helena seemed to be enjoying themselves very much. I began to wonder why I had been asked to tea as they made so little attempt to entertain me.

At last there was a pause and I made a remark about the books and images, asking if they belonged to Miss Clovis.

'Good Heavens, no,' said Miss Clovis. 'The late President's widow gave them. She could hardly wait to get them out of the house. I suppose they were just so much junk to her.'

'Oh, yes; I think I remember her.' The old woman nodding in her chair and falling asleep over her knitting. How she must have disliked those images, nasty malevolent-looking things, some with dusty unhygienic raffia manes. Perhaps they had even come between her and the man she had married. I wondered if she had had to have them in her drawing-room, though even if they had been relegated to his study they must have been a continual worry to her, especially at spring-cleaning time. 'I suppose you are glad to have his relics,' I said. 'Will his wife's name go up on the board among the list of benefactors?'

'I suppose it will have to,' said Miss Clovis, 'though I doubt if she will ever have the pleasure of seeing it there. I'm sure she won't attend any of our meetings now that her husband is dead.'

'I wonder if she feels a great sense of freedom,' I said, more to myself than my companions. 'Perhaps she never really understood the papers and wasn't interested, and now she need never come again. Or perhaps she feels lost without the discipline of sitting through them and will find nothing to take its place.'

'Well, she certainly hasn't got your churchgoing and good works,' said Helena quite genially.

'Oh, did he take even that from her?' I asked, shocked by the idea that she could now have been the backbone of some parish, one of the invaluable helpers of some overworked vicar, had not her husband made her an unbeliever. 'Oh, the wicked things men do, leaving her nothing for her old age, not even anthropology!'

'You put yourself too much in other people's places,' said Helena. 'I believe she is quite happy pottering about her garden and reading novels. To be free and independent, that's the thing.'

'But surely you don't want that when you're old?' I protested. 'Would you know what to do with freedom and independence if it came so late in life?'

'Well, all I can say is that I'm thankful *I* never got myself tied up with any man,' said Miss Clovis.

Helena looked at her doubtfully, perhaps wondering, as I was, whether Miss Clovis had ever had the opportunity of entering into this bondage.

'You will do better work without your husband,' said Miss Clovis. 'You will now be able to devote your whole life to the study of matrilineal kin-groups.'

I could not help pitying Helena, condemned to something that sounded so uninteresting, and she may have pitied herself a little as she said bitterly, 'You should have said higher things. Isn't that what one usually devotes one's life to? Come along, Mildred, it's time we were going now.'

I thanked Miss Clovis, who seemed unwilling to let Helena go, and went down the stairs with Helena's suitcase and a small evil-looking image, which was given to me to carry. I felt awkward when people in the bus started to stare and giggle and I had to sit with it in my lap, trying vainly to cover it with my gloves and handbag.

As we approached the house Julian Malory came towards us. I had imagined that the sight of Helena would frighten him away, but he stood his ground.

'I am sorry to hear of this trouble between you and your

husband, Mrs Napier,' he said. 'I think you should go back to him and talk things over.'

We were all – even Julian, I think – so taken aback at his boldness that for a moment nobody said anything. I myself was full of admiration for him, for I had not expected that he would speak so frankly. I had imagined he would make some trivial social remark and that our encounter would end with remarks about the weather.

'Well, he has gone into the country,' said Helena, without her usual self-possession. 'And there are difficulties, you know.'

'There are always difficulties in human relationships,' said Julian. 'You won't think I am trying to interfere, I hope, but I do think you should see him. And if there is anything I can do for you, please let me know.'

Helena thanked him in an embarrassed way and we went into the house. I felt almost as if I ought to apologize for Julian's boldness, as if he and all clergymen were my personal responsibility, and perhaps they were when I was up against unbelievers. I could not help feeling glad that he had spoken.

'I suppose he felt he ought to say something,' said Helena in a detached way. 'It must be a bore having to go about doing good, saying a word here and there. I didn't realize they ever *did* anything like that, though.'

'Oh, yes, Julian certainly has the courage of his convictions,' I said. 'I believe he and Rocky had a drink together the other night. I saw them going into the pub at the end of the square.'

'Really, Mildred, the things you see happening! Is there anything that escapes you?'

'Well, I couldn't help seeing them. I just happened to be passing. I expect they had a talk and Rocky would feel more at ease talking to a man than he would to me. I suppose there must be times when men band together against women and women against men. You and Miss Clovis against Julian and

Rocky, and I like the umpire in a tennis match.'

Helena laughed, but when we reached her sitting-room she exclaimed angrily, 'But my chairs have gone! Really, this is too bad. And the desk too! Mildred, why did you let them go?'

'I'm sorry,' I said meekly. 'Rocky gave me a list of the furniture that was to go and I just followed his instructions.'

'Oh, you were always on his side!' she burst out. 'Anyway, those chairs were a wedding present to both of us. He had no right to take them.'

'Yes, it is difficult, when something is given as a wedding present,' I said. But how could people foresee the separation of a happy pair and always give presents that could if necessary be easily divided? Surely that was too cynical a view for even the most embittered giver to take of marriage?

Helena darted here and there in the flat, missing objects which she claimed as hers. 'Mildred, you'll have to write to him,' she declared, sitting down in the one armchair that was left.

'*I* write to him? Wouldn't it be better if you did?'

'Oh, I certainly couldn't do it myself. You know him and he might take more notice of a letter from you. Otherwise I might ask Esther Clovis to do it, or even Everard.'

'Oh, I don't think you should ask *him*,' I burst out, suddenly remembering that I had never had the opportunity of telling Helena, as he had bidden me to, that he did not love her. But it hardly seemed to matter now. 'Anyway,' I went on, 'he's at a conference of the Prehistoric Society in Derbyshire, so it wouldn't be much use.'

'Oh, *that*,' said Helena impatiently. 'I can't think why he bothers with archaeology. All this dabbling won't get him anywhere.'

'I shouldn't have thought he dabbled,' I said. 'He gives me the impression of being a very definite kind of person.'

'How do you mean?' asked Helena suspiciously.

'Well, he knows what he wants or doesn't want,' I floundered. 'I should think he has – er – very high principles.'

'Oh, he doesn't believe in divorce, if that's what you mean,' said Helena in a light tone. 'And naturally he imagined that if I quarrelled with Rocky I should go rushing to him. That's why he went to Derbyshire, of course.'

I was a little taken aback at her summing-up of the position and must have shown it in my face, for she laughed and said, 'Oh, yes, men are very simple and obvious in some ways, you know. They generally react in the way one would expect and it is often a rather cowardly way. I should think Everard was most alarmed when he heard that Rocky and I weren't getting on very well. He doesn't really care twopence about prehistory, you know. He always uses the Society as an excuse, just because I don't happen to be a member myself.'

This seemed to me rather a waste of a subscription and there was something altogether comic about the thought of a man hiding from a woman behind a cloak of prehistory.

'I met his mother,' I said, hoping to change the subject. 'She seems rather odd.'

'Yes, she is odd, but then people's mothers usually are, don't you think?' said Helena. 'I suppose there's really no reason why Everard and I should ever meet again, except at the Society. It would be more dramatic, really, if we didn't for about ten years, and then we should be like the pair in that sonnet that people always think of when they part from somebody,

Be it not seen in either of our brows,
That we one jot of former love retain.'

'I dare say you wouldn't still love a person after ten years,' I suggested, 'so you wouldn't retain one jot of former love, anyway, and that would spoil the excitement of the meeting.'

'Yes, one would have nothing to conceal and would probably wonder how one could ever have felt anything at all. It would be better if I forgot all about Everard, I suppose, since he obviously doesn't intend to have anything more to do with me.'

'Yes, of course, it would. But forgetting isn't very easy,' I said doubtfully.

'I suppose you have perhaps had to forget somebody too?' asked Helena, equally doubtful.

'Oh, yes,' I said cheerfully, thinking of Bernard Hatherley, but unwilling to bring such a poor thing out into the open after so many years. 'I suppose everybody does at some time in their lives.'

'I was wondering if you were rather fond of Rocky,' said Helena, with what seemed to me unsuitable frankness. 'People do fall in love with him, you know.'

'Oh, you mean the Wren officers?' I said, with an attempt at laughter.

'Yes, they certainly did, but that was only to be expected. Rocky looked so fine in his uniform and was kind to them at parties and danced with them all in turn. But you have seen him much more as he really is. And I know he likes you very much. He has said so several times.'

This was very little consolation to me and the whole subject of the conversation was a most uncomfortable one, I felt.

'Perhaps I had better get down to writing that letter about the furniture,' I said firmly. 'If you could give me a list of things you want sent back, I might start it tonight.'

'Oh, yes,' Helena stood up, 'that would be a great help. I wonder if your vicar would take me out for a drink? He did say that I was to let him know if there was anything he could do for me, didn't he?'

'I'm not sure that was quite the kind of thing he meant,' I said, 'though if he takes Rocky to have a drink I don't see why he shouldn't take you. But I rather think tonight is his boys' club night.'

CHAPTER TWENTY

A LIST OF furniture is not a good beginning to a letter, though I dare say a clever person with a fantastic turn of mind could transform even a laundry list into a poem.

I sat for a long time at my desk, unable to put pen to paper, idly turning the pages of a notebook in which I kept accounts and made shopping lists. How fascinating they would have been, had they been medieval shopping lists! I thought. But perhaps there was matter for poetry in them, with their many uncertainties and question marks. 'Rations, green veg., soap flakes, stamps', seemed reasonable enough and easily explained, but why 'red ribbon'? What could I have wanted red ribbon for? Some daring idea for retrimming an old hat, perhaps; if so it had been stillborn, for I knew that I had never bought any and that it was unlikely anyway that I should wear a hat trimmed with red ribbon. As for 'egg poacher?' – that was an unfulfilled dream or ambition to buy one of those utensils that produce a neat artificial-looking poached egg. But I had never bought it and it seemed likely that on the rare occasions when I had a fresh egg to poach I should continue to delve for it in the bubbling water where the white separated from the yolk and waved about like a sea anemone. Sometimes I had noted down places or shops to visit. I came across the name of a well-known Roman Catholic bookshop, also with a question mark. I do not think I had ever bought anything there, but I remembered going into it at Christmas, when the basement, with its brightly coloured plaster figures, seemed to offer a peaceful refuge from the shopping crowds.

I went on turning the pages until I was reduced to studying old gas and electricity bills, but I knew that I could not brood over such trivia indefinitely and at last, after several false starts, I managed to produce some kind of a letter, beginning 'Dear Rocky', stating the facts and giving the list of furniture and ending 'I hope you are settling down well, Yours ever, Mildred.' The ending had cost me more anxious thought than was justified by the result, but I believed that 'yours ever' was the correct way to finish a friendly letter to a person for whom one was supposed to have no particular feelings. I dare say there would have been no harm in sending my love, but I could not bring myself to do this.

Rocky's answer, when it came, was characteristic and had obviously cost him no anxious thought at all.

> Dearest M. [he wrote], Helena is quite wrong about all this and the things I have taken are definitely MINE. As for the *Blue Casserole*, I admit that she bought it, but only to replace one of mine which Everard Bone broke. So let's have no more of this nonsense.
>
> I hope you are well and that the church is flourishing, also Father Malory – ought I to write Fr? All those Sundays after Trinity must be tedious but I suppose there will come an end sometime!
>
> You must come and see me some time and (if fine) I will give you lunch in my wild garden with an amusing wine.
>
> In haste and with lots of love,
>
> R.

I brooded over this letter with pleasure and sadness, but after I had learned its contents nearly by heart the chief impression that remained was one of surprise. I could not imagine Everard Bone breaking a casserole! It was a silly trivial thing, but every time I thought of it I smiled, sometimes when I was by myself in a street or in a bus.

As I had expected, Helena received the letter with indignation and decided that she would have no further communication with her husband but would go home and stay with her mother in Devonshire. I had not expected that she would behave in this conventional way and somehow liked her better for it. So it seemed that my part in the unhappy affair was at an end, and I could only hope that something would occur to make them come to their senses. I began to think that if I went to see Rocky I might be able to bring them together again; I saw myself playing a rather noble part, stepping into the background when they were reunited and going quietly away to make a cup of tea or do some washing or ironing. But although Rocky had said that I must go and see him some time, he had not suggested any definite date and I did not like to invite myself.

It was the middle of August now, a difficult time in the church. There were, as Rocky had pointed out, all those Sundays after Trinity; even the highest church could not escape them and it was sometimes difficult to remember whether we were at Trinity eight, nine or ten. Then too, Julian Malory was away, leaving Father Greatorex in charge, and we were like a rudderless ship. There was no sermon on Sunday mornings and little things seemed to go wrong – sparks came out of the censer and alarmed some of the older members of the congregation; one of the little acolytes tripped over his too long cassock and fell down the steps, causing the others to dissolve into giggles. One Sunday Teddy Lemon went to Margate for the week-end, and Mr Conybeare, looking like an angry bird, was called up out of the congregation to act as Master of Ceremonies. It was the organist's holiday too, and although Sister Blatt made a valiant attempt to take his place those peculiarly unnerving noises that only a church organ can produce would keep bursting out.

Julian and Winifred had gone on holiday with Allegra Gray to a farm in Somerset. I could not help feeling that they were an ill-assorted trio, but perhaps Julian had not thought it quite proper to go on a holiday alone with his fiancée and there was always the problem of what to do with Winifred. I could have offered to go somewhere with her myself had I not been pledged to go away with Dora Caldicote in September, as I did every year. I began to look forward to my holiday as never before. I felt that I needed to get away from all the problems – mostly other people's – with which I had been worried in the last few months. If I could look at them from a distance they might solve themselves. Helena would forget about the furniture. Allegra Gray would turn out to be the perfect wife for Julian, Winifred would marry or enter a religious community. Even the woodworms in the back of Rocky's desk would be destroyed and their ravages arrested by the application of that remedy Mrs Bone had been talking about.

One day towards the end of August I was coming out of my office at one o'clock when I saw Everard Bone standing looking in a shop window some distance away. My immediate reaction was one of irritation. What was he doing? If he wanted to see me, why couldn't he telephone and arrange a meeting in a normal way? I remembered the last time we had met, I in my old cotton dress and no stockings, with Cardinal Newman and a loaf in my string bag. Today I was at least wearing a respectable dress and had no domestic shopping with me. I had planned to hurry home and finish a dress I was making for my holiday, so, imagining that he had not seen me, I turned and walked briskly in the opposite direction. I heard the sound of somebody running after me but I did not look round. Then my name was called and I had to stop and feign surprise.

'Oh, it's you,' I said ungraciously.

'Yes, I've been waiting for you. I hoped you would have lunch with me.'

'Why didn't you write or telephone, then?'

'Well, it didn't occur to me till this morning. I've been away, you see. A little archaeological tour in the Dordogne.'

'Have you been hiding in a cave?' I asked.

'I have been in some caves, certainly,' he replied. 'But I don't know why you should think I have been hiding.'

'Oh, it doesn't matter,' I said, feeling rather ashamed. 'I was only making a kind of joke. I thought anthropology was your subject anyway.'

'Yes, but it all links up, you know. Archaeology seems to fit in better with a holiday.'

'There are stone circles in Brittany, aren't there?' I began, trying to show an intelligent interest. 'And then of course there's always Stonehenge.' I remembered that my father had been interested in Stonehenge, and I seemed to see us all sitting round the dinner-table, my mother and father, a curate – I could not remember which curate – and a canon and his wife. We were having a conversation about Stonehenge and suddenly all the lights had gone out. The curate had let out a cry of alarm but the canon's voice went on without a tremor – I could hear it now – just as if nothing had happened. My mother got up and fussed with candles and the canon went on explaining his theory of how the great stones had been carried to Salisbury Plain. It was an impressive performance and had been rewarded, or so it seemed to me, by a bishopric not long afterwards. Thinking about it after all these years, I smiled.

'Yes, there's always Stonehenge,' said Everard rather stiffly.

We walked on in silence until we came to an area where there were restaurants.

'You haven't said in so many words that you will have lunch with me,' said Everard, 'but as we seem to be going in the right direction I assume that you will.'

'Oh, well, I suppose so,' I said indifferently and then realized that I was not behaving very well. It seemed too late to apologize and I felt resentful towards him for bringing out the worst in me, but I made some attempt. 'You must think me very impolite,' I said, 'but the worst side of me seems to be coming out today. It does seem to have been coming out more lately.'

'I expect you are upset at all this happening,' he said.

'Yes, I suppose I might make that excuse. It is upsetting when things happen to friends.'

We went into a restaurant and were shown to a table. It was not until we were sitting down that I realized that it was the restaurant where I had had lunch with William Caldicote in the spring.

'What exactly *has* happened?' he asked casually.

'Rocky is in the country and Helena has gone home to her mother in Devonshire.'

'Oh, that is a relief,' he said, taking up the menu and ordering lunch with rather less fuss than William did.

'I don't really know that one should have expected anything else. Women who quarrel with their husbands usually do go home to their mothers, if they have mothers.'

'I certainly gave her no encouragement,' said Everard, almost in a satisfied tone.

'Oh, I'm sure you didn't,' I said, contemplating my *hors d'œuvres*. 'I can't imagine you doing such a thing.'

'Of course,' he went on, with a note of warning in his tone, 'I shall probably marry eventually.'

'Yes, men usually do,' I murmured.

'The difficulty is to find a suitable person.'

'Perhaps one shouldn't try to find people deliberately like that,' I suggested. 'I mean, not set out to look for somebody to marry as if you were going to buy a saucepan or a casserole.'

'You think it should be left to chance? But then the person might be most unsuitable.'

The idea of choosing a husband or wife as one would a casserole had reminded me of Rocky's letter and his allegation that Everard had broken one of his casseroles. I suppose a smile must have come on to my face, for he said, 'You seem to find it amusing, the idea of marrying somebody suitable.'

'I wasn't really smiling at that. It was just that I couldn't imagine you breaking a casserole.'

'Oh, that,' he said rather irritably. 'Helena had put it in the oven to warm and when I took hold of it it was so hot that I dropped it.'

'Yes, I could imagine it happening that way, with a perfectly reasonable explanation. It was a pity you didn't use the oven cloth,' I suggested.

'But it had only been in the oven a few minutes. Besides, I don't think there was an oven cloth.'

'I always have mine hanging on a nail by the side of the cooker.'

'Well, you're a sensible person. It's just the kind of thing you would have.'

Oh, dear, one was to be for ever cast down, I thought, brooding over the piece of fish on my plate. If I had been flattered by Everard's invitation to lunch I was now put in my place as the kind of person who would have an oven cloth hanging on a nail by the side of the cooker.

'Would you have married Helena if she had not been married already?' I asked boldly.

'Certainly not,' he declared. 'She is not at all the kind of person I should choose for my wife.'

'What would she be like, that Not Impossible She?' I asked.

'Oh, a sensible sort of person,' he said vaguely.

'Somebody who would help you in your work?' I suggested. 'Somebody with a knowledge of anthropology who could correct proofs and make an index, rather like Miss Clovis, perhaps?'

'Esther Clovis is certainly a very capable person,' he said doubtfully. 'An excellent woman altogether.'

'You could consider marrying an excellent woman?' I asked in amazement. 'But they are not for marrying.'

'You're surely not suggesting that they are for the other things?' he said, smiling.

That had certainly not occurred to me and I was annoyed to find myself embarrassed.

'They are for being unmarried,' I said, 'and by that I mean a positive rather than a negative state.'

'Poor things, aren't they allowed to have the normal feelings, then?'

'Oh, yes, but nothing can be done about them.'

'Of course I do respect and esteem Esther Clovis,' Everard went on.

'Oh, respect and esteem – such dry bones! I suppose one can really have such feelings for somebody but I should have thought one would almost dislike a person who inspired them. Anyway, Miss Clovis must be quite a lot older than you are, and then she looks so odd. She has hair like a dog.'

Everard laughed. 'Yes, so she has.'

I now felt ashamed at having made him laugh by an unkind criticism of the excellent Miss Clovis, so I tried to change the subject by commenting on the other inhabitants of the restaurant in what I hoped was a more charitable way. But he would not agree with me that this woman was pretty or that one elegant, and we lapsed into an uncomfortable silence which was broken by a voice behind me saying my name.

It was William Caldicote.

I introduced him to Everard and then William took command of the conversation.

'Thank goodness *some* of one's friends are unfashionable enough to be in town in August,' he said, 'then one needn't feel *quite* so ashamed, though I suppose nowadays women don't feel that they must go about veiled and in dark glasses and sit in their houses behind drawn blinds.'

'No, I think there are a good many people who have to stay in London during August,' I said, remembering the bus queues and the patient line of people moving with their trays in the great cafeteria.

'Yes, even people like ourselves,' William agreed. 'But *what* my poor mother would have said!'

I thought for a moment of old Mrs Caldicote sitting

comfortably in the ugly drawing-room of her villa in a Birmingham suburb, but I did not remind William of how she had liked to visit London in August – her 'annual jaunt' she called it – to stay at one of those garishly decorated hotels which used to be, and perhaps still are, the Mecca of provincial visitors, especially when the tips were often included in the bill and they were thus saved that embarrassment. My father had preferred a quiet depressing hotel near the British Museum, where he could be near the reading-room and perhaps meet another clergyman who had been up at Balliol in the very early nineteen-hundreds.

'Yes, August is not a pleasant month in London,' said Everard stiffly. 'So many libraries and museums seem to be closed.'

'One's club is being cleaned,' chanted William, '*so* inconvenient.'

'But Lyons Corner House is always open,' I reminded him, trying to remember which was William's club or even if he really had one. He could hardly be on his way there now, for I noticed that he was carrying two rolls in his hand.

'Bread for my pigeons,' he explained. 'I feed them every afternoon; Mildred knows the ritual. Well, Mildred, I suppose you will be going on your holiday with Dora, as usual. We must have luncheon together when you get back,' he added, with a suspicious glance at Everard.

In the autumn? I thought and nearly said it aloud, for our annual luncheon was always in March or April.

'Yes, that would be nice,' I said. 'Dora and I will send you a postcard.'

'Oh, I do like to be the kind of person people send postcards to,' said William, 'those anonymous "views" with too much sea or too many mountains, or your window marked with a cross, or even those rather naughty ones of fat ladies on donkeys.' He waved the rolls at us and hurried away.

'Who was that?' asked Everard politely.

'The brother of a school friend of mine. He's a civil servant in some Ministry. I've known the Caldicotes for years.'

'I thought he might be a friend of the Napiers. Have you any more news of them?' he asked rather too casually.

'Oh, Rocky is in the country and Helena has gone to her mother in Devonshire,' I began, 'but I've already told you that. And I have had to write letters about furniture and arrange for it to be moved.'

'There is no question of any – er – proceedings?' he asked delicately.

'You mean a divorce? Oh, I don't think so. I certainly hope not.'

'No, one doesn't approve of divorce,' said Everard, rather in William's manner. 'But it seems a bad sign, all this moving of furniture, if it's only a temporary quarrel.'

'Oh, dear, perhaps the remover's men will have to bring it all back again – I hadn't thought of that. And perhaps this time the worm-eaten desk really will fall to pieces.'

Everard looked puzzled.

'When they came to move Rocky's desk it was all worm-eaten at the back,' I explained. 'I nearly telephoned your mother to ask her what to do.'

'Oh, my mother has been in Bournemouth for the past fortnight,' said Everard quickly, as if he could not bear that any of the Bone family should be associated even with the Napiers' furniture.

'Then it would have been no use my telephoning her,' I said, putting on my gloves and gathering up my bits and pieces. 'Thank you very much for my lunch.'

'It has been so nice seeing you,' he said, rather too politely to be sincere, I felt. 'We must meet again after you come back from your holiday. I hope you will enjoy it.'

I thanked him but did not offer to send him a postcard, for Everard, unlike William, did not seem to be the kind of person one sent postcards to. Although, I reflected, if one should happen to come across something of anthropological or archaeological interest, some stone circle or barrow or curious local custom, perfectly serious, of course, no jokes about windows marked with a cross or fat ladies, it might be quite well received.

CHAPTER TWENTY-ONE

'OF COURSE it rains a great deal in Austria and Switzerland in the mountains and even in Italy at certain times of the year,' said Dora cheerfully, as we stood at the window of the hotel lounge gazing at the steady downpour.

'And in Africa and India, too,' I added.

'Yes, but there the wet and dry season are carefully defined,' said Dora in a schoolmistress's tone. 'It depends on the monsoons and other things.'

'We might go and look at the Abbey this afternoon,' I suggested, 'as it's so wet.'

'Oh, well, I suppose so,' said Dora, who did not really like looking at buildings but was an indefatigable tourist. 'We can go on the bus.'

The bus-stop was just outside the hotel and there were already a few people waiting when we got there. A crowd of little black priests from a nearby Roman Catholic seminary came and waited in the queue behind us. Dora nudged me. 'Like a lot of beetles,' she whispered. 'I hope we don't have to sit near them. I bet they'll try and push in front of us.'

The bus was half full when it came and some of the priests were left behind. Dora looked down gloatingly from our superior position on the top deck. 'Serve them right,' she said. 'The Pope and all those Dogmas of his!'

'Oh, poor things,' I protested, pitying the dripping black priests who would have to wait another twenty minutes. 'It's not their fault.'

'I suppose the Abbey will be swarming with priests and nuns,' Dora went on, with a fierce gleam in her eye.

'Well, naturally there will be a good many. After all, it must be like a kind of pilgrimage for them and it's certainly rather wonderful to think that the Abbey was built by the monks themselves. I expect there will be quite a number of ordinary tourists as well, though.'

After a ride of about half an hour we got off the bus and found ourselves in what seemed to be open country with no sign of an Abbey anywhere. A woman came up to me and asked me the way. 'I think it must be somewhere along here,' I said, indicating what seemed to be the only path.

'Oh, thank you,' she said. 'I hope you didn't mind my asking, but you looked as if you would know the way.'

I pondered on the significance of this as we walked along in a straggling file, led by Dora and me. Even the priests had accepted our leadership. This seemed a solemn and wonderful thing.

'You'd think they'd have a signpost saying "This way to the Abbey" or an arrow pointing,' grumbled Dora in a satisfied way. 'I wonder if we'll be able to get a cup of tea there? I expect they'll have thought of every way of making money.'

As we rounded the next bend in the lane we came upon a rather new-looking building of an ecclesiastical appearance.

'That must be it,' said Dora.

'Yes, I think so,' I said, relieved that it had shown itself at last, for it would indeed have been a dreadful thing if I had led priests astray. 'I suppose we can join a conducted party.'

'Oh, if you like,' said Dora, 'though I'd rather poke about by myself. You can be pretty sure they won't want to show us everything,' she hinted darkly. 'Like those tours of Russia.'

Parties of tourists arriving in cars and buses or on foot filled the space in front of the Abbey. There was a large car-park and Dora nudged me and pointed to a notice which said LADIES and another which said TEAS. 'I told you the whole place would be commercialized,' she said.

I did not answer, for by now we were inside the Abbey and I was almost overwhelmed by the sudden impression of light and brilliance. The walls looked bright and clean, there was a glittering of much gold and the lingering smell of incense was almost hygienic. Not here, I thought, would one be sentimentally converted to Rome, for there was no warm rosy darkness to hide in, no comfortable confusion of doctrines and dogmas; all would be reasoned out and clearly explained, as indeed it should be.

A neat-looking monk with rimless glasses took charge of our party or rather the group of people in which we found ourselves, for we were an ill-assorted company – a few young soldiers in uniform, a priest or two, middle-aged and young 'couples', a cluster of what seemed to be Anglo-Catholic ladies of the kind who might advertise their services as companions in the *Church Times*, and a crowd of nondescript or unclassifiable bodies, among whom I supposed I should have to include Dora and myself, though I dare say I should have been quite happy with the Anglo-Catholic ladies.

We moved from place to place with reverence and admiration while our guide explained the history and meaning of this or that in a kind patient voice.

'I don't suppose any of you are Catholics,' he said smoothly, 'so you may not understand about Our Lady.'

I saw the Anglo-Catholic ladies gather more closely together, as if to distinguish themselves from the rest of the group. They seemed to be whispering indignantly among themselves and one looked almost as if she were about to protest. But in the end, perhaps remembering their manners or the difficulty of arguing with a Roman, they calmed down and listened patiently with the rest of us.

Dora was looking particularly fierce, though for different reasons, and I was afraid that she might challenge our guide at any moment and start an argument, but evidently she too thought better of it and moved sulkily on to the next point of interest.

'Of course it's no use saying anything to them,' she muttered. 'They've got it all off pat and just recite it like parrots. I'm tired of being led round like this. I'm going to explore on my own.'

When we had finished our tour I found her waiting outside the Abbey, her eyes gleaming triumphantly.

'I hope you didn't put any money in any of those boxes,' she said. 'They've got a shop round the corner to sell rosaries and images and all sorts of highly-coloured junk. I can't imagine why anybody should want to buy such stuff.'

I tried to explain that Roman Catholics and even non-Romans found these things comforting and helpful to their faith, but Dora would not be convinced.

'Parts of the place are roped off,' she said in a low voice. 'One certainly isn't allowed to see everything here. I wonder what goes on *there*?'

'That must be the monks' enclosures,' I said. 'One would hardly expect to be able to go in among them.'

'Oh, I shouldn't want to,' said Dora huffily. 'Nothing would induce me to.' She grasped her umbrella and waved it like a sword.

'Well, then, we may as well find somewhere to have tea. After spiritual comes bodily refreshment.'

'I'm afraid *I* didn't get any spiritual refreshment,' said Dora. 'Quite the reverse, the smell of that incense made me feel quite ill. It would probably penetrate into the tea place here and anyway I don't fancy the look of it. Could we find somewhere on the way back, do you think?'

'Yes, there's a nice village we came through,' I suggested. 'It's where Helena Napier's mother lives, as a matter of fact, and Helena is staying with her now. Don't you remember that black and white café we saw from the bus?'

'Oh, Ye Olde Magpie? Yes, we might try that.'

'You never know,' I ventured, 'we might even see Helena.'

'Oh, you can't keep away from those Napiers,' said Dora good-humouredly. 'Though somehow I don't think it's *Helena* you really want to see.'

I could think of no suitable answer to make to this, so let Dora think what she liked. Rocky's easy and obvious charms were in themselves a kind of protection, for no sensible person could be supposed to feel anything for him. I had to admit to myself that the thought of seeing Helena did not please me particularly, but it seemed a kind of duty to Everard Bone to find out what was happening to her and what, if any, were the latest developments.

I had hardly expected to come upon her as quickly as we did, standing outside Ye Olde Magpie with a shopping basket.

After we had greeted each other with suitable exclamations of surprise and even a certain amount of pleasure, she said, 'Mother sent me out to buy cakes. The vicar is coming to tea.'

'That will be a nice change for you,' said Dora brightly, and, I thought, impertinently.

'Oh, but didn't you know? I get on splendidly with clergymen. Father Malory was quite taken with me – wasn't he, Mildred? – and asked me to let him know if there was anything he could do for me.'

'They always say that,' said Dora, 'and hope to goodness there won't be. It's part of their duty.'

'Oh, come,' I said, but feebly, I'm afraid, 'Julian Malory certainly does a lot of good and so do many other clergymen. He would even have taken Helena out for a drink if that was what she really wanted.'

'Only it happened to be his boys' club night and it always would be something like that, wouldn't it?' asked Helena rather sadly. 'Mother is a real holy fowl. She and Mildred would get on splendidly.'

'Like a house on fire,' said Dora inevitably.

'Won't you come in here and have a cup of tea with us?' I suggested. 'It's only a quarter to four and I don't suppose the vicar will be punctual,' I added, with no possible means of knowing.

'You should really come to tea with us,' said Helena, hesitating, 'but it might be a little embarrassing. Perhaps I will just have a cup, then.'

We went into the café and sat down at an unsteady little round table which was just too small for three people. After what seemed a long time, a young woman with flowing hair and dark red nails came to take our order.

Helena ignored Dora and began questioning me. Had I seen Rocky? Had he written to me? Had I visited him at his cottage? I answered 'No' to all these questions, and added, 'he did say something about my going to see him, but nothing has been arranged yet.'

'Oh, I expect he has forgotten all about it,' said Helena. 'That would be just like him.'

'Yes, I expect he has forgotten.' I bowed my head and peered into the teapot. It had been assumed that I should pour out and until the young woman brought us more hot water I could not have a full cup of tea.

'You must go and see him,' said Helena, 'or at least you must write. We really must make up this stupid quarrel or whatever it is. You can't imagine how bored and miserable I am here.'

'I expect your mother is glad to have you,' I said helpfully.

'Oh, yes! Nothing has been touched in my old room, so terribly depressing. The girlish white painted furniture and the hollyhock chintz – even photographs of old loves on the mantelpiece.'

'I think white painted furniture is nice in a bedroom,' said Dora. 'Do try a piece of this sandwich cake. It's really good.'

'Imagine finding photographs of old loves on the mantelpiece after all these years,' Helena went on, refusing the cake.

'Yes, it must be a little unnerving,' I agreed, seeing as usual Bernard Hatherley's face, the sepia print a little faded behind the glass, yet not faded enough to be romantically Victorian. 'Didn't you think of putting them away in a box or a drawer before you left home? It would seem quite decent and suitable to find them there.'

'Oh, you know how it was in the war. Things did get left.' Helena stood up. 'I must go now. Look, there's the vicar already. He must be on his way to our house.'

I looked through the window and saw a round jolly-looking little man hoisting himself up on to a bicycle. 'Does he,' I began, 'I mean, will he – have been told about things?'

'Oh, Mildred, your delicacy is wonderful!' Helena laughed for the first time that afternoon. 'I am sure Mother has already told him all. She can never keep anything from a clergyman.'

'Well, they are often able to help, as I've said before.'

'Oh, you can help much better than any vicar. Promise me that you will write to Rocky *soon* and tell him about me.'

I said I would try to do this.

'But *soon*, Mildred. I may already have lost him to one of the Wren officers. And think how noble your position will be, a mediator, a bringer-together of husbands and wives.'

I agreed that it certainly did sound noble, but like so many noble occupations there was something a little chilly about it.

Dora and I sat in silence for a little while after Helena had gone.

'Well, well,' said Dora at last, in her comfortable manner which seemed to dispose of difficulties, 'some people don't seem to know when they're well off. It sounds delightful, I think.'

'What sounds delightful?'

'Her room with the white painted furniture and the hollyhock chintz. Of course at school we have bed-sitting-rooms so one can't have anything really dainty-looking, but I was thinking of getting a new divan cover this autumn and possibly curtains to match. I've got a brown carpet, you remember, and my colour scheme has usually been blue and orange. What do you think, Mildred?'

'Oh, hollyhock chintz would look charming,' I said absently.

'You don't think it would be too much? Having curtains as well?'

'Oh, no, of course not.'

'I might not be able to get hollyhock, though I shall have to see what there is, of course.'

'Yes, you will have to see what there is.'

'There seems to be a little garden at the back here. Shall we go out and look at it?' said Dora, springing up from the table. 'It seems to have stopped raining now.'

We walked out through the back of the café into another room, also full of unsteady little round tables, but empty now. It was damp, cold and silent and the tables needed polishing. On one wall there was a spotty engraving of a Byronic-looking young man who reminded me of Rocky. The room led out into a romantic little garden, shut in with high walls covered with dripping ivy.

'Oh, what a gloomy place!' exclaimed Dora. 'You'd think they could brighten it up with a few striped umbrellas.'

'Oh, we do have umbrellas in the season, madam,' said the waitress in an offended tone. She had followed us in with our bill, as if fearing that we might escape without paying for our tea. 'But of course we aren't doing many lunches and teas now, you see, the season's really over.'

Yes, I thought sadly, the season was really over and in the little garden I could see the last rose of summer. 'This must be an old house,' I said, 'almost Elizabethan.'

'I don't know about that, madam, but of course it's called Ye Olde Magpie, so it must be *old*,' said the girl. 'It's a pity they don't spend a bit of money on it and make it more modern. The kitchen's terrible.'

'I don't feel like going in that garden,' said Dora. 'It looks a bit damp to me. You don't want to go out, do you?'

'No, not really.' I could see a little lawn and a stone cupid with ivy growing on it and it seemed rather too melancholy. 'I wonder if they have any picture postcards of this garden?'

'Oh, to send to William, you mean?'

'Yes, perhaps to William, but I've already sent him one.'

'Oh, you mustn't overdo it, or he'll think you're running after him.'

I agreed that I mustn't and imagined William's beady eyes, round and alarmed. But there were no postcards of Ye Olde Magpie at all, and even if I had been bold enough to send one to Rocky I should not have been able to say anything about the last rose of summer and the ivy-mantled cupid.

'We should just catch the five o'clock bus,' said Dora, 'if it isn't too full of those awful priests.'

When we reached the bus-stop we were a long way behind in the queue and when the bus came it took only half a dozen people. I noticed a group of priests looking down on us from the upper deck and I felt that somehow the Pope and his Dogmas had triumphed after all.

CHAPTER TWENTY-TWO

A WEEK LATER I sat at my desk trying to compose a letter to Rocky. It was one of those sad late September evenings when by switching on a bar of the electric fire one realizes at last that summer is over. I had been sitting for over half an hour, listening to the heavy rain falling outside rather than writing, for I did not know what to say. It had been difficult enough to write about the furniture but it seemed infinitely harder to know how to tell Rocky that Helena regretted their quarrel and that they must come together again, that he must take her back. And yet, who was to take who back? That was the point, for I had forgotten, if I had ever really known, who was to blame. The inability to wash a lettuce properly, the hot saucepan put carelessly down on the walnut table . . . it seemed now as if it had been nothing more than that. But there was Everard Bone – where did he come into it? His position now seemed to be merely that of an anxious onlooker, who did not want to become involved in any 'unpleasantness'. I smiled to myself as I remembered the carefully worded postcard I had sent him. A Dolmen on Dartmoor – at least the title was pleasing. 'We walked here today – I wonder if you know it? A lovely spot. Luckily it was a clear day so we had an excellent view. All good wishes – M. Lathbury.' With that ambiguous signature, which was one I never normally used, I might have been man or woman, though the wording of the card was perhaps not very masculine. William Caldicote had been luckier in my choice for him, a fine picture of the Diamond Jubilee band-stand, with a few little jokes which it would be tedious to repeat here. I had not been able to find a suitable card for Rocky.

'Dear Rocky . . .' I turned back to the letter with determination and wrote on a fresh sheet of paper. 'I have just come back from my holiday in Devonshire and happened to see Helena there.' That was a good clear beginning. I would say that she seemed unhappy and bored, then I might ask how he was and what he was doing. The next thing would be to introduce a more personal note – 'You may think it very interfering, but it does seem to me . . .' What seemed to me? I wondered, listening to the rain which had suddenly become heavier, and why should he take any notice of what I said?

The shrill sound of my door-bell made me start as if somebody had fired a pistol shot at my back. Who could be calling now? Not that it was very late – barely half-past nine – but I could not think of anybody likely to visit me unexpectedly and on such a wet night. I went down to answer the bell rather unwillingly, but hearing the rain drumming on a skylight I hurried, realizing that whoever it was must be getting very wet, standing by the door.

I had just started to turn the handle when I heard my name being called. It was Winifred Malory's voice. I had certainly not expected it to be her, for I had imagined that she and Julian and Allegra would all be cosily together in the vicarage, from which I felt myself to be somehow excluded these days.

'Oh, Mildred, thank goodness you're in!'

I drew her quickly into the hall and saw that she was soaking wet. Then I noticed that she was wearing only a thin dress without a hat or coat and that on her feet were what looked like bedroom slippers, now sodden with rain.

'Winifred! Whatever are you doing dressed like that? You must be mad coming out without even an umbrella.' I suppose I must have spoken sharply, for she drew back as if she would go out again and I saw that she was crying. So I led her up to my sitting-room and put her in an armchair in front of the fire. I found myself turning on the second bar and plugging in an electric kettle for a cup of tea, almost without thinking what I did.

'I couldn't stay in the house a minute longer with that woman!' Winifred burst out.

'What woman?' I asked stupidly, thinking as I did so how melodramatic Winifred sounded, talking about 'that woman' as if she were in a play or a novel.

'Allegra Gray,' she stammered in a burst of tears.

I was so astonished that I could think of nothing to say, but wondered irrelevantly if I was to be caught with a tea pot in my hand on every dramatic occasion.

'But I thought you were such friends . . .' was all I could say, when words came at last.

'Oh, we were at first, but how was I to know what she was

really like? It's such a terrible thing to be deceived by a person, to think they're something and then find they're not.'

Of course it all came out then, all I had always felt myself about Allegra Gray but with apparently no justification. It seemed that the friction between her and Winifred had started quite a long time before they went on holiday together.

'You remember those flowers Lady Farmer sent for the church at Whitsuntide?'

'Oh, yes, lilies, weren't they?'

'Yes. Well, Allegra and I were doing the altar and naturally I felt that the lilies should go there, but she had the idea of putting them on the floor at the side and having peonies and delphiniums on the altar. I told her we never had peonies on the altar and naturally Lady Farmer would expect the flowers she sent to be used for the altar . . .'

I suddenly felt very tired and thought how all over England and perhaps, indeed, anywhere where there was a church and a group of workers, these little frictions were going on. Somebody else decorating the pulpit when another had always done it, somebody's gift of flowers being relegated to an obscure window, somebody's cleaning of the brasses being criticized when she had been doing them for over thirty years . . . And now Lady Farmer's lilies on the floor and peonies on the altar, an unheard-of thing! But here, of course, there was more to it. The little friendly criticisms, the mocking which had gradually become less good-humoured – 'Winifred, you really must do something about your clothes . . . Have you made any plans for when Julian and I are married? Where are you going to live?' And then the suggestions flung out, the settlement in the East End, the religious community – 'Dear Winifred, you're just the kind of person who would have a vocation, I feel' – or the cheap and comfortable guest-house in Bournemouth, full of elderly people . . .

'But Mildred, I'm *not* elderly! I'm only a year or two older than she is.' Winifred's voice came at me plaintively and I reassured her that of course she was not elderly.

'I'd always thought we could live together so happily, the three of us. I never imagined any other arrangement. Julian never gave any hint of it.'

'No, he wouldn't, of course,' I said. 'This may sound a cynical thing to say, but don't you think men sometimes leave difficulties to be solved by other people or to solve themselves? After all, married people do like to be left on their own,' I said as gently as I could. 'Didn't it occur to you that perhaps you ought to find somewhere else to live after they were married?'

'No, I'm afraid it didn't, but then I haven't known many married people. And it never occurred to me that Julian would marry. Men are so strange,' she said, in a pathetic puzzled way, as if she were finding it out for the first time. 'He always said he would never marry. You see, Mildred, I always used to think it would be so nice if you and he . . .'

'Oh, there was never any question of that,' I said quickly. 'Where *was* Julian when all this happened this evening? Surely he didn't let you run out of the house in the rain?'

'Oh, no, it's his boys' club night and he went out immediately after supper, otherwise Allegra would never have said the things she did. She was always nice to me when he was there. He thinks she has such a sweet nature.'

'Yes, men are sometimes taken in. They don't ever quite see the terrible depths that we do.' The Dog beneath the Skin, I thought, and then remembered that it was the name of a clever play William Caldicote had once taken me to, so perhaps it didn't apply here.

We sat in silence for a while and I thought of the unfinished letter to Rocky lying on my desk. 'What time will Julian be back?' I asked. 'I had better come back to the vicarage with you when you're quite sure he will be there.'

'Oh, but, Mildred, I hoped I could come and live with you,' said Winifred with appalling simplicity.

For a moment I was too taken aback to say anything and I knew that I must think carefully before I answered. Easy excuses, such as the difficulty of finding a whole pair of clean sheets that didn't need mending, would not do here. I had to ask myself why it was that the thought of Winifred, of whom I was really very fond, sharing my home with me filled me with sinking apprehension. Perhaps it was because I realized that if I once took her in it would probably be for ever. There could be no casting her off if my own circumstances should happen to change, if, for example, I ever thought of getting married myself. And at the idea of getting married myself I began to laugh, for it really did seem a little fantastic.

Winifred noticed my amusement and smiled a little uncertainly. 'Of course it may be too much to ask,' she faltered, 'but you've always been so kind to me. I should pay, of course,' she added hastily.

The truth was, I thought, looking once more at the letter on my desk which could not now be finished tonight, that I was exhausted with bearing other people's burdens, or burthens as the nobler language of our great hymn-writers put it. Then too, I had become selfish and set in my ways and would surely be a difficult person to live with. I could hardly add that the bed in my spare-room was hard or that Dora might want to come and stay with me. I must obviously make a gesture towards helping Winifred.

'But of course you must stay for a night or two,' I said, 'at least until we see how things are going to turn out.'

She thanked me and then we were both silent for a time, as if thinking over the implications of the last part of the sentence. I felt better after I had made this offer and together we looked out a pair of sheets and some blankets. We had just finished making up the bed in the spare-room, when the front-door bell rang again, urgently and impatiently.

I went down and found Julian Malory outside the door. He was hatless and had flung round his shoulders one of those black speckled mackintoshes which seem to be worn only by clergymen. He looked worried and upset. I could not think why he should be carrying a couple of ping-pong bats in his hand, until I remembered that it was his boys' club night.

'Where's Winifred?' he asked sharply. 'Have you seen her this evening?'

'Oh, yes, she is here,' I said. 'She is going to stay a night or two with me – after what happened,' I added, feeling awkward.

'That's quite impossible,' said Julian quickly. 'You must see that it is.'

We were walking upstairs and as I switched landing lights on and off I racked my brains to discover why it should be impossible for Winifred to stay a night or two with me.

'Don't you see,' he went on, 'Mrs Gray and I cannot stay alone in the vicarage. It would be most awkward.'

'But she could keep to her own flat, surely?' I said, wondering why he was calling her 'Mrs Gray' and not 'Allegra'.

'Even so, we are still under the same roof.'

'Oh, don't quibble so,' I said, impatient of this talk of roofs. 'Nobody would think anything of it. You are both respectable people, and after all you *are* engaged to be married.'

'The engagement is broken off,' said Julian flatly, laying down the ping-pong bats rather carefully on the kitchen table.

I hardly know what happened next, but eventually we were all sitting down and I was trying to console both Julian and Winifred, who seemed to be in tears again. It occurred to me that I might have to put them both up for the night and I began to wonder how it could be managed. I should have to sleep on the narrow sofa in the sitting-room, unless I used one of the Napiers' beds.

Julian did not tell us very much about what had happened. It appeared that he had come in and asked where Winifred was and then the whole story had come out. I should never know exactly what had passed between him and Allegra Gray. There are some things too dreadful to be revealed, and it is even more dreadful how, in spite of our better instincts, we long to know about them. I found myself worrying about irrelevant details – who had actually done the breaking off, had she given him back the ring, and how did it come about that he was still carrying the ping-pong bats, which he had presumably taken from the boys' club to the vicarage, when he came to my flat? Had he perhaps been holding them in his hand all the time the dreadful scene was going on? I knew that things like that *could* happen . . .

At that moment the telephone rang. It was Mrs Jubb who looked after the Malorys at the vicarage. I handed the receiver to Julian and heard him say 'Yes' and 'No' once or twice in answer to what seemed like a great flood of conversation from the other end.

'Well, she's gone,' he said, turning towards us. 'She left the house ten minutes ago with a small suitcase. Mrs Jubb thought I ought to know.'

Winifred gave a kind of moan and began to cry again.

I looked at Julian questioningly and he nodded.

'Come, Winifred,' I said, 'you've had enough for tonight. You must go to bed and I'll bring you a hot drink and something to make you sleep.'

She came with me willingly enough and when I had settled her as comfortably as I could, I returned to Julian, who was sitting despondently by the electric fire.

'Where will she have gone at this time of night?' I asked almost fearing that the bell might ring and I should find her outside my own door.

'Oh, she has a friend in Kensington who will put her up. I expect she has gone there.'

'What sort of a friend?'

'Oh, an unmarried woman with her own flat. A very sensible person, I believe.'

I lay back and closed my eyes, for I was very tired. I wondered if Mrs Gray's friend was tired too. I imagined her in the tidy kitchen in her dressing-gown, just putting on the milk for her Ovaltine and being startled by the front-door bell ringing and wondering who on earth it could be calling so late. And now she would have to sit up half the night, listening and condoling.

'What does she do?'

'What does who do?' asked Julian rather irritably.

'This friend with the flat in Kensington.'

'Oh, I'm not sure. She is a civil servant of some kind, I believe, I think she has quite a good job.'

'I suppose Mrs Jubb knows what has happened?'

'Oh, I imagine she will have gathered that something is wrong. I suppose everybody will know tomorrow, but these things can hardly be concealed.'

'Are you going to put an announcement in *The Times*?'

'Oh, does one do that?' asked Julian vaguely. 'I should hardly have thought it was necessary.'

'Well, it might save embarrassment, and there is nothing dishonourable about it, I mean nothing to be ashamed of,' I said. 'It is much better to have found out now rather than later.'

'Yes, that's what people say, isn't it? I suppose one must bear the humiliation of having made a mistake. I obviously had no idea of her true character. You see, I thought her such a fine person.'

She was certainly very pretty, I thought, but I did not say it. I could not add to the burden of his humiliation by pointing out that he may have been taken in, like so many men before him, by a pretty face.

'Of course it was mostly my fault,' Julian went on. 'I can see that now.'

'Well, I imagine there are always faults on both sides, though one person may be more to blame than the other. But I'm sure you need not reproach yourself for anything you did.'

'Thank you, Mildred,' he said, with a faint smile. 'You are very kind. I don't know what we'd do without you.'

'Perhaps clergymen shouldn't marry,' I said, realizing that Julian was now a free man again and that we ladies of the parish need no longer think of ourselves as the rejected ones. But the thought did not, at that moment, arouse any very great enthusiasm in me. Perhaps I should feel differently in the morning when I was less tired.

'Some seem to manage it very successfully,' said Julian rather sadly.

I could think of nothing to say beyond suggesting that he could always have another try, but this did not seem to be quite the moment to say it.

'I know the kind of person I should like to marry,' he went on, 'and I thought I had found her. But perhaps I looked too far and there might have been somebody nearer at hand.'

I stared into the electric fire and wished it had been a coal one, though the functional glowing bar was probably more suitable for this kind of an occasion.

'I cannot see what flowers are at my feet,' said Julian softly.

Nor what soft incense hangs upon the boughs, I continued to myself, feeling that the quotation had gone wrong somewhere and that it was not really quite what Julian had intended.

'That's Keats, isn't it?' I asked rather bluntly. 'I always think *Nor What Soft Incense* would be a splendid title for a novel. Perhaps about a village where there were two rival churches, one High and one Low. I wonder if it has ever been used?'

Julian laughed and the slight embarrassment which I had felt between us was dispelled. He stood up and began to make preparations for going. He put on his speckled mackintosh, but seemed to forget about the ping-pong bats on the kitchen table nor did I like to remind him. I went to bed immediately after he had gone, but I did not sleep very well. In my dreams Allegra Gray came to my house with a pile of suitcases. Rocky stood by the electric fire and asked me to marry him, but when I looked up I saw that it was Julian in his speckled mackintosh. I woke up feeling ashamed and disappointed and made a resolution that I would take Winifred her breakfast in bed.

CHAPTER TWENTY-THREE

THERE WAS a kind of suppressed excitement about Mrs Morris's manner next morning and she went about her work smiling and almost nodding to herself, occasionally glancing at me and then at Winifred with an expression of triumph on her face. I could see that she was longing to get Winifred out of the way and when, after we had drunk our mid-morning cup of tea, Winifred asked if I would mind if she went over to the vicarage to see if Julian was all right, I was almost as eager as Mrs Morris to see her go.

'*Well*, Miss Lathbury, *now* what've you got to say?'

She stood with her back to the sink, her hands on her hips. I felt unequal to the note of challenge in her voice, as if I were about to perform before a critical audience and was certain that I should not fulfil expectations.

'It's all been so sudden,' I said feebly. 'I hardly know what to say.'

'Ah, but that's how it goes. Getting engaged and breaking it off. One minute it is and the next it isn't.'

I had to agree that this was certainly so.

'I hardly know what really happened,' I said.

'Oh, well, if that's it,' she said comfortably, 'I've had it all from Mrs Jubb. She heard every word.'

'Oh dear, I do hope she wasn't listening at the door.'

'Listening at the door? Goodness, you could hear it all over the house. Mrs Gray, that is, not a word out of the vicar. Only a sort of muttering, she said. Oh, it was terrible!'

I was glad that Julian had preserved his dignity, as, indeed, I knew he would, even with the ping-pong bats in his hand.

'She said she'd had quite enough being married to one clergyman, and something about them not knowing how to treat women and no wonder.' Mrs Morris paused, a little puzzled. 'I don't know what it was no wonder about, Mrs Jubb didn't say. And then she went on about Miss Winifred, oh, it was shocking the things she said.'

'What kind of things?' I found myself asking.

'Oh, well, Mrs Jubb didn't say exactly or maybe she didn't hear but she said it sounded something terrible. Not *bad* words, you know,' said Mrs Morris, lowering her tone and looking at me a little fearfully, 'if you see what I mean. Not the kind of things with bad swear words but dreadful things. And then Mrs Gray ran screaming upstairs to her flat and *he* went out of the house very quickly. And then *she* came running down again with a case packed and went away somewhere, Mrs Jubb didn't seem to know where.' Mrs Morris looked at me hopefully to supply this missing information.

'To a friend in Kensington, I believe,' I said, thinking that although I shouldn't be talking like this to Mrs Morris, it was better that she should know some of the truth.

'*Kensington, well*,' said Mrs Morris, sounding more Welsh than usual in her excitement. 'And when Mr Malory, Father Malory, I should say, got back he looked *terrible*, Mrs Jubb said. I should think he'd been walking the streets, distracted,' said Mrs Morris, adding something of her own. 'I shouldn't be surprised if he hadn't been down by the river.'

I could hardly believe that sitting quietly by my electric fire could have given Julian such a terrible appearance, unless, of course, he had not gone straight home when he left me. 'He was here with Miss Malory and me,' I said.

'Oh, he knew who to turn to,' said Mrs Morris, beaming. 'Didn't I tell you, Miss Lathbury? He knew who his true friend was, the poor soul. A pity he didn't see it before. But a thing often happens like that, some terrible calamity and we get some kind of revelation. Like St Paul, isn't it?'

'Well, perhaps, not quite . . .' I began, but I was unable to stem the flow of her Welsh eloquence.

'The scales fell from his eyes and he saw her for what she really was and you for what you really was, and oh, the difference! To think he'd been so blind all this time, *groping* in darkness . . .'

'I hardly think . . .'

'Not knowing black from white, but a lot of men is like that. And a clergyman's just the same as other men, isn't he, only he wears his collar back to front, that's all, really, isn't it?'

I did not think it worth pointing out that there were perhaps more subtle differences between clergymen and others than the wearing of the collar back to front.

'Well, look at us, this won't get the work done, will it, Miss Lathbury?' she said suddenly, seizing the wet mop and swilling it vigorously in the bucket. 'But I'm not surprised at this. I saw it coming.'

I was not quite clear as to what it was that Mrs Morris had seen coming, but I decided that we had talked enough about it. Was I then to marry Julian? Was that what she had seen coming? Would he propose to me, after a decent interval, of course, and should we make a match of it and delight the parish? It sounded ideal, but somehow morning had not brought any more enthusiasm than the night before. I still thought of myself as one of the rejected ones and I could not believe that he loved me any more than I loved him. Of course I liked and admired him, perhaps I even respected and esteemed him, as Everard Bone did Esther Clovis. But was that enough? In any case, it was indecent, wicked, almost, to be thinking of such things now. There must surely be some practical help I could give. What was to happen to Mrs Gray's furniture and possessions? Was a go-between needed, or a letter-writer? Letter-writing reminded me of the unfinished letter to Rocky Napier which was still lying on my desk. Gritting my teeth, as it were, I determined to get it out of the way, and sat down there and then and did it. I hardly knew what I wrote and spent no time on subtleties. I told him the news about Julian and Mrs Gray and made that an excuse for my careless writing.

When I had posted the letter, I walked towards the shops to buy some things to eat. I was walking back with my string bag full of uninteresting food, when I saw Sister Blatt advancing towards me on her bicycle. She lowered herself carefully off it and blocked the pavement, so that I could not help stopping and talking to her.

'Well, well,' she said, waiting for me to begin.

'Well,' I repeated, 'there really seems to be nothing to say. It's all very upsetting, isn't it?'

'Oh, I'm sorry for Father Malory, of course, though I never liked the woman, but good comes out of everything.'

'Yes, I suppose it does,' I said uncertainly, for although I believed that it did I thought that it was surely a little soon for any to be apparent yet.

'I am to have Mrs Gray's flat,' said Sister Blatt triumphantly. 'A friend of mine from Stoke-on-Trent is coming to work in Pimlico, so near, you see, and we have been wanting to get a place together and now this has happened.'

'A ram in a thicket, in fact,' I said, feeling like Mrs Morris and St Paul.

'Exactly.' Sister Blatt nodded vigorously. 'Just what I said to Father Malory this morning. I went to the vicarage as soon as I heard the news. You see, I realized that it might be awkward for them being under the same roof, so I put forward my idea as a solution to the difficulty. As it happened, she had gone away.'

'To a friend in Kensington,' I murmured.

'Yes, much the best thing for all concerned. You're looking tired,' she said suddenly. 'Your face is quite grey. You must take care of yourself.' And with these encouraging words, she swung herself up on to her bicycle and rode majestically away.

I am tired, I said to myself, as I walked upstairs, and my face is quite grey. Nobody must come near me. I would have a read this afternoon, for Winifred had gone back to the vicarage and was comforting Julian. I felt a little sorry for him, surrounded as he would be by excellent women. But at least he would be safe from people like Mrs Gray; Sister Blatt would defend him fiercely against all such perils, I knew. Perhaps it might after all be my duty to marry him, if only to save him from being too well protected.

I made myself what seemed an extravagant lunch of two scrambled eggs, preceded by the remains of some soup and followed by cheese, biscuits and an apple. I was glad that I wasn't a man, or the kind of man who looked upon a meal alone as a good opportunity to cook a small plover, though I should have been glad enough to have somebody else cook it for me. After I had washed up I went gratefully to my bed and lay under the eiderdown with a hot-water-bottle. I had finished my library book, and thought how odd it was that although I had the great novelists and poets well represented on my shelves, none of their work seemed to attract me. It would be a good opportunity to read some of the things I was always meaning to read, like *In Memoriam* or *The Brothers Karamazov*, but in the end I was reduced to reading the serial in the parish magazine, and pondering over the illustrations, one of which showed a square-jawed young clergyman in conversation with a pretty young woman, as it might be Julian and Mrs Gray, except that Julian wasn't square-jawed.

The caption under the picture said, 'I'm sure Mrs Goodrich didn't mean to hurt your feelings about the jumble sale.' I finished the episode with a feeling of dissatisfaction. There was some just cause or impediment which prevented the clergyman from marrying the girl, some mysterious reason why Mrs Goodrich should have snubbed her at the jumble sale, but we should have to wait until next month before we could know any more about it.

I turned back to the parish news. There was a warning from our treasurer about our financial position. Julian's letter to his flock was short and uninteresting. The servers had had a very enjoyable day at Southend; all those who had brought gifts and helped to decorate the church for Harvest Festival were thanked; there was to be a working-party to mend the cassocks, 'commencing on the first Tuesday afternoon in October.' I was distressed that Julian should use the word 'commence', but I suppose I must have dropped off to sleep somewhere here, for there was a long gap between the announcement about the cassocks and my next conscious thought, which was that I was thirsty and that it must be teatime.

I was just finishing tea when the telephone rang. I let it ring for quite a long time before I lifted the receiver warily and held it to my ear, wondering whose voice would come out of it and what it would ask me to do. It was a man's voice, a pleasant voice, but for the moment I could not think whose.

'Hullo, Mildred. This is Everard.'

I was instantly suspicious. I had hardly even realized that we called each other by our Christian names but I supposed that after all this time we probably did, though I was not conscious of ever having called him Everard.

After a few formal preliminaries, during which each asked how the other was, and gave and received an answer, there was a pause. What does he want? I wondered, and waited for him to say.

'I rang up to ask if you would come and have dinner with me in my flat this evening. I have got some meat to cook.'

I saw myself putting a small joint into the oven and preparing vegetables. I could feel my aching back bending over the sink.

'I'm afraid I can't tonight,' I said baldly.

'Oh, I'm sorry.' His voice sounded flat and noncommittal, so that it was impossible to tell whether he really minded or not. 'Perhaps some other time?' he added politely.

'Yes, that would be nice,' I said. But perhaps then he wouldn't have any meat. Although there was a telephone line between us, I felt embarrassed and ashamed at my lie and was convinced that he must know from my voice that I was not telling the truth.

There was another pause. He did not suggest any other evening but said he would ring again some time.

'Thank you for the postcard,' he added.

'Oh, it was nothing,' I said foolishly, for indeed it was nothing. 'There isn't any news,' I added.

'News?' he sounded puzzled. 'What kind of news?'

'About the Napiers.'

'Oh, would there be?'

'Well, there might have been . . .'

Our conversation seemed about to trail off very miserably and then I blurted out, 'Our vicar has broken off his engagement.'

'Oh, that's rather a good thing, isn't it?'

'Yes, I suppose it is, really.'

'I imagined you would think so.' His voice sounded as stiff and unfriendly as in the days when we had first met.

'I'm sorry about the meat,' I said, trying to infuse life into our now nearly dead conversation.

'Why should you be sorry about it?'

'Do you know how to cook it?'

'Well, I have a cookery book.'

There can be no exchange of glances over the telephone, no breaking into laughter. After a few more insincere regrets and apologies we finished and I hung up the receiver, thinking that the telephone ought never to be used except for the transaction of business. I paced about my sitting-room, feeling uneasy and yet not quite knowing why. I had not wanted to see Everard Bone and the idea of having to cook his evening meal for him was more than I could bear at this moment. And yet the thought of him alone with his meat and his cookery book was unbearable too. He would turn to the section on meat. He would read that beef or mutton should be cooked for so many minutes per pound and so many over. He would weigh the little joint, if he had scales. He would then puzzle over the heat of the oven, turning it on and standing over it watching the thermometer go up . . . I should have been nearly in tears at this point if I had not pulled myself together and reminded myself that Everard Bone was a very capable sort of person whose life was always very well arranged. He would be quite equal to cooking a joint. Men are not nearly so helpless and pathetic as we sometimes like to imagine them, and on the whole they run their lives better than we do ours. After all, Everard knew quite a lot of people he could ask to dinner and was probably even now ringing them up. If I could not come, no doubt somebody else would be only too glad to. But then another thought came into my mind. Why had I assumed that I was the first person he had telephoned that evening? I might very well have been the last. There must be many people whom he knew better than he did me and with whom he would rather spend an evening. For some reason that I could not understand for I believe I have always had a modest opinion of myself, I found this a disturbing thought. It seemed as if it was necessary for me to know that I had been the first choice, but I did not see what I could do about it. I did not look forward to my evening at home, and all the useful and half-pleasant things I had planned to do, like ironing and sewing and listening to the wireless, seemed uninteresting and unnecessary. In the end I decided to go over to the vicarage to see if there was anything I could do there.

CHAPTER TWENTY-FOUR

'MILDRED, *darling* . . . how wonderful to see you!'

I was quite unprepared for Rocky's effusive greeting and embrace. I was unprepared for his appearance at all at that moment, for I had had no answer to the letter I had written to him some time ago, and I had begun to think that I had offended him by my well-meaning efforts to bring him and Helena together again. It is a known fact that people like clergymen's daughters, excellent women in their way, sometimes rush in where the less worthy might fear to tread.

'Hullo, Rocky,' was all I could say.

'You don't seem very pleased to see me.'

'Oh, I am, but it's so unexpected . . .'

'Surely nice things always are?' He stood looking at me, confidently charming. I noticed that he was holding a bunch of chrysanthemums.

'These are for you,' he said, thrusting them at me. I saw that the stems had been broken very roughly and that they were not tied together at all.

'Are they out of your garden?' I asked.

'Yes; I snatched them as I was hurrying for the train.'

Somehow they seemed a little less desirable now. He had not chosen them, had not gone into a shop for that purpose, they had just happened to be there. If he had gone into a shop and chosen them . . . I pulled myself up and told myself to stop these ridiculous thoughts, wondering why it is that we can never stop trying to analyse the motives of people who have no personal interest in us, in the vain hope of finding that perhaps they may have just a little after all.

'Helena said that I must bring you some flowers and these happened to be in the garden,' he went on, leaving me in no doubt at all.

'Thank you, they're lovely,' I said. 'Is Helena with you, then?'

'Yes, of course. After getting your letter, I wrote to her and we met.'

'I hope you didn't think it interfering of me?'

'Of course not. I know how you love contriving things,' he smiled. 'Births, deaths, marriages and all the rest of it.'

Perhaps I did love it as I always seemed to get involved in them, I thought with resignation; perhaps I really enjoyed other people's lives more than my own.

We were standing in one of our usual talking places, the entrance to my kitchen. I could feel Rocky looking at me very intently. I raised my eyes to meet his.

'Mildred?'

'Yes?'

'I was hoping . . .'

'What were you hoping?'

'That you might suggest making a cup of tea. You know how you always make a cup of tea on "occasions". That's one of the things I remember most about you, and surely this is an "occasion"?'

So he did remember me like that after all – a woman who was always making cups of tea. Well, there was nothing to be done about it now but to make one.

'Oh, certainly,' I said. 'And anyway it is nearly teatime, I mean, the conventional hour for drinking tea.'

'You never came down to visit me at my cottage. Why?'

'Well, you didn't ask me.'

'Oh, but people mustn't wait to be asked. Other people came.'

'Did any of the Wren officers come?' Had they had luncheon in the wild garden with a bottle of some amusing little wine? I was very much afraid that they might have done.

'Wren officers?' Rocky looked puzzled for a moment and then laughed. 'Oh, yes, one or two. But of course they weren't in their uniforms, so one regarded them as human beings. Oh, lots of people came. I was very social. Had you imagined me there all alone?'

'I don't know, really. I didn't think.' I was unwilling to remember or to tell him how I had imagined him. 'Of course, men don't tend to be alone, do they? I think we talked about it before some time.'

'Oh, surely! Haven't we tired the sun with talking on every possible subject?'

The tea was made now and it was as strong as it had been weak on the day Helena had left him. I wondered why it was that tea could vary so, even when one followed exactly the same method in making it. Could the emotional state of the maker have something to do with it?

We sat in silence for a while, brooding over our strong tea, and then I began to ask him about the furniture which had been moved and whether he was going to have it all brought back again.

'Oh, no, we have decided to settle in the country,' he said. 'We don't really like this place very much.'

'No; I suppose the associations . . .'

'The rest of the stuff can quite easily be packed up and sent after us, can't it?'

'Oh, yes, that can easily be arranged,' I said in a consciously bright tone. 'I wonder who will take your flat?'

'Somebody respectable, I hope, as you have to share the bathroom. Couldn't you advertise in the *Church Times* for a couple of Anglo-Catholic ladies? That's really what you want.'

'Yes, I suppose it is.' I hoped I did not show how depressed I felt at the idea of this future. But then I remembered that it was not within my power to decide who the new tenants should be. The landlord would arrange that, though I suppose that had I known anyone in need of a flat I could put in a word for them.

'What news?' asked Rocky, taking the last chocolate biscuit. 'Has anything exciting happened in the parish?'

'Julian Malory has broken off his engagement,' I said. 'I think I told you that when I wrote.'

'Oh, of course, the vicar, *your* vicar. But that's splendid; now he can marry you. Isn't that just what we wanted?'

'If he had wanted to marry me he could have asked me before he met Mrs Gray,' I pointed out.

'Oh, not necessarily. It often happens that a person is rejected or passed over and then their true worth is seen. I always think that must be very romantic.'

'It could be romantic if you had been the person to do the rejecting, but one doesn't like to be the person to have been rejected,' I said uncertainly, feeling that I must be giving Rocky the impression that I really did want to marry Julian. 'Anyway, there has never been any question of anything more than friendship between us.'

'How dull. Perhaps you could marry the other one, the curate?'

I explained patiently that Father Greatorex was not really suitable, not the kind of person one would want to marry.

'Let me stay as I am,' I said. 'I'm quite happy.'

'Well, I don't know. I still feel we ought to do something,' said Rocky vaguely.

I got up and took the tea tray into the kitchen.

'Have you seen our friend Everard Bone at all?' Rocky called out.

Immediately he asked this, I realized that there had been a little nagging worry, an unhappiness, almost, at the back of my mind. Everard Bone and his meat. Of course it sounded ridiculous put like that and I decided that I would not mention it to Rocky. He would mock and not understand. It made me sad to realize that he would not understand, that perhaps he did not really understand anything about me.

'I had lunch with him some time ago,' I said. 'He seemed very much as usual.'

'I imagine he will be both relieved and disappointed when he knows that Helena and I have come together again,' said Rocky complacently. 'I think he found the situation a little alarming.'

'It was rather awkward for him,' I said. 'Or it might have been.'

'Poor Helena, it was one of those sudden irrational passions women get for people. She is completely disillusioned now. When he should have been near at hand to cherish her she found he had fled to a meeting of the Prehistoric Society in Derbyshire! Do you know how that happens?'

'You mean being disillusioned? Yes, I think I can see how it could. Perhaps you meet a person and he quotes Matthew Arnold or some favourite poet to you in a churchyard, but naturally life can't be all like that,' I said rather wildly. 'And he only did it because he felt it was expected of him. I mean, he isn't really like that at all.'

'It would certainly be difficult to live up to that, to quoting Matthew Arnold in churchyards,' said Rocky. 'But perhaps he was kind to you at a moment when you needed kindness – surely that's worth something?'

'Oh, yes, certainly it is.' Once more, perhaps for the last time, I saw the Wren officers huddled together in an awkward little group on the terrace of the Admiral's villa. Rocky's kindness must surely have meant a great deal to them at that moment and perhaps some of them would never forget it as long as they lived.

Rocky stood up. 'Well, thank you for my tea. Helena is coming back at the week-end. I must go and do some shopping at the Army and Navy Stores before they close. What are you doing this evening?'

'I have to go to a meeting in the parish hall to decide about the Christmas bazaar.'

'To decide about the Christmas bazaar,' Rocky mimicked my tone. 'Can I come too?'

'I think it would bore you.'

'Why do churches always have to be arranging bazaars and jumble sales? One would think that was the only reason for their existence.'

'Our church is very short of money.'

'Perhaps I should give it a donation as a kind of thank-offering,' said Rocky lightly. 'Though I should really prefer to give something more permanent. A stained-glass window – the Rockingham Napier window – I can see it, very red and blue. Or some money to buy the best quality incense?'

'I'm sure that would be most acceptable.'

'Well, perhaps I will. I must hurry now – good-bye!'

After he had gone I stood looking out of the window after him. I seemed to remember that I had done this before, and not so very long ago. But my thoughts on that occasion, though more melancholy, had been somehow more pleasant. Now I felt flat and disappointed, as if he had failed to come up to my expectations. And yet, what had I really hoped for? Dull, solid friendship without charm? No, there was enough of that between women and women and even between men and women. Of course, if he had not been married . . . but this suggested a situation altogether too unreal to contemplate. In the first place, I should probably never have met him at all, and I should certainly not have enjoyed the privilege of preparing lunch for him on the day his wife left him or of making all those cups of tea on 'occasions'. This thought led me to worry again about Everard and his meat and how I had refused to cook it for him, and it was a relief when the church clock struck and I realized that it was time to go to the meeting in the parish hall.

CHAPTER TWENTY-FIVE

PERHAPS there can be too much making of cups of tea, I thought, as I watched Miss Statham filling the heavy teapot. We had all had our supper, or were supposed to have had it, and were met together to discuss the arrangements for the Christmas bazaar. Did we really *need* a cup of tea? I even said as much to Miss Statham and she looked at me with a hurt, almost angry look. 'Do we *need* tea?' she echoed. 'But Miss Lathbury . . .' She sounded puzzled and distressed and I began to realize that my question had struck at something deep and fundamental. It was the kind of question that starts a landslide in the mind.

I mumbled something about making a joke and that of course one needed tea always, at every hour of the day or night.

'This teapot's heavy,' she said, lifting it with both hands and placing it on the table. 'You'd think one of the men might help to carry it,' she added, raising her voice.

Mr Mallett and Mr Conybeare, the churchwardens, and Mr Gamble, the treasurer, looked up from their business, which they were conducting in a secret masculine way with many papers spread out before them, but made no move to help.

'I see it is done now by the so-called weaker sex,' said Mr Mallett. 'I think Miss Statham has got everything under control.'

'Come on now,' she said, 'make room for your cups of tea. You've got the table so cluttered with papers and your elbows on it too. You'll be knocking something over. Anyone would think you weren't interested in having a cup.'

'Oh, we are that, all right,' said Mr Conybeare. 'Just you pour it out, Miss Statham, and we'll soon make room.'

Miss Statham and I served the men and the other ladies and

then sat down ourselves. Winifred Malory was at home with a bad cold and Julian had not yet arrived, which added considerably to the enjoyment of all present, as the broken engagement could be discussed freely and without embarrassment. It was the first time since it had happened that there had been any kind of parish gathering.

'Of course a man can carry it off with more dignity, a thing like that,' said Miss Statham, putting a knitted tea-cosy on the teapot. 'Anyone who wants a second cup can help themselves. A man doesn't feel the shame that a woman would.'

'After all, he can easily ask somebody else – after a decent interval, of course,' said Miss Enders.

'Once bitten, twice shy,' said Mr Mallett. 'I should say he was well out of it. Not that she wasn't a charming lady in her way. But if he's got any sense Father Malory won't go asking anyone else in a hurry. He'll know when he's well off.'

'Really, Mr Mallett, it's a good thing your wife isn't here,' said Miss Statham indignantly. 'Whatever would she think to hear you talking like that?'

'My good lady leaves the thinking to me,' said Mr Mallett, amid laughter from the men.

'What does the vicar want with a wife, anyway?' asked Mr Conybeare. 'He's got his sister and you ladies to help him in the parish.'

'Oh, well, what a question!' Miss Statham giggled. 'He's a man, isn't he, and all men are alike.'

There followed some rather embarrassing badinage between Miss Statham and the two churchwardens in which I was quite unable to join, though I envied her the easy way she had with them. Their joking was broken up by the arrival of Sister Blatt, looking very pleased with herself.

'*Well*,' she said, sitting down heavily and beaming all over her face, 'it's a disgrace, I never saw anything like it.'

We asked what.

'The way Mrs Gray left that kitchen in the flat. You know

the remover's men have been in today to take away her furniture. Oh, my goodness, there was food in the larder, been there weeks! And dishes not washed-up, even!'

'She left in rather a hurry,' I pointed out. 'I don't suppose she thought of washing-up before she went.' People did tend to leave the washing-up on the dramatic occasions of life; I remembered only too well how full of dirty dishes the Napiers' kitchen had been on the day Helena had left.

'But, Miss Lathbury, dear, that wouldn't account for the mess there was. Tins half used and then left, stale ends of loaves, and everything so *dirty* . . . *I* never thought she was the right wife for Father Malory and I often said so too. I'm afraid she was a real viper.'

'In sheep's clothing,' added Mr Mallett. 'Now, is the vicar going to honour us with his presence tonight or is he not?'

'I dare say he's forgotten and is playing darts with the boys next door,' said Miss Statham. 'Would anyone like to go and see?'

I said that I would, and, bracing myself to meet the pandemonium went into the main part of the hall, where Julian, surrounded by a crowd of lads, was playing darts. It seemed a pity to interrupt the game and drag him off to our dull meeting and the cold stewed tea and he seemed to come rather unwillingly.

'What is it, Mildred?' he asked. 'The bazaar meeting? Good heavens, I'd forgotten all about it!'

He took his place at the head of the table and accepted a cup of the stewed tea absent-mindedly. Everybody was quiet now as if out of respect for Julian's new status brought about by the broken engagement.

'I'm sorry to have kept you waiting,' he said. 'Now, what exactly is the purpose of this meeting?'

'It might have been to decide on a wedding present from the parish,' whispered Sister Blatt to me. 'What a good thing we hadn't started to collect the money!'

The treasurer cleared his throat and began to explain.

'Ah, yes, the Christmas bazaar,' said Julian lightly. 'Well, I suppose it will follow its usual course. Do we really need to have a meeting about it?'

There was a shocked silence.

'He's not himself,' whispered Miss Statham.

'Why not let us decide about the bazaar?' I suggested boldly. 'Why don't you go back to the boys? I could see that you were having a very exciting darts match with Teddy Lemon.'

'Yes, I was beating him for once, too,' said Julian. 'If you'll excuse me, I think I will go back.' He got up from the table and went off, leaving his tea unfinished.

'Well, really, I've never heard of such a thing,' said Miss Statham. 'The vicar has always presided at the meeting to arrange about the Christmas bazaar – it's been the custom ever since Father Busby's time.'

'Well, Miss Statham, if you can remember what went on in the eighteen-seventies when Father Busby was vicar, the rest of us must retire,' said Sister Blatt genially.

'But it's so irresponsible,' protested Miss Statham, 'especially when you consider how important the bazaar is in these days.'

'I am reminded of nothing so much as the Emperor Nero fiddling while Rome is burning,' said Mr Mallett.

'Now then, Mr Mallett, who said anything about Rome,' said Sister Blatt. 'We're not there yet, you know.'

'Not like poor Mr and Mrs Lake and Miss Spicer,' said Miss Enders.

There was a short silence as is sometimes customary after speaking of the dead, though in this case the people referred to might have been thought to have met with a fate worse than death, for they had left us and been received into the Church of Rome.

'Oh, well, I was speaking metaphorically, as is my wont,' said Mr Mallett.

'One might say that Father Malory's conduct this evening reminds us of the behaviour of Sir Francis Drake, going on playing bowls when the Armada was sighted,' suggested Mr Conybeare.

'But that was supposed to be a good thing, a brave thing,' said Miss Enders.

'I think perhaps Father Malory is doing a good thing,' I said.

'But he didn't even finish his cup of tea,' protested Miss Statham.

'Well, it was rather stewed,' said Sister Blatt.

'Perhaps this unfortunate affair has turned his head,' said Miss Statham mysteriously. 'We shan't know what to expect now.'

'He might take it into his head to enter a monastic order or to become a missionary,' said Miss Enders, almost gloating at the prospect.

'People often do strange things when they've had a disappointment,' agreed Miss Statham. 'He might ask the Bishop to put him in the East End.'

'Or in a country parish,' said Miss Enders.

There seemed to be no end to the things that Julian might do, from making a hasty and unsuitable marriage and leaving the Church altogether to going over to Rome and ending up as a Cardinal.

'Well, ladies,' said Mr Mallett at last, 'what about this bazaar? Isn't it the purpose for which two or three are gathered together?'

'Oh, well, as Father Malory said, it can just follow its usual course,' said Miss Statham rather impatiently. 'I imagine the stall-holders will be as usual?' There was a note of challenge in her voice as she looked round the table, for it was known that she herself had always taken charge of the fancy-work stall, which was considered to be the most important.

'Oh, yes, we leave it to you ladies to fight all that out,' said

Mr Mallett, recoiling in mock fear. 'We men will just do all the hard work, eh?'

'Of course we could ask Father Greatorex to preside,' said Miss Enders doubtfully.

'Oh, that man! A fat lot of good he'd be,' said Sister Blatt. 'I think we've really done quite well on our own.'

'Without benefit of clergy,' said Mr Conybeare.

'But we don't really seem to have *decided* anything,' I said. 'When is the bazaar to be? Have we settled the date?'

'Oh, well, it will be when it always is,' said Miss Statham.

'When is that?'

'The first Saturday in December.'

'Is it always then?'

'Oh, yes, it always has been as long as *I* can remember.'

'Since the days of Father Busby, eh?' said Mr Mallett jovially.

Miss Statham ignored him; perhaps she was tired of his joking or considered the date of the bazaar to be no matter for joking.

'It is not a movable feast, then?' asked Mr Conybeare.

'Well, there isn't any better date, is there?' said Miss Statham sharply. 'It must be on a Saturday and a week or two before Christmas.'

We agreed that no better date than the first Saturday in December could be imagined, and I felt rather guilty for having raised doubts in anybody's mind. But I still felt dissatisfied, as if the evening had been wasted. Surely there was something we could discuss, some resolution we could carry?

'What stall shall I help with?' I asked.

They looked at me with such surprise that I began to think that perhaps I had been infected by Julian's strange behaviour.

'Why surely you will help me with the fancy stall?' said Miss Statham. 'Like you did last year and the year before. Unless you'd prefer to do anything else?'

I hesitated, for there was an uneasy feeling in the air, as if umbrage were about to be taken. 'Of course I will help you, Miss Statham,' I said quickly. 'I was only wondering if there was anything else that needed doing. The hoop-la or the bran-tub,' I suggested feebly.

'But Teddy Lemon and the servers will look after that sort of thing,' said Miss Statham, as if it were beneath our dignity, 'they always do.'

'Yes, so they do. I'd forgotten.'

'Money needs to be spent,' said Mr Gamble, making himself heard for the first time. 'You must bring some of your rich friends, Miss Lathbury.'

'I dare say that Mrs Napier could afford to spend a bit of money on us,' said Miss Statham.

'I've often seen her smoking cigarettes in the street *and* going into the Duchess of Granby,' said Miss Enders, in a mealy-mouthed sort of way.

'Well, why shouldn't she?' I burst out. 'You can hardly expect her to come and spend money at our bazaar if that's the way you feel about her.'

'Oh, I didn't say anything, Miss Lathbury,' said Miss Enders huffily. 'I'm sure I didn't mean to offend.'

'I suppose these cups should be washed,' I said, standing up.

'Oh, yes, and the big urn ought to be refilled. The lads will want something,' said Miss Statham.

The men went on smoking and chatting while we gathered the cups together and struggled to fill the heavy urn between us. They belonged to the generation that does not think of helping with domestic tasks.

'Poor Father Malory. I suppose it was all for the best,' said Sister Blatt, waiting with a drying-cloth in her hand. 'We are told that everything happens for the best, and really it does, you know.'

'When one door shuts another door opens,' remarked Miss Statham.

'Yes, of course. Perhaps a door will open for Father Malory.'

At that moment a door did open, but it was only a group of lads headed by Teddy Lemon coming out of the hall. When they saw that we were washing up they withdrew hastily, with some scuffling and giggling.

'Perhaps he will throw himself into the boys' club,' suggested Sister Blatt. 'After all, it is a splendid thing to work among young people.'

I found myself beginning to laugh, I cannot think why, and turned the conversation to Sister Blatt's friend, who was to share the vicarage flat with her.

'I wonder if Father Malory will get engaged to her?' said Miss Statham in a sardonic tone.

'Oh, no, my friend isn't at all the type to attract a man,' said Sister Blatt with rough good humour. 'There won't be any nonsense of that kind.'

'Well, well, then everything will be as it was before Mrs Gray came, then.'

'Nothing can ever be really the same when time has passed,' I said, more to myself than to them, 'even if it appears to be from the outside. And didn't I tell you, the Napiers are leaving? So there will be new people in my house and things won't be at all the same.'

'Oh, I wonder who they will be?' asked Miss Statham eagerly.

'I don't know yet. Somehow I think they will be women who will come to our church.'

'Then there might be danger there,' said Sister Blatt in a satisfied tone. 'I shall have to keep my eye on Father Malory.'

'That's right, Sister,' said Mr Mallett, overhearing the tail-end of our conversation. 'Where would we be, I'd like to know, if you ladies didn't keep an eye on us?'

CHAPTER TWENTY-SIX

IT WAS EASIER saying goodbye to Rocky the second time. He and Helena seemed almost sorry to be going and were very nice to me. They asked me down to their flat the evening before they were to go and Rocky opened a bottle of wine. Seeing them together, gay, frivolous and argumentative, made me feel smug and dull, as if meeting them had really made no difference to me at all.

'You *must* look after poor Everard Bone,' said Helena. 'Oh, how he needs the love of a good woman!'

'I'm glad you are not claiming that your love was that, darling,' said Rocky flippantly. 'Personally, I can't imagine anything I should like less than the love of a good woman. It would be like – oh – something very cosy and stifling and unglamorous, a large grey blanket – perhaps an Army blanket.'

'Or like a white rabbit thrust suddenly into your arms,' I suggested, feeling the glow of wine in me.

'Oh, but a white rabbit might be rather charming.'

'Yes, at first. But after a while you wouldn't know what to do with it,' I said more soberly, remembering that I had had this conversation about white rabbits with Everard Bone.

'Poor Mildred, it's really rather too bad to suggest that the love of a good woman is dull when we know that she is so very good,' said Helena.

'And not at all dull,' said Rocky in his expected manner. 'But Mildred is already pledged to the vicar, and after his unfortunate experience you must surely agree that he has first claim.'

'Oh, he's surrounded by good women,' I said.

'I think he's nice,' said Helena, 'but it always seems to be his boys' club night, so one would never get taken out for a drink.'

'He and I had a drink together once,' said Rocky. 'We had a long talk about Italy.

Because it is the day of Palms,
Carry a palm for me,
Carry a palm in Santa Chiara,
And I will watch the sea . . .'

He began pacing round the room, touching the bare walls and looking out of the uncurtained windows. 'I wonder who will be sitting in this room a month from tonight?' he mused, 'I wonder if they will feel any kind of atmosphere? Should we carve our names in some secret place? One longs to have a bit of immortality somewhere.'

'You were going to give a memorial stained-glass window to the church,' I reminded him.

'Yes, but that's rather an expensive way of doing it. Besides, I feel it would be such a very hideous window.'

'Well, then you said you would give some money to buy incense.'

'Good heavens, so I did.' He took out his wallet and handed me a pound note which I put away quickly in my bag.

'That won't make you remembered,' said Helena; 'it will go up in the air and be lost. I suppose we should write something on a window-pane with a diamond ring. Here, Rocky,' she took a ring from her finger, 'try with this.'

'When my grave is broke up again
Some second guest to entertain,'

chanted Rocky, 'but perhaps a line of Dante would be better, if I could remember one.'

'I only know "abandon hope all ye who enter here," ' I said, 'which doesn't seem very suitable, and that bit about there being no greater sorrow than to remember happiness in a time of misery.'

'Ah, yes,' Rocky clapped his hands together, 'that's it!

Nessun maggior dolore,
Che ricordarsi del tempo felice
Nella miseria.'

'It seems an unkind way to greet new arrivals,' I said doubtfully.

'Oh, don't you believe it – people love to recall happiness in a time of misery. And anyway, they won't know what it means.'

'Quite a lot of people who were in Italy during the war must have learnt Italian,' I pointed out.

'But not Dante! The noble Allied Military didn't get much further than a few scattered imperatives, but they might have got as far as asking if dinner was ready and they probably knew the names of a few wines.'

'Unless they had Italian mistresses,' said Helena.

'Oh, then they domesticated them and taught them English,' said Rocky coolly.

'I don't suppose the new tenants will understand it anyway,' I mumbled quickly.

'Of course I haven't the patience to do this really properly,' said Rocky, looking at what he had written, 'the lettering isn't very good, but at least we shall feel we've left something to be remembered by.'

'But you don't need to. People aren't really forgotten,' I said, not wanting to be misunderstood but certain that I should be.

Rocky gave me one of his characteristic looks and smiled.

'What will you *do* after we've gone?' Helena asked.

'Well, she had a life before we came,' Rocky reminded her. 'Very much so – what is known as a *full* life, with clergymen and jumble sales and church services and good works.'

'I thought that was the kind of life led by women who *didn't* have a full life in the accepted sense,' said Helena.

'Oh, she'll marry,' said Rocky confidently. They were talking about me as if I wasn't there.

'Everard might take her to hear a paper at the Learned Society,' suggested Helena. 'That would widen her outlook.'

'Yes, it might,' I said humbly from my narrowness.

'But then she would get interested in some little tribes somewhere and her life might become even more narrow,' said Rocky.

We discussed my future until a late hour, but it was hardly to be expected that we should come to any practical conclusions.

The next day I saw them off and turned back a little sadly into the quiet empty house, wondering if I should ever see them again. Of course there had been the usual promises to write on both sides and I was invited to visit them whenever I liked.

It seemed that husbands and wives could part and come together again, and I was glad that it should be so, but what happened after that? It is said that people are refined and ennobled by suffering and one knows that they sometimes are, but would Helena have learned to be neater in the kitchen, or Rocky to share her interest in matrilineal kin-groups? It seemed as if this was at once too little and too much to expect from the experience they had been through, and I felt myself incapable of looking into their future. All I could do was to be prepared to receive Helena if she should ever appear on my doorstep with a suitcase, though perhaps that was Esther Clovis's privilege.

In the meantime, I began to think about Everard Bone and even to wish that I might cook his meat for him. I had a wild idea that I might join the Prehistoric Society, if only I knew how to set about it. It would probably be easier to belong to this than to the Learned Society, whose members must surely have some knowledge of or interest in anthropology. But anybody could scrabble about in the earth for bits of pottery or wander about on moors looking for dolmens, or so it seemed to me in my innocence. Then a more practical idea came into my head. I was supposed to keep Everard up-to-date with news about the Napiers; perhaps he did not know that they had become reconciled and left London to live in the country. Why had he not telephoned me? Was it possible that he had gone away, or was lying ill, alone in his flat with nobody to look after him? Here my imaginings began to follow disconcertingly familiar lines. Well, at least I should see him in Lent, I told myself sensibly, at the lunchtime services at St Ermin's. I remembered that there was a poem which began *Lenten is come with love to town*, and with a feeling of shame I hastened to look it up in the *Oxford Book of English Verse*. But it was one of the very early ones, 'c. 1300', and although there was a glossary of unfamiliar words at the bottom of the page, the poem did not really comfort me.

Deowes donketh the dounes,
Deores with huere derne rounes
Domes forte deme;

I read; that would teach me not to be so foolish.

Some days later I was walking near the premises of the Learned Society; in other words, I was doing what I had so often done in the days of Bernard Hatherley. The walk along Victoria Parade in the gathering twilight, the approach to 'Loch Lomond,' the quick glance up at the lace-curtained window, the hope or fear that a hand might draw the curtain aside or a shadowy form be seen hovering behind it . . . is there no end to the humiliations we subject ourselves to? Of course, I told myself, there was no reason why I shouldn't be walking past the premises of the Learned Society, it was on the way to a dozen places. So I did not bow my head in shame as I approached the building but even looked up to see a bearded man step out on to the balcony, and Everard Bone and Esther Clovis coming out of the front door.

Esther Clovis . . . hair like a dog, but a very capable person, respected and esteemed by Everard Bone, and, moreover, one who could make an index and correct proofs. I felt quite a shock at seeing them together, especially when I noticed Everard taking her arm. Of course they were crossing the road and any man with reasonably good manners might be expected to take a woman's arm in those circumstances, I reasoned within myself, but I still felt very low. I decided that I would go and have lunch in the great cafeteria where I sometimes went with Mrs Bonner. It would encourage a suitable frame of mind, put me in mind of my own mortality and of that of all of us here below, if I could meditate on that line of patient people moving with their trays.

'Mildred! Didn't you see me?'

Everard sounded a little annoyed, as if he had had to hurry to catch me up.

'I didn't think you'd seen me,' I said, startled. 'Besides, you had somebody with you.'

'Only Esther Clovis.'

'She's a very capable person. What have you done with her?'

'Done with her? I happened to come out with her and she was meeting a friend for lunch. Are you going to have lunch? We may as well have it together.'

'Yes; I was going to,' I said, and told him where I had thought of going.

'Oh, we can't go there,' he said impatiently, so of course we went to a restaurant of his choice near the premises of the Learned Society.

Naturally the meal did not come up to my expectations, though the food was very good. I found myself wondering how I could have wanted so much to see him again, and I was embarrassed at the remembrance of my imaginings of him, alone and ill in his flat with nobody to look after him. Nothing more unlikely could possibly be imagined.

The conversation did not go very well and I began telling him about the people with their trays in the great cafeteria and suggesting that it would have done us more good to go there to be put in mind of our own mortality.

'But I'm daily being put in mind of it,' he protested. 'One has only to sit in the library of the Learned Society to realize that one's own end can't be so very far off.'

After that things went a little better. I told him about the Napiers and he invited me to go to dinner with him at his flat. I promised that I would cook the meat and I felt better for having done so, for it seemed like a kind of atonement, a burden in a way and yet perhaps because of being a burden, a pleasure.

Just as we were leaving the restaurant two men came and sat down at a table near us. I did not need to be told who they were.

'Apfelbaum and Tyrell Todd,' said Everard in a low voice. 'I dare say you remember who they are.'

'Oh, yes, you and Helena met them once at one o'clock in the morning and you were all so surprised. I often think of that – it makes me laugh.'

'Well, nothing came of it,' said Everard rather stiffly. 'I suppose it was amusing, really. I expect they will be more interested to see me with somebody they don't know. You must come and hear Todd talking about pygmies some time.'

'Thank you – I should like that very much,' I said.

I went home rather slowly, imagining myself having dinner with Everard at his flat; then I saw myself at the Learned Society, listening to Tyrell Todd talking about pygmies. I was just getting up to put an extraordinarily intelligent and provocative question to the speaker, when I realized that I was nearly home and that there was a furniture van outside the door. As I approached it I was able to take note of some of its contents which were lying forlornly in the road. There were some oak chairs and a gate-legged table, an embroidered firescreen and a carved chest, the kind of 'good' rather uninteresting things that people of one's own kind might be expected to have. I guessed that the owners were probably a couple of women like Dora and myself, perhaps, though I had no means of knowing if they were older or younger.

I walked quietly up the stairs, not wanting to meet them yet but I was just passing what I shall always think of as the Napiers' kitchen when a sharp but cultured woman's voice called out, 'Is that Miss Lathbury?'

I stood transfixed on the stairs and before I had time to answer a small grey-haired woman, holding a tea-caddy in her hand, put her head out of the door.

'I'm Charlotte Boniface,' she announced. 'My friend Mabel Edgar and I are just moving in – as you can see.' She gave a little laugh.

Another pair of women, I thought with resignation, feeling a little depressed that my prophecy had come true, but telling myself that after all they were the easiest kind of people to have in the house.

'Edgar!' called Miss Boniface into the other room. 'Come and meet Miss Lathbury, who lives in the flat above us.'

A tall grey-haired woman holding a hammer in her hand came out and smiled in a mild shy sort of way.

'Come in and have a cup of tea with us, Miss Lathbury,' said Miss Boniface.

I went into the sitting-room which had a carpet on the floor and a few pieces of furniture spread about in an uncertain way. Miss Edgar was standing on a stepladder hanging pictures, dark-looking reproductions of Italian Old Masters.

'Do excuse me,' she said. 'I always have to hang the pictures because Bony can't reach. These walls don't seem to be very good, the plaster crumbles when you knock nails in.'

'Oh, dear,' I said conventionally, feeling relieved that there was nothing I could do about it. 'I hope you will like this flat.'

'Oh, it will be wonderful to have a home at last, to have

our own things around us,' said Miss Edgar. 'And I think we shall be happy here. We have found an *omen*,' she lowered her voice almost to a whisper and pointed in the direction of the window.

I saw Rocky's lines from Dante scratched on the glass.

'What is it?' I asked.

'Our Beloved Dante,' said Miss Boniface reverently. 'Could anything be happier? Those wonderful lines.' And she quoted them with a rather better accent than Rocky had managed.

'Whoever engraved them has made a small mistake,' said Miss Edgar. 'He or she has written *Nessun maggiore dolore* – it should of course be *Nessun maggior dolore*, without the final "e", you see. Still, perhaps this person was thinking of Lago di Maggiore, no doubt it was the memory of a happy time spent there. It would be interesting to know how the lines came to be engraved on the window – there must be a story behind it.'

I decided that I could not reveal the circumstances and the conversation turned to other things. I learned that Miss Boniface and Miss Edgar had lived in Italy for many years and were now eking out their small private incomes by teaching Italian and doing translations. They fired questions at me, speaking sometimes individually and sometimes, or so it seemed, in unison. I told them of a laundry, a grocer and a butcher where they might register, and we went on to discuss the bathroom arrangements in some detail. They were much more businesslike than the Napiers had been and insisted that we should have a rota for cleaning the bath.

'All right,' I said; 'shall I do it one week and you the next?'

'Oh, no, there are two of us. We shall do two weeks and you will do one, and so on.'

The question of the toilet-paper was not openly discussed as it had been with Helena, but I noticed later that a new roll had appeared, hung in a distinctive place. It seemed as if Miss Boniface and Miss Edgar were going to be very pleasant and cooperative, a real asset to the parish, in fact.

'And where is the nearest Catholic Church?' asked Miss Edgar.

'Oh, very near, not two minutes' walk away,' I said. 'Father Malory and his sister are friends of mine. He was engaged to be married, but it was broken off,' I added chattily.

I thought they looked a little surprised at this, and then it suddenly dawned on me that perhaps they meant *Roman* Catholic, so I hurried to explain myself.

'Oh, well, mistakes will happen,' said Miss Edgar pleasantly. 'Of course we know about Westminster Cathedral, but there must surely be a church nearer than that.'

'Oh, yes, there is – St Aloysius, and Father Bogart is the priest there. I believe he is a very nice man.' 'A lovely man' was how Mrs Ryan had described him at the jumble sale and I had often seen him on his bicycle, a fresh-faced young Irishman, waving to a parishioner or calling out 'Bye-bye now!' as he left one after a conversation.

I gathered that they had 'gone over' in Italy, which seemed a suitable place to do it in, if one had to do it at all.

'There was really no English church where we were,' said Miss Boniface almost apologetically, 'or at least, it was just a room in a house, you know, not at all inspiring.'

'There was an altar at one end, I suppose it was the east,' said Miss Edgar doubtfully, 'but you could see that it was just a mantelpiece with the fireplace below it.'

'We didn't care for the priest either – Mr Griffin – he was very *Low*,' said Miss Boniface.

'And the congregation was rather snobbish and unfriendly,' said Miss Edgar. 'You see, Bony and I were governesses and they were mostly titled people living in Italy for their own pleasure.'

'Oh, yes, I can understand that,' I said obscurely, and I did understand their feeling although their reasons appeared to be hardly adequate; no doubt there had been other and deeper ones, but I could not expect to be told about those.

'I do hope you will let me know if there is anything I can

do for you,' I said, as I got up to leave. 'Perhaps I can lend you cooking things and have you got bread and milk?'

It seemed that they had everything, but we parted on very cordial terms. I could see us having interesting religious discussions, I thought, as I went upstairs to get ready for supper with Winifred and Julian Malory.

'It seems a strange coincidence,' I said, 'but I remember coming to supper here just after Helena Napier moved in.'

'Yes, and Julian had just received the anonymous donation for the restoration fund,' said Winifred.

'Did you ever find out who gave it?' I asked.

'Oh, it was Allegra Gray,' said Julian lightly. 'Didn't I tell you?'

'No, I don't think I ever knew. And I don't think I should have guessed. I thought she was supposed to be poor,' I added, remembering the extraordinary delicate conversation about the rent which Julian had reported to us.

'That made the giving all the more praiseworthy,' said Julian.

At this moment an unworthy thought occurred to me. Supposing *I* had given an anonymous donation of, say, twenty pounds, would Julian have got engaged to *me*? Had Allegra Gray regretted the donation when the engagement was broken off or had she simply not thought of it? Perhaps she was one of those generous people who do not remember when they have given money or think about it when it is gone . . . I stopped suddenly, remembering Rocky thrusting a pound note into my hand on the evening before they left. I supposed I must have put it into my bag and forgotten all about it.

'Julian,' I said, 'I've done a terrible thing. Rocky Napier gave me a pound, he said it was to buy the best quality incense, and I forgot about it!' I rummaged in my bag and found that it was still there folded up among a jumble of ration books, shopping lists, old letters and the other things that collect in bags.

'How nice of him,' said Julian. 'I thought him a charming fellow. I'm so glad he made up that silly quarrel with his wife – she was very charming, too. Do you know, Mildred, I met her when I was coming out of church one evening and we went and had a drink together.'

'She never told me that. She complained that it was always your boys' club night,' I said, admiring Helena for having managed it. 'I shall miss them. The new people seem quite nice, though, two middle-aged spinsters.'

'Ah, yes, very suitable.' Julian nodded and became rather clerical again. 'Churchgoers, I've no doubt.' He seemed resigned to the prospect of them.

'I'm not sure about that,' I laughed. 'You'll have to ask Father Bogart about it.'

'Bogart, is it now? Are they after being Romans?' asked Julian, his relief making him break into an Irish brogue.

'I'm afraid so,' I said, almost as if it were my fault. 'But you wouldn't grudge him a couple of gentlewomen, I'm sure. He hasn't many such in his flock.'

'I thought they looked very nice,' said Winifred. 'I happened to be passing when they were down talking to the furniture men. I hope we shall be able to be friends.'

'They've lived in Italy for many years,' I said.

'Italy! Oh, how lovely!' Winifred clasped her hands and I heard the familiar note of enthusiasm in her voice. Looking forward a little, I could almost imagine a time when Winifred might want to become a Roman Catholic and I wondered if I should be there to help with the crisis. That was something that had not so far fallen within my experience of helping or interfering in other people's lives, and I wondered whether I should be capable of dealing with it.

CHAPTER TWENTY-SEVEN

SOME TIME before the evening when I was to go to dinner at Everard Bone's flat, the idea came into my mind that of course Esther Clovis would be there. It seemed the most likely thing in the world, especially as Everard was writing an article for a learned journal and was also busy on a book about his fieldwork in Africa. I should find her there correcting proofs or making an index, and the idea did not please me. I decided that I would try to make myself look like the kind of person who could not possibly do either, but it was not very easy. My normal appearance is very ordinary and my clothes rather uninteresting, but the new dress I had bought showed an attempt, perhaps misguided, to make myself look different. It was black, a colour I had never worn before except when I was in mourning after my parents' death. I had often seen Helena in black, but her fair hair and complexion set it off better than my mousy colouring, and she had the knack of enlivening it with some brilliant touch of colour or 'important jewel' as one was told to do in the women's magazines. I had no important jewels except for a good cameo brooch which had belonged to my grandmother, so I fastened this at the front of the little collar, brushed my hair back rather more severely than usual and looked altogether exactly the kind of person who would be able to correct proofs or make an index. Still, I reflected, Esther Clovis, with her dog's hair, would probably be wearing a tweed suit and brogues. At least I should provide a contrast.

As I was going out of the house, I met Miss Statham walking towards the church.

'Hullo, dear,' she said, peering at me with a doubtful expression on her face. 'What've you done to your hair?' she asked at last.

'I don't know,' I said feebly. 'Nothing, really.'

'It looks sort of scraped back as if you were going to have a bath,' she said cheerfully. 'If you don't mind my saying so, it looked better the way you did it before.'

'How did I do it before?'

'Oh, I don't know, really, but it was softer somehow, more round the face.'

Well, it was too late to do anything about it now and perhaps Miss Statham's opinion was not worth bothering about. Softer, somehow, more round the face . . . who wanted to look like that? Certainly she herself was no oil-painting, as Dora would say.

Suddenly she moved towards me and took my arm. 'I *knew* I had something to tell you,' she said. 'I just popped into Barker's on Saturday morning and who do you think I saw? You'll never guess!'

'Mrs Gray?' I suggested.

'There, and I thought I'd surprise you! Well, anyway,' she went on, recovering quickly from her disappointment, 'I felt a bit awkward and was going to walk past – she was looking at some underwear, you see – but, oh no, she came after me and began asking me what news in the parish and all about everybody and Father Malory, even – I didn't know what to say.'

'Well, you could have told her about the Christmas bazaar.'

'Oh, I did and she said she might even come to it! You'd think she'd have a little shame, wouldn't you? Anyway, it seems that she's found a flat already, in the *best part of Kensington*, that's what she said – oh, a *much* higher-class district than *this*. And there are three or four Anglo-Catholic churches, all within ten minutes' walk and less.'

'An *embarras de richesse*,' I said.

'What, dear? Anyway, the one she's decided to go to has a vicar and *two* assistant priests and they're none of them married! She told me that. They all live together in a clergy house.'

'Goodness me, I suppose they need to band together to protect themselves and each other,' I said.

'That's what I thought,' said Miss Statham. 'I'd almost feel like warning them to look out.'

'Oh, I expect she's tired of clergymen,' I said. 'To have been married to one and engaged to another, isn't that perhaps enough?'

'Well, I suppose you get a liking for a particular type of man,' said Miss Statham tolerantly, 'though they aren't all as nice as Father Malory, I must say.'

The bell started to ring for Evensong and Julian hurried out of the vicarage into the church.

Miss Statham clapped her hand over her mouth and giggled. 'Talk of the devil,' she exclaimed, and hurried into church after him.

I went on my way feeling a little less confident than when I had set out, though the interest of hearing about Allegra Gray helped a little to take my mind off my appearance. I felt more kindly disposed towards her now that she was removed from us and I did not grudge her the flat in the best part of Kensington or the three unmarried priests. I had no doubt that she would eventually marry one of them.

I got off the bus and turned into the street where Everard's flat was, only to find that I had walked straight into William Caldicote.

'Why, it's Mildred,' he said, 'but I hardly recognized you. You have a rather more *triste* appearance than usual – what is it?' He stood back and contemplated me. 'The hair, perhaps? The sombre dress?' He shook his head. 'Impossible to say, really.'

'Do you think it an improvement?' I asked apprehensively.

'An improvement? Ah, well, I should hardly presume to express that kind of an opinion. You mean an improvement on the way you usually look? But how do you usually look? One scarcely remembers. Where are you going now? Were you perhaps coming to see me?'

I thought I detected a note of alarm in his voice, so hastened to reassure him.

'Ah, perhaps it's just as well. I should not have been able to entertain you as I should have liked. I have a small bird *en casserole* in the oven, but it is such a *very* small bird, and now I am hurrying to my wine merchant, who shouid still be open, because I have just discovered, to my chagrin, that I have nothing but white wine in my little cellar!'

'How dreadful,' I murmured. 'I suppose you will buy a bottle of Nuits St Georges?'

'Well, possibly. He has one or two quite drinkable burgundies. My only fear is that it will scarcely be *chambré* by the time I shall want to drink it.'

'Well, why don't you put the bottle by the fire or into some hot water for a few minutes?' I suggested. 'That should warm it up.'

'Warm it up! Mildred, my dear, you *mustn't* say such things. One can't stand the shock. I might have expected such a remark from poor Dora but never from *you*.'

I felt obscurely flattered. 'If you are dining alone,' I suggested, 'nobody need know about it.'

'Yes, you're right, of course. There's sometimes quite a pleasure in secret vice. One can feel really rather wicked and at the same time have the satisfaction of not harming anybody else – if that is a satisfaction.'

'Oh, surely,' I said. 'And now I really must go. I'm supposed to be having dinner with somebody and I shall probably have to help with the cooking.'

'How very anxious for you,' said William. 'I always like to have *full* control of a meal or no part in it at all. I'd rather not *see* people adding Bovril to the gravy and doing dreadful things like that.'

We parted with mutual expressions of anxiety about the meal which each of us was going to eat, though William seemed a little complacent about his bird, I thought.

When I rang the bell at Everard's flat, I realized that I was late. Miss Statham and William had each delayed me a little, but it was better than being too early and having to walk slowly past the house in the dark, hoping I should not be seen from an upper window.

'Oh, there you are,' Everard said as he opened the door. Not exactly a welcoming speech but I knew him well enough now to realize that he never did appear pleased to see anybody.

'I'm afraid I'm a little late,' I said, taking off my coat and hanging it in the hall which had, I noticed with a slight shock, several fierce-looking African masks hanging on one wall. There was no looking-glass, which was just as well, and I waited with resignation for Everard to make some comment on my appearance. But to my relief none came, and after a time I realized that he evidently did not think I looked any different from usual. Unless, of course, he was too polite to say anything.

He led me into a sitting-room where I noticed a decanter of sherry on a low table and a bottle of red wine by the gas-fire. I suppose I must have looked at it rather pointedly, remembering my conversation with William, for Everard commented on it.

'I know what you are looking at,' he said, 'and I know it's one of the unforgivable sins. I can only hope you'll forget what you have seen and let it be a secret between us.'

'I think perhaps that everybody puts wine by the fire secretly,' I said. 'I don't think I should ever have known it was wrong if William Caldicote hadn't told me. But what about the meat? Oughtn't it to go in the oven?'

'Oh, the woman got everything ready for me. She has put something in the oven,' he said vaguely. 'A bird, a chicken or something. I expect it will be all right. Perhaps you would help to take it out – at about half-past seven, I believe.'

'Is it in a casserole?'

'Oh, would it be? Then I dare say it is.'

'And is there an oven cloth?'

He looked a little worried for a moment but then a smile broke through. We sat down by the fire and he gave me a glass of sherry.

'It should be hanging on a nail by the cooker, shouldn't it?' he said. 'I seem to remember that.'

Not an inspiring conversation, I thought, but it would do. We sat quite peacefully drinking sherry until I suddenly remembered about Esther Clovis. No doubt she would be arriving just before dinner, when I was taking the casserole out of the oven. No woman is at her best when taking something out of the oven, and I couldn't even correct proofs or make an index.

'Where is Miss Clovis?' I asked.

He looked surprised. 'At home, I imagine. Where else should she be?'

'I thought she might be coming to dinner.'

'To dinner? Would you have liked me to invite her? I'm afraid I didn't think of it.'

'I thought you respected and esteemed her.'

'Oh, certainly I do, but that doesn't mean that I should want to ask her to dinner.'

There was a silence, during which I looked round the room, which was pleasant but in no way remarkable or unusual. There was a large desk, a great many books and papers, but no photographs and nothing interesting on the mantelpiece, apart from a card announcing the autumn programme of the Learned Society.

'How is your mother?' I asked.

'Oh, quite well, thank you.'

'And Miss Jessop?'

'Miss Jessop?'

'You know, the person who was in the room that evening when I had dinner with you.'

'I'm afraid I don't know anything about her.'

'I think it may be time to see to that casserole,' I said, getting up. 'It's just on half-past seven.'

It turned out to be a very nice bird and I am sure that even William's could not have been better. The red wine was perfectly *chambré* and our conversation improved quite noticeably, so that by the time we were sitting drinking coffee by the purring gas-fire the atmosphere between us was a pleasant and cosy one.

'I should be interested to see the article you said you were writing for the Learned Journal,' I said.

'Oh, it's very dull; I shan't inflict that on you.'

'Well, what about your book, then? How is it getting on?'

'I have just had some of the proofs and then of course the index will have to be done. I don't know how I'm going to find time to do it,' said Everard, not looking at me.

'But aren't there people who do things like that?' I asked.

'You mean excellent women whom one respects and esteems?'

'Yes, I suppose I did mean something like that.'

There was a pause. I looked into the gas-fire, which was one degree better than the glowing functional bar into which I had gazed with Julian.

'I was wondering . . .' Everard began, 'but no – I couldn't ask you. You're much too busy, I'm sure.'

'But I don't know how to do these things,' I protested.

'Oh, but I could show you,' he said eagerly; 'you'd soon learn.' He got up and fetched a bundle of proof sheets and typescript from the desk. 'It's quite simple, really. All you have to do is to see that the proof agrees with the typescript.'

'Well, I dare say I could do that,' I said, taking a sheet of proof and looking at it doubtfully.

'Oh, splendid. How very good of you!' I had never seen Everard so enthusiastic before. 'And perhaps you could help me with the index too? Reading proofs for a long stretch gets a little boring. The index would make a nice change for you.'

'Yes, it would make a nice change,' I agreed. And before long I should be certain to find myself at his sink peeling potatoes and washing up; that would be a nice change when both proof-reading and indexing began to pall. Was any man worth this burden? Probably not, but one shouldered it bravely and cheerfully and in the end it might turn out to be not so heavy after all. Perhaps I should be allowed to talk to Mrs Bone about worms, birds and Jesuits, or find out who Miss Jessop really was and why an apology had been demanded from her.

'It should be interesting work,' I said rather formally and began to read from the proof sheet I was holding. But as I read a feeling of despair came over me, for it was totally incomprehensible. 'But I don't understand it!' I cried out. 'How can I ever know what it really means?'

'Oh, never mind about that,' said Everard, smiling. 'I dare say you will eventually. But don't you remember the late President's wife?'

'Why, of course, that's a comfort,' I said, seeing myself once more in that room at the Learned Society where the old lady was sitting in a basket chair in the front row with her knitting. The lecture flowed over her head as she sat there, her needles clicking and then dropping from her hand as her head fell forward on to her breast. She was asleep, but it didn't matter. Nobody thought anything of it or even noticed when her head jerked up again and she looked about her with unseeing eyes, wondering for the moment where she was. After all, she was only the President's wife, and she always went to sleep anyway.

And then another picture came into my mind. Julian Malory, standing by the electric fire, wearing his speckled mackintosh, holding a couple of ping-pong bats and quoting a not very appropriate bit of Keats. He might need to be protected from the women who were going to live in his house. So, what with my duty there and the work I was going to do for Everard, it seemed as if I might be going to have what Helena called 'a full life' after all.

Jane and Prudence

CHAPTER ONE

JANE AND PRUDENCE were walking in the college garden before dinner. Their conversation came in excited little bursts, for Oxford is very lovely in midsummer, and the glimpses of grey towers through the trees and the river at their side moved them to reminiscences of earlier days.

'Ah, those delphiniums,' sighed Jane. 'I always used to think Nicholas's eyes were just that colour. But I suppose a middle-aged man – and he is that now, poor darling – can't have delphinium-blue eyes.'

'Those white roses always remind me of Laurence,' said Prudence, continuing on her own line. 'Once I remember him coming to call for me and picking me a white rose – and Miss Birkinshaw saw him from her window! It was like Beauty and the Beast,' she added. 'Not that Laurence was ugly. I always thought him rather attractive.'

'But you were certainly Beauty, Prue,' said Jane warmly. 'Oh, those days of wine and roses! They are *not* long.'

'And to think that we didn't really appreciate wine,' said Prudence. 'How innocent we were then and how happy!'

They walked on without speaking, their silence paying a brief tribute to their lost youth.

Prudence Bates was twenty-nine, an age that is often rather desperate for a woman who has not yet married. Jane Cleveland was forty-one, an age that may bring with it compensations unsuspected by the anxious woman of twenty-nine. If they seemed an unlikely pair to be walking together at a Reunion of Old Students, where the ages of friends seldom have more than a year or two between them, it was because their relationship had been that of tutor and pupil. For two years, when her husband had had a living just outside Oxford, Jane had gone back to her old college to help Miss Birkinshaw with the English students, and it was then that Prudence had become her pupil and remained her friend. Jane had enjoyed those two years, but then they had moved to a suburban parish, and now, she thought, glancing round the table at dinner, here I am back where I started, just another of the many Old Students who have married clergymen. She seemed to see the announcement in the *Chronicle* under *Marriages*, 'Cleveland-Bold', or, rather, 'Bold-Cleveland', for here the women took precedence; it was their world, the husbands existing only in relation to them: 'Jane Mowbray Bold to Herbert Nicholas Cleveland.' And later, after a suitable interval, 'To Jane Cleveland (Bold), a daughter (Flora Mowbray).'

When she and Nicholas were engaged Jane had taken great pleasure in imagining herself as a clergyman's wife, starting with Trollope and working through the Victorian novelists to the present-day gallant, cheerful wives, who ran large houses and families on far too little money and sometimes wrote articles about it in the *Church Times*. But she had been quickly disillusioned. Nicholas's first curacy had been in a town where she had found very little in common with the elderly and middle-aged women who made up the greater part of the congregation. Jane's outspokenness and her fantastic turn of mind were not appreciated; other qualities which she did not possess and which seemed impossible to acquire were apparently necessary. And then, as the years passed and she realized that Flora was to be her only child, she was again conscious of failure, for her picture of herself as a clergyman's wife had included a large Victorian family like those in the novels of Miss Charlotte M. Yonge.

'At least I have had Flora, even though everybody else here has at least two children,' she said, speaking her thoughts aloud to anybody who happened to be within earshot.

'I haven't,' said Prudence a little coldly, for she was conscious on these occasions of being still unmarried, though women of twenty-nine or thirty or even older still could and did marry judging by other announcements in the *Chronicle*.

She wished Jane wouldn't say these things in her rather bright, loud voice, the voice of one used to addressing parish meetings. And why couldn't she have made some effort to change for dinner instead of appearing in the baggy-skirted grey flannel suit she had arrived in? Jane was really quite nice-looking, with her large eyes and short, rough, curly hair, but her clothes were terrible. One could hardly blame people for classing all university women as frumps, thought Prudence, looking down the table at the odd garments and odder wearers of them, the eager, unpainted faces, the wispy hair, the dowdy clothes; and yet most of them had married – that was the strange and disconcerting thing.

Prudence looks lovely this evening, thought Jane, like somebody in a woman's magazine, carefully 'groomed', and wearing a red dress that sets off her pale skin and dark hair. It was odd, really, that she should not yet have married. One wondered if it was really better to have loved and lost than never to have loved at all, when poor Prudence seemed to have lost so many times. For although she had been, and still was, very much admired, she had got into the way of preferring unsatisfactory love affairs to any others, so that it was becoming almost a bad habit. The latest passion did not sound any more suitable than her previous ones. Something to do with her work, Jane believed, for she had hardly liked to ask for details as yet. The details would assuredly come out later that evening, over what used to be cocoa or Ovaltine in one of their bed-sitting-rooms when they were students and would now be rather too many cigarettes without the harmless comfort of the hot drink.

'So you have all married clergymen,' said Miss Birkinshaw in a clear voice from her end of the table. 'You, Maisie, and Jane and Elspeth and Sybil and Prudence . . .'

'No, Miss Birkinshaw,' said Prudence hastily. 'I haven't married at all.'

'Of course, I remember now – you and Eleanor Hitchens

and Mollie Holmes are the only three in your year who didn't marry.'

'You make it sound dreadfully final,' said Jane. 'I'm sure there is hope for them all yet.'

'Well, Eleanor has her work at the Ministry, and Mollie the Settlement and her dogs, and Prudence, her work, too . . .' Miss Birkinshaw's tone seemed to lose a little of its incisiveness, for she could never remember what it was that Prudence was doing at any given moment. She liked her Old Students to be clearly labelled – the clergymen's wives, the other wives, and those who had 'fulfilled' themselves in less obvious ways, with novels or social work or a brilliant career in the Civil Service. Perhaps this last could be applied to Prudence? thought Miss Birkinshaw hopefully.

She might have said, 'and Prudence has her love affairs', thought Jane quickly, for they were surely as much an occupation as anything else.

'Your work must be very interesting, Prudence,' Miss Birkinshaw went on. 'I never like to ask people in your position *exactly* what it is that they do.'

'I'm a sort of personal assistant to Dr Grampian,' said Prudence. 'It's rather difficult to explain. I look after the humdrum side of his work, seeing books through the press and that kind of thing.'

'It must be wonderful to feel that you have some part, however small, in his work,' said one of the clergymen's wives.

'I dare say you write quite a lot of his books for him,' said another. 'I often think work like that must be ample compensation for not being married,' she added in a patronizing tone.

'I don't need compensation,' said Prudence lightly. 'I often think being married would be rather a nuisance. I've got a nice flat and am so used to living on my own I should hardly know what to do with a husband.'

Oh, but a husband was someone to tell one's silly jokes to, to carry suitcases and do the tipping at hotels, thought Jane, with a rush. And although he certainly did these things, Nicholas was a great deal more than that.

'I like to think that some of my pupils are doing academic work,' said Miss Birkinshaw a little regretfully, for so few of them did. Dr Grampian was some kind of an economist or historian, she believed. He wrote the kind of books that nobody could be expected to read.

'Here we are all gathered round you,' said Jane, 'and none of us has really fulfilled her early promise.' For a moment she almost regretted her own stillborn 'research' – 'the influence of something upon somebody' hadn't Virginia Woolf called it? – to which her early marriage had put an end. She could hardly remember now what the subject of it was to have been – Donne, was it, and his influence on some later, obscurer poet? Or a study of her husband's namesake, the poet John Cleveland? When they had got settled in the new parish to which they were shortly moving she would dig out her notes again. There would be much more time for one's own work in the country.

Miss Birkinshaw was like an old ivory carving, Prudence thought, ageless, immaculate, with lace at her throat. She had been the same to many generations who had studied English Literature under her tuition. Had she ever loved? Impossible to believe that she had not, there must surely have been some rather splendid tragic romance a long time ago – he had been killed or died of typhoid fever, or she, a new woman enthusiastic for learning, had rejected him in favour of Donne, Marvell and Carew.

Had we but World enough, and Time
This Coyness, Lady, were no crime . . .

But there was never world enough nor time and Miss Birkinshaw's great work on the seventeenth-century metaphysical poets was still unfinished, would perhaps never be finished. And Prudence's love for Arthur Grampian, or whatever one called it – perhaps love was too grand a name – just went hopelessly on while time slipped away. . . .

'Now, Jane, I believe your husband is moving to a new parish,' said Miss Birkinshaw, gathering the threads of the conversation together. 'I saw it in the *Church Times*. You will enjoy being in the country, and then there is the cathedral town so near.'

'Yes, we are going in September. It will all be like a novel by Hugh Walpole,' said Jane eagerly.

'Unfortunately, it is rather a modern cathedral,' said one of the clerical wives, 'and there is one of the canons I do not care for myself.'

'But I've never thought of myself as caring for canons,' said Jane rather wildly.

'One woman's canon might be another woman's . . .' began another clerical wife, but her sentence trailed off unhappily, giving an effect almost of impropriety which was not made any better by Jane saying gaily, 'I can promise you there will be nothing like *that*!'

'It is an attractive little place you are going to,' said Miss Birkinshaw. 'Perhaps it has grown since I last saw it, when it was hardly more than a village.'

'I believe it is quite spoilt now,' said somebody eagerly. 'Those little places near London are hardly what they were.'

'Well, I expect it will be better than the suburbs,' said Jane. 'People will be less narrow and complacent.'

'Your husband will have to go carefully,' said a clerical wife. 'We had great difficulties, I remember, when we moved to our village. The church was not really as *Catholic* as we could have wished, and the villagers were very stubborn about accepting anything new.'

'Oh, we shall not attempt to introduce startling changes,' said Jane. 'There is a nearby church quite newly built where all *that* has been done. The vicar was up here at the same time as my husband.'

'And we are to have your daughter Flora with us, next term,' said Miss Birkinshaw. 'I always like to see the children coming along.'

'Ah, yes; I shall live my own Oxford days over again with her,' sighed Jane.

There was a scraping of chairs and then silence. Miss Jellink, their Principal, had risen. The assembled women bowed their heads for grace. '*Benedicto benedicatur,*' pronounced Miss Jellink in a thoughtful tone, as if considering the words.

There was coffee in the Senior Common Room and then chapel in the little tin-roofed building among the trees at the bottom of the garden. Jane sang heartily, but Prudence was silent beside her. The whole business of religion was meaningless to her, but there was a certain comfort even in the reedy sound of untrained women's voices raised in an evening hymn. Perhaps it was because it took her back to her college days, when love, even if sometimes unrequited or otherwise unsatisfactory, tended to be so under romantic circumstances, or in the idyllic surroundings of ancient stone walls, rivers, gardens, and even the reading-rooms of the great libraries.

After chapel there was more walking in the gardens until dusk and then much gathering in rooms for gossip and confidences.

Jane ran to her window and looked out at the river and a tower dimly visible through the trees. She had been given the room she had occupied in her third year and the view was full of memories. Here she had seen Nicholas coming along the drive on his bicycle, little dreaming that he was to become a clergyman – though, seeing him standing in the hall with his bicycle clips still on, perhaps she should have realized that he was bound to be a curate one day. She could remember him so vividly, wheeling his bicycle along the drive, with his fearful upward glance at her window, almost as if he were afraid that Miss Jellink and not Jane herself would be looking out.

Prudence had her memories too. Laurence and Henry and Philip, so many of them, for she had had numerous admirers, all coming up the drive, in a great body, it seemed, though in fact they had come singly. If she had married Henry, now a lecturer in English at a provincial university, Prudence thought, or Laurence, something in his father's business in Birmingham, or even Philip, small and spectacled and talking so earnestly and boringly about motor cars . . . but Philip had been killed in North Africa because he knew all about tanks. . . . Tears, which she had never shed for him when he was alive, now came into Prudence's eyes.

'Poor Prue,' said Jane rather heartily, wondering what she could say. Who was she weeping for now? Could it be Dr Grampian? 'But after all, he *is* married, isn't he? – I mean there is a wife somewhere even if you've never met her. You shouldn't really consider him as a possibility, you know. Unless she were to die, of course, that would be quite all right.' A widower, that was what was needed if such a one could be found. A widower would do splendidly for Prudence.

'I was thinking about poor Philip,' said Prudence rather coldly.

'Poor Philip?' Jane frowned. She could not remember that there had ever been anyone called Philip. 'Which, who . . .?' she began.

'Oh, you wouldn't remember,' said Prudence lighting another cigarette. 'It just reminded me, looking out at this view, but really I haven't thought about him for years.'

'No, I suppose Adrian Grampian is the one now,' said Jane.

'His name isn't Adrian; it's Arthur.'

'Arthur; yes, of course.' Could one love an Arthur? Jane wondered. Well, all things were possible. She began to think of Arthurs famous in history and romance – the Knights of the Round Table of course sprang to mind immediately, but somehow it wasn't a favourite name in these days; there was a faded Victorian air about it.

'It isn't so much what there *is* between us as what there *isn't*,' Prudence was saying; 'it's the *negative* relationship that's so hurtful, the complete lack of *rapport*, if you see what I mean.'

'It sounds rather restful in a way,' said Jane, doing the best she could, 'to have a negative relationship with somebody. Of course a vicar's wife must have a negative relationship with a good many people, otherwise life would hardly be bearable.'

'But this isn't quite the same thing,' said Prudence patiently. 'You see underneath all this, I feel that there really is something, something *positive*. . . .'

Jane swallowed a yawn, but she was fond of Prudence and was determined to do what she could for her. When they got settled in the new parish she would ask her to stay, not just for a weekend, but for a nice long time. New surroundings and new people would do much for her and there might even be work she could do, satisfying work with her hands, digging, agriculture, something in the open air. But a glance at Prudence's small, useless-looking hands with their long red nails convinced her that this would hardly be suitable. Not agriculture then, but a widower, that was how it would have to be.

CHAPTER TWO

'I FEEL THAT a crowd of our new parishioners ought to be coming up the drive to welcome us,' said Jane, looking out of the window over the laurel bushes, 'but the road is quite empty.'

'That only happens in the works of your favourite novelist,' said her husband indulgently, for his wife was a great novel reader, perhaps too much so for a vicar's wife. 'It's really better to get settled in before we have to deal with people. I told Lomax to come round after supper, perhaps for coffee.' He looked up at his wife hopefully.

'Oh, there will *be* supper,' said Jane in a firm tone, 'and there may be coffee. I suppose we could give Mr Lomax tea, though it wouldn't be quite the usual thing. I wonder if we are well-bred enough or eccentric enough to carry off an unusual thing like that, giving tea after a meal rather than coffee? I wouldn't like him to think that we were condescending to him in any way because his church is not as ancient as ours.'

'Of course coffee does tend to keep people awake,' said Nicholas rather inconsequentially.

'Lying awake at night thinking out a sermon,' said Jane; 'that might not be such a bad thing.'

'What are we having for supper?' asked her husband.

'Flora is in the kitchen unpacking some of the china. We could open a tin,' added Jane, as if this were a most unusual procedure, which it most certainly was not. 'Indeed, I think we shall probably have to, but I know we've got some coffee somewhere if only we can find it in time. Will he be bringing Mrs Lomax with him?'

'No, he is not married as far as I know,' said Nicholas vaguely, 'though it is some time since we've met. Our conversation yesterday was mostly about parish matters. I remember at Oxford he rather tended towards celibacy.'

'I dare say he was a spectacled young man with a bad complexion,' said Jane. 'He may have thought there was not much hope for him, so he became High Church.'

'Well, my dear, there are usually deeper reasons,' said Nicholas, smiling. 'Not all High Church clergymen are plain-looking.'

'Nor all Moderate ones, darling,' said Jane warmly, for her husband's eyes were still blue and he had kept his figure.

They were in the room which was to be Nicholas's study, sitting in the middle of a litter of books which Jane was arranging haphazardly on the shelves.

'These are all theology,' she said, when Nicholas suggested that it might be better if he did them; 'as long as nothing unsuitable-looking appears among these dim bindings I don't see that the arrangement really matters. Nobody could possibly want to read them. You're sure you wouldn't rather have the room upstairs for your study? It looks over the garden and might be quieter.'

'No, I think this room is the best for me. It seems somehow unsuitable for a clergyman's study to be *upstairs*,' said Nicholas, and then, before Jane could enlarge upon the idea with her vivid fancy, he added hastily, 'I shall have my desk in the window – it is sometimes an advantage to be able to see people coming.'

'Then you must have a net curtain across the window,' said Jane, 'otherwise you will lose your advantage if they can see you too. But at the moment it seems as if nobody will ever come to see us. . . .' She looked out over the laurels to the green-painted gate. 'You would think they'd come out of curiosity, if for no nobler reason.' She turned back to arranging the books.

'But there *is* somebody coming,' exclaimed Nicholas in a rather agitated voice. 'A lady, or perhaps a woman, in a straw hat with a bird on it, and she is carrying a bloodstained bundle.'

Jane hurried to the window. 'Why, that's Mrs Glaze. It must be! She is to do for us. I quite forgot – you know how indifferent I am to domestic arrangements. I hadn't realized she was coming tonight.' She ran out into the hall and flung open the front door before Mrs Glaze had even mounted the steps.

'Good evening, Mrs Glaze. How kind of you to come to us on our first evening here!' Jane cried out.

'Well, madam, it was arranged, Mrs Pritchard said you would want me to.'

'Ah, yes; she and Mr Pritchard were so kind. . . .'

'*Canon* Pritchard,' Mrs Glaze corrected her gently, entering the house.

'Yes, of course; he is that now. *Canon* Pritchard, called to a higher sphere.' Jane stood uncertainly in the hall, wondering if perhaps such words were found only on tombstones or in parish magazine obituary notices, and were hardly suitable to be used about their predecessor, who was still very much alive.

'Well, if you will excuse me, madam—' Mrs Glaze made as if to pass.

'Oh, certainly!' Jane stood aside, for she had hardly yet grasped where the kitchen was and in any case it was a part of the house in which she took little interest. 'I don't know what we are going to have for supper.'

'Don't you worry about that,' said Mrs Glaze, raising her bloodstained bundle and thrusting it towards Jane. 'I've got some liver for you.'

'How wonderful! How did you manage that?'

'Well, madam, my nephew happens to be a butcher, and one of the sidesmen at the Parish Church too. I warned him when you would be coming and naturally he wanted to see that you had a good supper. He loves his work, madam. He's as happy as a sandboy when the Christmas poultry comes in – looks forward to it all the year round. Of course, he can't take the same pride in it that he used to, not every day, that is – meat has never been at such a low ebb as it is now, what with everything having to go through the Government; it's no wonder the butchers can't go on grinding out the ration, is it madam?'

'No, indeed, one does wonder how they grind it out,' said

Jane fervently. 'My husband is so fond of liver. But what about vegetables?'

'Why, in the garden, madam,' said Mrs Glaze in a surprised tone.

'Of course – "well-stocked garden". We didn't have much of a garden in London,' said Jane apologetically.

By this time they had reached the kitchen, which was at the end of a long stone passage. Flora was just putting away the last of the china. She had not inherited her mother's vagueness and looked very much like her father, tall and slim with blue eyes and dark smooth hair. She was eighteen and looking forward to going up to Oxford in the autumn.

'This is my daughter Flora,' said Jane. 'She's been putting away the china.'

'Well now, isn't that kind,' said Mrs Glaze; 'that's saved me a lot of work. And I see she's even got the vegetables; I can start getting supper right away. Then you will be ready for Father Lomax when he comes for coffee.'

It was almost soothing that she should know so much about one's life, Jane thought. 'Yes,' she said. 'I do hope he will be able to tell us something about the parish and what we should know about everybody. You see, we are like people coming into the cinema in the middle of a film,' she went on, losing consciousness of her audience. 'We do not know what, if anything, has gone before, or at the best we have a bald and garbled synopsis whispered to us by somebody on his way out; that's Canon Pritchard, of course.'

'Mother,' said Flora a little desperately, 'shall I put out the coffee cups on the silver tray?'

'Yes, darling, by all means.'

'Oh well,' said Mrs Glaze in an easy tone that promised much, 'I've lived in this parish all my life. If Mr Meadows, our curate, had been still here, he'd have been a great help to the vicar. But of course he left when Canon Pritchard did. He was married just before he went.'

'Married? Oh, how nice. Was his wife from this village?'

'No, madam. He was engaged when he came to us.' Mrs Glaze turned her back and busied herself at the sink. A certain flatness in her tone roused Jane from her own thoughts and caused her to look up. Engaged when he came to them. Oh, but that was bad! Bad of the Bishop to send them a curate already engaged. It was a wonder the ladies of the parish hadn't torn him to pieces. A married man would have been preferable to an engaged one, for a curate's wife was often a dim, manageable sort of woman, whereas a fiancée, especially an absent one, has an aura of mystery, even of glamour about her. Who else is there? she wanted to ask. Tell me all about everybody. But she couldn't put it as bluntly as that even though Mrs Glaze was obviously ready to do her part.

'Has Mr Lomax a curate?' she asked at last.

'Father Lomax, he calls himself,' corrected Mrs Glaze; 'but of course he isn't married. There's no woman sets foot in that vicarage, except Mrs Eade to clean, and the ladies of his parish, of course. No, madam, Father Lomax hasn't got a curate. Not more than twenty or so go to his church. You see, madam, it's the form of service. Romish practices, you know what I mean. Though I must say he's got Mrs Lyall going there and that's something. But *we've* still got Mr Edward,' her voice softened and she looked up from her vegetables, a smile on her face, 'and that's as it should be, isn't it, madam?'

'Mr Edward?' echoed Jane hopefully, for there was much here that she did not understand.

'Yes, Mr Edward Lyall, our Member of Parliament, such a nice young man. Of course his father was Member before him and his grandfather, oh, we couldn't have anybody but a Lyall as our Member. They've always lived at the Towers as long as anybody can remember and always come to the Parish Church, except this Mrs Lyall, that is. Some vicar in Kensington, London, got hold of her, madam, ten years ago she started going to Father Lomax's, but Mr Edward's always come to the Parish Church.'

'Does he read the lessons sometimes?' asked Jane. 'It seems right for a Member of Parliament to read the lessons in his constituency.'

'Oh, yes, madam; when he's here he does. But of course there's Mr Oliver too, he reads the lessons sometimes, though Mr Mortlake and his friends, oh, they don't like it, madam, but no doubt you'll be hearing about *that*. And they do say that Mr Fabian Driver would like to do it. Oh, he'd fancy himself standing up there looking like a lion above the bird, but we haven't come to that *yet*. Have you got a flour-dredger, Miss Flora? I'll just be flouring the liver.'

Mr Mortlake and His Friends . . . A Lion above the Bird . . . but these are the titles of new novels still in their bright paper jackets, thought Jane with delight. And they are here in this parish, all this richness.

'Mother, I think we'd better have supper as soon as we can,' said Flora firmly, 'wasn't Mr Lomax invited for half-past eight? We don't want him to arrive and find us in the middle of our supper, do we?'

'No, darling, especially as he may not have had liver.'

'He won't have done, madam. I can tell you that,' said Mrs Glaze. 'Mrs Eade didn't get any this week – she does all his shopping for him. Of course, my nephew shares out the offal on a fair basis, madam, but everybody can't have it every time. Father Lomax will have had his liver *last* time,' she concluded firmly. 'And he will have it *next* time,' she added on a note of hope.

'Which won't be much consolation to him now,' said Jane, 'so he had better not see us eating it. Like meat offered to idols,' she went on. 'You will remember that St Paul had no objection to the faithful eating it, but pointed out that it might prove a stumbling-block to the weaker brethren – not that Father Lomax would be that, of course.'

'In fact, Mother, the whole comparison is pointless,' said Flora, 'as our liver won't have been offered to idols.'

'No; but people in these days do rather tend to worship meat for its own sake,' said Jane, as they sat down to supper. 'When people go abroad for a holiday they seem to bring back with them such a memory of meat.'

'This certainly looks very good,' said Nicholas, putting on his spectacles to see better what he was about to eat. 'Mrs Glaze seems to be an excellent cook. Pritchard spoke very highly of her. Of course, I believe they had a resident maid as well.'

'Yes,' said Jane; 'somebody handing the vegetables, holding the dish rather too low. I remember that when we lunched with them. Quite unnecessary, I thought it.'

The Clevelands were still at the supper table when the front door bell rang, and a man's voice was heard in the hall.

Mrs Glaze appeared at the door.

'I've put him in the drawing-room, madam,' she announced. 'I'll be bringing the coffee directly.'

'I'm afraid our drawing-room can hardly be compared with Mrs Pritchard's,' said Flora. 'Mr Lomax is probably noticing that.'

'Oh, but it looks "lived in",' said Jane, 'which is supposed to be a good thing. I thought Mrs Pritchard's a little *too* well-furnished – those excessively rich velvet curtains and all that Crown Derby in the corner cupboard, it was a little overwhelming.'

'Shall I come in too, Mother?' asked Flora.

'Of course, darling. After all, it's really a social occasion, isn't it?' She stood up and brushed some crumbs from her lap, glancing at her dress in a doubtful way as she did so. 'I really meant to have changed into something more worthy, but perhaps he will understand and make allowances. I don't suppose he is anything of a ladies' man.'

Flora, who had changed her dress and tidied her hair, made

no comment. She knew her mother well enough by now to realize that Mr Lomax's understanding and making allowances really mattered very little to her.

When the drawing-room door was opened, Father Lomax was discovered standing with his back to the fireplace, whose emptiness was not even decently filled in with a screen or vase of leaves or dried grasses.

He was not at all the ascetic type of clergyman, and Flora felt a rush of disappointment at the first sight of him, fair and ruddy-complexioned, with the build of an athlete. She liked men to be dark, but in any case he was old, a contemporary of her father's, and therefore uninteresting and profitless.

'Well, Father Lomax,' said Jane pleasantly as she poured the coffee, 'it is very good of you to come along, especially as I suppose we are rivals, really.'

'Yes, you might say that,' Father Lomax agreed, 'but I expect your husband and I can come to some amicable arrangement not to poach on each other's preserves. After all, we were up at Oxford together, you know. I've been here several years and can probably tell him quite a lot about the parish. We neighbouring clergy get to know things about other parishes – a word or a hint here and there, a casual remark in the public-house, things have a way of getting around.'

'One hopes there isn't really anything to get around,' said Jane, 'or at least not in public-houses.'

'Oh, Lomax means the general way things go,' said Nicholas vaguely. 'Numbers of congregations, personalities and so forth.'

'Ah, personalities,' said Jane; 'that's really what one wants to know about.'

But Father Lomax did not take the hint and began reminiscing with Nicholas about college days in what seemed to Jane a very boring way. He then recalled how Nicholas's father had opposed his ordination and had even called round to see the Principal of their college to register a protest.

'You were never able to bring him round to your way of thinking?' he asked Nicholas.

'No, I'm afraid not. He died without believing in anything, I'm afraid.'

'I suppose old atheists seem less wicked and dangerous than young ones,' said Jane. 'One feels that there is something of the ancient Greeks in them.'

Father Lomax, who evidently thought no such thing, let the subject drop and then somehow he and Nicholas were talking about parish matters, parochial church council meetings, Sunday School teachers and visiting preachers. Jane lay back in her chair lost in thought, wondering about Mr Mortlake and his friends. Flora got up and quietly refilled the coffee cups, offering a plate of biscuits to Father Lomax. But he refused them with an absent-minded wave of the hand. Meat offered to idols, thought Flora scornfully, taking a biscuit herself and eating it. Then, as nobody seemed to be taking any notice of her, she ate another and another until the clock struck ten, and her mother, oblivious of their guest, stood up, stretching her arms and yawning.

'Young Francis Oliver rather fancies himself at reading the lessons,' Father Lomax was saying, 'and there may be trouble in that quarter from Mr Mortlake. I have heard that the atmosphere at the last P.C.C. meeting was very strained.'

'Dear, dear,' said Nicholas, who was a mild, good-tempered person and never saw why any atmosphere should be strained, 'we shall have to try and change that.'

'Both Oliver and Mortlake are extremely stubborn,' said Father Lomax with satisfaction. 'My own Council are very different – I never have any trouble.'

'Well, I don't see why either of them should read the lessons,' said Nicholas.

'Ah, but during the war, when Canon Pritchard had no curate, the custom grew up.'

'Couldn't Mr Fabian Drover read the lessons?' asked Jane innocently.

'You mean Driver?' asked Father Lomax. 'Oh, I hardly think *that* would be suitable. He isn't what one would call a churchman, you know. He occasionally goes to Evensong, I believe. He has even been to my church once or twice.'

'People always seem to like Evensong, don't they?' said Jane. 'I mean, it seems more attractive to them than the other services. The old Ancient and Modern hymns especially seem to have an appeal to something very deep in all of us – I don't exactly know what you would call it.'

Neither Nicholas nor Father Lomax had any ready answer to this, and as they had been standing in the open doorway for some time Father Lomax finally edged his way down the steps and disappeared into the darkness.

'A fine, upstanding man, isn't he?' said Nicholas absently. He was evidently thinking that perhaps they might have a round of golf together on Mondays.

CHAPTER THREE

ON SATURDAY morning Jane crept quietly into the church to have a good look at it. It had been so full of people at the induction service – the Bishop, robed clergy and inquisitive parishioners – that she had hardly been able to form any idea of what it was like, except that it was old. Dear Nicholas, he would no longer have to say to visitors in his gentle, apologetic tones, almost as if it were his own fault, 'I'm afraid our church was built in 1883,' as in the suburban parish they had just left. For here were ancient stones, wall tablets and carved bosses in the roof, and in one corner the great canopied tomb of the Lyall family – a knight and his lady with a little dog at their feet.

Jane moved quietly about the church, reading inscriptions on wall and floor, noticing, without realizing its significance, the well-cleaned brass. She was just standing in front of the lectern, almost dazzled by the fine brilliance of the bird's head, when she heard footsteps behind her and the sound of women's voices, talking in rather low, reverent tones, but nonetheless with the authority of those who have the right to talk in church. One voice seemed louder than the other – indeed, when she had listened for a minute or two, Jane decided that the owner of the louder voice was somehow in a superior position to that of the softer one.

'Harvest *Thanksgiving*, we call it,' said the louder voice. 'Harvest *Festival* has a rather different connotation, I feel. There is almost a pagan sound about it.'

'Oh, yes.' The softer voice sounded very demure. 'Festival is altogether more pagan – I could almost see Mr Mortlake in a leopard skin with vine leaves in his hair.'

'Hush, Jessie,' said the louder voice on a reproving note. 'We must not forget that we are in church. Ah, here are Mrs Crampton and Mrs Mayhew. Perhaps we had better start.'

The speakers had now come into view and Jane saw a large woman who gave the impression of being dressed in purple hung about with gold chains, and a smaller younger one in brown with a vase of dead flowers in her hands. They were greeting two middle-aged ladies in tweed suits carrying bunches of dahlias.

An English scene, thought Jane, and a precious thing. Then she realized that it was of course Harvest Festival or Thanksgiving, and the ladies had come to decorate the church. She slipped quietly away behind their backs and found herself in the porch surrounded by fruit, vegetables and flowers.

'Who was that?' asked Miss Doggett, the lady in purple, who was elderly with a commanding manner.

'I think it was the new vicar's wife,' said Jessie Morrow, her companion, in an offhand way. 'It looked like her, I thought.'

'But why was I not told?' Miss Doggett raised her voice. 'What must she have thought of us not even saying good morning?'

Mrs Crampton and Mrs Mayhew stood with their dahlias, expressions of dismay on their faces.

'She will surely want to help with the decorating,' said Mrs Crampton, a tall woman with what is thought to be an English type of face, fresh colouring, blue-grey eyes and rather prominent teeth.

'I wonder she didn't introduce herself,' said Mrs Mayhew, who looked very much like Mrs Crampton. 'Mrs Pritchard wouldn't have been so backward, would she? Of course, I did recognize her myself, but I was so surprised at her walking away like that that I couldn't even say good morning.'

Miss Doggett went out into the porch. 'Why, she is in the churchyard walking about among the tombs,' she exclaimed. 'That long grass must be very wet – I wonder if she is wearing goloshes?'

'Shall I go and see?' asked Miss Morrow seriously.

'Well, you could certainly ask her to come into the church,' said Miss Doggett. 'I mean, indicate to her that we should be very pleased if she would join us. After all, she may have her own ideas about how the Harvest decorations should be arranged.'

Miss Morrow nearly let out a shout of laughter. Even Mrs Pritchard, the last vicar's wife, who had been a forceful woman, had been unable to depose Miss Doggett from her position as head of the decorators. Mrs Cleveland, as far as one could see, looked as if she would be neither desirous nor capable of doing any such thing.

Miss Morrow padded through the long grass and tombstones, humming a popular song of the day. She picked her way carefully, for she had a feeling about walking on the older graves, and some were so overgrown that it was difficult to avoid them.

She found Jane contemplating a rather new-looking mound, which was decorated, not with the conventional vases of flowers or growing plants, but with a large framed photograph of a rather good-looking man with a leonine head.

'What a curious idea,' said Jane, looking up at the woman who approached her through the tombs and dimly recognizing her as the one in brown who had been holding the vase of dead flowers, 'to have a photograph of oneself on one's tomb. I wonder if it is usual. It seems to be rather a delicate thing – perhaps one would really prefer to be remembered for oneself alone, for one's simple goodness, though it might be a kindness to posterity if one were particularly handsome, as this man appears to have been.'

'Appears to have been!' Miss Morrow gave a short laugh. 'But he still is, or thinks he is. The photograph is of Fabian Driver, and that is his wife's grave.'

'Fabian Driver,' Jane repeated, something about lions and eagles going round in her head. 'Is his wife recently dead?'

'Nearly a year ago. We thought at first that the photograph was put there temporarily until he could get a stone put up, but he seems to have come to the conclusion that he need not go to that expense after all. People are used to seeing it there now.'

'Perhaps his wife would have liked it better than a stone,' Jane suggested.

'Well, it is something for her, poor soul. I suppose even a photograph is better than nothing. You see, her husband was more interested in other women than he was in her. I believe that does sometimes happen. Her death came as a great shock to him – he had almost forgotten her existence.' Miss Morrow imparted this information in a cool, detached tone; there was nothing secretive or gossiping about her manner.

'He takes flowers to the grave sometimes,' she went on, 'flowers of a particular kind that are said to have been her favourites, but I often wonder if they really were.'

'You think he may be confusing her preferences with somebody else's?' Jane asked in an interested tone.

'Well, it seems quite likely. He is one for the grand gesture and has no time for niggling details.'

'And what now? Does he live alone?'

'Yes. In a pretty house on the village green. He is an inconsolable widower.'

'What does he do for a living?'

'Oh, there is some business in the City which belonged to his father-in-law. Whatever it is it doesn't seem to require his attendance every day of the week. He is often here, apparently doing nothing.'

'I feel it a good thing that I should have this information,' said Jane, walking with Miss Morrow towards the church. 'Canon and Mrs Pritchard told us so little about the people here.'

'Yes, some things must be known,' said Miss Morrow. 'It is no use nodding and pursing lips and saying dark things, and as you were by the grave I felt I could tell you. It is not the sort of thing one can talk about in the church. I was to ask you if you would care to supervise the decorating, though I imagine that you would have stayed in church if you had wanted to.'

'It isn't really much in my line,' said Jane. 'I'm not very good at arranging flowers at the best of times and I have had little experience of fruit and vegetables. Coming from a town parish, we didn't really have much at Harvest Thanksgiving. Sometimes we even had to have artificial fruit – I see you look shocked, but I think there was some excuse for us; London suburban gardens don't burgeon as they do here.'

'Perhaps I was thinking of Roman Catholic churches in Italy and Spain,' said Miss Morrow apologetically; 'those dusty bunches of artificial flowers. But I can see that fruit might be different; it would be easier to keep it clean.'

'Something made me slip away when I saw everybody there in the church,' said Jane. 'I'm afraid it's a fault in me and a great disadvantage for a clergyman's wife, not to be naturally gregarious. But I should really like to meet them all,' she added with more confidence than she felt.

'Well, I am Jessie Morrow,' said the little brown woman. 'I suppose you would describe me as that outmoded thing, a "companion". Miss Doggett, my employer, is a vigorous old lady who has no need of my services as a companion but rather as a sparring partner. The other two ladies are connected with the church.'

'You mean they are deaconesses?' Jane asked.

'No, they are widows who do a good deal of church work. Actually they run a tea-shop with home-made cakes and that sort of thing.'

They stepped back into the church and introductions were made. The ladies had now been joined by others and there was a confusion of fruit, vegetables and flowers everywhere. Dahlias and chrysanthemums blossomed in unlikely corners, marrows tumbled off window ledges, spiked arrangements of carrots and parsnips flaunted themselves against stained glass.

'I hope we shall have *Let us with a gladsome mind*,' said Jane. 'It is such a fine hymn. In many ways one dislikes Milton, of course; his treatment of women was not all that it should have been.'

'Well, they did not have quite the same standards in the old days,' said Miss Doggett, frowning. 'Of course we shall have the usual harvest hymns, I imagine. *We plough the fields and scatter*,' she declared in a firm tone, almost challenging anyone to deny her.

The corners of Miss Morrow's mouth lifted in a half-smile. 'Not without our goloshes,' she murmured, looking down at her thin glacé kid shoes, damp from walking among the tombstones.

Mrs Crampton and Mrs Mayhew looked up from the font in surprise.

'Miss Morrow was telling me that you run a tea-shop,' said Jane. 'I do hope you do lunches too. I have to send my husband out for lunch at least twice a week!'

'Yes, it is difficult to manage sometimes,' said Mrs Crampton.

'And the clergy are always with us where meals are concerned,' sighed Jane.

'Of course, a man must have meat,' pronounced Mrs Mayhew.

'Certainly he must,' said a pleasant voice in the porch.

Jane looked up to see a tall, good-looking man of about forty, with a marrow in his arms, coming towards them.

'Oh, Mrs Cleveland, have you met Mr Driver yet?' asked Miss Doggett, taking command of the situation, as if the other ladies might not be equal to making the introduction.

'No, I don't think I have,' said Jane, taking in at a glance the rather worn, perhaps ravaged – if one could use so violent a word – good looks, the curly hair worn rather too long and touched with grey at the temples, also the carefully casual tweed suit and brogued suede shoes, which gave the impression of a town-dweller dressed for the country.

'This is a great pleasure,' said Fabian as they shook hands.

Jane looked up at him frankly and then lowered her eyes, embarrassed at being confronted by such an excellent likeness of the photograph she had just been looking at on his wife's grave. She felt that she knew more about him than one usually does on a first meeting, remembering Miss Morrow's words about his having been more interested in other women than in his wife and the possibility of his taking the wrong flowers to the grave. That might be a stumbling-block between them, she felt, the photograph and the infidelities, but perhaps there might come a time when they would speak frankly of these things and even laugh, though, when one came to think of it, neither graves nor infidelities were really any laughing matter.

'What a fine marrow, Mr Driver,' said Miss Doggett in a bright tone. 'It is the biggest one we have had so far, isn't it, Miss Morrow?'

Miss Morrow, who was scrabbling on the floor among the vegetables, mumbled something inaudible.

'It is magnificent,' said Mrs Mayhew reverently.

Mr Driver moved forward and presented the marrow to Miss Doggett with something of a flourish.

Jane felt as if she were assisting at some primitive kind of ritual at whose significance she hardly dared to guess.

'We are so much looking forward to hearing our new vicar's first sermon,' said Fabian gallantly, looking at Jane rather intently.

'Nicholas isn't one of these dramatic preachers,' she said quickly, feeling a little confused.

The ladies looked interested, as if hoping that she might be guilty of further disloyalties, but Jane recollected herself in time and said: 'Of course, he's a very good preacher; what I meant was that he doesn't go in for a lot of quotations and that kind of thing.'

'Much wiser not to,' agreed Miss Doggett. 'Simple Christian teaching is what we want, isn't it, really?'

Jane had to agree, but she was conscious that Miss Doggett's tone was a little patronizing and was not surprised when she went on to add that Canon Pritchard had been a very fine preacher, '. . . most eloquent. Such a fine mellow voice and never at a loss for a word. . . .'

'Nicholas is never at a loss for a word, and his voice is very mellow; I think one could call it that,' said Jane, feeling ridiculous now, and wishing she could think of some excuse to leave the gathering.

'I'm sure we shall find it to our liking,' said Fabian kindly.

'And now I really must be going,' said Jane. 'There is the

meal to see to,' she added vaguely, remembering that both Flora and Mrs Glaze were at the vicarage that morning, so that her presence there was really quite unnecessary.

'Yes, of course,' said Mrs Crampton sympathetically.

'Why, here is your husband now,' said Miss Doggett. 'How nice of him to come and see us. We shall work all the better for this encouragement.'

'Oh, there you are, darling,' said Jane, stepping backwards on to a heap of vegetables. 'I was just going to see about lunch. Goodbye, everybody,' she said, leaving Nicholas to make his own impression. She had noticed that he seemed a good deal more at ease with the decorators than she had been, but perhaps that was to be expected.

She hurried away down the church path and found Fabian at her side.

'I don't feel I can do much good there,' he explained. 'I too must see about lunch.'

'Do you cook for yourself then?'

'I live alone, you know. Since my wife died . . .'

'Yes, of course, Miss Morrow told me.'

'Really? What did she say?'

'Oh, how sad it was and all that sort of thing,' said Jane rapidly with her eyes on the ground.

'Yes, I think she knows. She is a very understanding person in her way.'

'And do you like cooking and looking after yourself?' asked Jane in a brighter tone.

'One manages,' said Fabian; 'one has to, of course.'

The use of the third person seemed to add pathos, which was perhaps just what he intended, Jane thought.

'You and your husband must come and have a meal with me one evening,' Fabian went on.

'We should love to,' said Jane, pausing to open the vicarage gate.

'Goodbye, then.' Fabian walked slowly away.

He is going back to cook a solitary lunch, thought Jane, or perhaps it will just be beer and bread and cheese, a man's meal and the better for being eaten alone.

'I've just met Mr Driver,' she said to Flora as she entered the house. 'He is a widower and lives alone. I felt quite sorry for him going back to eat a rather miserable lunch.'

There was a bark of laughter from Mrs Glaze, who was dusting in the hall.

'I don't think Mrs Arkright would thank you for calling it that, madam,' she said.

'Mrs Arkright?'

'Yes, she goes in and cooks Mr Driver's meals, and a very good cook she is. I dare say he'll be having a casserole of hearts today,' said Mrs Glaze in a full tone.

'A casserole of hearts,' murmured Jane in confusion, thinking of the grave and the infidelities. Did he eat his victims, then?

'My nephew the butcher had hearts and liver this week, madam, but I didn't know if you liked hearts. Not everybody does.'

'No, I don't think my husband does,' said Jane.

'The vicar doesn't like hearts? Oh, I must remember that.' Mrs Glaze nodded her head and stopped in her dusting as if to let the fact sink into her memory.

'But Mr Driver gave me to understand that he did his own cooking,' she said.

'Well, madam, I dare say he might make a cup of coffee or boil an egg; you know how men are.'

'Yes, of course,' Jane agreed. 'The church is going to look very nice, I think.'

'Oh, Mother, you always say that,' said Flora, Mrs Glaze having left them alone together. 'And you never really notice.'

'No, I notice the things one shouldn't,' said Jane.

She thought of this again the following evening when she

and Flora were sitting in their pew at Evensong and she found herself regretting that they were not sitting further back, where they could have had a better view of the congregation. Fabian Driver was on a level with them at the other side. When they came into the church he had looked up and half smiled at Jane; it was the sort of smile one could give in church or to a very intimate friend. Miss Morrow and Miss Doggett and a few elderly ladies in yellowish brown fur coats were in the front pews. But apart from them Jane could see hardly anybody. It was not until the time for the collection came and a bag was handed to her that she realized that it must be Mr Mortlake standing there, deferential yet expectant, appearing confident of the folded note or couple of half-crowns that would be slipped into it. But Jane had been taken unawares and a desperate fumbling in her purse produced only a threepenny bit and two pennies. She felt almost as if she should apologize to the tall, elderly man with the beaky nose waiting so patiently there, for surely he must have seen her miserable offering.

'Oh, dear,' she whispered to Flora, 'I hadn't got the right money. I'm sure he noticed.'

But Flora wasn't really listening to what her mother said. Her eyes were fixed on the back of the young man in one of the front pews who had read the second lesson. Tall, with fairish wavy hair and a thin, spiritual-looking face; he looked a little tired, perhaps even hungry. She must persuade her mother to ask him to supper some time.

I suppose that's the one Mr Mortlake doesn't like reading the lessons, Mr Oliver or some such name, thought Jane, trying to get him clear in her mind. But she soon lost interest, and found herself turning her attention to Mr Driver and wondering, though very faintly, if he might perhaps do for her friend Prudence?

CHAPTER FOUR

PRUDENCE, unlike Jane and her family, had attended no kind of Harvest Thanksgiving service, and got up on Monday morning thinking of nothing but the week's work ahead of her and the rapture and misery and boredom of her love for Arthur Grampian.

When she reached the vague cultural organization where she worked for him, she found that Miss Trapnell and Miss Clothier, who worked in the same room, had already arrived. Miss Trapnell was putting on her mauve office cardigan, while Miss Clothier arranged some leaves of an indefinite species in a jar on top of the filing-cabinet. Miss Trapnell's garment was shrunken and not altogether clean, but she did not believe in wearing 'good' clothes for the office. Prudence often wondered when she blossomed out in these so-called 'good' clothes which she was reputed to possess and what company was considered special enough to deserve them. Both Miss Trapnell and Miss Clothier were of an indeterminate age, though it was rumoured that Miss Clothier had passed her fiftieth birthday. There existed between the three of them a kind of neutral relationship and they banded together against the inconsiderateness of their employer and the follies and carelessness of the two young typists. Besides the three women and the two girls there was also a young man, Mr Manifold, a kind of 'research assistant' who had a little room to himself and kept to his own mysterious business.

Prudence sat down at her table and wished as she always did that she could have a room of her own. Her status, though somewhat indefinite, was higher than that of Miss Trapnell and Miss Clothier, but they had been there longer, which gave them a slight advantage. If one were asked point-blank it would really be difficult to say what any of them, even Dr Grampian, actually did; perhaps the young typists' duties were the most clearly defined, for it was certain that they made tea, took shorthand and typed letters which did not always make sense. However, on this Monday morning Prudence put on her pale-blue-rimmed interestingly-shaped spectacles, took a bundle of proofs and a typescript from a wire tray, and began to apply herself to them. Miss Trapnell went to the filing-cabinet and put some pieces of paper into a file, and Miss Clothier drew a small card index towards her and began moving the cards here and there with her fingers, as if she were coaxing music from some delicate instrument.

'I wonder if we might have one bar of the fire on?' asked Miss Clothier at last.

'Oh, it isn't cold,' said Miss Trapnell. 'Do you find it cold, Miss Bates?'

Prudence disliked being called 'Miss Bates'; if she resembled any character in fiction, it was certainly not poor silly Miss Bates. And yet how could Miss Trapnell and Miss Clothier call her anything else? And how could she call them Ella and Gertrude?

'No. It doesn't seem cold,' she said.

'Well, of course I have been sitting here since a quarter to ten,' said Miss Clothier. 'So perhaps I have got cold sitting.'

'Ah, yes; you may have got cold sitting,' agreed Miss Trapnell. 'I have only been here since *five* to ten.'

Prudence, who had arrived at ten past ten, made no comment and indeed none was necessary. The hours of work were officially ten till six, but Prudence considered herself too highly educated to be bound by them. Her fine brain, which was now puzzling over a misplaced footnote, could not be expected to function under such stupidly rigid conditions. She always expressed herself as very willing to stay long after six o'clock should Dr Grampian want her to, but he very seldom did, being only too anxious to hurry away to his club or even to his home.

And yet it had been on one of those rare late evenings, when they had been sitting together over a manuscript, that Prudence's love for him, if that was what it was, had suddenly flared up. Perhaps 'flared' was too violent a word, but Prudence thought of it afterwards as having been like that. She remembered herself standing by the window, looking out on to an early spring evening with the sky a rather clear blue just before the darkness came, not really seeing anything or thinking about very much; perhaps an odd detail here and there had impressed itself upon her mind – she liked to think that it had – the twitter of starlings, a lighted window in another building – and then suddenly it had come to her. *Oh, my love* . . . rushing in like that. And as there had been at that time a temporary emptiness in her heart she had let it rush in, and now here it was with her always, a constant companion or a pain like a rheumatic twinge in the knee when one neared the end of a long flight of stairs. It was also on that occasion that Arthur Grampian had for a moment laid his hand on hers and said for no apparent reason, 'Ah, Prudence . . .' She had thought at the time that he might be going to kiss her, but it had not come to that; he had merely taken his hand away and said in his usual flat tone, 'Well, thank you, Miss Bates, I'm afraid I've kept you rather late. You'd better run along home now.' And so she had gone through these last months with nothing more than this 'Ah, Prudence . . .' to hug to her heart and take out and brood over numerous times a day. For nothing had happened since and he had never again even called her by her Christian name. He had gone to his club and home to his wife Lucy and his children Susan and Barnabas, and Prudence, for want of better material, had built up the negative relationship of which she had spoken to Jane at the Old Students' week-end, the negative relationship with the something positive that must surely be there underneath it all.

'Surely it must be tea-time, or is the milk late again?' said Miss Clothier. 'I had a very early breakfast this morning and I'm just dying for a cup of tea.'

'You can hardly call it the cup that cheers,' said Miss Trapnell. 'If only those girls wouldn't pour it all out at once and then leave it standing for about ten minutes. I've told them I don't know how many times.'

'It would be better if we made the tea ourselves,' suggested Prudence.

'But, Miss Bates, we couldn't do that,' said Miss Clothier in a shocked tone. 'It wouldn't do at all.'

'No; I suppose it wouldn't,' Prudence agreed.

But at that moment a sound was heard outside the door and a pretty girl of about seventeen dressed in the height of fashion pushed her way through the door carrying a tray from which poured a stream of weak-looking tea.

'Oh, Marilyn, why don't you put the cups and saucers separately on the tray?' said Miss Clothier fussily. 'Then you wouldn't slop it all into the saucers.'

'Sorry, Miss Clothier,' said the girl cheerfully. 'I was hurrying to get tea over before *He* came in.'

'But Dr Grampian will want a cup when he comes,' said Miss Clothier.

'He's had it, then. We've run out of tea; that's why I had to make it so weak. I couldn't add any more water to what's left in the pot.'

'I'm sure that shouldn't have happened,' said Miss Trapnell sharply. 'It isn't the end of the ration period yet. We *can't* have used all the tea.'

Somebody was heard walking past the door.

Marilyn threw up her hands in a comical gesture. 'What did I tell you? There he is!'

'But surely there's some Oxo or Nescafé or something,' said Prudence in a faint voice. She had no wish to become involved in this trivial controversy, but the thought of Arthur having to go without his elevenses was quite unbearable. Not that the tea was even drinkable.

'Mr Manifold has a tin of Nescafé, but he always makes it himself and keeps it locked up in his cupboard.'

'Then somebody must go and ask Mr Manifold if he would mind Dr Grampian having a little of it,' persisted Prudence.

Miss Trapnell and Miss Clothier turned away and busied themselves with their files and card-indexes with an air of it being none of their business.

'Oh, Miss Bates, *I* couldn't ask Mr Manifold,' giggled Marilyn. 'I don't mind making it if you'll ask him, Miss Bates.'

'Very well, then.' Prudence rose from her table and followed Marilyn out of the room.

Miss Trapnell and Miss Clothier exchanged glances.

'Would you like a biscuit, Miss Clothier?' asked Miss Trapnell in a rather ceremonial voice. She opened a little tin and offered it to her companion. 'These are Lincoln cream. My grocer always saves them for me.'

'Thank you,' said Miss Clothier. 'I wonder if Dr Grampian would like one?'

'I shan't offer them. He gets a good lunch at his club and I expect he had a good breakfast.'

'Miss Bates might not like it if you were to give him biscuits,' said Miss Clothier obscurely.

'There would be nothing in it if I did,' said Miss Trapnell. 'I believe I have offered him one before now when the occasion called for it. Naturally, I shouldn't go out of my way to do it.'

'Oh, no. I certainly wouldn't take the trouble that Miss Bates does. Dr Grampian isn't really the kind of man I should fancy for myself.'

'You'd think Miss Bates could do better. After all, she's very good-looking and smart. Besides, Dr Grampian is married.'

'Well, what is there for her here?' asked Miss Clothier. 'She obviously thinks herself too good for Mr Manifold.'

Prudence knocked at Mr Manifold's door, and then was annoyed at herself for doing so. After all, it wasn't his bedroom; she had a perfect right to walk straight in.

He was a thin, dark young man in the late twenties who kept himself very much to himself, either because he was naturally of a retiring disposition or because he felt his position as the only man in the office apart from Dr Grampian. It was thought that he sometimes unbent with the typists, but Prudence did not like to imagine what form this unbending could take.

At Prudence's entry he looked up from his table, where he seemed to be sorting out sheets of paper covered with his spidery writing.

'I hear you have a tin of Nescafé,' she began rather aggressively.

'Yes, I have,' he said unhelpfully.

'Well, I was wondering if you would lend it for Dr Grampian to have some.'

'But isn't he going to have tea? The girls have only just made it.'

'No, there isn't enough tea. The ration was used up and no more water could be added to the pot. You see, there wasn't enough tea to begin with and it would be impossibly weak if water was added,' said Prudence, despising herself for going into such a long, tedious explanation.

'Well, personally, I like weak tea,' said Mr Manifold, 'when I drink it at all, which isn't often. Still I suppose Gramp should have some coffee to keep him awake,' he added on a sarcastic note, opening a drawer in his table and taking out a tin. 'Mind you return it, though.'

'Of course,' said Prudence scornfully. 'Thank you very much.' She didn't like the way Mr Manifold called Arthur Grampian 'Gramp'. It was just the kind of silly, obvious name he would think of, and she suspected that the girls also used it among themselves.

She took the tin to Marilyn, who made the coffee and went to Dr Grampian's door with it. Prudence heard her go in and presumably place the cup on his desk, but she was not to know that it lay there untouched until it was removed by the cleaner who came in that evening, and she returned to her proofs with the feeling of having done something more worthwhile than emending footnotes and putting in French accents.

The morning wore on and Dr Grampian did not send for her. At twelve Miss Clothier got up to go to her lunch, again remarking that she had been here since a quarter to ten and really felt quite hungry. Some time after that Miss Trapnell produced a packet of sandwiches from her hold-all and took out the green openwork jumper she was knitting. At half-past twelve Dr Grampian was heard to leave the office. At a quarter to one Prudence went out for her own lunch.

On her way to the restaurant she passed Arthur Grampian's club, with its noble portals, into which undistinguished-looking but probably famous men could be seen hurrying. She imagined Arthur himself in conversation with professors and bishops. But did they talk? she wondered. Wasn't it quite likely that they concentrated solely on the business of eating? Men alone, eating in a rather grand club with noble portals – and women alone, eating in a small, rather grimy restaurant which did a lunch for three and sixpence, including coffee. While Arthur Grampian was shaking the red pepper on to his smoked salmon, Prudence was having to choose between the shepherd's pie and the stuffed marrow.

While she ate she turned the pages of a book of Coventry Patmore's poems; the Blackbird was breaking the Young Day's heart as her fork toyed with her food. But the book remained open there, and after a while she stopped reading and became conscious of herself sitting alone at a table that could have held two. She was still young enough – and when does one become too old? – to wonder if people were looking at her and asking themselves, 'Who is that interesting-looking young woman, sitting alone and reading Coventry Patmore?' But it was altogether unlikely in this kind of restaurant, she realized, where it was obvious that people were eating seriously and with too much concentration to notice anybody else.

'Is this seat taken?' asked a man's voice.

Prudence looked up suspiciously. 'No,' she said in rather a nervous tone.

The man took off his raincoat and sat down. He was middle-aged with a small moustache. Prudence handed him the menu without looking at him. She felt she couldn't bear it if he should begin to talk to her.

'You must have a good lunch,' said a woman's voice from the next table. They were evidently together, but had failed to find a table for two. 'It'll be pretty late before you get your supper.'

'Well, I don't feel much like eating. Seven-thirty to eight the visiting hours are. I suppose I could get a snack before that.'

'Madge will be looking forward to seeing you,' said the woman. 'But you mustn't expect to see her looking too grand, you know.'

'No, it'll be a shock to the system, won't it, the operation? She won't feel like much, but I thought I'd take her a few grapes. . . .'

The lump in Prudence's throat made it difficult for her to speak, but she managed to offer to change places so that the man and woman could be at the same table. They thanked her and the change was made. Prudence sat for the rest of the meal, listening to her neighbours' conversation, her eyes full of tears. Disliking humanity in general, she was one of those excessively tender-hearted people who are greatly moved by the troubles of complete strangers, in which she sometimes imagined herself playing a noble part. The man sitting at her table, who had at first appeared to be a bore or even a menace, was now proved to be an object of interest. There was both nobility and pathos about him.

She was just walking to the cash desk to pay her bill when

she noticed a young man sitting at one of the tables. It was Mr Manifold. He was eating – perhaps 'tucking into' would describe it better – the steamed pudding which Prudence had avoided as being too fattening. She had never seen him eating before and now she averted her eyes quickly, for there was something indecent about it, as if a mantle had fallen and revealed more of him than she ought to see. Of course the women in the office had known that he lunched somewhere – indeed, they had even speculated on where he went; perhaps the vastness of the Corner House swallowed him up or the manly security of a public-house lapped him round. Prudence hurried out of the restaurant feeling disturbed and irritated. Had he ever been there before, she wondered? She hoped he wasn't going to make a habit of frequenting the places she went to. It would be annoying if she had to change her own routine.

When she got back into her room, Miss Trapnell and Miss Clothier were sitting virtuously in their places, occupied with the same rather indefinite tasks as before lunch. Prudence settled down to her proofs again and began to feel sleepy; she even took a few minutes' nap, covering her eyes with her hand. Outside all was quiet; Dr Grampian did not come in again. No visitors called. At a quarter to four Miss Trapnell and Miss Clothier began to speculate on the possibility of tea – whether it would be punctual or not. Eventually the clatter of the tray was heard and Gloria, the other typist, brought it into the room. Miss Trapnell opened her tin of biscuits, Miss Clothier took a slice of homemade cake from a paper bag; Prudence ate nothing, but lit a cigarette. And so the hours went on until it was a quarter to six.

'I think I am justified in leaving a little *before* six tonight,' declared Miss Clothier. 'I arrived here at *twenty* to ten this morning and was sitting down to work at a quarter to.' She looked at Prudence and Miss Trapnell as if challenging them to contradict her.

'Oh, certainly,' said Prudence in a bored way.

'Well, I think I shall stay till six,' said Miss Trapnell, 'although I was actually here between ten and five to ten this morning, so I could really leave a *little* before six. But I think I'll just finish what I am doing; it's rather unsatisfactory to leave a piece of work half-done.'

'I quite agree! But sometimes one has to make a break if a thing can't be finished within a reasonable time,' said Miss Clothier. 'I shouldn't at all mind staying until *half past* six if I thought I could finish what I've been doing, but to do that I should have to stay until about eleven o'clock' – she gave a little laugh – 'and I'm sure Dr Grampian wouldn't expect me to do that.'

Prudence swallowed down her irritation. How could they presume to know what he expected?

'He seems to expect little and yet much,' said Miss Trapnell obscurely. 'One wouldn't like to fall short.'

'He has never complained about *my* work,' said Miss Clothier in rather a huffy tone.

'Oh, I didn't mean to suggest anything like that,' said Miss Trapnell with a look at Prudence; they both found Miss Clothier a little 'difficult' at times.

'Won't you miss your train if you don't hurry?' suggested Prudence.

'There are other trains,' said Miss Clothier. 'I shouldn't like anyone to think I was a clock-watcher.'

'But surely we are all that to some extent,' said Prudence. 'We should hardly be human if we didn't notice when it was tea-time or feel glad when the end of the day came.'

'Well, I am certainly going now,' said Miss Trapnell, gathering her things together. 'Don't stay too late, Miss Bates,' she added in a jocular tone. 'We shouldn't like to think of *you* being here till eleven.'

At last they had both gone. Prudence finished the page she was reading and then began to prepare to go home. But she did it rather slowly. Sometimes Dr Grampian came in at six o'clock and worked quietly by himself until dinner-time. But tonight was evidently not to be one of those evenings. Prudence had given up hope as she went out of the door and heard a step behind her.

'Did you enjoy your lunch, Miss Bates?'

It was Mr Manifold. There was a hint of roguishness in his tone. So he had noticed her after all.

'Neither more nor less than usual,' said Prudence. 'It isn't the kind of place where one gets an *enjoyable* meal.'

'Well, I thought I'd try it,' said Mr Manifold, walking by her side. 'But I could have eaten it all twice over.'

'You men have such enormous appetites,' said Prudence, conscious of being rather kittenish.

'You seemed more interested in your book than in the food,' said Mr Manifold. 'What were you so deep in?'

'Just Coventry Patmore,' said Prudence coldly.

'Ah, Coventry Patmore. Just your cup of tea, I should think.

> '*My heart was dead,*
> *Dead of devotion and tired memory . . .*

Look, that's my bus and I think I can get it if I run. Do excuse me, won't you. Goodbye!'

Prudence remained rooted to the spot; really, there was no other way to describe it. That he should even have *heard* of Coventry Patmore! And then to quote those lines, those telling lines. What was it he had said? Just your cup of tea, I should think. . . . What exactly did he mean by that? It sounded almost as if he had studied her and thought about her and what her tastes were likely to be, as if he had noticed things about her, perhaps even her feeling for Arthur Grampian. It was most annoying and disturbing. She pushed her way angrily on to a bus and stood huddled with the others inside.

She had calmed down by the time she arrived at her flat. As if it mattered what Geoffrey Manifold thought about her! He was a dull young man who kept his private tin of Nescafé locked in a drawer. It was impertinent of him to ask her what she had been reading. She wished now that she hadn't told him.

There was a letter on the mat when she got in. It was from Jane, a bubbling, incoherent sort of letter full of underlinings.

> 'Dearest Prue, such *richness* here! I suppose you would say that we are really getting *settled*, though I still don't seem to have unpacked all my clothes and have just been *burrowing* in a trunk to find Nicholas a *clean surplice*! If only they could have them made of paper and just throw them away when they're dirty – or even of *nylon* – dare say American clergymen do. I always remember when I went to Dresden as a girl and attended the American church there, it was the best heated building in the town and there were little gold stars on the ceiling! Anyway, such *richness*! The secretary of the parochial church Council is called Mr Mortlake; he is a tall dignified gentleman with the look of an eagle about him and he is also a *piano tuner*. There seems to be a kind of feud between him and a young man, a bank-clerk who sometimes reads the lessons. Flora finds him rather attractive, I believe. Oh, to be young again! Then there is Mr Fabian Driver, a disconsolate widower but very fascinating. I believe he eats the hearts of his victims *en casserole*. He looks more like a lion, or *lyon*, so we are surrounded by the noblest of God's creatures.'

Prudence read on, for there was much more in the same strain. At the end she managed to disentangle the news that Jane hoped to come up to Town soon 'ostensibly to visit Mowbrays and buy holy books', but she insisted that Prudence should meet her for lunch somewhere, when she would tell her '*all* about *everything*'.

She put the letter back into its envelope and poured herself a gin and French. She always enjoyed getting home in the evening to her pretty little flat with what Jane called its 'rather uncomfortable Regency furniture'. When she had finished her drink she went to the kitchen and started to prepare her supper. Although she was alone, it was not a meal to be ashamed of. There was a little garlic in the oily salad and the cheese was nicely ripe. The table was laid with all the proper accompaniments and the coffee which followed the meal was not made out of a tin or bottle.

It had been a trying day, Prudence decided, though she could not have said exactly why. No sign of Arthur Grampian, the slightly upsetting lunch – that poor man would be sitting at Madge's bedside now, leaning slightly forward in his chair, waiting for her pale lips to move in speech – the impudence of Mr Manifold, the perpetual irritation of Miss Trapnell and Miss Clothier – any one of these things would have been enough and she had had them all. So she decided to go to bed early and read a book. It was not a very nice book – so often Miss Trapnell or Miss Clothier asked her 'Is that a nice book you've got, Miss Bates?' – but it described a love affair in the fullest sense of the word and sparing no detail, but all in a very intellectual sort of way and there were a good many quotations from Donne. It was difficult to imagine that her love for Arthur Grampian could ever come to anything like this, and indeed she was hardly conscious of him as she read on into the small hours of the morning to the book's inevitable but satisfying unhappy ending.

CHAPTER FIVE

JANE KEPT the thought of a day in London as a treat to buoy her up as she went about doing those tasks in the parish that seemed within her powers. She kept thinking of all the things she would tell Prudence when she saw her and even began to speculate on where they should have lunch and what they should eat. The day after she had written to Prudence, Mrs Glaze was, for some mysterious reason which Jane did not dare to ask, unable to come, so that the problem of meals had to be solved by Jane herself, as Flora had gone out for the day to visit a school-friend.

'I think, darling,' she said, going into Nicholas's study just before lunch-time, 'it would be better if we had lunch *out* today.'

Nicholas looked over the top of his spectacles with a mild, kindly look, obviously not having heard what she said.

Mild, kindly looks and spectacles, thought Jane; this was what it all came to in the end. The passion of those early days, the fragments of Donne and Marvell and Jane's obscurer seventeenth-century poets, the objects of her abortive research, all these faded away into mild, kindly looks and spectacles. There came a day when one didn't quote poetry to one's husband any more. When had that day been? Could she have noted it and mourned it if she had been more observant?

'What doth my she-advowson fly
Incumbency?'

she murmured. Unsuitable, of course, but she loved the lines.

'What, dear?' said Nicholas, not looking up this time.

'I don't know,' said Jane. 'I've forgotten what I wanted to say.'

'You did say something. Something about going out.'

'Yes, lunch. I really think it would be better if we went out today.'

'Why today especially?'

'Well, you see, Mrs Glaze isn't here and neither is Flora, and I really don't know what we should have,' said Jane a little desperately.

'Couldn't we open a tin or something?'

'A tin of *what*? That's the point.'

'Oh, meat of some kind. Spam or whatever you call it.'

'But, darling, there isn't Spam any more. It came from America during the war and we don't get it now.'

'Then there isn't anything to eat in the house? Is that what you're trying to tell me?' asked Nicholas quite good-humouredly.

'Yes, that is the position. Mrs Glaze did say something about there being sausages at the butcher if one went *early*, but I'm afraid I forgot, and now it's nearly half-past twelve,' said Jane guiltily.

'Well,' said Nicholas, standing up, 'we may as well go out. Should we go now?'

Jane put on an old tweed coat which hung in the hall – the kind of coat one might have used for feeding the chickens in – and they went out together. They stood uncertainly outside the front gate, wondering which direction to go in, and then wandered off past the church with no clear idea of where they were to have their meal.

'*I* know,' said Jane suddenly. 'Mrs Crampton and Mrs Mayhew! They run a café, don't they? The Spinning Wheel, I think it is.'

'The Spinning Wheel,' repeated Nicholas doubtfully. 'That doesn't sound as if it would provide us with lunch. Are you sure it isn't just one of those places that sells home-spun scarves and things like that?'

'No, I'm certain they do provide meals as well. In fact, I had a conversation with them about it in church when they were doing the Harvest Festival decorations.'

Eventually they came to the Spinning Wheel, and although there were a number of home-made-looking objects of an artistic nature in the window, there was also a menu written in a gentlewoman's flowing hand pinned up at the side of the door.

'It looks very quiet,' said Jane as they stood on the threshold; 'there's nobody here at all.'

'Perhaps people don't lunch till one,' Nicholas suggested.

'No, that may be it. Shall we sit in the window? Then we shall be able to see what happens.'

They chose a table in the window and sat down to look out at the deserted street.

'I expect they were all early at the butcher's and got sausages,' said Jane, 'and now they are all eating toad-in-the-hole.'

'I don't think I should like *that*,' said Nicholas in a more definite tone than his usual one.

There was a movement behind them, and Jane looked up to see Mrs Crampton herself standing by the table.

'Good morning, vicar, and Mrs Cleveland,' she said. 'What would you like?' She handed them a menu which offered them a choice between toad-in-the-hole or curried beef.

'Oh, dear,' Jane burst out, 'I'm afraid I don't like curry and my husband can't take toad, so could we just have the soup and a sweet, perhaps?'

'How would you like an egg and some bacon?' said Mrs Crampton, lowering her voice.

'That would be fine,' said Nicholas.

'Could you really manage that?' asked Jane.

'Oh, yes, we can sometimes, you know, but not for everyone, of course. And you'd like the soup, would you?'

They said that they would, and Mrs Crampton hurried away behind a velvet curtain at the far end of the café.

'Why did you say, "my husband can't take toad"?' asked Nicholas, shaking with suppressed laughter. 'It sounded so very odd.'

'I don't know. I think I wasn't conscious of having said it until I did. I must have thought she would expect me to say something like that.'

Mrs Crampton brought the soup, which they finished, and there was a long silence. Neither Jane nor Nicholas spoke and nobody came into the café. After a time Jane heard sounds from behind the velvet curtain, the low mumbling of voices and the hiss of frying. At last Mrs Crampton emerged from behind the velvet curtain carrying two plates on a tray. She put in front of Jane a plate containing an egg, a rasher of bacon and some fried potatoes cut in fancy shapes, and in front of Nicholas a plate with *two* eggs and rather more potatoes.

Nicholas exclaimed with pleasure.

'Oh, a man needs eggs!' said Mrs Crampton, also looking pleased.

This insistence on a man's needs amused Jane. Men needed meat and eggs – well, yes, that might be allowed; but surely not more than women did? Perhaps Mrs Crampton's widowhood had something to do with it; possibly she made up for having no man to feed at home by ministering to the needs of those who frequented her café.

Nicholas accepted his two eggs and bacon and the implication that his needs were more important than his wife's with a certain amount of complacency, Jane thought. But then as a clergyman he had had to get used to accepting flattery and gifts gracefully; it had not come easily to him in the early stages. Being naturally of a modest and retiring nature, he had not been able to see why he should be singled out.

'This is delicious,' said Jane, hoping that Mrs Crampton wasn't going to stay and watch them eat their meal.

'Do you find that many people come here for lunch?' asked Nicholas.

'Well, we have a few regulars, you know, and "casuals" as we call them. Mr Oliver is one of our "regulars" – he always comes at a quarter past one. He works in the Bank, you know, and I don't think his landlady does lunch for him; just breakfast and an evening meal.'

'Poor Mr Oliver,' said Jane, scenting pathos. He certainly looked very pale reading the lessons on Sunday evenings, but perhaps that was just a trick of the lighting. She hurried to finish her egg and bacon in case he should come in and see them at it without being able to have it himself.

'Ah, here he is.' Mrs Crampton opened the door with a gesture of welcome and Mr Oliver took his seat at a small table in the corner. He nodded and poured out a glass of water. She then disappeared behind the velvet curtain.

'Good morning, vicar,' said Mr Oliver, 'or good afternoon, perhaps, though it always seems morning until one has had lunch.'

Nicholas introduced Jane to Mr Oliver and they began a rather stilted conversation across the café. Jane was embarrassed because Nicholas had not yet finished his last egg, and hoped Mr Oliver wasn't noticing.

'You must come and have tea with us one Sunday,' said Jane. Flora would certainly like to meet him, though she might be a little disappointed in him. He did not appear to have much to say for himself and his suit was of rather too bright a blue to be quite the thing, Jane felt. Still, tea would be quite easy to manage, and they arranged that he should come the very next Sunday.

Mrs Crampton now returned and set down before Mr Oliver a plate laden with roast chicken and all the proper accompaniments. He accepted it with quite as much complacency as Nicholas had accepted his eggs and bacon and began to eat.

Jane turned away, to save his embarrassment. Man needs bird, she thought. Just the very best, that is what man needs.

'Does Mr Fabian Driver ever come here, I wonder?' she said to her husband.

'Fabian Driver? How on earth should I know?' said Nicholas indulgently.

They ate their sweet – stewed plums and rice pudding – and drank a cup of surprisingly good coffee. Then Nicholas called for the bill. 'I do hope you are coming to the whist drive,' said Mrs Crampton. 'I can sell you some tickets.'

'Whist drive?' asked Nicholas. 'Is there going to be a whist drive? I haven't heard anything about it.'

'Oh, not a *Church* whist drive,' said Mrs Crampton, smiling. 'This is just in aid of Party funds, you know. It is not until early in December, but there will be a big demand for tickets. Mr Lyall himself has promised to be there and even Mrs Lyall, if she can. It will be quite an occasion.'

'We should like to come,' said Jane. 'I haven't met our Member yet. May we have four tickets, please?'

'Miss Doggett is organizing it, and Mrs Mayhew and I are to be in charge of refreshments.'

'That is certainly an inducement for anyone to come,' said Nicholas in his best manner. They said goodbye and went out, leaving Mr Oliver to his bird.

'If only I could get Prudence to come for that week-end,' said Jane. 'It might be just the thing for her.'

'I hardly think a village whist drive could do much for Prudence,' said Nicholas. 'I've often wondered why she doesn't take up social work of some kind.'

'Now you are talking like a clergyman, or like Miss Birkinshaw, our old tutor,' said Jane crossly. 'You imagine Prue "fulfilling herself" by sitting on some committee to arrange amenities for the "poor".'

'She doesn't go to church at all, does she?' asked Nicholas tentatively. 'That seems a pity.'

'Well, I suppose it does,' said Jane; 'especially in London, when you think what a choice there is.'

Nicholas sighed and left the subject.

Fabian Driver, doing his pre-lunch drinking in the bar of the Golden Lion, looked out and saw Nicholas and Jane walking home. He had a confused feeling of irritation and envy as he watched them. It must have been Jane's smiling up at her husband and the awful old coat she was wearing, the kind of coat a woman could wear only in her husband's presence, he thought. For a moment he was tempted to call out to them, to invite them in for a drink, even. But the moment passed, and anyway it was half-past one, time for Fabian to go home to what he called his 'solitary meal'.

'That was the new vicar and his wife,' he remarked to the lady behind the bar. 'I might have asked them in for a drink.'

'Oh, Mr Driver!' she giggled.

'Well, what would have been so funny about it?'

'I was just thinking of the Canon and Mrs Pritchard. You wouldn't have had them coming in here.'

'No, certainly not. Perhaps the Clevelands wouldn't have come either. I dare say they've been having lunch at the Spinning Wheel.'

There was nobody left in the bar now except Fabian. He sat idly, contemplating his reflection in the looking-glass framed with mahogany and surrounded by bottles.

'Mrs Arkright'll be giving you what for if you don't hurry home to lunch,' said the lady behind the bar good-humouredly. 'I expect she's got something tasty for you.'

Fabian put down his glass. 'Well, yes, I may as well go.'

'That's it,' she said comfortably. 'I don't like to think of your dinner spoiling.'

No, Fabian thought, it wouldn't do for it to get spoilt. It did not occur to him that perhaps she was wanting to get her own meal.

He walked slowly down the main street, past the collection of old and new buildings that lined it. The Parish Church and the vicarage were at the other end of the village. Here he came to the large Methodist Chapel, but of course one couldn't go there; none of the people one knew went to chapel, unless out of a kind of amused curiosity. Even if truth were to be found there. A little further on, though, as was fitting, on the opposite side of the road, was the little tin hut which served as a place of worship for the Roman Catholics. Fabian knew Father Kinsella, a good-looking Irishman, who often came into the bar of the Golden Lion for a drink. He had even thought of going to his church once or twice, but somehow it had never come to anything. The makeshift character of the building, the certain discomfort that he would find within, the plaster images in execrable taste, the simplicity of Father Kinsella's sermons intended only for a congregation of Irish labourers and servant-girls – all these kept him away. The glamour of Rome was obviously not *there*.

There remained only the Church of England, and here there was at least a choice between the Parish Church and Father Lomax's church – in the next village, but still within reasonable distance. It was natural to Fabian's temperament to prefer a High Church service, incense and good music, vestments and processions, but Father Lomax discouraged idle sightseers and expected his congregation to accept the less comfortable parts of the Faith – going to Confession, and getting up to sing Mass at half-past six on a winter morning. So there was really nothing for it but to go to the Parish Church, where, even if the service was less exotic, the yoke was easier. Also, the Parish Church was older and had some interesting wall tablets and monuments. Fabian often imagined a tablet to himself put up in the church, though he never stopped to consider who should put it up or why.

His own house was one of several standing round the little green with its chestnut trees and pond which formed the real centre of the village. As he pushed open the gate and walked up the path, bordered now with fine pompom dahlias, he saw that Mrs Arkright in her hat and apron was standing in the open doorway.

'Oh, Mr Driver,' she said reproachfully, 'I was wondering what had happened to you. I've a piece of steak for you and I didn't want to start grilling it until you came. We can't afford to spoil meat nowadays, can we?'

Fabian went into the little hall and then out of the drawing-room french windows into his garden, which was a long stretch of grass with a fine walnut tree in the middle of it, and at the end a vegetable patch and a group of apple trees.

Next door to him on one side was the doctor and on the other Miss Doggett and Miss Morrow. Miss Morrow was in the garden now, cutting early chrysanthemums which grew near to the fence separating the two gardens.

'Ah, cutting flowers,' said Fabian.

'Yes, cutting flowers,' said Miss Morrow, in a bright tone.

Yes, she was undeniably cutting flowers, thought Fabian irritably. He wished he hadn't come out into the garden, for he found it difficult to make conversation with her. When his wife had been alive he had hardly noticed Jessie Morrow; indeed, if possible, he had noticed her even less than he had noticed his wife. Miss Doggett he knew, of course, but Miss Morrow had appeared always in her shadow, a thing without personality of her own, as neutral as her clothes.

Lately, however, he had become more conscious of her, though he could not have said exactly why or in what particular way. She did not seem to speak to him more than she ever had, but when he was with her he felt uncomfortable, as if she were laughing at him, or even as if she knew things about him that he didn't want known.

'Would you like some apples?' he asked, to break the silence. He glanced vaguely up at a tree.

'Thank you, but we really have plenty,' said Miss Morrow, indicating their own apple trees with a gesture.

Fabian felt rather foolish, for indeed Miss Doggett's garden had far more apple trees than his.

'Perhaps you would like some quinces when they are ripe?' she suggested. 'Our tree always does very well. You haven't a quince tree, have you?'

'Alas, no. Constance was so fond of quinces,' said Fabian sadly.

Constance was so fond of quinces! thought Miss Morrow scornfully. As if Fabian had known or cared what Constance was fond of – why, Miss Doggett had several times offered her quinces and she had always refused them!

'Mr Driver! Mr Driver!' Mrs Arkright came out on to the lawn calling. 'Your steak's ready!'

'Ah, my steak.' Fabian smiled. 'You will excuse me, Miss Morrow?'

'Of course. I shouldn't like to keep you from your steak. A man needs meat, as Mrs Crampton and Mrs Mayhew are always saying.' She waved her hand in dismissal.

Fabian hurried away, conscious of his need for meat and of the faintly derisive tone of Miss Morrow's remark, as if there were something comic about a man needing meat.

The dining-room was in the front of the house and was furnished with rather self-conscious good taste, a little too carefully arranged to be really comfortable. The general effect, as might have been expected, was Regency.

The steak was tender and perfectly cooked, as were the potatoes and french beans. Constance had not appreciated good food. She had been a gentle, faded looking woman, some years older than Fabian. She had been pretty when he had married her and had brought him a comfortable amount of money as well as a great deal of love. He had been unprepared for her death and outraged by it, for it had happened suddenly, without a long illness to prepare him, when he had been deeply involved in one of the little romantic affairs which he seemed to need, either to bolster up his self-respect or for some more obvious reason. The shock of it all had upset him considerably, and although there had been several women eager to console him, he had abandoned all his former loves, fancying himself more in the role of an inconsolable widower than as a lover. Indeed, it was now almost a year since he had thought of anybody but himself. But now he felt that he might start again. Constance would not have wished him to live alone, he felt. She had even invited his loves to the house for week-ends, and two women sitting together in deck-chairs under the walnut tree, having long talks about him, or so he had always imagined, had been a familiar sight when he happened to be looking out of an upper window. In reality they may have been talking of other things – life in general, cooking or knitting, for the loves always brought knitting or tapestry work with them as if to show Constance how nice they really were. But they would be talking a little awkwardly, as two women sharing the same man generally do; there would inevitably be some lack of spontaneity and frankness.

After lunch Fabian went upstairs and into the room which had been Constance's. It was almost like a room in a Victorian novel, where nothing belonging to the departed had been touched, but it was laziness and lack of enterprise rather than sentiment which had left clothes still hanging in the wardrobes and the silver-backed brushes and mirror still on the dressing-table. Perhaps he would ask somebody to help him to sort out these things and give them away. The new vicar's wife, Mrs Cleveland, might do it. She seemed to be a sensible sort of person. He could not ask Miss Morrow or anybody who had known Constance and his behaviour towards her to help him. He made up his mind to ask Jane Cleveland about it the next time he saw her.

By now he had moved over to the window and was looking out. Miss Morrow was still at the bottom of the next door garden. Surely she couldn't have been cutting flowers all this time? Suddenly, to his astonishment, he saw her glance up at his house and wave her hand, but the next time he looked she was gone, so that afterwards he was not sure whether she had really waved to him or whether he had imagined the whole incident.

CHAPTER SIX

'MOTHER,' SAID Flora the following Saturday, 'don't forget that Mr Oliver is coming to tea tomorrow. You said you'd asked him when you saw him having lunch the other day.'

'Why, yes, so I did,' said Jane. 'Well, I suppose Mrs Glaze might make a cake or we might get some from the Spinning Wheel.'

Mrs Glaze seemed a little uncertain about whether she would be able to make a cake and Jane thought she detected some unwillingness in her manner.

'I don't suppose he gets very good food at his lodgings,' she said, to encourage Mrs Glaze. 'I always feel so sorry for young men living in lodgings, especially on a Sunday afternoon. I wonder if he has a sitting-room with an aspidistra on a bamboo table in the window and a plush tablecloth with bobbles on it,' Jane mused, forgetting her audience, 'and some rather dreadful pictures, perhaps, even photographs of deceased relatives on the wall.'

'Mrs Walton has given him a very nice front room,' said Mrs Glaze, 'and there is a plant on a table in the window – an ornamental fern it is, a beautiful thing, better than he deserves.'

Jane changed the subject hastily. Perhaps it was not quite the thing to ask Mr Oliver to tea. Nicholas had seemed a little uncertain after she had done it. 'Are you going to ask all of them separately?' he asked rather fearfully. 'Shall we never have a Sunday afternoon in peace?'

'Of course, but Mr Oliver seemed quite a nice young man and as he lives by himself in lodgings I thought it would be a kindness,' said Jane. 'I certainly don't intend to ask all the Parochial Church Council, if that's what you mean.'

'Well, dear, I suppose you could hardly do that,' said Nicholas, 'I don't want Mortlake and Whiting and the others to feel in any way slighted, though.'

'Oh, we'll have a cup of tea and some buns after the next P.C.C. meeting,' said Jane airily; 'that will make up for it.'

'Can you eat and drink in the Choir Vestry?' asked Flora.

'We could have the meeting here, I suppose,' said Nicholas; 'there'd be plenty of room. Though,' he added doubtfully, 'it might be unsuitable to be lolling about in armchairs.'

'Well, they needn't loll,' said Jane; 'and there would probably be fewer disagreements and less unpleasantness if they were more comfortable. People don't realize the importance of the body nowadays – oh, I know the seventeenth-century poets did,' she added hastily, 'but not quite in the way I mean.'

'No, not quite,' said Nicholas, darting a fearful glance at her, for indeed he was not sure what she might quote, and with Flora in the room one must draw the line somewhere. 'Anyway,' he concluded, 'we shall have to see how things go.' He ambled off into his study conscious of having taken an easy way out, if it was a way out at all.

The next day after lunch Flora got out the best tea service and began washing the cups and plates, for it was some time since they had been used. Lovingly she swished the pink-and-gold china in the hot soapy water and dried each piece carefully on a clean cloth. Tea could be laid on the low table by the fire, she decided, with the cloth with the wide lace border. Mrs Glaze had eventually been persuaded to make a Victoria sandwich cake, there were little cakes from the Spinning Wheel and chocolate biscuits, and Flora intended to cut some cucumber sandwiches and what she thought of as 'wafer-thin' bread and butter. It would be a much better tea than was usually served at the vicarage; she only hoped her mother wouldn't spoil it all by making some facetious comment. She got everything ready, went up to change her dress and tidy herself, and then settled down by the fire with a nice Sunday afternoon kind of novel from the library. Jane was sitting on the other side of the fire with her feet up on a pouffe; there was a book open on her lap and the Sunday papers were spread out at her side, but she was not reading; she had 'dropped off', as she frequently did on a Sunday afternoon, and her head was drooping over against the back of the chair; her mouth was slightly open too. She had just been reading the review of a novel where a character was said to 'emerge triumphantly in the round', and somehow this had set her nodding. She was conscious of Flora coming into the room and she seemed to remember that she had said something about having cleaned the bath. 'But surely Mr Oliver won't want to have a bath at four o'clock in the afternoon,' she had said. After that all was blessed oblivion until the cruel shrilling of the front-door bell startled her into uttering a cry and sitting bolt upright in her chair.

'That must be him,' said Flora, her tone betraying signs of agitation also, 'but it's only half-past three.'

'Quickly, let me get out of the room,' cried Jane. Diana and her nymphs bathing could not have felt more embarrassed when surprised by Actaeon as Jane did at this moment. She gathered up the Sunday papers and fled from the room.

Flora hurried to the front door and found Mr Oliver standing there. He was wearing a dark suit, either in honour of tea at the vicarage or perhaps in anticipation of reading one of the lessons at Evensong. Seen at close quarters, he was naturally rather less pale and spiritual-looking than he had appeared in the kinder light of the church.

'I'm afraid I'm rather early,' he said. 'Mrs Cleveland just said tea and I wasn't quite sure what time to come.'

'Oh, you're not at all too early,' said Flora enthusiastically. 'Do come in. Perhaps you'd like to leave your raincoat in the hall.'

'Yes, thank you. I thought it safer to bring it. The sky looked rather overcast as I was leaving my lodgings, and I thought I felt a drop as I came up the drive.'

Flora looked up at the ceiling. 'I expect we need rain for the harvest,' she said.

'But the harvest is gathered.'

'Yes, of course, it must be. We've had Harvest Festival, haven't we?' And Mr Oliver had looked so beautiful against the autumnal background – the sheaves of wheat, the great jars of Michaelmas daisies and chrysanthemums, the grapes on the lectern.

Flora led the way into the drawing-room. It was empty.

'I'm afraid it looks rather untidy,' she said, going over to Jane's chair, plumping up a cushion and gathering up an odd sheet of one of the Sunday papers. 'I'm afraid my father isn't in yet – he's taking the Boys' Bible Class.'

There was a pause. What could she say next? Flora wondered. Mr Oliver did not seem to be very easy to talk to. She almost wished that her mother would come back; at least there would not be silence then.

Mr Oliver was looking round the room hopefully. He had noticed the table laid with a lace-edged cloth and a rather pretty tea-set, so there would be tea, and perhaps quite soon. He had not imagined himself alone with the vicar's schoolgirl daughter; in fact, he had hardly realized her existence until she came to the door. He had hoped to have a profitable talk with the vicar and perhaps with Mrs Cleveland too; otherwise he would have preferred to be in his lodgings, looking over the lesson he was to read that evening and perhaps practising some of it aloud. Mrs Walton, his landlady, always had her wireless on very loudly on Sunday afternoons, so that he could raise his voice without fear of being heard or of making himself ridiculous.

'I am going up to Oxford next week,' said Flora, to break the silence.

'Really, Miss Cleveland? Have you relatives there?'

'No. I mean I am going to the University.'

'Ah, to study. What subject, may I ask?'

'English Literature,' said Flora rather stiffly.

'Oh, I see.' Mr Oliver did not appear to have anything to

say about English Literature and Flora was glad when there was a sound at the door and Jane came into the room.

'Mr Oliver, how nice! I'm so glad you were able to come.'

Flora looked at her mother in astonishment. She had spent the time that had elapsed between her rushing from the room and her meeting with Mr Oliver in improving her appearance, or rather in altering it, for it was difficult to say whether the garments she now appeared in were any more suitable for the occasion than those she had been wearing before. Her dress, a patterned navy foulard with long sleeves, was really too light for October and was a little crushed, for, as Flora rightly guessed, it had been put away in a drawer since the last warm weather. She had also taken the trouble to change into silk stockings and a pair of very uncomfortable-looking navy shoes with pointed toes and high heels. Her face had been hastily dabbed with powder of rather too light a shade.

Mr Oliver rose to shake hands.

'I do hope my daughter has been entertaining you,' said Jane easily. 'I was suddenly called away,' she added, thinking as she said it that this was the kind of thing some clergy wrote in parish magazines when people had died. Called away or called home, they said.

'I expect you're very busy, and the vicar too,' said Mr Oliver.

'Ah, here is Nicholas coming in now,' said Jane, stepping carefully to the window in her tight shoes. 'Now we can have tea. Darling, go and put the kettle on, will you? I think everything else is ready.'

Flora went quietly from the room and Nicholas came in, rubbing his hands together and looking vaguely benevolent.

'Ah, good afternoon, Oliver, very glad to see you,' he murmured. 'Tea not ready yet?' he said, in the way men do, not pausing to consider that some woman may at that very moment be pouring the water into the pot. 'Teaching those lads is thirsty work.'

'Flora is just making it, dear,' said Jane, soothingly. 'Here she is.'

Mr Oliver sprang up to help her with the tray and soon they were comfortably settled round the fire.

Conversation did not flow very easily at first. There was too much passing of sandwiches and enquiries about who took sugar. Jane hardly ever remembered what even her own family's preferences were in this respect. When she had discharged her duties, she began to ask Mr Oliver about his work. It must be so interesting working in a bank, she thought.

'Interesting?' he echoed. 'Well, yes, it is in a way, I suppose.'

'I always think of the medieval banking houses in Florence; great times those must have been,' went on Jane rather wildly.

'I should think there have been a good many changes since then,' observed Nicholas drily. 'What department do you work in?'

'I'm in the Executor and Trustee Department at the moment,' said Mr Oliver.

'How that must put you in mind of your own mortality!' said Jane, clasping her hands under her chin in rather an affected way. 'You must see the worst and the best sides of people too – I believe it always comes out over money. Are you shut up in a room at the back of the bank, then? We shouldn't be able to go in and peer at you over the counter.'

'No, I am not visible to passers-by,' said Mr Oliver with a faint smile.

'What a disappointment,' said Jane, echoing her daughter's thoughts, for Flora had been very much cast down when she realized that it would not be possible to see him by going into the Bank on some pretext or other. It was not, unfortunately, the one where the Clevelands had their account. But it didn't really matter very much, she decided; she was beginning to fall out of love with him already. He was not so very interesting after all, and had hardly given her a glance. It had been nice of him to help her with the tray, but any man with reasonable manners would have done the same. Now he was talking to her father about the Parochial Church Council, a most boring subject. Something about Mr Mortlake and Mr Whiting. That was a kind of fish that always had its tail in its mouth, Flora thought, wanting to giggle. Apparently there was some complication about something, nothing 'overt', whatever that might be, nothing had been said but the feeling was there. Nicholas was just nodding and saying 'really' or 'oh dear' as if he didn't much want to be talking about it at all, but Mr Oliver's voice was going on and on. It was rather that kind of voice.

Jane wished he would go, so that she could have a fourth cup of tea, take off her tight shoes and finish reading the book reviews, but the party did not break up until Nicholas suddenly looked at his watch and it was discovered that they must all be getting ready for Evensong.

In church Mr Oliver again appeared glamorous, seen in the distance and the dim light; Flora's love came flooding back, so that she could hardly bear to look at him. His voice when he read the Lessons sounded different from when he was talking about the Parochial Church Council in the afternoon. She was reminded of a poem she had once read somewhere, something about my devotion more secure, woos thy *spirit* high and pure . . . . If she could find it, she would copy it out into her diary.

At supper afterwards Jane and Nicholas discussed what their visitor had been saying about Mr Mortlake and Mr Whiting.

'I couldn't quite follow,' said Jane; 'it all seemed rather obscure. For a moment I almost thought it was something to do with the men's lavatory in the church hall, the cistern or something, but how could that be?'

'Well, there is more to it than that,' said Nicholas guardedly. 'Though that does come into it. I'm wondering,' he went on quickly, fearing his wife's ready laughter, 'whether it was perhaps a mistake to ask Oliver to tea. If Mortlake and Whiting got to hear of it, there might be feeling.'

'Then we'll have them all to tea in turn,' said Jane comfortably, 'though goodness knows what we shall talk about. I should think they would be even more difficult than Mr Oliver.'

'Well, the Bank and the Church aren't always the easiest combination – I mean, the two together.'

'We should have asked him about his home,' said Jane regretfully, 'his mother and sisters. I'm sure he has sisters.'

'We didn't touch on his war career, either,' said Nicholas. 'That would have been a topic of conversation.'

'His triumphs in the Army,' said Jane.

'I don't think he served with any particular distinction.'

'I meant his triumphs with women,' Jane explained. 'He might have had those, but I suppose they were hardly suitable topics of conversation for a vicarage tea party. Even the water-tank in the church hall was more in keeping.'

Nicholas sighed. 'Yes, one does rather long for the talk of intelligent people sometimes – people of one's own kind, I mean.'

Jane laughed. 'Oh, that would be too much! Besides, we might not be equal to it now.'

CHAPTER SEVEN

JANE STOOD on the platform waiting for the train which was to take her to the junction where she would change to the London train. It was a cold November day and she had dressed herself up in layers of cardigans and covered the whole lot with her old tweed coat, the one she might have used for feeding the chickens in. Her hat, however, was quite smart, out of keeping with her other garments, since it had been bought for a wedding and seldom worn since. It was black and of quite a becoming shape, though the dampness of the day had made its veil droop rather sadly round her face.

She paced up and down the platform, humming to herself, looking at the gardens which bordered the station, wondering whether Nicholas really minded her missing the Mothers' Union tea. He had seemed quite amenable to her going up to London to have luncheon with Prudence, though he had smiled a little at her serious excuses, the visit to Mowbray's to buy suitable books for Confirmation presents and perhaps even to get some Christmas cards in *really good time*, and had told her to enjoy herself.

'After all,' Jane had said, 'I don't really feel so very much of a mother, having only *one* child, and you know how bad I am at presiding at meetings. It would be far more suitable if somebody like Miss Doggett were to do it, though I suppose spinsters aren't eligible, really.'

'Good morning, Mrs Cleveland . . .' A firm voice called out the greeting from some distance away. It was Miss Doggett herself approaching at a steady pace. But just as she came near to Jane, she seemed to hesitate. Her mouth opened and she glanced round as if to make sure that they were not overheard, then said in a low confidential tone, 'I hope you'll excuse me for mentioning it, Mrs Cleveland, but I thought you might like to know.' She lowered her voice still more and almost whispered, 'Your underskirt is showing a little on the left side.'

'It's this wretched lock-knit,' said Jane rather too loudly and gaily, so that Miss Doggett recoiled a little; 'it does *sag* so. Still, there's nothing I can do about it now. The train's coming.'

They got into an empty carriage together and sat rather

stiffly on opposite sides by the window. Miss Doggett produced a safety pin from her bag.

'You could take it up at the shoulder, perhaps,' she suggested, offering the pin.

'Thank you,' said Jane, who had had no intention of doing anything about her sagging slip, 'I suppose I ought to do something, especially as I am going to London. People might notice,' she added unconvincingly, for who among the many millions – six, was it, or eight? – would notice that a country vicar's wife had half an inch of underskirt showing on the left side?

'Well, it is feeling right oneself that's the important thing,' said Miss Doggett, stroking her musquash coat. 'I am going up to my dressmaker for a fitting.'

'How grand that sounds, having clothes specially fitted so that they are exactly your shape and nobody else's,' said Jane impetuously.

Miss Doggett, whose figure was rather an odd shape, known to dressmakers as 'difficult', seemed as if she did not quite know how to take Jane's remark, but she must have decided that she was obviously much too unworldly to mean any offence, so decided not to take umbrage.

'I suppose you have to go to London on business,' she said quite pleasantly. 'You will be sorry to miss the Mothers' Union tea. I believe it is quite an event.'

'Yes, I am sorry,' said Jane quickly; 'but you know, I feel so unlike a mother when I am at these functions. I am so very undomesticated. They are all so splendid and efficient and have really quite wonderful ideas. Do you know, a mother in our last parish had one of her hints published in *Christian Home*.'

'Really?'

'Yes. It was a use for a thermometer case, if you had the misfortune to break your thermometer, of course. A splendid case for keeping *bodkins* in!' Jane chortled with laughter.

An uncertain smile appeared on Miss Doggett's face. 'Well, well, I must remember that,' she said.

'Yes, do!'

There was a short pause. The last topic of conversation did not seem to lead very easily to anything else.

At last Miss Doggett said, 'I suppose you and the vicar are coming to the whist drive?'

'Oh, certainly,' said Jane. 'I do so very much want to meet our Member. I have heard he is very charming.'

'Yes, and his principles are very sound.'

'I often wonder whether people born into his station of life can really know how others live,' said Jane thoughtfully. 'I'm always reminded of that verse in *We are Seven* – something about a little child that lightly draws its breath, what can it know of death? Do you see what I mean?'

Miss Doggett obviously did not, but she went on to repeat that Edward Lyall's principles were very sound and that of course his father and his grandfather had been Members of Parliament before him.

'He is not married?' asked Jane, trying to keep her voice neutral.

'No, he does not appear to be.' Miss Doggett sounded puzzled for a moment. 'He is thirty-two, but of course a man in his position couldn't afford to make a hasty or unsuitable choice. His wife would have to be quite exceptional – one could hardly expect him to marry a very *young* girl, either,' she added with a glance at Jane.

'Certainly not,' Jane agreed. 'I have no hopes in that direction.'

'Well, it would *hardly* be suitable,' said Miss Doggett. 'Your daughter . . .'

'Has just gone up to Oxford, where she is surrounded by young men. A man of *twenty*-two would seem old to her,' said Jane gaily. But was she failing in her duty as a mother, she wondered, by not entertaining hopes of Edward Lyall as a possible husband for Flora? He would be more suitable for

Prudence, if anybody, but the truth was that one hardly considered members of his Party as being within one's own sphere; it would have seemed presumptuous to regard them as possible husbands for one's relations and friends.

'What is Mrs Lyall like?' asked Jane bluntly.

'Well, of course she is not one of us,' said Miss Doggett. 'You may have heard that she goes to Father Lomax's church, which seems a pity.'

'Oh, well, Nicholas is the last person to mind a thing like that. He and Father Lomax were at Oxford together. I often think I would prefer a High Church service myself, but of course clergy wives have to be very careful, you know. They have to be sitting there in their dowdy old clothes in a pew rather too near the front – it's a kind of duty.'

Again Miss Doggett had no ready answer. 'Of course,' she went on after a while, 'Mrs Lyall is not very sound politically either. I have heard that there are tendencies the other way. . . .' She moved her hands about in a vague gesture.

'The other way?' Jane echoed. 'Yes; I see what you mean. Rome and Russia.'

'Oh, not *Russia*,' said Miss Doggett in a shocked tone. 'After all, her son was educated at Eton and Balliol, and Mrs Lyall herself is of quite good family.'

'Well, thank you for telling me,' said Jane in a reassuring tone. 'I shan't indicate in any way that I have heard when I meet Mrs Lyall.' Then, seeing that Miss Doggett was looking very puzzled, she added, 'About the tendencies the other way, I mean.'

They sat in silence in their corners for a moment or two, then Jane said, 'I do like your companion, Miss Morrow, so much.'

'You like Miss Morrow?' Miss Doggett sounded surprised. 'Well, she is really a distant relation more than a companion. Her mother was my cousin. I felt I had to do what I could for her when she was looking for a post.'

'That is a difficult position to be in, especially when there's a relationship,' said Jane. 'She seems such a bright, intelligent sort of person – she told me quite a lot about the village.'

'You mean about the people in the village?' said Miss Doggett sharply. 'Yes, Jessie certainly has her eyes open.'

'She told me a good deal about Mr Driver,' said Jane. 'About his wife and other things.'

'Ah, the other things,' said Miss Doggett obscurely. 'Of course, we never *saw* anything of those. We *knew* that it went on, of course – in London, I believe.'

'Yes, it seems suitable that things like that should go on in London,' Jane agreed. 'It is in better taste somehow that a man should be unfaithful to his wife away from home. Not all of them have the opportunity, of course.'

'Poor Constance was left alone a great deal,' said Miss Doggett. 'In many ways, of course, Mr Driver is a very charming man. They say, though, that men only want *one thing* – that's the truth of the matter.' Miss Doggett again looked puzzled; it was as if she had heard that men only wanted one thing, but had forgotten for the moment what it was. 'Ah, here we are at the junction,' she said, gathering her things together with an air of relief. 'You will need to hurry to catch the London train – they don't allow much time.'

The remainder of Jane's journey was shorter and less interesting. She thought idly about Fabian, turning him over in her mind as a possibility for Prudence, but in no time the train was slowing down under the great glass roof of the London terminus and she was gathering together her bag and umbrella and unread book and newspaper.

She was to meet Prudence at a quarter to one and found that when she got to Piccadilly she still had some time to spare. So, in anticipation of lunch or perhaps to tantalize herself by looking at dainties she would most certainly not be eating, she wandered into a large provision store and moved slowly from counter to counter, her feet sinking into the thick carpet, her senses bemused by the semi-darkness and the almost holy atmosphere. She finally stopped in the middle of the floor before a stand which was given over to a display of *foie gras*, packed in terrines of creamy pottery, some of them ornamented with pictures.

A tall man, rather too grandly dressed for his function, Jane thought, came up to her.

'Can I help you, madam?' he asked quietly.

'Well, now, I wonder if you could,' said Jane.

'I shall certainly endeavour to, madam,' said the man gravely.

'The point is this. How can a clergyman's wife afford to buy *foie gras*?'

'It would seem to be difficult,' said the man respectfully. 'Let us see now.' He took down a card from the stand. 'The smallest size is fourteen and ninepence.'

'Yes,' said Jane. 'I saw that. But I shouldn't really want the smallest size. Those large decorated jars have taken my fancy.'

'Ah, madam, those are one hundred and seventeen shillings,' said the salesman, rolling the words round his tongue.

'Well, I'm sorry to have wasted your time like this,' said Jane, moving away. 'I should like to have bought some.'

'To tell you the truth, madam, I don't care for it myself,' said the salesman, bowing Jane out of the door, 'and my wife doesn't either.'

And, comforted by these words, Jane moved out into the street feeling that she had been vouchsafed a glimpse of somebody else's life. She wondered about the man as she walked to meet Prudence – perhaps he was a churchwarden or sidesman somewhere, there had been something about his bearing that suggested it; in a way he had reminded her of Mr Mortlake.

Jane realized that she had killed too much time and was now a little late, for Prudence was already waiting at the vegetarian restaurant where they were to have lunch. The place was crowded and they found themselves sitting at a table with two women, under the photograph of the founder of some system of diet in which the restaurant specialized. He was bearded and wore pince-nez, which seemed suitable.

Prudence ordered a raw salad while Jane chose a hot dish of strange vegetables. Conversation was a little difficult at first, since the women already at the table were engaged in an interesting family tale which Jane and Prudence could not help listening to. Indeed, it would have seemed impolite to start a conversation of their own, and they contented themselves with murmurs and glances. Jane noticed a woman wearing heavy silver jewellery and an orange jumper – she looked the kind of person who might have been somebody's mistress in the nineteen-twenties. She was also interested in two foreign gentlemen at the next table, arguing vigorously.

'Prue,' said Jane when they were at last alone at their table, 'I do so want you to come down and stay with us the week-end after this one. Flora will just be back, and there's going to be a kind of political whist drive where you'll meet simply everybody.'

Prudence hoped that her horror did not show in her face. She disliked going away from home in the autumn and winter. Other people's houses were so cold, and she knew from experience that Jane and her family lived in an uncomfortable, makeshift way. The food wasn't even particularly good; it seemed that Jane would stop to admire a smoked salmon in a window or a terrine of *foie gras*, but in the abstract, as it were; her own catering never achieved such a standard even on a lower scale.

'I don't know if I shall be able to manage *that* week-end,' she said warily. One's married friends were too apt to assume that one had absolutely nothing to do when not at the office. A flat with no husband didn't seem to count as a home.

'Oh, Prue, do come! I'm sure it will be fun, and it will do you good to get away from London.'

'Well, I dare say I could – though the idea of a whist drive fills me with dismay.'

'But we needn't play – or at least not seriously,' said Jane. 'You know I'm no good at anything but patience, and not always very good at that. But I feel it will be a drawing-together of the threads – we shall see the place all of a piece as it were.'

'Have you met any interesting people – people of one's own type, I mean?' asked Prudence cautiously.

'Yes, in a way. There's Miss Morrow and Fabian Driver – I think I told you about him in my letter.' Jane was too wise to appear anything but casual in her tone as she mentioned this eligible widower. She knew that the pride of even young spinsters is a delicate thing and that Prudence was especially sensitive. There must be no hint that she was trying to 'bring them together'.

'Yes – you said something about him eating the hearts of his victims,' said Prudence, equally casual. She realized that Jane might have some absurd idea in her mind about 'bringing them together', but determined not to let her see that she suspected or that she entertained any hopes herself. So they were both satisfied and neither was really deceived for a moment. The conversation went on smoothly – Jane revealed that Fabian was good-looking and quite tall, about five foot eleven which was really tall enough for a man, and that he had a nice house.

At last Prudence looked at her watch and said she must be getting back to her office.

'Are you supposed to take only an hour for your lunch?' Jane asked.

'Good Heavens, no,' said Prudence impatiently. 'I can take as long as I like – Arthur never minds and I'm not answerable to anyone else.' It gave her a peculiar pleasure to speak of Dr Grampian casually by his Christian name – Jane was the only person with whom she could do it.

'Funny how I thought his name was Adrian,' said Jane, as they walked out into the street. 'Won't the other women who work with you be jealous, though, if you take a longer lunch-time than they do?'

'I don't know. I'm not really interested in what they think.'

'I'm sure I should be horribly conscious of it,' said Jane rather complacently. 'I should feel their eyes on me. I should pretend I'd been in the lavatory or something.'

'One has to have the courage of one's convictions,' said Prudence.

'I suppose they are like the weaker brethren,' said Jane. 'One ought perhaps to think of them like that, being led astray by one's own actions or example.'

'Really, Jane, you talk as if I were doing something wrong,' said Prudence crossly. 'And anything less like the weaker brethren than Miss Trapnell and Miss Clothier couldn't possibly be imagined. They certainly wouldn't like to hear themselves described like that.'

They stopped outside the building where Prudence worked and made some final arrangements about the week-end. They were just about to part when a man came up to them and said 'Good afternoon' to Prudence.

'Jane, I don't think you've met Dr Grampian,' she said rather nervously. 'This is a friend of mine, Mrs Cleveland,' she explained.

Jane said 'How do you do' and shook hands, her glance resting with interest on the man before her. So this was Arthur Grampian. Certainly, now that she saw him, she realized that the name Adrian, with its suggestion of tall, languid elegance, would have been entirely unsuitable. He was of middle size, almost short, and gave an impression of greyness, in his clothes and face and in the pebble-like eyes behind his spectacles. Whatever did Prue see in him? she wondered, conscious as she asked herself of the futility of her question. Arthur Grampian and his wife Lucy – one mustn't forget his wife Lucy, though it was obvious that Prue did. But this insignificant-looking little man . . . Oh, but it was splendid the things women were doing for men all the time, thought Jane. Making them feel, perhaps sometimes by no more than a casual glance, that they were loved and admired and desired when they were worthy of none of these things – enabling them to preen themselves and puff out their plumage like birds and bask in the sunshine of love, real or imagined, it didn't matter which. And yet Prudence's love didn't seem to have had any very noticeable effect on Arthur Grampian; he made nervous conversation about the weather, and smiled and nodded in a rather vague way, as if he didn't really know who either of the women really were.

At last Jane broke away and went off in search of suitable books for Confirmation presents. Prudence stood in the lift with Arthur Grampian, holding herself rather stiffly apart from him as if afraid that their sleeves might touch.

'Getting on all right, Miss Bates?' he asked as the lift stopped and they got out at their floor.

No, no, nothing is all right, everything is wrong, Prudence wanted to call out, but instead she merely answered, 'Yes, I think so. Do you want to see me about anything?'

Perhaps a note of hope had sounded in her tone, for he looked startled and seemed to clasp his brief-case to his breast and step backwards and away from her as he said, 'Want to see you about anything? No, I don't think so. I'm sure everything is going all right.'

And so he hurried into his room and Prudence into hers.

Miss Trapnell and Miss Clothier were in their places, their appointed places it seemed, like something in a hymn, or the wise virgins in the Bible. Not much hope of *them* sparing any oil from their lamps.

O, happy servant he,
In such a posture found,

thought Prudence with irritation, noticing Miss Clothier's casual glance at her watch.

'I was meeting a friend I haven't seen for some time,' she heard herself say weakly, 'so I'm afraid I'm rather late. I shall have to stay on a bit to make up for it.'

'Oh, meeting a friend is rather different,' said Miss Trapnell with excessive geniality. 'I'm sure Dr Grampian would have no objection to any of us taking a longer lunch-hour for a reason like that.'

'As a matter of fact, I met him coming in,' said Prudence, 'so I was able to introduce my friend.' She disliked the way she kept referring to Jane as 'my friend', almost as if she hoped to give the impression that she had been lunching with a man.

Jane, in the meantime, was wandering round a religious book-shop, glancing at their selection of new novels; so absorbed was she that half an hour passed by like a minute and then it was time for her to go to the station for the train back. It would have been nice to have tea in the Corner House or gone, rather wickedly, to a Solemn Evensong with lots of incense, she thought. But as it was, she hadn't even time to buy the Confirmation presents. Really, except for looking at the jars of *foie gras*, having lunch with Prudence and seeing Dr Grampian for the first time, her day had been wasted.

CHAPTER EIGHT

PRUDENCE WAS in the train on her way to spend the week-end with the Clevelands. It was Friday evening and she sat rather crushed up in her corner, for the half-empty carriage which she had chosen so carefully for herself had filled up at the last moment with men in bowler hats and overcoats, carrying despatch-cases and evening papers. Prudence looked at them with resentment, almost with loathing; she wished she had a spray of freesia or lily-of-the-valley to hold under her nose so that she wouldn't smell their horrible pipe smoke – she hated men who smoked pipes. As it was, she had drenched her handkerchief in expensive French scent, for going to stay with Jane always drove her to extremes, and she would take her best clothes rather than her most suitable. Besides, there was this whist drive at which they were supposed to appear, with its promise of a young Member of Parliament and an eligible widower; presumably one would have to dress up for that.

Although she disliked going away in the winter, it was a relief to be leaving London and her flat. The blankness of the last few weeks, with Arthur Grampian taking even less notice of her than usual, combined with the approach of winter, had brought her down to a rather low state. I have given him the best years of my life, she thought, and he doesn't even know it. He was immersed in his work and his club and going home every evening – or so one imagined! – to his wife Lucy, and she was saying, 'Well, dear, had a good day?' or whatever it was that wives said to their husbands when they returned home in the evening.

The train slowed down and Prudence gathered her things together rather fussily, for this was the junction where she had to change. She stood up and prepared to lift her suitcase down from the rack, but before she could do so the man sitting next to her had jumped up and taken it down for her. Prudence thanked him, experiencing that feeling of contrition which comes to all of us when we have made up our minds to dislike people for no apparent reason and they then perform some kind action. Now she gave him her most charming smile and thought of him enjoying a pipe in the train on his way home, a good husband and father. She noticed that he had some cakes in a white cardboard box – taking them home for the children, she supposed; she could hardly bear it . . . she left the carriage, her eyes full of tears.

Jane was to meet her at the junction, ostensibly to 'show her the way', but really because she loved an excuse to go on a little journey. She peered at the people stepping down from the train and then ran forward to greet Prudence and to hurry her over the bridge.

'The train won't be a minute,' she said. 'How lovely it is to see you and how lovely you smell. What is it?'

Prudence murmured the name a little self-consciously, for she knew that her French accent was not good and the name was of an amorous kind that sounded a little ridiculous when said out loud. Anyway, it would convey nothing to Jane. She gritted her teeth for Jane's peal of laughter, which came almost before she had finished speaking.

'What names they think of! And really they're all made from coal-tar. Does Dr Grampian like it?'

'I don't know – I don't use it in the office, really.'

'No, of course not, just a little eau-de-Cologne or a light toilet water – you see, I read the women's magazines when I go to the dentist. How *is* Dr Grampian?'

'Oh, just as usual,' said Prudence evasively.

'Which seems to be rather sad and shy, unless he was frightened of me,' said Jane.

'Wasn't he as you'd imagined him?' asked Prudence in a stifled voice.

'No, but of course people never are. It reminds me of that poem about two men looking out through prison bars, one seeing mud and the other stars – do you know it?'

'Yes.' Prudence couldn't help smiling at Jane's absurdity. 'But it doesn't seem very appropriate.'

'Well, perhaps not, but it conveys the general idea. Obviously you see him quite differently from me – I'd imagined a big, tall, dark man, a sort of Mr Rochester.'

'He is rather good-looking, though, don't you think?'

'Yes, in a way, but if you think him so that's the main point after all. Some hollow in the temple or a square inch of flesh on the wrist, that's all it need be, really . . .'

A little train came puffing along the platform, and Jane and Prudence got in.

'The vicarage is some way from the station,' said Jane, 'but I've asked one of Nicholas's lads to meet the train and carry your case for you.'

The boy took hold of the case, swung it up on to his shoulder and ran off with it at a great pace. Jane and Prudence followed more slowly, picking out landmarks, or rather Jane enthusiastically pointed them out while Prudence dutifully peered through the moonless darkness at the shapes of buildings – the gasworks, the Golden Lion where Fabian Driver did his pre-lunch drinking, the chapel with the Temperance Hotel next to it and the Spinning Wheel Café opposite; then on to the older part of the village with the church, the village green, the pond and the more picturesque houses, and at last to the vicarage with its green-painted gate and the laurels in front of Nicholas's study window.

'Here we are,' said Jane. 'It's quite a nice house, though not as old as the church. Of course, it's enormous, with too many rooms, impossible to heat adequately.'

Prudence shivered. She was wondering if there would be a glass of sherry or a drop of gin waiting; she was so used to that little comfort at the end of a day's work and one seemed to need it even more in strange surroundings.

They were in the hall now with the old coats hanging up and the piles of parish magazines waiting to be delivered. The place felt damp and chill. Nicholas came out of his study with his spectacles pushed halfway down his nose and greeted Prudence.

He used to be so attractive, she thought, but being a clergyman and a husband had done their worst for him, rubbed off the bloom, if that was the right word. He murmured something conventional about the journey and the shortening days so that Prudence was reminded of the silly old joke about winter drawers on.

'You'll want to see your room,' said Jane. 'We haven't put

you in the *proper* spare room – it seemed so very vast and cold – but in one of the smaller ones. Here we are.' She flung open the door of what seemed to Prudence, who was used to a boxlike, centrally-heated flat, a very large, bare-looking room with a bed in one corner, a chest of drawers, a chair and an old-fashioned marble-topped washstand. There were a few books on a little table by the bed, but no reading lamp, Prudence noticed quickly, just a light hanging rather too high up in the middle of the room. The floor was covered with shabby linoleum on which two small rugs had been placed in strategic positions, one by the bed and the other before a little looking-glass which hung on one wall.

Darling Jane, thought Prudence, noticing a rather rough arrangement of winter flowers in a little jar on the bedside table, a solitary rose, a few Michaelmas daisies and a dahlia.

She lit a cigarette and began to unpack her case. She felt happier with her own possessions around her, her hot-water bottle in its pink cover, her turquoise blue wool housecoat, her bottles and jars on the chest of drawers and Arthur Grampian's photograph, cut from some learned periodical, on the bedside table.

'Prue,' Jane's voice called, 'supper will be ready in a minute! I've just been trying to open a bottle of sherry, but the corkscrew's gone in all crooked – do be an angel and help me with it.'

Prudence ran downstairs with a lighter heart. It was a good sherry, too, the kind one would hardly have expected Jane to buy.

'I remembered you liked it like this,' said Jane, 'so I asked the man for a very *pale* sherry and he said, "You mean very *dry*, madam" – of course, I always forget these things.'

'Aren't you going to have any?' asked Prudence, seeing Jane fill glasses only for herself and Nicholas.

'No, I don't really like it, you know. I've got out of the way of drinking. It seems rather terrible, really.'

'Not at all, my dear,' said Nicholas conventionally.

'I've been such a failure as a clergyman's wife,' Jane lamented, 'but at least I don't drink; that's the only suitable thing about me.'

'Well, clergymen's wives don't really drink, do they?' said Prudence, contemplating the topaz colour of her drink under the light. 'That doesn't seem to be one of their vices.'

'So even my not drinking isn't an advantage,' said Jane. 'I might just as well take to it, then.' She poured herself a full glass of sherry.

'I shouldn't have it if you don't like it,' said Nicholas in an anxious tone. 'It seems a pity to waste it.'

Jane flashed him a look which Prudence caught. She supposed that marriage must be full of moments like this. She looked round the large, cold drawing-room, inadequately furnished, and imagined what she would do to such a room.

'These curtains aren't quite long enough,' said Jane, following her glances, 'and they don't really meet across the windows. Canon Pritchard was rather a wealthy clergyman – they had long crimson velvet curtains and a curtain over the door too; of course, they *would* keep the draughts out, but luckily we don't feel the cold.'

Prudence remembered other houses where Jane and Nicholas had lived and the peculiar kind of desolation they seemed to create around them. They certainly did not appear to feel the cold, but she was glad that her black dress had a tartan stole to wrap round the shoulders.

'Ah, there is supper,' said Jane. 'I can hear Flora taking it in. Mrs Glaze doesn't oblige us in the evenings.'

'Flora is shaping very well as a cook,' said Nicholas. 'I don't know where she gets her talent – certainly not from either of us. She will make a good wife for somebody one of these days.'

'But men don't want only that,' said Jane, 'though perhaps the better ones think they do. I was talking to Miss Doggett in the train the other day . . .' Her sentence trailed off vaguely, for perhaps she too had difficulty in remembering what it was that men wanted.

'How has Flora enjoyed her first term at Oxford?' Prudence asked.

'One hardly knows,' said Jane in rather a flat tone. 'I had expected her to be so enthusiastic. The new work, the wonderful atmosphere of Oxford in the autumn, the walks up to Boar's Hill and Shotover and all those lovely berries we used to gather, and then going to St Mary's on Sunday evenings . . . Oh, it was all so thrilling!'

'But, darling, it's probably different now,' said Nicholas.

'Yes, I suppose it's a mistake to think one can live one's youth over again in one's children,' said Jane sadly.

'Has she fallen in love?' Prudence asked.

'She doesn't say. Of course, she's met a lot of young men, but there doesn't seem to be anyone special yet.'

Prudence smiled a little complacently, remembering her own first term. Why, the very first week somebody had fallen in love with her, poor Cyril, saying rather pompously, 'Male and female created He them,' when she had refused to kiss him goodnight. And after that, barely a month later, Philip, sending flowers every day . . . .

'Well, shall we go in to supper?' Nicholas suggested. 'Prudence, you had better sit with your back to the fire. Only one of the bars seems to be working, I'm afraid. Something must have gone wrong with the other, but I have no idea what it can be.'

Flora had prepared a very good meal, a chicken casserole with rice and french beans followed by a lemon meringue pie. Prudence had hardly seen her apart from a brief greeting on the doorstep, and was surprised to find her attractive-looking and nicely dressed, almost a grown-up person. She did not join very much in the conversation, but was busy with the food. Prudence could see that she was growing away from Jane, leading her own secret life. Afterwards the women went into the kitchen to wash up, leaving Nicholas in his study, preparing Sunday's sermon. At least Prudence supposed he must be doing this, for her imagination was unequal to the task of penetrating behind the closed door of a clergyman's study.

Later, when she was in her hard bed, reading by the light of a candle which Jane had given her, she heard the murmur of him and Jane talking together in their room, which was next to hers. Husbands took friends away, she thought, though Jane had retained her independence more than most of her married friends. And yet even she seemed to have missed something in life; her research, her studies of obscure seventeenth-century poets, had all come to nothing, and here she was, trying, though not very hard, to be an efficient clergyman's wife, and with only very moderate success. Compared with Jane's life, Prudence's seemed rich and full of promise. She had her work, her independence, her life in London and her love for Arthur Grampian. But tomorrow, if she wanted to, she could give it all up and fall in love with somebody else. Lines of eligible and delightful men seemed to stretch before her, and with this pleasant prospect in mind she fell into a light sleep.

Later, however, she awoke with the realization that married people did not understand the importance of the full hot-water bottle. Hers was now thin and cold and she had not had her usual hot bath before going to bed. For a moment she wondered whether she could creep downstairs and refill her bottle, but it seemed to be too much trouble and she did not want to wake anybody up. So she draped her fur cape over the bed and then, a sudden inspiration, one of the little rugs from the floor over her feet and lay curled up under the weight of all these clothes, waiting for sleep.

CHAPTER NINE

'SHOULD WE have something to eat before we go, do you think?' Jane asked. 'I believe refreshments are provided, but they may not be till rather late.'

'Perhaps a glass of sherry and a biscuit?' suggested Prudence hopefully. 'One doesn't really want much to *eat* . . .' but *how* we need a drink, she continued to herself; the idea of facing this whist drive without one was quite terrifying.

'Oh, yes, that would be the thing,' said Jane quickly, with her head bent. She found herself quite unable to look at Prudence, whose eyelids were startlingly and embarrassingly green, glistening with some greasy preparation which had little flecks of silver in it. Was this what one had to do nowadays when one was unmarried? she wondered. What hard work it must be, always remembering to add these little touches; there was something primitive about it, like the young African smearing himself with red cam-wood before he went courting. The odd and rather irritating thing about it was, though, that Nicholas was gazing at Prudence with admiration; it was quite noticeable. So it really did work. Jane studied her own face in the looking-glass above the sideboard and it looked to her just the same as when Nicholas used to gaze at it with admiration. Would he look at her with renewed interest if she had green eyelids? she wondered, but her thoughts were interrupted by his voice asking about the glass of sherry. Were they going to have one or not?

'I've got it here,' said Flora; 'and a few sandwiches. I think we'd better start soon.'

'Why, how nice you look, darling,' said Jane in a surprised mother's voice. 'That's the dress you made, isn't it?'

'Yes. I did make it,' said Flora quickly, embarrassed by her mother's comment and fearing worse to come. 'Does anybody want a sandwich – they're only cheese, I'm afraid.'

'It's a charming dress,' said Prudence, wishing she could feel more natural with Flora. It was awkward when one's friends' children suddenly became grown-up people. 'You look like, oh, something Victorian, that striped silk and the locket and the way you've done your hair. There was a picture very like that in last month's *Vogue*,' she went on, anxious to please.

'Oh, but your dress is much nicer,' Flora burst out, 'and the colour of your nail varnish is so lovely. What is it?'

So we're two women talking together, thought Prudence with surprise and a little dismay. She was glad when Jane made some joking remark about not liking Flora to use nail varnish, thus turning her into a child again.

'We really ought to be going,' said Nicholas. 'It starts at eight, you know.'

'We can be a *little* late,' said Jane, 'though not as late as the party from the Towers. It would be a serious social error if we were to be later than the Lyalls.'

'I suppose the villagers will be there already,' said Prudence, glancing at her watch.

'Yes, the old order hasn't changed that much. Edward Lyall isn't one of these new-fangled Members of Parliament. His ancestors have represented this place for generations.'

They set out, Jane in her old tweed coat, Prudence in a fur cape. The hall was practically next door to the vicarage, so there was little time in which to compose oneself. Suddenly a door was pushed open and there was a noise of talk and laughter and chairs scraping on the wooden floor. Looking around her, Prudence realized at once that she was overdressed. Her green-and-gold shot taffeta cocktail party dress was out of place here, where most of the women were in long-sleeved wool or even coats and skirts. Her fur cape was the only one in the little cloak-room where they hung their coats.

'I think I'll wear it round my shoulders,' she said. 'It doesn't seem very warm.'

'You'll be boiled,' said Jane cheerfully. 'And it will get in the way of the cards.'

They went out into the hall and stood vaguely around, but only for a moment. Mrs Crampton and Mrs Mayhew were upon them, Prudence was being introduced, and within a matter of seconds she found herself sitting down at a table with three others.

'You must be Mrs Cleveland's friend that's come to stay,' said a woman in a dark felt hat trimmed with a bird's body. 'I'm Mrs Glaze and this is my nephew' – she indicated a fresh-faced young man – 'and this is Mr Mortlake. We're all great churchgoers and we like the vicar so much.'

'Oh, good,' said Prudence nervously.

'Canon Pritchard was a good man in his way, but we didn't care for his lady,' said Mrs Glaze. 'Much too interfering. There's none of that from Mrs Cleveland.'

'No, I don't suppose there is,' said Prudence. 'She usually gets on well with people.' She wished they wouldn't talk quite so much, for it was many years since she had played whist and she found she had to concentrate. Her partner, Mrs Glaze's nephew, the butcher, was taking no part in the conversation, but the others kept up a continual flow, most of it about people she didn't know or had just heard Jane mention.

It was a relief to find herself at a table with Jane, and Mr Oliver and Mr Whiting, who were also apparently church-people.

'They will be arriving soon,' said Mr Whiting, 'the party from the Towers, I should say. I hope Mr Edward will give us a few words. We need that bit of encouragement these days.'

'Does he usually give a few words?' Jane asked.

'Yes, Mrs Cleveland; he usually has a message. And then we adjourn for refreshments. After that he takes a hand himself and Mrs Lyall too, but the poor lady has very little notion of how to play.' He shook his head, and gathered in a trick.

'She's a good sort, though,' said Mr Oliver. 'She's got the

right ideas, though of course she can't go against the Party openly.'

'If you can call them the right ideas,' said Mr Whiting, glaring at Mr Oliver. 'Personally, I shouldn't.'

'Well, you know my views,' said Mr Oliver truculently.

'We've certainly heard them often enough,' said Mr Whiting.

Jane and Prudence exchanged a look.

'Well, we all have different views,' began Jane, but fortunately it was not necessary for her to continue with her platitudes, for at that moment a hush seemed to strike through the hall, cards were laid down and faces turned towards the door.

A slight, dark young man, with a pale, interesting face and hair worn rather too long, stood on the threshold. He was accompanied by a middle-aged woman in a black lace dress, who looked about her anxiously.

'There they are!' said Mr Whiting, raising his hands and bringing them together in a clap which was taken up by the rest of the hall.

'Is it usual to clap one's Member?' whispered Jane to Prudence. 'I should have thought the time would be *after* he had said a few words or given his message.'

Edward Lyall acknowledged the applause by a wave of his hand and a charming smile which seemed to include everybody.

'Thank you, my friends,' he said in a ringing voice; 'thank you. It gives me great pleasure to be among you tonight and to see so many of you here in this good cause. As I drove down from the House this evening to be with you I found myself wondering what I could say to you, what encouragement I could give you.'

'He might well find himself wondering,' said Mr Oliver in a low tone, but he was silenced by an angry look from Mr Whiting.

Edward Lyall's smooth voice flowed on. Political speeches at such gatherings tend to have a certain sameness about them, and Edward Lyall's message to his constituents had nothing particularly original about it. Jane found herself noticing his continual references to the 'burden' and began to wonder whether this word was more used by clergymen or politicians. Indeed, after Edward had been speaking for about ten minutes, she came to the conclusion that his words might almost have been coming from a pulpit. Would he perhaps end with a prayer?

'And now, my friends, I have talked long enough. You didn't come here to listen to me, I know. And I'm not ashamed to admit that as I drove down from the House tonight I found myself looking forward to Mrs Crampton and Mrs Mayhew's excellent refreshments' – he turned to those ladies and smiled – 'so I won't keep you from them any longer.' He ended with a reference to 'these austere days' and flung in an extra burden for luck, as it were, and then he really had finished. Jane and Prudence found themselves being borne forward on a tide of people surging towards the refreshments and their beloved Member.

'I suppose we should wait to be introduced,' said Jane, looking over to where Edward Lyall and his mother were waiting, as if to receive presentations. 'It's a pity they're standing right in front of the refreshments, though. We could at least have made a start on those.'

'Surely not before *they* start,' said Prudence. 'They aren't eating anything yet.'

'Ah, Mrs Cleveland . . .' Miss Doggett, in her purple woollen dress, seemed to take command of the situation. 'Let me introduce you to our Member.'

Jane followed meekly and shook hands first with Mrs Lyall and then with her son. He had an appropriate word for her, if not exactly a message, and she found herself liking him very much, falling a victim, as she put it, to his easy charm of manner. Refreshments now began to be offered and many ladies came up to him with plates of sandwiches and other delicacies. Jane saw Mrs Mayhew offer a plate rather furtively and heard her say in a low voice, 'Oyster patties – specially for you. I know how much you like them.' The situation interested and amused her; there was something so familiar about it and yet for a moment or two she could not think what it was. The hall, the trestle tables, the good-looking young man, the ladies surrounding him . . . where had she seen all this before? Then it came to her. It was usually curates who were accorded such treatment, but this parish had no curate. Edward Lyall, therefore, was a kind of curate-substitute. The idea pleased her so much that she wanted immediately to tell somebody about it, but she found herself standing next to his mother and felt she could hardly reveal her thought. What should she say to Mrs Lyall, a gentle-looking person with a rather long, melancholy face?

Fortunately, Mrs Lyall started first.

'Edward is so tired,' she said; 'it's really a nice rest for him to come down here. That speech yesterday took a lot out of him.'

That speech? Jane never followed the proceedings of Parliament, but she could imagine quite well what a young man of his Party might have said, so she said cheerfully, 'Yes; it must have done. Very fine, I should think it must have been. That bit about Youth and the Empire,' she hazarded.

'Yes, everyone was very pleased. I'm glad to see him doing so well, though of course, as you may have heard, I don't always agree with everything he says.' There was a little worried frown on Mrs Lyall's face, which made Jane say in a hearty reassuring voice, 'Oh, no, of course one doesn't. There's good and bad on each side, isn't there?'

'I'm so glad to hear you say that, because it's just what I feel.'

'After all,' said Jane, warming to the subject, 'Members of

Parliament are only human beings, aren't they? We all make mistakes, even the best of us, whichever the best may be.'

She realized that she had spoilt her little message of cheer by throwing in this last obscurity, for the worried frown appeared again on Mrs Lyall's face.

'If only one could take the good from *both* sides,' said Mrs Lyall sadly. 'Still, I do feel that things are not quite as they used to be.'

'No,' Jane agreed. 'There have been many changes in the last few years.'

'Especially since the war,' went on Mrs Lyall. 'I think of it often, especially at breakfast-time.'

'At breakfast-time?' Jane echoed.

'Yes, all those dishes on the sideboard. When my husband was alive, we'd have three or four different hot dishes and cold ham when there were only the three of us at breakfast.'

'Ah, yes,' said Jane eagerly; 'kidneys and bacon and scrambled egg and boiled eggs, perhaps haddock too, not to mention porridge. I used to read about it in novels about Edwardian country house parties.'

'Now we've done away with all that,' said Mrs Lyall, 'and it's such a relief. I just have tea and toast. Edward likes coffee and a cereal of some kind. He might have a boiled egg or a rasher of bacon occasionally. . . .'

Jane turned away, feeling that she was not worthy to receive these sacred revelations of his tastes. Others ought to have been listening and they apparently were, for Miss Doggett's voice chimed in, saying, 'I think a man needs a cooked breakfast, especially after an all-night sitting in the House. I can imagine Mr Lyall needing a cooked breakfast then. Can't you, Jessie?' She turned to her companion and spoke rather sharply for, as Jane had noticed, Miss Morrow was smirking a little as if there were something funny being said.

'Men seem to need a lot of food at all times,' said Miss Morrow in a rough, casual tone.

'Sometimes,' said Mrs Lyall, on what seemed a reproachful note, 'Edward is too tired to eat breakfast when he's been in the House all night.'

'Oh, dear . . .' Mrs Mayhew and Mrs Crampton had now joined the little group round Mrs Lyall.

'Perhaps a nourishing milk drink would be best at a time like that?' suggested Mrs Crampton. 'Benger's or Ovaltine . . .'

'Or a more drastic remedy,' said Miss Doggett boldly. 'Brandy, perhaps?'

'Yes, one does feel that in cases of fatigue, something really strong is needed,' said Mrs Mayhew.

'I always think one should have brandy in the house,' said Mrs Crampton.

'Does she mean in the house or in the House?' said Miss Morrow to Jane. 'I think we can safely leave them to their worship now, don't you?'

'Yes,' Jane agreed. 'Why, what have you got there?' she asked, seeing that Miss Morrow appeared to be secreting a paper bag behind her back.

'Oyster patties,' whispered Miss Morrow. 'I like them too. I thought I would eat them when I got home in the privacy of my bedroom. I took these when nobody was looking, or, rather, nobody who mattered. I think Mr Oliver saw me, but with his views he could hardly disapprove. Would you like one?'

'No, thank you,' said Jane. She looked rather anxiously round the hall to see that Prudence and Flora were all right. The latter was talking to Mr Oliver, but Prudence was standing in an incongruous little group, which consisted of Mrs Glaze, Nicholas and the two churchwardens. She did not look as if she were enjoying herself very much, and she had been promised at least a glimpse of Fabian Driver, Jane realized, and there was no sign of him as yet.

'I wonder what can have happened to Mr Driver?' she said to Miss Morrow. 'Doesn't he usually put in an appearance at these affairs?'

'Oh, yes,' said Miss Morrow. 'He will be coming along when he judges the time is ripe.'

'Ripe?' echoed Jane in a puzzled voice. 'How can it be ripe, and for what?'

'A good entrance. He has to time his appearance carefully – it mustn't be too soon after the arrival of Edward Lyall, otherwise he wouldn't be noticed.'

'Surely he wouldn't consciously think of it like that,' said Jane, laughing. 'I expect he likes to have a leisurely dinner and then come along.'

'Yes; Mrs Arkright has left him a cold bird – pheasant, I believe – with a salad, and he will take his time over the meal, but he will take more time than is really necessary.'

'What a lot you know about him,' said Jane, looking at Miss Morrow with new eyes. What she saw was unremarkable enough; the birdlike little face with long nose and large bright eyes, the ordinary dark blue crepe dress with a cheap paste clip at the neck.

'Well, living next door, you get to know these things. I knew Constance, his wife, of course. One can know a lot about men through their wives.'

'Oh, dear . . .' Jane considered herself ruefully. 'Yes, I suppose one can. What was she like?'

'Older than he was, not a very interesting person really; she was a good needlewoman.'

Miss Morrow's tone was dry and Jane did not feel she had gleaned very much about Constance Driver from this bare description. Surely he will come soon, she told herself, anxious for Prudence's evening, and very soon after this he did come, walking in slowly, his leonine head held rather high, looking around him with an air almost of surprise.

Miss Morrow smiled sardonically. Jane advanced towards him and he greeted her.

'I want you to meet Miss Prudence Bates,' she said. 'She is staying with us for the week-end.'

So this is Fabian Driver, thought Prudence, putting on a rather cool social manner. She had a natural distrust of good-looking men, though they seemed to offer a challenge which she was never unwilling to accept. Fabian's glance when they shook hands was so penetrating that something of her poise deserted her. She had often enough had men look at her like that, and perhaps it is a thing that women cannot have too much of. She returned his glance and held it.

'How do you do?' he murmured.

Jane, watching from the side, thought 'Oh, goody,' in a childish sort of way. It was going to be all right. The way he had looked at her was most promising. *By our first strange and fatal interview* . . . she said to herself.

Prudence and Fabian drew a little apart from the whist players, who had now started again, Edward Lyall and his mother among them.

'Have you been playing?' Fabian asked.

'Only a little,' said Prudence, with a laugh. 'I'm afraid I've forgotten all I ever knew about it, though.'

'I like to look in at these affairs,' said Fabian. 'One has a certain responsibility, living in a small community.'

'Yes, I suppose so.'

There was a pause. It's like being at a cocktail party without anything to drink, thought Prudence.

'Would you like a sandwich?' she asked, offering a dejected-looking plate.

'No, thank you. I had dinner before I came. I was wondering, though,' he looked deeply into her eyes, 'whether we might slip out and have a drink? Would you like one?'

'Yes, I certainly would. The strain of making conversation with so many people has quite worn me out.'

'Had you a coat or something? It's rather cold outside.'

'I had a little fur.' Prudence made a helpless gesture round her shoulders. 'We left it somewhere when we came in.'

Fabian retrieved her cape from a pile of tweed coats and

they went out together. The pub was just the other side of the pond. They seemed almost to run towards it and were soon sitting by a blazing fire. Most of the villagers were at the whist drive and the bar was deserted. Fabian asked Prudence what she would like to drink and she told him with no false modesty or beating about the bush. Mild-and-bitter or light ale, which she did not like, anyway, would have seemed unworthy of the occasion. But their conversation did not improve very much even with strong drink, though they gradually became more relaxed and their eyes met so often in penetrating looks that it did not seem to matter that they had little to say to each other, or that Prudence found herself doing most of the talking. She had spent many such evenings in her life and always enjoyed them; the time passed pleasantly until it was time to go home.

'I'm afraid it's rather dark in the country,' said Fabian, taking Prudence's arm. 'I shall have to guide you.'

'I can see quite well, thank you,' said Prudence in her cool voice. 'I like walking in the dark.'

'I will see you to your door,' said Fabian.

'Well, that is kind of you. I'm not quite sure where the vicarage is from here.'

'Just the other side of the pond. But it's quite easy to get lost in a strange place. My house is just here.' He indicated a gate.

'How nice. Jane tells me it is a lovely house.'

Fabian sighed. 'Yes, I suppose it is, but I'm a lonely person.'

Prudence, her perception a little blunted by whisky, did not smile. She looked up at his face and found his profile pleasing. Poor, lonely Fabian. . . . She began to wonder if he would kiss her outside the vicarage gate.

'Good night, Mr Driver,' a loud countrywoman's voice broke in on her thoughts, and she realized that they were passing the village hall, from which a crowd was now emerging. So it was unlikely that he would have the opportunity to kiss her good night. She wondered if she would have enjoyed it if he had.

'We must meet in London,' Fabian was saying as he let go of her arm. 'Perhaps you could have lunch with me or something? Or we might go to a theatre and have dinner.'

'That would be very nice.'

'May I write or telephone you, then? Is your name in the book?'

'Oh, yes.'

'Miss Bates – Miss Prudence Bates.' He took her hand as if he would kiss it, but his gallant gesture was interrupted by the appearance of Miss Doggett and Miss Morrow, who called out 'Good night' and went on their way muttering.

Fabian sighed. 'Ah, well . . . good night, my dear,' and Prudence walked up the vicarage drive alone.

Inside the vicarage the family had assembled in Nicholas's study.

'We felt like a cup of cocoa,' said Jane brightly. 'Would you like one?'

'No, thank you,' said Prudence, blinking her eyes in the light.

'No, perhaps not – you had a drink with Fabian, I imagine.' Jane tried to keep her voice flat and uninterested.

'Yes, I did.'

'What did you have?'

'Whisky.'

Jane made a face. 'How horrid! Was Fabian in good form?' she asked, yielding to temptation.

'Good form? Well, I don't know. We talked about Italy and Coventry Patmore and Donne and various other things.'

'Coventry Patmore and Donne! He has never talked like that to me – you *must* have got on well.'

'I thought him rather pleasant,' said Prudence in an off-hand way. Really, now she came to think of it, though, it was she who had brought Coventry Patmore and Donne into the conversation.

I wonder if he kissed her, Jane thought. She was surprised to hear that they had had what seemed to be quite an intelligent conversation, for she had never found Fabian very much good in that line. She had a theory that this was why he tended to make love to women – because he couldn't really think of much to say to them – but she could hardly reveal her thought to Prudence.

'Edward Lyall is charming, don't you think?' she went on. 'I thought he looked rather tired tonight. It must be exhausting to be admired like that, and one feels that politicians aren't quite so used to it as the clergy are.'

Nicholas smiled down into his cocoa.

Prudence agreed that Edward Lyall was good-looking. Flora busied herself removing the cups, but said nothing. Tonight she had known the exquisitely painful sensation of a moment's unfaithfulness to Mr Oliver, whose place in her affections had not yet been taken by any undergraduate. Edward Lyall's pale, even slightly hollow, cheek had touched her imagination. But everyone had been rather horrid to Mr Oliver, and that had touched her heart. She scarcely knew which she would think about before she went to sleep that night.

Jane stood up and stretched her arms. She hoped it had been a good evening. Perhaps Fabian and Prudence could meet in London. She began to plan lunches and dinners for them. Really, she was almost like Pandarus, she told herself, only it was to be a courtship and marriage according to the most decorous conventions. Fabian was a widower and Prudence was a spinster; there wasn't even the embarrassment of divorce. No, when she thought it over, Jane decided that she was really much more like Emma Woodhouse.

CHAPTER TEN

'DO YOU suppose Miss Bates has any love life?' asked Marilyn idly one morning after Prudence had been staying with Jane. 'She's quite attractive still, really.'

'I wonder how old she *is*,' said Gloria. 'About thirty, do you think?'

'Oh, yes, must be. I hope I die before I'm thirty – it sounds so old.'

'Forty must be worse,' said Gloria sensibly. 'I shouldn't like to be forty. Miss Trapnell's over forty, I should think, and Miss Clothier too.'

They brooded silently for a moment over this horror.

'Manifold's thirty,' said Marilyn in a brighter tone. 'It doesn't seem so bad for a man.'

'And Gramp's forty-eight this year,' said Gloria. 'I looked him up in *Who's Who*.'

'Fancy him being anybody,' giggled Marilyn. 'You wouldn't think it to look at him. Forty-eight! That makes him nearly twenty years older than Miss Bates. When she was a baby, he was grown-up. Fancy that! How do you think the passion's going these days?'

They discussed Miss Bates's passion for Dr Grampian for some moments, after which they came to the conclusion that any feeling one might have for such an elderly man – and in the office too – could hardly be counted as love life. They regarded themselves as much more fortunate in having friends of their own age who had nothing to do with their work.

'I suppose I'd better make the tea,' said Gloria, getting up and taking the kettle to fill it. 'It's my turn today.'

'Are you going to make Manifold's Nescafé?'

'No, he can make it himself if he wants it. I don't mind boiling water for him – he can have what's left over from the tea.'

In another room Prudence sat with Miss Trapnell and Miss Clothier, discussing the possibility of tea being ready within the foreseeable future.

'Five-past eleven,' said Miss Trapnell. 'I hope they've put the kettle on.'

'I thought I heard a sound,' said Miss Clothier, opening her tin of biscuits.

'What kind of a sound?' asked Prudence idly.

'The sound of running water.'

'Did you say rushing water?' asked Miss Trapnell seriously.

'No, no; *running* water,' said Miss Clothier impatiently. 'As if somebody was filling a kettle.'

Footsteps were heard outside the door. They paused for a moment.

'Ah,' said Miss Trapnell.

'Look here, Miss Bates!' Mr Manifold burst into the room and confronted the three women.

I suppose he hides his feeling of inferiority under this blunt and rather ill-bred manner, thought Prudence, hardly looking up from what she was doing. After a moment she did glance up in what seemed to him her cool, maddening way.

She saw him standing by her side, holding a bundle of galley proofs. Corduroy trousers, plaid shirt and tweed jacket – why must he dress like an undergraduate? she thought with irritation. And the dear boy was so cross about something. His eyes were blazing.

'Have I done something?' she asked.

'Yes, or at least I think so,' he faltered, disarmed by her coldness. 'Didn't you write up these notes of mine for Gramp?'

'I may have done. Let me see.' Prudence held out a hand for the proofs. 'What's it all about? Ah, yes,' she smiled. 'It was most obscure – Dr Grampian and I had a very difficult time with it. We couldn't make out what you meant.'

'Well, it wasn't what you've put,' said Mr Manifold rather more meekly now. 'Perhaps I didn't make it quite clear.'

'No, I don't think you can have done. Oh, good, here's tea. Stay and have yours here and then we can talk it over.'

'I don't want any tea.'

'Oh, no. You don't like it, do you? Gloria will make you some Nescafé, won't you, Gloria?'

'All right, Miss Bates,' said Gloria rather sulkily.

'I don't want anything, thank you,' said Mr Manifold. 'I'll make it myself later, if I do.'

'You really ought to have something,' said Miss Clothier. 'Won't you have a biscuit?'

'Thank you. I am rather hungry as a matter of fact.'

'I'll just slip out and tell Gloria to make you some Nescafé,' said Miss Trapnell.

Mr Manifold sat down by Prudence and together they discussed the corrections that would have to be made.

'You see, it isn't really quite what's written here,' he explained. 'You've over-simplified it.'

'Really?' Prudence assumed an interested tone and looked up into his clear hazel eyes as if she understood every word he was saying. 'I'm afraid we've got it wrong, then.'

'One doesn't want to be misrepresented.'

'No, of course not. I'm sorry.'

'Oh, that's all right. I only thought for a moment . . .'

'What did you think?' Prudence looked up at him again. Really, his eyes were beautiful, she thought. Her voice had taken on an absent-mindedly intimate note as if she were not in the office at all.

Mr Manifold looked surprised. Then he smiled and something like a blush flooded into his pale cheeks. Prudence turned away to hide a smile and he hurried out of the room.

'Why, he didn't finish his Nescafé,' she exclaimed after he had gone.

'I suppose he forgot it,' said Miss Trapnell.

'Being with you must have put it out of his mind,' said Miss Clothier.

'Being with *me*?'

'Yes, I always think he rather likes you, Miss Bates.'

Prudence laughed. 'Well, really, what an extraordinary idea!' But, why not? What could be more natural? She was attractive and intelligent, even 'desirable'; it was not at all surprising that Geoffrey Manifold should find her so.

When the telephone rang and she was summoned into the presence of Dr Grampian she went to his room feeling light-hearted and confident, ready to be admired by him too.

He was sitting at his desk with a glass of water and some tablets before him. Prudence felt a pang that she was not as moved at the sight as she would have been a few weeks ago.

'Ah, Miss Bates,' he said, opening the bottle and shaking a few tablets out on to the desk.

'Aren't you feeling well?' asked Prudence, her tone softening. We must love them all, she thought, and perhaps we should make a special effort with those for whom our love is growing cold.

'I suppose I am as well as I ever am,' said Dr Grampian in a colourless tone. 'But things have been rather trying lately.'

Prudence wondered what things. Men did not have quite the same trials as women – it would be the larger things that worried him, his health, his work, perhaps even his wife Lucy. Was she being unsatisfactory in some way? Prudence felt that she could hardly ask.

'I think you and Manifold between you could manage to do something with this . . .' he went on, taking up a thick folder of typewritten foolscap, turning over the pages and marking certain paragraphs with a pencil. Prudence appeared to be attending to him, but her thoughts were wandering to the evening she was to spend with Fabian. Their acquaintance had prospered since the evening they had met at the whist drive. Luncheons and dinners, with the appropriate foods and wines, had turned it into quite a romantic love affair.

When the time came to leave the office, Prudence was ready to go before six o'clock had struck.

'Being with Dr Grampian always takes it out of me,' she explained. 'I'm really quite exhausted.'

Miss Trapnell nodded sympathetically. 'Contact with a brilliant mind like that must be very tiring,' she agreed. 'You have to be so very much on your mettle.'

Prudence remembered the bottle of tablets and the fingers turning the pages of the typescript and her own silence, filled with thoughts of Fabian, and had the grace not to pursue the subject further.

She was to meet Fabian at a Soho restaurant which they usually frequented, but luckily there was time for her to go back to her flat first to change her dress and give herself a suitable evening face.

He was waiting for her with a spray of red roses, her favourite flowers. He found it pleasant to be taking an attractive woman out to dinner again – ten months was a long time to be away from it all, he had hardly realized how much he had missed it, and was gratified to find that he had not lost his old touch. And this time there was the added pleasure of a clear conscience; it was a very long time since he had been able to take out another woman without the nagging guilty feeling at the back of his mind, the picture of Constance, sitting in a deck-chair under the walnut tree, doing her needlework.

'My darling,' he said as they sipped cocktails, 'how very lovely you look tonight. I've been so longing to see you again.'

Prudence took a larger gulp of her drink. She had thought his words rather banal, disappointing, even. Her imaginary evenings with Arthur Grampian had not been quite like this, but probably he would have been just as dull when it came to the point. Perhaps nothing could be quite so sweet as the imagined evenings with their flow of sparkling conversation, but it was not the kind of thing she could very well say to Fabian. All the same, she told herself sensibly, he would probably make quite a good husband for her. He was the right age, they had tastes in common and she enjoyed his company. Also, and this was not unimportant, he was good-looking. They would make a handsome couple.

'Now we must have something nice to eat,' said Fabian, studying the menu. 'What would you like, my dear?'

Prudence chose what she would have, perhaps more carefully than a woman truly in love would have done, and Fabian made his choice, which was equally deliberate and not quite the same as hers.

The chicken will have that wonderful sauce with it, thought Prudence, looking into Fabian's eyes. She had ordered smoked salmon to begin with, and afterwards perhaps she would have some Brie, all creamy and delicious.

'Have you seen Jane lately?' she asked.

'Oh, yes. I quite often see her,' said Fabian. 'We are great friends. I find her a most delightful person.'

'Yes; dear Jane. She is rather wonderful, and yet in a way she's missed something. Life hasn't turned out quite as she meant it to.'

Fabian looked blank.

'She seems quite happy,' he ventured.

'*Seems*, well, yes . . .'

Fabian found Prudence's tone disconcerting; it was as if no woman could be really happy even when she was being taken out to dinner. He felt he ought to say something profound, but, naturally enough, nothing profound came out.

'I mean, she leads a useful kind of life – work in the parish and that kind of thing,' he went on vaguely.

'But she's really no good at parish work – she's wasted in that kind of life. She has great gifts, you know. She could have written books.'

'Written books? Oh, good heavens!'

'Well, what's wrong with that?' asked Prudence rather sharply.

'I always think women who write books sound rather formidable.'

'You'd prefer them to be stupid and feminine? To think men are wonderful?'

'Well, every man likes to be thought wonderful. A woman need not necessarily be stupid to admire a man.'

Prudence thought a little sadly of her admiration for Arthur Grampian, now perhaps in the past. She could not pretend that she really admired Fabian in quite the same way. But when the wine came, golden and delicious, her heart warmed towards him and by the time they were drinking black coffee and brandy she felt that perhaps she really did admire Fabian. After all, what was a brilliant mind and some rather dull books that nobody could be expected to read? Not so very much really when compared with curly hair, fine eyes and good features.

'I shall have a dark, lonely journey home,' said Fabian softly. 'It seems very sad that we have to part.'

'Yes, it does,' said Prudence thoughtfully; 'but evenings have to come to an end.'

'They need not,' Fabian began, but then he remembered that Prudence could not be quite like all the others. There was the complication of her being a friend of Jane Cleveland's. Somehow one did not play fast and loose with the friend of one's vicar's wife, he thought solemnly.

'Perhaps some other time . . .' said Prudence uncertainly.

'I'll see about getting you a taxi, then.'

While Prudence was waiting in the foyer, a tall young woman in a tweed suit came up to her.

'Hullo, Prue! I saw you in the distance, but you wouldn't look at me.'

'Why, Eleanor, what are you doing here?'

'My dear, I've been having dinner with J.B. He's off to the

Middle East tomorrow. We didn't leave the Ministry till after nine – there were *things to see to*, you know.'

Eleanor's tone, mysteriously important as always, made Prudence a little envious. How wonderful it must be to work for somebody who really needed you, who couldn't get off to the Middle East unless you were there to see to things. J.B. couldn't do anything without Eleanor. She stood now, beaming, tweedy and efficient, while J.B., a tall worried-looking man with an excessively bulging briefcase, got his coat from the cloakroom.

'We must lunch one day,' said Prudence rather feebly.

'Oh, yes, let's. Give me a ring some time.'

Going home by herself in the taxi, Prudence thought of Eleanor and her other contemporaries at Oxford, all neatly labelled in Miss Birkinshaw's comfortable classification. 'Eleanor, with her work at the Ministry, Mollie with the Settlement and her dogs, and Prudence . . .' Well, what about Prudence? Prudence with her love affairs, that was what Jane used to say, and perhaps, after all, it was true. She would put the red roses in a glass on her bedside table and take them into the office in the morning.

CHAPTER ELEVEN

NOW THAT there was a feeling of spring in the air, Fabian decided that he really ought to do something about 'poor Constance's things'. Also, the entry of Prudence into his life made it seem unsuitable that nothing should have been done about them before.

It was Mrs Arkright who managed to spur him to some definite action. She was always saying to her friends what a shame it was that all those good things of poor Mrs Driver's should be still lying in the drawers and wardrobes, and now that another spring with its attendant cleaning and tidying was approaching it really did seem as if she ought to say something to Mr Driver. Last spring it had been different, of course; the bereavement was too fresh in his mind, poor man, but now it really was time that he pulled himself together.

Jane Cleveland heard all about this from Mrs Glaze.

'It's just over the year now,' she said. 'I was looking in the paper last week to see if there'd be anything, but there wasn't.'

'In the paper?' Jane asked. 'But why should there be?'

'In Memoriam,' said Mrs Glaze rather stiffly. 'It's nice to put something.'

'Oh, in the local paper, of course,' said Jane, remembering the long column of pathetic, limping verses commemorating Gran and Dad and the rest of the dear departed.

'You'd have thought there might be something,' went on Mrs Glaze. 'Mrs Arkright passed the same remark to me only yesterday. You'd think he'd remember her.'

'I don't suppose he forgot,' said Jane, 'but people don't always show their feelings in the same way, do they.' And sometimes, she added to herself, they don't have the feelings one would expect.

A long sad year has passed today
Since my dear Connie was taken away . . .

Was that the kind of thing Mrs Glaze and Mrs Arkright would have found suitable, nodding their heads and saying it was 'nice'?

'That sort of thing shouldn't really be necessary for Christians,' she began firmly; 'if we believe, as we should . . .' But then, she thought, weren't we all, even the most intelligent of us, like children fearing to go into the dark, no better than primitive peoples with their ancestor cults, the way we went to the cemetery on a Sunday afternoon, bearing bunches of flowers? But she couldn't say all this to Mrs Glaze, standing at the kitchen table in her hat and apron, making pastry.

'At least he's going to get her things sorted out; that's something,' said Mrs Glaze. 'Mrs Arkright said why not let Miss Doggett and Miss Morrow do it – they're nice ladies and they were friends of poor Mrs Driver.'

'Or Mrs Crampton and Mrs Mayhew,' suggested Jane, 'though they might be too busy at the Spinning Wheel.'

'Well, four ladies might be a bit too much even for Mr Driver,' said Mrs Glaze with a laugh. 'Perhaps there should be a married lady, though. He might have asked you, but I told Mrs Arkright, I didn't think you would be much of a one for tidying.'

Jane hung her head. 'No, not for tidying, perhaps,' she agreed. But was her status as wife of the vicar of the parish to count for nothing? She could hardly add that her insatiable curiosity might also render her eligible for the position. 'When are they going to do it?'

'On Saturday afternoon – that seemed the best time.'

'I should have thought a morning might be better,' said Jane.

Mrs Glaze looked a little shocked. 'We have our work in the morning, madam,' she said importantly. 'Mrs Arkright will be there to do the tea, of course.'

'So tea is to be provided?'

'Well, they'll need tea. There's a lot of things to be sorted.'

'Yes, of course,' said Jane slowly, her mind on plans for being there herself. A casual call? A request to borrow a lawn-mower in the depths of winter? How was she to manage it? No doubt something would occur to her when the time came.

On the chosen Saturday afternoon Miss Doggett and Miss Morrow left their house at about a quarter past two. Miss Doggett had considered the occasion important enough to give up her afternoon rest and was rather more grandly dressed than a call next door seemed to warrant, in a skunk cape and large hat of the type known as 'matron's', trimmed with brown velvet and little tufts of feathers. Miss Morrow wore her grey tweed coat and had a plaid scarf over her head.

They went up to Fabian's front door and rang the bell. Mrs Arkright in her apron and a purple turban opened the door and showed them into the dining-room, where Fabian was still at the table drinking his coffee. He sat with his head bowed, gazing into his cup, one cheek resting on his hand. It seemed a suitable position for him to be in, making it appear that a mere week or two and not a whole year had elapsed since poor Constance's death.

'You will forgive me if I don't join you,' he said in a low voice. 'I should find it . . .'

'Oh, very painful, of course. We quite understand,' said Miss Doggett briskly. 'We'll get to work straight away.'

'Most of the things are upstairs,' said Fabian in the same low voice. 'In the large room overlooking the garden and some in the room next to it. I shall stay here . . .' He drew towards him a bowl of white hyacinths which stood on the table and began to sniff at the flowers absent-mindedly.

Miss Doggett and Miss Morrow went quietly out of the room. Once out of his presence, however, their steps became noticeably brisker and there was an eagerness about their bearing which they did not attempt to conceal.

'Now for it,' said Miss Morrow, almost running up the stairs.

'Really, Jessie,' said Miss Doggett, whose step was slower than her companion's only because she was a much older and heavier woman. 'I wonder if Mr Driver would object to our lighting the gas-fire,' she said as they opened the door and sensed the chill of the big room overlooking the garden. 'It's rather cold in here. Poor Constance always used to say this room was damp.'

'He'd jolly well better not object,' said Miss Morrow, lighting the fire and then removing her coat and scarf. 'On what principle are we to sort out these things? Distressed gentlewomen and jumble? Or should there be more and subtler distinctions?'

'No. I should think that is what Mr Driver would wish, and what poor Constance herself would have wished,' said Miss Doggett, opening the wardrobe. 'Oh, dear, here is her musquash coat! She never had it remodelled, though I often suggested to her that she should. Mr Rose could have done it for her as he did my cape.' She stroked the strands of skunk which still hung from her shoulders, for the room had not yet warmed up in spite of the flaring and popping gas-fire.

'I can just see her in that coat,' said Jessie, looking at the long brown coat with its narrow shoulders and old-fashioned roll collar. She remembered Constance's long, pale face with the worried grey eyes and the fair, wispy hair drawn back into a rather meagre little knot on the nape of the neck. 'And, oh dear, here are all her shoes, long and narrow and of such good leather. Just the thing for the gentlewomen.'

'She was much too good for him,' said Miss Doggett, taking a pair of the shoes into her hand. 'I often wondered how they ever came to be married. These lizard courts – they cost eight guineas, I remember Constance telling me. She had to have them specially made, such a very narrow foot she had.'

Miss Doggett was still holding the shoes when Jane came into the room carrying a khaki canvas hold-all.

'I came round on the off-chance of getting a bit of jumble,' she said, bringing out the words she had been rehearsing on her way from the vicarage. She had decided to appear in the simple role of a vicar's wife seeking jumble, and hoped it sounded convincing. Mrs Arkright, who had opened the door, had looked a little suspicious, but Miss Doggett and Miss Morrow appeared to accept her without question.

'Jumble's on the bed,' said Miss Doggett. 'We have put the things we think might do for the distressed gentlewomen on the chaise-longue.'

'How very suitable to put them there!' Jane burst out. 'I suppose this was Mrs Driver's room?'

'Yes, and she had the little room next door as a kind of workroom – she kept her sewing-machine there and her embroidery things.'

'These were her books?' Jane asked, going over to a small bookcase which was fixed on to the wall near the bed.

'I suppose so,' said Jessie, 'though Constance didn't seem to be much of a reader. She had a novel from the library sometimes.'

'Or a good biography,' added Miss Doggett.

'You mean a life of Florence Nightingale or the memoirs of some Edwardian diplomat's widow,' Jane murmured. 'But these are mostly books of poetry. Was this what she read secretly, I wonder?'

'Oh, I don't think Constance was the kind of person to go in for that sort of thing,' said Miss Doggett in a shocked voice.

'People do seem to be ashamed of admitting that they read poetry,' said Jane, 'unless they have a degree in English – it is permissible then. It has become a kind of bad habit, but one that is excused. I wonder what she made of Mr Auden and Mr MacNeice? Perhaps the seventeenth century was more to her taste, as it is to mine. Odd to think that we may have had that in common.' She took a book from the shelf and began to examine it in the hope of finding an interesting inscription on the fly-leaf. Nor was she disappointed, for on it was written in a fine, intelligent-looking hand:

F. from C., 18th April, 1935

My Love is of a birth as rare
As 'tis for object strange and high . . .

She closed the book quickly and slipped it into the canvas hold-all. This must not go to the jumble sale. Marvell – *A Definition of Love* – had poor Constance's love been begotten by Despair upon Impossibility? Jane wondered. But then of course when writing an inscription one did not always consider the appropriateness or otherwise of the rest of the poem. 1935 – Fabian would have been in his early twenties and Constance some years older – it must have been at some moment during their courtship. Jane wondered when she had taken her gift back, if it had been a conscious action performed on some special occasion, perhaps after some particularly painful infidelity on Fabian's part, or whether the book had just got into the shelf of its own accord, as it were, as books do when they are no longer particularly treasured.

'Do you suppose he really wants any of these books?' she asked in a rather rough tone.

'Well, perhaps we had better ask him,' said Miss Doggett, 'though he did say he'd rather we used our own judgment.'

'I'll go and ask him if you like,' said Jessie, hurrying from the room.

She found Fabian downstairs huddled over the fire in the drawing-room. He did not seem to be doing anything in particular, though *The Times* was folded back at the crossword and there were a few words filled in. It was difficult, Jessie thought, for him to know what he ought to be doing while she and the others were upstairs. There was rugby football or dance music on the wireless, but neither of these would be suitable listening, and the Third Programme had not yet started. Perhaps some Bach on the radiogram or a little work in the garden, but the earth was still bare and hard and it did not look as if anything would ever grow again.

'Mrs Cleveland wants to know about the books,' she began.

'What books?'

'On the shelf by the bed.'

'Oh, let her do what she likes with them – take them herself or have them for a jumble sale – I don't care.'

'Poor Fabian. What are you doing?' Jessie laid a hand on his head and looked down into his face. 'Just brooding?'

'I don't know what to do,' he said. 'The whole thing is most painful to me.'

'Yes, you are having the pain now,' Jessie said. 'Women are very powerful – perhaps they are always triumphant in the end.'

'What do you mean?'

'Oh, you wouldn't understand!' She dropped a light kiss on his brow and hurried away.

If Fabian was surprised by her action he gave no indication of it. After all, it was by no means the first time that a woman had paid him a little spontaneous tribute; it might be considered as no more than his due. He stood up and looked at his face in the mirror framed in a design of gilded cupids which hung over the mantelpiece. Its dim surface gave back an interesting, shadowy reflection. He began to think about Jessie Morrow – more in her than met the eye – a deep one – his thoughts shaped themselves into conventional phrases. She had an unexpectedly sharp tongue; there was something a little uncomfortable about that. She was so badly dressed, usually in tweeds that had never been good. It would be interesting to see her transformed in the way that the women's magazines sometimes glamorized a dowdy woman. No doubt Prudence would be able to make some suggestions. . . . Fabian's thoughts now turned to her, but his evenings in her company, though delightful, seemed to have little reality at the moment. Wine, good food, flowers, soft lights, holding hands, sparkling eyes, kisses . . . and upstairs those three women were sorting out poor Constance's things. Altogether he was glad when Mrs Arkright announced that she had laid tea in the dining-room.

'I thought the ladies would prefer to sit round the table,' she explained.

They were summoned from upstairs and came down eagerly enough. Jane began to wonder if they were to have a meat tea or fish and chips as a reward for their hard work, but she was quite satisfied when she saw the hot buttered toast and sandwiches and several different kinds of cake.

'We're nearly through,' said Miss Doggett briskly. 'There are one or two small personal trinkets, we thought perhaps . . .'

'Oh, no . . .' Fabian bowed his head into his hands, 'not that . . .'

'Somebody had better pour out tea,' said Jane sensibly, wondering when Fabian would raise his head.

'You, of course, Mrs Cleveland,' said Miss Doggett.

'I always do it rather badly,' said Jane. 'The ability to pour tea gracefully didn't come to me automatically when I married. I wish you would do it, Miss Doggett.'

'Very well, if you wish,' said Miss Doggett.

Fabian had by now raised his head and was taking a piece of hot buttered toast.

Mrs Arkright came into the room bearing an iced walnut cake on a plate. 'Mrs Crampton and Mrs Mayhew have just called,' she explained. 'They thought Mr Driver might like this cake. It's his favourite, I know.'

'How kind,' said Fabian, rousing himself. 'Are they at the door? Do ask them to come in so that I can thank them.'

'No, sir. They hurried away,' said Mrs Arkright.

Jane reflected how much more delicate their behaviour had been than hers and bowed her head. Still, she had perhaps done some good by saving poor Constance's gift from prying eyes, and she had certainly collected a lot of useful jumble.

Miss Doggett and Jessie too could feel that they had done something both for Fabian and for the distressed gentlewomen, and Jessie had privately earmarked one or two garments for herself and planned to alter them suitably and add them to her wardrobe.

Conversation at tea was not very brilliant. Jane was thinking too much about Constance and the book, Jessie about Fabian, and Fabian himself about the oppressive presence of three not particularly attractive women at his table, and also about Jessie's strange behaviour earlier in the afternoon. He hoped she wasn't going to become a nuisance in any way. They still had a little more sorting out to do, but he decided against offering them sherry when they had finished. It might go to their heads, he decided, and then they might all behave foolishly. He could easily make it understood that he was really too much upset to prolong the painful business any longer. He would have a half bottle of St Emilion with his dinner, and after that he might write a letter to Prudence.

'Well, it's a very satisfactory thing to have done,' declared Miss Doggett as they stood outside Fabian's gate in the cold night air. 'I expect Mr Driver is very relieved to have it settled. We shall be going in tomorrow to parcel up the things for the gentlewomen.'

'Well, I suppose I must be getting home,' said Jane. 'Poor Mr Driver – it seems unkind to leave him all alone this evening.'

'Yes,' Miss Doggett agreed. 'One does feel that men need company more than women do. A woman has a thousand and one little tasks in the house, and then her knitting or sewing.'

Jane, who did not seem to have these things, made no answer.

'A man can have his thoughts,' suggested Miss Morrow.

'Perhaps they do not care to be left alone with those,' said Jane. 'I often wonder when I leave Nicholas in his study.'

'But surely, Mrs Cleveland, a clergyman must be different. He would be thinking out a sermon or a letter to the Bishop.'

'Yes, he ought to be doing things like that,' said Jane vaguely. 'Well, I mustn't keep you talking in the cold. Good night.' She wandered away in the direction of the vicarage, but when she reached the church she lingered a while by the churchyard wall, thinking of eighteenth-century poets and charnel-houses and exhumations by the light of flickering candles. Then she saw that there was a light in the choir vestry. No doubt Nicholas was doing something there; there was a meeting of some kind or perhaps a choir practice. Then she remembered that he was away from home that evening, at some ruridecanal conference, something that went beyond the narrow confines of the parish. Mrs Glaze was to have left her something simple and womanish for her evening meal, the kind of thing that a person with no knowledge of cooking might heat up.

She crept up to the window where the light was and stood outside it for a moment. People seemed to be talking inside – men's voices were raised in what sounded like an argument. Jane felt like some character in a novel by Mrs Henry Wood. But she was the vicar's wife and as such surely had a right of entry to the choir vestry. So she went boldly up to the door and opened it.

'Good evening,' she said. 'I saw a light and heard voices so I thought I'd look in.'

'Good evening, Mrs Cleveland.' Mr Mortlake stood before her, obviously angry at being disturbed and looking rather terrible.

'Good evening.' Mr Oliver stood up and looked a little taken aback. The third member of the party, Mrs Glaze's nephew, the butcher, said nothing. Tomorrow, thought Jane, we may have to face each other over a tray full of offal or a few chops scattered between us, so perhaps silence is the best thing.

'I could hear your voices from outside,' she observed pleasantly. 'Were you having an argument about something?'

'We were discussing a little matter,' said Mr Oliver in a soothing tone; 'nothing of any importance, really.'

'There was some disagreement,' said Mr Mortlake.

'A difference of opinion, you might say,' ventured Mrs Glaze's nephew.

'Well, I'm sure you ought not to disagree about things,'

said Jane. 'After all, you are all members of the Parochial Church Council, and in a way I suppose you are on hallowed ground here.'

'I wouldn't go so far as to say that, Mrs Cleveland,' said Mr Mortlake indignantly, so that she feared he must have misunderstood her.

'Well, perhaps not,' Jane faltered, for she was not really certain whether the choir vestry was in fact regarded as part of the church, 'but one doesn't like to think of any unpleasantness here. I know my husband would be sorry to hear about it.'

'I am not aware that there has been any unpleasantness,' said Mr Oliver in a hostile tone. 'We all have our own opinions and are entitled to them, I suppose.'

'Of course,' said Jane. 'Perhaps an outsider could help you to make up your minds, though.'

'Well, Mrs Cleveland, we can hardly regard you as that,' said Mr Mortlake unctuously. 'But we cannot burden you with our little petty differences. It is a matter altogether out of your sphere.'

Really, thought Jane, it was like one of those rather tedious comic scenes in Shakespeare – Dogberry and Verges, perhaps – and therefore beyond her comprehension. She suddenly saw them all in Elizabethan costume and began to smile. 'Oh, well, I suppose I shouldn't interfere,' she said. 'We women can't always do as much as we think we can.' She had imagined herself mediating and bringing them together so that they all went off and settled their differences over a glass of beer. She turned to go, half hoping that they would call her back, but they watched her in silence, until Mr Oliver bade her good night and the others followed his example.

When she got home she found that Mrs Glaze had left her a shepherd's pie, a dish she particularly disliked, to put in the oven. She waited hopefully for Nicholas's return, but when he eventually came she found herself talking only about the afternoon they had spent at Fabian's and not mentioning the episode in the choir vestry.

CHAPTER TWELVE

IN HER EARLY days Jane had once had a book of essays published and had somehow managed to become a member of a certain literary society of which she still sometimes attended meetings. These usually took place in the evenings, and were another excuse for Jane to absent herself from parish duties and to stay a night with Prudence at her flat. This particular meeting was to be a rather special one; it was the centenary of the birth of an author whose works Jane had never read, but who had died recently enough to be remembered by many persons still alive. This seemed a good reason for a literary society to be gathering together, as Jane explained to Nicholas, who had protested, though mildly enough, at her missing a meeting of the Parochial Church Council.

'I shouldn't do any good there,' said Jane guiltily, remembering her intrusion into the choir vestry a few weeks ago of which she had told him nothing.

'I should have thought the time could be more profitably spent in encouraging young authors rather than in celebrating dead ones,' Nicholas declared.

'But it does encourage them,' Jane said. 'They imagine that one day such a meeting might be held about them, and I suppose they wonder what will be remembered and hope it won't be something they'd prefer to be forgotten.'

Nicholas sighed and did not argue further, for he knew it was likely to be as profitable as most arguments with his wife. His poor Jane, he must let her go where she wanted to.

The society met at a house with vaguely literary associations, for it was next door to what had once been the residence of one of the lesser Victorian poets, who is, nevertheless, quite well represented in the *Oxford Book of Victorian Verse*.

Jane entered the house with rather less awe than on her first visit many years ago, and made her way to a room on the first floor where the meetings were held. It was a pleasant room with the air of a drawing-room about it, though the rows of chairs were set a little too close together for comfort. Jane stood in the doorway, looking to see if anyone she knew had arrived, and soon noticed her old college friend, Barbara Bird ('Miss Bird has her novels and her dogs,' as Miss Birkinshaw put it), sitting in the back row. She was wearing a shaggy orange fox fur cape and smoking a cigarette which she waved to Jane, indicating a vacant chair at her side.

'Freezing cold in here,' she said. 'Nice to see you, Jane.'

Jane sat down and looked around her. Here again, as when she went back to her old College, she found that she did not really look any more peculiar than the majority of the women present, most of whom were dressed without regard to any particular fashion. But it was a cold evening, so perhaps they had more excuse than the graduates who met in the summer. Jane herself was wearing her old fur-lined boots and a tweed coat, underneath which an assortment of cardigans and scarves concealed a red woollen dress that Prudence had once given her.

'Better gathering than usual,' said Miss Bird; 'quite a few critics.'

'Such mild-looking men,' said Jane, seeing one of them taking his seat rather near the front. 'Perhaps they compensate themselves for their gentle appearance by dipping their pens in vitriol.'

Miss Bird then went on to tell Jane about what the critics had said about her latest novel, during which Jane's thoughts wandered, 'much incident and little wit' she heard dimly, and then Miss Bird's wheezy smoker's laugh ending in a paroxysm of coughing.

Why was it, Jane wondered, that there were usually more women than men at these gatherings? Were men less gregarious, less willing to listen to a lecture or talk from one of their kind, or was it something really quite simple, such as the lack of alcoholic refreshment, that kept them away? Certainly there were some men who attended regularly, and each had his little circle of what were presumably admiring women. Jane had not so far attached herself to any group; she preferred to wander freely and observe others with what she hoped was detachment.

Tonight there were three speakers, an elderly female novelist, a distinguished critic and a beautiful young poet. Or perhaps he was not really so very young, Jane decided, though he was certainly beautiful, with brown eyes and a well-shaped nose. It is a refreshing thing for an ordinary-looking woman to look at a beautiful man occasionally and Jane gave herself up to contemplation, while the talk of the critic and the novelist flowed over her. The poet spoke last and had a soft, attractive voice which was totally inaudible at the back of the room. Miss Bird shamed Jane at one point by demanding in her gruff voice that he should speak up, which he did for the rest of his sentence, afterwards lapsing into soft inaudibility.

As the time drew on towards the usual hour for closing the meeting, Jane saw through a glass door at the back of the room the faces of two women anxiously peering. One of them was holding a coffee-pot. Perhaps they made their presence felt to the speakers in some way, for shortly after this the talk finished. There was a short, appreciative silence, a hasty vote of thanks and then the crowd proceeded to squeeze itself with as much dignity as possible through the narrow door to the room where the refreshments were to be served. Miss

Bird again embarrassed Jane by pushing herself forward, knocking against a novelist of greater distinction than herself and seizing a plate of sandwiches and making off with it to a comparatively uncrowded corner.

'Didn't have any dinner,' she explained.

'Aren't you Miss Barbara Bird?' said a tall, youngish woman with large eyes and prominent teeth, addressing Jane.

'No. *I'm* not Barbara Bird,' said Jane. 'You won't ever have heard of me. This is Barbara Bird.' She indicated her friend.

The woman then gave her name, which was unknown to both Jane and Miss Bird, and the titles of the two novels she had published, neither of which seemed familiar.

'I think I've heard of them,' said Jane kindly. 'And now I shall look forward to reading them.'

'Oh, they're nothing, really,' said the young woman.

'One's first two books are really rather more than that,' said Miss Bird. 'After the first two or three one must be unselfish and consider one's public and one's publisher. I have just finished my seventeenth – "Miss Bird's readers know what to expect now and they will not be disappointed." '

Jane thought the young woman looked a little cast down, so she said, 'Oh, but I think one develops as one goes on. I feel sure I shouldn't have had Barbara's attitude if I had written more than one book. It was nothing you could possibly have read,' she went on hastily, seeing the puzzled look on the woman's face. 'A book of essays on seventeenth-century poets about fifteen years ago. The kind of book you might put in the bathroom if you have books there – with Aubrey's *Brief Lives*, and *Wild Wales* – really, I wonder why, now! It would be an interesting study, that.'

'It's been lovely meeting you and Miss Bird,' said the young woman. 'I was wondering, do you think I *dare* speak to *him*?' She indicated the young or not-so-young poet, who was surrounded by a little group. 'I found his talk so wonderfully stimulating.'

'Was it? We couldn't hear a word at the back,' barked Miss Bird.

'But do you think I should *dare* to tell him how much I enjoyed it?' the woman persisted.

'Of course,' said Jane sympathetically, realizing how much she longed for a glance from those brown eyes. 'I expect he is used to being admired.'

'It was what he *said* really,' protested the young woman, though rather faintly.

'Yes, go on,' said Barbara Bird, almost giving her a push. She and Jane turned and watched their former companion approach the poet, linger on the edge of the circle and then plunge boldly in with an apparently paralysing effect, for the others immediately broke away, leaving her alone with him.

'The evening will have been made for her now,' said Barbara Bird not unkindly.

'Oh, yes,' agreed Jane enthusiastically, stepping backwards into a critic and causing him to upset his coffee over himself.

'I think it will be better to pretend I didn't notice,' she whispered to her friend.

'Yes, by all means. Look, he is being attended to. A woman is mopping at his trousers with her handkerchief.'

'This seems a good time to leave,' said Jane. 'The last impression will have been good – one woman rendering homage to a poet and another mopping spilt coffee from the trousers of a critic. Things like that aren't as trivial as you might think.'

Rather to Jane's surprise, their decision to leave seemed to break up the other little groups, and once outside in the dark square they were groups no more, but isolated individuals, each one going his or her own way. Barbara Bird took a taxi, the critic made his way to the Underground, the poet walked quickly away, while the young woman who had admired him, after a regretful glance after him, stood rather hopelessly at a request bus stop. Perhaps she had hoped that they might stroll to a pub together or continue their conversation – if such it had been – walking round the square. But once outside the magic circle the writers became their lonely selves, pondering on poems, observing their fellow men ruthlessly, putting people they knew into novels; no wonder they were without friends. Jane was reminded of Darley's *Siren Chorus* and found herself thinking of the last verse:

In bowers of love men take their rest,
In loveless bowers we sigh alone;
With bosom-friends are others blest,
But we have none – but we have none.

The swans in snowy couples and the murmuring seal lying close to his sleek companion. . . . Jane almost forgot where she was supposed to be going and came to herself just as she reached the stop for the bus that would take her to Prudence's flat. She enjoyed riding on the top of the bus, smoking a cigarette and looking into the lighted windows of the houses they passed, hoping that she might see something interesting. Mostly, however, the curtains were discreetly drawn, except occasionally in a kitchen where a man was seen filling a hot-water bottle (for his invalid wife or for himself? Jane wondered) or a woman laying the breakfast ready for the morning. Once they stopped outside a high, dark house and Jane found herself looking through the uncurtained window into an upper room, dimly lit, where a group of men and women were sitting round a large table covered by a dark green cloth. The glimpse was too fleeting to reveal whether it was a séance or a committee meeting. Would she ever pass that house again? Jane wondered. She doubted in any case whether she would have recognized it again.

Prudence's flat was in the kind of block where Jane imagined people might be found dead, though she had never said this to Prudence herself; it seemed rather a macabre fancy and not one to be confided to an unmarried woman living alone. Prudence came to the door quickly in response to Jane's ring; she was wearing a long garment of dark red velvet, a sort of rather grand dressing-gown it seemed to Jane, who supposed it was a housecoat, the kind of thing to wear for an evening of gracious living. Not the sort of garment a vicar's wife could be expected to possess.

'Jane, how lovely to see you! Was it a good meeting? Let me take your bag – then perhaps you'd like a drink or some tea or Ovaltine?'

Prudence prided herself on being a good hostess and tried to think of everything that a guest could possibly need. Jane, while appreciating this and benefiting from it, thought the flat a little too good to be true. Those light striped satin covers would 'show the dirt' – the pretty Regency couch was really rather uncomfortable and the whole place was so tidy that Jane felt out of place in it. Her old schoolboy's camel-hair dressing-gown looked as unsuitable in Prudence's spare room as Prudence's turquoise blue wool housecoat did at the vicarage.

'You've got a new dressing-gown,' she said, trying to keep out of her tone the accusing note that women are apt to use to each other, as if one had no business to spend one's own money on nice clothes.

'Yes, I have. Red seemed a good colour for winter and people seem to think it suits me. You're quite sure you wouldn't like whisky? I actually have some – but then I know you don't really like it.' Prudence was fussing a little, almost as if she were nervous.

'No. Ovaltine for me, thanks,' said Jane. 'I hate the taste of whisky.' Had she entertained Fabian in her red velvet dressing-gown? she wondered. 'People' seemed to think it suited her, and 'people' said in that way often meant a man.

'Does Fabian like you in red?' she asked bluntly.

'Yes. I think so,' said Prudence rather vaguely.

'Has he seen you in that?'

'I can't remember really – he probably has.'

'I suppose it's all right in London,' said Jane, thoughtfully stirring her Ovaltine.

'How do you mean?'

'Well, to entertain a man in one's dressing-gown.'

'It isn't a dressing-gown,' said Prudence rather impatiently; 'it's a housecoat. And in any case I don't know what you mean by "all right".'

'No, it's a very decent garment really, with long sleeves and a high neck.' Jane picked up a fold of the full skirt and stroked the velvet. 'I suppose what I meant was would people think anything of it if they knew.'

Prudence laughed. 'Oh, really, Jane! It certainly isn't like you to worry about what other people would think.'

'No. I suppose it isn't. I was just thinking of you, really. A married woman does feel in some way responsible for her unmarried friends, you know.'

'Really? That hadn't occurred to me. In any case, I'm perfectly well able to look after myself,' said Prudence rather touchily.

'Darling, of course! I only wondered . . .' Jane paused, for really it was difficult to know how to ask what she wanted to know, assuming that she had any right to ask such a question. 'I suppose everything is all right between you and Fabian?' she began tentatively.

'All right? Why, yes.'

'I mean, there's nothing *wrong* between you,' Jane laboured, using an expression she had sometimes seen in the cheaper women's papers where girls asked how they should behave when their boyfriends wanted them to 'do wrong'.

'But I don't understand you, Jane. Did you think we'd quarrelled or something? Because we certainly haven't, I can assure you.'

'No, it wasn't that. I don't seem to be putting it very clearly, what I was trying to ask was, are you Fabian's *mistress*?'

As soon as she had said it, Jane found herself wanting to laugh. It was such a ridiculous word; it reminded her of full-blown Restoration comedy women or Nell Gwyn or Edwardian ladies kept in pretty little houses with wrought-iron balconies in St John's Wood.

Prudence burst into laughter, in which Jane was able to join her with some relief.

'Really, Jane, what an extraordinary question – you *are* a funny old thing! Am I Fabian's *mistress*? Is there anything *wrong* between us? I couldn't imagine what you meant!'

Jane looked up from her Ovaltine hopefully. 'I don't really know how people behave these days,' she said.

'Well, I mean to say – one just doesn't ask,' Prudence went on. 'Surely either one is or one isn't and there's no need to ask coy questions about it. Now, Jane, what about a hot-water bottle? Did you bring one with you?' Prudence stood up, slim and elegant in her red velvet housecoat.

Jane said, 'No, but I don't mind about a bottle, really I don't, though if you have a spare one it might be a comfort.' She felt a little peevish, as if she had been cheated, as indeed she had. She also felt a little foolish – naturally, she should have known that Prudence was (or wasn't) Fabian's mistress.

'What about Arthur Grampian?' she asked. 'Is there still that negative relationship between you?'

'Oh, poor Arthur,' said Prudence lightly. 'He's a dreary old thing, in a way, but rather sweet.'

Jane clasped her hot-water bottle to her bosom and went to her room. She felt out of touch with Prudence's generation this evening.

CHAPTER THIRTEEN

JANE RETURNED home feeling quite pleased with the result of her visit to London. The meeting of the literary society had been interesting, it had 'made a change', as people said, and she had enjoyed staying with Prudence. Though she was really no wiser than before about the exact relationship between Prudence and Fabian, it seemed that things were going well; the position was satisfactory, and no doubt their engagement would be announced quite soon, perhaps when the real spring weather came. Jane began to imagine Prudence settled in the village as Fabian's wife. It would be such a comfort to have her near and she would certainly make an admirable mistress – in the right sense, Jane told herself smilingly – of his house. She could give cultured little dinner parties with candles on the table and the right wines and food. She might even wear that becoming red velvet house-coat, which Jane had mistakenly called a dressing-gown. It would be perfectly suitable to receive guests in.

On the afternoon following her return, Jane received a message from Miss Doggett asking her if she would very kindly help her and Miss Morrow to pack up poor Mrs Driver's things, which were to go to the distressed gentlewomen. Naturally, Jane accepted the invitation eagerly; they were to start at half-past three, after Miss Doggett had had her rest, so it could be assumed, Jane decided, that there would be tea at some time during the proceedings.

She found Miss Doggett and Miss Morrow already sorting out the clothes in the drawing-room when she arrived.

'I am going to send most of these things to the Society for the Care of Aged Gentlewomen,' said Miss Doggett. 'Not that poor Constance was aged herself, but one does feel that they need *good* clothes, the elderly ones.'

'Oh, yes,' Jane agreed; 'when *we* become distressed we shall be glad of an old dress from Marks and Spencer's as we've never been used to anything better.'

Miss Doggett did not answer, and Jane remembered that of course she went to her dressmaker for fittings and ordered hats from Marshall's and Debenham's.

'Miss Morrow and I, that is,' she added, hardly improving on the first sentence.

'*I* don't intend to be a distressed gentlewoman,' said Miss Morrow airily, 'though I have been one for the first part of my life, certainly.'

'Well, Jessie, I don't know that there is much that you can do about it,' said Miss Doggett comfortably. 'Of course, there may be something for you when I have passed on.'

'She may make a good marriage,' said Jane quickly, folding up a black wool dress rather badly. 'People can do that at any age, it seems.'

Miss Morrow looked almost smug, but said nothing.

'Oh, that reminds me,' said Miss Doggett. 'I had a letter from Mrs Bonner who works at the Aged Gentlewomen headquarters and she told me a piece of interesting news. That nice Miss Lathbury has got married – what do you think of that?'

'Well, I never knew her,' said Jane. 'Did she work for the gentlewomen? And ought one to feel surprised at her marrying?'

'Yes,' said Miss Doggett. 'I was surprised. She seemed to have so much else in her life. Her work there and in the parish – it seems that she was the vicar's right hand.'

'Who has she married?' asked Miss Morrow.

'An anthropophagist,' declared Miss Doggett in an authoritative tone. 'He does some kind of scientific work, I believe.'

'I thought it meant a cannibal – one who ate human flesh,' said Jane in wonder.

'Well, science has made such strides,' said Miss Doggett doubtfully. 'His name is Mr Bone.'

'That certainly does seem to be a connection,' said Jane, laughing, 'but perhaps he is an anthro*pologist*; that would be more likely. They don't eat human flesh, as far as I know, though they may study those who do, in Africa and other places.'

'Perhaps that is it,' said Miss Doggett in a relieved tone. 'I read Mrs Bonner's letter rather quickly. But the main thing is that he seems to be *most* suitable, good-looking and tall, Mrs Bonner said. Over six feet tall, I think.'

'I never quite see why tallness in itself is so much sought after,' said Jane, 'though I dare say he has other qualities. I hope so for her sake.'

'He is a brilliant man,' said Miss Doggett. 'She helped him a good deal in his work, I think. Mrs Bonner says that she even learned to type so that she could type his manuscripts for him.'

'Oh, then he had to marry her,' said Miss Morrow sharply. 'That kind of devotion is worse than blackmail – a man has no escape from that.'

'No, one does feel that,' Jane agreed. 'Besides, he would be quite sure that she would be a useful wife,' she added a little sadly, thinking of her own failures.

'I will go and get tea,' said Miss Morrow, slipping quietly from the room.

'Talking of marriages,' Miss Doggett began, 'I often wonder whether Mr Driver will ever marry again.' She seemed to toss her sentence into the air hopefully for Jane to catch and throw back.

'Well, I suppose it is to be expected,' said Jane warily.

'That friend of yours, Mrs Cleveland.' Miss Doggett hesitated. 'I was wondering . . .'

'Now, what were you wondering, Miss Doggett?' Jane asked.

'Whether they might marry,' said Miss Doggett firmly, winding up a ball of string.

'I really don't know,' said Jane. 'Of course, they have met

and I think they like each other – it is difficult to see further than that.'

'I believe it would be an excellent thing,' said Miss Doggett. 'Mr Driver is a lonely man.'

'He always seems to be telling people that he is,' said Jane.

'And your friend, Miss Bates – isn't that her name? – seems to be a very charming young woman.'

'Yes, she is certainly,' Jane agreed.

'You see, poor Constance was older than he is,' said Miss Doggett thoughtfully. 'One feels that if he were married to a young, attractive woman there wouldn't be any of those little – er – *lapses*. You see what I mean, of course.'

'Yes, I do see.'

'We know that men are not like women,' went on Miss Doggett firmly. 'Men are very passionate,' she said in a low tone. 'I shouldn't like Jessie to hear this conversation,' she added, looking over her shoulder. 'But you and I, Mrs Cleveland – well, I am an old woman and you are married, so we can admit honestly what men are.'

'You mean that they only want one thing?' said Jane.

'Well, yes, that is it. We know what it is.'

'Typing a man's thesis, correcting proofs, putting sheets sides-to-middle, bringing up children, balancing the housekeeping budget – all these things are nothing, really,' said Jane in a sad, thoughtful tone. 'Or they would be nothing to a man like Fabian Driver. Therefore it is just as well that Prudence is an attractive young woman.'

There was a rattle of tea-things outside and Miss Morrow pushed open the door with a tray.

Conversation became more general during tea and ranged over parochial subjects, including the forthcoming meeting of the Parochial Church Council, of which Miss Doggett was a member. After tea the parcels were finished off and addressed and it was felt that a useful task had been accomplished.

As she walked out into the dusk of the March evening, Jane suddenly realized that spring was coming. Its arrival was less thrilling in the country than in London, and she wondered if Prudence was sensing it as she walked out of her office, noticing that the sky was a strange electric blue, that the starlings were twittering more loudly on the buildings; perhaps she was meeting Fabian that evening and he would have a bunch of mimosa for her.

But the next moment she knew that her fancy could not be reality, for she saw Fabian coming towards her through the blue dusk. Perhaps a sight of his beautiful, worn-looking face was what she needed on the first evening of spring. Her heart lifted for a moment in quite an absurd way as she prepared to greet him.

'A lovely evening,' she said; 'the first evening of spring. Have you been for a walk?' She raised her eyes to his.

'Yes, a short stroll. The rain seems to have kept off.' He tapped his umbrella on the ground.

'You take an umbrella for a country walk?' said Jane in astonishment.

'Yes, of course, if it looks like rain.'

'And you're wearing a hat and an overcoat and gloves,' Jane went on, and probably woollen underwear too, she added to herself.

'Yes, one is apt to catch cold at this time of year, I find,' said Fabian, slightly on the defensive, for he sensed her hostility.

'Oh, I never think of things like that,' said Jane, tossing her head. 'You'd better hurry in or the night air will harm you.' And with that she left him.

He looked after her as she went through the vicarage gate. No hat and that wild hair and that awful old coat and skirt. And lisle stockings too, he noted maliciously. He regarded it as an insult to himself that she should appear so carelessly dressed; he might perhaps have forgiven her if she had appeared at all confused or conscious of her shortcomings.

Even Jessie Morrow, sharp though she was, did not take it amiss if he suggested some improvement in her appearance. He went in to his own house, smiling to himself, glad that he had not invited Jane Cleveland in for a glass of sherry.

When Jane got into the house she found Nicholas standing in the hall with a parcel in his hand. The absurd first-evening-of-spring feeling came back to her suddenly and she wondered if he had perhaps felt it too and brought her a present.

'Look,' he said undoing the wrapping. 'I thought I'd put them in my little cloakroom downstairs.'

On the table stood four soap animals in various colours, a bear, a rabbit, an elephant and a tortoise.

'Kiddisoaps, for children, really,' he explained. 'I shall arrange them on the glass shelf.' He went happily away, humming to himself.

If it is true that men only want one thing, Jane asked herself, is it perhaps just to be left to themselves with their soap animals or some other harmless little trifle?

'Darling,' she called out, 'what do you think . . .?'

'I shall use the tortoise *first*,' her husband was saying in his little cloakroom.

'Fabian Driver takes an *umbrella* with him on a country walk and wears a hat and gloves.'

'Does he?' Nicholas emerged, beaming over his spectacles.

Beamy and beaky, mild, kindly looks and spectacles, Jane thought, whether in the Church or in the Senior Common Room of some Oxford College – it's all one really.

'There was a letter from Flora,' he went on. 'I haven't opened it yet.' He handed it to Jane.

Ah, Oxford in the spring, she thought, tearing open the letter to read Flora's news. Her letters were more interesting now than they had been. Work seemed to be going well, Miss Birkinshaw was 'rather remote', but next term she and her friend Penelope were to go to Lord Edgar Ravenswood for tutorials, which would be 'most stimulating' – 'imagine doing *Paradise Lost* with Lord Edgar!' Jane felt herself unequal to the effort of imagining it and passed on to the end of the letter, which was concerned with Flora's social life. She had been meeting a great many young men, as one still apparently did at Oxford; her favourite appeared to be somebody called Paul, of whom the letter was rather full. 'He is reading Geography and is rather amusing. . . .'

'Just imagine,' Jane called out to her husband. 'Flora has a young man called Paul who is reading Geography. And yet he is rather amusing!'

Nicholas appeared to find nothing strange in this, and Jane was left to ponder alone on the strangeness of anyone choosing to read Geography, which seemed to her, in her ignorance, a barren, dry subject, lacking the excitement of English or Classical Literature or Philosophy. Things are not what they were, she thought sadly, and at supper she felt very low, her spirits well damped down after the lift which the spring evening had given to them.

'Oh, I can understand people renouncing the world!' said Jane rather wildly as they sat down to a particularly wretched meal.

'Well, I should not mind renouncing cold mutton and beetroot,' said Nicholas evenly. 'That would be no great hardship.'

'We should not mind what we eat,' said Jane, 'and yet we do. That shows how very far we are from that state where we *might* renounce the world.'

Nicholas helped himself to more beetroot and they finished the meal in silence.

After supper Jane began rummaging in the drawer of her desk where her Oxford notebooks were kept, in which she had recorded many of her thoughts about the poet Cleveland. Creative work, that was the thing, if you could do that nothing else mattered. She sharpened pencils and filled her fountain-pen, then opened the books, looking forward with pleasurable anticipation to reading her notes. But when she began to read she saw that the ink had faded to a dull brownish colour. How long was it since she had added anything to them? she wondered despondently. It would be better if she started quite fresh and began reading the poems all over again. Then she remembered that her copy of the *Poems on Several Occasions* was upstairs and it seemed too much of an effort to go up and get it. How much could she remember without the book? A line came into her head. *Not one of all those ravenous hours, but thee devours . . .* If only she were one of these busy, useful women, who were always knitting or sewing. Then perhaps it wouldn't matter about the ravenous hours. She sat for a long time among the faded ink of her notebooks, brooding, until Nicholas came in with their Ovaltine on a tray and it was time to go to bed.

CHAPTER FOURTEEN

THE NEXT meeting of the Parochial Church Council was to be held in the vicarage drawing-room as an experiment, for Nicholas, encouraged by his wife, imagined that an informal setting with comfortable chairs, the opportunity to smoke and possibly a cup of tea at some suitable point in the evening might create a more friendly atmosphere in which there was less likelihood of any unpleasantness.

It was arranged that Jane should slip out at a propitious moment and give the signal to Mrs Glaze, who had consented to be in the kitchen that evening to make the tea and assist with the sandwiches and cakes. She had also agreed to answer the door-bell and admit the members as they arrived, while Jane and Nicholas waited, or perhaps cowered, in the dining-room until the time should come for them to emerge.

Mr Mortlake, the Secretary, was the first to arrive, followed closely by the Treasurer, Mr Whiting. They took their seats at the table facing the row of chairs and looked round the room critically, appraising the furnishings, which were less costly than those of their own homes, though in better taste, which they were unable to appreciate, since they noticed only the worm-eaten leg of a table or the broken back of a Chippendale chair.

'Chairs from the bedrooms,' said Mr Mortlake laconically, pointing to a couple of white-painted, cane-seated chairs in the back row. 'Dining-room chairs would be more in keeping.'

'I expect they're sitting on them now, having their dinner,' said Mr Whiting.

'Dinner isn't what they have,' said Mr Mortlake. 'They have the big meal midday. Mrs Glaze leaves something for them, whatever can be heated up, or a salad.'

'Ah, it was very different in Canon Pritchard's time,' said Mr Whiting on a note of lamentation which seemed excessive for the triviality of the subject. 'Even during the war years they had the big meal in the evening. It seems more in keeping.'

'The dignity of the office,' said Mr Mortlake. 'But then Mrs Pritchard filled her position well. And she was a wonderful cook. I know that. They say Mrs Cleveland hardly knows how to open a tin. It isn't fair on the vicar.'

'You never know, it might hold him back from promotion,' said Mr Whiting. 'A man is often judged by his wife.'

'That evening she came to the choir vestry. It was most importunate . . .'

'She may have thought she was doing good,' said Mr Whiting rapidly, lowering his voice at the sound of approaching footsteps. Although it was not the vicar or his wife but Miss Doggett who came into the room, the conversation could not be continued along its former lines, and changed to more uninteresting topics – the approach of spring, the drawing out of the days. By the time Mrs Crampton and Mrs Mayhew and Mr Glaze had arrived, they were on to the subject of summer holidays.

It was at this moment that Jane and Nicholas chose to make their entry, Nicholas, as Chairman, taking his place at the table and Jane sitting down on one of the bedroom chairs at the back near the door.

'Well, is everyone here?' Nicholas asked in a brisk tone which he seemed to have assumed specially for the meeting.

'Mr Oliver hasn't arrived yet,' said Mr Mortlake.

'Oh.' Nicholas looked at his watch. 'Well, it is after half-past eight. Perhaps something has kept him. I think we should begin.' He stood up. 'Shall we say a prayer?'

They rose to their feet and bowed their heads. Jane tried very hard to realize the Presence of God in the vicarage drawing-room, but failed as usual, hearing through the silence only Mrs Glaze running water in the back kitchen to wash up the supper things.

The meeting began with Mr Mortlake's reading of the minutes. During this Mr Oliver came in and sat by Jane at the back on the other bedroom chair. Mr Glaze then stood up and gave a report on the water tank at the church hall. Something was blocked, dead leaves and dust had formed some kind of an obstruction; it was all highly technical. Jane could see that there was a puzzled frown on Nicholas's face as he tried to follow. She herself had given up any attempt to take an intelligent interest in the proceedings. It seemed that there was a particular kind of hat worn by ladies attending Parochial Church Council meetings – a large beret of neutral-coloured felt pulled well down to one side. Both Mrs Crampton and Mrs Mayhew wore hats of this type, as did Miss Doggett, though hers was of a superior material, a kind of plush decorated with a large jewelled pin. Indeed, there seemed to be little for the ladies to do but observe each other's hats, for their voices were seldom heard. Occasionally Nicholas would interpose with some remark, such as 'Now what do you feel, Miss Doggett? I am sure we should all like to hear your views on this point,' but as it was usually a matter such as the taxation of the Easter Offering, on which ladies could not be expected to have any sensible views, their comments amounted to very little and were soon disposed of and even made to seem slightly ridiculous by the men.

'And now we come to the parish magazine cover,' said Nicholas, gently but firmly curtailing Mr Mortlake's dissertation on Income Tax. 'I believe everybody is not quite happy about it.'

'No, certainly not.' Jane, who was sitting by him, was quite startled by the violence of Mr Oliver's protest. 'I must say I was most surprised to see the photograph of the lych-gate on the new cover. I was under the impression, and I may say that I believe others were too, that we had definitely decided to use the photograph of the high altar.'

'Yes, that was so,' said Nicholas hastily, 'but we did feel – the standing committee, that is – that as both photographs were equally suitable – you will remember I'm sure, Mr Oliver, that we had great difficulty in deciding which we liked best – the Council would have no objection to our using the photograph of the lych-gate.'

'But why couldn't we have the high altar?' asked Miss Doggett bluntly. 'It seems to me to give a better idea of our beautiful old church.'

'Well, there were certain difficulties,' said Nicholas rather too weakly for a Chairman.

'Not to put too fine a point on it,' said Mr Mortlake, 'the vicar and the churchwardens did feel, after considering the matter, that there was a danger of the cover of our magazine looking too much like that of St Stephen's.'

'Well, really,' Jane burst out, 'I never heard anything so ridiculous. Even if the covers looked alike, there could certainly be no confusion over the contents. High Mass, Confessions and all that . . .'

Nicholas, who had thought it wiser to keep this matter of

the magazine cover from his wife, smiled unhappily. She would never learn when not to speak, he thought, with rather less affectionate tolerance than usual. Not for the first time he began to consider that there was, after all, something to be said for the celibacy of the clergy.

Jane realized from Nicholas's laugh and the uncomfortable silence that followed that she ought not to have spoken. 'I wonder whether a cup of tea would help us to see things in better perspective,' she said quickly. 'I will just go and see Mrs Glaze about it,' she added, hurrying from the room.

'A cup of tea always helps,' said Mrs Mayhew in a rather high, fluty voice. 'It can never come amiss.'

'I shouldn't like to contradict a lady,' said Mr Oliver, 'but I do feel that this is perhaps not quite the moment.'

'If you wouldn't like to contradict a lady, then why do it,' said Mr Whiting, in something of a quandary, for he would have liked to agree with Mr Oliver that this was perhaps hardly the time and place for a cup of tea.

'I think the best thing we can do is to take a vote on the matter of the cover,' said Nicholas hastily; 'then we can have the matter settled before the tea arrives.'

Everybody seemed willing to accept this suggestion, with the possible exception of Mr Oliver, who sat looking sulky. There was a show of hands and the result was that everybody except Mr Oliver voted in favour of having the photograph of the lych-gate on the magazine cover. Miss Doggett, who had raised a mild objection, confided to Mrs Crampton and Mrs Mayhew that of course she quite saw that it wouldn't do to have the picture of the high altar if there was any danger of their magazine being confused with that of Father Lomax's church.

'What a nice idea to have refreshments,' said Mrs Crampton as the rattle of china was heard outside the door. 'We never had them in Canon Pritchard's time.'

'Well, it seemed a good idea,' said Jane from the open doorway. 'I always think when I'm listening to some of these tense, gloomy plays on the wireless, Ibsen and things like that, oh, if only somebody would think of making a cup of tea!'

'I hope our meeting doesn't strike you in that way,' said Mr Whiting. 'They have usually been friendly affairs. There was never any necessity for a cup of tea in Canon Pritchard's time. We never had any unpleasantness then.'

'The Canon did have the knack as you might say of keeping certain people in their places,' observed Mr Glaze.

'Do you mean blundering vicars' wives?' asked Jane pleasantly. 'Why, Mr Oliver seems to have gone,' she exclaimed, standing with a cup of tea in her hand.

'I think he slipped out when you were bringing in the tea, Mrs Cleveland,' said Mrs Mayhew.

'He might have excused himself,' said Mr Mortlake; 'but then one has ceased to expect these small courtesies from young men now.'

'I am sure I heard a nightingale the other night,' said Nicholas rather loudly. 'Would that be possible, Mr Mortlake? Is the bird known to occur in these parts?'

Jane, who was sitting rather gloomily on a bedroom chair at the back, brightened up at the expression her husband had used – did birds *occur?* – but then lapsed into brooding silence again.

O for a beaker full of the warm South,

she thought sadly, clasping her hands round her teacup and looking into its depths. She sat thus for several moments, trying to see how much of the Ode she could remember, but the few lines that came to her did not bring her comfort –

Fade far away, dissolve, and quite forget
What thou among the leaves hast never known,
The weariness, the fever, and the fret
Here, where men sit and hear each other groan . . .

but in the next moment, they were all standing up and Nicholas was giving the Blessing and the meeting was over.

'Was it a success, having it here and with refreshments?' she asked him as the last footsteps scrunched away down the drive. 'Do you think it came off?'

'My dear, I wish you had not said what you did,' said Nicholas gravely.

'I, say anything?' Jane looked bewildered for a moment. 'But I always say what I think, and it *was* ridiculous all that fuss about the magazine cover and Father Lomax.'

'Yes, it was a small thing, but Mortlake and Whiting seemed to think it important. You cannot expect them to see things as we do.'

'Why should we always do what they want,' Jane burst out. 'Oh, if I had known it would be like this . . .' She ran from the room and into the downstairs cloakroom, where the sight of Nicholas's soap animals reminded her of her love for him and she might have wept had she not been past the age when one considers that weeping can do good or bring relief.

Instead she came back into the drawing-room and began moving chairs about rather aimlessly, not remembering where they had come from.

'If only you could have been a chaplain at an Oxford college,' she lamented. 'You're wasted here.'

'But, darling, you always said you wanted to be in a country parish. You were so pleased.'

'I know, but I didn't think it would be like this. I thought people in the country were somehow noble, through contact with the earth and Nature, I suppose,' she smiled; 'and all the time they're just worrying about petty details like water-tanks and magazine covers! – like people in the suburbs do.'

'We must accept people as we find them and do the best we can,' said Nicholas in too casual a tone to sound priggish. He stood up and began pacing about the room. 'Now I have thought of a wonderful idea. I am going to grow my own tobacco. Don't you think it would be interesting as well as a great saving?'

'Certainly, darling; what interests you do have in your life,' said Jane humbly. 'Shall we try to finish these sandwiches?'

And so they sat down on either side of the fire, two essentially good people, eating thick slices of bread spread with a paste made of 'prawns (and other fish)', Nicholas reading a book about tobacco-growing, and Jane wondering how she could make up for her tactlessness this evening. Perhaps by going to see Mr Oliver and trying to reason with him, perhaps by visiting Mr Mortlake, though even she shrank from that. She began imagining herself being shown into the front parlour, waiting, examining the photographs and ornaments . . . No, she had better leave well alone and concentrate on the things she *could* do, whatever they might be.

CHAPTER FIFTEEN

WHEN MISS Doggett reached home, she found, rather to her annoyance, that Miss Morrow was not there. Then she remembered that it was her evening out, for Jessie had insisted on having a definite free evening of her own, and that she had said she would probably go to the cinema. She had evidently gone out in a hurry, Miss Doggett decided, looking through the open bedroom door at the clothes flung down on the bed and the litter of cosmetics on the dressing-table. It seemed as if Jessie had been in doubt as to what to wear and also as if she had taken considerable trouble over her appearance, a thing she did not usually do. In this Miss Doggett was perfectly right, for no sooner had she left the house at a quarter to eight to go to the Parochial Church Council meeting than Jessie had hurried upstairs to her room.

Tonight she was going to see Fabian. Not by invitation, for it would not have occurred to him to invite her in formally, but as a surprise. He often sat listening to the wireless in the evenings after he had had his dinner – she knew that. Sometimes he went out to the pub or the Golden Lion, but she would have to chance that.

She had a special dress she was going to wear, a blue velvet one which had belonged to Constance and which she had altered to fit herself. She knew that men did not notice things like that, but even if he did she was confident that she would be able to carry off any embarrassment successfully.

As she sat at the dressing-table, she felt like a character in a novel, examining each feature, the sharp nose, the large grey eyes and rather too small mouth. She worked carefully, smoothing on a peach-coloured foundation lotion, blending in rouge, powdering, outlining and filling in her mouth, shading her eyelids with blue and darkening her lashes. When she had finished she was quite pleased with the result. She was thirty-seven, older than Mrs Cleveland's friend, Prudence Bates, but younger than poor Constance and than Fabian himself. She had always loved him, but it had not occurred to her until that autumn day in the garden when she had seen him looking out of the window that anything could be done about it. She was not the person to cherish a hopeless romantic love for a man, especially if he were free and lived next door, and now that Prudence Bates had come into his life Jessie felt that she must act quickly. It seemed to her entirely appropriate that she should lay her plans while Miss Doggett was at a meeting of the Parochial Church Council, discussing the parish magazine cover.

At a quarter to nine she left the house, looking carefully as she stepped out of the gate to see whether anyone had observed her; but it was dark and there was nobody about. She opened Fabian's garden gate and then slipped quietly down the side of the house to the back, where the drawing-room french windows opened on to the garden. This evening they were lighted and the curtains not yet drawn; she saw Fabian in a velvet smoking-jacket, sitting by the fire with a glass of some amber-coloured liquid – whisky, perhaps – on a small table at his side. There was a blotter on his knees and he appeared to be writing a letter.

Appeared to be writing was a correct impression, for he sat with his pen in his hand adding nothing to the few words he had already written. He did not find it easy to write to Prudence. To begin with, he had never been much of a letter-writer, and then her letters were of such a high literary standard, so much embellished with suitable quotations that he found it quite impossible to equal them. He felt that this was wrong; the man should be the better letter-writer, not the woman, though he remembered that he had never been able to equal Constance's either. It was ironical to think how much better she would have been able to answer Prudence's letter than he could himself. He thought that perhaps he should give up trying for this evening; he might stroll round to the Golden Lion for a nightcap later on; it was possible that the walk might give him some inspiration. It seemed to be quite a pleasant evening, he thought, going to the windows to draw the long dark green brocade curtains.

As he stood there he saw a figure move out of the shelter of a rhododendron bush – a woman whom he did not recognize stood there looking at him. For a moment he felt alarmed, and she smiled and he saw that it was Jessie Morrow.

'Why, what are you doing there in the gloaming?' he called out in a rather forced way. 'Won't you come in? Is Miss Doggett with you?' He was conscious as he said it of the incongruity of Miss Doggett lurking in bushes.

Jessie stepped in through the open french window and he shut it and drew the curtains behind her. 'No. I am alone this evening,' she said, 'and I wondered if you were too, and if I would have the courage to call on you. Well, I did have, so here I am.'

'Sit down,' said Fabian, drawing up another chair to the fire. Now he could not possibly go on struggling with his letter to Prudence. 'What would you like now, a cup of tea or a hot drink of some kind?'

Jessie said nothing, but her eyes were fixed on the amber-coloured liquid on the little table.

'Would you like whisky?' Fabian's eyes lighted up and he fetched another glass. 'Somehow I didn't imagine you as liking it.'

'What did you imagine that I liked?'

'I don't know. I suppose I never thought.'

'You mean you never thought of me as a human being at all? As a person who could like anything?'

'Well, I don't know . . . but you seem different tonight.' Fabian looked at her, a little puzzled, appraising her. 'Your dress is becoming.'

'Yes, I think it is, and I'm glad you think so.'

'Constance had a dress rather like that once. Velvet, isn't it?'

'Yes – I think I remember it.' But fancy *him* remembering, she thought. It was a little unnerving the way men sometimes did – not that she feared he would recognize the dress as being the same one altered to fit her; it was just that an unsuspected depth had been revealed in him, and she realized that she might not know him quite so well as she had imagined she did.

'I think Constance would like to think of us sitting here together,' said Fabian. 'She was always very fond of you. You were very good to her.'

'Was I?' said Jessie in a rather brisk tone. 'I suppose I was better to her than you were. That wouldn't have been difficult.'

'What hurtful things you say! As if I didn't realize it. I am not quite so insensitive as you seem to imagine.'

'I'm sorry. My sharp tongue runs away with me sometimes.' Jessie noticed without surprise but with a kind of comfortable satisfaction that Fabian's arm had somehow placed itself round her shoulders. She leaned her head back against his sleeve.

'It seems sometimes that we must hurt people we love,' said Fabian, stroking her hair. 'Oscar Wilde said, didn't he . . .?'

'Let's not bother about him,' said Jessie. 'I always think he must have been such a bore, saying those witty things all the time. Just imagine seeing him open his mouth to speak and then waiting for it to come out. I couldn't have endured it.'

Fabian smiled. He hadn't been quite sure what it was that Oscar Wilde had said, anyway.

Was he thinking of Constance or of Prudence? Jessie wondered. He had hurt one and he might be going to hurt the other. How strange their names were, when one came to think of it, Constance and Prudence . . . Jessie was somehow a more comfortable name, without any reproach in it. Did he love Prudence, anyway, and did she love him? Oh, well, thought Jessie as Fabian bent his head to kiss her, even if she did she would soon get over it.

CHAPTER SIXTEEN

JANE WAS making the beds, a humble task that she felt was within her powers. The window-cleaners had arrived shortly after breakfast and it was a kind of game trying to evade them. If I go down to the uttermost ends of the earth, Jane thought, seizing a flattened pillow and beating it into roundness, there they will find me. And sure enough here was the ladder propped up against the sill, the sound of footsteps mounting and then the face at the window, surprised, perhaps, to see the vicar's wife making a bed. Mrs Glaze should do the beds really, but then she couldn't come very early, and by the time she arrived there was the breakfast washing-up, the vegetables to do for lunch and the drawing-room to be sketchily mopped and dusted in case anyone should call. . . .

The face at the window was impassive now, but that seemed more unnerving than the surprised look, and suddenly Jane fled, leaving the bed half made and her husband's striped pyjamas lying on the floor. I suppose it may interest him to see the vicar's pyjamas, she thought, but was the window-cleaner a churchman? Now that she came to think of it, she couldn't remember ever having seen him in church. Perhaps he was a Roman or Chapel or went to the little tin-roofed Gospel Hall by the gasworks; or perhaps he was *nothing* – a frightening thought, like seeing into the dark chasm of his mind. Of course, it was just possible that he was merely High and carried a candle or swung a censer at Father Lomax's church. Yes; that was it. Jane saw him now through a cloud of incense, his rugged features softened . . .

'Nicholas!' she called out, but there was no answer from the study, and then she remembered that he had gone out immediately after breakfast, she couldn't remember where. Somebody was ill or dying; he had gone to play golf or perhaps to the church to see how the decorating was going; he had taken to looking in on a Saturday morning to encourage the ladies, and Jane felt that they really welcomed that more than her own uncertain help. Anyway, he was not here, so she could not confide her thoughts about the window-cleaner to him. . . .

'Madam!' Mrs Glaze appeared at the foot of the stairs in her hat and flowered pinafore. 'Mr Mortlake is here.'

'Mr Mortlake? Good heavens!' Jane called out in agitation, her thoughts going back to the meeting of the Parochial Church Council and her outspokenness about the magazine cover. Had he come to see her privately about it? To reproach her for her interference?

'I have shown him into the drawing-room,' went on Mrs Glaze.

'The drawing-room? Yes, certainly.' Jane smoothed back her tousled curly hair with her hands. 'I will come down.'

'Well, madam, I don't think you need disturb yourself.'

'Why, is the vicar with him?'

'Mr Mortlake has come to tune the piano,' said Mrs Glaze in a surprised tone.

'To tune the piano – of course!' Jane almost shouted.

She ran downstairs into the hall. There was his hat, a bowler of rather an old-fashioned shape, lying on a chair. Oh, the relief of it! He had come not to scold her, but to tune the piano! She wanted to rush in to him, to greet him with some exaggerated mocking gesture, '*Buon giorno, Rigoletto*,' posturing and bowing low. But he would not appreciate it or understand. So she seized his hat and placing it on her head, pirouetted round the hall singing,

O Donna Clara,
I saw you dancing last night . . .

From inside the drawing-room came the sound of Mr Mortlake striking out single notes, cautiously, then rather impatiently. It would be some time before he ventured on to the rich chords and harmonies peculiar to his profession. Jane replaced the hat on the chair and opened the front door.

A young man, who had evidently been about to ring the bell, stood on the doorstep. He was rather flashily dressed and carried a large suitcase.

'Good morning, madam,' he said. 'Are there any old clothes for sale here?'

'This is the vicarage,' said Jane in a rather vague tone.

'Oh, I see . . .' His confidence seemed to leave him for a moment.

'So you wouldn't really expect any, would you?' Jane asked. 'Unless the ones I'm wearing would do?'

'The ladies like to keep old things to wear in the mornings,' he said, recovering his poise. 'I know that.'

'I expect I shall go on wearing these all day,' said Jane. 'My days don't really have mornings as such, not in that way, I mean.'

The young man edged away from her.

He thinks he has come to a private mental home, thought Jane, the patients are not dangerous, but are allowed to take walks in the grounds. 'I'm sorry I can't oblige you,' she said pleasantly. 'What a lovely morning it is,' she added as he wished her a hasty good morning and hurried out through the gate. And it certainly did seem to have improved, after that shock about Mr Mortlake.

She would wander in the garden, thinking about what she should write. It was good to be alive, in the spring. Daffodils were out in the grass under the chestnut tree, which was showing sticky buds, and in the lane at the back of the church a plant with bright leaves and greenish flowers was flourishing. Dog's mercury – Jane remembered the name from childhood, a strange, rather sinister name . . . what was its derivation? she wondered. Was it perhaps a corruption of some other name? She went up to the chestnut tree and leaned her head against its trunk. Perhaps she could hear the sap rising and the flowers preparing to burst out of the buds. *Not one of all those ravenous hours, but thee devours?* Well, yes, that was true still, but it mattered less on a spring morning. She would cut some buds and bring them back into the house. They should stand in a great jar on the hall table, to show callers that there was hope at the vicarage. But she would need something to cut them with, some implement from the potting-shed, where the tools were kept. She ran over the lawn and round to the back of the house, but then she stopped.

A woman in a tailored costume and a fur was looking over the back gate, as if about to enter it. Behind her stood a stout, rosy-faced clergyman with white hair.

'Ah, Mrs Cleveland. Good morning!' The man's voice

rang out. 'Do forgive us for calling so unceremoniously, but one usually finds the womenfolk round at the back of the house these days, especially in the mornings.'

Womenfolk, thought Jane irrelevantly, how silly that sounded. And all this emphasis on the mornings.

'In the kitchen, doing the cooking,' went on the clergyman as if in explanation.

'Mrs Glaze is doing that,' said Jane. It now occurred to her to wonder who her callers were and how they could know about the back gate, which was not immediately apparent. The clergyman, surely, was Canon Pritchard; therefore the woman must be his wife. They had thought to creep round the back and peer in at windows to surprise her in the kitchen, perhaps catch her in the very act of stubbing out a cigarette in the tea-leaves in the sink basket. She felt almost triumphant that they should have failed.

'Do come in,' she said, trying to sound gracious. 'My husband isn't in at the moment, but he should be coming back soon.'

They walked round to the front of the house and into the hall. From the drawing-room came the sound of somebody playing the piano in a rather florid Edwardian style. Mr Mortlake was on his last lap. The arpeggios flowed; the chords rippled and modulated from major to minor and back again.

'This *is* like old times,' cried Mrs Pritchard, 'to hear Mr Mortlake playing again. His style is so very much his own.'

The door opened and Mr Mortlake came out, emerged almost, a tall, dignified figure.

'Well, Daniel,' said Canon Pritchard, 'this is a pleasant surprise.'

Jane noticed that Mr Mortlake's face really did light up. 'Why, it's the Canon,' he said. 'And Mrs Pritchard. This is indeed a pleasant surprise. And how are you both keeping?'

'Very well, thank you, Daniel; and you're looking very fit too.'

Jane waited for Mr Mortlake to say something about it not being like the old days with Canon Pritchard gone, but the Canon, perhaps realizing that something of the kind might come and wishing to spare Jane's feelings, had contrived to dismiss him in a very gracious kind of way that could not possibly give offence.

The party moved into the drawing-room. Jane wondered what time it was and what, if any, refreshment she could offer to her visitors. There was no sherry; she knew that. Presumably there could always be a cup of tea or even coffee, but were there any biscuits?

'Ah, you have your summer curtains up,' said Mrs Pritchard, looking round the room. 'We always found this room so draughty even in summer that I often waited until May before I took down the velvet ones.'

'Yes, these are quite light ones. It has been a mild spring,' Jane observed. 'My husband likes air, of course.' In the daytime when the curtains were drawn back they looked better. Had the Pritchards called in the evening they would have noticed the shortness and skimpiness of the curtains, which did not even cover the windows in places.

'I find the curtains we had here a little too large for my new drawing-room,' went on Mrs Pritchard.

'Really?' said Jane. This was not much of a conversation for the Canon, she thought, wishing that Nicholas would appear.

'Do you find your new position congenial?' she asked, trying to draw him into the conversation.

'Well,' he smiled, 'it could hardly be otherwise. The Bishop and I were at Rugby together, you know.'

'No, I didn't know. How nice. Arnold of Rugby,' Jane murmured.

'He was a *little* before my time, of course,' said the Canon.

'But the tradition still remains?' asked Jane. 'The lines on Rugby Chapel . . . I wish I could remember some of them now, but English Literature stopped at Wordsworth when I was up at Oxford, and somehow one doesn't remember things so well that one read since.'

Mrs Pritchard stirred a little restlessly in her chair.

There was a knock at the door and Mrs Glaze came in bearing a silver tray with a coffee-pot and cups upon it.

Jane turned to her gratefully. She would never have believed that Mrs Glaze could show this treasure-like quality. No doubt it was for the Canon and his wife rather than for herself, but it had saved the situation. She had been feeling that things were pretty desperate if one found oneself talking about and almost quoting Matthew Arnold to comparative strangers, though anything was better than having to pretend you had winter and summer curtains when you had just curtains.

'Would you like me to pour out, madam?' Mrs Glaze asked.

'Yes, please do, Mrs Glaze,' said Jane, relaxing, and noticing with surprise that there was a plate of bourbon biscuits on the tray. Now wherever had Mrs Glaze found those? she wondered.

'Black for you, madam?' asked Mrs Glaze, turning to Mrs Pritchard, 'and white for the Canon?'

It appeared that she had remembered correctly.

Conversation flowed more smoothly now. Various people in the village were asked after and discussed, though in not quite such an interesting way as Jane could have wished. Also she was very careful with her own comments, remembering how her tongue and curiosity were apt to run away with her.

'Has Fabian Driver married again?' Mrs Pritchard asked.

'No, not yet,' said Jane.

'Not yet? Do you think he has anyone in mind?' Mrs Pritchard leaned forward a little in her chair.

'Oh, I don't think so, but I suppose he will some time. After all, he is still a young man; barely forty, I believe.'

'Of course, there is nobody here for him,' went on Mrs Pritchard. 'He would have to look further afield.'

'Yes, one does feel that he must be rather lonely here . . .'

There was a pause and the Canon stood up. 'Well, my dear,' he turned to his wife. 'I think we shall have to be on our way.'

'We are to have luncheon with the Bishop,' Mrs Pritchard explained. 'We left the motor outside.'

Going out to luncheon and in a motor, thought Jane, seeing a high Edwardian electric brougham and Mrs Pritchard in a dust-coat and veiled motoring cap. But well-bred people talked like this even today, Jane believed. She hoped they would get a good meal at the Palace, but was prudent enough not to make any enquiries.

In the hall Canon Pritchard paused and held out his hands with a vague gesture. Jane thought for one wild moment that he was attempting to give her some kind of a blessing, but it appeared that he wanted to wash.

'Yes, of course,' said Jane, showing him into the little cloakroom. 'I wonder if there is a clean towel?' she added, knowing that there could not possibly be one.

'Yes, thank you, there is,' Canon Pritchard called out. Jane supposed that Mrs Glaze must have put one there when she heard them arrive, and she now realized that had they been able to stay to lunch an adequate meal would have been provided. Mrs Pritchard would have been able to say, 'We drove over to the Clevelands in the motor and stayed to luncheon.'

Mrs Pritchard did not appear to want to wash. No doubt the Palace offered better amenities, Jane decided, as they stood rather uncertainly in the hall.

'You must come over to luncheon one day,' Mrs Pritchard observed, 'and bring your husband.'

'Thank you. We should like to very much,' Jane said.

Canon Pritchard came out of the cloakroom and the three of them went out to the motor, which was not of an Edwardian type, rather to Jane's disappointment.

'Have the Clevelands a young child?' the Canon asked his wife as they drove away.

'I believe their daughter is about eighteen. She is at Oxford, I think.'

'A strange thing that,' said the Canon, changing gear. 'One would have thought there was a child about the place. The soap in the wash-basin was modelled in the form of a rabbit, and there were other animals, too, a bear and an elephant.'

'And you washed your hands with a soap rabbit?' asked his wife seriously.

'Certainly. There was no other soap. I wonder if Mrs Cleveland put them there; she seems rather an unusual woman.'

'Yes, there is something strange about her.'

'I think Cleveland is quite sound,' went on the Canon. 'None of this Modern Churchman's Union or any of that dangerous stuff . . .' He hesitated, perhaps meditating on the soap animals and what they could signify.

Jane and Mrs Glaze were also talking about them. Jane had thanked her for bringing in the coffee and biscuits at such an opportune time and for providing the clean towel.

'Oh, madam,' said Mrs Glaze, 'but I couldn't find a new tablet of soap.'

'Wasn't there any in the cloakroom?'

'Only the animals, madam.'

'Well, I believe it's quite good soap. I expect the Canon would enjoy using them. Men are such children in many ways.' Though perhaps not all in the same way, Jane thought. He may have regarded them as some dangerous form of idolatry.

'I was hoping he might think they belonged to Miss Flora,' said Mrs Glaze.

'Yes, he might have thought that. After all she is still a child, really.' And yet even she was old enough to enjoy doing

Milton with Lord Edgar Ravenswood and to fall in love with a young man called Paul who was reading Geography. Could children do these things?

Nicholas appeared just before lunch and Jane told him of her eventful morning. They had a good laugh about the soap animals.

'I wonder if he will tell the Bishop,' said Nicholas.

'It would be rather ominous if he kept it to himself,' said Jane; 'it would seem as if he considered it rather important, not a matter for joking.'

'Oh, Pritchard has no sense of humour. I'm glad I managed to avoid him.'

'Yes, it was rather heavy going,' Jane agreed. 'I suppose he just came to have a look at things. Perhaps they would peep into the church when they were sure we weren't looking to see if they could detect any smell of incense or other Popish innovations.'

'I saw their car outside just as I was coming through the gate,' Nicholas admitted, 'so I slipped into the tool-shed till they'd gone. In any case, I had to see to my tobacco plants,' he added, looking a little ashamed.

'Well, really, Nicholas,' Jane protested, 'you might have come and helped me out.' But secretly she was rather pleased to have managed so well on her own.

CHAPTER SEVENTEEN

WHITSUNTIDE came and went, the weather grew warmer, and Prudence appeared at her office in elegant dark printed silk dresses; Miss Trapnell and Miss Clothier in cottons or rayons of rather dimmer patterns. The conversation began to be about holidays. Even Dr Grampian raised the subject one morning when Prudence was in his room, and asked her when she would be taking hers.

'Not that it matters,' he added vaguely. 'I was wondering if it would coincide with mine. That is sometimes easier.'

A year ago Prudence would have seized on his words and twisted them into an 'Ah, if only we were really going on holiday together!' She had often imagined herself with him in the South of France or the Italian Lakes – she in the most elegant beach clothes and he wonderfully bronzed and mysteriously improved in looks and physique. But today, looking at him in his grey suit and dark tie, his shoulders hunched narrowly over his desk, it seemed quite fantastic to imagine him lying on a beach stripped to the waist.

'My wife wants to go to St Tropez in September,' he said, as if reading her thoughts. 'We both feel the need for the sun.'

'Oh yes, sun,' Prudence agreed. 'I haven't really fixed my holiday yet. I can go any time that suits you.'

'Well, the summer is a slack time,' he said, as if other times were busy, 'so please yourself.' Then he turned to a file of papers on his desk and Prudence felt that she had been dismissed.

She went into her own room, where she found Mr Manifold talking to Miss Trapnell and Miss Clothier.

' . . . walking in the Pyrenees,' he was saying. 'In late September – otherwise it will be too hot.'

'It sounds fascinating,' said Prudence in what seemed to him a cold, scornful tone, 'but terribly energetic.'

'I don't like luxurious holidays,' he said rather fiercely. 'I haven't any use for that kind of thing. I like to be on the move, seeing different places.'

'My idea of a holiday is just to sit somewhere in the sun drinking,' retorted Prudence, aware as she said it that she was being rather ridiculous.

'Oh, I like drinking too,' said Mr Manifold, 'but not in chromium-plated bars and hotels.'

Prudence felt anger rising within her, but could not think of anything to say.

'I'm very fond of Torquay myself,' said Miss Trapnell in an even tone. 'You always meet nice people and there's plenty to do if it rains.'

'I can't bear meeting people on holiday,' said Prudence childishly.

'Then you must be a lone wolf, like Mr Manifold,' said Miss Clothier.

The idea of Mr Manifold being any kind of a wolf made Prudence want to giggle, and she feared that he also had seized upon the vulgar meaning of the word, which was probably unknown to Miss Trapnell and Miss Clothier.

'I dare say that both Prudence and I have had our moments,' he said, leaving the two older ladies somewhat mystified.

Prudence! He had dared to call her by her Christian name! Had it just slipped out, she wondered, or was it deliberate?

'Really, he gets more insufferable every day,' she said, when he had gone out of the room.

'He's a nice young man, really,' said Miss Trapnell. 'And he's so good to his aunt. I happen to know that. I do think it's nice when a young man considers older people.'

'Good to his aunt?' Prudence asked, a little annoyed that Miss Trapnell should have this unlikely information about Mr Manifold.

'He lives with his aunt,' Miss Trapnell explained. 'His parents are dead, you see.'

'Oh?' Prudence was curious in spite of herself.

'He is an orphan,' interposed Miss Clothier by way of explanation.

'The poor little poppet!' said Prudence in a light, offhand tone. Of course, lots of people of his age were orphans, she told herself. There was really nothing pathetic about it. She took out some work, determined to dismiss him from her mind, but Miss Trapnell seemed disinclined to return to her card index and would not leave the subject.

'Miss Manifold is a great one for church work,' she was saying. 'And she's very artistic. I've never seen the flowers looking so lovely as they did on Whit Sunday. She'd put red and pink flowers on the pulpit, rhododendrons and peonies with some syringa and greenery. Red is the colour for Whitsuntide, of course.'

'But how did you see them?' Prudence asked. 'Do you live somewhere near?' She tried to imagine Miss Trapnell's North London suburb, and Geoffrey Manifold and his aunt living somewhere near.

'Yes, quite near,' said Miss Trapnell. 'A threepenny bus ride away. I'm not actually in the same parish – St Michael's, that is – but I'm on the electoral roll there. I'm afraid St Jude's, that's the church whose parish I'm really in, is much too high for me. They have Asperges and all that kind of thing, and the vicar hears Confessions.' She lowered her voice.

'Does Mr Manifold go to church?' Prudence asked.

'Well, no, Miss Bates, and that is a great grief to his aunt, I happen to know. But you know how these young men are, think they know the answer to all life's problems. But he is so good to her, so I suppose you can't have it all ways.'

'He's had a hard life too,' Miss Clothier interposed. 'You'd think he might have found consolation in going to church.'

'A hard life?' Prudence asked.

'Both his parents were killed in a motor accident when he was eighteen,' said Miss Trapnell, almost with a hint of triumph in her tone.

'Oh, *no* . . .' said Prudence in a strained voice. 'The poor boy . . .'

'Just when he was starting out on his University career,' said Miss Trapnell, piling it on.

'Well, I suppose he had scholarships and things,' said Prudence rather roughly. 'People usually do.'

'Yes, he was clever, of course. But it was a hard struggle.'

'Didn't his aunt help him?'

'Yes, I'm sure she did, but it was difficult for him.'

'He seems to have got over it now,' said Prudence, forcing herself to remember his rather bold manner and the fact that he had called her Prudence. But obviously he wasn't the kind of person to show his feelings . . . it was all over and done with, about ten years ago, she supposed; there was certainly nothing pathetic about him now. And no doubt he had had his moments – he had as good as told her so. All the same, the conversation had left an uneasy feeling at the back of her mind. She felt that she might wake up in the middle of the night and remember it. She would see him in his raincoat with the collar turned up, going to have lunch in Lyons, standing in the queue reading the *New Statesman*.

'Have you fixed your holidays yet, Miss Bates?' asked Miss Trapnell.

'I expect I shall go somewhere with a friend,' Prudence answered rather evasively.

Naturally, her holiday plans now included Fabian, bronzed and handsome, lying on a beach or drinking on a terrace, and this required less of an effort of imagination than when her companion had been Arthur Grampian. But so far Fabian had said nothing definite about it. His last letter, indeed, had been unsatisfactory, perfunctory almost – it was difficult to describe exactly what was wrong. It had begun affectionately enough, but after that it had meandered on about nothing very much, the weather, even, and then come to an abrupt end, with half a sheet left blank. But then Fabian was not at his best as a letterwriter. Prudence had been uncomfortably conscious for some time that her letters were much better written and fuller of apt quotations than his were. She remembered one of his some weeks back in which he had started to quote Oscar Wilde and then evidently thought better of it and crossed it out. This seemed a little ominous, for Wilde had said so many things that one would hardly have wished said to oneself. Perhaps the truth was that Fabian was a man of deeds rather than words, though he was certainly very slow in coming to the point.

This next week-end she was to go and stay with Jane. Perhaps things would come to a head then. The country would be looking at its best; there would be the long evenings, the lanes with wild roses and meadowsweet, and above all Prudence herself, adorning Fabian's house and garden and looking so perfect there that he would surely wonder how he could ever imagine the place without her.

The guest-room at the vicarage was more attractive now than it had been in November; its very bareness gave it a cool, almost continental look. Prudence's summer housecoat, a white cotton patterned with roses and frilled at the neck and elbows, seemed less out of place than her turquoise blue wool or crimson velvet. Jane had put a vase of roses on the little table by the bed, but this time there was no photograph of Arthur Grampian to set it off. Prudence had as yet no photograph of Fabian and she felt that it would somehow have been in bad taste to flaunt him there at the vicarage, when he was to be seen in the flesh, walking about the village. So the table held only the roses, a book of poems that Fabian had given her and a novel of the kind that Prudence enjoyed, well written and tortuous, with a good dash of culture and the inevitable unhappy or indefinite ending, which was so like life.

It was the end of the Oxford term and Flora and her young friend Paul, who was to spend a few days with them, were expected in time for supper on the Friday evening. Jane, or rather Mrs Glaze, had provided a boiled chicken, and Prudence offered to make a salad and see to the finishing touches.

'We mustn't treat this young man as if he were a curate,' Jane explained, 'but I don't want Flora to feel ashamed of her home.' She burst into a peal of laughter. 'Isn't that just the sort of thing they say in the answers to correspondents in a woman's magazine?'

'Have you some garlic?' Prudence asked.

'Garlic?' echoed Jane in astonishment. 'Certainly not! Imagine a clergyman and his wife going about the parish smelling of garlic!'

'But it does improve a salad.'

'Let the lettuce leaves be well washed,' said Jane airily; 'that's the main thing. I should have liked the kind of life where one ate food flavoured with garlic, but it was not to be. I don't suppose Flora's young man will mind. Geography and garlic don't seem to go together somehow. Of course Fabian may not be satisfied, but it should be enough pleasure for him to see you, without bothering whether the salad bowl has been rubbed with garlic.'

'You've asked Fabian? You didn't tell me.'

'Yes; I thought it would make up the numbers,' said Jane rather grandly. 'And he promised to bring some wine – I hope he won't make too much fuss about it – the wine, I mean. We do happen to have a bottle of sherry, not the very best, but I have poured it into the decanter, so nobody will know. The decanter at least is a good one.'

When they had finished their preparations they went into the drawing-room, which in summer appeared to be a pleasant, airy room with french windows opening on to the lawn and the winter's draughts turned to cooling breezes most refreshing on a hot evening.

Fabian advanced over the lawn with the bottles in his arms, carrying them as carefully as if they had been new-born babies. He saw Jane and Prudence sitting inside the room before they saw him. Jane was in a kind of 'best' summer dress of indeterminate pattern and cut, the kind of thing worn by thousands of English women, but Prudence wore something black and filmy, chiffon perhaps, which looked deliciously cool and elegant.

'Why, there is Fabian!' exclaimed Jane. 'Now he will make his entrance just like a character in one of those domestic comedies that have french windows at the back of the stage. I wonder what his first words will be.'

'Good evening,' said Fabian, bowing slightly over his bottles.

Jane sprang up to take them from him, while Prudence raised her hand in a rather languid gesture and smiled up at him.

'Hullo, Fabian,' she said.

'Prudence, how nice to see you,' he replied. 'Now, do be careful of those bottles,' he said, turning to Jane. 'They don't want to be shaken up too much – and put them in a cool place, if you can.'

'Give him some sherry, Prue,' said Jane. 'I must take these away.'

'Well, darling,' said Fabian, bending down to kiss Prudence, but rather gingerly, as if afraid of disturbing her face and hair, 'you're looking very lovely tonight.'

He always says that, thought Prudence with a flash of irritation. But of course it might be that it was always true.

They sat a little awkwardly sipping their sherry until Nicholas came in, and then the sound of a car was heard and Jane's exuberant greeting to Flora and Paul.

The beginning of the meal was a little awkward, but Jane soon carried them forward on a rush of conversation.

'Paul is reading Geography,' she explained. 'It must be a fascinating subject. All those tables of rainfall and the other things – vegetation, climate, soil . . .' She waved her hands about, seeming unable to go any further into the delights of Geography.

Paul, who was a quiet, mousy-looking young man with very blue eyes – a typical undergraduate, Prudence thought – did not appear to be at all embarrassed at having attention drawn to himself. Geography was a fascinating subject to him and he was able to discourse at some length about what he was doing. Flora gazed at him with obvious devotion and occasionally made an intelligent comment as if to draw him out still further.

Oh, the strange and wonderful things that men could make women do! thought Jane. She remembered how once, long ago, she herself had started to learn Swedish – there was still a grammar now thick with dust lying in the attic; and when she had first met Nicholas she had tried Greek. And now here was her own daughter caught up in the higher flights of Geography! He seemed a nice young man, but that was only the least one could say. Was it also the most?

Prudence regarded the young couple with something like envy. To be eighteen again and starting out on a long series of love affairs of varying degrees of intensity seemed to her entirely enviable. She began to recall some of her own past triumphs, at Oxford and afterwards, and to compare them with her present state. Had there perhaps been a slight falling off lately? When Paul looked at her a kind of startled expression came into his eyes, so that she wondered whether she had overdone her make-up and the elegance of her dress and appeared formidable rather than feminine and desirable. Fabian and Nicholas, however, showed their appreciation by their glances and the wine soon put everybody into a more mellow mood.

'If only we could have wine at the Parochial Church Council meetings,' said Jane. 'We have tried tea and sandwiches and more comfortable chairs, but somehow it didn't make much difference. Wine is *really* what maketh glad the heart of man, isn't it?' She raised her glass to Fabian rather gaily.

Flora looked at her mother a little anxiously. Indeed, the younger members of the party seemed altogether more solemn than the older ones. It was difficult to keep Paul away from the higher flights of Geography, but eventually they were all recalling their Oxford days and Fabian his Cambridge ones, and it seemed that life had been much gayer then.

'Ah, we flung roses riotously!' said Jane. 'Nicholas, do you remember that evening when we serenaded the Principal from a punt on the river? Of course, when she came to the window we all moved on!'

Prudence smiled rather enigmatically as if she had subtler memories of the river, as indeed she had.

'Is there a strong revival of religion among the undergraduates today?' Nicholas asked, turning to Paul. 'One hears that there is.'

'I'm afraid I wouldn't know about that,' said Paul quite politely. 'Naturally, my interests lie in other fields.'

'But haven't you observed?' said Jane.

'People might like to keep it to themselves,' said Prudence.

'My friends are mostly geographers and anthropologists,' said Paul.

'Anthropologists,' echoed Fabian on a puzzled note. Prudence wondered if he were going to ask what they were and felt irritated with him for the small part he was playing in the conversation. If only Arthur Grampian had been there! she thought suddenly, hearing his rather flat, measured tones discoursing. Or even Geoffrey Manifold being rather aggressive about bars and holidays and his 'material'.

After dinner they had coffee, and then Flora said she would show Paul the village. Nicholas and Fabian began talking about gardening, so that Jane and Prudence somehow found themselves at the kitchen sink, faced with the washing-up for six people.

'Of course, I could leave it for Mrs Glaze,' said Jane rather vaguely, scraping some bones from one plate to another. 'You certainly can't wash up in that pretty dress, Prudence. Wouldn't you like to go back and talk to the men?'

'No; I'll dry, if you can lend me an apron,' Prudence said.

She watched Jane plunging dishes and glasses indiscriminately into the water without any attempt at a scientific arrangement or classification.

'Flora's young man might have done this quite well,' she said. 'Do you approve of him?'

'Well, I hardly know,' said Jane. 'One rather hopes that he will be the first of many. I have been trying to see how he could be described as "rather amusing", which was what Flora said about him in her letter.'

'He didn't really show it,' Prudence agreed, 'but perhaps he was shy and felt he had to go on talking about Geography. I dare say he is better when they're alone. Perhaps he is a wonderful lover.'

'Oh, dear!' Jane looked up from the sink anxiously. 'One doesn't want that kind of thing. Flora is only eighteen. What should be my attitude?'

'Flora is very sensible,' said Prudence. 'I shouldn't worry.'

'Yes, she isn't like me. Somehow Paul isn't quite what I'd hoped for her. I know it's silly – but I'd hoped that Lord Edgar might fall in love with her – when they were at tutorials, you know.'

'But he hates women, surely?' Prudence asked.

'I know, that's the point. I'd imagined Flora breaking through all that.'

Prudence laughed and then looked a little apprehensively at Jane, who was swishing the wine-glasses about in an inch or two of brownish water at the bottom of the bowl. 'You really need clean water for the glasses,' she pointed out.

'And they should have been done first,' said Jane rather sadly. 'Look, the twilight is coming; we'd better have the light on.'

The light over the sink was a dim but unshaded bulb and added a kind of desolation to the whole scene, with its chicken bones and scattered crockery. Jane went on washing in an absent-minded way, looking out over the sink to the laurels outside.

'We have laurels outside Nicholas's study window and here,' she said thoughtfully. 'No doubt Nicholas and Mrs Glaze deserve laurels, a whole wreath of them, but I don't. Oh, Prudence,' she said, turning to her friend with a little dripping mop in her hand, 'you and Fabian must make a fine thing of your married life, and I know you will. You'll be a splendid hostess and such a help to him in everything.'

'He hasn't asked me to marry him yet,' said Prudence.

'Why don't *you* ask *him*?' said Jane recklessly. 'Women are not in the same position as they were in Victorian times. They can do nearly everything that men can now. And they are getting so much bigger and taller and men are getting smaller, haven't you noticed?'

'Fabian is tall,' said Prudence rather complacently. 'I must say I like a man to be tall.'

'Ah, you like a rough tweed shoulder to cry on,' said Jane scornfully. 'Now, why don't you go and interrupt Fabian and Nicholas in the rather dull conversation they must be having, and suggest a walk in the twilight?'

'You mean I should ask if *I* may see *him* home?' said Prudence derisively.

'Well, why not? Why shouldn't a woman take the initiative in a little thing like that?'

Prudence went on drying forks, and soon the sound of men's voices was heard in the passage.

'Can we help?' asked Nicholas in the tone of one who hopes he will be too late.

'Yes, we really should have offered sooner,' said Fabian, 'but I never feel I'm much good in a kitchen – not at the sink, anyway.'

'I never see why men should be good at cooking and yet not able to clear things up,' said Prudence rather acidly.

'Why don't you and Fabian leave the finishing touches to us,' said Jane. 'Husband and wife at the sink – that's very fitting.'

Fabian sighed. Jane wondered if he had bitter-sweet memories of washing-up with poor Constance.

'Good night, then,' he said. 'It has been such a pleasant evening.'

'Well, if you're sure I can't do any more,' said Prudence, hanging her damp drying-cloth on a line in the kitchen.

She walked into the hall with Fabian. The front door was open and she went out on to the steps.

'Perhaps I should be going now,' said Fabian. 'It seems rather a dismal end to the party, to leave them washing up.'

'Oh, I don't think Jane had anything else in mind. It was the meal that was the main thing.'

'I shall be seeing you tomorrow, darling,' said Fabian. 'You are all coming to tea with me. We shall have it in the garden under the walnut tree.'

'How nice,' said Prudence.

They had reached the gate by now and were standing rather aimlessly by it. Some bats were wheeling about in the dusky air and Prudence put her hands up to her head and uttered a little cry.

'What is it, darling?' asked Fabian anxiously.

'All these bats! I loathe them.'

'Then you'd better go indoors,' he said sensibly. 'It would have been rather pleasant to go for a little walk, but I expect you are rather tired and it wouldn't really do.'

'Wouldn't it?'

'Well, you see the village people walk about at night, but we don't,' he declared.

'What a strange idea! Paul and Flora have gone for a walk, haven't they?'

'Ah, young love,' said Fabian fatuously. 'They make their own rules. It is quite probable that I may be elected to the Parochial Church Council next year,' he went on more seriously. 'You see what I mean.'

'Oh, yes,' Prudence laughed rather hysterically. 'Naturally

you couldn't be seen walking in the dusk with a woman.'

'Well, it might look a little odd. Good night, darling,' he bent and kissed her hand. '*A domani!*'

Prudence walked back into the house and found Jane, her shoes off, lying on the drawing-room sofa.

'I didn't feel like going for a walk,' Prudence said. 'I'm rather tired, really.'

'How do you think it went – the evening?' Jane asked.

'Very well,' said Prudence politely. 'It was a lovely chicken.'

'A lovely chicken!' Jane laughed. 'Yes, it certainly was; and the wine and the conversation about Geography and then the washing up – you and Fabian, Flora and Paul, me and Nicholas.'

'Fabian isn't what you'd call a brilliant conversationalist,' said Prudence half to herself.

'Oh, who wants that!' said Jane. She yawned and got up from the sofa. 'Nicholas is out seeing to his tobacco plants – I shall fall asleep if I lie here any longer. Shall we go up before the "young people" get back? It might be rather daunting for them to be faced with me when they come in – of course, you would be different.'

'No; I think I'm quite ready for bed,' said Prudence. 'May I have a bath?'

'Yes, do!' said Jane enthusiastically.

Most of the hot water had been used for the great washing up, but it was a warm evening and Prudence lay for some time in the tepid water, contemplating the dingy ceiling of the vast room with its stained-glass window and the bath cowering in a corner. It was like having a bath in a chapel. I am drained of all emotion and nothing seems real, she thought, certainly not Fabian. Tea under the walnut tree tomorrow . . . and then what?

'Have you got something nice to read?' Jane asked, coming into Prudence's room.

'Yes, thank you; a novel.'

'And what could be better,' said Jane, 'particularly Mr Green's latest, or is it Mr Greene? I never know. Both are delightful in their different ways. And you have a book of poems too, if Mr Green or Greene should fail to charm or soothe.'

'Yes. Fabian gave me that,' said Prudence rather quickly.

'A very nice anthology,' said Jane, turning the pages. Of course, it was the same as the one poor Constance had given to *him* which Jane had rescued when the 'things' were sorted out. Perhaps he did not know of any other. She turned back the pages quickly until she came to the fly-leaf. He had written, 'Prudence from Fabian,' with the date, and then,

My Love is of a birth as rare
As 'tis for object strange and high;

the same inscription as Constance had written for him fifteen years ago.

How strange that he should have remembered that, thought Jane. Had it been somewhere in the back of his mind for all these years, to be brought out again, as a woman, searching through her piece-bag for a patch, might come upon a scrap of rare velvet or brocade?

She closed the book quickly. 'Does Fabian read much poetry?' she asked.

'No. I don't think so. He knows one or two tags,' said Prudence casually. 'Men don't really go in for that sort of thing like women do.'

'No,' Jane agreed; 'one has to accept that, together with their other limitations. Listen, I can hear Paul going up to his attic. I wonder if they had an amusing evening? One assumes that he has other conversation apart from Geography.'

'*O my America! My new-found-land*,' said Prudence. 'I wonder if he quoted that to her?'

'Oh, geographers don't read poetry,' said Jane confidently. 'Good night, Prue dear. Sleep well.'

CHAPTER EIGHTEEN

THE NEXT day was Sunday, and Prudence was awakened early by Nicholas's voice calling from what seemed to be the depths of the linen cupboard on the landing.

'Jane, there's no clean shirt *here*! What did you do with the laundry?'

Then Jane seemed to come, there was a good deal of rushing up and down stairs and agitated conversation. It was not at all as Prudence had thought it would be. She had imagined that she might perhaps hear the quiet footsteps of Nicholas and Jane creeping out to Early Service. She might almost have wished that she could have joined them herself. Was every Sunday morning like this? she wondered. Looking back to the other occasions when she had stayed with them, she decided that it probably was. If *she* were married to a clergyman, she would see that everything was put out ready for him on the Saturday night. . . . She dozed off again and was woken by a knock at the door and Jane in her hat and coat coming in with a cup of tea in her hand.

'Good morning, Prue. I thought you'd like a cup of tea,' she said, standing by the bed. 'How interesting you look, even at this hour of the morning. The whole effect is very Regency.'

Prudence had bound up her hair in a kind of emerald green turban, a shade darker than her nightdress, which was of a very transparent material, a little shocking, Jane thought. It was perhaps a good thing that Nicholas had not brought in the tea.

'We are going to church, of course, but Flora will start getting the breakfast,' she said, thinking how wonderful it was that Prudence should have taken the trouble to curl up her hair after what had seemed to be rather an unsatisfactory evening with Fabian.

'Oh, then I'll get up and help her,' said Prudence without much enthusiasm.

'Well, thank you, Prue, but I dare say Paul will be doing that. I believe he is quite useful in the house.'

After Jane had gone, Prudence drank her tea and then turned over on to her side. She felt disinclined to get up and face penetrating glances from Paul's blue eyes. Did he talk about Geography at breakfast? she wondered. At the best of times it was not a meal she enjoyed, and the prospect of the company of a young man under twenty-five and Jane's bright conversation seemed altogether too much to be endured. However, when the time came, Paul and Flora seemed to be engrossed in their plans for the day and little notice was taken of her. She attended Matins out of politeness to her host and hostess and noticed with a kind of scornful interest that Fabian was in church. She determined to look her best when they met in the afternoon, and to behave rather coldly towards him.

Jessie Morrow knew that she could not hope to equal Prudence in elegance, so she made no special preparations for the tea party under the walnut tree to which she and Miss Doggett, perhaps because they were next-door neighbours and could not be left out, had been invited. Her strength would have to lie in the deepening intimacy that was growing up between her and Fabian on the evenings when Miss Doggett was out. Besides, did men really notice one's clothes as much as all that? She had certainly made an effort to appear more striking on the first evening when she had called on Fabian in Constance's old blue velvet dress, but at other times she had gone to him in whatever she happened to be wearing and he had not appeared to be any less affectionate towards her. She had almost welcomed Prudence's visit this weekend, for she felt that it might give Fabian a chance to straighten things out. Perhaps last night he had taken a walk with her in the dusk and they had talked about the situation. But then it occurred to her that perhaps it would be better if he waited until Sunday, which would be Prudence's last evening. She could then go back on Monday and it would be much less awkward. After that things would just take their course. But the first thing was to get rid of Prudence, Jessie thought ruthlessly.

'Just imagine how lucky!' Miss Doggett was saying. 'Mr Driver has persuaded Mr Lyall and his mother to come to tea.'

'However did he do that?' asked Jessie abstractedly. 'I suppose he just asked them and they had no excuse. He fancies himself dispensing hospitality to the great.'

'It should be a delightful party,' Miss Doggett purred. 'And such a fine day. I shall wear my navy and white and my new hat. I suppose you will wear your flowered crepe?'

'I had thought I would go in this,' said Jessie, pulling out a crumpled fold of her faded blue linen dress. 'I can't compete with Prudence Bates.'

'Compete with Miss Bates!' Miss Doggett's laugh rang out. 'I should think not, indeed. But you can at least wear a cleaner-looking dress. Our Member is going to be there, after all.'

'Well, I am not a supporter of his Party,' said Jessie.

'Now, now, Jessie; none of that nonsense. . . . Look.' They were standing by an upper window which overlooked Fabian's garden. 'Mrs Arkright is putting out chairs under the walnut tree. She has been at it all morning, seeing to the food, Mr Driver was to have only a light lunch – a salmon salad with cheese to follow. Not *tinned* salmon, of course,' she added hastily.

'No, one could hardly give a man tinned salmon,' said Jessie ironically.

'It is very popular among the working classes, of course, but that's another matter. I see no reason why we shouldn't be the first to arrive,' continued Miss Doggett on a different note. 'Somebody has got to be first after all.'

'Shall I watch out for a propitious moment?'

'Well, yes; we don't want to arrive too early, of course, not before the preparations are fully completed.'

Jessie waited at the window and saw Fabian, in a light grey suit of some thin material, step out on to the lawn. She drew back into the shelter of the curtain and observed him, moving a chair here and there, standing back and surveying the scene. He looked just a little common in the grey suit, she thought; perhaps the colour was too light or there was something not quite the thing about the way it was cut. She could almost imagine that he might be wearing brown-and-white shoes, like the hero of a musical comedy in the twenties, but that was hardly possible. Yet she felt, as we so often do with somebody we love, that any little defect could only make him more dear to her.

'I think we could perhaps go now,' she said aloud. 'Mr Driver seems to be surveying the stage as if he expected somebody to make an entrance very shortly.'

At the gate they met Jane and Nicholas and Prudence, in a lilac cotton dress of deceptive simplicity.

'I'm glad we've met you,' said Jane. 'We were afraid we were too early.'

Fabian welcomed them and they lowered themselves cautiously into deck-chairs on the lawn.

'Your daughter isn't coming?' Miss Doggett asked.

'No; she has a friend staying and they have gone off somewhere for the day, to see a bit of the countryside.'

'I expect she has made some nice friends at Oxford,' said Miss Doggett.

'This is a young man,' said Jane obscurely.

'Oh?' Miss Doggett's eyes brightened.

'A geographer,' said Nicholas in a bluff kind of voice.

'Oh.' There was a slight falling-off of interest in Miss Doggett's tone. 'Of course, she will meet lots of young men,' she said reassuringly.

'I certainly hope so,' said Jane heartily. 'After all, she is only eighteen.'

'Ah, to be eighteen again!' said Fabian sentimentally.

'Is that a good age for a man?' Prudence asked, swinging her sun-glasses in her hand, like a picture in *Vogue*, Jessie thought, her eyes riveted on the crimson toe-nails that peeped out through the straps of her sandals.

'Yes, I think it is,' said Nicholas. 'You have your whole life before you, or so it seems.'

'All the things one was going to do, the books one was going to write,' said Jane dreamily, 'the brilliant marriages one was going to make.'

'Marriages?' said her husband. 'Well, well . . . Ah, here is Mrs Lyall and her son.'

'Strange how different it sounds said like that,' said Jane. 'Usually one says Mr Lyall and his mother.' He had timed his arrival well, she thought, but perhaps he had by now had enough practice, knowing that he must always be last.

The ladies almost rose from their deck-chairs at the sight of their beloved Member, who shook hands with them all. There were enquiries about his health, the word 'burden' was mentioned by Miss Doggett, Jane noticed, and Mrs Arkright came hurrying out with the tea.

He will ask Prudence to pour out, thought Jessie, a sudden agony of fear breaking through her carefully schooled indifference, and indeed at the sight of the silver teapot Prudence had sat up a little in her deck-chair and taken off her sun-glasses again.

'I have asked Mrs Arkright if she will kindly pour out for us,' said Fabian. 'It is rather troublesome to have to do it oneself, and I am really no good at it.'

'A splendid idea. Then there will be no hard feelings among the ladies,' said Nicholas in his best vicar's manner.

'Would there be hard feelings?' asked Edward in an interested tone. 'Do people *like* pouring out tea?'

'I don't, dear,' said Mrs Lyall. 'I get very flustered, as you know.'

'Well, it has a certain meaning, sometimes,' said Miss Doggett archly, with a glance at Prudence.

'Miss Bates shouldn't undertake it,' said Jessie brusquely. 'She might spill something on that pretty dress.'

'I'm sure Miss Bates would manage admirably,' said Edward.

'There is no need to spill anything, unless the teapot drips,' said Prudence.

'And we know that teapot,' said Miss Doggett in a warm, sentimental tone; 'it has never dripped in its life.'

Oh, we can't bring the dead into this, thought Jane, imagining Constance Driver presiding over the tea things. 'Our teapots always drip,' she said cheerfully. 'They are china ones with broken spouts.'

Mrs Arkright handed round cups of tea and cucumber and tomato sandwiches, and then seemed to melt away. It was as if she had somehow changed into a bush or plant to efface herself from the company, and then miraculously become herself again just at the moment when cups needed refilling and plates were empty.

'What a fine walnut tree!' said Edward, looking up into its branches. 'It is so deliciously restful here. I can't think how long it is since I sat lazily in a garden, and it's really one of my favourite ways of spending time.'

'Don't you often have tea on the terrace at the House of Commons?' Jane asked. 'I've always thought that sounded very pleasant.'

Edward gave her one of his charming, weary smiles. 'One is usually entertaining constituents,' he said, 'and can't really relax.'

'Well, I do hope you will relax *here*,' said Miss Doggett vigorously.

'We are your constituents,' said Nicholas, 'but you need

not feel that you must entertain us. Rather, *we* should entertain *you*.' He paused and a worried expression came on to his face. For how was it to be done? Country vicars are perhaps not used to entertaining Members of Parliament. Still, the women would see to it, he thought, relaxing again in his deck-chair.

'If only we knew how to,' said Fabian, with a smile only a shade less weary than Edward's.

'Edward just likes to sit quietly,' said his mother. 'That is really a change and a treat for him.'

'Yes, one does find it a great relief just to be able to relax in a garden,' said Fabian. 'I find the bustle of the City quite intolerable.'

'What is your work?' asked Mrs Lyall.

'Oh, it is quite unspeakably dull,' said Fabian. 'I really couldn't discuss it here. I suppose it is the dullness of it all that makes me feel so exhausted.'

'Exhausted?' said Jessie rather sharply.

'Yes, exhausted.' Fabian closed his eyes for a moment.

'Life is certainly tiring these days,' Nicholas observed.

There was silence.

'A gloom seems to have fallen on the party,' said Jane. 'Perhaps it would be better if we all sat in silence. If the men find life so exhausting, our chatter might disturb them.'

The women made a gallant attempt to carry on the conversation among themselves. Mrs Lyall talked all the time about her son and how she was hoping that he could be persuaded to take a real holiday. Miss Doggett listened sympathetically and recommended a guest-house in the Cotswolds which seemed to Jane hardly the kind of place for a Member of Parliament as exquisite as Edward, though, had he been of another party, perhaps, he might have considered it. Certainly he would be surrounded by doting middle-aged women, and perhaps that is not unpleasant to a member of any party or indeed to men in general, whether politicians or not.

The conversation about the guest-house became general among the women, for Prudence and Jessie had been unable to think of anything to say to each other, Prudence having no idea that they had anything at all in common and Jessie finding herself incapable of making any suitable use of her superior knowledge.

Fabian and Edward seemed to be trying to outdo each other in weariness, and even Nicholas was making some attempt to compete, detailing the number of services he had to take on Sundays and the many houses he had to visit during the week.

Suddenly there was a diversion. Jessie Morrow, getting up to pass a plate of cakes to Mrs Lyall, knocked against the little table on which Prudence had put her cup of tea, so that the cup upset all over the skirt of her lilac cotton dress.

'Oh, Jessie, how could you be so clumsy!' stormed Miss Doggett. 'You have ruined Miss Bates's dress – that tea will stain it!'

'It doesn't matter,' said Prudence, stifling her first impulse of anger towards Miss Morrow's clumsiness. 'It's only cotton – it will wash.'

'You must take it off at once and soak it in cold water,' said Miss Doggett.

'Yes, come into the house,' said Fabian.

'She had better come into my house,' said Miss Doggett, 'and then I can lend her something to wear.'

'I have my car outside,' said Edward. 'We could easily drive to The Towers.'

'I think it would be more practical if she went back to the vicarage,' said Jane, 'and then she could change into one of her own dresses.'

Prudence felt foolish and irritated at being the centre of so much fuss. Edward and Fabian were perhaps a little annoyed at having attention diverted from their weariness, and it seemed inevitable now that the party should break up, especially as Nicholas began murmuring about it being time for Evensong.

'Yes, I suppose I should go,' said Jane.

'Well, we shall be meeting again in church,' said Miss Doggett.

'I am to read one of the lessons, I believe,' said Edward with a touch of complacency. 'Thank you, Driver, for a most pleasant afternoon. An interlude for rest and refreshment.'

'I am worried about Miss Bates's dress,' said Miss Doggett to Jane. 'If you don't put it to soak in cold water at once that tea will stain. I'm very much afraid it may leave a mark.'

'It seems to be leaving a mark already,' said Jessie in an unsuitably detached tone for one who had been responsible for the disaster; 'rather the shape of Italy. I wonder if that can have any significance?'

'We shall consult *Enquire Within* about removing the stain,' said Jane. 'It is sure to have a good remedy – something to do with ox-gall or wormwood, so practical.'

'Well, Prudence,' said Fabian, rather at a loss, 'I expect I shall be seeing you soon in Town.'

'Oh, possibly,' said Prudence casually. 'Ring me up some time.'

Not a very satisfactory leave-taking, thought Jane. There seemed to be some want of enthusiasm, some lack of proper sadness, unless their casual manner was merely a way of disguising their deeper feelings.

'That silly little woman,' said Prudence crossly as they walked home, 'upsetting my tea like that. And then everyone made such a fuss. I don't think I shall come to Evensong, Jane. I really don't feel in the mood.'

'Oh, don't you? What a pity,' said Jane. 'I love Evensong. There's something sad and essentially English about it, especially in the country, and so many of the old people are there. I always like that poem with the lines about gloved the hands that hold the hymn-book that this morning milked the cow. We have the old hymns here, you know. Ancient and

Modern. *Sun of my Soul, thou Saviour dear . . .* the congregation love it and Nicholas wouldn't change it for the world.'

But Prudence did not want to be made to feel sad, and offered to stay at home and get the supper ready. After she had changed her dress she sat in the drawing-room, hoping that perhaps Fabian would telephone or call. But then she realized that of course he too would be at Evensong. A melancholy summer Sunday evening is a thing known to many women in love, she thought, seeing herself as rather ill-used, left alone in the big, untidy vicarage kitchen, opening a tin of soup and preparing things to go with spaghetti. Jane hadn't even any *long* spaghetti, she thought, the tears coming into her eyes, only horrid little broken-up bits. Oh, my Love, she said to herself, sitting down at the scrubbed kitchen table, thoughts of Fabian and Arthur Grampian and others, Philip, Henry and Laurence from the distant past, coming into her mind. Then she thought of Geoffrey Manifold and how good he was to his aunt, and a sense of the sadness of life in general came over her, so that she almost forgot about Fabian refusing to walk with her in the twilight in case it should prejudice his chances of being elected to the Parochial Church Council. When Jane and Nicholas came back from Evensong they found her crouching on the floor in the dining-room, delving in the dark sideboard cupboard among the empty biscuit barrels and tarnished cruets for the sherry decanter.

CHAPTER NINETEEN

THE TUESDAY following that week-end the weather broke, and on Wednesday it was still raining when Jessie Morrow set out for her afternoon off.

'I shall go to the pictures,' she said in answer to Miss

Doggett's enquiries, 'and have a high tea at the Regal Café.'

'Why not call and see Canon and Mrs Pritchard?' Miss Doggett suggested. 'You know we have an open invitation to visit her house any time.'

'The kind of invitation that includes everybody in the parish and means nobody,' said Jessie scornfully.

'I'm sure Mrs Pritchard would give you a cup of tea.'

'But not plaice and chips, which is what I usually have after the pictures – plaice and chips, a fancy cake or two and a pot of good strong tea.'

'Mrs Pritchard always had her own special blend, something between Earl Grey and Orange Pekoe,' said Miss Doggett rather wistfully. 'I suppose she still has it there, in those exquisitely thin cups. Poor Constance was fond of China tea, too.'

But Fabian likes Indian and a good strong cup, thought Jessie gleefully. Now that they had spent several of her half-days together he even enjoyed the fish tea which he had at first thought rather vulgar and had got over his anxiety lest anyone they knew might see them together. He still ate his plaice and chips a little furtively, though, and did not help himself to tomato ketchup as liberally as Jessie did.

'Well,' she said when she had poured out their second cups of tea, 'have you told her yet?'

'Told who?' asked Fabian nervously, glancing round the café. Perhaps it was not such a bad place to choose for a clandestine meeting after all. It was certainly not the kind of place where one was likely to meet Canon and Mrs Pritchard or Edward Lyall and his mother.

'Why, Prudence, of course. You said you would break it to her this week-end.'

Fabian sighed heavily and plunged his fork into his cake with a dramatic gesture, so that a piece of it shot on to the floor.

'No, I'm afraid I didn't. What can I say to her? She'll be so hurt.'

'Hurt? And would it be the first time you'd ever hurt a woman?'

'Well, no; one has had to hurt people, I suppose,' said Fabian, tilting his head to one side. He had just realized that the distinguished-looking man sitting at that distant table was himself reflected in a mirror at the far end of the room. No wonder one had had to hurt people, he thought, resting his forehead on his hand.

'Now stop trying to look like Edward Lyall with his burden,' said Jessie sharply. 'Do you mean to tell me that you have said nothing at all to her?'

'We had very little conversation about anything. After dinner on Saturday we stood outside the vicarage gate, I remember, and she was frightened by a bat. I think she would have liked a walk in the twilight if it hadn't been for the bats. And then I felt I really couldn't suggest it. She would have expected me to kiss her, and one can't do that in the village.'

'Only behind locked doors,' said Jessie mockingly. 'It doesn't matter what you do in the privacy of your own home.'

'Oh, my dear . . . don't speak of that here. It isn't a worthy setting.' He pushed aside the vase of dusty pink paper artificial flowers and took hold of her hand.

'You had better not hold my hand,' said Jessie in a low voice. 'Flora Cleveland and that young man of hers have just come in. I suppose they've been to the pictures too. *He* is not holding *her* hand. Perhaps middle-aged lovers are more sentimental – a beautiful thought.'

'I wonder if we could slip out another way without them seeing us?' asked Fabian anxiously. 'After all we don't want the news to get about too soon.'

'Not before you have finished with Prudence. Quickly, now, Flora has gone to the ladies' cloakroom and the young man will not recognize us, or certainly not me.'

'I will write to Prudence tonight,' said Fabian firmly as they hurried along the street. 'This deception is intolerable. Poor Prudence, she has always been loved. It will be a sad blow to her pride.'

'Look,' Jessie stopped outside an antique shop and looked in the window. 'I wonder if you would perhaps buy me some little token?' she said, feeling perhaps that Fabian was not likely to suggest it himself.

'This is rather an expensive shop, my dear,' he said cautiously. 'I have kept one or two of Constance's rings, and I was thinking . . .'

'Certainly, since I am to take her place I should have one of her rings,' said Jessie. 'Perhaps you have even kept her wedding ring with the inscription she told you to have engraved inside it?'

'Well, yes; I did not feel I could sell it. But I think you would probably prefer to have a new wedding ring,' said Fabian seriously. 'In any case, it might not fit you. But let me buy you some little trinket here. Today seems to have been rather a special day, doesn't it? Look, there is a tray with an interesting assortment of things. Is there anything there you would like?'

'All on this tray, 15*s*.' Jessie read. Well, that was something, to have him spend fifteen shillings on a useless sentimental object for her. 'That little brooch with *Mizpah* on it. I think I should like that.'

'It's rather ugly, isn't it?' said Fabian doubtfully. '*Mizpah* has a depressing Biblical sound about it.'

'But it has a meaning. And it might be quite appropriate for us. It means "The Lord watch between me and thee when we are absent one from another." '

'Well, yes,' Fabian smiled.

They went into the shop and Fabian bought the brooch, which the shopkeeper wrapped in a piece of tissue paper, evidently not thinking it worthy of a box. When they had got outside, Jessie unwrapped it and pinned it on to her mackintosh.

'Thank you, dearest,' she said, taking his arm. 'Now I really feel somebody.'

It had always been their custom to leave and return to the village by different trains so that they should not be seen at the station together, but this time, perhaps because of *Mizpah*, they decided to return together and, if necessary, to pretend that they had met accidentally.

But now, although they were not to know it yet, it did not really matter what they did, for Miss Doggett, alone in the house, had come upon the truth about them. Stumbled on it, was how she put it to herself.

Ever since the week-end when Jessie had upset the tea on Prudence's dress, she had had a feeling that there was something different about Jessie. She had noticed her smiling to herself and had several times caught her at the window, looking down into Fabian's garden.

After Jessie had gone out for the afternoon, Miss Doggett felt restless and dissatisfied. She put her feet up as usual for her after luncheon rest and listened to a woman's programme on the wireless, but somehow its competent little talks about breast feeding, young children's questions, and a housewife's life in Nigeria did not seem to be planned for an elderly spinster. Her library book also failed to hold her attention, for although, according to the mystifying jargon of the publishers, its fourth large impression had been exhausted before publication, its effect on her was that of exhausting without granting the blessing of sleep. When at three o'clock, therefore, she had not managed to drop off, her thoughts turned to Jessie. Why had she deliberately upset a cup of tea over Miss Bates? For it seemed now as if the action had been deliberately calculated. What could she have hoped to gain by it? Miss Doggett pushed away her footstool, flung her book down on the floor and walked upstairs.

Jessie's room was without any definite character apart from that given to it by the miscellaneous pieces, unwanted in other rooms, with which it was furnished. In all the years that she had lived with Miss Doggett, Jessie had not succeeded in stamping it with her own personality. One would have imagined that a gentlewoman would have her 'things', those objects – photographs, books, souvenirs collected on holiday – which can make a room furnished with other people's furniture into a kind of home. But Jessie seemed to have none of these. The only photograph was of her mother – Miss Doggett's Cousin Ella – a plain-looking woman with an unsuitably sardonic expression for a Victorian. She had married late and had made an unfortunate marriage – Miss Doggett's thoughts lingered with satisfaction on this theme for a few minutes, for Aubrey Morrow had left his wife and child after a few years – and then continued her examination of the room. The only books to be seen were the library book Jessie happened to be reading at that moment, a paper-backed detective novel that anybody might have and, rather oddly, an old *A.B.C.* There were no books of devotion, not even a Bible or a prayer-book, which one might certainly expect a spinster to possess. The 'objects' were even more unpromising – an ugly little china dog of some Scottish breed attached to an ash-tray, an old willow-pattern bowl with no apparent purpose, some dusty sea-shells in a box – it seemed almost as if Jessie had been at pains to suppress or conceal her personality. For there was no doubt that she had personality of an uncomfortable kind; she had inherited her mother's sardonic expression, and who could tell how much of her father there might be in her? These things always came out eventually. It was quite likely that she herself might make an unsuitable marriage. But who was there for her to make an unsuitable marriage with? That was the point. Miss Doggett's thoughts ranged rather wildly from the man who delivered the laundry and was rather free in his manner, to the Roman Catholic priest of the little tin church, whom Jessie had once admitted she thought handsome. Certainly the latter would be quite disgraceful. He would be unfrocked, no doubt. . . . Miss Doggett moved over to the wardrobe and opened it.

She knew all Jessie's clothes, the sage green jumper-suit, the grey tweed overcoat and the skirt that didn't quite match it, the blue marocain 'semi-evening' and the flowered crepe which had been her 'best' summer dress for some years now. It had a band of plain colour let into the skirt to lengthen it which dated it as having been new some time before 1947. Miss Doggett's hands moved idly among the fabrics, jersey, tweed, crepe, wool, cotton, until they suddenly touched velvet. Had Jessie a velvet dress? She tried to remember one, but failed, and so took down the hanger and brought the dress out. It was a blue velvet, long, with a square neck and tight-fitting sleeves. But when had she bought it? It was a good material, better than Jessie could have afforded. Constance Driver had once had one very like it, made specially for her at Marshall's. Surely it was this very dress! Jessie had shortened it and altered the neck in some way.

Miss Doggett stood with the dress in her hands, trying to think what this discovery could mean. Jessie must have hidden it away when they were sorting out poor Constance's things. Well, perhaps there was nothing much in that. She may have had a secret longing to possess a velvet dress, though she did not usually show any interest in clothes at all. Nevertheless, it gave Miss Doggett an uneasy feeling, which made her go over to the dressing-table and open the drawers. The bottom one was full of underclothes and stockings, quite unremarkable, nothing at all daring or unsuitable. There was a new pair of nylon stockings in a cellophane envelope, but everybody had those nowadays. The left-hand top drawer held handkerchiefs, gloves and one or two scarves. Miss Doggett lifted the pile of handkerchiefs and took out a larger one from the bottom. It was a man's handkerchief, the kind a woman might use when she had a cold. It was neatly marked with the initials, F.C.D. *Fabian Charlesworth Driver* . . . with an agitated movement Miss Doggett tugged at the handle of the right-hand drawer, but it would not open. It was locked.

She sat down rather heavily on the bed, still holding Fabian's handkerchief in her hand. The locked drawer, she thought, what could be in it? And why should Jessie have one of Fabian Driver's handkerchiefs? Had he dropped it accidentally when he was visiting them, or had it come into Jessie's possession in some other way? Could it be that there was something between him and Jessie?

Miss Doggett was now in a state of considerable agitation. She was angry at what seemed to be Jessie's deceit and yet excited at the same time. She went downstairs and made herself a pot of tea, hardly knowing that she did so. She longed to confide her discovery to somebody, to discuss, and brood over it, and began to consider the suitability of people she knew in the village. Most were married women too busy with their children and household cares; Mrs Crampton and Mrs Mayhew were stupid fluttering creatures; widows, she thought scornfully, with a silly, sentimental view of life. Mrs Cleveland seemed to be the only person who might be at all suitable, and who, indeed, could be more so than the vicar's wife? One should always be able to take one's troubles, hopes and fears to the vicarage.

Miss Doggett finished her tea and took the tray into the kitchen, leaving it on the draining-board. Then she put on her mackintosh and a top-heavy-looking maroon felt hat, took her umbrella from the stand and set out.

It was raining heavily as she opened the vicarage gate and the laurels outside Nicholas's study window were dripping wet. The garden wasn't what it used to be in the Pritchards' time, she thought. The grass was ragged and there was nothing in the front beds but a few straggling asters and nasturtiums.

Jane Cleveland herself came to the door. She was wearing

an apron, and hastened to explain this unusual circumstance by telling Miss Doggett that she was bottling plums.

'Or, rather, trying to,' she added. 'Nicholas is doing most of the work. The jars are just due to come out of the oven and have the boiling syrup poured into them. Then the tops must be put on – it's all very nerve-racking.'

Miss Doggett, who knew all about bottling plums, was hardly listening to what Jane said. It was most disconcerting to find her doing anything at all, and she wondered whether it might not be better to postpone the real object of her visit and come back at a more propitious time.

'I really wanted to ask your advice about something,' she began.

'Ask *my* advice?' Jane's face brightened. 'But how splendid! Do come in. Perhaps you wouldn't mind sitting with us in the kitchen while we finish these bottles? They won't take long!'

Miss Doggett followed Jane rather unwillingly down the long stone passage that led to the kitchen.

'It's Miss Doggett, dear,' said Jane, flinging open the door. 'She wants to ask my advice about something.'

Really, thought Miss Doggett irritably, this is most unsuitable. For not only was the table covered with all the paraphernalia of bottling – jars, metal caps, rubber rings, plums, jugs, kettles, and sheets of newspaper – but the kitchen itself seemed to be festooned with enormous green leaves which hung down from everywhere that things could hang down from, the mantelpiece, the dresser, the clothes airer and the hooks in the ceiling which had once held hams and sides of bacon. Miss Doggett held her hands up to her hat, feeling as if she were in some Amazonian jungle and that poisonous snakes and insects might drop on to her from the great hanging leaves. To make matters worse, the vicar now emerged from behind a screen of leaves, his usual mild expression betraying that there was nothing at all extraordinary about the situation. He too was wearing a flowered apron which somehow took away from the dignity of his clerical collar, Miss Doggett felt.

'Ah, Miss Doggett, how nice to see you.' He advanced towards her with his hand outstretched. 'My wife has probably told you that we are bottling plums. And I am trying to dry some of my tobacco leaves – ideally it should be done outside, in the sun, of course.'

Miss Doggett was quite unable to think of anything suitable to say. There did not even seem to be anywhere to sit down until Jane had removed a plate of plum stones from one of the kitchen chairs, and she found herself forced to chatter about trivialities, while the jars were being taken from the oven, filled up with boiling syrup and sealed.

'There now,' said Jane, screwing up the last cap. 'I wonder if I shall have the courage to test these tomorrow. It seems to require such a very great deal of faith to lift them up just by their glass tops. I suppose it is like going over to Rome – once you see that it works you wonder how you could ever have doubted it.'

'Really, Jane . . .' protested her husband, 'I hardly think . . .'

'But of course they don't always work,' Jane went on. 'Sometimes the top comes away in your hand.'

'Personally, I find the other method more satisfactory,' said Miss Doggett. 'I don't think I have ever had a failure.'

'Well, well. We must try that next year,' said Nicholas. 'But it seemed rather more complicated.'

'I always think it's worth taking that little extra bit of trouble,' said Miss Doggett complacently.

'Oh, my leaves,' said Nicholas anxiously, putting up a hand to touch them. 'I wonder how dry they are or how dry they should be?'

Neither of the ladies seemed able to answer his question, and Jane suddenly turned to Miss Doggett and reminded her that she had wanted her advice on some matter. 'I think you said you wanted to ask *me*?' she added.

'Well, there is no objection to the vicar hearing what I have to say,' said Miss Doggett.

'I feel I can almost count as another woman,' said Nicholas, perhaps rather too lightly, for he was still thinking more of his tobacco leaves than of Miss Doggett's mission.

'The matter concerns a man and a woman,' said Miss Doggett obscurely, for she hardly knew how to begin. The plums and tobacco leaves and the general scene of disorder in the vicarage kitchen had taken words away from her. She had imagined herself coming out with it on the doorstep, almost. It was to have been the spontaneous overflow of powerful feelings rather than emotion recollected in tranquillity.

'Has there been some trouble in the village?' Jane asked. 'Some girl in the family way?'

Miss Doggett shuddered. She had certainly not thought of *that*. And yet who could tell where Jessie's behaviour might have led her?

'No; it isn't that,' she said firmly. 'I may as well say quite plainly what it is.'

'Yes, it doesn't really help to know what it is *not*,' said Jane seriously.

There was a short pause, and then Miss Doggett said in a kind of burst, 'I think there may be something between Jessie and Mr Driver.'

'Between Fabian and Miss Morrow?' repeated Jane, not quite echoing her words. 'But what could there be?'

'An understanding, a friendship, something more than that, perhaps. I hardly know – I feel I hardly *wish* to know.' This last sentence was not strictly true. There was nothing Miss Doggett wished to know more.

'Well, I suppose they could be friends,' said Jane doubtfully. 'But he is engaged to Miss Bates – unofficially, of course, but I think it is generally understood.'

'My dear, I don't think so,' interposed Nicholas. 'I think that was an arrangement you and Prudence made between yourselves. I don't think it is in Driver's mind at all.'

'But how do you know what is in his mind?' Jane asked indignantly. 'How can you?'

'We had some conversation the other evening when he was here to dinner. I understood then that he was not thinking of marrying again.'

'So that is what men talk about when they're alone together,' said Jane angrily. 'While Prue and I were struggling with the washing-up for six people you and Fabian were planning that he should not marry again!'

'Well, dear, hardly that . . .'

'I suppose he decided that once was enough and you encouraged him by pointing out that the Church frowns on the remarriage of widowers?'

'My dear Jane, I could hardly have done that. You know quite well that there can be no objection to a widower remarrying. In any case, I feel we are getting off the point. After all, Miss Doggett hasn't yet told us her reasons for supposing that there is an – er – understanding between Driver and Miss Morrow.'

Miss Doggett was in a difficulty here, for she did not feel that she could admit to having found one of Fabian's handkerchiefs among Jessie's. So she had to content herself with vague hints, indicating that she had had a 'feeling' for some time, that she had 'noticed things', which were not really very convincing.

Nobody could quite see what was to be done at the moment. Jane was concerned only with Prudence, and the effect the news – if it was news – might have on her. Nicholas, perhaps unconsciously taking the part of men against women, felt that it was hardly anybody's business to interfere at this stage. In any case there was nothing that *he* could do.

'After all, I'm not an intimate friend of Driver's,' he

pointed out. 'Jane really knows him better than I do. I could, of course, say something if it appeared to be necessary, though I hardly know what . . .'

'Don't you worry about that!' said Jane vigorously. 'I shall have no hesitation in facing him with it, if I feel that he has been trifling with Prue in any way. And why shouldn't we go now?' she turned to Miss Doggett. 'The sooner the better, *I* think. Perhaps you would come with me, Miss Doggett?'

'I should be very careful what you say, dear,' said Nicholas in a warning tone. 'After all, it isn't really any of our business. . . .' But the women were out of earshot by this time, and he turned back to his tobacco leaves with a feeling of relief. The whole thing seemed to be of very little importance, the kind of mountain women were apt to make out of what was hardly even a molehill. He went to the window and saw that it was still raining. He wondered whether Jane had remembered to take a mackintosh.

She had snatched up the first one she saw hanging in the hall, which happened to be Nicholas's black clerical one and came nearly down to her ankles. She wore nothing on her head, but having naturally curly hair she seldom did, and brushed aside Miss Doggett's offer of a share of her tartan umbrella. Miss Doggett could have wished that she did not look quite so odd, almost ridiculous. There must be nothing comic about the scene that was about to be enacted. It was altogether a most serious business, she had not until now stopped to consider its possible implications. 'Something between Jessie and Mr Driver . . .' something disgraceful, that possibility immediately sprang to mind when remembering Jessie's strange personality and her mother's unsuitable marriage. On the other hand, it might be something depressingly respectable and above-board, no more than a friendship . . .

'Prue will be *so* upset,' murmured Jane, tramping through the rain in the long black mackintosh. 'Miss Doggett, I'm sure you must be mistaken. Is Miss Morrow at home? Couldn't we ask her? Though,' she went on, 'it might be better to ask Fabian right out. Women do occasionally get the wrong idea – imagine that there is more in a man's feelings for them than there really is.' As perhaps poor Prudence had done. But then she remembered 'Miss Bates and her love affairs'. . . . Surely *she* could not have been mistaken?

'Jessie has had her half-day today,' said Miss Doggett. 'She usually goes to the cinema. I doubt whether she will be back yet.'

'Then perhaps we had better call on Fabian,' said Jane, faltering a little, for even her courage was beginning to ebb. What were they going to say to him? Wouldn't he regard them as a couple of interfering busybodies and be perfectly justified in so doing?

Fabian's house looked very quiet and unoccupied as they approached it. Mrs Arkright would have gone by now, leaving him a cold supper, with perhaps some soup that he could heat up himself. Jane and Miss Doggett were not to know that Fabian and Jessie were in the drawing-room having an argument about how Prudence should be told and who should do it. It was almost a relief to Fabian when the front-door bell rang and he saw Jane and Miss Doggett standing on the doorstep in the rain.

'Ah, come in,' he said, almost in a welcoming tone. 'It's a horrid evening to be out.'

He showed them into the drawing-room. Miss Doggett let out a kind of cry on seeing Jessie there.

'So it's true,' she said, sinking down into a chair. 'There *is* something between you!'

Jessie did not answer, and Fabian, who had his back to them, was busy with glasses and bottles which he took out of a corner cupboard. He supposed that the occasion was one which called for a drink; indeed, in his life there was hardly any occasion which did not.

'Sherry or gin?' he asked in a rather neutral voice, ignoring Miss Doggett's question.

'Oh, gin, thank you,' said Jane indignantly.

Miss Doggett did not answer, so he placed a glass of sherry near her.

Jane took a great gulp of her colourless drink and then gasped and coughed. She had forgotten how unpleasant it was.

'Fabian and I are going to be married,' said Jessie calmly. 'We were going to tell you, but you seem to have forestalled us.'

'Yes, we are to be married,' said Fabian. 'It seems to have come to that.'

For an instant Jane bridled indignantly on Jessie's behalf. It seems to have come to that! What a way to announce that you loved a woman and were going to marry her! Could men do no better than that these days?

Then she remembered Prudence in her red velvet house-coat and her evasive answers to the questions Jane had put to her about her relationship with Fabian.

'And what about Prudence?' she asked. 'You seem to have forgotten her.'

Fabian clasped his hands together in a despairing gesture. 'Oh, what am I to do,' he moaned, pacing about the room. 'I haven't had the courage to tell her yet. I blame myself for this.'

'Yes, I think you should probably shoulder *this* burden,' said Jane. 'It is better to finish with one thing before you start another.' And yet, she thought, how hopeless to say a thing like that; it was like telling a child to put away one toy before he took out a new one to play with.

'It was not much really between Prudence and me,' said Fabian lamely; 'perhaps less than you thought. We had dinner together once or twice and went to a few theatres. I certainly thought her very attractive and charming, but she could never take Constance's place.'

'So Jessie has done that?' asked Miss Doggett in an interested tone. 'And yet in many ways they are so unlike. Who would ever have thought . . .?'

'Prudence would have wanted so much,' Fabian went on, pacing about the room and giving the impression that he was talking to himself. 'Her letters, wonderful letters in a way, but so difficult to answer. And then she would have wanted to change everything here. She used to go to Heal's and look at curtain materials – she even chose a new wallpaper for Constance's old room.'

Poor darling Prue, thought Jane, how sure she must have been. 'I suppose *I* could tell her what has happened,' she said. 'I could write to her.'

Fabian stopped his pacing and stood in front of Jane.

'*Could* you?' he said gratefully. 'That would be such a help. I shall of course write as well. I feel that I must do that.'

'Yes, Fabian, you must,' said Jane firmly. 'Men can't expect women to do quite everything for them.'

'Poor Miss Bates,' said Miss Doggett perfunctorily.

'Oh, she has plenty of admirers,' said Jane brusquely.

'Then she will soon get over this,' went on Miss Doggett, for she had now lost interest in Prudence and was already planning Jessie's wedding from her house. There could be no possible objection to a church wedding, for although Fabian had not always behaved very well when poor Constance was alive, there had been no question of divorce or anything disgraceful like that. Obviously, Edward Lyall and his mother would expect an invitation to the wedding. It would be quite an event in the neighbourhood.

'Well, Jessie,' she said in a satisfied tone, 'I think Constance would have been pleased at this news.'

'Yes, wouldn't she,' said Fabian, also with some satisfaction. 'I think it would have been just what she would have wished. Perhaps she does know and is giving us her blessing in some way. I feel very strongly that perhaps, in some way . . .' His sentence petered out rather feebly. Perhaps he was conscious of Jane's eyes upon him, and she now stood up, pushing aside her unfinished glass of gin with an impatient gesture. She had no sympathy with Fabian's sentimental theology, and indeed felt that her part in the proceedings was over. Nobody took much notice of her as she said goodbye and let herself out of the house.

When she reached home she found that Flora and Paul had returned and were in the kitchen getting supper. Nicholas was wandering about among his tobacco leaves, occasionally fingering one to see if it was drying well.

'How did it go?' he asked anxiously.

'We found them both at Fabian's house. Miss Doggett seems to have been right. Fabian and Jessie are to be married, apparently.' Jane sat down wearily, still wearing Nicholas's black mackintosh.

'Are you talking about Mr Driver and Miss Morrow?' called Flora from the gas stove. 'We saw them having tea at the Regal Café, didn't we, Paul?'

'Did we? I remember your saying something about a man and a woman sitting there. Wasn't it that man who came to dinner the other evening who didn't seem to know what an anthropologist was?'

So that was how Fabian was to be known to Paul, thought Jane with a flash of amusement. He would hardly have been very pleased.

Supper was rather a gloomy meal. Nicholas and Jane did not say much, for Jane was brooding about what she should say to Prudence, and the young people spoke in low whispers, as if there were a death in the house. After the meal was over Jane retired to write her letter and Nicholas to his study for some unspecified purpose.

Paul and Flora settled themselves to the washing-up and could be heard singing in the back kitchen.

'Poor Prudence,' said Flora. 'We did hope that *this* time . . . what did you think of her?'

'Rather attractive in a way, but she looks about thirty, you know,' said Paul solemnly.

'I wonder if I shall get like that,' Flora mused.

'How do you mean?'

'Oh, falling in love with people and casting them off and then being cast off myself in the end.'

'But need it be the end for her?'

'Well, the supply of suitable men isn't inexhaustible when one reaches her age – not like it is at Oxford.'

Paul, who was nineteen and had already had several romances, made no comment. 'Do you think this Fabian man attractive?' he asked at length.

'Yes; I suppose so, in a rather used-up, Byronic sort of way. But he's rather middle-aged, really.' Flora squeezed out the dishcloth and draped it neatly over the papier-mâché washing-up bowl.

'Let's go into the garden,' said Paul; 'it's stopped raining now.'

Looking through her bedroom window, biting the end of her pen, Jane saw them walking hand-in-hand down the path between the clumps of Michaelmas daisies. She remembered noticing the title of a play on the wireless, *Love and Geography.* She had wondered at the time what possible connection there could be between the two. Well, it was a nice evening now that the rain had stopped, she thought absently, turning back to the blank sheet of paper before her.

In the damp, earwig-infested summer-house, which was an old-fashioned wooden structure with diamond-paned windows of crimson, orange and royal blue stained-glass, Paul put his arms around Flora and began quoting Donne,

O my America! My new-found-land . . .

as Prudence had suggested that he might. But Jane, the anxious mother, was now deep in her letter and the sentences were flowing quite easily.

CHAPTER TWENTY

SO PRUDENCE had not been Fabian's mistress, after all. This was the thought that seemed uppermost in Jane's mind as she sat trying to think of what she could say to Prudence, and she was displeased with herself that it should be so. But thinking over Prudence's guarded answer when she had put the question to her plainly and Fabian's remarks of a few hours ago, it did seem as if the worst – which was what Jane called it in her own mind – had not happened. This should certainly make the situation easier. Prudence's feelings would be less deeply involved and there could be no chance that she might be going to have a baby. Though it seemed, Jane thought, as if that kind of thing didn't happen nowadays. It would have been a help if she could have known what Fabian was going to say in his letter, but he had given no indication, beyond promising that he 'would write a line'. Yet his whole bearing, hand clasped to brow, tragic eyes and ruffled hair, pointed to his taking the attitude that this would hurt him more than it hurt Prudence. Jane felt that he would write from the depths of a wretchedness that would not necessarily be insincere because its outward signs were so theatrical. Presumably attractive men and probably women too must always be suffering in this way; they must so often have to reject and cast aside love, and perhaps even practice did not always make them ruthless and cold-blooded enough to do it without feeling any qualms.

Of course, Jane told herself, in an effort to relieve her own misery and her feeling of guilt for the part she had played in bringing them together, Prue hadn't really been in love with Fabian. Indeed, it was obvious that at times she found him both boring and irritating. But wasn't that what so many marriages were – finding a person boring and irritating and yet loving him? Who could imagine a man who was *never* boring or irritating? It had all seemed so very suitable, so very much the thing for a woman of twenty-nine, and there was no doubt that Prudence's pride would be seriously wounded when she realized that it was plain, mousy Jessie Morrow who had taken Fabian away from her. Perhaps this was after all what men liked to come home to, someone restful and neutral, who had no thought of changing the curtains or wallpapers? Jessie, who, for all her dim appearance, was very shrewd, had no doubt realized this. A beautiful wife would have been too much for Fabian, for one handsome person is enough in a marriage, if there is to be any beauty at all. And so often there isn't, Jane thought, drawing little houses on the blotting-paper, remembering the grey and fawn couples one saw so often in hotel lounges, hardly distinguishable, men from women, in their dimness.

Difference of sex no more we knew,
Than our Guardian Angels do . . .

she thought, suddenly smiling to herself at the way a not quite appropriate quotation would come into her mind on nearly every occasion.

Then she returned resolutely to the matter in hand, and after marshalling her confused thoughts succeeded in writing a loving and sympathetic letter which brought the tears to Prudence's eyes more readily than Fabian's scrawl, stressing *his* wretchedness and how much better off she would be without him.

Both letters had arrived by the same post, when Prudence, in her rose-patterned, frilled summer housecoat, was preparing breakfast in her neat little kitchen.

The blow was none the less shattering for being not entirely unexpected, for although Prudence had noticed a falling off in Fabian's affection the last time she had seen him, she had attributed it to his preoccupation with the Parochial Church Council and what people would think if he were seen walking in the village with her at night. She had not really doubted that they would meet again in London and that all would then be well.

She stood holding Jane's letter in one hand, while the other automatically moved the toaster from under the grill.

'You know so much more than I do about the making and breaking of love affairs,' Jane had written, 'so I hope you will not long be unhappy over this, or not *too* long. But on the morning when you get this letter you will be alone, darling Prue, so be sure and give yourself a *good breakfast*, if you possibly can . . .'

Dear Jane, Prudence smiled; it was really unlike her to be so practical. Well, the toast was not burnt and the coffee was just starting to bubble up into the top of the percolator, there was no reason why she should snatch it off the gas before it had had a chance to get as strong as she liked it. She would have some orange-juice, too, and perhaps even a boiled egg. Later she might not feel like eating.

It was a hot day. Prudence dressed with her usual elegance and painted her face and eyes with almost more than her usual care. It was at once force of habit and a kind of defiance. But as she stood waiting to cross the road to the bus she felt curiously detached, as one sometimes does in a time of great happiness or misery, and began to wonder whether she would even be able to negotiate the traffic safely.

She arrived at the office without mishap, however. Miss Clothier was on holiday, and although Miss Trapnell seemed in some way incomplete without her, the conversation was exactly the same as if they had both been there.

'Such a lovely day!' said Miss Trapnell. 'I always find I wake earlier on these fine mornings. In fact, I was here and had started work at a quarter-past nine this morning.'

'Then you will be able to go at a quarter-past five,' said Prudence absently.

She turned to her work almost with relief, hoping to lose

herself in it. She even began to type out some tables of figures, work which she normally considered beneath her, and found it very soothing. Occasionally, however, other thoughts broke through the careful barrier she had put up. What was she going to say to Fabian when she answered his letter? Who would go with her on her summer holiday now?

At about a quarter to eleven Miss Trapnell looked at her watch and remarked, 'I hope Dr Grampian hasn't called Marilyn in for dictation this morning.'

'Why? What difference can it make to us?'

'Well, don't you see, Miss Bates, with Gloria on holiday there is only Marilyn to make the tea, and if Dr Grampian is dictating to her it may be delayed. He would not realize that it was getting to be time to put the kettle on.'

'No. I suppose he would consider that he had a mind above such things,' said Prudence.

'Well, Miss Bates, it's hardly a question of being *above* them. They are very important, vital, you might say. Somebody must be thinking about them or we should soon notice it, and men would be the first to complain.'

'I'll go and make the tea if Marilyn is with Dr Grampian,' said Prudence apathetically.

'*You*, Miss Bates? Well, I hardly think you could, you know. It isn't your place to, or mine, for that matter. It's rather difficult, really.'

'It seems impossible,' said Prudence.

They went on with their work in silence for a few minutes and then Miss Trapnell said, 'I think I'll just go and see what's happening. I might perhaps put the kettle on.'

When she had gone out of the room Prudence's control seemed to give way. She leaned her forehead down on her typewriter and felt the cold metal against her brow.

The door opened and Geoffrey Manifold came in.

'Well, and how is Prudence today?' he asked in a rather jaunty tone.

Prudence did not answer, but began to cry.

Perhaps she was hardly conscious of him standing there by her table and would have cried anyway, but if she had expected to find his arms around her, consoling her, she was disappointed. He just stood by awkwardly, embarrassed as men often are at the sight of a woman in tears.

'You'll spoil your make-up,' he said in what seemed a callous tone. 'Gramp will probably summon you in any minute now, and it will be rather difficult to repair the damage, won't it? Doesn't that stuff come off your eyelashes when you cry?'

'It's supposed not to,' sniffed Prudence, taking out her handkerchief and mopping her eyes very gingerly. 'But I believe you're right; it *has* run.' She looked up at him and noticed with a slight shock that the expression of his eyes did not match the indifference of his tone.

'Is there anything I can do?' he asked.

Do? thought Prudence, rather wildly, contemplating his plaid shirt and tie. 'Well, you might help me with these tables. I don't seem able to get them right somehow.'

They sat quietly side by side, until Miss Trapnell, rather flustered, came in carrying a tray with three cups on it.

'Marilyn is still in there with him,' she said, 'so I had to make the tea myself, there was nothing else for it. *Most* inconsiderate of him, I think. I went in with his cup and he didn't even look up to say thank you.'

'Well, we'll say thank you,' said Mr Manifold, putting on a certain amount of charm. '*We're* most grateful, aren't we, Miss Bates?'

'Yes, we certainly are.'

'I don't know whether I've made your Nescafé as you like it, Mr Manifold,' said Miss Trapnell fussily. 'I wasn't sure how much milk you liked, so I brought it separately in a jug.'

'Thank you. That's very kind of you, but I usually have it black.'

Miss Trapnell sat down in her chair and sighed, exhausted with the exertions of tea-making.

'Dr Grampian did say that he wanted to see you, Miss Bates, when you were free.'

'When *I* was free?' asked Prudence. 'It isn't like him to be so considerate.'

She went upstairs and paused outside his door. His voice droned on, dictating endless sentences without verbs.

Prudence tapped on the door.

'Come in, come in,' he said crossly, for he was not feeling very well this morning. Lucy had given a party the evening before which had gone on rather too long; the company had been boring and the drink strong and abundant. They could not really afford to give parties on such a scale. . . . 'Go away now,' he said, dismissing Marilyn, 'and bring that back to me when you've typed it. Now, Miss Bates, what is it?'

'I thought you wanted me,' said Prudence, feeling utterly forlorn. She was too much wrapped up in her own desolation to realize that he had a hangover. A year ago, she would have thought: Ah, one of Lucy's parties. Poor darling, I must humour him. But today it was she who must be humoured.

'Well, I don't think I did,' he said brusquely. 'Unless you've got anything to show me?'

'No, I haven't. But you told Miss Trapnell . . .'

'Oh, whatever it was, I've forgotten now.' Her heavy expensive scent, totally unsuitable for the office, reminded him of the party last night. He was only very slightly gratified to notice, when he looked up to dismiss her, that her eyes seemed to be full of tears. But over lunch at his club, the high, querulous voice of a Bishop complaining because there was no more Camembert left made him smile. And all because the tears in Miss Bates's eyes proved that he still retained his old power over women.

Prudence had hurried into the lavatory, where she had cried noiselessly for a few moments and then gone out to what she felt must be a solitary lunch. She chose a restaurant which was rather expensive, but frequented mainly by women, so that she felt no embarrassment at being alone. Here, she knew, she could get the kind of food she deserved, for she must be more than usually kind to herself today. A dry Martini and then a little smoked salmon; she felt she could manage that. There was a certain consolation in the crowds of fashionably dressed women, especially as Prudence felt that she could equal and even excel some of them. Had they too suffered in love? she wondered. Were some of them suffering even at this moment? Or had they passed through suffering to something worse, the blankness and boredom of indifference? It was impossible to tell from their smooth, well-groomed faces, and Prudence wondered whether she too looked as indifferent. Or might somebody ask, 'Who is that interesting-looking young woman, with the traces of tears on her cheeks, eating smoked salmon?'

'And what would you like to follow, madam?' asked the waitress. 'I can recommend the chicken.'

'Well,' Prudence hesitated, 'perhaps just a slice of the breast, and a very few vegetables.' No sweet, of course, unless there was some fresh fruit, a really ripe yellow-fleshed peach, perhaps? And afterwards, the blackest of black coffee.

There was Saturday to come and Sunday, she thought. Jane had offered to come up and spend the week-end with her if it would be any help, but she felt that having to cope with Jane might be too much for her. She would have to face her loving questions; she might even be asked again whether she had been Fabian's mistress.

Fabian had not been so much to Prudence's flat as to have left behind any particularly poignant memories. He had admired the rose-coloured curtains, they had sat together on the rather uncomfortable little Regency sofa and he had kissed her there, but he had never stayed for a night, pottered about in the kitchen, put up a shelf or mended a flex. Indeed, with his own elegance, he had seemed to fit into the general scheme of furnishing rather too well, like a turbaned blackamoor holding a lamp, so that he might have been no more than just another 'amusing' object.

In the evening Prudence wrote to him, a sad, resigned letter, a little masterpiece in its way, which he was to shed tears over as he stood in his garden reading it, with the first leaves beginning to drop down from the walnut tree.

Life with Jessie suddenly seemed a frightening prospect, unless it could be like life with Constance all over again, with little romantic episodes here and there. But Jessie was too sharp to allow that. It was as if a net had closed round him. He went into the house and put Prudence's letter away in a secret drawer of his desk, where, years later, he might come upon it, and either wonder which of all his many loves she had been, or brood regretfully over it as a wonderful thing that had come into his life too late.

CHAPTER TWENTY-ONE

SATURDAY PASSED somehow for Prudence in a rather fanatical tidying of her flat, in much polishing and dusting, and in buying herself all the nicest things she could think of to eat and drink. In the evening she had asked her contemporary, Eleanor Hitchens, to dinner, and quite enjoyed herself, hinting at tragedy, while Eleanor, her good-natured face beaming, said with a kind of rough sympathy, 'Oh, Prue, you and your men and all these emotional upsets! Doesn't it make life very wearing? Still, you were just the same at Oxford, I remember. Whoever was it then – Peter or Philip or Henry or somebody?'

Prudence smiled. It had been Peter and Philip and Henry

at one time or another. Not to mention Laurence and Giles.

'You ought to get married,' said Eleanor sensibly. 'That would settle you.' She hitched up her tweed skirt and stretched out her legs, clad in lisle stockings, to the warmth of the gas-fire, which Prudence, who wore only a thin dress, had thought necessary on this warm evening. 'Look at my awful stockings. I didn't have time to change after golf. I suppose I'll never get a man if I don't take more trouble with myself,' Eleanor went on, but she spoke comfortably and without regret, thinking of her flat in Westminster, so convenient for the Ministry, her week-end golf, concerts and theatres with women friends, in the best seats and with a good supper afterwards. Prue could have this kind of life if she wanted it; one couldn't go on having romantic love affairs indefinitely. One had to settle down sooner or later into the comfortable spinster or the contented or bored wife.

'We were going on holiday together,' said Prudence, perhaps not very truthfully. 'Now I suppose I shan't go anywhere.'

'Come to Spain with me, end of September,' said Eleanor brisk and practical. 'Even if you got bored with my company, you'd get some decent food and sunbathing. It would do you good – you must have a holiday, you know. Besides, you might meet some handsome Señor.'

Prudence smiled and thanked her, saying she would think about it and let her know. People were being so kind to her. Dear Jane and dear Eleanor, what would one do without the sympathy of other women?

The next day was Sunday, and Prudence woke up in tears. She supposed that she must have been crying in her sleep, before the consciousness of what had happened came beating down upon her. Her life was blank and the summer seemed to have gone. She lay listening to a church bell ringing and the rain pattering on the leaves in the square, wishing that she had the consolations of religion to help her. Now, at ten minutes to eight, she thought, Anglo-Catholic women with unpowdered faces and pale lips would be hurrying out to Early Service, without even the comfort of a cup of tea inside them. And at about nine o'clock or a little before, they would come back, happy and serene, to enjoy a larger breakfast than usual and the Sunday papers. The Romans, too, would slip into a convenient Mass at nine-thirty or some late and sensible time, and feel that they had done their duty for the day. Perhaps that would be the best kind of faith to have. Prudence imagined herself on holiday in Spain, a black lace mantilla draped over her hair, hurrying into some dark Cathedral. Perhaps she could do something about it even now. She remembered a poster by the Church she passed every day on her way to the bus. TALKS ON THE CATHOLIC FAITH FOR NON-CATHOLICS, BY FATHER KEOGH. Tuesday evenings, at 8. But then she imagined herself sitting on a hard, uncomfortable chair after a day's work, listening to a lecture by a raw Irish peasant that was phrased for people less intelligent than herself. Better, surely, to go along to Farm Street and be instructed by a calm pale Jesuit who would know the answers to all one's doubts. Then, in the street where she did her shopping there was the Chapel, with a notice outside which said: ALL WELCOME. The minister, the Rev. Bernard Tabb, had the letters B.D., B.Sc. after his name. The fact that he was a Bachelor of Science might give a particular authority to his sermons, Prudence always felt; he might quite possibly know *all* the answers, grapple boldly with doubt and overcome it because he knew the best and worst of both worlds. He might even tackle evolution and the atomic bomb and make sense of it all. But of course, she thought, echoing Fabian's sentiments as he walked in the village, one just couldn't go to Chapel; one just didn't. Nor even to those exotic religious meetings advertised on the back of the *New Statesman*, which always seemed to take place in Bayswater.

These thoughts gave her strength enough to get up from

her bed and make herself a pot of tea and some toast. As she lay back against her pale green pillows she could see her reflection in the looking-glass on the wall opposite. She was not quite at her best at this hour, but rather appealing in her plainness, sipping her favourite Lapsang Souchong, at ten and sixpence a pound, out of a fragile white-and-gold cup.

When she had finished her breakfast and read the Sunday papers, she took up a volume of George Herbert's poems which Jane had once given to her. The book opened at a poem called *Hope*, and she read:

I gave to Hope a watch of mine; but he
An anchor gave to me.
Then an old Prayer-book I did present;
And he an optic sent.
With that I gave a vial full of tears;
But he, a few green ears.
Ah, loiterer! I'll no more, no more I'll bring;
I did expect a ring.

It puzzled and disturbed her and she lay quietly for some time, trying to think out what it meant. Yet she was comforted too and it reminded her of Jane and Nicholas, Morning Prayer and Matins and Evensong in a damp country church with pews, and dusty red hassocks. No light oak chairs, incense or neat leather kneelers. Perhaps the Anglican way was the best after all. It was the way she had been brought up in. Should she perhaps go up to see her mother in Herefordshire and revisit the scenes of her childhood? The idea was attractive, but then she saw how it would be: the wet green garden, her mother and her friends all looking sadly older, playing their afternoon bridge, their eager eyes full of the questions they did not quite like to ask. Why didn't she come and see her mother more often? What did she do in London? What was her work with Dr Grampian? Why wasn't she married yet?

Lunch was a rather sad meal, hardly up to Prudence's usual standard. She had not the heart even to cook the small chicken she had bought for herself. Afterwards she tried to read a novel and fell asleep for a while, but at three o'clock she woke and there seemed to be nothing to do but to lie brooding in her chair, looking at the few letters Fabian had written to her, until it was time to make a cup of tea. Now the Lapsang Souchong tasted smoky and bitter, rather like disinfectant, she thought. As if she were putting an end to herself with Lysol.

At five o'clock the telephone rang. Prudence supposed it might be Jane, anxious to know how she was getting through the day, but when she picked up the receiver and a man's voice answered the thought leapt into her mind that of course it was Fabian. The whole thing had been a terrible mistake, a bad dream.

Her illusion was shattered in a second and the voice announced that it was Geoffrey Manifold, and asked how she was.

'Oh, all right, thank you,' said Prudence, very much taken aback.

'After tea on Sunday is always such a depressing time,' he went on. 'I was just wondering if you were free and would like to come out to dinner and perhaps see a film?'

'That's very sweet of you. I think perhaps I should.'

'Good. Then I'll call for you at half-past six.'

How kind of him! It gave Prudence a warm feeling to realize that perhaps he had been thinking of her today when she had been so unhappy. 'Mr Manifold is so good to his aunt.' For the first time that day she felt like laughing, and went quickly to change and decorate her face and finger-nails. Then she set out drinks on a tray and waited for him to come.

They were both a little shy at first. They had not met out of working hours before, and his neat dark suit looked less familiar than the plaid shirt and corduroy trousers which Prudence had expected.

He looked round the Regency elegance of Prudence's sitting-room with a half-nervous, half-scornful expression on his face.

'Just the sort of place you ought to live in,' he said at last. 'Very *Vogue* and all that. Not quite my cup of tea, I'm afraid.'

I'm not asking you to live with me, thought Prudence angrily; merely to have a drink. 'What would you like?' she asked, indicating her collection of bottles. 'And don't say you prefer beer, because I haven't any.'

He smiled. 'I'm sorry,' he said. 'I'm afraid I was rather rude about your flat. After all, I'm supposed to be here to comfort you, aren't I?'

'To comfort me?' asked Prudence rather indignantly. 'How do you know that?'

'I thought your heart was broken,' he said looking into his glass of gin. 'Never mind; it will pass.'

'How do *you* know it will?'

'Oh, I'm always having trouble with my girlfriends,' he said lightly.

Prudence felt a little stab of jealousy. How ridiculous this was! She wanted to ask in a formal tone 'And have you many girlfriends at the moment?' but pride held her back. How dared anyone be unkind to him! she thought fiercely.

'Where would you like to have dinner?' he asked rather stiffly.

As usual on the occasions when this question was put to her Prudence was unable to think of anywhere except Claridge's or Lyons, neither of which seemed really suitable. But in the end it seemed that Geoffrey knew of a quiet place in Soho where the food wasn't bad.

They were sitting studying the menu when a man at the next table came up to them and gazing intently at them with his bright beady eyes, said in a low voice, 'I do *not* recommend the *pâté* here tonight, but the *bouillabaisse* is excellent. An odd thing that – I felt I couldn't bear you to order the *pâté*.'

Prudence and Geoffrey thanked him in a rather embarrassed way.

'Oh, it is such an *anxious* moment,' he said, 'that first glance at the menu, will there be *anything at all* that one can eat? *Then felt I like some watcher of the skies*, on first looking into Chapman's Homer, you know. . . . I always feel that if I can do *anything* for my fellow diners. . . .'

'Mr Caldicote,' said a waiter, approaching with a bottle, 'I think you will find this sufficiently *chambré* now, sir.'

'Ah, Henry, you naughty man! You've just plunged it into a bowl of hot water, *I* know. . . .'

'Oh, Mr Caldicote, *sir* . . .' They both laughed.

'A not entirely unworthy little Beaujolais,' said the strange man, and, waving his hand in a friendly manner, he returned to his table.

'Well, now,' said Geoffrey, 'I wonder if we dare eat anything after that?'

'Is there *anything at all* that we can eat?' laughed Prudence.

She was surprised to find that she was quite hungry, and enjoyed her roast duck and red wine. 'You know,' she said, after a while, 'I'm not sure that I really want to go to a film. Would you mind if we didn't?'

'Not at all. I only suggested it because one can't expect a girl to be satisfied with nothing more than one's company as an evening's entertainment.'

'That was nice of you,' said Prudence. 'So many men think one should be delighted with just that.' But perhaps the girlfriends expected more?

'There is a new film at the Academy,' said Geoffrey.

'Le something de Monsieur something,' said Prudence.

'I expect it begins in a fog on a quay and a ship is hooting somewhere.'

'And a girl in a mackintosh and a beret is standing in a doorway.'

'And then she and a man who emerges out of the fog go into a café full of that tinny French music.'

'And a little later on there's the room with the iron bedstead and the girl in her petticoat. . . .'

'So we've really seen the film,' said Geoffrey.

'Talking of France, have you planned your holiday yet?' she asked. 'All that grim walking and no lazing in the sun drinking?'

'Yes. I've arranged it all. What about yours?'

'I'm probably going to Spain with a friend,' said Prudence rather mysteriously. Again she saw herself slipping into Mass with a black lace mantilla arranged becomingly over her hair.

'I shall be very near Spain. Perhaps we may even meet? I may see you sitting drinking on the terrace of a luxury hotel while I walk by with my rucksack.'

'And I'll invite you to share a bottle of wine with me!' Prudence laughed. It was all most unsuitable, she told herself. Fabian barely cold in his grave, and here she was laughing with Geoffrey Manifold, of all people. Whatever would Jane say?

Jane would hardly have known what to say, but when she rang Prudence's flat at about nine o'clock, she was rather disturbed to get no reply.

'Whatever happens, one always imagines that people will listen to the nine o'clock news,' she said. 'I do hope Prue is all right.' A dreadful picture came to her of gas-ovens and overdoses of drugs, and of how she had always thought the block of flats where Prudence lived the kind of place one might be found dead in. 'Oh, Nicholas, you don't think she would do anything *foolish*, do you?'

'Oh, but she is always doing foolish things,' he said mildly.

'Yes, but you don't think she would do anything to *herself*, do you?'

'Certainly not, darling. Prudence is much too fond of herself for there to be any danger of that.'

'I know. I expect she's having dinner with Dr Grampian!' said Jane suddenly. 'That's why she wasn't in. What a terrible week this has been, everything going wrong like this. Thank goodness we are to have our holiday soon. I only hope your *locum* doesn't fail.'

'Well, I shan't know if he does, and we shall certainly be too far away to be able to do anything about it,' said Nicholas comfortably.

'They'll all be waiting there,' said Jane, warming to the subject. 'Eleven o'clock will strike. There will be agitated whisperings among the congregation and then a hurried consultation between the churchwardens. I suppose Mr Mortlake and Mr Whiting would be able to take some kind of a service?'

'Certainly. It is the ancient right and duty of the churchwardens to recite the Divine Office of Morning Prayer,' said Nicholas. 'I suppose they would be perfectly justified in exercising it.'

'But wouldn't the Bishop have to be consulted first?'

'My dear Jane,' said Nicholas, now with a tinge of exasperation in his tone, 'I'm sure Mr Boultbee of the Church Missionary Society will be perfectly reliable. There is no need to worry about it.'

CHAPTER TWENTY-TWO

THE CHURCH in the Cornish village where the Clevelands were spending their holiday was a little Higher than either Jane or Nicholas had been used to.

'What a good thing you aren't having to assist in any way,'

said Jane after they had attended the Sung Mass on their last Sunday morning.

'There's nothing to it, really,' said Nicholas rather touchily. 'One soon gets into the way of ritual.'

'But supposing it had been sprung on you unexpectedly,' Jane persisted, 'would you really have known what to do?'

'A clergyman of the Church of England should be ready for every emergency, from Asperges and Incense to North End Position and Evening Communion.'

'Ah, yes; our weakness and our glory,' said Jane. 'Was that what St Paul meant about being all things to all men?' she mused. 'Of course, if we had had Mowbray's *Church Guide* we could have seen that this was not quite on our level. I wonder if anybody has ever thought of compiling a guide of *Low* churches – putting "N" for North End Position and "E" for Evening Communion against them?'

'People who want a Low church don't usually have to search so hard as those who want Catholic Privileges,' Nicholas pointed out.

'I do wish Prue had decided to join us,' said Jane. 'I'm rather worried about her being in Spain. She says she's never seen so many priests in her life.'

'Well, there could hardly be much danger from them.'

'No, perhaps not. But think of all those shops full of rosaries and statues. You know how impressionable she is. She also says that she has visited the birthplace of St Ignatius Loyola, and that she had an English-speaking Jesuit all to herself to show her round.'

'I think that a Jesuit would be even less likely than an ordinary priest to fall for Prudence's charms,' said Nicholas reassuringly.

'But don't you see, it's Prue falling for the charms of Rome that I'm afraid of,' said Jane. 'And that's not the worst. Listen to this! "Geoffrey and I went to see a bullfight at Pamplona. We had to get up at four a.m., but it was well worth it." Now who on earth is Geoffrey? I've never heard her mention him before. I quite understood that she was going with Eleanor Hitchens, and she's such a very sensible, solid sort of person.'

'She may have met this Geoffrey in Spain,' suggested Nicholas. 'Perhaps she and Eleanor quarrelled and separated, as people quite often do on holiday.'

'Well, I do hope it really *is* all right. I shall be quite glad to be home and back to normal again.'

They arrived home on a Saturday evening to find the garden like a jungle and Mrs Glaze welcoming them almost as if they had been Canon and Mrs Pritchard, Jane felt.

'Well, I *am* glad to see you back, madam, and the vicar too,' she said warmly. 'It'll be a nice change, we all feel.'

'A change?' said Jane. 'But Mr Boultbee was only here for three Sundays. You can hardly have got tired of him in so short a time.'

'It's tired of Africa, *we* are,' said Mrs Glaze firmly. 'Six sermons about Africa, we've had. It's more than flesh and blood can stand, madam. I was really shocked at some of their customs.' She paused, and then added in a brighter tone, 'I've got some nice chops for your supper. I expect you'll be ready for it. Mr Driver is having chops too. Mrs Arkright was going to braise them for him with some vegetables. It was a pity about him and Miss Bates.'

'Oh, yes,' said Jane hurriedly. 'I suppose it was. But of course there was nothing official, no engagement, you know.'

'Well, they both tried hard in their different ways, Miss Bates and Miss Morrow, and Miss Morrow won. What Miss Morrow *had*, we shall never know. She may have stooped to ways that Miss Bates wouldn't have dreamed of.' Mrs Glaze looked at Jane hopefully, but Jane was unable to throw any light on the matter. She felt she did not quite like to think of what Jessie might have done to get what she wanted. Perhaps *she* had been Fabian's mistress? Well, they would never know that now.

'It *is* nice to be home, just the three of us,' she said, as they sat down to their dish of chops with tomatoes, runner beans and mashed potatoes.

'Oh, Mother, you *always* say that after a holiday,' said Flora impatiently.

'Do I, darling? Yes, I suppose I'm getting to the age when one doesn't realize how often one says the same thing and doesn't really care,' said Jane complacently. 'I suppose it's one of the compensations of growing older.'

'I can hear somebody coming to the door,' said Flora. 'I suppose I'd better go and see who it is. Mrs Glaze will have gone by now.'

The bell rang and she opened the door to find Mr Oliver on the doorstep.

'Good evening, Miss Cleveland,' he said. 'I wonder if I could see the vicar for a moment?'

However could I have thought him interesting? Flora asked herself, ashamed at her lack of taste rather than her fickleness. That thin face, like some underfed animal, the fair hair with a curly bit in front . . . forgotten were the exquisite Evensongs when his face had appeared so spiritual in the dim light. Oh, Paul, *darling* Paul, she thought, as she showed Mr Oliver into the study, how was she going to bear the weeks until Oxford term began and she would meet him again after a lecture outside the School of Geography?

'I hope things are going well at the Bank?' she asked formally.

'Yes, thank you, Miss Cleveland. I shall be taking my holiday soon.'

'In October? That seems rather late. I do hope you will get some good weather. I'll tell my father you're here.'

'I suppose you put him in the study,' said Jane as Flora came back into the room. 'What a pity we can't all hear what he has to say.'

Nicholas left the room and Jane and Flora began to clear the table.

'I can't hear raised angry voices,' said Jane regretfully. 'Mr Oliver seems to be very subdued tonight. I wonder what he can have called about? It must be something rather important if it has to be discussed when we have been back from our holiday barely an hour.'

'They seem to be coming out of the study now,' said Flora. 'It hasn't taken long, whatever it was.'

Jane hurried out into the hall. 'Good evening, Mr Oliver,' she said. 'I hope you are well?'

'Very well, thank you, Mrs Cleveland; and I hope you have had a good holiday.'

Jane thanked him and waited hopefully.

'I have just been telling the vicar that I am afraid I shan't be seeing so much of you in the future.'

'I'm sorry to hear that. Are you leaving the district?'

'Well, not exactly that, Mrs Cleveland. Not to put too fine a point on it, I have joined Father Lomax's congregation.'

'Oh.' Jane hardly knew whether to express regret or to congratulate him. One got the idea that he had somehow been promoted. Friend, go up higher, she thought.

'I have been going to the services there for some months, off and on, you know,' declared Mr Oliver. 'And I find the form of the service, the ritual, you know, really more to my liking, with all due respect to you and the vicar.'

'Oh, I *quite* see,' said Jane sympathetically.

'And then there has been a certain amount of friction on some matters, as you may well be aware,' he continued.

'Yes, of course. That evening I found you all in the choir vestry . . .'

'Of course, Mr Mortlake has his point of view, but things can't stand still. Life isn't what it was fifty years ago.'

'No, of course not,' said Jane in a rather puzzled tone. 'But you will miss reading the lessons, won't you?'

Mr Oliver smiled in a rather superior way. 'Well, Mrs Cleveland, I am fortunate enough to have found a little niche waiting for me at St Stephen's. The post of thurifer has fallen vacant and I have been asked to fill it. The gentleman who used to do it has embraced the Roman Faith.'

'Well I never,' said Jane. 'You will be quite busy, then.'

'Yes, Mrs Cleveland. There will be the Sung Mass at eleven and Solemn Evensong at half-past six, and sometimes a Sung Mass during the week, on Days of Obligation, you know.'

'We must all come and see you swinging the censer,' Jane began before she realized that it would hardly be practicable. 'Good night,' she said quickly and hurried back into the dining-room, where Nicholas stood rather disconsolate, looking down at the chop-bones now congealed in their fat.

'Oh, dear, I feel I have failed there,' he said.

'Darling, you have done no such thing,' said Jane warmly. 'You can't help it if he quarrelled with Mr Mortlake and Mr Whiting and likes incense and all that sort of thing.'

'What was that you said about finding them all in the choir vestry one evening?' Nicholas asked.

'I just happened to be passing and heard them all squabbling in there. So I went in to see if there was anything I could do.'

'My poor Jane,' – he put his arm around her shoulders and they gazed down together at the remains of their supper – 'what can any of us do with these people?'

'We can only go blundering along in that state of life unto which it shall please God to call us,' said Jane. 'I was going to be such a splendid clergyman's wife when I married you, but somehow it hasn't turned out like *The Daisy Chain* or *The Last Chronicles of Barset*.'

'How you would have stood by me if I had been accused of stealing a cheque,' said Nicholas. 'I can just imagine you! Oh, now who is this coming to the door? Quite a crowd of people. Do you remember our first evening here and how you thought a crowd of parishioners ought to be coming up to the door to welcome us?'

'And nobody came except Mrs Glaze with a parcel of liver

for our supper!' Jane laughed. 'Well, now I can't complain. It seems to be Miss Doggett with Jessie and Fabian. I will go and ask Flora to make some coffee.'

'Ah, how nice it is to have you back,' said Miss Doggett, advancing into the room with her hand outstretched in welcome.

'Mr Boultbee seems to have done us a good turn,' said Nicholas. 'I gather his sermons were not much liked.'

'No; we got very tired of Africa and I didn't feel that what he told us rang quite true. He said that one African chief had had a thousand wives. I found that a little difficult to believe.'

'Well, we know what men are,' said Jane casually, surprised that Miss Doggett, with her insistence on men only wanting one thing, should have found it difficult to believe.

'Oh, come now,' protested Fabian, for she seemed to have glanced in his direction. 'And in any case, it was in the olden days, before Mr Boultbee got to work there.'

At this point Flora brought in the coffee, and Jane began to pour it out rather carelessly.

'Jessie and I were thinking that we might as well get married as soon as conveniently possible,' said Fabian. 'After all, we are neither of us very young.'

'I can arrange that for you at any time,' said Nicholas. 'You know about banns and licences and that kind of thing, I imagine?'

'Nicholas usually gives a talk to young couples before they marry,' said Jane hopefully. 'But perhaps it will hardly be necessary in this case.'

'He might just take Fabian aside,' said Jessie.

Nicholas began to talk to them about arrangements, and Miss Doggett said to Jane in a low voice, 'He has at last decided to do something about a stone for poor Constance's grave.'

'I'm very glad to hear it! What is it to be like?'

'Something quite plain and dignified. He thought Cornish

granite, with a suitable inscription. They spent their honeymoon in Cornwall, you know.'

'Stay for me there; I will not fail
To meet thee in that hollow vale.
And think not much of my delay;
I am already on the way . . .'

quoted Jane softly. 'What a good thing there is no marriage or giving in marriage in the afterlife; it will certainly help to smooth things out. Is Jessie to wear a white dress?'

'No; we thought white would hardly be suitable. Something in a soft blue or dove grey, we thought, with a small hat; and a spray of flowers, not a bouquet.'

'Brides over thirty shouldn't wear white,' said Jessie, who had now joined them.

'Well, they may have a perfect right to,' said Jane.

'A woman over thirty might not like you to think that,' said Jessie quickly. 'There can be something shameful about flaunting one's lack of experience.'

Jane, as a clergyman's wife, hardly knew how to answer this. Also, she was remembering Mrs Glaze's hint that Jessie might have 'stooped to ways Miss Bates wouldn't have dreamed of'. It was a subject best left alone, especially with Flora in the room.

Before they went, Fabian managed to manoeuvre Jane into the conservatory leading out of the drawing-room.

'I had to have a word with you,' he said. 'How is she, my poor Prudence?'

'Well, at the moment she seems to be on holiday in Spain with somebody called Geoffrey,' said Jane sharply.

'Oh, really?' Fabian looked decidedly crestfallen. 'Can she have forgotten so soon?'

'I expect so. Haven't you?'

'*I – forget?* My *dear* Jane . . .' He put one hand up to his brow with a characteristic gesture, while his other hand seemed to wander along the slatted wooden shelves of the conservatory, with the flower-pots full of old used earth and dried-up bulbs with withered leaves, until it came to rest on what felt like a piece of statuary. He looked down in surprise at feeling his hand touch stone, and started at seeing the headless body of a dwarf which had once stood in the rockery in the front garden.

'I can't understand Mrs Pritchard having that thing in her garden,' said Jane. 'She always struck me as being a person of taste, if nothing else. The head is here,' she said rather brightly, lifting it up by its little beard and holding it out towards Fabian.

'Don't.' He shuddered as if she had indeed offered it to him and he were rejecting it. 'Life's such a muddle, isn't it? How can we ever hope to do the right thing?'

Jane wanted to agree and to offer him the broken dwarf, perhaps for Constance's grave, as a kind of comment on the futility of earthly love, but instead she said gently, 'You must make Jessie happy. That will be the right thing for you now.'

'Yes, I suppose so,' he sighed.

'What plot are you two hatching?' said Miss Doggett's voice. 'Come, it's nearly dark, and we shall need Fabian to escort us home.'

'Rather a sad little procession,' said Jane, hearing the last scrunching of their footsteps on the gravel. 'Fabian being led away captive by the women.'

'Like *Samson Agonistes*,' observed Flora.

'*Oh, dark, dark* . . .' said Jane, laughing rather wildly. 'I told him that Prudence had forgotten him. I wonder if she has?'

CHAPTER TWENTY-THREE

IT APPEARED that Prudence had forgotten Fabian to the same extent as she had forgotten Philip, Henry, Laurence and the others. That is to say, he had been given a place in the shrine of her past loves; the urn containing his ashes had been ceremonially deposited in the niche where it would always remain. Philip, Henry, Laurence, Peter, Fabian and who could tell how many others there might be?

'I feel really that it *may* have happened for the best,' she said to Jane as they lunched again at the vegetarian restaurant.

'Well, yes; things do turn out that way really,' said Jane, glancing round the room, and seeing what looked like the same people eating the same food as before. She remembered rather sadly that she had not lunched here with Prudence since she had first had the idea of bringing her and Fabian together. Here were the same bearded and foreign gentlemen, and the same woman, dressed in orange and wearing heavy silver jewellery, who looked as if she might have been somebody's mistress in the nineteen-twenties. At the idea of being somebody's mistress, Jane became embarrassed, and began scrabbling about rather violently in her shredded cabbage salad.

'I wonder if one ever finds a caterpillar or anything like that,' she said in a loud, nervous tone.

Prudence did not answer, so Jane went on, still in the same tone, 'Now tell me, who is this Geoffrey? You mentioned him in your letter, but I'd never heard of him before.'

'Hush, Jane. Don't talk so *loud*. He's a young man who works for Arthur Grampian. I've known him for quite a long time. He was very kind to me when Fabian . . . you know . . . and then we happened to meet on holiday.'

'And do you like him?' asked Jane, lowering her voice and trying not to sound at all eager or interested.

'Well, yes, in a way,' Prudence hesitated. 'We get on quite well together. It was pleasant in Spain. I suppose it's the attraction of opposites really. But of course it wouldn't *do* at all.'

'Why wouldn't it?' asked Jane bluntly.

'Everything would be spoilt if anything came of it,' said Prudence seriously. 'Don't you see what I mean? That's almost the best thing about it.'

Jane felt very humble and inexperienced before such subtleties.

'Do you mean it's a kind of negative relationship like you once had with Arthur Grampian?' she asked, trying hard to appear intelligent and understanding.

'Oh, there's nothing *negative* about it. Quite the reverse! We shall probably hurt each other very much before it's finished, but we're doomed really.' There was a smile on Prudence's face as she said these words, for the experience of being in love with such an ordinary young man as Geoffrey Manifold was altogether new and delightful to her.

'Therefore the Love which us doth join
But Fate so enviously debars,
Is the Conjunction of the Mind,
And Opposition of the Stars,'

said Jane. 'Is that it, perhaps?' How much easier it was when one could find a quotation to light up the way; even Prudence seemed satisfied with Marvell's summing-up of the situation.

As they approached the building where Prudence's office was, Jane noticed a thin, dark young man wearing a raincoat standing in the doorway, and Prudence introduced him. And so Jane shook hands with Geoffrey as she had shaken hands with Arthur some months ago, and was amazed as she had been then at the wonder of love. What object could Fate possibly have in enviously debarring love between Prudence and such an ordinary and colourless young man as this appeared to be? But of course, she remembered, that was why women were so wonderful; it was their love and imagination that transformed these unremarkable beings. For most men, when one came to think of it, were undistinguished to look at, if not positively ugly. Fabian was an exception, and perhaps love affairs with handsome men tended to be less stable because so much less sympathy and imagination were needed on the woman's part?

But there was no opportunity to say any of this to Prudence, and soon she had left her turning to Geoffrey with every appearance of pleasure. Must it not be rather depressing to embark on a love affair that one knew to be doomed from the start? And yet, Jane supposed, people were doing it all the time, plunging boldly in with no thought of future misery.

She stood by a bus-stop, wondering what she should do. Then she remembered that there was a religious bookshop nearby, and it seemed very suitable that she should go into it and choose presents for the Confirmation candidates. Little holy books, she thought vaguely, stopping by a table and taking up what appeared to be a manual of questions and answers about points of ceremonial.

'Why do the Psalms end with a pneuma?' she read, wondering what it could mean and pondering on the answer. Her hands moved over to another pile and she found herself among books about Confession, the Answer to Rome and the mysteries of the Alcuin Society.

'Can I help you, madam?' asked an assistant, a kindly, grey-haired woman.

One's life followed a kind of pattern, with the same things cropping up again and again, but it seemed to Jane, floundering about among the books, that the question was not one that could be lightly dismissed now. 'No; thank you. I was just looking round,' was what one usually said. Just looking round the Anglican Church, from one extreme to the other, perhaps climbing higher and higher, peeping over the top to have a look at Rome on the other side, and then quickly drawing back.

'Thank you. I wanted some little books suitable for Confirmation candidates,' said Jane in a surprisingly firm and thoughtful tone. 'Not too High, you know.'

'I understand, madam,' said the assistant. 'I think you will probably find what you want on *this* table.'

Jane set to work with concentration and in ten minutes had chosen a number of little books and even a few early Christmas cards.

By now it was almost tea-time, but Jane, in her newly-acquired virtue, did not feel disposed to linger in Town, listening to the music at a Corner House or eating expensive cakes in the restaurant of one of the big stores. She would go without tea, as a kind of penance for all the times she had failed as a vicar's wife. Also, by catching a train now, she would avoid the rush hour.

But at the junction where she had to change she found that she had some minutes to wait for a train, and decided that she had perhaps earned a cup of railway station tea and a bun.

She stood waiting in the orderly little queue, contemplating the window at the back of the counter, which had stained-glass panels showing a design of grapes. They imagined us drinking wine here, she thought, and longed to share her thought with somebody. She turned away to carry her cup to a table and there behind her in the queue was Edward Lyall.

'They imagined us drinking wine here,' she said, pointing to the grapes on the window. 'I was thinking of that when I saw you and wondered if anybody else had ever noticed it.'

'No, I can't say that I had,' Edward admitted.

'I don't suppose you often drink tea here,' said Jane. 'It seems unsuitable for you to be here now.'

'I often have a cup of tea while I'm waiting for a train.'

'You don't always drive down from London in your car, then?'

'Oh, no. I feel I ought to travel by train sometimes.'

'You mean you want to know what your constituents have to endure? The tea too weak or too strong, the stale sandwich, the grimy upholstery, the window that won't open, the waiting on the draughty platform . . .' Jane could have gone on indefinitely, feeling like one of our great modern poets, had not Edward interrupted her with an embarrassed laugh.

'You want to carry our burden as well as your own?' went on Jane relentlessly.

'Now you're making fun of me,' he said with a very sweet smile. 'But at least let me carry your parcel. Look, here's the train.'

'I wasn't really making fun of you,' said Jane as they settled themselves in the carriage. 'I was seeing you as a human being for the first time.'

'Do I appear so unlike one, then?'

'It isn't your fault if you do. As Our Beloved Member you are naturally put on a pedestal, and when you come down it's a bit like a clergyman going into a pub wearing his clerical collar. You see what I mean?'

'One does want to get to know people,' said Edward. 'There is little opportunity for the sort of friendly conversation we are having now. It was very pleasant that Sunday afternoon at Fabian Driver's, wasn't it?'

'Ah, yes; tea under the walnut tree. How long ago it seems!'

'Your friend Miss Bates lives somewhere near Regent's Park, doesn't she?' Edward asked. 'I was wondering if I might run across her one day.'

'She has been on holiday,' said Jane, a sudden hope rising within her. 'But I expect she will be coming to stay with us again quite soon.'

'Then I shall look forward to meeting her again.'

They parted at the station, but Jane was a little absent-minded in her leave-taking, for she was full of a wonderful new idea. Edward and Prudence . . . Why hadn't it occurred to her before? Prudence living at the Towers, a much more worthy setting for her than Fabian Driver's house. The sound of footsteps hurrying behind her and Edward's voice calling that she had forgotten her parcel broke into her dream.

'My parcel?' she said in a dazed voice. 'Why, of course! Thank you so much.' Her parcel, the proof of the good work she had done in the bookshop, nearly left behind, and all because she had been matchmaking again!

'Well, dear,' said Nicholas, appearing at the front door, 'how was Prudence?'

'Oh, *very* well,' said Jane enthusiastically. 'And look, I've remembered to get books for the Confirmation candidates. The assistant was so helpful.'

'Splendid, dear,' said Nicholas. 'And I'm glad Prudence isn't taking this business too much to heart.'

Jane looked at the clock in the hall. It said five-past six.

'Dear Prue,' she said. 'I suppose she will be waiting in the bus queue now, or going out somewhere with Conjunction of the Mind and Opposition of the Stars.'

But in this she was wrong, for at five minutes to six Prudence had received a summons to Arthur Grampian's room.

'Well, really, Miss Bates,' said Miss Clothier. 'I call that *most* inconsiderate. Whatever can he want at this time?'

'I should be inclined to go in wearing your hat and coat,' said Miss Trapnell. 'Then he will see that you are not to be trifled with.'

'I shall be quite firm,' said Prudence. 'In any case, I have an engagement this evening.'

'She and Mr Manifold are going to the cinema,' said Miss Clothier to Miss Trapnell. 'I happen to know that.'

'I wonder if she has met his aunt yet?' asked Miss Trapnell in a tone full of meaning.

Prudence went to Arthur Grampian's room and looked in through the open door. He was sitting at his desk wearing an overcoat, although the gas-fire was full on and all the windows shut.

'Did you want me for something?' Prudence asked.

'Ah, Prudence' – he came towards her and took her hand – 'the melancholy mood is upon me this evening.'

'Is something the matter, then?'

'Not more than usual, but I have a desire for charming company. I hoped that you might be able to dine with me.' He looked at her intently, but could not see if there were tears in her eyes.

'I'm afraid I have an engagement this evening,' said Prudence firmly. 'You had better go and have dinner at your club. Perhaps we could go out some other time?'

She stooped to turn out the gas-fire and then began tidying his desk. Let him go among the bishops tonight, she thought, suddenly overwhelmed by the richness of her life. We have many more evenings before us if we want them.

All Pan Books are available at your local bookshop or newsagent, or can be ordered direct from the publisher. Indicate the number of copies required and fill in the form below.

Send to: Macmillan General Books C.S.
Book Service By Post
PO Box 29, Douglas I-O-M
IM99 1BQ

or phone: 01624 675137, quoting title, author and credit card number.

or fax: 01624 670923, quoting title, author, and credit card number.

or Internet: http://www.bookpost.co.uk

Please enclose a remittance* to the value of the cover price plus 75 pence per book for post and packing. Overseas customers please allow £1.00 per copy for post and packing.

*Payment may be made in sterling by UK personal cheque, Eurocheque, postal order, sterling draft or international money order, made payable to Book Service By Post.

Alternatively by Access/Visa/MasterCard

Card No. | | | | | | | | | | | | | | | | |

Expiry Date | | | | | | | | | | | | | | | | |

Signature ____________________

Applicable only in the UK and BFPO addresses.

While every effort is made to keep prices low, it is sometimes necessary to increase prices at short notice. Pan Books reserve the right to show on covers and charge new retail prices which may differ from those advertised in the text or elsewhere.

NAME AND ADDRESS IN BLOCK CAPITAL LETTERS PLEASE

Name ____________________

Address ____________________

____

____

____

8/95

Please allow 28 days for delivery.
Please tick box if you do not wish to receive any additional information. ☐